SO IT BEGINS

Gina Maria

To Teresa
for my woosie wu
I will always love you
Your Sister.

Gina

Order this book online at www.trafford.com
or email orders@trafford.com

Most Trafford titles are also available at major online book retailers.

Printed in the United States of America.

ISBN: 978-1-4269-5886-1 (sc)
ISBN: 978-1-4269-5887-8 (hc)
ISBN: 978-1-4269-5885-4 (e)

Library of Congress Control Number: 2011902953

Trafford rev. 02/22/2011

 www.trafford.com

North America & international
toll-free: 1 888 232 4444 (USA & Canada)
phone: 250 383 6864 ♦ fax: 812 355 4082

Dedicated to my husband for his hard work in helping me.
To my sons and mother because I love them.

"You there!" the order came from Simion. "Put that there, we will move it later." Simion couldn't believe his great fortune. He could see the tides changing in the world and had been working for years on his pet project.

The purchase of the old mine shaft was just the beginning. He had so much work to do and had done so much already. Most of his equipment had to be helicoptered in. This place was so remote, but that was the beauty of it.

The workers had to be hand picked for this project and had their families with them. The truth was not to be told to them. It was a project for the future. They were told to build a place as if it were a great spaceship getting ready to travel to a distant planet. Everything had to be considered from food, shelter, power and so on. Simion was sure it would be a haven when the war came. It had to be far enough away from the hoards of people escaping from the cities as their food and resources ran out, to find it.

Simion was brilliant beyond his years. The mine was perfect. Most of the heavy digging had been done, now it was getting the power, water, and air and making sure that no one could see it from the outside. He thought of everything, water purification, recycling, everything. The underground spring water was just one of the blessings he had with his old mine.

When they had been excavating the animal area near the spring they discovered huge caverns carved by years gone by. These caverns would serve as the growing domes and the animals could be housed down another tunnel.

Simion felt like Noah getting ready for the great flood, but this had to go far beyond that. Deep in his heart, when the time came, all these people may be the last left on the planet and he was going to make sure they survived.

As he did the hiring, he looked at all kinds of different races and professions. Genetic diversity was maybe the only hope.

"Zack" Simion yelled. Zack was a good man and an excellent foreman.

Zack went over to the edge and started barking orders. The men complied.

The sun was high in the sky when the lunch bells rang.

The women had been cooking all morning for the men. The children had been in the school that was almost complete now.

The Agro tunnel was well on its way and the women and children had put up the ideas for recreational space.

The helicopters kept coming and so did the supplies, everything from plants to seeds, to wiring. The water would generate power. Simion the ever protective boss overseeing the things he ordered did in fact arrive.

Simion was leaning over a makeshift desk examining some maps when Zack arrived to tell him the masons were well on to finish the outside wall.

Simion smiled. "Look here Zack. Do you know why I chose this location?"

Zack glanced at the map looking over the topography and realized this mountain range was almost in a full circle and in the middle of a huge valley. He thought for a minute. Simion had made an error in judgement. Why were they on the other side of the range when such a splendid valley was over the top of this mountain? He was about to mention this to Simion when he heard the lunch bell again.

"Bells, why bells," he said to Simion?

Simion smiled. "Some things in life just have beauty and bells are far nicer than a horn blasting your eardrums out."

They both laughed as they made their way into the old mine.

"Well," Zack asked Simion "What do you think of the cavern?" "They found fresh spring water and from the tests it appears to be as fresh as the world is old."

Simion smiled. "Yes indeed" he replied, "Seems it even has a current to it." This had possibilities. His mind was beyond this. He was planning water wheels for electricity that would be further help concealing this place.

"Simmy, Simmy, there you are sweetie." Up the hall came Simion's wife Rainie.

Zack couldn't believe this woman. She was no asset to Simion. Simion's dear wife was selfish to the bone. Whatever beauty may have been there was erased by her self-serving over bearing self-righteousness.

"Hi there Rainie," Zack said trying to smile. She as usual, gave him the cold glance up and down as if she was asserting her superiority over him. After all, she was the wife of the benefactor of this whole project.

"Simmy, when are you taking me to see my friends in the Alps, we have a skiing trip planned and all this construction is so dreary?"

"Soon Rainie soon," He couldn't bring himself to tell her that the political state of the world was in a desperate state. Three major countries were all threatening each other. There were so many things the masses were kept blind to. Mass panic would be the result so they had to keep a lot of it quiet.

"Let's go get our lunch. I have worked up a hunger like no other I've had for a while." Simion smiled at them and they made their way to the lunchroom.

The sound of the helicopter drifted down the valley to Simion and Rainie. She was beaming and hugged Simion. "Don't worry Simmy, I'll be back soon," she giggled. "I can't wait to hit the slopes and relax later in the spa." She watched the chopper land and this was the last dust she would have blown in her hair for a while she thought. She blew him a kiss and couldn't get into the helicopter fast enough.

Simion stared at her as she climbed in and waved at her. He had a foreboding feeling it wouldn't be for much longer. She would adapt he told himself. He had faith in her.

He turned and headed into the tunnel. The cavern they had exposed was perfect for the Agrodome. He had workers non-stop getting it ready for the garden.

Everything had to be considered, the lights, the humidity and the air, if he was to grow an Eden it had to be perfect. The underground water could be used for a fish farm. Maybe he could give that some thought.

"Sir, sir a moment, please" Dirk said. He was a short fellow and Simion thought oddly featured, but when it came to animal waste, the man was a genius.

"What is it Dirk?"

"Well sir."

"Please Dirk, call me Simion."

"Well Simion, the tanks for recycling the animal waste are completed. The tunnels growing the feed Alfalpha and grasses have proven exceptional, as well as productive. We can soon house the animals. The methane from the tanks can provide the gas for everything you want it piped to. The remaining waste can be used for nutrients for future planting. The bio waste from the people can be used as well and the water purifiers are in place now."

"What about the workshops Dirk? Has the waste from there been piped in?"

"Yes sir and it's a go."

Things are falling into order. The place was coming together well. The air filters would have to be cleaned and monitored. If the air was going out all the time, nothing could get in, but the outside air would still need to be monitored for radioactivity, he thought "Thank you Dirk."

Dirk looked up "When are you expecting the animals, sir?"

"Soon, soon, just a few more things then the trial runs. Outer space look out, we are almost out there. If this works, we can travel to distant planets my friend." He hated lying to them, but what other way would it be believable?

Simion headed to the library. "Andy my friend how goes it?" he asked.

Andy peered up from the books he was working on. "Well sir, all the people here is registered. It will be a great honour to be in this book of construction."

"Be sure all the members' families are there. Without the women and children here, the men couldn't get the work done. Make sure the women that are technicians are also named in there with the men. List them in order of status not gender."

"Already done," Andy replied.

"Thank you my good man," Simion added as he left the library and headed to the workshops.

Dee was there with her work clothes covered with sawdust. She was one of the best carpenters he had ever seen. She had a flare for design. He watched as she smoothed the wood with a sander, then stopped and felt the texture with her hand as if she was touching some delicate flower petal. She stopped and turned towards him. The bright smile told him she was pleased with her project.

"Hi there Sim," Dee beamed.

"Hi Dee, are you making any progress?

"Yes indeed," she replied. "Im just putting the finishing touches on the living quarters, might as well get the feeling of home in here. All this stone in here doesn't have the homey feeling that a few sticks of furniture can get you." "Hey Sim, why are you flying all this wood in with all the wood there is in the valley?"

"Now Dee, where would the bears sleep if we used up their forest?"

"Point taken," she smiled.

Simion went down to the labs. This was his domain. This is where it all would be held together. He had doctors and a full medical centre set up. He had a library full of medical books. They would be the teachers for the next generation. It never hurts to have the doctors ranging in ages. He had the cream of the crop, the best of the best. Things are almost ready. It would be here in the science study tunnel that any problems would be solved and he felt at ease here. He could think without the buzz of the activities going on around in the tunnels. He was thinking of the monorail of some sort driven magnetically, pure, clean and possible. The tunnels one day would be a honeycomb in this mountain. It would be too far to walk.

Just then, Zack strolled in. "Hey Sim, look at what I found here in your own kitchens."

Simion looked up and before him were two glasses and a chilled bottle of wine. Zack poured out two glasses and held one to Simion. He took the wine and Zack proposed a toast. "To all here and a project worthy of mankind completed."

Simion tapped Zack's glass and Drank. "So Zack are you staying on for the trial run? I could use you here."

Zack stared at him "Why not? He said? It's been a good project might as well see it through to the end. With all the construction near completion, I wasn't sure you wanted me to stay."

"Zack my dear friend, without you it never would have gotten this far." They tapped their glasses and proceeded to finish the bottle. About halfway through the bottle, Zack looked at Simion and said "So what got you started here? Was it a military project or government? You never did say."

Simion sat back in his chair. "Well, it's my project. I have paid for the works."

Zack couldn't believe his ears. He knew Simion was wealth, but this, this was immense and the cost must have been at least a billion or more.

Simion looked at Zack. "Come on, I want to show you something." Simion got up and headed out of the office and down a different tunnel.

Zack downed his glass of wine and soon was right behind Simion.

They soon entered the Communications room. Five people staffed it.

"Good evening Sir," Warren spoke.

Zack glanced around. There was a TV screen covering one wall. All had news bulletins and various battles going on all over the world. Zack for the first time realized there was far more to this project than just a case study on interplanetary travel.

Simion crossed his arms and then one hand reached up and ran his fingers through his hair. "Here we can see via satellite everything going on in the world."

Warren, status, please."

"The present talks in the east are going well. The west and east are at a stand still. The countries in the north have been developing nuclear power as were some smaller countries."

"Thanks Warren. Everything is still okay then?"

Simion turned to Zack. "You see my friend" he said as he turned and started walking down the hall, "it is my belief that the greed for oil and gold will soon drive one of these countries to start a war." "When this happens the world will fall into chaos."

Zack was kind of stunned. "Are you telling me the world on the verge of a nuclear war?

"I believe so Zack, yes I do believe so."

"So, this whole thing is a nuclear shelter then?"

"Something like that Zack, yes, something like that."

Zack stood looking at this man. He wasn't sure if he was losing it or if he was telling the truth.

"I would appreciate it if you kept this to yourself Zack. I can trust you in this?"

Zack was still not sure what to think, but he agreed. He pondered what he had just been told and though, Well, Simion could do what he wanted with his money. People had been predicting doomsday for ever. Simion was still a good guy and his money was as good as anyone's. It paid the bills.

Simion looked up and said "I have a few things to do. I will talk to you later." He walked down the tunnel and entered his office again. Before closing the door, Zack heard him say "Get my wife on the line please" and the door closed.

Zack wasn't sure what to think about what was going on here for real. He had agreed to keep quiet and headed to the carpentry tunnel.

Dee, as usual, was looking over some plans. Zack loved how her brow furrowed when she was designing something. She was charming. He loved her matter her fact ways and how she called a spade a spade. It was refreshing to have a woman so straightforward. She had deep green eyes and auburn hair. It was shoulder length and bounced a little when she walked. Her slim figure was always concealed in her coveralls and steel-toed sneakers.

He walked up behind her and slowly encased her in his arms.

With a start, she turned and that bright smile Zack so enjoyed beamed at him. He kissed and he felt her melting. Oh, how he loved her and knew she loved him.

"You know relationships between co-workers are not in the best taste?" she whispered. He laughed and she did too. Then out of the blue, she looked at him and said "we need to get married and the sooner the better."

He stood there holding her close when he realized what she was saying. He hugged her tight and lifted her a few inches off the ground. He said "I love you."

"I guess it's I love you too" she smiled. In her mind somewhere it was a relief. She wanted what was happening. "Let's keep this quiet" she said to Zack and smiled. "Whatever you want my woodcarver." They laughed.

"Why don't you go get some rest," Dee said to Zack? "I have to figure this out and you look like you need some."

Zack kissed her on the cheek and headed out the door.

Boy, this was the day for things to happen, Simion first and now Dee. With all these secrets, I think I need another drink.

Zack headed to the kitchen. He had some brandy there and he could use one.

Down two more tunnels and he was there. He rounded the corner and there sat Simion. He was drinking coffee and talking with the head cook about the amount of stores in the back. Paula assured him everything was in order and he sat back down looking at the papers before him. Zack could see the strain.

"Zack", Simion said, "Come look at this will you?"

Zack sat down across from him and glanced at the paper work. "What do you think?" "How long to build this do you think?" "Well, three weeks at least, if we have to excavate more tunnels." "No, no, no we can build it here. This is still all open." Zack had to agree it was a better spot closer to the living area. "I want people to have the ability to do whatever crafts, hobbies they wish."

Simion thought of everything. Zack couldn't believe he was so devoted to this. Maybe he knew something most of the rest did not.

Out of the blue, Simion said "Rainie is coming back thank goodness." "I don't like her flittering here and there." "She wastes her time so much." "With so much to do, she still wants to play. "Well" Zack said, "She is younger than you Simion and women will be women."

A smile crossed both their faces.

"Did you know that Rainie could sculpt and paint wonderfully Zack?" "She is amazing."

Zack couldn't see how this man could love her so much, but then to each their own. He asked Simion, "So when were you married?" "We've been married ten years now and it's the best move I ever made."

Zack didn't like Rainie much, but she wasn't his wife thank everything Holy.

Simion stared at Zack, "When are you going to bite the bullet and get yourself a wife?" "Actually, there is someone and we are going to get married as soon as we can. Speaking of which, Simion, I need to have a few weeks off."

Simion looked at Zack "Do I know this lucky lady?" Zack smiled, "Well, here's a secret for you. It's Dee and we need to get married as soon as possible."

Simion laughed, "You and Dee, that's grand. You have picked a wonderful person. She's a doll. I like her," Simion said.

"How come you need to get married?" Before the words left his mouth the realization hit him. "Well, well, well" he said. "I think I understand. You two come to my office in the morning."

Zack's mouth fell open. He wasn't sure if he should have told him. Before Zack could say anything, Simion got up and said "See you two in the morning."

Zack thought, well I guess its walking paper time. How is he going to tell Dee? She asked him to keep it quiet, because she lover her job here.

He did need that drink.

Zack headed for the living quarters, he had to talk to Dee. She was going to be furious. I just best tell her and be done with it. If they had to go, his parent's farm would be a good place until they could get something better. Dad was getting up in years and mom was not that spry anymore. They wanted him home for sometime now. The farm was great; peaceful and quiet. I wonder if it still had the old phone line or if mom had upgraded to cell phones yet?

It was at this time he arrived at Dee's dorm. Tap, tap "Dee, Dee" he said. "Doors open Zack come in". "I was just ready to jump into the shower. Pour yourself a drink and make me one too. I think there is some Mango juice in the fridge, Hun." With that Dee turned on the shower.

Zack poured two drinks of juice and moved to the table. How do I tell her He thought as he got up; running his hands over his head? He paced while Dee showered.

The water turned off. Dee said "Did you get some time off?" "What did Sim say?" "Was he ticked off about you leaving?" "I'll see him tomorrow. I ran late tonight, got a wall unit for the school I want to finish."

Dee stepped out of the shower room, towel drying her hair and wearing a purple fuzzy wrap. "Dee, sit down please" Zack said. From the look on Zack's face, she said "What's wrong?" "Simion want us both in his office in the morning. I kinda, well sort of...told him, Dee. It just slipped out. I'm sorry."

Dee looked at Zack. "Well, she said, to the office we go. If he fires us, it's not the only job in the world. We are great at what we do. I'm not worried, besides I will have to leave soon anyway. I didn't want to work full time till the baby comes."

Zack knew now why he loved her. Relief spread over him. "I love you" he said and leaned over the table and kissed her.

"Ah, get out of here you; I'm calling it an early night. If Simion wants to fire me he is going to be firing a woman that's had a good night's beauty sleep."

They laughed.

"Ok sweetie, I'll pick you up at eight sharp." With that he clicked his heals and saluted. Dee threw a towel at him. "Go on with you then."

He opened the door and headed towards his office. Well that never hurt at all he thought smugly.

On arriving at his office he sat at his desk and gave out a sigh. If nothing else it had been a great project. Simion had been a great boss and he had found Dee; losses and gains.

He started thinking about what Simion said about the state of the world affairs. Simion was a brilliant man and his wealth had afforded him contacts the world over. Zack hadn't paid much mind of the news in the past few years. He had been too busy here. He yawned, maybe he should head to bed, and it's been a long day. He leaned back in his chair with his feet on his desk and drifted off to sleep.

Simion had been up for hours. Rainie was due to arrive at noon. He had a surprise for Zack and Dee as well. He stood up, ah yes I put it there he thought. It was a ring from his mother, just a small band and intricately carved. Rainie was not fond of his mother's jewellery, so why not give it to Zack for Dee? She would appreciate that he knew that.

Tap, tap on the door. "Come in" Simion said.

Zack and Dee walked in.

"Sit down" Simion said. "Simion" Zack started. Simion looked at him. "Before we get started here, I want to give you something." Zack stood, staring at him confused.

Simion opened a small ring box and gave it to Zack. "It was my mother's and I want you and Dee to have it. You will need to get married here. Did you know that I'm a justice of the peace Zack?" Simion beamed at Dee, "Ok, over here you two."

Simion read the vows and had the papers signed. When the ceremony was over, Simion brought out a tray with three glasses on it. After the toast to the bride and good health, long life, etc…they drank. To Dee's surprise it was apple juice. What a day. Married and still employed she thought. What will happen next?

Warren appeared at the door. "Zack, there is a message in the communications room for you. I hate to interrupt, but it's important." Zack looked at Dee, then at Simion. "I guess I had best see what it is."

Zack followed Warren to the communications room, "Here it is sir" Warren said. Zack read the following words. Come home, father is in a bad way. I don't believe he is long for this world, son. Please hurry, love mom. Zack couldn't believe his eyes. He sighed and thanked Warren. He then headed back to Simion's office.

When he arrived, Simion and Dee were laughing. Simion looked over and said "not bad news I hope?" Dee knew by the look on his face that something was wrong. "What is it?" Dee asked. "Yes what is it?" Simion asked.

"It's my father, he is in a bad way and my mother wants me to come home." "I'll start packing" Dee said. "No, no Dee, you stay here. It might be mother is over reacting."

Simion spoke up "Well Rainie is due shortly. You can go back out on the chopper that's bringing her in." "Fine, Simion, thank you." "Dee I need to speak to you, excuse us Simion please and thank you for everything. You are a good man." Simion smiled, "you get back here, and we need you."

"I will, I promise you that." He looked at his wife Dee. When he got out in the hallway, Zack looked at Dee. "It will be probably be ok, but if not I will send for you right away." Dee looked at him and replied "Ok, but let me know right away." She hugged him. "I have to pack, that chopper will be here in 30 minutes."

He was throwing his shaving gear into his bag as Dee watched. "Some wedding night for you" Zack said. "No worries" she replied. "You will be back soon, we are not eighteen years old and moonstruck you know." "Yes I know Dee, but it wasn't really how I thought it would be." "Variety is the spice of life" she said. It was just like Dee to be so cool and collected.

They were approaching the chopper pad. Zack looked into Dee's eyes and knew he would never love another like he loved her. He pulled her to him and kissed her.

"Simmy, Simmy" Rainie stopped in her tracks and looked at Zack and Dee. "Well, well" she said as she passed. Simion met her at the door and they went inside.

"Come on Sir, we've got to go, a storm is moving in and we have a four hour flight ahead of us."

Zack threw his bags in and kissed Dee one more time. She turned and walked into the complex. Dee was not a wishy washy, but she did think she got a bit ripped off on her wedding day.

She walked down the hall, Simion, who had been talking to Rainie, told her to hold up. "Minute dear" Simion said to Rainie. Simion walked over to Dee and hugged her. "It's ok Sim" Dee said. "He will be back before we know it." Simion smiled and said "yes he will."

Rainie stood there looking, what's going on here? One skiing trip and she moves in on the men she thought. "Simmy, are you leaving me standing here all night?" "No dear, not at all" he replied. "You go rest Dee, we will talk later." Dee nodded and headed for her dorm. "Well finally I have your undivided attention" Rainie said. Simion smiled "You must tell me what's been going on around here." "Let's get some lunch" and at that the bell rang. "It's good to have you home dear" Simion said and kissed her on the cheek. He tucked her arm under his and they headed to the lunch room.

The chopper pilot was right, the cloud cover was thick. Zack never paid much attention to the scenery, he always seemed to be reading something that was work related and now he had the chance to look, but the clouds were covering everything.

11

"You do much flying out here?" Zack asked the pilot. "Yes sir, a lot of heli-logging in this area; not much else. A few souls looking for remote fishing spots, but that's about it."

Zack sat back and let his thoughts drift. He started thinking about his dad, how happy he always was. Zack was a success although he never took to the farm his father was proud of him. Mother never seemed to mind, not much riled her. She was a rock, steadfast. Dee reminded him of her.

What a turn of events, things never seemed to stop amazing him. He thought of the baby; hope it's a girl and it looks just like Dee.

It wasn't long before the pilot said "we will be landing soon, sir." It was Simion's private landing strip and a jet was waiting to take him further. Then a three hour drive to his hometown and we will see how dad is.

The day passed and Zack finally arrived at Cambry. It was a small little town of no consequence. He left his rental car in the driveway and made his way to the house. He strolled through the door and no one was home. Mom must be with dad.

He went out to his car and grabbed his luggage and put it in the hall foyer. It was a long day, jet lag still got him. He went to the fridge, grabbed a cold soda and lay on the couch. It wasn't long before he was sleeping.

"Zack, Zack, dear Zack." Zack opened his eyes and there was his mom. He sat up, smiled and hugged her. ""How is dad" he asked? "Not doing well sweetie. I've been told to get his affairs in order" his mom told him; Zack sighed. Then this is it, dad was passing. He could feel the tears welling up inside, but he had to be strong for his mom. "We will go see him tomorrow" Zack agreed. He got up and said "Want some tea mom?" "That would be lovely dear, I'm so tired tonight. It's been a long day." Zack headed for the kitchen.

He wanted to tell his mother about Dee, but thought he would wait a few days. The next days would surely be a strain. He took the tea and they sat in the living room as mom talked of father's condition.

Zack and his mother spent the next day visiting father and getting things in order. He could see the strain it put on her as she spoke with lawyers, of course she would have to notify the friends and the few relatives of this. When she walked out of the post office after posting the mail to the ones who lived in York, Zack thought how pale and frail she had become. He had been gone too long he thought.

Zack helped her into the car and headed east to the farm. On their arrival, mom soon had the kettle on. Then it came, the phone call they were dreading. Mother answered and after a few moments he heard her say "Thank you for the call, yes I will be fine, my son is here with me."

Zack went to the kitchen and sat at the table with his mom. She wept softly. "It's done then" she said. "I'm glad he passed so quickly. I don't think I could have endured him to linger for a long time." They spoke little, both understanding each others pain. Finishing her tea, his mother said "I think I'll go lay down for a while." She went to her room and closed the door. Zack knew she needed to be alone.

He got up and went to the porch. Looking out over the farm he thought of Dee. I better fill her in on what's going on. He got out his cell phone and it wasn't long before Dee was on the other end. "Hi sweetie, are things going ok? Is father alright? Your mom?" she inquired. "Dee are you sitting down?" "Oh dear!" she said. "Go ahead Zack." "Well father passed away today, we will be having the funeral in three days." Dee said "I'll start packing." "No, no Dee you stay there, I'll be back soon." "I don't want you to come at the moment." "It's pretty hectic and I haven't even told mom about you yet." "With everything that's been going on I couldn't just blurt it out." "I will miss and love you." "I love you too Zack, I guess I could make the school furniture while you are gone." Zack smiled "Dee, never mind I will call soon. I love you." "Love you too. Bye, Bye."

Zack wondered if she would like it here. He never cared for the farm. Not enough to do, other than just work, but then Dee would make home happy wherever it was.

He was now strolling around the farm. Father had sold most of the animals. They only had a few chickens left. Mom loved her chickens. He smiled to himself. He spent the evening of the porch, thinking of the days he had spent here when he was young.

The next few days passed quickly and mom never had to cook anything. The neighbours and people from the church brought plenty. Zack was glad there were so many people coming and going, it kept his mind off the funeral.

"Tomorrow we bury him" mom said. Zack looked at her. "Tomorrow will be a long day" she said "and with the wake after." "Yes" was all Zack could say, there wasn't much too say and too much talk would just make them cry. So they just sat in quiet contemplation of things that had been and never would be again.

Zack had phoned Dee several times in the last week. She told him how Simion had the place busy as ever with all the animals and plants. They were just working out the last minute details before he started up full force. Simion had assured Zack that he still needed him, but told him to take his time.

The funeral went well and his dad was laid to rest. Zack had fears of them dropping the casket. Thank goodness nothing happened for mom's sake.

The wake was hectic, full of old stories and the good times they all shared. After the last person left, mom closed the door, went to her chair and cried her heart out. After an hour or two, Zack wasn't sure how long, she went to bed.

Zack, alone now did his crying, being quiet so as not to disturb his mom. He lay there for hours before sleep finally took hold.

Zack was up late, his mom was up early and they sat at the table not saying much. "The farm is yours now" she said. Zack told her "No it's yours." "So you are leaving again?" she said. "Mom I need to talk to you, but it just didn't seem like the right time." "What is it Zack?" she replied. "Well I'm married." He said. "Married, my goodness Zack, why didn't you tell me?"

It was then the phone rang. "Is your mother there?" the voice said. "Yes, yes, I will get her, one moment please." "Yes," "yes," "yes," "we are feeling fine," "Ok thank you Frank." Mother hung up the phone. "Oh my, it seems there is a flu epidemic, lots of folks are sick. Gee, when it rains it pours."

The phone rang again; it was Zack's cell this time. "Zack it's me Simion, you had better get to the TV and see what's going on. Some things are not right" he said. "People are getting sick, seems its world wide." Zack said to Simion "do me a favour and keep her there with you my friend." "Sure, no problem, but you better get back here soon Zack." "I don't like what's going on" Simion said. "Yes, I just need a couple more days. I have to get my mother to town, she will probably be better off there." "Right, call me and keep me informed, my good man" Simion replied "Sure will." "Don't waste too much time Zack."

Zack wasn't sure what to do. "Mother, that was my boss, he seems to think this is more than just a flu epidemic." "Who has a TV around here?" Mother thought for a moment "that would be Hazel, the third farm on the right." "Let me get my purse."

It wasn't long before they were at Hazel's and she was more than glad to have company. She had been a widow for many years now. "Hazel" mom said "We need to watch your TV for a while." Hazel just looked at them and said "Sure, come into the living room."

Zack turned it on and went through the channels until he found the news broadcast. "This is SKTS news broadcast." "People are being advised to stay in their homes." "It appears we are having a nation wide pandemic going on." "Do not go to the city." "Only go to seek medical help." "The military has been called out to keep the riots under control." "Please stay at home." "If you the flu like symptoms, only then seek medical help." "We will update this bulletin in one hour."

Zack cell phone rang again, it was Dee. "Simion closed up the project." "He has told everyone if they wished to go, now is the time." "I want to come to you Zack" she was crying. "Oh my God, no Dee, stay there." "You will be safe there." "I'll get back to you as soon as I can." "I just have to get mom closer to town." "Oh Zack I want to be with you" she cried more. "It's ok Dee you stay where you are."

It was then his mother said in a loud voice "You listen to him; this is your mother talking." "Did you hear her Dee?" "Yes, yes" she said still weeping. "I'll be back soon" he told her and "Hugs too" he said as he heard the click of the phone.

Hazel, mom and Zack sat on the couch. "My goodness, what is happening in the world?" Hazel said "It's just like after the wars, we had many sick then too." "Yes that's the truth" Zack's mom said. "They said to stay home, guess that may help not spread it more."

"Oh my goodness, Freda said Hazel, how unkind, I'm sorry for your loss." Zack's mom smiled slightly at Hazel "Thank you lets make some tea."

The two women headed for the kitchen. Hazel looked at Zack "Are you going to look at that idiot box all day?" Zack smiled "yeah, I want to see the next bulletin." "I will bring you some tea," Zack nodded.

The hour passed and the next bulletin was worse than the first. People in the big cities were panicking. There were riots and now it seemed that the whole world had out breaks. The scientists were working around the clock.

Zack, Freda and Hazel stood in the living room, stunned. Hazel spoke first "good God, what's the matter with people? All that crazy business will not help." "They are afraid" Freda said. "Folks get crazy when they are afraid."

Zack was stunned, he knew there was more to this than they knew. The two old women had no idea what really was going on. It was Cambry, all the cities, major cities in all the countries. This was not just a simple flu outbreak.

Zack got on the phone, "Simion, my God, what's going on?" Simion replied "They did it, they finally did it. It's a virus, man made. They let is loose." "Zack are you sick?" "No, no, not yet" Zack said. "Then get masks, this is going to be bad, really bad." "Any idea what might help?" Zack asked. "As far as we can tell, it's attacking everyone, only some are not affected. Not sure yet, but will keep you informed." "Thanks" Zack said. "Get back here" Simion said. "I have to get my mom safe." "Zack, don't wait too long, it's getting worse. I'll keep in touch."

Zack looked at the two women in the kitchen, and couldn't believe what was happening. He just couldn't leave them. He wanted to get back to Dee, to safety. This was turning really bad.

"Mom, we have to go" he said abruptly. Hazel looked at Freda, "Ok, ok let's go home." Freda said "Thank you Hazel, I'll call you tomorrow." He knew his mom had no idea what was going on. How would she? Oh, my God, he thought.

Zack was driving back to the farm too fast and his mom made him slow down. "Zack just what do you think you can do today? This day's half over." Zack looked at her "We are leaving as soon as we pack." His mom just looked at him. She chose not to argue in the car, but when they get home she thought.

It wasn't long before Zack pulled into the farm. He helped his mom out of the car and they made their way to the house.

Once inside Zack started to get his things together. "I'm not going," his mother said. "What, what did you say?" "I'm not going anywhere" she replied. "Mom there is a virus loose out there and it's killing people" Zack said. "I'm not going" she announced again. "Look mom, maybe you don't understand, we have to leave." "We can go to where I work its safe there." Zack I'm not going. The TV said stay put. Do you think for one minute that they would say that if they want people travelling, passing it to others?" "Everything I know is here; I'm not going to run away because of that flu bug. We worked hard to build this place. I'm not going to run; besides I'm too old and tired."

Zack was beside himself with frustration. How could he make her understand? "Well we will talk in the morning, it will be alright" she told him and closed the door to her room.

Zack could have screamed with frustration. He pulled out his cell phone. "Argh", the batteries were dead. He went to his mom's phone, picked up the receiver and thought, maybe she was right. What could they do tonight, really?

He sat down. How did things get so out of order? He was so happy, Dee, and now the baby. He still wished for a girl, then dad and now this. I need a drink; there was just cola, water and tea. Pick one he thought.

He grabbed a cola and headed for the porch for some fresh air. What was he doing? Simion said, get a mask. He needed a list. He had to try and get some masks, batteries and gas. He had to phone Simion. He would have to send the jet and chopper. He lingered over the list. What would mom need? By now it was late and tomorrow was going to be tough.

He woke to the telephone. His mom answered, "Yes", "Oh dear", "Yes, now Hazel, I'll be right there."

"Zack" she said, noting that he was awake. "That was Hazel. Drive me over there would you?" "Mom we have to pack, we need to go." "You are driving me to Hazel's. I don't want to hear another word."

She grabbed her shawl and purse and was already at the door. Zack thought, I will get what we need from town, while she is there. Then we are going he thought no more excuses.

Zack pulled in the drive and stopped the car. "I'm running into town while you are here." "No" she said. "What" Zack replied? "No, come in."

Zack turned off the car. His mom was already on her way in. She never knocked, just walked in. There inside was Hazel. She sat in a chair by the phone. "Zack, make some tea please" his mom said.

As he passed, he knew Hazel was sick. After an hour or so, Freda had convinced Hazel to go to the hospital. Zack helped her get into the car. Zack was scared; he didn't want to touch her. She had the virus. This was getting worse by the minute.

"For crying out loud Zack, help me," his mom hollered at him. He did and they soon had her in the car and on their way to the small medical centre in Cambry.

"It's ok Hazel, I won't leave you" Freda assured her. She wasn't sure she could hear what she had said, but she pulled the blanket around Hazel; it will be ok, you'll see."

They had driven what seemed to be ages and finally arrived at the medical centre. It was pandemonium, there were sick people everywhere. All sick, Zack couldn't believe it. How could it spread so fast? He knew he was in trouble, big trouble. He sat there with his mom and Hazel, looking at the people.

"We have to leave mom, now." "I'm not leaving Zack." It was about then he realized that his mom was sick too. Good God, she had the virus too. He wanted to run, but he couldn't leave her.

He looked around and knew he was going to die. It seemed forever before a nurse finally came over to them. She said "I'm sorry, but there are no doctors available at present." Zack said "I beg your pardon. Where are they? Is this not a hospital?" The nurse looked at Zack and said "They are all sick, sir." She was looking at Hazel. "Oh dear", then she looked at Freda. "Please bring this woman" Zack looked at the nurse "but they both are sick." She looked at Zack "There is nothing we can do for this one." It was then Zack realized that Hazel was dead.

He picked up his mom and followed the nurse, there were people everywhere. The nurse stumbled, she almost fell. "Are you ok" Zack asked? "Put her here" and Zack laid his mom on a stretcher. He noted that the nurse did not look well. "Are you ok?" She looked up and said "I'm dying like the rest, the doctors are gone and there is no one to help."

"Is this woman a relative?" "Yes, she is my mom." "She is passing, I'm sorry; there is nothing I can do." She started to leave. Zack grabbed her arm, where are you going" he demanded? "Just here" she said and sat down and closed her eyes. "You best talk to her, she hasn't long."

Zack was horrified. He couldn't leave his mom as she lay dying. He stood beside her for the longest time. She never spoke, she never opened her eyes again; she just died.

He wasn't sure how long he stood there, but when he turned to the nurse, she was dead. He had to get out here. He lovingly wrapped his mom in the blankets. He headed to the door and stumbled over the people coming in. He made his way to the parking lot and placed his mom's body in the back seat. He got into the car and regrouped. He said to himself, ok I have to get to Dee. There is nothing left here now. He needed to call her, pay phone, batteries and gas.

The town looked deserted as he pulled out of the parking lot. He saw the most horrible sights. They were putting bodies outside. He couldn't see how many but, it was rows and rows. My God he thought. His hands were shaking as he drove through the deserted streets.

He needed a phone, every pay phone was damaged or not working. He knew he needed gas, but the line-ups at the pumps were crazy. The people were sitting outside their cars yelling and screaming, some looked dead. Most of the stores were cleaned out. Windows were broken. The one and only police car he saw was just sitting, lights flashing and the officer looked dead on the ground. He needed to get out of here and back to the farm. Gas, he would have to have gas, maybe batteries.

He started to head out of town. It was then he saw a young woman running and two men chasing her. He pulled passed the men to her and frantically motioned to her to get in the car. She did, while the car was still moving. She was shaking, "they took my car and they took everything." She started to sob. "I just wanted some gas. I would have paid." "Calm down" Zack said. So much for that idea he thought.

Zack reached into the back seat and grabbed his mother's shawl. "Here, wrap up, it will make you feel better." "Are you going to die like the others" she said? It was a plea for help and he could not do anything. "I have no idea and by the way I'm Zack." "Hi" she said, "I'm Jo Ann, my friends call me Jo." Zack smiled, "Jo it is." "We need gas soon or we will be walking, any ideas Jo?" "We can try another farm" she said. "I just got a bad one and you are here now." Zack had to give her credit; she didn't want to give up.

"Well my folks have a farm about an hour away; at this point Im not sure what to do." "There, there, let's try that one" she said and Zack pulled down the drive. This time they were lucky, it had a gas tank. He pulled up and noted money on the ground by the tank. "Hello, hello, is there anyone here?

Zack saw a small house and started towards it. "That's far enough" he heard. He stopped in his tracks. "I need some gas" Zack said. "Well, it's over there, leave the money on the ground." "Don't come back up here or I will blow you away." "No problem, no problem, I just want some gas." He back up all the way to the pump. He opened the gas cap and started to put in the gas. There wasn't much left, but he got some, it was better than none. He took out his wallet and added his twenty to the money on the ground. "Your tank is empty now" Zack yelled and made his way to the driver's seat. It didn't take long to turn around and soon they were on the road again.

"We have half a tank that will get us to my farm" he said. He looked over to Jo, she seemed lost. She had red hair and he thought she was fairly tall; not all that slim, maybe she worked, he thought.

It was Jo who spoke next, "Are we going to die like all the rest?" Zack hadn't really believed he was going to live, but she was right. They weren't sick yet and enough people around them had died already. What was going on? He had to get to a phone. "I don't know Jo, I really don't know." "Thanks for saving me" Jo told him. "The only consolation I have for those two men is that they looked sick too." Zack thought how cold that sounded, but it was the truth down to the bone. They were considered the dregs of society. Society, what society? At the rate people were dying was there going to be a society when the smoke cleared?

"Jo, how many folks did you see that were not sick?" Zack asked her. "Two, maybe three in the past day", "that includes you" Jo replied. "Do you feel sick too?" "No, no, not at all, just maybe sick and tired of being afraid." Zack could understand that. He was afraid, terrified was more like it.

The farm was in sight and relief fell over Zack as they got closer. He pulled up the drive. "I need a phone." He ran in and picked up the receiver. The line was dead. After a few moments he realized that there were no operators to connect them. My God, it has spread that far. He hung up the receiver and started rummaging through the drawers, looking for batteries.

Jo, by this time was standing in the doorway, looking, watching him. "What are you looking for?" "Batteries, just some darn batteries" he said. "She lived out here with dad all this time and have no batteries." Jo could see the strain was getting to him. "Sit down please, sit down" Zack said. "Maybe some tea or something might help and then we can look together."

Zack sat and looked out the kitchen window. He was going to go crazy, he thought. Jo, talking in the background was just there; he never heard words, just the sound of her voice. Zack wasn't a quitter, at work, if the problem seemed too big; he always found avenues around them. He had to do that now; he had to think of a way back to Dee. It was life.

Just then he noticed mother's chickens, they were dead too. What had they done with this virus? Had they not thought it through? They have killed off the world. Simion was right, he knew it all along. The masses were just fodder for the powerful, he thought.

"Zack, Zack did you hear me?" Jo said. "No, what did you say?" Zack replied. She stood her hands on her hips "Look, we have to get something together here." "It seems to me we have to think of somewhere to go." "There are a lot of folks that have to be left, don't you think?" "There must be somewhere they are gathering." "Look Zack, we are not sick. There must be others in the same boat."

"Sit down here Jo; I want to talk to you." Zack began with the story of Simion building the station. He related to her most of the things going on there. After that he began to tell her what he thought would happen next. "People will be moving from the cities and will take what they want along the way. Of course, if there are any people left. There probably will be survivors as they were still alive. In my best judgement, I feel we should start making our way there. A question I have at this point is where are some stupid batteries so I can call there?" She laughed and he smiled.

"Ok, a systematic search is my suggestion" Jo replies. "Right" Zack said. After searching for an hour, Zack said "This is useless, there isn't any here." "Ok" Jo piped up. "Then we have to get some kind of survival pack going." Zack had been placing items on the table: a flashlight, a compass, several maps, a first aid kit and other things. "Your powers of deduction are great" Zack smiled "We need some better clothes and bed rolls." "Just remember what we will probably have to carry what we have. The gas is almost out in the car." "Right, Oh!" Jo replied. Jo was in the cupboards now looking for food, light, easy to carry and nutritious. Can goods were out, but a few to start would help.

By evening they had accumulated almost everything they might need.

Zack was studying the old road maps. He tried to remember the maps Simion had shown him. What he could remember seeing, from the plane and chopper. From here he was sure it was at least 800 miles west and 400 miles north. The mountains all looked the same. Simion's maps were topographical, not regular ones like these. He stared for a long time, looking for what he saw on Simion's maps that day.

Jo finally said "Zack get some rest, tomorrow will be a long day." "Yeah, you're right. You rest too Jo." Then Jo said "You won't leave me, will you Zack?" "I, well, you won't leave me until we get to our folks?" Zack looked at her and said "Jo, it's Ok, I won't leave you." He smiled and they settled in for the night.

Jo took his mom and dad's room. Zack knew he had to bury his mom. He headed outside and dug her grave. He carefully placed her into the ground and cover her over. This was the end of everything he had known.

Chapter 2

$\mathcal{S}$imion had his hands full; he was in constant contact with Warren. The reports of the complex kept him sorting through the continual files on his computer. He would have to let everyone know the seriousness of the events outside.

All chose to remain after the broadcast; many feared returning to the outside. Simion knew that there was enough work to keep their minds occupied. Still he felt sorry for the ones out there.

Warren stepped in to Simion's office and said "You better come and see this."

Simion made into the next room. Simion glanced at the screens, some just static and others reporting massive deaths or pleading for help.

Warren looked at Simion "Four more screens down, mean the cities are falling fast." "I'm surprised we still have these few, with mass power outages everywhere out there shutting down. Simion looked at Warren "They won't last long. I fear there won't be enough people left to operate anything." Thank you Warren" and Simion returned to his desk.

Simion thought of Zack. What a shame, he should have contacted them by now. Dee would be asking about him and he had nothing to tell her. How unfair this was for her. He couldn't even say if he was alive.

It was Rainie that appeared next, "Simmy", she cooed. Simion's patience was near its end with her. Since he closed the complex, she had pestered him continually. "Rainie please, I have so much work to do." "Work, work, work" she was yelling. "That's all you do, you never want to have any fun."

That was it; Simion stood up, walked over and grabbed her arm. He half dragged her to the communications room, "Look here" he dragged her to the screens. "You see that one and this one?" "Look at this one, Rainie, doesn't it look like fun they are having?"

Rainie looked at the pile of bodies; the panicked newsmen; the riots. She tried to look away, but Simion held her there.

He finally pulled her through his office and into the complex. He waved his arm across the room. "This is it, this or that, Pick one."

She just stood and started to cry. Simion took a couple breaths and drew her into his arms. She was such a child for being such a woman. She sobbed "I'm sorry, I will be an asset Simmy, really I will." "Rainie you must stand with me. You must help me, because you my dear are all I have. Do you understand?" She just hugged him, "Yes Simmy, I do now" and sobbed more.

Simion gave her a few moments he could and said "Rain, I need to get back to work." "Alright Simmy, I'll be in our dorm." She almost ran as she walked on her way there.

Simion berated himself. He sort of let the people believe it wasn't as bad as it was. He was going to have to tell them the complete truth. He returned to his office.

Rainie was in their dorm now, crying her heart out. She felt so sorry for herself. Everything she was and dreamed of was gone. Her friends, her family were all gone she thought. All but Simmy and now he hated her as well.

It was her parents almost last wish she marry him. He was older, but wealthy and at that time, she thought it was just as easy to love a rich man, as one with less money. She had grown up having just about what ever she wanted. Her parents were sixty when she was twenty, by the time she was thirty they had both passed away. Now here she was thirty-three and what did she have? She cried more. What good was the complex anyways? They would die too, she thought after seeing the screens.

Soon she had cried herself out and headed for a bath. She filled her tub and climbed in. What was going to happen? She was a fraud. She had never really worked. Well, she said to herself, she would show them, show Simion that she was a woman of quality if she had to lose everything. She would make them respect her yet.

Just then she felt so foolish. She had embarrassed herself in front of Simion and Warren, the others as well. How could she ever save face? She started to weep again. Everything had been such a game for her and cold, hard reality was terrifying. Life could be such a cruel task master and she had just a taste of it.

Dee was always busy and busy she planned on staying. No word from Zack, well she knew he would make it back. If he was gone she would know it. She knew he was alive and on his way home. He would find a way, she knew that as well.

Dirk had sent her requests for the things in the animal shelter, as had Karen for the Aggro center. The school always needed things as well as personnel dorm items folks wanted. Work was the best therapy, she told herself. Even at night when she was alone, she patted her belly and told her and Zack's child, he would be home soon.

The complex was running smoothly considering what was going on, emotionally for everyone. Most were well educated and realized this was their best bet. The labourers and their families probably had the best deal. Most had always had had to work hard, not having education or the privileges of most of the people in charge.

Simion had decided to get on with the truth. It seemed now, as only two screens were still televising on the last reports. It was time to let the people in the complex know.

He called a general assembly. Almost everyone was there. He started out by telling them the basic truth of the virus and the catastrophe that had befallen them all. When it was clear to him that the world outside as they had known it was gone. He proposed the advantages of the complex. Through here, they could find the cure and in the future rejoin the ones outside. He noted that his teams, correction, our teams of researchers would continue on. He was now the owner of the complex that it would belong to them all and a committee would be set up to handle most major decisions. Their voice would be the voice of the complex. Without the extreme efforts of them all, the complex would not survive. A cheer went up for him. Simion thanked them all and returned to his office.

Warren was waiting for him when he got there. "The last of the screens have gone blank" he told Simion. "Well, keep trying for anything Warren. There are people out there, let's find them." Warren nodded "Yes sir."

Simion wanted to see Dee. He just wanted to keep her informed. He wished Zack had called. He was beginning to think the worst. Dee was going to have the first baby born here, the beginning of the complex's future. He wanted to talk to Rainie too, she needed to start helping out and there would be no slackers. Everyone was going to work for the good of all. Simion knew Rainie had talents and felt she spent far too much time expecting others on her.

He reached their dorm and Rainie was sitting at her desk. "Hi Simmy, come here" she said. "I have been working on something and I want you to see what you think." "I have been thinking about a lot of things and I think I have come up with something that might boost moral some" she smiled at Simion.

He walked over to see what she was doing. "You see this is the area for the community living, I think I could make statues that represent each family there." He glanced at the sketch "My dear that's a massive project and your talents might be used elsewhere to more advantage." "It does have merit though and it would give people a great sense of belonging." "Well, if I was needed elsewhere I would go. I thought the masons and any other of the younger people might want to learn to sculpt."

Simion picked up the sketch "you might just have something here Rain; this is more like the woman I know." "I could present it to the new committee, if you like?" said Rainie. Simion smiled "You never cease to amaze me." He kissed her forehead. "I must go see Dee. There's still no work from Zack. I'm beginning to think he has not made it."

Dee was always busy. She ran the carpentry tunnel like she did her equipment, with confidence and authority. Dee saw him coming. She flipped her eye protection and slid down her face mask. "What's up Sim?" she smiled. "Just wanted to tell you there's no word from Zack yet," Simion said. "No worries Sim, he'll call and find a way back" Dee replied. Simion raised an eyebrow "Dee, I'm concerned" he said. Dee just looked at him and said "He will call." Simion wasn't going to push the point. He smiled "If anyone could make it, it would be Zack." He smiled and headed for his dorm.

He stopped and looked back at Dee. She was already adjusting her face mask and pulling down her eye protectors. He turned and continued to his dorm.

"Zack, where are you? Why did he not phone, he had a cell phone. Simion feared still the worst.

Zack and Jo had enough gear together to begin their move west. The half a tank of gas left in the car, Zack knew he must find more.

As he was driving out of the driveway he looked into the rear view mirror and murmured "Good bye mom." On that statement they were on their way.

Zack figured on taking the back roads, they would be safer. The main roads may have hoodlums making trouble. He didn't want to mess with that. They stopped at any farm they could and finally late in the afternoon, they found one empty.

While looking for anything useful, Jo piped up and said "Bob's your uncle." Zack stared at her as she waved two batteries she had found at him. He couldn't believe it. "Woo hoo" he yelled as he fumbled them into his phone.

He dialled and with what seemed and eternity Warren answered. Warren, Warren it's me Zack. I'm on my way back; I'm on my way back." Just then the phone's low battery red light came on. "Warren old man, tell Simion and Dee, I'm on my way back." He heard "Yes sir," and the phone went dead.

He sat down and sighed "Well, at least they knew I'm alive." He would find more batteries. Then Simion could give him more coordinates to follow.

Jo by now had finished the search and said "Let's go Zack; this place gives me the creeps." He agreed "We need to find more gas as we are running on fumes."

Back on the road and not long after the car's engine stopped and the car rolled to a stop. He looked at Jo "We are on foot now." He could see the mountains now in the distance.

They unloaded the car with everything they could carry and started walking. Zack had to admit he felt a lot safer in the car, but there was nothing he could do about it. They walked for the rest of the day, taking short breaks.

Jo spoke up, "I've had enough let's make camp." Zack's shoulders were killing him and his feet were blistered. He agreed, but said to Jo "No fire, ok? I don't want any uninvited guests." Jo agreed.

Zack thought they would need to find water tomorrow and they ate from the few canned goods they brought. The only consultation in the meal was tomorrow the packs would be lighter. They didn't talk much after the trials of the last two days; both were content in their own thoughts.

Jo woke to Zack studying the maps. He still couldn't make out where the valley Simion had chosen was. He calculated in the jet and chopper rides, but still nothing looked familiar.

Zack handed Jo a choice of beans or peaches, she took the beans. He also gave her the first aid kit so she could treat her blisters. "We'll try to make it to the mountains. I think it's roughly forty miles" Zack said. Jo never said much. If this guy knew of someplace safe, she was going too. She wouldn't give him any reason to leave her behind.

They had walked through the morning until about two in the afternoon and then they saw a small group of people. Zack wanted to avoid them, but Jo thought there was something odd about them. It was not long before she replied "Oh my God, Zack, its children, there were four children there." Zack sighed. What he wanted now was to make time. This was going to slow them down, big time, but he just couldn't leave them wandering. His thoughts went to Dee and his visual of her nicely rounded with child.

"Zack" Jo said which brought him back to reality. "What are we going to do, we just can't leave them." "I know, I know" he replied. It was Jo that approached them. They were dirty and tired. It wasn't long and with the mention of food, they were with Zack. After making sure they understood, the food had to last, he gave Jo the last of the canned goods to them to share.

Nothing was going right Zack thought. At this rate he would never get to the complex.

After a while, the eldest of the four informed Zack and Jo they were headed for their auntie Helen's home. She lived by the ocean. Their mom said she would love to have them come. Their mom and dad had gone to sleep and never woke. He was nine and the others were seven, six and five years old.

MY God Zack thought, there must be others that they might find to take them.

He took Jo aside "Jo we can't pick up every straggler we meet. What will we do with them? We barely have enough for ourselves."

Jo looked back at Zack. "I realize that Zack, but what do we do, just leave them? They are alive; I can't turn my back and walk away. They have lost everything like us." Jo's temper was rising "Walk away if you want, I'm not going to leave them here." "Just hold on" Zack said. "I never said that, I just said we can't take everyone we meet along with us."

Jo looked at him. "I won't abandon them." Zack just said "No more, we have to look out for us, the six of us. It will be tough enough."

At night fall, they made camp. It was not far from a creek, the mountains were getting larger on the horizon to the west.

Jo made a pot of porridge for dinner. The children ate every bite and before bed, Jo washed them up. It wasn't long and the children were all sleeping.

Zack stayed up late this night. His mind wandered to Dee.

After the fire died down, Jo said to Zack "thank you for helping the children." Zack gave her a weak smile. He knew this was going to be a long journey, now with the children and whom ever else they may find; his chances of getting back started to get cut down.

Chapter 3

Warren by now informed Simion of Zack's call. Simion was happy to have heard from him. He sent Warren to tell Dee.

There was a problem in the small animal tunnels, so Simion headed down there. On the way he met Dirk, who explained that the amount of animals they had at present would soon be more than they could accommodate. It was Simion's idea to keep the people vegetarians as much as possible. Dirk showed Simion the progression on the computer. In twenty years there would be more animals than people. Simion smiled at Dirk, "I have a plan for the extra animals. Put your mind at rest Dirk."

Dirk asked if the food for the animals would continue as usual. Simion said that it would.

"Seems there will be new borns soon that will cut into our milk production" Dirk smiled. "I could use some help when they start birthing Simion, that's what I wanted to ask." Simion smiled "Dirk, you will get what help you need. Please never fear asking for help or things you require. We depend on you for so much." Dirk smiled "Thank you Simion."

"Might I suggest you look to the agro tunnels? They probably need some input on the amounts of feed you will need for your stock." With that Simion turned and headed back to his office.

Yes they needed a committee to handle this stuff. Simion knew this with every crisis, he would be called upon. He also knew he was just one man.

Dee was in her dorm when Warren caught up with her. "Dee, its Warren" he said as he knocked on her door. "Come in Warren," she replied. Warren relayed the message from Zack. He could see the relief on her face. "He will make it back, Dee; don't give up hope in him. He got this far." Tears were running down her face now, she couldn't contain them. "Thank you Warren."

Warren preferred Dee to Rainie, he thought as he made his way back to the communications office. He was going to spend the night trying to find any military instillations that might have bunkers. With the virus out there, they may have made it to one. Had Simion not closed the complex when he did, they too would have succumbed to it.

The doctors in the lab had found out it worked on everyone's DNA code. If you lack a certain tier on a segment, you got the virus and died. When the reports hit Simion's desk, he realized that a cure most likely was not possible.

Dirk wasted no time in getting to the aggro tunnels. He wanted his animals to have the best available food. Karen assured Dirk there would be ample food for them.

The smell of the plants in bloom, the vibrant colours and the hum of the bees were all heaven to Karen. She had brought flower seeds with her when she came. Simion might be a genius, but so many forget pleasure or joy, the simple beauty of a Daffodil or a crocus can bring. Karen lost herself in the growing of things. David, her husband often came to the tunnels to tell her to call it a night.

Since the disaster of the virus, Karen found some solace there. Dave often said she was more at home with plants than with people. She didn't mind him saying that because it was true.

David, her hearts desire was like a great oak tree in her life. He was strong, never wavering; giving her the steadfastness she needed.

Karen knew there was a danger of Ecolli with hydroponics growing, so she carefully monitored the water regularly. She was working on a pond for the common living area, with a small waterfall of some sort. Running water always made her feel mellow and she thought it might have a calming effect for others as well. It would bring some beauty to the place too she thought.

David was more interested in insects, so her relationship between her plants and him with his bugs drew them always closer. He had to keep enough bugs going for pollination as well as a food source for some of the song birds that Simion had agreed to welcome into the complex, not to mention the honey from the bees.

David and Karen had accepted what had happened in the world. After a few lengthy conversations they decided the future was on their thought list, although they were saddened to the core of their being by it. Life must go on; they were still alive and still wanted to live on. They worked hard together. The last vegetables of their world were here in the complex, without them they would die too.

Dirk was back with his animals. He was always a caretaker for them it seems. His whole life was wound around animals in some way. He had the care of his father's sheep and goats from such an early age. He didn't mind, he felt a kindred spirit for them. His wife Carla was forever nursing some poor creature that he managed find and bring home. She didn't mind, she loved them as well.

Dirk was always thinking of what could be of advantage for the complex, like the methane for the waste. He believed in recycling and reusing, a waste not, want not approach.

Carla agreed with Dirk on many things. She thought he was the most charming of men. She had studied to be a vet and it helped them in many situations. She never forgot the day they met. He brought in a lamb with a blockage, it was starving. After she corrected the problem she was amazed how he had convinced another ewe to adopt the lamb, after its mother died. She never would have thought of wrapping the new lamb in the skin of the dead lamb and thus convincing the ewe it was her own lamb.

Yes they were a pair. They had two children themselves and both boys had followed their examples. Chase spent as much time as he could with Dirk and Derek spent his time with her.

Noon and the lunch bell rang.

Paula had the kitchen running like a well oiled clock. Those that had not taken lunches to their station would be hungry. Paula was the best cook most had ever seen. She could make a salad or soufflé without skipping a beat. Most folks loved her grand sense of humour. She told one young man; be a good cook my mother said and you will get a man. What I did get was fifteen years of washing pots and cleaning grills. It wasn't true, Paula's husband, Eli was a good man. Folks liked him as much as they liked her.

It was surprising with just ten kitchen staff how Paula could cook for everyone in the complex.

Paula's family had been large, she was one of seven siblings and there had been many children from them all. It was painful for her to think how they were all now gone. Simion was a man of foresight she thought, but he could never know the sorrow she and so many felt. She was thankful she was here, but on the same vane felt such sadness for family and friends lost to her now.

She thought respectively now, maybe Simion did know. She just had no outlet for her grief and taking out on Simion wasn't fair. She had no right to believe he did not suffer as well as the rest. The more she thought, the more she felt sorry for him, just because he had no family didn't mean he couldn't understand. She reprimanded herself for being so thoughtless and walked back to the kitchen.

Eli, her husband was a machinist; his work kept him long hours in the tunnels. Sandra and Drew, their children spent as much time watching him at his work as they did at their school work. Eli didn't mind, he figured they were scared since the virus and he let them stay. He had to keep his family together. So much was lost and it was a shame. He worried for their future; would they ever make it outside or would the tunnels be all there ever would be.

He glanced at his children and pangs of sadness went through him. Tomorrow was another day he thought and went back to work. At least there was a tomorrow for them.

Simion, Rainie, Andy and Warren all sat at a table in the lunch room. Rainie was conversing with Andy on his work listing all the families in the complex. Her interest was a surprise to Andy.

Simion was taking to Warren and was disappoint with no contact with anyone from the outside world. Zack's message had been forwarded to Dee. Simion said "If he calls again find out where he is." Simion realized Zack would need help in finding the complex. Warren agreed.

After lunch Rainie and Andy headed for the library and Warren back to the communications room. Simion however needed a rest. He had been pushing himself to hard and was going to get a hot bath and a rest. He was going to relinquish some responsibility of the complex to others. He felt more at ease.

He made it to his dorm, poured a drink, sat in his favourite chair and thought about everything. He wondered if bottling all these people up in the complex was such a good idea. Things seemed okay at present, but he knew things could get easily out of hand as well. It was surprising that the end wasn't nuclear, but in a way this was worse. To be able to go out side again, they had to have the right genes. Clever jerks they must have been to have come up with that he thought.

Then he let his mind wander over all the events that had taken place and in his heart, he raged. He remembered the pleas for help, the piles of bodies and the riots. Although he had no family, but Rainie, he was so hurt. His way of coping was to keep working. Maybe, he thought it would be like anthraxes that lay dormant till disturbed. If after a long period of time they could return outside. He thought of Zack again. He must have the right genes, but the horror he must be seeing and what he was yet to see. Something told him that Zack would never make it back, but for Dee's sake he would hope. He would help in the labs; maybe he would see a solution the others did not. At that he went and drew his bath.

Chapter 4

$\mathcal{M}$orning was hectic with the children in tow. It took Jo a while to get them ready. Zack then would give them all jobs. Each carried a little bundle to ease Jo and Zack's weight some. They continued to the mountains, the silence was eerie with no birds' songs or bugs. Zack knew without bugs and bees, food would become scarcer.

It was Jo who spotted the farm house first. Zack's hopes lifted a bit as they made their way towards it. It was deserted like the others. Outside there were three graves.

Zack went to check out the barn before they went in. He found the owner, but wished he had not.

Jo and the children waited for the Ok from Zack, after going through the house, he called to them. There was plenty of food in the pantry and he asked Jo to feed everyone. He was going through the drawers and cupboards, taking anything of use, shirts for the children, aspirins, band aids and blankets.

He fitted the children with a pillow case. "You will have to help us carry now" he said. They never complained.

Jo found rice, puffed wheat, honey, elastic bands and salt. Zack was disappointed not to have found batteries, but the food had increased all their chances.

It wasn't long before they were on the move again. Jo was concerned about the children and told Zack "if you push them too hard they would loose more time if they had to be carried."

Zack knew she was right. After several breaks Zack called it a day, Jo and the kids plopped down. Zack began searching for some firewood and soon had a small fire going.

The children, wrapped in their blankets they salvaged from the house soon were eating a bowl of puffed wheat.

Zack sat watching for anything unusual out there and then also settled down. He thought of Dee, God he missed her.

They had travelled maybe ten miles today. It was going slow. Zack knew that everyday they held up, it reduced their chances. It was mid summer and with a long trek ahead, they had better move or winter would be on them.

The sun was going down and soon dark would overtake them.

Zack sat looking over this rag-tag group and thought we have to make it.

He woke to the youngest child as he snuggled next to him. After gently rolling away and covering the child with his blanket, he stood and walked out the kinks as he collected some wood.

It wasn't long before he had the fire going and the group was awake.

Jo fed the children, repacked and soon they were on the move again.

Zack's mind was on finding water again.

It was not quite noon when they came across another farm. As planned, Jo and the children would stay back as Zack investigated. Unlike the other farm, this one was not abandoned. There was an old man sitting on the porch.

"What do you want?" he called to Zack. "Just some water" Zack said. The old man pointed to the well.

Zack asked if there had been others by. The old man replied "Yes some." The old man further added "I told them to go north to the old fort about fifteen miles down the road." Zack's heart leaped. An old fort, there they would find people. Maybe there they could leave the children.

"Thank you sir" Zack said and made his way back to Jo and the children.

He relayed what the old man had told him and he could see the relief on her face. If they kept up the pace, they would make it there tomorrow mid day. He wondered why the old fellow stayed at the farm, but then why not he thought. He probably lived alone there for a long time. Zack couldn't help to think he was placing himself in danger, not everyone was like him.

The rest of the day passed uneventfully and when dusk fell it was a relief for all to rest.

Jo talked little since they found the children. She wondered if they would be safe at the fort. She said to Zack "he was pretty smart to send folks to the fort, with no power, etc... What a better place than the one the first settlers used." Zack agreed.

The fire was crackling and after a hot drink and some boiled rice, the children soon slept.

Jo asked Zack what he thought the amount of time they needed to get to the complex. The question set Zack back a bit. He thought she would stay at the fort too.

"Jo" Zack said, "I'm making my way back to my wife, you do realized that right?" Jo replied "yes Zack I know, but if this place is as you say, it seems to me a better bet then at the fort. Besides, I have nothing holding me anywhere now. Not likely I'll be a secretary or part time librarian anymore." Zack nodded, "this is true" he said. "Are you going to tell the people at the fort about the complex?" Jo asked. "No" Zack replied. "You see its set up for the folks there already. I can't go bringing who knows how many there. They haven't been exposed to the virus as well and for two or three to go in would be fine, but more would endanger them and I can't do that." Jo understood. "Get some sleep, a long day tomorrow" Zack said.

Morning came too soon and it was raining. They bundled up what they could and Jo gave each a garbage bag to wear. She found ball caps for the children at the last farm they were at and the garbage bags made good raincoats.

Zack pushed them on and they reached the fort by noon. There were about twenty people there. After a time, Zack found some young women there who had lost their children and were willing to take his foundlings.

Zack was amazed at how these people had been making the fort home and using everything there to help them survive.

Eager to go on, Zack realized he would be needing things before venturing further. He would need an axe and ropes to start.

The men bunked in one house; the women and children in another. Zack almost felt like he was going back in time. He traded with the other men for things he would need and Jo was doing the same with the women. She traded salt for some dried fruit and after some other trades she was off to find Zack.

They had made a big house their gathering place, a lot of commotion there, all presenting ideas of different things. Jo and Zack listened, but soon made their way back to their bunkhouses. Zack told Jo to meet him a 6 AM at the main gate and Jo agreed.

Zack wanted to study his maps and Jo wanted to rest.

Morning came too soon for Jo. Her shoulders and her back hurt, not to mention her feet. Oh her poor feet. She packed her belongings, a few women gave her a couple small items; a bar of soap, some safety pins, a hair clip, just some little things. Jo accepted them gladly.

She wanted to see the children before she left, just to put her mind at ease. She made her way to the other side of the fort and stopped. She had changed her mind. Let them go she told herself. Their road would be hard enough and getting attached to them would only cause them pain and to herself as well. She turned and went to meet Zack at the gate.

She knew this guy was going to find the complex and she wanted to go with him. Jo never told Zack that she saw him bury his mother at the farm It was a private moment for him; she silently buried her family there as well. She was glad to see him there ready to go. She sighed and thought, here we go.

Zack watched her approaching and was glad to have her company for the journey. She would do well at the complex he told himself. Simion would find her something to do, maybe with Andy in the library. "You ready Jo?" Zack asked. "Yeppers" she replied.

They started walking towards the mountains. They were getting closer; the prairies were turning to rolling hills. "How far are we planning to walk each day?" Jo asked. "I think it might be better if we set goals for distance" she added. "That's a good idea Jo" Zack answered. "For now the goal is to reach the mountains" he laughed and she joined his laughter.

They kept a steady pace and by noon they had covered a fair distance before stopping. Zack took off his pack, sat it down and sat on it. After a few gulps of water he told Jo "We should maybe stick to the river running through the mountains. We will probably make easier travelling." "We wouldn't have to search for water either" Jo added. Zack smiled.

As they walked, Zack kept a constant eye for other people and any animals that might be about. He knew the chickens had died, but all the other animals may have survived. Jo just kept on track trying to keep up.

When they stopped in the afternoon, Zack unloaded a few things from his pack and said "We'll make camp here." Jo could see that he was tired. "I'll get a fire going" she said.

Zack was already gathering poles and things to make a lean-to for the night. "Hope the weather holds, we don't need rain, it will make the going tough" Zack told her.

Jo decided it might be a good idea to gather some moss and small sticks. They could be light enough to carry, but small enough to carry in a bag to keep dry. The mention of rain was not on the top ten things she wanted.

Zack worked for an hour or so and had made a small shelter for them.

Jo had the fire going and had made some rice. Zack was starving and he ate his rice without any complaints.

"Zack, how long will it take to get to the complex?" Jo inquired.

Zack took out his map and told her of his plane and chopper ride. He pointed to where he thought the complex was. "Oh my God Zack" Jo leaned back. "It's so far away, our food will never last that long." Zack responded, "I was hoping to find something to eat along the way." "That's a bit iffy" she said.

Zack knew it was a long shot, but if he had to eat grass and tree bark. He was going to make it back. "Don't worry Jo, we'll make it." "Ok Zack, I trust you, just don't leave me. I'm afraid of being alone, not so much in town, but out here…"

Zack put a hand on her shoulder "We'll be ok Jo, get some rest, tomorrow will be a long day."

As Zack lay there "We'll be in the mountains tomorrow Jo" he said. Jo replied "Yeah, I try to think of this as a backpacking trip, it helps me keep my sanity." She was excited about travelling, but scared at the same time. How did everything get so crazy she thought? Well she was in it now; all she could do is pray that the future with Zack would be better than what she had seen over the last week.

"Zack" Jo asked, "How many people do you think are still alive?" "I have no idea, but from what we have seen so far, not many" Zack said.

Zack watched as Jo rolled over and heard her cry silently. "Get some sleep Jo" Zack said. He hoped that tomorrow, things would go well. He just hoped it would. He had to get a grip, as fear out here could cost them their lives. Think of Dee; with that he closed his eyes and went to sleep.

They made it over the ridge of the first mountains and as Zack guessed, there was a river in the valley.

Jo managed to find some nuts, berries, cat tail roots, wild onions and garlic to eat. She gathered as they paused for breaks and if it was a berry bush, they both picked.

The water in the river was cool and clear, probability glacier fed, Jo thought.

After three days they made little distance. Zack was getting frustrated, but walking in the mountains was not like walking in a park. They had not even travelled a quarter of the way. It was more like one eight of the way if they were lucky. They would not make it before the winter hit and Zack knew it.

"Jo, we will have to hold up somewhere soon for winter." "The next pass and we will see what's there." "There is no way we can travel in winter over these mountains" Zack told her. Jo knew he was right. The next pass might have more food and resources as well, she thought.

They crested the mountains and below they could see a few houses. Zack looked at Jo "see" he said, "We are destined to make it." Jo smiled.

There didn't seem to be anyone around as they got closer. It was what appeared to be a small farm. Zack and Jo approached with caution. There was no one around. They went into the house and the smell gagged Jo right away. Seems they found who lived here after all. Zack looked towards the barn. Jo stayed outside.

Zack entered the barn, this time he was the one who gagged, liquid animals he thought.

The wind was blowing away from them or they would have smelled it sooner.

Zack knew to stay here he would have to bury all of it. He headed back to Jo.

Jo was sitting on the ground under a tree and the look on Zack's face was not good. "Well, the good news is we can take shelter; the bad news was we have a lot of digging ahead of them." Jo looked at Zack "I am not afraid of a shovel" she said. Zack thought that she had a lot of spunk, she definitely had spunk. "Ok, first the one in the house. Have you any suggestions where to bury him?"

Jo looked around and picked a spot. "I think here, I think he would have liked it here."

Zack went to the barn and grabbed a couple shovels. He was gagging as he came out. They dug the grave for the poor fellow and after wrapping him a bed blanket, they buried him. Zack went and started digging more holes.

"Zack I have to air out the house" Jo said and Zack agreed.

She carried out the mattress, it would have to be burned she thought. After opening the windows she decided to wash what she could to help with the smell.

The next mistake was to open the refrigerator. She decided to bury it with the garbage. She started digging at the back of the house. She saw Zack with a wheeled barrow. He dumped it and leaned over and got sick. He worked constantly for about five hours.

When he made his way back to the house, Jo had a tub of water waiting for him. He washed himself with zeal. The smell of death was all over him and he wanted it off. Jo had tea ready and food, real food. She opened cans of potatoes, corn and a ham; fruit cocktail for desert, what a feast. The two of them ate, but the joy of the meal couldn't help but be dampened by the events of the day.

Zack told Jo it would take at least two more days to bury the rest. Jo took no pleasure in that statement. She knew from here they could plan the trip further and they would be safe from the winter elements. The house still smelled, but Jo felt sure she could clean it up. Zack took no pleasure in what he had to do, but thought the same as Jo. It would give them time to get a better plan together. So far they had been lucky and Zack didn't want to be lucky, he wanted to be sure.

After a few days the house was clean and the barn was empty as well. Zack had found a couple bags of lime. He spread some all over and saved some for later. He noticed a lot of things they could use, but how to carry it all was the problem.

Jo had been looking over the farm and found a lot of things still good in the garden and an apple tree. She had been drying as much food as she could. She had Ziploc bags full of many things.

Zack set out the map. He made lines and paths to follow and dates to try to keep. It would take at least two springs to cover the area as long as things went smoothly. He thought about a canoe, but carrying that was too much. He could ferry some goods up the pass for them to pick up as they went.

He would check the river later. Right now chopping wood was the priority. This would be their first winter here and he didn't want to be cold.

Jo had gone through the house and listed all the canned goods that would be eaten after all the fresh stuff was gone. Things like porridge, rice and powder milk, etc... was all the food for the trip, along with berries, nuts, now dried apples and strips she made from raspberries. She found honey and coffee, along with tea. She found a tooth brush and tooth paste, she didn't care if they had been used. She would soak it in vinegar and then hot water; it was so nice to be able to brush her teeth. She saved everything that they could use and when she had it bagged and ready for the trip, it was put in a box with the other things, gloves, hats, and socks. She even found a hot water bottle.

They both had hunting knives now and real back packs, this would help a lot. Zack gave up looking for batteries, but kept the phone just in case.

They found plastic tarps and real sleeping bags.

Jo found extra sheets and towels and when she rolled her sleeping back up, they went inside. She did the same to Zack's sleeping bag.

It wasn't long before they settled into a nice routine. Zack still pondered the ferry idea; it was Jo that said maybe tying stuff to a couple poles and pulling them along might work. Many ideas were passed between them.

The old man had kept books about things that grew wild. Jo was always reading them. She gathered things like marigolds for poultices and willow for pain. She kept busy as did Zack.

Although Dee was always on Zack's mind, he tried to keep thinking of anything that would make the trip there easier. She would be having the baby in late spring, early summer. Zack wanted it to be a girl, just like his precious Dee.

Chapter 5

After the commotion of the start up of the complex and the terrible tragedy of the virus on the outside world, life seemed to fall into a routine. Rainie met often with Andy and began her project. She had spent many hours with the masons as they helped her find the suitable stones to carve. She had spent many hours with Nick, the head mason. His family was always glad to see Rainie and she felt at home around them. Her passion for carving and the history of Nick's family working with stone; they were bound artistically and that was fine by all.

Rainie's passion for clothes also drove her to the tailoring stations in the tunnels. She watched for hours as Thomas designed clothes. His wife Leah loved knitting and weaving wool, she spent countless hours with a spinning wheel.

Rainie was surprised to see all the people work together and how they shared a mutual understanding of each others talents.

It was interesting how the human instinct to survive had pulled everyone and to work for the common welfare of all.

There was no competition for housing or food, it gave everyone work and time to be more creative.

The committee had been set up and they handled most of day to day issued that Simion found tiresome.

Rainie was on her way to the school and on her way she stopped to see Dirk. She had an idea of carving some animals and wanted to see if she could sketch some of animals he was caring for.

Dirk was always happy to share his knowledge and his ideas with her. He was a strange person, but Rainie liked him. She had spent several hours watching him calm distressed animals, which made her have an appreciation for him.

After sketching for a while, she decided to find Simion. He had locked himself in the labs and she knew he was driving himself too hard. She would save her visit to the school for later.

Simion was in the labs as she suspected. She walked in to find him looking slides under a microscope.

"Simmy" Rainie said.

Simion looked up, "what is it dear?"

"Simmy, I don't mean to be a bother, but can I drag you away from here for a while?"

He leaned back and rubbed his eyes, "What's up Rainie?" Simion asked.

She walked over and started to rub his shoulders. "Well" she said. "I'm not here looking for fun," she stung from their last episode at the labs and communication rooms. "I think you need a hot meal and an hour or so away from here" she said. "I need to discuss a few things with you, if you don't mind?" She almost sounded like she was pleading with him.

Simion looked up at her and smiled, "Rain I believe you are right. I do need a break." He stood, tucked her arm in his and left the lab.

Rainie assured him not to work so hard. If he got sick the complex would be without a critical member of the staff.

"Simmy, I've been doing a lot of thinking about things" Rainie told him. "That day you made me look at the reality of things. I was so angry with you" she continued, "but I have to tell you, if you had not, I might not have opened my eyes to what was here. I have been stupid, selfish and vain" she said. "I didn't appreciate people" she added.

"Rainie, don't be so hard on yourself" Simion said to her. "I'm glad you have started to realize, this may not be the world outside. We can make it liveable until we can venture outside again."

"Simmy you were right to do what you did. I guess I just wanted to tell you that and I'm sorry" Rainie said. "How about something good to eat and drink, then if you wish to go back to the labs, fine" Rainie said. "I just miss you Simmy" Rainie looked at him.

"My dear, I shall endeavour to spend more time with you" he smiled.

"You may be right to take a break away can be good sometimes, if you get to close to things, you can miss something obvious to others." He patted her hand and they walked into the kitchen.

Rainie discussed many issues with him. She told of her plans and that she had been helping in the medical stations. She had proposed a first aid class to the doctors as a lesson for the children. Rainie had thought a lot about people getting trained in other jobs, rather than sticking with the one they had been hired for.

Simion was happy; she seemed to have found a use for her talents. Now, here was the woman he knew all along. The others would learn to appreciate her as he did.

After a lovely dinner they returned to their dorm. They spent the evening just being close and mended a few fences they had broken.

Dee was always keeping busy; she had Paula make some things help with the sickness in the mornings.

She missed Zack terribly and was becoming worried. She knew winter was coming and she believed he would be in a bad way, if he got stuck in the mountains when the snow begins. She tried to be hopeful, but her courage was waning sometimes. Dee chalked it up to hormones and shed a few tears then got on with things. She thought of how awful things were for him; his dad dieing, the virus and the horrors he had to endure, again the tears escaped. She wiped them away. Dee imagined Zack holding her and longing for his touch, his embrace, his presence. Tears flowed now; Dee just wiped them away again.

She went to her dorm and wandered around in it looking for baby cradle designs and patterns for baby clothes. "Zack where are you?" she mumbled, "I need you. I am so lonely."

It was then a tap, tap came to her dorm door. Quickly she wiped her face and called "Come in."

Andy was standing there. "Hi Andy, what's up?" she asked.

"Nothing much" he told her. "Mind if I come in?"

"No, no, not at all" she said.

Andy came in a sat on the couch. "Dee, how have you been?" Andy asked.

"Ok, I guess" she replied.

"Mind if I bend your ear for a bit? I sometimes need one" Andy said.

"Sure shoot, I'm all ears" Dee was interested.

"As you know I spend a lot of times in research and sometimes it gets, well lonely. I just wanted to know if you might be interested in some company at a meal or during a walk sometimes." "I mean just since the virus I don't have anyone to talk to." "I thought with you waiting for Zack, well never mind," he got up. "Wait" Dee replied. "I would very much like your company." Andy smiled.

"Could I interest you in a glass of juice in the kitchen?" Andy asked her.

"I think I would like that" Dee replied.

"You know Dee, you remind me of my cousin" Andy stated. Dee just smiled.

They made their way to the kitchen and Dee decided hot chocolate was what she needed. Andy talked for some time and Dee let him. He told her of his interests in a young woman here, but he didn't know how to approach her. Dee gave him some pointers and they laughed.

She knew the woman he spoke of. She was a young woman helping Karen in the agro tunnels.

After a time, Andy said that he was sure that Zack would get back. He was smart and resourceful.

Dee thanked him for his confidence in Zack and for visiting with her.

He walked her back to her dorm and bid her good night.

Dee was glad for his company. He brightened her spirits.

She glanced at the cradle designs and picked the one she would make.

She lay on her bed and hoped Zack was okay. It wasn't long before she was sleeping.

Warren stayed in the communications labs. He tried everything he could. Every transmition he sent via satellite he prayed for an answer, but nothing. He had tried scanning the outputs for any signal that the satellite mad, but there just wasn't any.

The world they had known was gone.

Warren suggested to Simion to shut down the systems, might as well save the power and Simion agreed.

Warren had found, with his job severely cut back he could spend time teaching the next generation about communications. He enjoyed the children and was totally surprised how fast they picked up the way things worked. Warren like the children, they were honest. He was surprised how they enjoyed everything from the plants and animals to the computers. It didn't hurt that he enjoyed the company of Jane the teacher. He helped with the children a lot and found it a pleasure.

Warren did spend three or four hours a day still trying to contact outsiders. He decided that though life outside may never recover, he had the complex and the people here were going to survive.

He still waited for Zack to call, but it had been a week and that was not a good sign.

Warren liked Zack and Dee. He held a hope for him even though it seemed hope would be not enough.

Chapter 6

Zack and Jo slipped into what seemed like a quiet domesticity. He spent his evenings searching the maps for passes and Jo found more books. The days were spent looking for food near the farm and drying what they could.

Jo knew the fort was about four days away and often thought of the women there, sometimes longing for their friendship. She thought about the children and wondered how they were getting along.

Zack thought about the complex and Dee. He had told Jo of how Simion had planned everything and when they reached it things would be so different.

There still was the problem of food for their journey. Zack knew they would have to forage the valleys for everything they could find in order to make the trip over the mountains and into the next valley.

He had such dreams of reaching the complex sooner, but the hike had proven to be a lot more strenuous than he thought.

Maybe they would find more farms along the trek. They may also be claimed by other folks that managed to escape the range of virus.

Jo worried for Zack, she knew there was a complex, but making it there might be another story. He had gotten us this far so she decided to hang tight with him, besides, she like Zack.

Jo squirreled away bars of soap and things she would need when they were travelled. The weight to carry them was always an issue. She practiced packing, when Zack was out chopping wood, this time she wouldn't lag behind.

Winter blew in with a fury. Zack always praised her on her meals, etc…

How different life had become. Jo now knew how hard the first settlers must have had it. She admired them for their adventurism and strength of will. Determination was the key, she thought.

She could understand the term cabin fever. Winter had just begun and already she longed for people.

Zack had a much harder time of things, he only thought of Dee and the complex. It was Jo who got him to focus on other things. She was right; he needed to pay attention to what was happening now, not the future so much.

They never talked of the past much; both thought it was too painful.

Jo found a deck of cards and my midwinter Zack owed her over two hundred and fifty thousand dollars. Jo laughed as Zack accused her of stacking the deck. Through all the trials they had become great friends.

Chapter 7

$\mathcal{D}$ee was getting larger with each passing week. So many in the complex did what they could for her. She found out, although her baby would be the first born in the complex, there were other babies on their way as well.

She would walk into the living area of the complex and it was never long before the children were near her.

She watched them play and fight, then their mothers would step in and restore order.

On this particular day it was Rainie that came and sat near her.

"Dee" Rainie said "can I talk to you for a little while?"

"Sure Rain, what's the trouble?" Dee asked.

"Oh nothing, I mean, it's just, well, I'm going to have a baby too" Rainie finally managed to get it out.

"Oh Rain, that's wonderful!" Dee said.

"Dee" Rainie looked at her "I'm afraid" she said.

"Oh Rainie whatever for?" Dee asked.

"I'm not exactly a spring chicken anymore, I'm nearly thirty-four years old" Rainie told her.

"Oh my goodness, you are so lucky" Dee said. "You have Simion, who truly loves you and you have beauty and talent. Everything will be just fine. Follow what the doctors say and it will be just fine" Dee told her.

"Dee, would you mind if I call you now and then just to talk?" Rainie asked.

See just smiled, "You can call me whenever you like, but just remember I'm not sharing my pickles and ice cream."

At that they both laughed.

"Rainie would you like to see some of the things I have for my baby? If you like them I can make some for you as well" Dee asked.

"Yes Dee I would like that very much, Thank you" Rainie replied.

The two women left the living area and made their way to Dee's dorm.

On their arrival Dee showed Rainie the furniture she had made and designed for others.

Rainie looked at the designs and picked out a couple. As she glanced around she saw pictures of Zack and Dee together. She knew she was lucky to have Simion with her.

Rainie thanked Dee again and left her dorm.

Simian wasn't making any progress with his studies of the virus. They just didn't get enough information before it did its damage on the outside world.

He sat back in his chair and thought about the people here and what might happen if the virus made its way in. It was a scary thought, but Simion never the less ran the scenario through his head. He liked to have back up plans even if they never get used. He tried different angles to the scenarios and the outcome was not good. He hadn't contemplated death of anyone here, but it would be an eventuality. He would have to speak to the masons.

There would have to be a tunnel turned into a tomb for the people here.

Simion thought, how grim, but it was a reality none the less.

It was about then that Rainie arrived.

"Come in my dear, so what have you been up to?" Simion asked.

"Well, I have been at the medical station" Rainie told him.

"You're not feeling well?" Simion asked.

"No, no just a check up" Rainie replied, "but they did tell me something interesting."

"What's that dear?" Simion said.

"Simion, looks like you are going to be a father" she told him.

Simion looked at her and just as smooth as silk, he smiled and said "I thought you were looking extra beautiful lately."

"Oh, Simmy" Rainie said "I didn't know if you would be happy about this."

She walked over to him and as she got closer he stood up and hugged her softly when she arrived.

"I was worried" she said.

"Rain, I love you" he told her "I'll always love you Rain."

Simion held her for quite some time before letting her go. "This is a grand day" he said and smiled at her.

"I'm going to go lay down for a bit" Rainie told him, "I've been tired lately."

At that she left and went to their dorm.

Simion stayed in the lab and contemplated the thought of having a child. He thought it all came down to it's a grand day today and smiled.

Dirk had kept busy with the animals. They all appeared to be preparing for new life. It was fall and they all had mated. Now the gestation time would be like a big clock for him until the young started arriving. He would have the older children help and the younger ones observe.

Sara the teacher had asked what he wanted and with his mind now made up he would have to tell her.

Carla and Dirk's family had so much to do. He might have to call on others to observe the births. As problems seemed to present themselves, it would be easier with more to help.

Rainie had mentioned it at a committee meeting about others learning more about the different functions the complex needed was sound. Dirk thought.

He wanted to learn a bit more about the agro tunnels; not so much about clothes, but shoes. Who would believe he would like to learn to make shoes.

He started off for the school, about half way there he ran into Andy who was just leaving from seeing Sara. Dirk smile to himself, seems the animals were not the only ones seeking mates.

It was not his intention to interrupt the class, but his arrival was unannounced and it did.

Sara of course turned the visit into a proposed field trip to see the animals and the children couldn't wait.

Dirk made the field trip date and after talking with all the kids, made his way back to all the animals.

As he stood at the railing and watching for a while, he decided to find Carla. He just wanted to keep her up to date on the animals' progress.

Jo and Zack got on famously. It was Jo that spoke first, "Zack, without bees and bugs the food will not grow next year." It was more of a statement rather than a question.

"Jo, I think the wind can pollinate as well if it's a field or something. I don't think there would be as much food, but some would grow. Why do you ask?" he said.

"I have been thinking of the people at the fort. Just wondering how they were getting on" Jo replied.

All Zack said "They are closer to Cambry, I think they will go get what they can, by now the chaos will be over."

Jo thought it seemed like so long ago that the virus killed so many.

"So when do you want to start out again?" Jo asked.

"As soon as the weather turns and things thaw some." Zack said.

"It is exciting" she told him. "I hope we make good time, with the things we have now it should be easier." Zack nodded in a agreement. "If we manage to find old roads, etc... it would be of great help and we will make good time."

"My wife will be having our baby soon. You know Jo, I miss her so much. I must admit you have been a great friend to me and so much help. You have kept me together and I want to thank you for that."

Jo looked at him, "Thanks Zack, after all you did save my live and I don't think I could have made it this far without you, so thanks back." Zack smiled.

"Have you thought about names for your little one yet?" Jo asked.

Zack smiled, "No, I just want the child to be alright and Dee too, she can name the child; it would end up with a title like Sue or Bob if it was up to me." They laughed.

"Well you know" said Jo, "Bob is a good name; everyone has a Bob in their family it's almost a sure thing."

Zack looked at her "Oh my God and Bob's your uncle." They both laughed again.

"Yes, I can't believe you remembered that Zack" Jo said.

"It was pretty hectic then" Zack replied, "but it's going to be great to get to the complex. You will be so amazed Jo you really will."

Jo wondered what it would be like. She was so excited, but a little afraid too.

Winter was passing quickly and everyday it was getting closer to the time they would be moving on.

Jo had to admit it saddened her somewhat. She kind of liked it here and moving on into uncertainty was nerve racking. She knew it was the plan from the beginning so she adjusted her thinking to it.

Zack was like a cat on a hot tin roof, the days couldn't pass quickly enough for his liking. He had to pick the right time; too soon and they might get stuck in the snow and too late they might lose time.

It was always his mental picture of Dee that drove him on, their baby, gees a baby; a new soul for them to cherish. He marvelled at how life could twist and turn from great sorrow to great joy. He couldn't wait to see them all in the complex again.

"Zack come have coffee" Jo asked.

"I'll be right there Jo" Zack answered.

The evening was spent pleasantly drinking coffee and talking of their adventure that lay ahead.

Chapter 8

Time passed slowly for the people in the complex. Getting used to being inside continually was hard. Systems ran well and many found time to enjoy themselves.

Simion found himself the Justice of the peace and others found themselves in need of his services. Everyone helped wherever they could.

No one doubted that the complex was their home and as long as they all worked together they would survive. It was always thought of, but never talked of often, the fact they may never be able to leave with the virus outside, no one knew for sure.

Dee was large with child now, her time was growing near. She knew Zack was still alive, she could feel it, but where was he? She needed him so much. So many times she wanted him there with her, for all her strength Dee was losing her ability to hold back the tears. Everything had been so wonderful and in a matter of a week it was gone. She felt sorry for her loss of Zack, but wept for the hardships he must be facing out there. Her poor Zack, come home to me.

She decided to have a bath. She needed to relax; thinking of Zack always thrilled her immensely and totally saddened her at the same time.

She decided, she would go into the living area after and watch the children play.

Dee soaked for a long while, it was when she was getting ready to leave that the pain started. She decided to stay in her dorm; it would be a while yet. Zack where are you was all she could think of?

She paced in her dorm between pains and mentally went over all the things for the baby. It was getting close to the baby's arrival; the pains were about twenty minutes apart.

She headed for the medical labs and Dee arrived with time to spare.

As she lay there having the child, visions of Zack troubled her.

It wasn't long before Dana arrived and Dee was exhausted. She wanted to sleep in a desperate way. It was against this need that Dee realized something was wrong.

The doctors were hustling about, but sleep overtook her. Her mind had her in Zack's arms, dancing when she fell asleep.

Dee never woke up. The doctors could not stop her bleeding. She passed quickly and the people in the medical labs despaired when her heart stopped.

Dee was gone and Dana was all that remained of her and Zack.

It wasn't long before everyone knew and it brought great sadness to all.

It was a true love story that so many knew and most grieved openly.

Dee was the first they lost in the complex and it sent a wave of people's mortality to all there. How sad, it was poor Dana; no mother and a father lost outside.

It was Warren that took control of the situation. He had time on his hands now that there was no communications from the outside. He requested to be Dana's caregiver till something could be arranged.

A meeting was called and Warren was allowed to care for her.

The funeral they prepared for Dee was a solemn affair. She was taken to the tunnel with tombs and was placed in her place of rest. Many cried openly as they spoke of her life and of her contributions to the complex. She would surely be missed.

Most went to their dorms after the ceremony. It was time to reflect for many there.

Rainie took the news the worst. Dee had become her friend and they shared many things together. It scared her, what had happened especially since she to was expecting. Rainie ran her memories of Dee over in her mind, over and over again.

Simion worried for her well being.

"Rainie you must try not to think of the worst with what happened to Dee" Simion told her, "most women have no trouble at all."

"Oh Simmy, what do you know of it?" Rainie sighed. "Have you ever had a child or carried one inside you?" She started to weep. "It's not that

Dee was my friend, she was the only one that… well I'm having trouble with folks. I didn't really start out here with a great attitude" now she was crying.

Simion went to her and held her. "It will be ok, you'll see" Simion told her.

Warren had his hands full with Dana. He had been to Dirk and had got goats milk for her. In the moments he held her, Warren marvelled at how perfect she was, so tiny and new, innocent truly innocent. He thought this was maybe the only time in ones life that you were indeed pure of soul.

Warren was surprised many wanted to care for the child, but the point was he did and so far he was doing a great job.

Warren told Dana that Zack would be back to take over, he wanted that for Dee and Dana. He knew it was becoming harder and harder to believe as time passed.

Warren was surprised how many women in the complex had sent things to Dana. He became aware of the network of women with children and how extensive it was.

Jane was in his company more and more and he liked it.

Dana was changing his life in ways he never would have dreamed of.

Chapter 9

$\mathcal{T}$he melt was on for Jo and Zack. Zack was chomping at the bit to go. Jo was pulling together the last bits of things they might need. When she was packed, her last item was a book. The book was of things to eat and use in the wild. It had become a main stay for her.

"You ready Jo?" Zack called.

"Yeah, yeah I'm coming keep your shirt on" she yelled back.

As they stepped onto the porch, she felt sadness at leaving. This had been their home for the past winter.

Jo looked back and then they were on their way.

Zack walked with determination. He was going back to Dee and by now she would have had the baby. He smiled to himself.

The day was crisp and cold which was good for them. It was work to carry everything they owned with them.

When they reached the crest of the mountains, the sight was awesome. Jo stood staring over the next valley and beautiful was all she could say.

From their view point they could see the next valley over. Zack pulled out his maps and pointed to the distant ridge, "That's the way we go Jo."

Jo soaked up the beauty as they started their descent. Half way down they found themselves on a plateau of sorts and Zack took off his pack.

"We can rest here Jo" Zack told her.

She dropped her pack too and looked around. "It's so nice here Zack", she said "almost like a picture post card." Zack agreed.

He was already gathering wood and Jo rummaged through her pack for something to drink and eat.

"We have made good time today Jo" Zack smiled at her. "With luck we will be half way by next winter, maybe further" Zack told her.

Jo soaked in the sunshine and began noticing the plants around her. The wind was gently blowing. It was an eerie feeling not to hear anything but that.

She wondered how many plants would cease to be without bugs and bees to pollinate them.

"You have told me so much of your wife Zack" Jo said. "I will be happy for you when we get back to her" she smiled. "Thanks Jo me too, you have no idea" Zack said.

After they ate and had a hot drink. Jo said "Let's get this show on the road."

They put out the fire and pulled on their packs. The trip down to the valley took the rest of the afternoon. Zack knew they needed a shelter for the night and began a lean-too.

Jo prepared food after she got the fire going.

They called it an early evening and climbed into their bed rolls.

It seemed cold tonight Jo thought and she hoped it wasn't going to snow.

It was a good day of travelling Zack thought and soon drifted off to sleep.

It was well into the morning when they woke. The sky was overcast and both dreaded it might rain or worse snow yet.

They gathered their stuff, ate some of Jo's homemade trail mix and started off again.

It was cold; they could see their breath as they walked. Jo called to Zack "Keep an eye out for nut trees; we might see some on the ground." "Will do" Zack replied.

He set a hard pace but Jo kept up.

Going up a hill was harder than going down one. There were no broken trails through the bush which made walking difficult.

They made it up a ways and Jo told Zack she needed a rest.

"No problems" Zack said. He was going ahead to see if he could find an easier path. Old animals' trails were good, but there were none around. It wasn't long before Zack needed to rest too.

Jo was on her way up again. She could see Zack above her. The valleys below were so much easier to travel in.

"How much further Zack?" Jo called out.

"Not far" he replied.

He reached the top before Jo and below he could see what looked like the remains of a logging outfit.

By the time Jo made the top, Zack had already found a path down. "Let me go look around when we get down there, Ok Jo?" She nodded and they made their way down.

It was early afternoon when they got off the ridge they had just come over. Jo hung back with packs and Zack went to have a look.

It was an old logging camp; not much left here, but would be shelter for the evening.

He went back and got Jo.

They wandered around the camp looking for anything useful, but found nothing.

"There might be some kinds of roads here" Zack said, "It will make travelling a lot easier." Jo agreed.

It had been abandoned long ago, but to Jo it was good so see something man made out here.

Zack looked at the hills around the camp and found what looked like an old road.

"There Jo, we will go that way, follow the road tomorrow" he said.

Jo smiled; it was going to be an easier time she thought.

They put their packs in an old building and got the bed rolls out.

Soon they had a fire going and then came the rain. It rained and poured all night, by morning it was just drizzling out.

This was going to be a long day Jo thought.

They donned their rain wear and started down the road. It was miserable out and they both felt it. They followed the old road; it took them around the mountain and into the next valley before it petered out to the wilderness.

There was a river in this valley and that night after they made camp, Zack searched his maps.

"Jo, look her!" he said to her.

She came over and he pointed out where they were. For all the climbing and walking they had not gone very far.

"We will have to cross the river" Zack told her.

Jo looked at him, "Just how are we going to do that? This is no small creek."

She was cold and cranky.

"We'll have to cross somewhere" Zack said. "I'll look tomorrow, Ok?' Zack told her.

Jo was fine with that. He could scout and she would look for any food that might be out there.

Jo dried out her clothes by the fire. It felt good to be dry and warm.

Zack seemed to be so at home out here and J wasn't. She didn't like being dirty and sweaty all the time.

Tomorrow would be another long day. Jo covered up and went to sleep.

Zack couldn't sleep; he was making his way back to Dee, his thoughts kept him going. He wanted so to hold her and the new baby. He would find a way over the river, it was what had to be done and he would do it.

Zack finally was able to sleep.

Zack was up early and woke Jo. "I'm off, don't wander far Ok?" he said to her.

Jo stirred the coals and decided it was a tae and porridge morning. She ate and enjoyed the break. Soon she dressed and made her way into the valley a ways. She didn't find food, but she did enjoy the beauty of it all.

She returned to camp and soon Zack returned, smiling.

"I found a cable car going across the river, Jo. It was probably used to count fish during the spawn. We can use it to cross." Zack was pleased with his discovery.

Jo was relieved to hear the news. She had no desire to swim in a fast moving river.

"That's great Zack" she told him.

"Let's get going, it would be nice to be on the other side and on our way a bit today" he smiled at Jo.

They packed up and Zack led the way to the old cable car.

It took four trips to get all their stuff across. Jo had to admit she was glad they were finally across.

Zack led the way. They made good time after the crossing; the ridge they were climbing was not as steep as the previous one. Soon they were on top and below they saw people, what were they doing there?

Jo looked at Zack, "People, woot!" she said.

"Don't get to ahead of yourself; they may not want strangers near."

They made their way down and soon were in the settlement.

Jo was ecstatic. These people welcomed them in and after a few conversations they learned they too were almost wiped out by the virus. The good news was there seemed to be enough of them to carry on. The women out numbered the men, but they didn't seem to mind. About three quarters had passed away and most of the young were left.

They were determined to go on and had enough food and resources to carry on.

After a hot bath, Jo was enjoying the company of the women and Zack the men.

He asked about the mountains around the area, but was surprised they didn't travel much. They stayed put close to where they were. Zack was evasive as to where they were going. He told them stories of the things he had seen so far. They spent the night and ate wonderfully.

The folks asked about the animals, as theirs all died. Zack had to relay that it seemed all animals were gone and insects as well.

Jo slept well in her bed there and was glad to have it.

Soon as the sun rose they would be on their way again.

Zack asked about batteries, but they had no use for modern contraptions. The situation being as it was, it was a good thing they lived close to the land with a hands on policy rather than relying on machines.

After a wonderful evening, great company Jo and Zack wished them well and headed out again.

It was mid afternoon when Zack told Jo they would rest. The terrain turned bad, it would be slow going now.

They rested for about twenty minutes and were on their way again.

Jo watched as Zack climbed over the next few boulders and then he was gone. Oh my God she thought, she dropped her back pack and ran to where she last saw him. She looked down and saw Zack sprawled out down the hill a ways.

"Zack, Zack!" she cried out as she climbed down to him. He was unconscious and both his legs, she could see were broken. A bone was sticking from one of his legs. She had to do something. She looked for some strong straight pieces of wood for splints. On her way to him she checked his head and breathing. How could this have happened she thought? She would have to set his legs, but was terrified. She was glad he was not conscious to feel the pain. She grabbed one foot and pulled, the bone slid back into the leg and it appeared to be straight. She bound it with the wood she found and then she set the other leg.

"Okay, okay" she said, the bleeding stopped, bones set and immobilized; shock would be next. Jo started to cry. How did he fall? She thought and wept for a while. She wrapped him in blankets and a tarp to keep in the heat. She would have to go back for help, but she didn't want to leave him.

What if he woke and no one was here or went into shock, she thought. She left a canteen of water and some aspirins and made sure he was secure. She left her pack, grabbed a ball of string from it and secured a tarp over him to keep him dry.

She placed her hand on his head, "I will be back as soon as I can Zack. I will not leave you out here" she whispered. She got up and started back to the settlement.

They hadn't gone that far and she knew her way back. It took her about two hours of hard work to get back. It didn't take long before she had a few men to help her get Zack.

Jo led them to Zack and it appeared that he was still unconscious. Zack was looking very good she thought.

The men soon had Zack on a stretcher and on the way back to the settlement. It was dark when they arrived at the settlement. The woman, who tended Zack, never left his side. They sewed the wounds and checked his legs. The woman told Jo, it was a good thing you set his legs, but we will not know for some time if he will ever walk again. If the bones didn't mend he will die and if they mend the wrong way, he will probably be crippled.

Jo's heart did a flip flop in her chest. "He has to walk" she cried. "He has to" and she cried more.

"Now, now" the old woman said. "He will need you now, if infection sets in it will be his life." "You must be strong for him" she told Jo. Jo nodded. "When will he wake up?" Jo asked.

"The longer he sleeps the better. He will be in great pain so don't wish it too soon."

Jo couldn't believe it. How could this have happened? She just wept.

The old woman took her to a room where a warm bath awaited. "You have a bath and you will feel better" she said.

"Thank you" Jo replied.

She soaked for a while and then got dressed in clean dry clothes. She made her way back to Zack and sat in a chair beside his bed. She took his hand and told him "I will never leave you Zack, so just get well. Do you hear me?"

When she realized what was going on, her neck was stiff. She had fallen a sleep leaning on the edge of his bed.

When she looked up at Zack, he was wet with sweat.

It was about then; the old woman appeared with some hot water and a cloth.

She looked at Jo "Go, I will tend him now. He will not have an easy time of it."

Jo looked at her "I will not leave him" she said.

"You will do him no good if you don't have your strength. Go eat and the others will get you settled. You will be here for some time now."

Jo knew she was right and she made her way back to her room.

Chapter 10

*I*t was Karen from the agro tunnels that found Rainie in her dorm. Rainie heard a tap, tap at her door and called "Come in."

Rainie's friendship with Dee was well known and Karen made the move out of sympathy for Rainie, as she knew all to well the pain of losing someone close.

"Hi Rainie" Karen said, "I just wanted to stop and tell you how sorry I am about Dee. I know you two got on well."

Rainie looked at her "Thank you Karen, Dee was so good to me. I shall miss her so much."

"I want to show you something, if you are up for a small trip?" Karen asked her.

Rainie was glad for an opportunity to get out of the dorm "Sure" she said.

Karen walked with Rainie to the Agro tunnel and told her "Anytime you like you are welcome here" Karen said.

Rainie smiled "Thank you Karen."

They turned a corner and Rainie couldn't believe what she saw; flowers, lots of flowers of all colours and kinds.

She turned to Karen "Oh my goodness, this is wonderful!"

Karen blushed, "I kinda smuggled them in. I do so like blooms, they make you feel better" she smiled at Rainie.

"I thought some for Dee and some for you to take home," Rainie hugged Karen.

"You are a dear; I would love to take some to Dee and my dorm. It is such a welcome sight, thank you so much."

Karen smiled and helped her pick some. "Do you think we can put some in the main living area? I know they would be appreciated."

"As long as Simion says Ok" Karen replied.

"You don't worry about him" Rainie smiled. "He's really a big teddy bear under all that bark."

Karen smiled "How long until you have your baby Rainie?"

"In about three months."

Karen knew by her tone she was frightened after what had happened to Dee.

"Don't worry" Karen told her, "Women have been having babies for a long time. What happened to Dee was tragic, but not the norm."

Rainie was a little comforted. After she had picked two bouquets, she thanked Karen and made her way to Dee's tomb.

She lovingly placed the flowers down, in a vase that Karen given her. She told Dee not to worry, Dana would be fine and Zack would soon be here to care for her.

Rainie headed back to her dorm and when she arrived, she placed the flowers in the middle of the table.

Karen was right; it did make her feel better.

Warren was surprised at how having little Dana caused women to flutter over him. They would give him tips on rearing and cooking.

He had an eye for Sara the teacher until he met Elsa. Why had he not noticed her before? She was a worker in the tailor station. She wasn't over attractive, but she just oozed with something and it struck Warren's fancy.

The two were spending a lot of time together. Sara never minded, she preferred Andy, so all worked it's self out in the daily wash of daily living.

Life was moving on, as it will do; Rainie had her baby, a boy who was named Erik.

Warren and Elsa married and kept Dana, who now was growing fast.

Andy and Sara finally got together after the time they spent with Dirk and the animals.

Watching all the new life was contagious and things moved on as it should.

Chapter 11

Zack had been in a delirium for about two weeks before he pulled through, to Jo's relief. Now the reality of never walking again frightened him.

He thought this will not happen and with Jo's help and the others, he would regain the use of his legs.

Spring was here and everyone had the job of planting food. Jo helped where ever she could.

Zack watched from the porch. His mind was never far from Dee and his baby.

The old woman that helped him drew Jo aside on afternoon.

"Jo" she asked "he talked of a woman named Dee and a child in his fever."

Jo looked at her "yes he has a wife and a child" she told her. "They are far away; we were on a journey to them when this happened."

The old woman looked at Jo "he will never be able to travel hard in the mountains again. The young men here have gone several days away and found nothing."

Jo told her they were going further away then that.

"I must tell you that he will not accept this, you must help him come to terms with that. It is not an easy task ahead for you or for him."

Jo knew she was right "Thank you" Jo told her.

Zack of course had no intention in staying here or giving up. Jo knew now was not the time to tell him. She felt he must come to realize it on his own. In the mean time healing was the important thing, disappointments would come too soon as it was.

Jo worked hard and learned many things from the people here. Jo came up with a method of pollination that the folks agreed might work. It was time consuming, but with no animals it would be the grown food that would have to sustain them.

When the garden was in bloom they would pick some blooms and would rub all the other blooms with the picked ones. If they did this daily, it might work.

Zack was up and about. Jo watched as he struggled to walk. He was doing a lot better she thought, but she could see the pain in his face. He was feeling useless and soon the men found him things he could do. At first he was whittling simple utensils and soon he was building small household chests and benches.

Jo gave him space and spent more time with the other women. It wasn't long before she decided to have a heart to heart talk with him.

It was odd that the others seemed to be busy away from them. Jo thought that they must have known the time had come.

"Zack" Jo said as she walked towards him. "I would like to talk to you if it's ok?"

Zack looked up "Sure Jo" he replied.

"How are you feeling?" she asked.

"How do you thing I feel Jo?" he said.

"I don't know" she replied.

"I can see the writing on the wall, it's not likely I will ever see Dee or my child again, if that's what you were wondering?" he snapped.

"That's not fair Zack" she said "I never caused this and I did save your life" she said.

"For what???" he said almost yelling. "Why did you bother, everything is gone. What's left?" he looked at Jo. "There are you satisfied now?" that was a blow below the belt for Jo.

She looked at him, "For your information mister, it's not what I wanted; none of this is what I wanted. You never asked me once what I wanted, why should it matter now? I'm sorry you can't get back, but unfortunately life goes on as we are reminded of daily. I'm alive, God knows why, but I am and I'm going to survive. If you want to feel sorry for yourself, fine. You aren't the only one that lost and don't you forget it." Tears streamed down her face as she turned and walked away.

Zack just leaned over and held his head. She was right, it wasn't her fault. She had been a good friend and he had just told her she was worthless, when it was his own self pity that was driving his emotions.

It wasn't long before a few men approached him. "Zack you will have to live in this world as it is. Not many get choices on how it will be for them. Maybe before you throw away a good woman and a friend, you should put some real thought into it."

Zack just nodded and hobbled to his room.

His performance to Jo was uncalled for, but he had to vent. He had no more avenues to get to the complex and dieing right then wasn't going to happen. He had to think of some way of finding peace of mind.

Jo walked out to the garden and then beyond. Why should she care about him? She knew from day one that he was married and had a child. What difference did it make to her, but it did matter to her. It mattered a lot.

The women seemed to sense her feelings and it wasn't long before they were near, but they never intruded on her private space.

Zack was churning up inside. His life with Dee was over and he knew he would never make it now. He also knew the men were right. Life goes on and really not many get a chance to choose how that life would be. He was going back and now he was going no where. The world that he and everyone knew was gone. Zack cried openly.

It was a knock came to the door. It was the old woman that nursed him through the fever.

"Please I would like sometime to myself" Zack told her.

She looked at him and came in.

"Zack" she started "do you think you are doing the right thing?" she asked.

"What do you mean?" Zack asked.

"Most things happen for a reason. How many things do you think I have had to face in my life?" she said. "Life is ever changing, just like the seasons. Things appear to be going good and one good storm brings much change. You can bent like a young tree and weather the change or not bent and break, never to regain what was lost. Nature replenishes its self, life does too if you let it. The last storm took most of my friends and family, but that is the way. At first I wished I too was taken, but what of the younger ones left? Without guidance, how would they learn how to bend? You may not know it, but Jo loves you. I am not sure she is aware of it herself, but you could do worse I can tell you that. All is not lost for you only changed. Think of this before you cast yourself into the mercy of the wind. It may blow you into a place far worse." With that the old woman got up and left.

It was two days before Zack sat on the porch again.

Jo did not go near him. She worked all day, everyday. Winter soon would be on them and at this point working made her think less and feel less.

Zack watched her often. Maybe the old woman was right, it was time to bend; then he would think of Dee and bending was not possible.

Jo had decided to make her way back to the fort. There was nothing here for her she thought. After the harvest she would go. She wanted to see if her idea of pollination worked and she would take some food with her.

She slowly started to get her things together. It was four days to the farm and another three days after that to the fort. She needed the maps and compass from Zack. She would have to talk to him.

After the harvest was in and it was a good harvest, Jo went to talk with Zack.

"Zack" she called from his porch. She heard him get up and hobble to the door.

"What is it Jo?" he asked. He was glad to talk to her, which surprised him.

"I need to talk to you" she said.

"Come in, come in" Zack told Jo.

"I'm going back to the fort Zack" she said.

It hit him like a ton of bricks, he did not think of Jo ever leaving.

"I would like the maps and compass if I might?" she said.

Zack just stared at her.

Then he said "Sure Jo, if you really want them?"

"Yes" she told him.

"Why are you leaving?" he asked. "I thought you were happy here" Zack said.

"There you go again" she said, "Happy here? Why would I be happy here? What's here for me, work and more work? I have no prospects here" she told him. "Do you think I want to be alone until I die? Well Zack I don't. I have needs, wants and dreams too. May I have the maps, yes or no?" she asked.

Zack felt like he had been burned with hot coals.

"Yes Jo you can have them" he told her.

"When are you leaving? He asked.

"In a few days" she told him.

Zack gave her what she came for and she left.

The next few days past and Jo never saw Zack.

Jo packed up her stuff and left the village heading for the farm. To her surprise she saw Zack standing on the trail just outside the settlement. As she approached him, she could see he had been weeping. He said to her "I need you Jo, please don't leave me; please don't leave me."

It was what she had said to him, what seemed so long ago. He was crying and so was she, then she hugged him and said "I won't leave you Zack, don't worry I won't leave you."

They made their way back to the settlement; folks didn't say anything to them, as they passed the old woman, she smiled at them.

Jo knew that this was probably one of the hardest decisions Zack ever made. She also knew she would never be Dee, but life will prevail and if she took second place that was okay. Zack was a good man and after everything that had happened, the situation for both could be worse.

It wasn't long before they fell into a routine. Zack was learning to appreciate Jo more and more everyday. He put Dee into the back of his mind and only thought of her and the baby when he was alone. When he thought of Dee and Jo always knew, but as time passed it became less often.

The following year Jo had a son with Zack. They called him West.

The journey for West was just beginning. His life would be filled with love from Zack and Jo, but also adventure fuelled by finding the complex that Zack talked of so much.

Jo and Zack worked hard at the settlement and with the help of all West grew into a nice young boy.

The settlement was getting large. Jo and Zack often talked of moving into the next valley. It would take a few families, but it would also relieve the pressure on the existing farms here.

Jo mentioned to the other women, how she would like her own place in the next valley. She found there were others that felt the same way.

Zack got around better now, still not great but a lot better than just after his fall.

West was a fine boy. He helped Zack carry things and was always near to lend his dad a shoulder to lean on when needed. Jo never had any more children, but the fact she had West was good with her.

It was in early spring when Zack and Jo were approached by two other couples. They wanted to make the move to the next valley. They were thrilled with the idea, but Zack wasn't sure if he could make the trip.

The two young men spoke up and told Zack that they would build a large cabin the first year. They would build one cabin for each family the next year, if he would consider going with them. Gary and Brad knew Zack could design fine functional homes. They had seen his work and wanted his knowledge for their buildings. Zack was proud they wanted his help.

He couldn't do much manual labour, but he could design, that he knew well.

"Let me discuss this with Jo and we will let you know soon" Zack told him.

That evening Jo, West and Zack sat at the table. "What do you think about moving to the next valley?" Zack asked.

Jo said "I want to, but for West it will not be so easy. There would not be the children there like he has around him at present."

West just smiled "I want to go" he said, "It's and adventure. Nothing happens here much and I think I would like to see what's over that mountain' he beamed a smile.

"Well that's that then" Zack said. "You do realize the work there will be there Jo?" Zack commented.

Jo looked at him "work here, work there, that never changes, but it would be nice not to have so many to worry about. Of course if they need us or if we need them, they wouldn't be that far away" Zack smiled.

Gary and Brad arrived the next day. Zack talked many hours with them. He wanted to go see the lay of the land and the best places to build. The young men agreed.

It would be a long arduous trip for Zack, but one which he relished. West was to go as well and he nearly jumped for joy at the prospect of being with the men.

What should have been a two or three day trip took them a week to get there. The valley was adequate. Zack made drawings of the layouts and the best places to build the cabins as well as the best places for farming. West was always at his side, learning much from his dad. After he had all the areas mapped to his liking, they made their way back to the settlement.

Jo and the other women started preparing for the move. The move would be in the following year. Anything they wanted to take they would have to carry.

There had been one trip to the fort by the men; they brought back tools and a few items like salt, etc...

The fort had a forge and tools were made of metal that had been found. Food worked as a trade item and as at the settlement, the fort too was growing in population.

The people, who survived after the outbreak of the virus, had given up fighting over and stealing food. They realized that working together was better after all.

On Zack's arrival back at the settlement, he was exuberant. The trip had done him well. He of course had to rest, but that night at the table he told Jo of the valley.

"Jo" Zack said, "When you are done with the dishes come see this."

Jo smiled to herself "Yes, I will hurry" she replied.

She was glad to see Zack excited about something again, it had been so long.

West and Zack were looking over the papers, talking and laughing. It made Jo's heart glad to see the merriment between them.

West was growing; he was almost eight years old now, He was such a little man, with Zack's aliments he had been forced to mature faster than the other young boys.

It didn't take Jo long to finish the dishes and she was at the table with them.

Zack proceeded to show her his drawings of the valley. He showed her his place of choice for the cabin. Jo agreed.

West wanted to help with the drawings of the cabin. Jo and Zack let him have a piece of paper. Jo had made paper with flax pulp. It was not bad, bur not like the paper from before the viruses. Jo and Zack never talked of the time before the virus much. West heard stories, but never asked too many questions.

Gary and Brad were regular visitors after the trip. They went to the valley every weekend. Each time, they were loaded with stuff.

Jo often thought they would be so glad when the hiking and packing would be over.

They were good fellows with kind hearts and manners.

The three families move caused much commotion in the settlement. Over a few weekends several men went along. The women tended the gardens and worked on things for the families leaving.

It was sad and happy at the same time. Leaving the settlement for Jo was a relief in some ways, but in other ways sad. The good thing was with all the previous trips there would be a better path going there. Remembering Zack's fall sent a shudder through her. She knew others would come visit them as well. She felt sad at saying goodbye to a place she called home for the past decade.

Zack was contented with life now. He loved designing things and doing their home made him think of many of things. Maybe a future project could be a forge for them and the settlement.

He designed a fireplace that would warm the house and would be more convenient for Jo to cook. Running water, Zack smiled, to have hot water from a tap, it seemed like so long ago.

Zack shook his head does no good to dwell on it he thought.

He glanced at the drawings and smiled, Jo would like her new house.

West always wanted to go with the men on the weekends. Jo relented a few times. It gave Zack and her time to share alone.

Jo asked Zack "Are you sorry we got together?"

Zack looked up from the table "Jo don't be silly, what was before is not now. I am quite reconciled with it. I do think of them, but I know I will never get back, so that's that."

"Do you think we should tell West? I many ways I think he should know that he has a brother or sister," Jo said.

"Maybe, but for now let him enjoy being a boy. After we move and get settled maybe then we can tell him of the journey" Zack stated.

Jo went and sat at the spinning wheel. She found much more comfort spinning than weaving or knitting.

Zack watched her from her table. As she pulled her shawl over her shoulders Zack made a mental note to make sure there was room near the fireplace at the new cabin.

He thought how nice it would be to have windows.

"Jo what do you think of a kiln? I did see some clay by the river and it might be fun to make some things."

Jo smiled "You'll have me make a brick house before long. Best watch, too many ideas or you'll never rest, just work, work." They both laughed.

The idea never occurred to Zack, but it was worth some thought.

He was building a wagon for West. It was too bad there were no animals, Zack thought. West would love to have a pet.

A wagon would help him when he got wood. Watching West made Zack think of his own growing up on the farm.

For such a little fellow he worked hard. He made Zack's life easier in the things he now did to help. Zack missed him when he was gone on the few weekends they let him go. He did enjoy the time with Jo; he had given up on playing with her. She always won when they played.

"Jo, I think it's time to start teaching West to read and write" Zack said.

"Yes I agree, but he may not want to sit still long enough to learn" Jo replied.

"This winter would be a good time for him to start" Zack told her.

"You can take the first shift teaching him" Jo smiled.

"Have Brad and Gary's children started yet, do you know Jo?" Zack asked.

"Not sure" she replied, "but, I will find out, might be a good time for them all to learn."

West would be home tomorrow and just bursting to tell how everything went.

After a pleasant evening Zack and Jo retired to bed.

West had given Brad and Gary the fifty million questions drill all the way to the valley.

The trail there was becoming well worn, the weekends that all the men went were spent clearing it and making it better to travel on. West of course helped them, he knew it would be a great help for his dad if the trail was much easier to follow. The men always gave West a lot of praise.

When they got to the valley there was the cutting of trees for the cabins. The stumps were burned out and West had the job of clearing what branches were around and putting them on the burning stumps. Any usable wood was stacked.

It was surprising how much work two men could do. It was mid summer now and all the wood needed had been cut. The building of the cabin would begin now and by winter they would be living in the new valley.

West was looking forward to adventuring and seeing what was there. As they made their way back to the settlement they cleared rough spots on the trail as they always did.

After the long trail trip, West was home. He spent the evening telling Zack and Jo everything he had done over the weekend.

Jo was relived to have him home.

West was always chattering endlessly about everything. Jo and Zack always listened attentively. It was Brad and Gary that highlighted the conversation as always.

Zack never took offence, he was happy that West had role models. It was hard to survive and Zack was glad they had taken West under their wings so to speak.

Since Zack had his accident, the contributions made by Jo and him made many things easier for the settlement. They had great respect for them.

Brad always showed that in the new things that Zack had ideas for and put many into practice.

Gary appreciated the ideas Zack had for keeping existing things in good working order.

The women showed Jo many ways to help keep her family healthy. Jo's ideas for pollination and finding wild things to transplant and grown never went unnoticed or unused.

Jo found Brad's wife Susan shy and reserved, but she weave and was always willing to give new things a try.

Gary's wife Lily preferred hands on. She liked the garden and took much interest in the remedies for all ailments.

The children of the three families got on well, West led the way for the rest.

Jo noted that the three oldest stuck together a lot and the younger two as well.

It was exciting to be moving, but she knew there would be much work to do. The children would have to help next spring to get the garden in.

The clearing of the land would also be hard as well as burning the brush, picking the rocks and digging the dirt. A horse sure would be blessing, but there were no animals.

How different West's life had been compared to her's, she thought and went back to weeding her garden.

Zack was on the porch watching Jo. He was lucky to have her. Why she ever stayed with him was beyond him. He knew it was because she loved him, but he always felt that her life would have been much easier had she chosen to leave that day, but she stayed and to his luck she cared for him all this time. He had the deepest respect for her and was sure he loved her, but the passion he shared with Dee was never forgotten.

Jo knew Zack would never love her like he loved Dee, but he did love her. Maybe Jo was right, maybe they would tell West, but Zack wanted to wait. Jo never pushed the subject.

Fall was in the air, the trees started turning and the harvest was always busy for everyone.

The cabins had been built and would be in use this winter. It was after the harvest was in when the whole settlement told Jo and Zack that they would help carry all the things they would need to their new homes. The three families couldn't believe that they had planned all this for them. There were many gifts, stocks of food, household items and raw materials to make what they would need.

The families packed what they could and with the help from members of the settlement, the trek into the new valley began.

Zack and Jo were happy to see there was a decent trail now; it would make travel between them much easier.

The caravan of people through the forest was like a big parade and the children enjoyed it the most. It was an event that most of them would never forget. Since it was the first move of people from the settlement, it was done with the hopes that people would soon be in all the valleys. It brought hope for them all.

When they reached the valley, Zack and Jo couldn't believe they had all the cabins built, not just one. Brad and Gary accepted the adulation that was well deserved.

The folks from the settlement stayed the night and celebrated. It was such an event for them all.

Zack found the trek much easier than the first time. The trail made all the difference. He too enjoyed the festivities.

The next day after many handshakes, tears and hugs the folks started their trek home, but assured them they would visit.

The three families got to work getting settled, they worked some to get the ground ready to be turned in the spring and the snow came.

Zack was surprised that Brad and Gary had been able to get them built. He thought they did a great job.

Soon after, the routine was more familiar here. Zack decided it would be time for West and the other children to learn to read and write.

Jo sate by the fire and spun flax, Zack sat near. She would smile and thought this was their home and it felt good.

After a few words from Zack, West settled down to learning. He was smart and picked up things easily. He had an inquisitive mind.

Jo left the education to Zack, when she tried West would never sit still.

Gary and Brad's children would follow West and before long the lessons would turn to chaos.

Zack never had problems; Jo figured the children feared him. What ever it was the children settled down and go on with learning.

Jo was surprised to see that the more they learned the more they wanted to learn.

Zack didn't mind teaching them; it was something he didn't need his legs to do.

Jo got caught up with many of the household things. She was forever spinning and weaving for West. He was growing in leaps and bounds.

Jo stepped out to get some wood and watched the snow gently fall. She always wondered hat the miracle of snow It muffled all the noise and covered the ground with its protective blanket, holding all plants at bay until spring. She got her wood and stepped back into the cabin.

Zack made a cold room off the cabin so Jo didn't have to go out to get veggies. She decided to make vegetable stew with fried bread. The men needed a good meal.

After Jo got West to bed, her and Zack shared some tea.

Spring would come soon; they discussed what things took precedence. The garden was always first on the list. Zack was still rolling the kiln idea around.

Jo mentioned a workshop. She want a shed to work in to make paper and store her things needed for weeding.

Zack mentioned that he had found a pond that cat tails grew in abundance. Jo smiled, one always needs baskets and roots were a food source. It was soon dark and they retired.

Jo lay in bed and thought of the coming spring. She was happy to have the other women to share the work with. She had seeds from apples she wanted to plant. It was not just her future here; it was West's too. Zack slept peacefully and Jo was soon asleep.

Chapter 12

$\mathcal{S}$imion and Rainie had Erik and he was growing fast.

Simion doted on him as did Rainie. She had been working the statuary for the living area. Erik didn't show much interest, he was more interested in the agro tunnels.

The first statues were of Zack and Dee. It was her tribute to her for being her friend in the beginning. Rainie often worked on her statues and brought Dana with her. Rainie told Dana how her mother was a talented carpenter and how her father helped design the complex. Dana spent long hours watching Rainie carve their statues. She so wished she had met her mom and dad. She knew that, although she never got to meet them they were loved by the people here. Dana also spent time with Dirk and Carla. She loved the animals and spent many happy hours learning about them. She was doing well in school, but at this point she had no clear idea what she wanted to do. Warren and Elsa had three other children, Hetti, Carl and Jake. Dana being the oldest always had the other three follow her around. She never minded, just sometimes she wanted to be alone. Hetti being the closest in age to her was her constant companion. Hetti wanted to go everywhere with her. When Dana visited the animals, Hetti was entertained by the oldest of Dirk and Carl's children. They didn't mind and it gave Dana more time to herself while she was with the animals.

Andy and Sara had two children as well, Tyler and William. They were younger than Dana and she spent little with them. Carla and Jake, more their age were always with them.

The children were being born regularly in the complex. This was good. Many of the workers older children were now getting into positions of work, often dreamed of, but most never had the opportunity.

There didn't seem to be a lot of people that longed for the outside. It did make it easier for all, not having to deal with the ones who felt closed in here.

The population of the complex was growing as was the need for tunnels to accommodate, the growing of food, making of clothes, etc…

Simion did not spend much time in the labs anymore. He knew a cure for the virus may never be found, but he still worked on genetics. He had some of the children from the school show interest in many stations of the complex. He spent time helping them find the ones they enjoyed the most and excelled at. They were the future and Simion knew that.

It was Dirk that found him on the way to his dorm. Dirk asked "Simion do you remember how I told you that we would be over run with animals in the future?"

"Yes Dirk I do remember" Simion said.

"It's getting close to the time. We will have to let some out" Dirk told him.

"Okay Dirk, leave it with me for now and I will see what we can do" Simion told Dirk.

They would have a council meeting and get everyone's opinion on the matter, Simion thought as he continued to his dorm.

Dana as usual was with Dirk and the animals. Dirk was looking over the animals, since the council meeting agreed to let the surplus go outside. Dirk wanted to make sure the breeding stock was the best and that the ones to be let out would have the best chance. Any animal that seemed unable to survive would be processed for the animals they needed for meat. Dirk never favoured the meat eating animals, but realized they were needed in order to keep the balance outside.

Dana was startled by snakes. She wasn't sure if she liked them, but after seeing how many mice could be born in a season and Dirk's explanation on their ability to keep the numbers in check in the world. Dana understood the nature of their existence and the need for them.

Dana was growing up and as she gained in age, she gained in wisdom of things. Often she sat in the living area and started at the statues of her mother and father. How often she wished she had known them. She had things that her mother and father had made which she treasured.

She was their love child and when she felt lonely or scared, she thought of them and surrounded herself in the love they shared and their love for her. Her thoughts drifted to Rainie and her memories of her mom carving the statues. How she would carve and then sit back and look at her work. Rainie would smile as if she remembered some moment she would share with them. Sometimes Rainie would cry and stop work. Dana would sit beside her and Rainie would pat her hand. Dana its okay she would say, Dee always made me feel better. I just miss her sometimes. Then she would tell Dana that was enough for one day.

Simion was a mystery to Dana. He watched her from afar, but she always knew he was there like a watchful guard.

When they had time together Simion would tell Dana of Zack, how much he respected him. The haven would never have been built without him. He was a talented man Dana, Simion would tell her and he was my friend.

Simion made sure Dana had everything she needed and worked behind the scenes to get most of the things she wanted. It surprised Simion how easy it was to please her, she found pleasure in things most people never saw.

He watched her one day in the butterfly atrium after a hatch, all alone with the butterflies. The glee in her face warmed Simion to the core. He felt for her and was glad Warren provided the home and stability she needed.

Simion's mind wandered to his son Erik, how different the two were. Erik excelled in sports and he was smart. He could see him in the labs before long. He was self assured. He could see problems and work out a solution.

Dana seemed to look beyond the problem, where Erik didn't. He loved them both. Erik never took offence to the caring they gave to Dana. He liked her too. He was younger than her, but she never dominated him.

Dana watched Dirk preparing animals to be let out. He had a little bit from all different species. Soon Dana would see if they would survive the outside.

Simion and the council had many reservations about opening anything to the outside. Fear of the virus was still fresh in the adults' minds. Most of the children had no memory of the virus. The adults would never forget. After many hours of discussion they agreed to let the animals go. Simion had not agreed, but the council's decision was hat mattered.

Dirk and Carla spent the next few days preparing, David was the first to arrive with his insects. They would be the first to be set free. It would be a good indication if the other animals would survive.

The tunnel was filled and the doors opened.

They watched the monitors at first, the insects, and birds and finally the mammals were set free. After a few days the monitors showed many dead, but some did survive.

Simion was hopeful that with the survivors there would be hope.

It was when they were cleaning the tunnels and carelessness of the worker that let in the virus. It took about a week before the full devastation was realized. Many perished; they lost about a third of the population and over half of the birds and animals. Simion and Warren were among the first to die, but there wasn't a family left untouched. Andy was among the living left to pull the people together. The dead needed to be entombed ad the living needed to maintain the tunnels to survive.

The sadness of the children that died was felt throughout the complex. The missing adults must have the work they started completed.

Andy reviewed the complex's population status and realized they had lost a lot but nothing the loss to the outside world.

Simion had picked the right people for the complex. Whatever DNA code was, there was a lot of it here.

It took months for the people to pull the complex into some sort of order. The council met and the outside was again locked out. They didn't fear the virus now. It had taken its toll, but that was not the only sickness that could get in. Until they had enough people, the outside was off limits.

Dirk had survived as did his wife Carla, but they lost two of their children.

Dana was at the funeral, she attended them all. She was one of the oldest children in the complex and the other children drew strength from her.

She took on many responsibilities, like finding young people to work in the stations that had lost too many to function. It was Dana that believed in the younger folk. With help and instruction from a few of the adults, they would soon have things up and running.

Erik often talked with Dana; he was concerned for his mom. Erik knew there was a bond between them and begged Dana to help his mom.

Dana did what she could. Rainie was alone, like she was. Dana would not have wished that on anyone.

Dana on her first visit to see Rainie stopped where she had her carvings. She wandered around her studio looking at the pieces left undone.

"Rainie" Dana called "You here?"

"Come in Dana" Rainie replied.

"So how are you today?" Dana asked.

"Fine Dana" Rainie replied.

Dana handed her a list. Rainie looked at it, then her.

"What is it?" Rainie asked.

"It's your to do list" Dana told her.

Rainie looked at her again "What's the point?" Rainie said and looked away.

Dana sat facing Rainie and took her hands. "Do you remember when I used to watch you carve?" Dana asked her. "Do you what I thought about as I watched you" "When you carved my mother and father it was a gift you were giving me. Oh, I know it was for all, but in me I felt them", "You Rainie no one else. It was you that gave them to me. After that life was different. I never felt so alone."

Rainie had tears on her face. Dana looked at her "Everyone here has lost so much. They need to know what's gone is not lost. You can give them that."

Rainie cried "I can't, I just can't!"

Dana hugged her. When she was leaving Dana looked back and said "Can't or won't?" She looked at one more time and left her studio.

Rainie just sat and stared into nothingness. Dana, she thought, for not knowing her mother how so alike they were. Dee would have been so proud of Dana and disappointed in me, she thought. So would have Simion. She cried now, and then when no more tears came, she went and had a bath.

As she soaked, she recalled when she had first come here, when she made a fool of herself. She recalled a lot of her past. On finishing her bath she went to bed.

The next day Dana saw Rainie in her studio. The two women shared a glance and a smile. Rainie was back and Dana was relieved because she needed her, more than Rainie might have known.

Dana made her way to the tailoring station. She had begun lessons on running the weaving machines. She liked it there, the steady clacking of the machines; the spindles running back and forth and the softness of the material. The wooden materials did not hold the same fondness Dana had for cotton.

It was late before she left there. On her way to her dorm she thought about many things. Dana wanted to see Dirk and Carla, but that could wait till tomorrow.

Chapter 13

*T*he snow had melted and spring was underway.

Jo, Susan and Lily had been out since early morning looking over the garden area. They worked edging the area that would be worked up today.

The children picked rocks and took them to a pile that had been started. Zack, over the winter had made them all wagons.

Jo thought the children could move mountains if left to their own devices, then smiled as she watched them.

All the bushes were burned, digging them out was unnecessary. The charcoal was good for the ground.

Zack was making plans for his kiln and for a blacksmith shop.

They took a few hours at noon to rest a bit. After they ate, Jo took West and his wagon to look for wild plants. West enjoyed these trips; it gave him a chance to adventure.

Today he made a great find, an old bee's nest. He hollered to Jo and she came to see. This was a great find. She knew they would not get honey, but they would get wax. Jo gathered every piece of wax like it was gold. She would make preserves and share it with the three families. What a treat. She made West promise not to breath a word, as at Christmas they would receive the gift. What a lovely surprise for them. West was proud as a peacock at his discovery and promised his mom he would say nothing.

She tussled his hair, "You are my dear of dears" she said to him and they continued on.

Jo noticed the maple trees and made a note of their location. They would supply maple syrup.

It was time to head back. Jo looked over their treasure, a bunch of wild onions, sage and some wild flowers for her pleasure and the wax and a bunch of reeds for baskets.

West pulled the wagon; he took his job seriously, but with pride as well.

The work that afternoon was hard; when dusk fell she was glad for it. When Jo arrived at the cabin, Zack had a tub of water for her to bath in.

"Oh Zack I do love you so" Jo told him.

He smiled and sent West to the smaller tub.

Zack bathes West. He was pretty grubby after all that picking that day. After cleaning him up, he had supper ready for him.

Jo soaked in her tub. Zack added more hot water for her.

He sat down and relaxed. West soon finished eating and after a hug headed for his room. He knew night was when mom and dad had their time together.

Jo talked of the day and Zack showed her his ideas after she got out of the tub. She ate the food Zack made and drank the tea.

It was getting dark and soon the light from the fire would fade.

Jo emptied the tubs and went to bed. Tomorrow would be another busy day.

Dawn came early for Jo. She got up and started the fire. It wasn't long before Zack joined her and then West. They talked of many things, but all too soon it was time for work.

"West, put your sweater on there's still coolness in the air" Jo told him.

Jo and West headed to the garden. West was big enough to move some of the big rocks, any he couldn't manage, and then Jo, Gary and Brad moved. The women digging and turning over the soil made good progress. They would have the garden ready soon.

They still needed the fields for flax and wheat, they would be next. Brad and Gary would help with those. The two men were building some out buildings for storage and a workshop. The endless wood for fires kept them more than busy. Zack had built a station to make it easier for him to chop wood.

Jo marvelled at how he managed. He tired easily, but managed to keep enough wood cut, West of course stacked it for him.

It was a happy time Jo thought. She was happy to have a place they called their own, she was content.

Zack on wet days kept on with West and the other children's education.

They had grown over the winter and Zack could see the growth in their minds. He wondered how long it would be before the children would change into young adults.

When Zack was alone he mapped the area. He and West walked and Zack was always drawing or writing. West would soon be picking up these habits. West loved his father; he never minded that he had trouble walking; it just was and it never seemed a problem for him.

West roamed the valley. He was inquisitive and enjoyed discovering. On this one particular day he discovered a walnut grove. He picked up a sack full and headed back to the cabin. Zack was the first he saw. He was by the river examining the clay. "West, my dear boy where have you been? Your mother has been looking for you" Zack said to him.

"OH just out and about" West replied. ""Do you know what's over the next ridge father?" West asked.

"No West I don't" Zack looked at him. "I never made it that far. You are as far into the mountains as I ever was" Zack told him.

"Father, don't you wonder what's there?" West asked.

"Not anymore West" Zack replied.

West could tell it was not the time to pursue that line of questions. "What are you looking for here?" West asked.

"Oh, just looking at the clay. I want to use it to make things" Zack told him. "Let's go back to the cabin West" Zack said and the two headed back.

Zack could hear the nuts in West's bag. "What's have you got in your pack?" Zack asked.

"Oh, just something for mom" West smiled.

Jo was happy t see them coming. She had water on to make tea.

West was soon showing Jo his cache of nuts and as usual talking a mile a minute about what he had seen.

Jo looked at the nuts "You must take me there West" she told him.

Zack had a small ball of clay and he threw it into the fire. "We will see if that brick house is possible now" Jo smiled.

West was soon in bed. Jo sat and opened the walnuts. She was surprised to find that most were still good.

"Zack: Jo said as she fumbles opening the nuts.

"What my dear?" Zack replied.

"West is going to be asking questions he needs to know" Jo looked at Zack.

"I know, he was asking questions today. I will tell him soon" Zack told her.

Jo nodded "I'm tired tonight Zack."

He looked at her "I'm tired too, seems like an awfully long day."

Chapter 14

Dana was with Dirk and Carla. She was glad they were spared. She wished they had suffered no loss, but they lost two of their children.

"Dirk, do you know if the animals survived outside?" Dana asked.

"Well with the ones that survived in here, they may have."

"Do you have enough stock in here to meet the needs of the complex?" Dana asked.

Dirk thought for a moment "Yes I believe so, we have enough Dana. We lost a few lines, but with the cross breeding I believe we can get the diversity back." Dana was relieved.

""How is it that we had so many live Dirk? From what I read of my mother's journals they all died outside." "I don't know Dana, Simion picked the best animals and we did give them top of the line food. Maybe all the hormones and genetic breeding they did alter them too be resistant."

"Humm" Carla said "I think Simion mentioned that it was more than that Dirk. He did say it was something with genetics."

Dana sat for a moment and after she thought about it, "then my father might still be alive?" she said. "He never died with the other people; my mother's journal said he was on his way back."

Dirk put his hand on Dana's shoulder "This complex is so remote, if he is alive he may never make it back, but then" Dir smiled, "You just never know. Let's go and see if our animals are still okay." Dana got up and they headed for the animal tunnels.

There were a lot of empty pens. It broke Dana's heart to think how many animals had died.

Dirk was always checking the ones left over. "Yes Dana, I believe we will be just fine."

Dana was relieved "I need to go see Andy; I'll be back later if I can."

Dirk looked up "Okay Dana" he said.

Dana made her way to Andy. He had survived also, too Dana's relief.

He kept a written record of all the people in the complex. She always enjoyed Andy's company. Dana was more interested in who could fill the empty stations. They still needed machinists and people for the labs and the carpentry stations. Dana just took the job on, of finding people for the different stations. So many passed due to the virus and as such all was in a total upheaval. She had done well, everything was running again, but training was needed in many lines of work. The young had to fill the posts and it was Dana that encouraged them to do it.

Andy, as normal was in the library when Dana arrived. She sat down next to Andy "What is it my dear?" Andy asked.

"Andy have you finished updating the complex's family tree?"

"Almost Dana, you want to see it again?" he said and smiled at her.

"Yes please" she said.

He showed her the family tree and noted all the red lines. It made her sad to see some families gone. She did see many survivors. It seemed to follow a pattern; she just could twig what it was. After studying it for a while, she thanked Andy and went to her dorm. Dana took a bath and rested.

She got settled and was reading Dee's journals when a knock was at her door.

"Come in" Dana called out.

It was Erik, "Hi Dana" he said.

"Hi Erik, want some tea or hot chocolate?" Dana asked.

"No thanks, I just wanted to thank you" he said.

"Thank me? Thank me for what Erik?" Dana asked.

"For giving me back my mom" he said.

"Oh, she never left Erik, she just needed to sort some things through is all" Dana replied.

"Since dad passed, it's been awful" Erik started "he really made the difference around the place. Mom missed him so much, I do too. How do you do it Dana? How do you put it away and carry on?"

Dana looked at him, "Erik it was hardly the same for me. I never knew my parents. I miss them and have so much, but it's not the same.

You had Simion all your life. He was always that rock for you and your mom, strong, steadfast and he was so smart. I envied you so many times" Dana told him. "I know Simion is in you Erik. You are much like him you know?" Dana put a hand on his arm "He taught you strength you know. You must draw on it to help your self and your mom. She's strong too you know, just listen to her when she wants to talk to you. It will be a while before you both find your own peace with all of it."

Erik looked at her "Father was right about you." Dana looked at him "He was?"

"Yes Dana" he said "He said you looked at things differently and he was right. I have been t busy in solving a problem. I need to look beyond it, that's what he said that you did."

"Thanks again Dana" Erik told her.

"I'm glad we are friends" Dana said.

"Me too" he told her and made his way to the door. "We will be okay" he said.

"Yes, I think we will be" Dana replied.

Dana sat there and thought about Erik, he really was a nice fellow.

Dana's mind wandered over all the people and she cried when she thought of Warren. He had cared for her from day one. He was gone, if what she felt for Warren was anything like what they felt for Simion. Then they will take a long while to get over them. Simion and Warren echoed in her mind, keep the complex going; it is the key for all here and maybe for the outside as well.

Dana crawled into bed and went to sleep.

Chapter 15

Summer was hot and West loved it. He had now wandered over most of the valley.

During the week he helped with the farming and building.

Jo had the vegetable garden well worked and planted with the help of the other two women. Sara and Lily worked tirelessly along with her. They had spent the summer digging and preparing more land for next year's crop. The flax field needed to be at least twice as big.

Zack found the clay good to fire after the ball he threw into the fireplace turned red. He made a kiln from the rocks in the rock pile. From there he started making pottery.

The women were glad for the crock pots and water jugs.

He made a potters wheel he could spin with his good leg.

They had a well for water.

Brad and Gary worked hard. They built the work shop.

Zack rolled plans for a forge over in his head. He wanted to make bricks, but mortar might prove harder to make than the bricks. He wondered if some of the few older men at the settlement might have some ideas.

He decided this winter to tell West of Dee and the complex. He could see that West was an adventurer. His curiosity of what was over the next ridge might lead him to find it.

Zack made a surplus of things. They would make good trade items and the settlement women would need them as well.

A young man had brought news from the settlement. There would be visitors before snow fall.

The women excitedly prepared for the visit. Life was going on and Zack was comforted by it. He thought of his mother not wanting to leave the farm. He understood how she felt now. As he potted, he rolled the plans of pipes and other things in his mind. They needed a forge, yes they did he thought.

He finished with the clay. He had and wanted to surprise Jo with a tub of hot water. She loved to bath and he didn't blame her. The hot water always eased the pains in his legs.

He washed up and headed into the cabin. It wasn't long before West was there.

Zack looked at him and said "You look like you has a grand day, by the dirt on you", they both laughed.

He would be ten soon and for such a little fellow he was a great help. "How's the field going for your mom?" Zack asked.

"Oh it's okay, we have nearly all the rocks gone" West told him.

"That's good" Zack said "I your mom misses her flax, she does like to weave."

West watched as Zack dragged out the tub. "Want me to get the water?" Zack looked over his shoulder "Yes my boy that would be a big help."

West hurried outside to the well and brought in two buckets. When Zack filled the pots to boil it, West got two more for the next ones.

"You better get cleaned up or she will have you in one also" West looked at Zack "That's okay, I think I need one." Zack laughed.

"Dad" West said. "Yes what is it?" Zack replied.

"When I get older could I make a trip to the fort?" Zack looked at him in surprised. "What do you want to go to the fort for?" "Oh I just want to go see that's all" West told him.

"We'll see West, we'll see" Zack told him. "Brad and Gary may make a trip there. If they do I'll talk to your mom about it, alright West?" West beamed.

Zack soon had the tub full and one for West. Jo arrived at dusk and was glad to see something to eat and the tub of water. Jo was soon soaking and West was off to bed.

Zack chatted about the extra pots and things for the visitors from the settlement. Jo too told him of the dried herbs she had.

"How goes the fields Jo?" Zack asked her.

"Oh sometimes I feel like I'm digging to China, that it will never end. They are coming. This is the worst part, breaking new ground. It will be easier after this." Jo told him.

Zack felt for her. She worked hard. "Our boy wants to take a trip to the fort" Zack told her. "What does he want to go there for?" Jo asked. "He told me to just see it." "He is like someone else we know" Jo said and smiled.

Zack sat at the table and smiled.

"Think it will rain soon?" she asked.

"By the aching in my bones I would say yes" he said. "I do hope it does rain. I don't relish packing water to the gardens again." Jo said.

"You work too hard Jo" Zack told her.

"I don't mind, it keeps me sane. Beside, come harvest everyone will be happy. This winter I have some surprises" she smiled.

Jo wrapped herself in the clothes that Zack had hung by the fire to warm them. She wrapped her hair and gathered her work clothes and West's and threw them into the tub of water.

Zack was up now and said "Let me do that, comb out your hair" Jo smiled.

Zack washed the clothes. Jo told him not to be so fussy. They would just get grimed out tomorrow again. He hung them by the fire.

Jo started to empty the tubs. She watered her flowers outside with some and her herbs. The rest she tossed into the yard. The tubs were empty now and she sat by the fire.

It burned to embers and Zack said "Let's hit the hay" Jo agreed.

The morning always came too soon, but today the rain was falling. The garden work was on hold. "Hear the rain Jo? No packing water today." She was happy for that. The rain barrels would fill and that was always nice. Today she could catch up with things in the house. She wanted to use some things that Zack had made. It wasn't long before she had breakfast done and sat to do the mending. Zack and West talked of making bricks.

She could hear Brad and Gary in the workshop. She was glad they had a dry place to work now.

Jo watched Zack and West. She was glad she never left that day. Zack looked over at her "What's up, you like a cat that just swallowed a mouse?" Jo laughed.

"What's a cat dad?" West asked.

"Now you started it" Jo laughed. "I'm going over to see Sara. I'll be back in a while." Jo told them and Zack nodded.

Jo knew Sara was with child and even though she didn't say she was.

"Sara" Jo told her "You need to rest more. I don't want you digging anymore" Sara smiled. "It's okay Jo I'll be okay" Sara replied.

"No you can start picking berries and dry them. Soon the garden will be ready and you'll have work enough there."

"Alright Jo I will do that" Jo was relieved, she patted Sara's hand. "I'm off to Lily's" Jo said as she went out the door.

Jo looked back "No heavy anything" and pointed her finger at her. Sara smiled.

Jo made her way to Lily's. When she arrived she was spinning flax.

She stopped and made them some tea. Jo sat down "You know that Sara is in the family way?" Lily looked at her "Well she had better lay off garden digging then" Lily said.

"Yes I have been to see her. She can start gathering berries and nuts will soon be falling." "That's good" Lily said. "It will give us a jump start on that. Harvest will be upon us before we know it. Next year we will have flax and oats. I will be glad when we get this done." Lily told her. "Yes the first year is the hardest" Jo replied. "Yes, but this is a good valley and it's full of good things to eat." Lily said. "Well" said Jo, "I just wanted to talk to you about Sara." Lily smiled.

As Jo left, she walked in the rain and looked at Sara's fruit trees. They had grown a lot. With winter around the corner she hoped for a good snow pack to cover them.

It would be at least three or four years before they start to bloom.

Jo made her way back to the cabin and found comfort there with Zack and West.

Rainy days always made her reflect on things and soon, Zack her convinced to pop some corn. The rest of the afternoon and evening were spent talking and kidding West.

Chapter 16

*D*ana had been watching the outside monitors. She could see that indeed some things had survived. It warmed her to think that someday they might go outside.

The council voted to close it up for the time being, until the complex was running smoothly again.

Dana found herself at a loss for something to work at. She had not found what she wanted to do yet. Of all the stations she favoured tailoring the most. Of course the animal station was a close second.

Dana was nearly sixteen now. The young men watched her more than before. She found it unnerving. When she told Dirk, he just smiled at her "It was as it should be" and smiled again. Dirk knew that she wasn't ready to be with a young man yet, but soon the time will be upon her.

Carla had kept the remaining animals in good shape. Soon they too would be paired off for the next season. Carla and Dirk were getting older, now their children had taken over most of the work. Like Carla and Dirk they had a way with the animals. They too, soon would be thinking of families of their own.

Carla was relieved that the virus was over. It had taken so many, but the people left would be free to go back outside. It surprised her that so many people and animals did survive.

Carla asked Dana "Would you like to help when the animals are birthing?" Dana smiled and said "Yes I would." Carla smiled because she knew Dana was happy when the new animals arrived.

Dana left Carla and Dirk and went to the agro tunnel. She wanted some flowers to take to the funeral tunnel.

Karen and David had been spared by the virus. Dana made regular visits to see Karen for flowers.

"Karen" Dana asked when she saw her, "Would you go and see Rainie sometimes?" "Yes Dana I think that could be arranged" Karen replied. Dana told her that Rainie was back in her studio, but that she worried about her.

Karen watched Dana as she walked around the flower beds. "Are you going to take some flowers to our lost ones?" Karen asked.

"I want to if you might spare some?" Dana said to her.

Karen said "Come with me." Dana followed her and as they rounded the corner Dana smiled. "I have grown these in pots so they can be placed there." Karen you think of everything" Dana said.

"The flowers will have to be watered and when they finish blooming you will have to bring them back, okay?" Karen said.

Dana hugged her.

Karen knew that the loss was hard for most. Flowers would make them feel a little better.

Karen decided that she would see Rainie soon. It was time for her to get away from work a bit. David would be happy. He always tells her to go out more, but he was just as bad with is bugs.

Dana took a few baskets and made her way to the tombs. Before the virus outbreak there were not many that went there. Now there always seems to be someone there. It did not make Dana feel good that others had to feel the pain of losing someone.

Dana placed the two baskets near the entrance. Then she went in and sat near her mother's tomb. "Well mom the virus got in and as you see you are not alone anymore. I wish you were here now, more than ever before. Simion, Warren, Dirk's children and so many more are no longer here for me to seek solaced with mother. Help me be strong."

Dana sat quietly for about and hour more and then made her way to her dorm.

Karen and David survived the virus, but one of their children did not. Since the death of Noel, the small family kept together. They worked and studied anything to get through the days. Petra seemed to miss her brother so much. She found working with her father gave her the stability she needed.

Karen knew it was David not the work that was the help. David talked little of Noel, but she knew he loved him. It was his way. When the outside suffered, they decided through the loss that life must continue. Karen believed David felt that way now. He told her that we have to be thankful that we survived and that we have Petra. All is not lost, just changed. David looked at her and said "Changed yes changed." "I will miss him so Karen" he told her. After that they spoke little of Noel, but Karen knew he was with them now and always.

It was then that Karen began to pick some flowers for Rainie. As she picked out the blossoms she thought of Simion, than of Rainie and Erik. She was glad Rainie had Erik. After Dee's death Rainie was terrified to have her child, but all went well. For Rainie there were no more children, she feared it too much. Simion didn't mind, Erik was enough for him. The child was perfect to him. How he loved Rainie. So different they were, but what they shared brought them close together,

Karen thought of David then and how they felt for each other. Her mind drifted to Petra and Dana. They soon would find partners to share their life with.

Rainie saw her first and was delighted to see her, their visits were not often enough.

They sat drinking hot chocolate and talking of daily living. Rainie was going back to the art studio, but Karen asked her to go to the funeral tunnel with her. Rainie looked at her and agreed. It was on the walk there, they asked each other how things were, and Karen told her how she felt about losing Noel. How she was having trouble finding something to fill the void he left.

Rainie understood too well. "Do you think the emptiness will ever be filled?" Rainie asked her. "No Rainie, I don't think so, but each passing month I find the loss easier to deal with. It doesn't go away. I just find different ways of coping."

Rainie looked at Karen "I do understand." The two women walked arm in arm to the tombs. They stayed there for about and hour and after they went to Rainie's dorm.

"Karen you have been good to me, thank you" Rainie said.

"It's good to have another woman to share some things with" Karen said. "I must get back Rainie, David worries for me. He is good to me, but this has not been easy for him or Petra." Rainie thought of Erik. "I know Erik has been such a steadfast tower for me too." Karen added "Rainie, promise me to not forget his feelings. He is not a tower, just a young man."

Rainie nodded.

"We must do coffee soon." Karen told her. Rainie agreed.

Karen left; Rainie would be fine she thought, Dana always worried about everyone.

It did take Rainie long to start crying after Karen left, but they were more tears of relief than sorrow. Relief that she would be okay, she knew that now.

Chapter 17

Summer turned to fall and it wouldn't be long before winter would be upon them.

Zack with the help of West had put things they needed to be stored for the winter away.

The harvest had been great. There was plenty of food to hold them through until next spring. The people from the settlement had been, they brought oats and flax for them and Zack presented many pottery items for them. Jo had herbs that she shared and the gathering had turned to a festive time for all, but too soon the returned to the settlement.

West had taken up the studies with Zack in earnest and the other children followed suit.

Jo, thankful to have received the flax, sat and spun as she listened to their progress.

The days passed and soon the snow was falling in the valley they made their life in.

Zack had promised to tell West of the complex and of his other child.

Jo had been weaving when Zack brought out his maps and things from his past with what they started their journey into the valley. When Jo realized he had chosen this time to tell West, she told him she was off to visit Sara.

Zack looked up from the table and told her to take her time.

West had been filling the wood shed when Zack called him in. West was a good child and Zack wasn't sure how he would react to the story he was about to tell him. He had made tea and sat at the table which was now covered with maps and different items. West sat down and drank his tea.

Zack decided to start at the beginning. "West I must tell you of life a little. There are a few things I would like you to know."

West sat listening "Okay Dad" he told him.

"Okay let's start before the viruses were let loose. I worked with many people; I was a foreman for building projects which many I designed as well. There were lots of people in the world and animals. I grew up on a farm with my mother and father. It was not that different from here, this place." West sat quietly. "I didn't live at home with them. I travelled to many places over the world. We had many ways of travelling, by boat, trains and cars. We had planes that flew in the sky." Zack shared his memories of many things in the cities he had been to. West sat and listened. Zack proceeded to tell him of the complex where he worked and how Simion had known things in the world that were not right. He told him of Dee and how he felt for her.

West looked at him "How did she die, like the others Dad?"

Zack then told him how he was called away from the complex to help his mother as his father was dying. It was when he was there that the virus was let loose on the world. He told him of the deaths, the panic of the people and animals. How they perished and how the people in hunger killed any animals they found still living. He told West how he met Jo, his mother and saved her from the men who were chasing her.

He went on and told him how he and Jo started their journey to make it back to the complex. How he wanted to get back to Dee and that she was with child. It was well into the evening when he told him how he had fallen and how Jo saved his life. How Zack knew his journey was at the end and it was Jo that made him find reasons to keep on living. He told West although he loved Dee and missed her to this day and the child he never got to see, that Jo was his partner in life now and would be until he passed. He told West that he was blessed beyond his dreams. It was Jo that gave him the reasons to live on and she had given him, you West.

West sat looking at his dad. He had just heard a story that would forever be with him. He knew that Zack loved him and his mother, but he knew he had lost some people were equally dear. West never asked many questions just went over to Zack and hugged him. "I love you dad and I love mom, but I will tell you something, I will look for this place and maybe someday we will be together." Zack was relieved he had told him, but he knew in his heart that if West did look, he would likely not find them and he would not live to see it.

Zack now felt at ease. "Look here West" Zack told him. "This is the map I have of the mountains, here and further on. This is our valley here and the settlement is here." He pointed to the map. "I believe the complex to be in this area.

West carefully looked at the map and told Zack. "Well dad, that's an awful long ways to there. I wish I had a plane to fly there." Zack smiled "So did I West, so did I."

Zack let West look over the map and play somewhat with the compass. He told West that the compass was maybe one of the most important items he would need if ever he decided to go on a journey. West looked at him "I will father, I will" and he put the compass back in its case.

It was late and Zack was beginning to wonder where Jo was.

Jo sat with Sara and let her talk of things that troubled her. This child seemed to be the hardest of all her children to carry so far. Jo knew she had worked to hard, but she was younger than Jo and had that advantage. Brad had been busy making items for her. He made a cradle, high chair, a crib for later and a dresser and a chest to keep the new baby's things in. Jo thought Sara looked tired and she still had a few months to go.

Jo brought some diapers and a blanket she had made. Sara was happy and thanked her very much. Jo had been making paper and thought that maybe keeping a record of everyone was a good idea.

"Sara" Jo asked "Do you remember much before when the virus was let loose on the world?"

Sara smiled "Yes I remember the settlement and how we had animals. We had milk and eggs and so many other things. Oh the foods we made and the things the animals provided like wool and leather. I remember many things and then when everything died, so many passed and sadness, when the people stopped dieing and the fear of things, with us so few of us left. When the animals were gone it was awful, but our remaining elders got us working and they helped us get organized. Had it not been them I fear we would not have survived. It was not long after that I remember you coming to the settlement. You gave us all so much hope and how you helped us save the crops. You have always been a good person Jo and Zack, oh how terrible it was. When it was us that came here, I was so proud and well Jo, I looked upon you as my dear friend; a friend as my own sister would have been."

Jo got up and hugged her. "I feel the same way about you too Sara. You and Lily have been so wonderful. I would not like to think of my life without both of you in it."

They shared stories of their lives before the virus and since.

It was dark when they decided to call it a night. Jo asked Sara to take it easy and Sara smiled.

Jo made her way back to their cabin. Zack was still up waiting for her. West had gone to bed.

After Jo settled she asked Zack how it went. Zack calmly told her they had a wonderful child in West and that he loved her.

Jo never pursued the subject further.

Zack felt like a weight had been lifted from him. He silently wished West luck and hoped he would someday find the complex, someday.

Morning came all too soon, but it being winter there was no hurry on waking up. The days that followed found Jo caring for her men and visiting Sara and Lily. The time was approaching fast for Sara's baby to arrive.

West was excited too. He had watched Sara grow in size and when Sara placed his hand on her swollen stomach, he would beam a smile at Sara when he felt the baby move.

The three families were almost as one, each caring and watching out for the others.

Jo took West aside one day and told him that when Sara's time came it would be his job to care for the other children. West smiled, it would be good that he would have a job.

It was now near spring and the thaw had begun. Jo got West and told him to get the sled that Zack had made; she dressed warmly and headed to Lily's. Jo didn't take long in getting Mark and Cassy ready to join them. They had several baskets with them. The children were excited.

Jo took them to the trees about a mile away. She had Zack carve wooden spouts that could easily be pounded into the trees. She had West place the buckets under each spout. This was a fun time for the children. They had never tapped the maples for sap and it was going to be a pleasant surprise for them. They left the sleigh there and hiked back. Tomorrow they would collect them. It would take several days, but the bounty was going to be delightful.

The next day they were back collecting the sap. Jo had them pour it all into one bucket, them two and then they brought the sap home.

After a fire was built in the workshop, Jo boiled the sap to remove the water. Soon it was thick and gooey. She took a ladle full and poured onto some clean snow. She gave all the children a piece of the hardened male syrup and watched as they delighted in it. She soon had plenty of syrup and filled the clay pots that Zack had made.

The sleigh again was taken out and the spouts and the buckets were removed. Jo told the children the trees needed to heal. Next spring they would again come and harvest them. The syrup was a great treat and all the families shared the bounty.

It was mid afternoon when Brad appeared at their cabin. "It's Sara Jo" he told her. Jo looked at him "Her time?" Jo asked. "Yes" Brad responded. "Okay I will be there shortly."

Jo dressed and was soon Sara's side. Jo checked on Sara and child. She soon had West take Amy to their house and Brad off to get Lily. As she boiled the water, she prepared Sara and for the new arrival. Lily was soon there and the two women eased Sara through the birth. It was a boy and he was perfect. Lily cleaned him and wrapped him in warm cloths. Sara had an addition to her family. It was an easy birth and Jo helped her to bed. After she settled Jo gave her the child to nurse, while Lily and Jo cleaned up.

West had all the children in tow and they were talking of great adventures they were going to make, when Jo arrived at their cabin. All the children wanted to hear. "It's a boy and they are both fine." Brad, Gary and Zack were all relieved and the children were happy to have a new playmate.

Gary gathered up his children and headed home.

Lily could not leave Sara until Brad arrived. Jo convinced him to leave Amy for the night and he went on to see Sara.

Jo sat with Zack and watched West and Amy. It was Zack that popped the corn this night, as he and Jo thought of the new life.

The next day with Amy's hand in hers they went to Sara's. Brad had things well in hand and Amy went straight to her mom. The baby and Sara looked well. Jo asked if they had chosen a name. It was Brad that piped up "We are calling him Sean" Brad smiled.

Jo went over and picked up the baby, "Well welcome Sean" she said and gave him back to his mother. Amy looked and touched his small head, then crawled up on the bed next to Sara. She kissed her mom and said "I like him" and then crawled off the bed and went and sat on her dad's knee. He let her stay and soon told Jo tea was ready.

Jo came out and asked him to boil some water. Brad smiled "Already done." He looked over to where the hot water was, "West you visit with Brad for a while."

With that Jo closed the door and helped Sara wash. Jo changed the bed linens. He had a good set of lungs as he bellowed through his bath. After clean wrappings, he was soon contented at his mother's breast.

Lily was there then and the two women soon had the linens washed and hung to dry.

Sara's strength was returning and Jo was relieved.

Jo told Sara that she would check on her the next day and called to West as she made her way home.

Chapter 18

Dana was on her way to the fish farm, when she met a young man carrying too many boxes, more than he could handle. She stopped and took two from him and asked him where they were to go. "Those two go to the labs, for Carla the vet. Do you know where she is?" he asked. "Yes" Dana told him. "Good that will save me some leg work" he replied.

Dana turned and was about to go, when he said from behind the boxes that he was able to manage, "Do you work here at the farms?" "No I haven't ye found what I want to do" Dana replied. "Ah" the young man replied "I am the same, but my folks think I should choose something soon. So in the mean time I get to be an errand boy" and he laughed. Dana smiled; the young man asked "Do you know where I might find Dirk? I have something for him too? They told me that he may be in the animal tunnels." Dana said "Just follow me; I was on my way there anyways."

The young man chatted on and Dana found him funny. "So what's your name?" he asked. "Dana" she told him. "Oh that's a nice name" he said "You are lucky, some girls have awful names." "Dana" he said "I like it." Just then Dirk appeared. "There you are Todd, what took you lad?" "They had trouble making what you asked for in the shop. Dad worked for awhile to get it right." "Thank him for me will you Todd?" Todd nodded, "Was nice to meet you Dana" and Todd was on his way.

Dirk watched Dana watch Todd.

"Dana, Dana!" Dirk called her. She turned and looked at him. "Oh, oh" Dana said, "These are for Carla." Dirk took the boxes from her. "You okay Dana?" Dirk asked.

Dana blushed from head to toe. "Yes I'm fine Dirk" she replied. Dirk never pursued the conversation further, he just smiled.

"So have you come to see the new arrivals? We have quite a few" Dirk smiled.

"Yes I would love to see them" she said. "Any lambs?" she asked.

"Yes" Dirk told her and watched her smile.

They spent the next few hours checking them over and then Dana told him she wanted to check on the birds. Dirk nodded and Dana made her way over to the aviaries.

There were very few birds left after the virus, but it seemed they were nesting and Dana was pleased. She passed the hawks and the owls and was soon at the smaller birds. She liked the song birds, Finches, canaries, warblers and sparrows. She watched as they flew in the cages.

She then went to the communications room. It was a long ways, but she always went, somewhere, in her heart she wished that one day there would be a face or voice coming through. There never was.

She made her way down to the living area. She wanted a tea and liked to watch the people. She was surprised to see Rainie there and Erik with a few friends.

Rainie called her over and they drank their tea together. Rainie started telling Dana of her plans for the statues of Simion and Warren. Dana was happy that Rainie was renewing her talents. "Oh Rainie I think that's wonderful." Rainie smiled "I was just sitting here looking to see where she they should be put, any suggestions?" Rainie asked.

"Oh my" Dana said. Rainie had done five statues to date and Dana suggested they be placed near the fountain. "I think that's the place. Want to come with me to pick out the stone?" Rainie asked her. "I think I would like that." Dana said.

Rainie and Dana headed to where the masons were. With the deaths, the masons had kept busy in the tombs. They were opening another tunnel for the future. Although many did not relish the idea, it was the elder mason Nick that said it was a necessary evil.

Nick lost his wife Sophie to the virus and his daughter Mary. When Nick saw Rainie, a big smile swept across his face. "Rainie it's so good to see you." He went over and hugged her. "I'm so glad to see you again." "It's good to see you too Nick." Rainie told him. "I have come to see some stone" she told him. "Ah" Nick replied "Come this way my dear, I'm sure we can find something." He smiled.

They walked down the tunnel and into another; here were the blocks of stone. Rainie was pleased. "Do you have plans for it?" Rainie asked. "Most would be used for pillars. Pick what you want" he said.

There were stacks of stones that they were using to close individual tombs, pillars that were well on there way to being finished, marble for tablets and counter tops.

"What do you think? We found another vein of marble. It's a good if not better than the last one." Nick said.

Just then Dana saw him again. He was carving a pillar. Dana watched him carve then smoothed over some rough spots. Dana watched him and how he moved as he worked the stone. Todd was unaware of her watching him and then he stood back for a moment and looked at the pillar. He seemed satisfied.

"Dana, Dana!" Rainie called her. At that time Todd looked over and smiled at her and she blushed. She turned to see Rainie watching her. "Yes!" she said to Rainie.

Rainie was looking past her and saw Todd.

Nick was the one that broke the silence, seeing them looking at Todd. "That's my sister's boy, Good lad and a hard worker. Now Rainie do you want these pieces brought to your studio?" he asked. Rainie said she did and Rainie and Dana made their way out.

It was Rainie who spoke first. "Have you met Todd before? He seems to know you." Rainie asked.

"Yes I met him earlier today" Dana replied. "He has a feeling for stone" Rainie told her. "He has been to my studio to ask my opinions on stones he has worked on." "Oh" Dana replied.

"He is a very nice young man, but I think he needs direction in life. I would like to see him carve, but I don't think he wants to for a living." Rainie said.

Dana then said "I know the feeling. I am having the same trouble. I just don't know which I like best, tailoring station or the animals."

"Well you know Dana, you could do both. There's no law that says you must have only one avenue of profession. I have always believed that everyone should learn to do many things. It was a good thing too; after the virus went through here we lost many of our key people. Had others not learned more than one position, I fear we would have been in trouble."

Dana believed her to be right. She was glad she had Rainie to talk with.

They walked and talked more. Then Dana told Rainie that she was heading for the tailoring station. Rainie told Dana to be careful around the machines.

As Dana walked there, her mind wandered back to Todd. How come she never noticed him before? He was about two or three years older than her. He was tall and well built. Dana noticed his dark hair and he had blue eyes. His face was strong, but with kindness in it.

She rounded the corner and walked right into Todd. He caught her as she stumbled.

"Oh it's you!" Dana said.

He was covered with dust from the stone he was carving. "Yes it's me" he smiled.

"I'm sorry" Dana told him "My mind was elsewhere" she replied.

"No problem" he commented "I had to pick up new aprons for the cravers. What are you doing in this neck of the woods?" he asked her. "Oh, I was just on my way to the weaver station." "Oh, is that where you work?" he asked. "Yes, there and with the animals" she stated. "I thought about working in the machine shop and thought I might try carpentry." Oh, my mother was a carpenter." Todd looked at her "What does your father do?" he asked. "He was a designer." "Oh sorry" Todd said "Did you lose him when the virus got in?" "No, no" Dana replied. Todd didn't ask anymore questions. He could see she was nervous. "Well, I'll be off. Nick will be wondering if I got lost."

They both smiled and they went on their way. Dana was glad, he made her nervous, but it was a strange kind of nervous. Who was he anyways she thought. How come she had not noticed him before? Soon she was at the tailor station. Dana started to weave, but her mind was on Todd.

Todd made his way back to where the masons were working. Nick was there "Well Todd, what took you s long?" "Oh nothing much I was talking with Dana."

Nick looked at Todd "You best be good to that girl, she's not had an easy time of things." Todd asked Nick "Who is she? I have never noticed here about before." "She's a nice girl. She spends too much of her time alone I think" Nick said.

"Who is she?" Todd asked again.

"She is Dee and Zack's daughter." "Who were they?" Todd asked.

"Come and sit here and I will tell you" Todd sat down.

"Zack and Dee, they were such a pair" Nick said as his mind wandered back to the first days of the complex. "Her father helped build the complex.

He was the main foreman. He designed much of what is here. He was a good man and never once did I ever see him abuse his power. Dee his wife, Dana's mother was a lovely woman. If I wanted a straight answer, Dee was the one you would have asked. She carved wood. It was her passion. Almost all the wood, everything here has her touch on it. When the virus was first let loose Zack was not here. He was with his dying father. Simion closed the complex to protect us and Zack was locked outside. We know he was trying to get back. He managed to contact us here twice. Then we never heard from him again. It was devastating for Dee, she was with child. We all tried to comfort her, but I can tell you she never recovered the loss of him. When Dana was born Dee died, it was a terrible thing. I remember sealing her tomb. She was the first one that perished here. It was Warren that took Dana and raised her as his own. Everyone that knew Zack and Dee cared for Dana. She has grown into a beautiful young woman, so listen. You had better not hurt that child; she has carried hurt with her all her life." Nick meant what he said and Todd knew it.

"That's awful" Todd said.

"Yes" Nick told him "It has been lonely for her, but she is a nice young woman."

Todd looked at Nick "I like her. She's not pushy like the other girls I have met. There is a kind gentleness to her. I really like her." Todd said. "You had better treat her right Todd. I'm not the only one that looks out for her. Now you better get back to work." Nick told him.

Dana couldn't weave today. Her mind was just not on weaving. She decided to go talk with Dirk.

It wasn't long before she was with Dirk. "Dirk, can I talk with you?" she asked.

"Sure, what's the matter?" he asked.

"Oh nothing is wrong; I just wanted to talk a bit."

Dirk sat down. "You come sit here" he told her. "Well what's troubling you?" he said. "Oh it's not troubling I just want to ask about someone." Dirk nodded and "Who is this someone?" Dirk asked.

"Do you know Todd? He carves in with the masons." "Hmm" Dirk said "Todd you say? Ah that's Nick's nephew, his sister's boy. Has this boy offended you? If he has I will speak with Nick." "Oh no" Dana told him. "He has done nothing. He has been very nice. I just wanted to know more about him that's all."

"Well" Dirk said "I just know he is Nick's nephew. He has worked often with him. What I have seen he is a good young man." "Oh" Dana said "What does his mom and Dad do?"

"Lars, his dad helped the masons. I think his mom, Andrea that's Nick's sister worked nursing until the virus went through. I think she stays at home more than anything. After the virus, Andrea didn't go to the nursing station much. We all think she saw too much death and didn't want to work there anymore. Todd is a good fellow and works hard from what I've seen."

"Thank you" Dirk Dana smiled.

Dirk looked at her and thought that she has finally found a companion. He was not displeased with her choice as he liked Todd.

"So what do you want to talk about Dana?"

She smiled and said "Thank you Dirk. I'm going home. I feel restless today. I will see you tomorrow."

Dirk stood and went back to the animals. As he went he smiled at Dana and thought Dana, little Dana is growing up.

Dana made her way to her dorm. When she arrived, she made some tea. As she sat, slowly sipping her tea, her mind drifted back to Todd. She picked up the weaving samples she had been working on. She thought Rainie was right, why not do both. She drew a bath and soaked, it would help her unwind before bed.

Todd wanted to get to know Dana better. He just didn't know how. He had finished the pillar he had been working on and went to his dorm. He still lived with his mother and father. After he showered he sat beside his mother.

"Have you decided what you want to do?" his mother asked.

"I can think of a lot of things worse than working with stone." His mother smiled "Your father will be happy."

Todd smiled back "So how are you today mother?" Todd asked.

"Fine, fine" she replied "What has brought on this concern for me Todd?"

"Oh nothing, I was just thinking of the complex. You lived outside before didn't you?" Todd asked.

"Yes, but you knew that" she replied. "Do you ever think we will ever live in the outside world again?" Todd asked.

"All we can do is try. The complex is our haven. We can stay alive here until it's safe to go out." She told him.

"Do you think anyone survived out there? I have a hard time believing it. If anyone did, there would be issues of food and just living through any other illnesses that might have happened. Without doctors, life would hang on a thin thread."

"What has got you interested? Take my advice and don't think about it. We must replenish the people here and take care of ourselves before opening the doors again." Todd's mother said.

"Mother I met a girl."

"Oh well I now understand what's troubling you." She smiled "So tell me about this girl."

"Her name is Dana" he said. His mother looked at him "Dana is a good child."

"You know her then?" he asked. "Yes I do." "Well tell me about her."

"I think if you want to know Dana, you better ask her." His mother smiled.

Todd was getting more frustrated. Everyone seemed to know her, but didn't want to discuss her at all. He decided to get to know her more.

After a quiet evening with his parents Todd went to bed, tomorrow he would start a new pillar and he was going to see Dana.

Chapter 19

Spring came with all its work. Jo, Lily and West soon had the garden in. The digging of the fields for the oats and flax was started. Jo forbade Sara to dig, so West got the job, but he didn't mind. He felt more a part of the adult group. He removed the larger stones the younger children could not and the boulders were left for Brad and Gary to move.

West was in their company a lot more. Jo knew the children did not hold the interest with him now. He was getting older.

Cassy found helping Sara with Sean occupied her time. Mark, Chad and Amy were still found playing the best past time. They still had their choirs, but were let to play. West worked nearly as hard as Jo did. It surprised her just how strong he was. Lily was happy for the help digging as well. If they got this field done they could plant it and get a crop.

After two weeks of digging they planted what they turned over, and then they dug further. West had calluses on his hands now so it made it easier. When he stopped and rested, he would look at the mountains. Jo knew him and his adventurous spirit. He needed a break from work, he was still young.

That night Jo talked to Zack. "Do you remember that farm we stayed at before we reached the settlement? I wonder if it's still there."

"Why do you ask?" he asked.

"Oh I just wondered if the books were still there."

"Book?" Zack asked.

"Yes he had a great collection". Jo then said "I often thought of the fort too."

"Why is there something special you need?" Zack asked.

"No, no I was just wondering is all" Jo replied.

Zack stopped and looked at Jo "Okay Jo what's up?"

"Well, I was just thinking about West. He needs to…well I don't know" Jo said.

Zack smiled "I know he needs a break. I've seen it in him too. Gary is going to the settlement. Maybe West should go with him."

Jo smiled "Yes I think he should go, by the way Zack. Did I tell you that I love you?"

"Yes dear and did I tell you that I love you too?" Zack stood and looked at Jo. He thought that he really did love her.

It was Zack that talked to Gary about taking West. Gary didn't mind, he agreed the company would make the walk more enjoyable. When West found out he was happy. He enjoyed hiking and going to the settlement was exciting. "Is there anything you need mother?"

"No not this trip: she replied.

West knew he would have things to bring back, but he asked anyways. It was settled, Gary wanted to leave early. West never faltered with work, he dug in the field until dusk when Jo finally called him in.

"You must not push yourself so hard West" she told him. "Its okay mom I just wanted to get a bit more done." he smiled at her. West would soon be a man. In the past year Jo saw a big change in him.

They wasted no time in the morning. Gary laughed at West, always bounding everywhere. After the hike to the settlement his energy would be curbed. It would be late afternoon before they arrived and West was always full of questions.

"Gary have you ever been to the fort?" "Yes a few time." "Have you ever been beyond that?" West asked. "No, I never needed too. Besides the stories I heard about the places are kind of creepy." "What do you mean?" West asked. "Well, after the viruses went through there, the people died and with no one to bury them. They were just left. The folks say there are towns, towns of the dead."

"Do you remember times before that?" West listened. "I guess I was about your age West, when it happened. My mother and sister died, lots died at the settlement. Let's talk of more pleasant things." Gary said. West made no fuss about it.

As they hiked, West tried to think what is was like before. He thought about what Zack had told him. It was on that day, he promised to find the complex.

West was soon back to the hike and talked little after that. Gary noted his lack of conversation, but never pushed it.

They arrived at the settlement and everyone was glad to see them. West had noticed there were new people there and soon found out folks from the fort had been slowly moving into the valleys between them. With the coming and goings of people, the small paths were becoming well worn trails.

They stayed at Gary's brothers place and listened to them talk. With the new people in the settlement, the food resources would suffer if they didn't find new valleys to farm. Gary said he would talk Brad and Zack. The valley could sustain more, but there would be no free rides. If they didn't work they would not survive.

West never spoke, he just listened. He made his way to the door, went out and sat on the porch. He never considered more people coming to the valley. He knew Gary was right; there is room for more families.

Gary had the salt they came for. That evening there were a lot of things brought to give to Sara and Brad. It was a very old woman that came and Gave West a parcel for Jo. He thanked her.

The next day they headed back to the valley. The hike back was harder with all the goods they had. West talked little and Gary asked "So what do you think of the new folks in the valley?" West struggled then spoke "I never thought about more people, but I guess as more children are born, the older ones marry and move on. They need to have places to live too." "West" Gary said "You are growing up." There wasn't much talk after that. A quiet understanding had passed between them.

When they arrived home the gifts were passed out and Jo opened the parcel from the old woman. In it she found the journals the old woman had written from the times before the viruses and after. She found a letter telling Jo that she hoped there would be things she had written that may help them in their struggles in life. Jo carefully folded the letter and replaced it with the journals. She would have to thank her, but Jo knew the woman wouldn't have parted with them if her time was not near.

After West washed up he spent a little time chatting about the trip and mentioned seeing the new people.

The trip Jo and Zack hoped would fulfill his needs seemed not to have helped. Zack mentioned to Jo after West went to bed, "He will need to sort things for himself. Give him time Jo." Zack said. Jo was right.

Tomorrow would arrive soon enough and all the work with it. Jo wanted to read the journals as well. She would make the time to do so.

Jo worked endlessly; there was always something that had to be done. The flax was growing well and Jo examined how large the field was and if it was large enough for their needs. After looking intently at she decided it was, but with little to spare.

Her mind wandered to the old woman's journal and she thought about the recipe for soap. How Jo wished she could have had a bubble bath. She smiled; well she thought a bubble bath is not going to get this work done. The flax and the oats fields were still being dug.

West was digging when Jo approached him. Jo watched him work intently on the field. How he had grown she thought. Soon he would be looking for a partner. Zack and Jo had survived the viruses and through West she had hope for the future.

"West" Jo said "You should not work so hard." "It's okay mom." he replied.

He looked at her "You know there are more people arriving from the settlement?" "Yes West I do, I believe they are from the fort." "Do you think our valley might soon have more people?" West asked.

"Yes West I do. It's a good thing." Jo told him. "People have survived and they need to spread out to live. Soon this valley will be home for many as the settlement as." West said "Well I like it better like this, just all of us."

Jo smiled "Well my son, you are an adventurer that's why you're independent, but must remember no one is meant to live alone. You must find someone that shares your feelings for the wilderness."

West went back to digging and Jo started back to the cabin. "Don't work too long West we have all summer to get the field ready for next spring."

West watched Jo walk to the cabin. This valley would soon be filled with people. Soon he knew they would accept a few families from the settlement. As he dug and turned over the sod, he decided to venture into the next valley. He was going to build a cabin there and live there when he was a bit older. With his mind set, the digging was less arduous. He would talk to Zack and Jo this evening about it. He knew his mother would like it, but he would tell her he might find new food sources. His father would encourage him to find his place in the world, but probably side with his mother. He was coming on fifteen years old, but with a plan they would relent.

West knew his journey to look for the complex was about to begin and he was excited.

That evening when he came in for the night, after he washed and ate, he sat with his dad. He started the conversation about building in the next valley. He was young when they came here and Gary and Brad had done most of the work. Zack told West to take the time to talk with them. Clearing the area would be hard for a lone man. West was not deterred of course. Jo was not so sure she wanted him so far away alone. After what happened to Zack, Jo always was upset with any travelling done by someone alone.

West told Jo "Mom relax, I need to make a trail first, that will take a summer for sure. Then maybe you could come with me." He smiled and looked at Zack, he too was smiling. Zack then told her "The break will do you good." He said "You have been working non stop since we got here and you could use the break."

Jo then smiled "You might be right, you just must be right." They spent a quiet evening talking of the adventure and Zack talked to West about what he wanted for a cabin. Soon the family was planning and working towards a new settlement in the next valley.

The next day Brad and Gary got in on the plan. After West got a workable path into the next valley, they would go and help after the work was finished in this valley.

It was thrilling for West. He was finally going to be able to start his life's adventure.

Spring rolled into summer. West had made several trips to blaze a trail into the next valley. West never minded and he blazed a trail that was easy to walk with no great declines. The natural formation of the mountain provided an almost lazy path inching down to the valley below. He found a creek formed by the run off from the mountains. It would give him the water he would need in the future. West called it his valley and the place was in for some change.

Jo and Zack were both feeling their age. On the weekends that West was away they talked of life and many things from the past. Zack wondered why he had been spared and the thought often crossed his mind. He thought of Dee and the child. He thought of Jo and West and pondered that all things lost could be found again, if you look for them. He thought of Jo and how she rarely complained, hoe he had West and the joy the boy had given him. He thought of how his adventure was just beginning.

Jo was busy, she hid her fears. She kept busy and it was there she found her solace she needed. She had been alone most of her young life and Zack filled many voids that had been vacant for as long as she could remember.

West was her joy, in him life continued. She often thought that life now in some ways was better. Before, too many thought of profit. The society was fast and unfeeling. It was a throw away society, greed always won over charity. Now folks stuck together and there was no doubt that everyone needed the other to live. It was death to someone that did not have help. The lack of food and medicine was ever present for all. Jo missed the conveniences of the old world, but she admitted that she preferred it now. The human bond was their hope and the hope for all.

West was always his own man. The ideas of Jo and Zack, along with the basic facts of life had instilled an honour and sense of living. This had made him see things in a truer light than most. He was educated by his father and he was thankful for it. It gave him an advantage and any advantage would be needed. He knew people and life was hanging on by a thin line, any new thing might wipe out what was left.

He had made a trail into the valley that was good to travel on now. West thought of the settlement and of the people. He would need to travel to the fort fro tools. It would be a journey he was looking forward to. He would make it after the harvest and before the snow came. West had fallen almost all the trees he would need for his cabin. In the spring he would begin to build it. Gary and Brad would help after the gardens were in.

Brad and Gary's children were growing. Lily and Sara this year would each be having another child.

When harvest was ready they all worked to bring it in. Lily and Sara prepared the flax for weaving. Jo and the men, as well as the children brought in and stored the food.

West sat at the table with Jo and Zack. Mother, father" he said "I am making a trip to the fort. I thought of going beyond to see the places of before the viruses." Jo and Zack knew that telling him not to go was beyond them at this point. He was not asking them, he was telling them. West was becoming his own man and they had to let him discover things for himself.

Zack asked West "Why now, winter will be upon us soon? I fear that you will be snowed in at some other place than here. Might I suggest you wait till after spring planting? If you wish to travel further, I can give you the information about it out there." West sat there for a few moments and finally said "I believe you might be right father."

Jo was relieved, she did not want him to go, but she knew she could not stop him. Jo realized this would be her last winter as a doting mother.

West asked Jo "What did you like about the world before the viruses?"

Jo laughed "Bubble bathes." "What about you father?" West asked. "Pens and paper" Zack said "and running water" Zack smiled at Jo and then at West.

"Mother what do you need from the settlement? I will travel there this week." Jo wrote a small list and gave it to him. Zack gave him some pots to use as trade items. "I will ask Sara and Lily if they need anything as well" West told them. "That's thoughtful" Jo replied. "Father I would like to make a bigger wagon this winter. One I can haul more things with" West asked. Zack nodded "Okay son, we will work on it soon, but let's relax tonight my legs are paining me." Jo went to the pantry and got Zack a cup of wine. She knew it helped easy his pain.

"The weather will change soon" Zack told her "My legs always tell me that" he smiled.

West often felt for his father. Tomorrow he would travel to the settlement and see if he could gather information about the land beyond the fort.

The sun rose and there was a chill in the air. West smiled, father was right. He headed to Brad and Sara's cabin.

When he got there Amy and Sean followed him around the cabin. Sara was large again. After a tea and some conversation West had a small list from them.

Soon enough he was at Gary and Lily's. Cassy was helping her mom. Mark and Chad were busy on a building project. Gary had them helping with the new baby's cradle. They gave West a list of their wants and West smiled. He was happy to help. He left and was soon back gathering his things at home for his hike.

It wasn't long before he was on his way ad glad for the solitude. West was determined to make good in this world and he knew he could.

As he walked, he thought of the tales of the old world and of the things others had told him about.

It was late afternoon when West got to the settlement. He liked all the hustle and bustle, but couldn't live here. The elders of the settlement were glad to see him. They asked when some might move into the next valley and West told them after winter. This was good news. The settlement worked together and the people had done well this year.

West spent time with the old folks and asked them of the old world. He spent the evening talking of all at home and the next valley he was preparing to move to.

The evening was full of laughter and advice. It wasn't long before West felt the weariness of the long trip and called it a night.

West woke to find the day warm. It was a good day to travel. He accepted the tea made for him and began to pack his gear.

After he packed he headed back home. He had the salt and the new pick head and shovels. West wasted no time on the path, it was a long trip and he wanted to be home before nightfall. Mother would be happy as would the other women.

West stopped; he could hear someone in the forest. He looked and then saw her. She had a basket and it was full of mushrooms. He watched as she searched for more. West was struck by her graceful movements. She entered the small clearing and the sun shone on her reddish hair. She had it tied back in a braid. Her tunic was hand embroidered. West watched as she made her way to the settlement. He waited until she was out of sight before continuing on his way. He must see her again, he thought. She looked his age, next spring he would go see her.

He walked towards home, his steps lighter and his mind was on the girl he had watched.

Jo was glad to see him home.

After he delivered all the items on the lists he was given, he settled in to a quiet evening with his parents.

Zack had started designing a wagon. Jo and West shelled the bounty of nuts they had collected. West told them of the families ready to come to the valley.

Zack told West "You must talk to Brad and Gary to get the lumber cut this fall before the snow falls."

West replied "but, I need to cut the trees for my cabin." Zack looked at him. West rarely talked back to Zack and after the look, West gave in. He told him he would see to it the next day, the rest of the evening passed without incident.

The following day West talked to Brad and Gary. Zack went with him and two sites were picked for the new cabins.

After two weeks of cutting trees they had the lumber cut. The stumps were burned and the logs were left to dry. Zack had talked with Brad and Gary. They agreed to hike with West to the next valley and help him cut his trees for his cabin.

West was happy. His father was the best man he ever knew and he was proud to be his son.

"Father, father" West called as he hurried his pace to catch up to him.

"What is it West?" Zack said. West hugged him "Thank you father." Zack looked at him "I know your cabin is important to you." Then Zack smiled "We had best get you packed if you are going to make it before the snow falls." Zack told him.

The next day the three men headed to the next valley to cut the lumber for West. The travelling was easy; West had carved a good trail. Brad was interested in the place West had chosen and Gary was amazed at the work West had already done.

"Your father will be able to travel this Path West, you have done a grand job." And Gary placed a hand on his shoulder. Brad agreed and told him he should consider taking a partner soon.

West laughed "and be surrounded by children and work forever?" they laughed.

"Yes and you will see it is well worth it to." Both told him.

West wanted to search for his father's complex. The cabin may be one of many he would build in the valleys. He was sure of that and what woman would want that?

The men worked hard and within a week the trees were cut into lumber and they were on their way back home.

They arrived home just before the first snow came and the three families settled in for the long winter.

The babies were born soon and the women kept in close contact. All the children came to Zack for education. West planned his cabin and pondered a trip to the fort in the spring. The valley settled into its normal routines.

Brad appeared at the door with the news that Sara was having the baby. Jo wasted no time and soon Lily and she were at Sara's side.

Cassy took charge of the two children and by nightfall the baby arrived, it was another son. Brad, the ever proud father beamed. Sara had an easier time with this child and Jo was glad. After things were taken cared of, she laid the baby with Sara. "What will you call him?" Tayler was the name picked. Jo added Taylor to the family tree.

Jo and Lily cleaned and hung all the linens and hung them to dry.

Lily wanted to stay with Sara and Jo made her way home.

Zack had all the children drawing when she arrived. "It's a boy, Tayler is his name" she told them.

Jo made some tea and soon settled in to her chair and picked up her sewing. "Zack" Jo asked "Did you ever miss not having more children?" Zack smiled "No Jo, West was perfect and besides I have lots of children" as he gazed at the children drawing at the table. Jo smiled "Well who is popping the corn tonight?" Zack asked and all of them spoke at once "Me, me, me!" After the corn was popped and eaten, they were put to bed. Soon Lily's baby would come and the scene would be repeated.

West was happy his trees were now lumber, although there was much work still to do the hardest part was almost done.

"Father would you make some bricks for me?" West asked him. Zack told him "Sure."

West then told him he wanted some large flat stones to if it was possible. Zack smiled.

West went to his room and took the plans for his cabin with him.

Zack and Jo headed for bed as well.

The next day found the cabin full and after some porridge the children went home with Cassy in charge of them.

The quiet was nice to have again. Winter was well entrenched in their valley.

Gary was the next one that approached. Lily was having her child. Jo went alone as Sara still needed her rest. Lily did not have an easy time. The delivery was long and tiring. Any further children probably wouldn't be a good idea. After many hours the baby arrived. It was a boy.

Gary was happy for the child, but was concerned for Lily. After helping Lily clean up, Jo asked what they were calling him. Thomas was his name and he was added to the family's tree. Jo washed and hung all the linen. She told Gary that they would keep the other children for a few days to give Lily a chance to rest. Gary was thankful. He never left Lily. He would stay close to her until Jo told him she would be okay.

Sara came over after and thanked Jo for helping Lily. Jo went home and this time she went to rest after she arrived.

Zack kept the children occupied and after a few days they went home.

The winter days got shorter and the families waited for spring. Soon work would start and life would renew.

Chapter 20

*T*odd went to Nick. He was going to meet Dana, but first he wanted to find out more about what she liked. When he arrived Dana was there. He watched as she helped Nick and Carla with the animals. She had a way of calming the animals. She looked totally at ease with them.

It was Carla that noticed Todd and called for him.

"Todd can you come and give us a hand?" Carla asked. "Sure" he said. Todd was wondering just what he could do. He went into the pen and Carla gave him a lamb to hold. The ewe had given birth to three and one was sickly. After Carla took blood from all and insured the ewe was fine, she left to do her tests. The two stringer lambs had no trouble getting to the milk, but the one Todd had held was in troubled.

Dana asked Dirk "Want me to care for it Dirk?" "It most likely will not survive Dana" Dirk told her. Then it baaed a bit and Todd looked at her, "Mind if I help? If it has a chance I would like to help." Dirk and Dana both looked at him. "Well?" Todd said. "It will probably be sickly and not survive" Dirk told him. Todd picked up the lamb and said "If Chester wants to live then let's help him." Dana giggled. Todd looked at her "Okay what's so funny?" Dana looked at him "Well I hate to tell you, but Chester is a girl." At they all laughed. Dirk relented; Dana and Todd were given stewardship over Chester.

With surprise from Carla and Dirk Chester did well. The lamb was never far from either Todd or Dana. She followed the two everywhere. Through Chester the bond formed Dana and Todd grew stronger. They were always together.

Dirk had never seen them happier and he smiled at them. He understood how an animal could bring happiness between people.

Todd became interested in many aspects of the rearing of Chester. It surprised him on many occasions how much Dana knew about animals. He spent much of his time sharing Dana with them and grew to appreciate them as well.

Chester grew fast and soon it was time he was sheared. Dana had kept the sheep in good shape, always washing them and happy when different colours appeared on their wool. She had shown him from start to finish the process of taking raw wool, to soft yarn, to weave and knit. Dana spent most of her spare time with Todd. The two were a match.

Todd found his job working with stone much more satisfying since he and Dana got together and it did not go unnoticed by his father. Todd's mother also noticed he was more contented and knew that it was Dana had given him this. Dana spent many happy hours with the family and they loved her.

It was Dana that went to Dirk and asked his opinion on Todd. Dirk liked him and that gave comfort to her. Elsa and Rainie both agreed he was a kind and compassionate man.

Todd was never as happy and he knew that Dana was going to be his life's partner. He had carved her a lamb that was the image of Chester. He had to ask her to marry him and soon he would do just that. His mother gave him her wedding rings. Todd had an evening planned and now, just to get Dana to marry him. Why he had doubts he didn't know, but he did and that bothered him. She just had to say yes.

Dana met Todd in the butterfly atrium, she liked it there. Dana had been so happy since she met Todd. Her life seemed to be going somewhere, if one could go anywhere in a series of tunnels. When Todd came in he brought a basket of food. Dana always liked his surprises. They had a favourite spot to sit and often they could be found there. Todd had already spoken to Elsa and had received her blessings, now Dana just had to say yes.

It was Dana that noticed that he was fidgety "What's the matter Todd?" Dana asked.

"Nothings the matter, I just need to ask you something and well I'm not sure how." Todd said. "Nothings wrong is it Todd?" Dana was now becoming concerned. "Oh no Dana, it's just I want to, well would you?" Todd stopped talking. He looked at Dana, "Dana!" He said "I love you so much and I would be honoured if you could agree to be my wife?" Dana looked right at him and then smiled. He could see her tears forming. "Todd" she said "I will be your wife, I will. I love you." Dana told him.

Todd held her and softly kissed her. He almost cried himself with happiness and relief. He didn't even want to think of what he would have done if she had said no, but she said yes and with that thought he smiled. They spent the rest of the evening talking of their future. Todd walked Dana to her dorm and then he headed to his.

When he arrived, his mom took one look at him and smiled. His father shook his hand and hugged him. She was so happy. Todd was a good man; they had done well by him. Dana is a wonderful woman; they make a good match.

Dana filled up her tub and added a ton of bubbles. She was getting married, She! Dana! She got into the tub and soaked. Her mind wandered to her mother and father. She wondered how Dee felt about Zack. She wished they could be alive and here now. Then she thought of Warren and Elsa, how they loved her. They were not her parents by blood, but in every other way they were. She would see Elsa first thing tomorrow. She just wanted to soak in the satisfied feeling she had at the moment.

After her bath she lay in bed and dreamed of what her life was to be now. She smiled and soon fell a sleep.

The next day the complex was a buss with the news. Dana and Todd were the couple of the hour. Everywhere either went congratulations went with them. Dana went to see Rainie. She needed to have her blessing and wanted to ask her about Dee.

When she arrived at Rainie's dorm, she found Rainie involved in her art sketches. Rainie hugged Dana and told her right off how happy she was for her. She was glad that Rainie approved.

"What is it my dear?" Rainie asked. "Well I guess I'm just nervous." Dana told her. "Don't worry, everything will be fine." Rainie smiled. "I wish my mother was here." Dana said. "Well Dana, so do I, so do I. So many times I have missed your mother. Elsa and I will just have to do." Rainie smiled as did Dana. "Thank you." Dana told her. "Rainie were my mother and father truly in love or did they marry because of me?" "Oh my goodness Dana, has that been troubling you? Let me set your mind at ease. Zack and Dee were so in love. When Zack got locked out of the complex, Im sure it was the reason Dee lost her life having you. She so loved him it broke her heart. You are that love and every time I look at you it warms my soul. Not many have it and I'm sure you and Todd shine with it. So be happy sweetie and revel in its glow." Rainie smiled at Dana. Dana felt better, Rainie always made her feel better. "Rainie I'm off to see Elsa." Dana stated. Rainie told Dana to enjoy her happiness.

Dana made her way to See Elsa. Elsa was getting old and the bond with Dana was strong. When she arrived they hugged. "So my dear you have found him? That is good. I always wanted you to have a good man that would care for you." Dana smiled "I have always had the care in you" she told Elsa. "Why did you take me Elsa?" Dana asked.

"At first it was out of respect for Zack and Dee, but when I held you for the first time, it was for you. You touched something in my heart. I guess I loved you from the very first." Elsa smiled and Dana hugged her. "Todd is worthy of you Dana. Care for him and he will care for you." Elsa told her. As Dana left she thought that Elsa was aging and it pained her to see that in her.

It wasn't long before she entered the animal tunnels. Dirk was there as always. "Well my little dear, how are you?" Dirk said when he saw her. "I'm doing okay Dirk" Dana replied. "Well?" she asked. "Well what?" Dirk replied. "You know what I mean." And they both laughed. "Yes dear he's the right one Dana." At that moment she beamed.

Dana sighed, thank goodness everyone approved. It will make things so much better.

"Why did you let that worry you? We all just want you to be happy." Dirk told her

"Yes I know, but I would have felt uneasy if I had to feel bad around everyone. I love him and I will marry him, but to have everyone feel bad would have dampened my blessing."

"Dana you are a special person." Dirk said to her.

Dana smiled "I must go; I'm to meet Todd for dinner at his house tonight."

She got up and he watched her as she left. Dirk thought, with the children now growing the complex would survive, if people like Dana and Todd took over the reigns of control their future was safe. .

Todd of course was getting his share of hand shakes and he liked it. Dana was his other half and he knew it. Soon they would be married and living on their own. In some ways he would miss living at home, but knew Dana was his home, his life and his very being.

He headed to his dorm. When he arrived Dana was already there with his mother. She was happy for them and looked forward to having them often for dinner. Dana was happy, truly happy and with Todd she felt her life was complete.

They all sat for dinner and talked easily of things.

Life in the complex was thriving again and there was a safe secure feeling for all.

Chapter 21

The snow was a few feet deep already when the big storm moved in. It was an awful blizzard, for two days it wrecked havoc outside. When it finally blew itself out the cabins were near covered with drifts. All the men work laboriously to clear paths to every home. The children romped in it and built snow houses and men.

Jo enjoyed the serenity of the valley when covered with nature's blanket. She was on her way to Lily's house and it was a good thing she did. Jo sent Brad and the children to her house.

Before long, Jo had water boiled. Lily did not have an easy time of it. The baby was large and Jo had to sew stitches. Jo finished with Lily. She helped Lily into fresh nightwear and with clean sheets and blankets, put her and the baby to bed.

Sara could not help Jo as she was at home with her own baby. Jo spoke with Lily "You do know that having more children might not be a good idea?" Lily weakly smiled "Yes I know Jo, but if it happens, it happens." The two women exchanged a glance and the both understood.

Jo was happy to return home after she finished at Lily's. She knew the baby would be well now that it had arrived. Gary was a good man and he would care for her while she recuperated.

Zack was happy they both made it. "Gary will be glad of another son to help with things in the future." Zack said.

"True enough" Jo said "It always helps to have men do the hard labour."

"You know Jo; I am surprised that there are as many people still alive. There may be hope for us yet." He smiled at Jo. "It's not so far fetched to think, if we can get people educated we might be able to start some industry to get power and water running." Zack said.

"A hot bath would be nice." Jo smiled "I'm not getting my hopes up for running water yet, but it sure would be nice."

Zack and Jo spent the rest of the evening chatting and relaxing.

West was busy doing his own thing planning out his home place in the next valley. The excitement of searching it out and the valley beyond was his cup of tea. He wanted to travel the old world to the city of the dead. It sounded awful, but dead people couldn't hurt you. He wanted to see the places his mom and dad lived. He would one day and it was coming sooner than Jo and Zack would have preferred.

Spring had touched the valley. The trip to the maple trees was the first start of the food harvesting and one the children all helped with. After all the sap was collected, the women poured some syrup onto the snow and it froze into candy for them.

Jo, Lily and Sara knew it would be all too soon before the gardens would have to be in.

With the two new families moving into the valley, the men would be busy helping build the new dwellings. West, Jo's stand by was always a welcomed help with the digging. Cassy minded all the children so Sara and Lily could help dig.

The new families would have to work very hard this year. They needed to get gardens growing. The garden for all would be worked by all. Private gardens were on time left over. The flax fields would be finished this year. Jo was happy about that. After four years, it was overdue.

The week days they all worked hard. The new families seemed to be good people and West found a companion his age.

It didn't take long for the cabins to be built and when they were done the men joined in working in the fields. The men got wood ready for winter and West was eager to get to his cabin in the next valley. The young woman from one of the new families was called Willow. She and West spent all the time they could together. Jo knew her boy was becoming a man and she would soon lose him.

Zack never saw it as a loss, more like more. He and Jo weren't losing a son, they were gaining a daughter.

It was West that told Willow that he had seen her long before she had come to live here.

"Oh stop teasing West" she said "I never saw you at the settlement." Willow said to West.

"Never the less, I saw you." He teased her. She had a basket full of flower plants for her mother and as she kneeled down to did another, she glanced over to West. "Okay then, where did you see me?" She asked.

"I saw you in the forest. You were gathering mushrooms" West told her. "You spied on me?" she asked. "Oh no" West told her. "Nothing like that, I just saw you and watched till you were out of sight. I was on the path back here. You were busy and I didn't want to startle you." West smiled. "Thanks I think." Willow said.

"I want to show my cabin in the next valley. Think you can get away?" West asked her.

"No probably not. Too much work here. Mother depends on me really." Willow told him.

West just smiled and said "I'm going there in a few days. I need to clear some land for the gardens."

Willow smiled and said "I must go and help with dinner." And she headed to her family's cabin.

West made his way home and found Zack, as usual teaching the children. He admired the patience his father had. "Dad" West told him "I'm off to my cabin. I'll be gone a couple of days." Zack nodded "You should start packing the bricks I made you. It will take a few trips to get them all there. Zack told him. "Yes you're right I want to work on the trail a bit too." West smiled. He knew Zack would want to come see it, but travelling over the rough terrain was not possible for him.

It was about then that Jo arrived and West wasted no time in getting her to pack up some food for him. Jo didn't mind, life had afforded him a few pleasures. If he had such joy from the next valley and cabin, she obliged.

"When are you going to be back?"Jo asked.

""I'm planning three or four days. I want to get all the stumps burned out and work on the trail a bit. I still have to dig the well, etc…There are a lot of things for sure." West smiled. "I will be up and gone before you even wake." He said to her.

Jo just raised an eyebrow; she was always the first one up. Then a devilish smile crossed his face and they both laughed.

The morning came quickly and West was ready to go. He hugged his mom and told her to tell dad that he would be back soon. He gathered his gear and headed out.

The ground was wet with dew and before long his feet were soaked. He moved quickly on the path even with the weight he was carrying. It wouldn't take him long to reach the other valley, another hour and he would be at his cabin.

It was just passed midday when he arrived. He unloaded his pack and got as fire going. The first thing was to dry his footwear. He made a trip for water and washed while he was at the creek.

Back at the cabin, he fed the fire and soon had some good coals going. He headed out and decided to burn a few stumps before dark. He laboured hard for a few hours and soon had the area around the cabin raked up and started burning it with the stumps.

He liked his cabin looking cleaned up. Tomorrow he would cut down some dead snags he spotted in the brush near by. He wanted to get his wood stockpiled. He still needed to pick rocks in the field he was preparing. He thought about the trail and that it needed a lot of work. Soon it would be clear enough for his wagon to be pulled along it. He would bring most of his things then.

Night fell too quickly. West had dug a trench around each stump and as they had been reduced to coals, he felt safe in calling it a night.

He washed up when he got into the cabin and soon had some tea going. He slept near his fire. He was the master here and he did as he pleased.

Dawn arrived too soon. West stretched out and decided the dead wood could wait some. He wanted to check out the valley a bit first. As he prepared for the day he decided to see what kind of trees were about. With some luck there might be some maples here as well.

His first stop was at the creek for water. He had to get that well dug too, he thought, and soon too. After filling up the water barrel he was free to explore some.

Following the creek he soon found maple trees and not far away hazelnuts. Mom would like those he thought. The day was clear and warm to the point of almost being hot. As he scanned the trees he saw quite a few dead ones. Good for fire wood he thought.

West explored until noon and then headed back to the cabin. He decided to take out the dead wood. It wasn't going away and it was dangerous.

After reaching the cabin he made some lunch. He sat outside eating and thinking of the complex. How wondrous it must be to have to have all the things from the old world. He was going to see the city of the dead. His mind was made up.

He scanned the trees and picked out the ones he would cut down. West got busy and started cutting them down. He was bear chested and sweating by mid afternoon. The tree he was chopping was bad; every chop caused higher dead branches to break off and drop. No wonder the women called them widow makers. If he got hit by one of the falling branches it would be serious. West was fully aware of this, took his time and soon had the dead tree down. When it hit the ground it broke open revealing a huge old bee's nest. There were three or four pounds of wax in it. West smiled, mom would be thrilled. He gathered up the wax and took it to his cabin.

It wasn't long before he was back cutting up the wood. He would stack it tomorrow.

West thought about Willow. He wished she could have come, next time maybe. He understood that she had to help in the garden and her parent's cabins. When everything was planted and dug he was going to travel to the fort and beyond.

He continued cutting and stacking for the next few days. He knew he had to get back, but he was going swimming first. After all his hard work it felt good to swim.

The weather was holding, but he knew it could change fast. After his swim he packed up his gear and headed back. On his way back he stopped often and cleared things on the trail.

When he arrived back that evening Jo was relieved to see him "Did you get lots of things done West?"

"Yes I did. I think I like it there more every time I'm there." West replied. "Oh and I found this mom" and he took out the wax from his pack.

Jo smiled "That's enough wax for all the preserves. How did you find it?'

"Oh I didn't find it mom, It found me" West said. Jo looked at him. "I was cutting down some dead wood and it was inside one of them." He told her.

"You should not cut dead wood without someone else there." Jo told him.

He just smiled at her and said "Where's dad?" West asked.

"He's at the kiln. He has been making bricks for you." Jo told him. "Hmm" West was out the door before she could say anything else. She took the wax and put it away as it was starting to melt. After that she would let it harden, anything foreign would settle to the bottom after it melted.

West found Zack stoking the fire to the kiln, "Hello son" Zack said "Was the trip worth it?" he smiled at West. "Yes it was father" West told him. "Willow was asking about you" Zack smiled. "Really, she knew I was going to the cabin" West replied. "She's a good girl and she's coming of age. If you have plans for her in the future you had better say so and if not say so." West was kind of stunned by that remark. Zack looked at him "If you have no feelings for the girl you should let her know." "Well" West said "I do like her. I like her a lot. I never thought about it." "That's right" Zack said "You need to think about it." "But, what about the complex father?" West said. "Life is a long time and being alone is not good. I want you to look for the complex, but I also want you to be happy. Willow is smart and resourceful. The two of you could look for the complex together. She would like the woods almost as much as you do. West my boy, you need to make some decisions. The sooner you get things in order the better."

West was dumbfounded, "Okay dad" and he headed back to the cabin.

"What's troubling him?" West asked his mom. "What do you mean" She asked. "Dad is telling me to get my life in order, like I was floating around doing nothing." "Well" Jo said "Let's say he is concerned for Willow. You do know she is learning to read and write for him and speaks of you often. It doesn't take a genius to figure out that she is in love with you. I guess your father feels you should do something about it. She shouldn't be left dreaming about something that may not happen."

"Gee, I go away for a couple days and everything gets all weird. I'm going to my room for a while." West told her. Jo just smiled "Yes okay West."

Jo prepared their dinner and called Zack when it was done.. Zack washed up and soon was at the table. "West not eating?" he asked Jo. "He's working out some things" Jo told him. "Let him do it in his own time."

West lay on his bed and thought. Man yesterday I was content and now I'm not sure what I am. Willow yes I admit she is nice, really nice, but do I want to spend the rest of my life with her? Yes I do, but I want to look for the complex and I want to see the city of the dead too. I think I need to talk to Willow and ask her what she wants. West's mind rolled around these thoughts until he fell asleep.

West woke to Willow voice, she was reading to Zack. It was a soothing sound to West. He would talk with her after her lessons.

It was about an hour later when he heard her leave, West got up and Zack was at the table. He was clearing the papers away from the lesson. "So you have decided to join the living?" Zack said to him. "Dad, can we talk?" West said to him. "Want a tea, some is made here?" "Sure" West replied.

"Dad, what's up with all this with Willow?" West asked.

130

"West do you like this girl?" he asked point blank.

"Yes I believe I do dad" West said.

"Why are you leaving her hanging then?" Zack replied.

"What do you mean?" West said.

"There are only so many people. If you find someone that you can care for and can love as well, you best, and you had best hold on to it. If you don't tell her she may look for another. I happen to like her a lot." Zack told him.

"Well father I do too. I will talk to her later, it's just I have a few things I want to do before I settle down." West told him. "Where's mom?" "Oh she is in the garden as usual."

"I will be making another trip, something I need to do Dad." Zack looked at him. "You remember dad, you told me you would make me a map?" "That I did, you planning to go soon?" "I will speak to Willow later; first I want to speak to mom."

West got up and headed to the garden. Jo saw him coming and knowing as she did, knew he had made up his mind. "Well son, what have you decided?" Jo asked him. West smiled, his mom knew him well. "How long until the harvest mom do you think?" he asked. "I would say six weeks at most." Jo told him. "Mom would you pack me enough food for about three, maybe four weeks hike?" Jo knew he was not going to the fort. "Have you talked to Willow yet?" "No mom, I'm on my way there now. Thanks mom." West said and headed to Willow's cabin.

When he got there her mom told him she was out collecting mushrooms. He nodded and she pointed him in the direction Willow had gone.

West made his way into the woods. It wasn't long before he found her. It reminded him of the first he saw her. He watched her gracefully weave her way through the woods, stopping to collect the mushrooms. Then suddenly she stopped and turned right to where he was standing. "West are you spying on me?" she said. "No just watching you. I didn't want to startle you." He said to her. Willow walked over to him "How was your trip West?" she asked. "Oh the valley is looking great" West told her. "Willow do you fancy me? I mean would you consider being my wife when I get back?" West asked her. "West what are you talking about? You just got back." Willow said. "I have to make a trip to the fort. When I get back I want to talk to your father." He told her. "West where are you going there for?" "Well Willow, do you want a life of travel and excitement or do you want to stay here forever?" Willow didn't know what to say. "West do you want me because you feel something for me or because you feel sorry for me?" Willow asked.

It was then that West pulled her close and kissed her.

"Until today I never knew I loved you, but I do. I want you as my wife. I just need to make this trip first. It's something I have to do, I hope you understand?" West said.

"West, I would wait for you forever. If it's just another month, I'm sure I can make it." "Come spring Willow, we are moving to our cabin. Is that okay with you?" West asked her. "Yes West you can say so." Willow just smiled and for an instant she reminder him of his mother. West walked her out of the woods and then headed to see his father.

Zack was sitting at the table. He had completed the map and on it he marked the location of his family farm, Cambry and its basic layout. Zack knew, until West went it would be a need unfulfilled. It would be an adventure in some ways he wished he could share with him. Jo, of course was not keen on the idea. She did not like people to travel alone, but she also knew West would not be held back. She could just pray everything would be okay. She had packed him the trail mix and tea; some oats, a tinder box for fire and a small first aide kit.

West sat with Zack most of the evening. They talked of the trail, the fort and beyond. Jo sat spinning and let the two men talk.

Before long it was dark and with the glow from the fire gone, the only light. They all called it a night. Morning would arrive all too soon.

Jo was worried and she told Zack. He patted her hand "It will be fine. He's travelled the woods his whole life. He is not some foolish man like his father, leaping before he looked." Jo hugged Zack "It was an accident" Jo said. "One I'm reminded daily of." Zack replied. "He will be fine. It will cool his heals. He and Willow will settle into a good life in the next valley."

Jo was not sure. Since he was a child he was adventurous and now that the complex was out there it would drive him on. Jo knew his personality.

West wasted no time in making his way to the fort. His first stop was at the settlement. All the folks were eager for news of his family and the new families that moved there. West filled them in and found out any information on the next valley over. The path was good he was told.

He spent the night talking to the old timers about what was beyond the fort. West could see the looks they had, how some missed it so and others never spoke.

He would make an early start. He would travel to the valley his mom and dad first stayed at on their way here. The cable car that crossed the river had been maintained.

Sleep did not come easy that night. He was going, he was actually going. He pondered Cambry and his father's farm. He thought about the virus and how many died. It must have been awful for them. His mind wandered to the complex; how they could live there and how he had family too. Then he thought of Willow and how they would search together. They would find the complex. It was after a few hours of these thoughts that sleep finally came.

The day dawn and he was surprised at the noise in the settlement for having only four or five families there. The noise made of just daily living astounded him.

He had breakfast and packed up his gear. The day looked glum; it was over cast and soon no doubt it would be raining.

West didn't mind the rain for travelling, but it makes for miserable sleeping. He was good at making shelters so it would just be the drying of his clothes, etc…

He met no one on the trail. There was travel between the fort and the settlements, but more just messengers.

It was late in the afternoon when he reached the cable car. He crossed the river and looked for a place to build a shelter. It wasn't long before he found a spot. West moved quickly and efficiently and soon had the shelter built. His feet were soaked now. This is one thing he didn't like. His fire was going in no time and soon he was warm and his gear was drying. It rained for most of the night. West listened to the rain and to the storm; there was no lightning which he was glad. A fire out there could be dangerous. It was good there was rain, things burn less when wet. After hot tea and something to eat, West slept better.

Morning came too soon and with it more rain. West knew he has a few days walk to the farm that was his mom and dad's first stop. Zack had told him how ill prepared for travelling they had been and how finding the farm may have saved their lives. No doubt people had moved into it and were using it for a home now.

He soon packed his gear and was on the move again. As he made his way along the path he marvelled at the forest around him. His mind recalled his dad telling him of the animals that once lived in the forest. Now, only the trees held the memory of them. The older folks from time to time told of the outbreak, but they were passing and soon any memory of these times would be gone. West wondered what Cambry looked like if people were right when they called it the city of the dead? He thought of the farm that Zack grew up on, what did it look like?

Although, West's mind wandered, he was keenly aware of his surroundings. He had lived all his life in the mountains and wanted to see the plains Zack had told him of.

His thoughts ceased as he reached the crest of the mountains he had been climbing, the view was wondrous, and he could see the different ranges. He marvelled at how much territory was really out there.

The rain had stopped and the clouds were breaking with patches of blue sky and sunlight showing through. He thought this was not getting him closer to the farm.

The path he followed was good and it made travelling through the valley so much easier. What took Zack and Jo two days to travel might only take West one day.

He just had eaten some trail mix as he walked, but he knew night would soon be there so he scouted for a good place to make a shelter for the night. It was well into the late afternoon when he decided to stop.

As usual he moved as a skilled woodsman and had his shelter made in no time. It didn't take him long to gather some firewood for the night's fire. He had some tea and something to eat. He opened the maps that Zack had made and he knew he was close to the farm. After he ate he settled back and was thinking of Willow. He wondered what she was doing and how his life would be when he got back. He was going to have a wife to share his cabin with. Willow was a hard worker and that would help a lot when they got there. The dream of the complex was ever present and he knew Willow would help him look for it. With Zack's help, she would be well versed in reading and writing. She was a wonderful woman and West was beginning to realize just how lucky he was to have her.

He slept well that night and dawn came too early. He stirred the coals and made tea.

The dampness could out a chill on you, but by noon it was stifling hot. He would reach the farm today and wondered what his folks would be like there. It was from that orchard the fruit trees in his valley came from. The ones that Jo had grown would soon be producing fruit in abundance. He would have to get a few on the way back for his valley. Willow would be happy about that.

It was mid morning when he arrived there. He had messages from the settlement for folks at the fort, but passed them out them out here as well. There were several families there now.

He was approached by a young man that heard he was from beyond the settlement. "Excuse me, but you said you're from beyond the settlement? Have you ever met a couple named Zack and Jo?" the young man asked.

West smiled "Yes I know them very well" he said.

"Oh that's wonderful. Would you do me the kindness and tell them that my brothers and sisters are all well thanks to them and we hope they are as well. Tell them we have a great family and they are always welcome."

"How is it that you know them?" West asked.

"After the outbreak we were lost, our parents died by the virus. Zack and Jo took us in tow. They left us at the fort. A woman that lost her children cared for us."

West had no idea that his parents had done this. "I will be sure to convey the message." "Thank you" he said and headed for one of the cabins. West was amazed at how the people had changed the farm, but he was glad to see folks just the same.

It would be a couple days before he reached the fort. The people had built a small cabin for travelers and it was a welcome abode for West. He got water from the rain barrel and washed. He donned his clean clothes and washed what he had been wearing. He sat at the table and looked at the maps his dad had drawn. He then added the new buildings to it. Zack would be interested to see how it had changed. He carefully rolled up the maps and put them back in his pack.

Tap, tap at his door. West said "Yes" and opened the door. There was a young woman there.

"I brought you a bowl of vegetable stew; my brother said you were going to relay our message to Jo and Zack? I just wanted to thank you as well."

"Oh here, just leave the bowl I will get it later." And with that she left.

West was hungry and the veggies hit the spot. It was the first real food he had in the past few days. Tomorrow he would be on his way to the fort. He wanted to really look over the set up they had there. If he could apply any of what they had it could help all back home.

He rested easy that night and at first light he was on his way again. It felt good to have clean cloths on and to know he had a fresh set in his pack.

West followed the path. This one was more travelled. It was three days travel to the fort. As always he was well aware of his surroundings. He scanned his view continually. There was no one, just him and the trees again. The wind had picked up some and often made howling noises through the trees. West wondered how many people really did survive the outbreak. As far as his folks in the valley, there couldn't be more than two hundred or so. He guessed there would be a lot more near the fort now.

He knew that life was hanging on and that they would make it. He wondered how many children he and Willow would have. Children would be a lot of help in the valley when they got older. Then he stopped in his tracks. Children would not be a great help for a few years and what about the complex? He then decided, if it had been there all this time he was sure it would be there for a few more years. Besides he would only be able to look for it a month out of each year anyways. He continued on his way.

The forest was serene, a gentle breeze blew through the boughs now and West loved how it smelled. He could tell the different trees in the area by their scent.

As he crested the ridge he could see what used to be a camp of some sort. It must be the logging camp his dad told him about. He made his way down to the camp. There wasn't much left after all these years, but it was interesting. He spent a while examining the rusted works and tried to visualize what it was like when it was working. The buildings were falling apart so he never went far into them. The wood was rotten and would be dangerous. He looked over the area and picked a spot to have something to eat. He soon found one with a view of the camp. He pulled out his maps and knew the fort was at least a day, probably two away. He rolled the maps up and put them away and started to gather his gear together. It wasn't long before he was in the next valley. Night would be here soon so he looked for a good campsite.

By late afternoon he made his way to the creek in the valley and in no time he had his shelter built. He was tired tonight, it had been a long day and he covered a lot of country. He still had a ways to go. He settled in and made dinner. His thoughts went to Willow. He couldn't believe the hold she had on him and it wasn't in the least upsetting. The next time he travelled here he would bring her. He wondered if she was thinking of him and how their life would be when he got back. He was resolved to make as good as he could for her. He had no idea what was in store for him and that's what was exciting about this trip. He laid back and watched the stars. He watched the satellites cross and starred into the vastness of space. It was truly wondrous to be alive.

Morning dawned with a downpour. West was dry in his shelter, but dreaded a day with soggy feet again. He was in no hurry and hoped the rain would let up. He made some porridge and added wood to the fire. Still no people passed on the trail, not even a messenger. He would be at the fort today with luck. He was interested to see how many new things there were to make life easier. The folks at the fort were always trying new things. After that he would venture onto the plains. He looked at his dad's drawings of the land and wondered what if anything remained.

The rain did let up to West's pleasure and he packed up his gear. He started out and breathed deep, the air had been washed clean by the rain. The forest had a scent of its own. He wondered what the plains would smell like if at all.

He had walked a good four hours when he met a messenger from the fort. He made a fire and he shared news and tea. All too soon it was time to get moving. He bid the messenger farewell and started for the fort. He decided one day at the fort and he would move on.

After an uneventful afternoon he arrived at the fort. There was all the regular commotion that came with populated areas. West stopped and watched the children, they were flying kites. He thought they were the future and smiled. He head to the public lodging house and found it not to be full. Folks had been moving out into their own homes. He got a room and soon had a tub full for a bath. After the bath he washed his cloths and hung them to dry. He decided to see the blacksmith and see what he was making. There was always the public market where food and other items were traded. He wanted to see if any books available so he headed to the school house.

After a few hours of reading he started towards the smithy. He watched him smelt iron and watched him work it into everything one could think of.

"If I was to bring you some iron could you make something for me? If I half the iron with you?" West asked. "Sure" the smithy replied. On that note West left.

He was glad to see the smith was teaching his trade to a few young men. West stopped at the public house and had some food and listened to the talk. There wasn't much news, the same talk of new fields, what grains were needed, new cabins to be built and new additions to the families. West soon finished and headed to his room. A good nights rest and he would be off to see if dad's farm was still there.

He slept well that night. The morning was bright and sunny. It was nice, but he knew it would be a long dry walk. He packed his gear, but before he left he looked over his maps. He wanted to be sure he would have water. He decided to follow the river across the plains to the farm. Cambry was still a day away, if not two, He rolled up the map.

He headed out of the fort area and was soon far away walking in the valley. He noticed the rolling hills. He looked behind and saw the mountains. They were majestic and for the first time he realized how massive they were. He followed the river for most of the day and in late afternoon he made some mental notes on how far he had come. He kept an eye out for a good spot to make camp. The river was a slow moving and a warm sight to see.

West was well into the foothills by late afternoon. He found a good campsite and set up for the night. It seemed strange to be in such open ground. He wondered what the plains would be like to live on.

The wind blew a lot here he thought. Not like in the mountains. West cooked some food and settled in. He liked the full open skies. He could watch the clouds for miles. Tomorrow he would be at the farm, the place where his dad grew up. West loved his folks and he knew they loved him too. He was surprised that Zack took such a shine to Willow and his mom as well. He was going to walk where is ancestors had and for some reason this was important to him. He had studied the maps and stoked the fire. He knew tomorrow was going to be a fulfillment of many things for him. He had listened to his dad talk of the farm; his mom and dad and of Cambry. His mom never spoke of her folks only how much she missed them. They had passed when she was a bit older than he was now. The thought of losing either of his parents was beyond him. He depended on their knowledge and love. Soon he would wed to Willow and he then would be king of his household, of course when Willow let him. He knew his mom really ruled the roost at home as did most women. The thought of having children was kind of frightening in some ways. He was the only child of Zack and Jo. He wondered if he would be the father that Zack was to him. With that thought he went to sleep.

West woke at the crack of dawn. He watched the sun rise over the horizon and with this beauty he sighed. After he ate, he packed his gear. Today he would see the farm if it was still there. He followed the roads or what was left of them, they stretched for miles. Mother Nature was well on her way to reclaiming them.

West followed the maps his father drew for him and soon the farm was in sight. The buildings were still there, but dilapidated. The barn was falling down as was the house. West picked up his pack and in no time was there.

The house was still intact enough to go in and West did. He looked at all the furniture and the pictures on the wall. He marvelled at all the things that were there, the phone, the refrigerator, clocks and the store, it was surreal. A lot of the windows were broken, but still in the frames. He went to the bedroom and opened up the dresser drawers. He found pictures and trinkets of jewellery. He put them in his pack. He knew that Zack left in a hurry and he wanted to bring some things back for him.

He wandered back to the kitchen. He looked in the cupboards and drawers. After choosing some silverware and a couple of pots, he went outside. He wandered around outside and couldn't find much else. He was happy to see the farm and yet he was terribly sad at the same time. How had things gone so wrong? How had man done this to themselves? They had everything and they threw it away. This would all be soon gone and with it the memories carried by the older folks.

West started for Cambry. He looked back at the farm and knew he knew he would never return there. The maps that Zack drew were almost exact. West had no trouble finding his way. He passed a few, what looked to be farms and knew he was getting closer to Cambry.

It was early evening when he arrived in Cambry. It was nothing at all like what he had expected. It was shattered ruins, any buildings left were just shells of burned out waste. The town was burned, West wondered if it was deliberate or just a series of events that caused the fires. He walked around. It was deserted and had been so for a very long time. Rusty vehicles and then he began to see bones. Had these been the folks from this area and town? He walked further through the rubble and came to a big building that was also burned. Nearby he saw a pile of human bones; there were thousands of them, West just stared at them. He had no thoughts just a great feeling of sadness, so many people gone forever. It occurred to him why the old folks called this place the city of the dead. His mom and dad lived through this he said aloud. Then he continued to look around, there was nothing there. Why did he want to see this he thought? It was as if he didn't believe what he had been told somehow. They must be wrong he told himself, but there was no denying it everything was true.

He had seen enough. He started out of town. He wanted to get some distance between him and Cambry. He now decided to tell his mom and dad little of what he saw. It gave him and insight into how they thought and felt. He realized how hard it must have been for them. He never had all the things they did, so he never missed them, but they must miss many things. He felt in awe of their bravery and steadfastness. He felt sad for all the things they lost from their past.

It didn't seem to take long until West saw an old farm house. He would camp there for the night. When he got to the farm night was falling quickly. He decided to sleep under the stars, it was a clear night and there was not much about to build a shelter with. He made a small fire and pondered everything he had seen. This must never happen again. Mankind must endeavour to solve problems and not destroy themselves. West ate and stared into the night sky. It had been a long walk and now it had not been in vain. He thought about the complex and how his father had searched until his accident. West knew he would search for it and with luck he would find it.

The day came too soon and West looked around the farm. He found some wax in the house and a wet stone for sharpening his knives. He found some bars of soap in a plastic bag were still good, his mom could decide. He did find three books just of fiction, but he knew his mom would enjoy them. He picked up some porcelain bowls and a mirror from the barn. He found some glass pains and decided to bring them, along with a few jars. It was about all he could carry and home was a long ways away. His great adventure had turned into sort of a flop. What he thought was going to be an exciting thrill turned into a trip of realization. It showed just what mankind had done to themselves and how they were their remnants. It was not what he had expected to come to the conclusion of at all. He moved closer to the fort, he would go as far as he could before making camp. Soon he was at the river and followed it up stream.

Willow was as happy as a lark. She had been busy putting together her things to take to the next valley. She, Willow was soon to be a married woman. She would have her own home to care for. The older women all presented her with things to take with her. Willow worried for West, it was a long journey he had undertaken. She had been working hard trying to get as many things done as she could, to help her mom. It would some time most likely till she would see her again. That saddened her, but she knew it was the beginning of her life. The next children she cared for would be her own and not her siblings.

Willow never wavered from her education with Zack. There were many things she asked about the old world. She never asked her father, he would just refuse to talk about it. Her mother was the same. Zack spoke of many things. His stories were wondrous and she them to be true. Willow even looked forward to the hard work there was going to be, digging gardens and the harvest. With West to help it would not seem like a choir. She had never seen the cabin, but she did see the drawings of it. Willow had put all her things in her room and as she sat on her bed she looked around; yes she was happy, truly happy. She needed to talk to Zack and made her way there.

Tap, tap "Zack" Willow asked. "Come in my dear" Zack replied. Willow went in.

"Come sit here" Zack told her. Willow sat down. She wasn't sure how to start the conversation. Zack noted her uneasiness "Well my dear, you are taking away my West."Zack said. "Oh I'm not taking him away" she said. Zack smiled "I know dear." Willow now felt more at ease. "I just want to ask you about, West I mean." Zack wasn't sure what was troubling Willow "West is a strong young man in mind, spirit and in body. He's a deep thinker and I've never known him to do anything he didn't think was right." Willow looked at Zack "I guess I'm worried about you" she said. "Me!" Zack raised an eyebrow "Why are you worried about me?" Zack asked. "I know you so depend on him and if we move to the next valley, well he won't be here to help you."

Zack smiled "Willow, don't forget there are enough people here now to work the fields and bring in the harvest. Most of the hardest work has been done and don't forget I have Jo. It's a good thing, as she has been my guardian angel. I would never have survived had it not been for her." Willow just listened. "Did I tell you how I had my accident?" Zack asked her.

"No it had not been talked of" Willow said.

"Long before West was born, I was married to another. When the virus broke out, Jo and I were heading to find the complex in the mountains I had once worked on. There, they were completely self sufficient and they sealed themselves off when the virus hit. In my haste to get back there I wasn't paying attention and fell. It was Jo that saved my life. My legs were badly broken; the bones were sticking out through the skin. Jo set them and got help. I woke up in the settlement. It was a terrible time. I was so ill and then I started to heal. Jo was steadfast, she never wavered. When I had healed enough to move around I almost lost her. I said awful things to her in pain and anger at the fact I would never get back to the complex. She was going to go back to the fort. It was then I realized that I needed her and that she was more than a friend to me. I also know that I had come to love her. So you see Willow, we will be just fine." Zack told her.

Willow was relieved and couldn't believe how awful all of that must have been. "Thank you Zack." Willow said. "I had no idea you suffered so. You mentioned a complex you were going to find." Willow asked.

"Willow that is something I wish you to keep to yourself. West knows everything and he will tell you. You see, if everyone knew about it they would not try and make a life for themselves. I fear many would perish trying to find it. It is a wondrous place Willow and I pray that you and West find it someday."

Willow always enjoyed her conversations with Zack. She knew her life was about to break free and where it would lead she did not know. Willow went over and hugged Zack.

Willow headed out to find Jo. There was always some work to do outside.

She found Jo weeping in the garden. When Jo saw her she stopped and smiled. Willow asked if she needed help and Jo told her all was okay.

"Willow there is something you can do for me" Jo said.

"Sure" Willow replied.

By now Jo had walked over to her. "Let's sit in the shade, it's to hot today." Soon both were enjoying the coolness the shade provided.

"Willow I just wanted to talk to you about West. West has a way of working things right in his mind. I have always given him room to do this. To tell you the truth he's very much like his father in that sense." Jo smiled. "West will be a good husband and father that I'm sure and in many ways I envy you." Willow was startled "You envy me?" she said. "Yes" J told her. "You see you have a fresh look on the world. Your minds are not clouded with memories of the past." Jo smiled. Willow said "But all things must not have been bad" she couldn't believe that. "This is true" Jo smiled "I do so miss a hot bubble bath and running water. I miss a nice big turkey roasting in the oven and brandy to sip while it backed. There are many things but, they are no more and that is that. I am quite reconciled with that fact. This life has many virtues to it. One's feeling of worth and accomplishments at hard days work and when winter comes, the bounty stored to enjoy then. There is something in knowing that your work has some meaning to it and not some mindless tasks that benefit no one, but some rich corporation.

Anyways Willow I guess I'm just telling you to be happy. Life can be good if you work towards making it that way." Jo smiled at her.

Willow felt so close to Jo and Zack. Her mother was always too busy with all the children, to talk much. Willow often felt like her built in child care. She never minded her mother working hard. They always had clothes and food. Her father always made sure they had a home. There was a difference between them. Zack and Jo had accepted life, her mom and dad always seemed resentful. She had hear her mom say to her father once, why had we survived? We lived to see all that we lost and that was a sadness they both carried. She was sure the solace they found in each other was a temporary moment of comfort.

"Well" Jo could see Willow was deep in thought. "I must get back to work. Would you see if you could find some of those lovely mushrooms for me?" Jo asked.

Willow smiled and said "Sure" and headed to the storage shed for a basket. She picked one out and headed into the forest. Willow like the peace of the woods. She moved through it with the grace of a butterfly. She often challenged herself not to make any sound as she passed through it. She loved the smell and in some spots the suns rays shone through the openings above to laminate small areas. There was something magical about them she thought. She often sat in them and let the sun warm her when she was cool. It didn't take long for her to find what she was looking for. Soon she had a basket full of mushrooms. Willow was soon in the open valley and on her way to give Jo her mushrooms.

Jo was delighted and set them out to dry. Willow was happy after her visit headed home.

Her mom was glad to see her and soon had Willow busy doing various choirs. She didn't mind and it was as Jo said that. She knew soon her life would be just that, hers. She was not bitter or sad about everything as it was now, it just was. West was the shining star in her path now, lighting a way she couldn't begin to imagine.

Night always came too soon for Willow. She had been weaving when there was not enough light to continue, she climbed into bed after she washed. Soon sleep had its hold on her.

The next morning found her doing household choirs. Willow knew what had to be done and knew that if it wasn't done all would suffer for it along the way. Her mom was in the garden and her father was working in the wood shop. She washed all the linens and hung them out to dry when she saw Zack and Jo.

Zack was making tiles and Jo was sitting on the porch mending. She had a table out and Willow knew she was drying herbs and nuts. The mushrooms would be almost dry by the end of the day. After she finished the laundry she headed to see what Zack was doing.

She was surprised to see how many tiles he had made. "What on earth are you going to do with all those tiles?" Willow asked.

Zack smiled "I'm going to make a nice walkway around the house for Jo." He told her. Willow smiled "That's a grand idea. That would stop a lot of mud going into the house." She said to Zack. "I think it will be easier to shovel in the winter as well." Zack said. "I believe you are right" Willow agreed. Zack smiled. "Where are you off to dear?" he asked her. "Oh I just thought I might go and see if the nut trees are getting ready to drop some nuts." "Don't be gone too long; your laundry will be dry in no time with all the wind and heat." "I won't be" and Willow headed out to the grove of walnuts.

Jo was busy with her home things and as she sat there, she looked at her apple trees. The first one she planted had so many apples, the second had some and the third had none yet. Next year it would produce.

She watched Zack work at his kiln and knew he was up to something, but she let him do his thing. She would find out soon enough. She wondered how West was. He had been gone a week now and soon would return. She thought of Cambry and what might be left, if anything. He was bound and determined to see, that alone would drive him to go there. She thought of the day she met Zack and how glad he was there, out of no where to save her.

She got up and checked the progress of her herb drying and decided to put on some tea. She had grown roses close to the house for hips for tea. It had been a good idea. She decided that once the kids were settled she would bring some clippings from her herbs and flowers.

Jo went back to the porch and sat in her rocking chair. The air was warm and sweet with the smell of summer and a soft breeze was blowing. Jo closed her eyes and soon was sleeping.

It was Zack that woke her in the late afternoon. "Jo, Jo, you okay?" Zack asked her.

She opened her eyes and smiled "Yes" she said "Perfectly fine Zack." Zack sat down "That's not a usual thing for you to do" he said to her. "Oh, it was just so nice and warm and this chair is a dream." Jo replied. "Well as long as you are okay" he said. "Well I just didn't want to say I'm getting old and just wanted to take a cat nap." At that they both laughed.

They spent the next few hours chatting and then the coldness of the evening set in, they retired into the house.

The house would not be the same without West, but that too is as it should be.

Chapter 22

$\mathcal{T}$he big day had arrived; Dana and Todd were both nervous. The wedding was minutes away and Dana beamed. It was just friends and close family to attend. Todd checked and double checked everything. He wanted this day to be the best for Dana. It was his day too; he wanted her to have a day she would look back on and remember as the day she was no longer alone. She was no longer a single soul passing through the world. Todd loved her and knowing that she loved him was all he needed.

The ceremony was beautiful and Todd lingered at the get together after as Dana wanted to. He knew this was the first day of the rest of their lives together and was in no hurry. Dana could never have been happier. She loved Todd so and knew she too was complete now as a person. Throughout the party she glanced at him often and knew she was safe and that was a feeling new and glorious.

The older folks sat together and talked of many things, some things of the past and many new things for the future.

It was a merry time and all enjoyed it. Tomorrow most would go back to life as normal, but Todd and Dana. It would be new and full of discoveries about each other. The love the two shared was like a warm glow that followed them wherever they went. All too soon the dinner, dance and songs were over for the guests.

Todd took Dana to their dorm. That evening was theirs and the sharing they had was the mark of their inseparability. Todd and Dana were one and nothing would ever change that.

They spent the next two weeks enjoying intimate moments together in their favourite spots. They talked of what they wanted for the complex and its future. They dreamed of living outside again. It was all too soon, they had to come back to reality and get back to work. Everyone had to pull their share for all to survive and they knew it.

Dana headed to see Dirk. It seemed ages since she had been to see the animals. After the virus went through they lost some, but they were coming back now and that pleased her. Since this was the stock of the future and they would let the surplus go again when they had recovered enough.

Dirk as always was happy to see her. "Well my sweet." Dirk said when he saw her. "What brings you here?" he asked her. "Married life driving you crazy already?" he asked her. "No, I just wanted to see you." She told him. "Dirk" Dana asked "How long before you think we can start letting some animals out again?" "That depends" he said. "On the birth rate, if it keeps at this pace, about three years I'd say."

Dirk shared Dana's opinion about regaining life outside the tunnels, although he had doubts that he would ever see it. Carla and he were not young anymore and time was taking its toll. He taught his children everything they needed to know, with Dana and the others interested in the welfare of the animals he felt secure in knowing that they would continue t be in good hands.

Dana asked Dirk "Have you seen any life outside through the monitors? I was just there and I didn't see any." Dirk replied "I did notice a few last week and thought I saw a couple birds, but that's it." Dana sighed. "Look" Dirk said, "It's an awfully big valley out there. I'm sure more are there just hidden, so don't fret."

He could see that brightened her some. Dana wandered in and around the pens of the sheep. She often went to see them; sheep were so lovely, so calm she smiled. She never went to see the predators much. She knew they would be needed to keep the populations of game in check outside, but they still were not her favourites.

"Dirk!" Dana said "I am so content now. Do you feel that around Carla?"

Dirk smiled "Yes dear and it will keep growing, that's contentment." He told her.

"I am happy Dirk and somehow I feel the world is a new place." Dirk smiled "It is my dear and everyday will be more wondrous than the day before, just remember, you will have differences of opinions, but that is how we learn. It's how we resolve those differences that will make the following times better. Just remember you two are just people and folks are not perfect. Help each other over the hurdles life will through in your path."

"Thanks Dirk you always make me feel better." Dana told him. "Not that I was feeling bad or anything. Just you do make me feel things are just right." Dirk smiled "Where is Todd today?" he asked. "He has to help finish some pillars with dad. He works hard." Dana said. Dirk laughed "He's young and strong, hard work is good for him." "I don't want him to burn out." Dana said. "If he seems to be on too long, make him take a break then."

Dana decided to go see Karen and David. They still ran the agro tunnels and the virus didn't seem to hurt the plants. "Im off Dirk" and she started towards the agro tunnels.

She found Karen tending her plants with Petra. After losing Noel, Petra was near her a lot. David spent even more time with the bugs. The loss of Noel hurt him dearly, but Karen and David knew that is part of life and kept their sorrows within the family.

When Karen saw Dana she stopped and welcomed her.

"Hi Karen, Petra" Dana said. "Hi" they replied together. Dana looked at them and they burst into laughter. "What brings you here Dana?" Karen finally asked. "Oh, just the usual, checking on your plant growth and how David's bugs are doing" Dana replied. "The plants are all fairly well, but you will have to ask David about the insects." "Have you managed any new breeds of flowers yet Karen?" Dana inquired. "As a matter of fact Petra has been in charge of them" Karen smiled.

Petra beamed "I have a new colour of Gardenia. It's white with a pale blue line edging the bottom" Petra told her. "Oh really, it sounds beautiful" Dana said. "You two have done such wonders with everything here." Petra told Dana "We lost so many insects with the virus we were worried that there would not be enough for pollination left. Father said for us not to worry, but I think if we lose bees and a few others, we might be in big trouble." Dana looked at her one consolation; the virus has done its worst. I think if anything else was going to die from it, it would have by now. I think your father was right." Dana told her.

Karen was amazed at how Dana managed to keep many fingers in many fires it took to run the complex. She seemed to be aware of many aspects of the workings of everything in the complex. Karen was glad she was just concerned with the agro tunnels.

Petra spent almost as much time with the plants as Karen. It was good that she wanted to learn everything, but Karen also knew soon the plants would not be enough. She would have to find someone to share it all with.

"I think I will go and find David" Dana told them. "I want to know as soon as he has a surplus." When the time came Dana would like to see the animals and bugs whatever they were, let outside. "He said he would be in his lab" Karen told her." "Alright, later then" Dana said as she waved.

Karen watched her go and then said to Petra "When are you going to get married?" Petra replied "Not for a long while yet, no kids for me not yet anyway." Karen smiled knowing when she found the right partner, children would come. They went back to tending the plants.

Dana made her way to where David was working. She found him reading. "David" she said and he looked up. "Oh hello Dana, what brings you here my dear?" David replied. "I'm checking on the surplus of the insects if you have any." Dana smiled. "As a matter of fact I do. There are several species that are doing very well." "Oh that's wonderful." Dana said. "You are the best, are there and bee queens?" Dana asked. "Yes I have three or four and enough bees to start new colonies. You are looking to let them out then?" he asked. "Yes David, I want to live out there someday." David smiled. "As do most of us and you are right, if we keep letting them go they will replenish the world. I have earthworms, spiders and flies as well." Dana was pleased.

"Dirk has deer, fish and soon we might let some birds go. Hummingbirds first, when there is enough bugs and bees, then maybe some seed eaters as well." David smiled. "Well I'm off. I want to go to the monitor room. I keep hoping there will be something there some day."

With that she started towards the labs. Simion always thought more made it and Dana prayed her father was one of them.

Todd worked hard that day and it was in the tomb tunnel. He never cared for that job, too many passed already. They had to make the tombs there were many of the original folks here and they were getting older. Todd dreaded the day when his folks passed. He knew many others that would be such a loss to the complex.

When he arrived at their dorm Dana wasn't there. He headed for the shower, she would be back soon. He wasted no time. He liked to wash the dust off. It had been a long day.

Dana had watched the monitors for some time and as usual nothing. She looked at the ones pointing into the valley and watched the trees in the breeze. She caught a glimpse of something, she hoped was a deer, but it was gone. She sighed and decided to go home. Tomorrow she would see

Dirk and start making arrangements to let the animals go. She headed home and realized that Todd would be there already. She hurried.

When she arrived, Todd was in the shower. "Todd, I'm home" she called. "Hi sweetie, I'll be out in a few minutes." Dana smiled. She put the kettle on and decided a nice dinner would be in order. She started preparing it when Todd arrived at her side from the shower. He wasted no time getting her into his arms "I missed you today" he said. Dana held him close "Had a hard day then?" she asked. "No not all that hard, just a job I didn't care for." "Ahhh you were working on the tombs again." "Yeah" he told her. "It always makes me sad even though I know I'm making a place for them to rest, that's got beauty and is...well you know what I mean." "Yes I do Todd" Dana said. "I want to talk with you, so let me finish making us dinner and you get dressed." Todd smiled "Yes dear" he said and they laughed.

Dana in no time had the meal done and they shared it as they talked. "I have been to see Dirk and David. There's a surplus again. Tomorrow I want to start making the arrangements to let them out. Todd, do you think we will ever live outside?" Dana asked. "I hope so" he replied. "I went to the labs today and there was nothing." Dana told him. Todd knew that she always hoped her father would find a way to send a message. "Maybe tomorrow, there's always tomorrow." Todd said to her. "Yes maybe." She said, but in her heart she knew that message would never come.

"Do you think there are many people alive out there?" Dana asked. "There has to be. We survived in here. Dana, mankind is strong." "I know" she said. "But they wouldn't have the advantages as we do here." "This is true, but I still think they made it and just think, with us letting out animals and insects, we will be helping them."

Dana smiled "You always make me feel better." Todd smiled "That's because you love me." And he smiled too. "Let me help clear these dishes. So tell me Dana, any plans for tonight?" "No not really." She said. "Well then, how about a walk in the atrium then?" Todd said. "Sure" she replied.

They went there and both enjoyed it. Todd sat and watched Dana wander through the plants. He hoped someday she would walk in the woods outside. He had watched the monitors too and thought it would be a dream like. Outside, would be a wonder indeed. The council was against any of it since the virus got in. So many had died they feared any more contact with the outside, but his Dana never gave up. She always presented her arguments to them. "We are not meant to live in the tunnels forever. Simion never wanted that." She would say, but they were too fearful yet.

The complex was just now starting to get back to some kind of normal functioning. They would relent and Dana would be there.

She made her way back to him and beamed, when he smiled at her. "Let's go home." She said. Todd stood and took her arm. "Lead on my dear lady." He said to her and she giggled. "You are a card, you know that?" she said and placed her hand on his cheek and kissed him. They soon were on their way home. Todd teased her and laughed.

Before they knew it, they were soon home and soon in bed. They both had a lot of work to do the next day and it was late. They loved each other and soon fell into a peaceful slumber.

It was Todd always first to rise in the morning. He made coffee and woke Dana. It was a big day for her. "Oh thanks Todd, the coffee is just what I need." He was already finished his and was heading for the shower. He glanced back and said "Join me when you're done." she smiled over her cup at him.

It didn't take long before she was showering. It was a big day; a lot had to be done. She washed and almost dressed when Todd finished. "I want to come with you today Dana." Todd said. "Sure we can use all the help Todd, hurry up and get dressed." Where are we off to first?" he asked. "Let's go and see David first, then we can visit Dirk and Carla afterwards." "That sounds good to me." He replied.

Karen and David were always pleased to see them. Petra was there to help too. "Well" Dana smiled "Let's do this." It took them about three hours to get all the creatures, from bugs to mice into the cages. These cages would be opened automatically from safe inside. They would open them one at a time to make sure they all had time to escape before the next one was opened. Anything that had wings wasted little time when freedom presented itself. The others took their time.

Karen had a little lunch packed and all shared the food. They all talked of living outside again and what it would be like. Petra had to leave early; she always had a fancy for books and spent a few hours in the library.

After the last creature was freed they cleaned all the cages. Then it was off to see Dirk. He would have his ready to go with the help of the children and Carla. Dana wondered what animals he would be releasing.

They wasted no time in getting to the animals tunnels. On arriving, just as Dana had expected they had many animals ready to go. Dirk had weasels, ground hogs, squirrels and to her surprise he was going to let out some canaries and humming birds as well.

Dirk said "Let's see if they make it, with luck they will." Dana smiled.

They spent the rest of the day and it was early evening before they had the rest of the cages cleaned. It was then Dirk said to Dana "Dana, come with me. I want to show you something."

Dana and Todd followed Dirk down a new tunnel. There were animals there that Dana had never seen before, bison, moose, boar and elk. Dana just looked at Dirk "They are wonderful" she said. Dirk just smiled "I wanted to let some out. How about we do it tomorrow?" he said. "You think we should? Do you think they will survive?" Dana asked. "I'm hoping." He smiled. Dana watched and looked at Dirk. "This is going to be a big job." And with that they all laughed.

Carla had dinner brought in and it was very welcomed. Dana asked Dirk if he had other animals that no one knew about and he looked at Carla "Hmm." "I take that as a yes" Dana said.

Dirk rubbed his chin "Yes there are animals here, but they are not from this area. They would only survive in the tropics." "Really?" said Dana. "Would you show them to me Dirk?" Dana asked. "Yes, but not tonight. I have as little contact as possible with them. I have been trying to keep them as wild as possible." Dana thought about that and realized that he was right. After all Dirk was still surprising her. He was an amazing man.

Todd was already cleaning up the table and Dana knew it was time to call it a day. "Tomorrow will be upon us before we know it" Todd said "and I want to see those beasts outside." He knew if they survived, life was on its way again. "We will see you tomorrow." Dana said and her and Todd left.

Todd held her arm in his and he led her to the labs to watch the monitors for a little while. She knew why she loved him so. There was nothing on them and no recorded messages. They were locked on the valley outside and both were glad to see birds flying. "Come ob Dana lets go home. We will look again tomorrow." Dana looked up at him and nodded. They walked home in silence and after showering, went to bed.

Todd again, was the first to rise and made coffee. Danna knew he would and stretched in bed. It was delicious; she loved it and soaked it up like a big sponge. She never knew that anyone could make her feel the way she did now. "Coffee is on love" he told her "Get up Love" he called to her.

Slowly she got up and made her way to the shower. It was a quick one because she knew Todd wanted to get going. After the coffee she cleared the table and made their way to the animal tunnels.

It was Dana that started the conversation first "Todd, how many children do you want?" she asked. "However many God gives us, if it's one okay, if it's ten I will be happy." He smiled at her. "You know I never thought about children too much before, but with you it seems like the right thing." Dana said. Todd smiled at her, "Don't fret sweetie if it happens it happens, if not, then well not. I want to think about getting the world ready for all the children to come in the future." He told her. "I love you Todd." Dana told him. "Well I love you more." He said and they both smiled.

They had arrived at the animal tunnels and Dirk was there to meet them. Mark, his son and Ann, his daughter were also there to lend a hand.

The animals took awhile to get into the cages. Dirk smiled when the last ones were ready to go. Mark started to clean the stalls and Ann did the last of the paper work to be given to the council.

Dirk was ready to set them free. He knew they would survive. The deer that first were let go had made it and he felt sure these would be fine. The first winter would be the hardest, after that they would be on their way to regaining the outside world. Dirk looked over to Mark and Ann and knew it was in their lives that freedom would be gained.

It was Carla that made the final inspection. She had the final say on their health etc…with a nod the cages were transported to the exits.

They were locked in the tunnel and the doors to the outside opened. The bison and elk wasted no time venturing out. The moose moved slower, the bears were the last.

Dirk knew the next year a different genetic line would have to be released. Ann kept track of all that. She knew every line of the entire animal tunnel.

Dirk was proud of his children. He and Carla had done well. The loss of the two others still broke his heart if he dwelt on it too much, so he tried not to.

Todd and Dana clean the cages after they were empty. The work was not like work to them, more of a pleasure.

Dirk was glad to see the work and as a reward he took them to see the animals he kept a secret.

Dana and Todd watched in amazement at the monkeys and antelope. The larger animals died with virus. Dirk was sad at the loss of the water buffalo and crocodiles, but then there were still so many still alive. There were wild pigs and rodents and even a platypus, peccary and many more.

It was too soon when Dirk decided to leave. He stopped them outside and asked them to keep it under their hats. Todd and Dana both knew the reason why. "Listen you two; we are having a bit of a get together. It seems my children decided to announce some news, will you come?" Dana and Todd both agreed to be there. Dirk smiled and Dana hugged him before they left.

Chapter 23

Willow was worried about West. He had been gone a week, but to Willow it seemed like forever. She was studying with Zack daily and it was a distraction. Jo was there often when the lessons were on. After, the two women often spun flax or chatted about cooking or designs for the new clothing. Willow always liked to learn about anything Jo would teach her. Jo was a mother that most would have loved to have and Willow felt blessed.

Gary and Brad had made her and West so many household furnishings. It was all so exciting. Willow had never had so many, be so kind to her.

She helped her mom most afternoons after lessons. The days Willow spent with Jo, her mother never minded, she was happy that Willow was going to have a life and she was glad of it. Her life would be hard work, but it would be worth it. West was a good man and that was a relief. She prayed her other children might find happiness that Willow found. The happiness she had before the viruses were let loose.

The next morning Willow had her basket and was looking for forest tidbits as she called them. Everyone loved the mushrooms and Willow shared them with all. She loved the woods and picking them let her wander in the woods. She let her mind wander to West, he might be home today she thought. How nice it would be to have him back, next time she would go with him. Next time she would be his wife. Willow smiled, where was he? She thought. He would have so much to tell her and she could hardly wait to hear all of it. Where were Cambry and the farm like? She thought about the settlement and the fort. It was Jo calling to her that got her attention as she left the cover of the forest. "I'm coming" she called back.

Jo made tea and was glad for the mushrooms Willow gave her. "I will be making paper tomorrow, want to learn?" Jo asked her. "Oh yes" Willow said "I would like that very much." Jo smiled. Willow was always willing to learn new things that would help them a lot in their future. "Alright in the morning then, I know you have laundry day at your mom's in the afternoon." "Yes I do" Willow said. "Okay" Jo said "when you stop at Sara and Lily's ask them if they need paper too. I want an idea of how much to make." Jo asked her. "Yes I will" Willow replied and with that she made her way home.

The walkway between all the houses had been made of bricks. Zack had been busy. It was so nice for the women and far less mud tracked into the houses. When she got home, her mom had plenty of things that needed to be done. Willow was almost thankful for all the work; it was less stressful than worrying about West. Why was he not back yet? She did not feel uneasy, just him being gone made her miss him all the more. She knew he would notice the walkways right away. Willow wondered if he would have the same for them, she hoped he would.

The day passed quickly and night soon took hold. She sat on the porch and stared at the sky. West please hurry home I do miss you so. Willow then rose and headed to bed. Jo would be expecting her early.

Dawn came too soon. Willow had worked hard the day before and was having a time getting going. When she arrived at Jo's, she still was not fully awake. Jo handed her a tea and was gathering things together. The two women soon were in the shop they had made for Jo to do her projects in.

Jo said "First we need to fill this tub with water" and they packed at least thirty buckets to fill it. Then they beat flax over a board that had claws open at the top and soon had the flax down to fibres, like it was ready for spinning. "Now we cut it up" Jo told her and soon it looked like a pile of fuzz. "Now we mix this with water," Willow was fascinated. The water was like a thick soup, almost.

Jo then produced several frames with lightly woven cloth in them. "The trick" Jo told her "is to keep the water mixed well." Jo dipped each frame into the soupy mix and then laid them on a press. She placed cloth material between each frame and turned the press down. The water was then squeezed off. Jo carefully peeled the cloth off and the paper was laid out to dry. The remaining water was run through a filter so it could be used again and the filter was hung to dry.

It was mid day now and Willow knew how to make paper. Jo smiled at her "Want some tea?" she asked and Willow was glad to have some.

"Jo, how did you learn to do so many things?" Willow asked. "I read most of it in books Willow" Jo replied. "Were there many books before?" Willow asked. "Oh yes" Jo told her. "There were books about anything you wanted to know or about places, about people and their history." Willow sighed. "Why did they destroy so much? It's just so senseless to me. What did they think when they let loose the viruses?" Willow asked. Jo sat there for a moment "I think they didn't think. It wasn't the everyday person; it was the people in positions of power. They got greedy and one thing led to another. I really believe they had no idea of the storm they let go and just what would happen. It makes no never mind, we are here and this is our life." Jo smiled. "You're not unhappy are you?" Jo asked. "Oh no, I'm just curious." She replied. "Jo shouldn't West be home soon?" she asked. "Yes he is due. Don't worry; West is a strong young man and he will be home soon." Jo told her. "I hope so; it's not the same here without him." Jo smiled "I know what you mean."

Willow at that point felt sad they were moving into the next valley. "You must miss him too and when he gets back it will be me that takes him away." Willow told Jo. "That's not the same and we will visit. It's not like you will be days and days away." Jo told her. "I must go. There is a huge pile of clothes waiting to be washed at home." Willow told her. "You never mind working so hard. I don't want you sick and miss your own wedding." Jo smiled at her. Willow smiled too "I wouldn't miss it even if I was sick" and they both laughed. "Alright dear, I will see you tomorrow. The garden is calling me, time to weed it again." "Now don't you over work Jo. I want you around for a long time yet." Willow said to her and Jo smiled. "I will come for tea tomorrow." Willow told her and headed down the path for home.

The sun was warm and she saw Zack cutting wood at the table he made to help him do it. She waved and was soon at home getting water to fill the wash tub. If she finished before nightfall she would take a walk by the river. Willow wanted West to come home. She missed and needed him. Where was he she thought? He said a week and it's going into the second week. Willow's thoughts went to him kissing her. How he always made her feel important to her, her holding him and him holding her. She missed his closeness and just being able to reach out and touch him; his company and his laughter. She just plan missed him.

It was too late when she finished the wash to go walking, so after it was all hung to dry, she went to bed. Willow was lonely and it was West she was lonely for.

West wasted no time in getting to the fort. He had a few treasures for all and in some ways he was glad he had made the journey. It brought him down to earth and helped him realize what was important. He knew Willow would be waiting as would his mom and dad. He would be glad to see them. The city of the dead truly was and he could see why most left and never talked much of it.

He would be at the fort today it would be good to see people. He never found anything for the smithy, but that was okay. He wouldn't have been able to carry it with everything he had at the moment anyways. He would be able t get some nails and spike though. He wondered how long it would be before the young men he was training would move to the next settlement. Moving any iron would be awfully hard work unless they did something with the path there. West would mention that to folks and see what their reply would be. A road would sure improve travel, but it would be a lot of work.

West looked over the flat plains and wondered if his life's journey would ever bring him back again. He might make a trip just to show Willow. The constant wind, although refreshing from the heat was also annoying.

He still was following the river and soon he would meet the road to the fort. His pack was getting heavy; it would be a relief to rest there and get something different to eat other than trail rations. He wanted to see Jo's face when he gave her the books. He liked giving her things she enjoyed. She had little from the old world and never seemed to mind that. His mom was maybe the finest woman he had ever known and Willow was next to her.

The thoughts of Willow brought a smile. He remembered when he first saw her. He thought of her flaming red hair and emerald green eyes, how delicate her facial features were. He thought of how it all came together in a small strong sturdy frame and with a kind loving heart. West knew her parents and how unhappy they were. The past was what they wanted and everyday was a struggle for them. They never took out their anger on the children, but they were not the means to make it easier for them. He was glad he would be taking Willow away from that. His parents never lived in the past; they lived for the future and often saw the humour of daily life. How different the two sets of parents were.

Jo and Zack made many overtures to Willow's parents of friendship and kindness, but they chose to stick to each other, letting few or none get close. His mom and dad gave them room to be themselves.

West couldn't turn off his mind. He could see the fort in the distance and was glad of it. Dusk would soon be falling and his pack was starting to wear on him. He picked up his pace and was soon there.

He got a room in the common house and the first thing he did was wash. He changed his clothes and washed the clothes he was wearing. He ventured downstairs and smelled a veggie stew cooking. He wasted little time getting some for himself. It was great and he was starving it seemed like.

As he ate he listened to the talk and to his surprise the families were planning to start a new settlement. He didn't know why that surprised him. He himself built a cabin in the valley next to their settlement. He was sitting near the older and listened to them talk. They spoke of being young again so they could adventure out, but their aches and pains kept them near the fort. West smiled, he wondered if they really wanted a life of hard work. That's what it was, hard work. From what his father told him of the past, some worked hard and others bought what they needed/wanted with money. Now folks traded for what they needed as there was no money. It seemed it was one thing most left alive after the virus went through the world that held no further meaning.

"Excuse me sirs" West said to the men who were talking. "What valley have you chosen to start your new settlement in?" "South, my boy" One man replied. "Seems the young are spreading their wings" another added. "Yes it will relieve some of the burden on some of our food stores." Yet another said. "Why did they pick south?" West inquired. "They feel it might give a longer growing season and I tend to agree with them." The men then broke into chatter about the weather and such, West just sat quietly and listened. There might be some validity to them moving south, West thought.

"Well thank you gentlemen" West said and rose to leave. The old men bid him well and West went outside and sat on the porch. He stared into the sky and wondered where life would take him and Willow. He also wondered what adventures awaited them. He soon felt waves of tiredness and headed for his room. He stretched out on his bed and was soon asleep.

West woke to the commotion downstairs. He dressed quickly and went to see what the noise was about. There was a runner downstairs. He had come from the settlement ten days out on the prairie. People were all talking all at once. How many folks there? Where is it, are there others beyond? The runner told them, the settlement had two hundred now, but they knew of none beyond. "What brought you out this way?" someone asked. "Well we knew there had to be others because we survived; crops had not been good. Some have died from lack of food. It was an old-timer that spoke of the fort. I came across a few towns, but nothing there just bones." West what he was talking about. "Why did you not look for us before?" "We did, we had been to Cambry and saw what was left. The choice was to stick where we were and try to survive. With our food shortage we had to try and find the fort and hope there were folks. You have no idea what a relief it is to find more people." "Well we have enough food for us, but not for that many people."

West spoke up "They could work the valley south and maybe beyond. I can take the word to the other settlements to start a stock pile for the winter." "Aye, Good plan" one of the older men said. "If we all work together we just might do it. It will be a long winter and your people will have to be settled before winter. We have a common house, but it can not hold 200."

The runner looked around "I must get back and tell them it will be two or three weeks before we can make it back here. I am thankful, so thankful to find people like you who are willing to help." "We are what are left of the old world and this might be a start of a new beginning for all of us. Two hundred people, that's a huge increase in population. It would put the fort and the surrounding area now near a thousand. This is good, hope is ever there and opportunity is knocking for new things." The runner was given a room and food.

West by now had his gear packed and was ready to leave. He worked his way through the fort and listened to the buzz of the people talking about the new folks coming. West hiked his pack and headed to the smithy. He got his spikes and nails, after a talk with the smithy about the new arrivals, he headed for home. He knew the way and had the runner from the fort with him part of the way. He was taking the news to the settlement further out. He was weighed down with things for the settlement that his mom and dad came from. West didn't mind the company.

He soon found out that Carry had no wife and children and was the eldest son of the cook at the fort. "So what made you want to be a runner?" West asked. Carry looked at West "Have you ever been in a cook house in the summer?" he replied. "No I haven't" West said. "It's hot and tons of work. I guess I just wanted some freedom. Being a runner seemed like a good idea and well it has been. Folks get their news and items I carry. I get away and others get what they need" and with that he smiled. West agreed with him. "So what brings you out this way West?" Carry asked.

"Curiosity mostly, my mom and dad had a family farm not far from Cambry. I just wanted to see it and Cambry; sometimes I wish I had not." West told him. "I have never been so far from the fort really" Carry told him "Listening to the old men talk about Cambry, I never had a desire to see it. I've seen too much death in my life to suit me." He told West. West just nodded, he wondered how many had such tragedy and still strove to make good lives for themselves and others around them. He liked Carry. West knew he would have a good life; he had a good attitude.

"I will marry when I get home." West told him. "Really! Wow! You must want to get home quick then?" Carry said. "Yes I miss my girl a lot. Next time it will be together when we come to visit the fort. The talk, all the new folks will be interesting to find out how they survive." West replied. "Well interesting to you means work to me." Carry told him. "All those people eating, the cook house will be in full force." West just nodded "I see what you mean." "I wonder if I can be a runner till winter?" and they both laughed.

The journey to the settlement didn't seem to take the day that it was with West and Carry sharing their thoughts on many things. Carry was going to move south when they started the new settlement, but with all the new people coming maybe west would be a better direction.

When they reached the settlement West looked for the common house and Carry went to deliver his messages. It didn't take long before the news of the new people were the talk of the settlement. The older folks were called on for their opinion on sharing stocked food and other material things they may need. The whole settlement soon was organized and bringing all the extra things to the common house to be stored for them.

Carry soon joined West for a hot dinner. After they ate, they said good night, West was glad to be in his room and as usual he washed his clothes and crawled into bed.

Morning came and found West tired. He could hear the rain outside. Great he thought; wet feet. He packed his gear and headed downstairs for breakfast, before he would start out again. It would be a two day hike to the next settlement. After he had eaten he started on his way. "West, West hold up there." He turned to see Carry. West waited for him to catch up. "Do you feel like some company?" Carry asked. "Sure" West told him. "I thought you would be here for a few days." "I thought a day, but they want news taken quickly to the next settlement." Carry replied. "It looks like we are in for a soggy walk." West said. "Yeah" Carry said "I guess one can't have it perfect all the time. I don't mind the rain. You know when you get to the next settlement; just think how nice a hot meal and dry room will be." Carry told West. West smiled, he was right there.

His feet were already wet. The trail to the river was in good shape. The travelling was easy; he knew he was getting close to where is father had fallen, just after the settlement. They walked in silence, West always surveying his surroundings. Carry never seemed to pay attention to anything, but the path in front of him. West was sure he would get lost if he ever left the trail. West's mind wandered to the stories that Zack told him of the animals, bears, cougars, bobcats, and lynx. He was glad they had no threats especially for the night, but it would have been a thrill to see one just the same. West thought even a deer or bird would be exciting. The forest was quiet, no buzzing of bugs, nor chirps from birds; nothing just the breeze in the tree tops and the sound of water dripping down.

West soon located a sheltered spot to make some tea. He wanted to change his foot wear and try and dry what he had on. Carry was a big help, someone had taught him to build shelters. Soon they had a fire going and tea brewing.

West asked him who taught him to build shelters. "When we want to be runners, the older men take us out and teach us. After all if we are taking messages, etc we have to sleep out here." Carry replied. "Ahhh, it was like training for you guys then?" West said. "Yes, but not all runners are men, some women are too." West looked up "Lots of women are suited to being out in the woods." He thought of Willow, he knew she was a survivor and if she wanted she could be anything she set her mind too. Carry and West had both been born after the virus had done its worst. Until West saw Cambry, he never really realized just how devastating it had been.

After they had eaten and warmed their soggy bones they were ready to go. It would be a long afternoon. The rain made the travelling a chore. Just before dusk they picked a spot to camp. Soon they had the camp made and they would be dry for the night.

It was after midnight when the two were awakened by thunder. West never cared for thunder storms, he always worried about forest fires. He was not long in his thoughts, Carry spoke first "I sure hope the forest is wet enough, so we don't have a fire." "I agree" said West. "Have you ever seen a forest fire West?" "No, but I know I don't want to." West told him. "I saw a prairie fire; it almost made it to the fort. Everyone worked to protect the fort. I wouldn't want see a forest ablaze, the grass burning was scary enough." Carry told him.

The rain was coming down fairly good and that put the two young men more at ease. The storm moved over the mountains and soon both found sleep.

West woke and Carry had a fire going already. "Decided to join the living again?" Carry smiled. West got up and worked the kinks out. "Yeah, I didn't sleep well after the storm." West replied. "So when do you think we will be at the settlement?" Carry asked. "Oh probably by dusk" West replied. "I figured so" Carry said. They had tea and West put on his dry foot wear. With the storm gone, the day was starting better.

They packed up and were soon making tracks towards the settlement. It wasn't long before they realized each was trying to out pace the other. By mid-afternoon exhaustion was starting to take its toll and the two called it a draw as to who was travelling the fastest. By dinner time they had the settlement valley in sight. They never stopped for dinner, with dry beds and hot food the goal.

They wandered into the settlement at dusk. West headed for a room and Carry made his way to see the elders of the settlement. West was relieved to be close to home; one more day he thought. He got his room and was soon looking for some hot food.

He met up with Carry in the common house and the news once again had everyone talking. Carry sought out West and sat with him. "Well my friend, it was a great journey and I just wanted to thank you for the company. Promise me when you bring your wife to the fort that you will stop in and see me." West shook his hand and told him that he would. He made a friend in Carry and knew their paths would cross again.

West headed for bed, he was tired and tomorrow he would be home. He and Willow would marry and a whole new life would be theirs. He wanted to see the cabin and valley. It was so different from the valley they now lived. He told Carry he would pass the news on and wondered what they would think at home. West couldn't imagine how all these people lived on the prairies. From what they had seen there wasn't much there. How relieved they would be when their runner returned with the news he had found people. West wondered if they survived, how many more would be alive and thinking they were all that was left. Sleep finally took West, he really needed it.

Dawn came too soon; this trip was too arduous and had an effect on his emotions West had not counted on. He was happy to get home. Home he thought would never sound so good. He got up and packed his gear. He sat at his table eating his hot and listened to the talk of the new people. He wondered what his mom and dad would feel as well as the others at home. He looked at Carry, but didn't see him. He wanted to say a final farewell, but he was not around. West finished eating and started for home.

The sky was overcast, but it wasn't raining yet. He was thankful for that. His mind wandered to Willow and he was glad he was on his way home to her. She was a bright spot in his life and he needed that at the moment.

The path was still good he thought, soon though the men would have to spend a weekend clearing a few spots before they got out of hand. West soon could hear the river and it was a welcomed sound. The trip home seemed to be going slowly. He wasn't sure if he was just tired or what he had seen and heard the last week just weighed on him. Willow would be excited to hear everything. His mom and dad knew what was there and misgivings about him going in the first place. He understood so much more about the older folks now. In 20 years most would be gone and with them a wealth of knowledge, some good and some bad.

West soon crossed over the river and was on the final part of his journey home. His pace quickened, he wanted to be home now and his legs moved faster. The sun had come out, to West's relief. As he gazed around the forest he could see the sun's rays shine through any open spots above. It almost looked magical. One more range to cross and he would be back. First thing he was going to do was take a bath. Then he was going to spend some time with Willow. They would have to start packing things for the cabin. His adventuring would be on hold until he knew Willow and himself had enough food stores to hike around. It would be at least three years he thought, but then the search for the complex would begin in earnest. He thought about building another cabin for when his folks came to visit. There was no shortage of things that could be done.

It was just after noon and West took time to make tea and have something to eat. In about 4 hours he would be back.

Willow was getting worried, West should be back by now, where could he be she thought? She had spent the morning collecting mushrooms and now was with Zack. She sat at her lessons and Zack could tell her mind was elsewhere. "Don't fret Willow" Zack told her "He will be home soon," Zack smiled at her. "Oh I know" she said "but I miss him and Im worried. He said 6 days; we are going into 8 days and tomorrow will be... you know? Aren't you worried" Willow asked. "No not yet, many things can hinder travel. The weather being a big part and each settlement there, he will be visiting, etc...so you see my dear, you are fretting for nothing." Zack told her. Zack didn't tell her he was beginning to worry. His fall reminded him daily of one foolish moment of not paying attention, but then he reminded himself that there were trails now. West was wise about the woods.

Jo as usual was in the garden with Sara and Lily. This year the crop was going to be good and plenty with much for trading. Jo always liked the extra; it was a security thing for her. The fruit trees were loaded with fruit and Jo would always make some treat with the windfalls. She was a good woman and Zack thanked his lucky stars he had her.

It was lunch and Jo was at home, she had a basket full of things to be dried or cooked. She washed up and began to prepare for lunch. She stopped suddenly, looked at Zack, then Willow and said "West will be home today" she stated so matter of fact. "How do you know that?" Zack asked and Willow waited to hear. "I can feel him dear. It's a mother thing" and she smiled. Willow felt almost relieved at that comment. "I must go help mom" she told them and closed her books. Zack smiled as she cleared the papers up. She headed for the door and with a wave goodbye she headed home.

"Well my dear" Zack said to Jo. "You brightened her day" Zack smiled. "Oh he will be home" Jo said "I told you, I can feel him." Zack raised an eyebrow "Looks like you made a proverbial haul on the garden goods." Zack said to Jo. "Oh yes this year there is plenty. All the past years of hard work are finally paying off." Jo replied and smiled.

"Yes it has been a time since we came here. You have worked extremely hard and I am proud of you Jo." Zack said. "Well all of us have had a hand in it, without you my dear we never would have gotten this far. It's been your ideas that have made the work a lot easier." Jo smiled. Zack knew it was with great effort on all to get this valley to function this well. It seems the future would be secure now for the children here.

"Maybe we should build a couple more cabins just for the future. I'm sure the settlement will have some wanting to move out and the valley could accommodate at least three more families. What do you think Jo?" Zack asked her. "Well" she said "You're the designer and I'm sure Gary, Brad and West would have them built in no time. It will give you something to work on this winter." Jo told him. "True, very true" Zack replied.

Jo had lunch ready; the two ate and talked about where the cabins should be built.

Willow had made lunch for her siblings and after feeding them, cleared up the mess. Her mom and dad stayed working in the garden, so she prepared lunch for them and took it to them. Jo had said West would be home today and the thought of it thrilled her. She was finding it hard to contain her happiness.

West was now coming to the rise on the mountain before the decent into the valley. He hiked the pack on his shoulders and sighed. Why was the last mile or two of a journey always the longest? The weight of the pack made West sigh. Just as he reached the top of the crest he saw the sun creep out from behind a cloud and it shone down on the valley. It really was a breath taking sight, the familiar trails of smoke rising from the four cabins; the slow winding river and sight of the fields. He was home and he smiled.

He walked do the path and it wasn't long before Willow saw him. She wasted no time in making her way to him. He was a sight for sore eyes. He swung his pack off when he saw her and before he knew it she was in his arms. "Oh West I have been so worried, but you are home now" she said to him. He kissed her softly and just held her close. He could feel her heart beating and he knew she was the only love in the world for him. "I missed you too" he whispered in her ear. "Do you have any idea how much I love you sweet Willow?" She sighed and just relished him holding her. It was too soon when he said "Let's go home, I want to show you what I have found and I also have some news." West said told her.

Willow picked up the smaller items and found them to be of considerable weight. "How on earth did you carry all this stuff West, it weighs a ton?" West smiled. They arrived to Zack and Jo on the porch. Jo had water and fruit out for him and had a bath tub in the living room. She knew he would want a bath. Zack looked at Jo "Looks like you were right, he's home." Jo smiled. West kissed his mom on the cheek and then hugged her and Zack. "I have news; better get everyone here to hear it." Willow said she would get everyone and West went to wash up.

By the time West finishing washing everyone was at the house. After the good to see you home was over, West began telling them of the runner that appeared at the fort. He came from a settlement ten days out on the prairies. There are about 200 people there and are starving. The people at the fort have agreed to have them come there. Runners have been sent to the settlements asking for any extras that could be given to help. There was a silence. Zack spoke first "Well it seems to reason that others survived. This is good news" he said "but 200 people and for them to be sick and starving, this is not good. Is there any reason for them being starving?" West nodded "Yes it's apparently been a fire. The settlement had several in the past years. It wiped out their food." West told them.

"That would do it for sure. Did they saw anything about where they are all going?" Zack asked. "From what I found out, there is a new settlement starting south of the fort. They will take some as will the two other settlements from here to the fort will also." West told them.

Gary and Brad spoke "We could take a few families more in the valley." They all agreed.

Jo having not said too much knew what extra they had would now be gone. The fact they were sick was never a good thing. She agreed that the three families would be the most they would be able to accommodate.

West sighed and said "If need be the next valley could hold a few as well." With all in agreement, Jo said she would travel to the settlement and tell them. West told her he would travel with her and he and Willow would marry there. It was set; tomorrow Jo, Willow and West would head to the settlement. They all returned to their cabins and the women began searching for extra things to be given.

The storage shed was cleaned out by Brad and Gary that used to stock pile the extras.

Willow's mom and dad had little to offer, but her mom told the women she would help with the spinning and weaving of the flax. Being new to the valley they were still trying to get their stores set up.

Zack and Jo went in to give West and Willow some time together. They sat on the porch for a few hours and West told her all about his journey. Willow sat attentively and listened. She was amazed at how he described the plains and was devastated at the thought of the piles of bones in Cambry. He talked of Carry and the farm his dad grew up on. He told her someday he wanted to show her the farm.

After he rested he started to empty out his pack. First was the two windows, he gave one to mom and one to Willow. He produced a mirror for them both and a new knife for Zack. The pots and silverware were shared between them. He pulled out some books for Jo. She hugged him. The last parcel was from the farm and he handed it to Zack. He carefully opened it and found it contained some pictures and some of his mom's jewellery, a few knick knack things that Zack remembered of his mom. Zack tried not to be emotional, but a few tears escaped. "Thank you West, you have no idea what these mean to me. Was the farm still intact after all this time?" Zack asked. "Yes and no." West replied. "Time has taken its toll on the place and Mother Nature is well on the way to reclaiming it." West told him.

Zack sighed "Had we not been in such a hurry to leave, we might have brought more things with us." Zack told him. "Oh and there's a family at the farm settlement that know you. I was to tell you that had you not saved them when they were children they most certainly would have perished. They are well and send you best wishes." Jo looked at Zack "Oh my goodness the children, I almost forgot about them." Jo said "It was so long ago now."

"Who are they?" West asked. "When the virus broke out it was total chaos, panic and frightened people. On our journey here we came across them on the road, hungry, dirty and I think the oldest one was just 9 years old. Their parents died and the mother sent them in the direction of the fort." "How awful that must have been" Willow said "to have known you were passing and that there was no one to care for your children." "It was an awful time Willow." Zack said. Jo finished the tale by telling them of the woman at the fort that had lost all her children and took them in. "I am glad to hear they are all well." Jo said. "As for you my son, you need a bath." Willow and Jo got up and went to get the water.

"Dad, are you going to be okay here while we go to the settlement?" West asked. "Yes son I will be, beside there is Gary and Brad and Willow's folks. Don't think for a moment Sara and Lily would let me starve." "I noticed the brick walkways, excellent job dad." West said. "Thank you, Jo liked them too" he said "less mud in the house for her to clean." Zack smiled. "I'm off to see the men. I will leave you with the two women, they both missed you." West smiled.

Before long West was in the tub and Jo and Willow relaxed on the porch. "Where were you going to put your window?" Willow asked. "I think I would like to look out while at the table." Jo told her. "You know I think that's the best place." Willow replied. "I think I will get West to do the same." They both laughed.

It wasn't long before West appeared washed and refreshed. "That bath felt good, thanks." He smiled at the two of them. Jo got up and told them not to stay up too late; it is a long walk to the settlement tomorrow. They nodded and Jo went in to start her preparations for the trip the next day. Willow lingered with West as long as she could. She too had things that had to be done. After many moments together as they could have, she hugged and kissed him good night. He watched her walk home and smiled. He was tired now, but he still needed to get a pack together as well for the next day.

Before long Zack returned and the plan had been put into motion for more trees to be fallen. Three cabins would have to be built and before winter. Zack would make what furniture he could, while Brad and Gary logged. The women would all do the food with Willow's dad doing the heavy lifting for them.

West knew he would have to start in the next valley as well. She would have to dig the garden and he would fall the trees. The aim would be for one more cabin. Next spring another could be built if needed. There was the settlement to the south as well and the valley would take folks and the fort had big common houses. It would be alright they would have new people and soon have them located.

Night was falling and the only light would be from the fire. West knew the oil from corn could be burned in a small lamp, but there never seemed to be a lot extra for such frivolous use. Before long everyone was sleeping and West couldn't remember his bed feeling any more comfortable as it was that night.

Jo was up early and had things well organized by the time her sleepy headed men woke. Willow soon arrived and before long they were ready to go. Willow was excited; she had not been to the settlement in so long, since they came to the valley and she was interested to see her how her friends were that she had left behind. Not to be mentioned that she was to be married.

Jo smiled at her and could pretty much figure out what thoughts were flowing through her head. West was slow moving this morning. He had just made it home and now was back on the trail again. At least he would not be carrying the heavy packs he had before. The weather was fair and Jo once again smiled knowing how much West hated travelling with wet feet.

It was about three hours till mid day when they finally headed to the settlement; West and Willow walked close together which suited Jo alright. It gave her time with her own thoughts. West was telling Willow of the farm and the prairies again. She heard him speak of Carry, the runner and all the commotion the runner had created from the distant settlement. There was much to do before the people started arriving. The only giving grace was that they were so far away, but that would be a horrid trip for anyone sick. Jo knew that the fort would be the best point to get them well and start to help them settled elsewhere in settlements, the thought of 200 more people, that was a big increase. She was happy they had survived, but at the same time sad for them to be in such dire straights. Once she spoke with the elders, a bigger plan would be able to be devised.

She brought as many medical herbs as she could spare, hoping they would be helpful. Jo also knew that there were not many folks that knew the herbal remedies as she would have liked. Willow was learning, but had her plate full just learning the basics of reading and writing. Jo never understood why her parents never sent the children to learn before they came to live there. Zack made sure they were going to read and write now.

The group was travelling in silence now and Jo looked over the forest as they travelled. It was West that broke the silence. "This path needs work. We will have to get on it next spring." He said. "Yes I agree" Jo told him. "How did you like the brick walkways West?" Jo asked. "I like them, I think we will do the same." he said. Willow smiled. "This sure is a lot nicer walk without a heavy pack." West told them and the two women smiled. "Just hope we don't find a ton of things at the settlement" they kidded him, West smiled. "It's too bad you didn't get to meet Carry. I liked him" West told them. "Maybe one day" Jo replied.

It was noon and they found a spot to make lunch, the one West used the day before. "You know" West said "this would be a good spot to build a small shelter to be used as a relay spot between settlements." "That's a good idea West. You should, it is a good idea for runners. Winter would be the time they would find them most useful I think." said Jo. "Oh I don't know" said West "a rainy day or night might be another." Jo smiled "You are right; it's always nice dry spot to be in."

They had tea and fried bread with jam made the previous year for lunch. Jo was sure that West and Willow did not comprehend the enormity of 200 sick and hungry people coming. She knew the tasks that would be needed and it would not be easy. If the runner left the next day as did West from the fort he would be half way back almost. That means they had about a week to get things ready to house them until they could be situated.

They packed up and were soon on their way; they would be at the settlement that night. They picked up the pace somewhat. West and Willow chatted about all the things they were going to do in the future. Jo was glad they had a future to plan. They pulled out the shawls and light jacket for West. The settlement should be in sight. Willow was excited and

Jo was happy for them. First thing was to talk to the elders and get them married in the morning. Then start the work for the new folks

They crossed the river and soon after had the settlement in sight. They walked into the settlement and went to the common house. Jo soon had her messages to the elders sent and they went to get cleaned up.

It wasn't long before Jo was invited to the council house. West and Willow stayed in the common house. They talked of how they would transport the bricks to the next valley for their walkways.

The news of Willows arrival soon found the ears of her friends and before long West was surrounded by women. He leaned over and kissed Willow's cheek and told her he wanted to go rest. She understood, he had been travelling for over a week. "Okay West" she told him "I won't be long. I just want to visit a bit." West had no troubles with that and headed to lie down.

Willow was chatting up a storm. They were all happy to hear that she was to be married in the morning. Willow was still with her friends when Jo got back. She told Willow that she needed to talk and not be too long with her friends. Willow bid her friends goodnight and joined Jo at the table.

"Where is West?" Jo asked. "He went to lie down, he was awfully tired." Jo agreed. "There's good news and bad news. The good news is you will be married early in the morning," Willow smiled. "The bad news is that I must go to the fort and I want you to come with me." Willow was dumb struck. "Who will tell the others at home?" "I am sending West back." "What about food and clothes?" Willow asked. "The elders here have seen to our needs. I just want you to know that I need your help. You will be away from West until we get the new people well and situated. If it is too long we might have to spend the winter there. Travelling in the mountains in the snow is out." Willow couldn't believe her ears. She had waited so long to marry West and now she would not even see him for weeks. She almost cried. "It will be okay Willow" Jo told her. "We will be just fine I must go to the food store house and give them my list of things we are taking. Two runners have been assigned to carry the packs for us." Willow nodded, the whole thing was upsetting. West was supposed to be the one to take her to the fort. He was going to be the one to share her first impressions.

Jo disappeared out of the building and Willow was alone with her thoughts. She thought of West, of home and then of the sick people. She knew the right thing was to go and help them. With Jo being one of the few knowledgeable healers she would be necessary there. Willow was glad she asked her to help, it made her proud she had learned the things Jo taught her and Jo had felt her worthy enough to ask her for her help. Poor West she thought, all their plans had to be put on hold. She sighed and soon Jo was back with her. "Willow you need to get some rest. I will tell West in the morning if you like. I'm not sure how he will take the news." Willow agreed and they both headed to bed. It would prove to be an adventure Willow thought and not one she would have planned.

She woke to Jo packing gear. "Good morning" Jo said to her. "Get dressed, West is waiting downstairs. I want you to have a good meal before we leave." "Have you told West yet?" Willow asked. "No, not yet" Jo told her.

Willow washed and got dressed. They went down to eat and found West in the company of a young man. When West saw them he smiled. Willow and Jo made their way to his table. "Mom, Willow this is my friend Carry I told you about." Carry stood up and shook both their hands. "I thought you would be back at the fort by now." Jo smiled. "I'm not that good of a runner, but I did go a day when I met the runner bringing the message for the elders. I brought it back and so here I am. West tells me he is to marry this young lady. He spoke of little else when we travelled together." Willow blushed and West smiled.

Willow and Jo had their meal and then Jo told them to follow her to the elder's house. Carry stayed behind, as he had things he had to see to. Willow and West were to be married and all West could think of was getting home and starting living their lives. Jo took him aside and told him she needed to talk to him after they were married.

It didn't take long for the two to say their vows and they left the house bound together in life as one soul. It was magical for them, they had waited so long and now they were finally married. West picked Willow up and spun in a circle while holding her. He kissed her and she almost melted on the spot. Jo let them take their moment "Let's go back to the common house." Jo said. They held each other, arm in arm. It was West that asked "What's up?" "I have bad news and it's not pleasant." West's heart sank "I will tell you when we are sitting down."

They all had tea when they got there and Jo broke the news to West. He just sat there and stared at her. "What do you mean both have to go?" West said. It was one of the few times Jo heard anger in his tome of voice. "Well what would you have us do?" Jo asked. "How many can you count that have the knowledge of healing and herbs?" West sat and looked at them. Jo continued "There will be 200 people more than what's here West and they are starving and sick." she paused. "If you prefer we can go home and leave it to them to make it or die on their own." West felt like his mom just slapped his face. Willow never spoke. His expression changed and he said to his mom "You're right, I know you are right." He said "but I just wanted to go home with my wife." Jo leaned over and patted his hand "I know dear, I know, but it's not forever just till they are mending and on their way to better health. I need to take care of your father for me. I know he will not be impressed either." "How will you two be travelling? Not alone I hope." West said. "No we are to have two runners with us." "That's good, when do you leave?" he asked. "As soon as we are ready to go" Jo said. West couldn't believe it. His wedding day and he would not even to get to spend it with his wife. Jo looked at the two of them; she was going to finish packing.

West took Willow's hand and kissed it "I love you Willow, don't you ever forget that and don't you go and get sick and let the runners carry your stuff and…" "West please!" as tears filled her eyes. "It's not fair, but I can't get past all those sick people. They thought they were the only ones left and they are dying a slow painful death." West looked at her and then went over and hugged her. He smiled and said "They will be well long before the first snow and I'll have the cabin waiting for the lady of the manor to return." Willow smiled and thought he was such a good man.

Jo made the final arrangements to go and West was relieved when he found out Carry was to go with them. He spoke to Carry to take care of them and he was more than happy to help "I will see to it that they eat well at the fort as well. After all I have connections there." And they laughed. "Good man" and West shook his hand "Thank you." West told him.

West watched the runners hike up the packs and after hugs and a soft kiss for Willow, they were off. Jo told West to hurry home and tell Zack and to take care of him for her. West nodded and they headed out.

Willow looked back several times and Jo put a hand on her shoulder "It will be okay Willow, you will see." Jo knew that these people would bring more changes for all and right now getting them healthy was the main objective. The population was now growing to over a thousand and Jo knew they had a better chance to survive now.

The runners carried most of the gear and Carry did his best to keep the conversation going. It helped to pass the time. Jo could see why West liked him and he catered to her and Willow. Willow never spoke much she just wanted to go home. The trip to the fort was not pleasant for her. Her mind never wavered from West. Jo knew that once at the fort she would get into a routine and it would help time pass for her. The needs of so many would be considered over Willows at this time. They walked until late afternoon when Carry picked a spot to rest for something to eat. The next spot would be for the night and Carry was trying to make good time travelling.

West didn't stay long at the settlement, he headed for home. He felt angry at the fact he never even spent one night with Willow before she left. He knew she didn't want to go, but knew she had to. West would make her homecoming the best and began plans to have a lot of bricks hauled to the new valley. He would have to help Brad and Gary build the cabins. As life was, there was never a shortage of things that had to be done. He knew that Zack would not be happy about having Jo there, but West knew the lives of the new people were in their hands. Everyone knew the next few years would be hard. He kept up a fast pace; by late afternoon he crested the rise to home and the familiar scene below, a sight for sore eyes and feet.

It didn't take him long to make it down and into the valley. He went to the cabin and dropped his pack. Zack wasn't in and was found in his work shop. He was cutting lumber for beds for the new cabins. When he realized West was there he stopped. "So what's your mom making for supper?" Zack said with a smile. "Nothing" said West. Zack looked at him "What do you mean nothing, she sick?" Zack asked. "She's not here" West replied. "Where is she?" Zack inquired. "Her and Willow are on their way to the fort." West told him. "What!!!" Zack said. "Seems the elders and others have decided she is needed at the fort to help tend the sick" West told him. "Well isn't that just peachy" Zack said. "So where's my new daughter then?" Zack asked. "Willow went with her" West said. "We never even got to spend one night together and they were off." West replied. That comment shook Zack to the core of his soul. All the memories of Dee just flooded his mind. How they too married and how he too never had the chances to tell her how much he loved and cared for her. West looked at Zack "You okay dad?" he asked. "Oh yes, yes West you go to the fort. You look after our women" Zack told him. "Dad I can't leave you here." West said. "Never mind me. I'll be okay; you just get packed and head for the fort." Zack told him. "Mom will freak out if I leave you here." West said. "Well I'm not a child and I'm not going to have you suffer something you may never be able to get over.' Zack said. West just looked at him, "Come to the cabin West I want to talk to you" Zack said.

He followed his dad and after tea was hot Zack sat down. "What's with everyone?" West asked. "Since the news of the new people everyone has been acting almost crazy." He looked at his dad, and the Zack said "This has nothing to do with the new people. Do you remember me telling you about me leaving the complex to help my mom with my dad?" West nodded. "Well the day I left was the day Dee and I married. I never saw her again." Zack said. West looked at him "That's hardly the same as this dad. They just went to the fort to help." Zack looked at him "Do you love Willow?" he asked. "Of course I do dad, don't be daft." West said. "Then go to her and stick to her like glue. Too many things can turn ugly fast in life. What if she gets sick there or hurt on the trail? Don't you tell me that can't happen." Zack said. "Alright father, I'll leave in the morning." "Good" Zack said. "I have to clean up the shop. You get some rest West tomorrow you will be on the road again." West nodded

After he washed he flopped on his bed. His mind was filled with all kinds of thoughts. Things had gotten out of hand, life wasn't simple now and it was changing too fast. West was getting a head ach. He would go to the fort to help. The fact that Zack was so worried did not help. Everything would be fine, Willow was with mom and she would be fine also. He did want to be with her, but dad did not make the situation better by expecting peril to befall them. He appreciated his father's misfortunes as being awful and tragic, but he was not his father and Willow would be just fine.

He slept, but it was an uneasy sleep and morning found him more tired then when he went to bed. Zack was up, West washed and sat at the table. "Why are you so worried something bad was going to happen to them?" West asked. "I don't think anything awful is going to happen. I just think you should be with Willow. So many times before your mother and I got together I looked back and wished I never left the complex, not only for myself, but for Dee as well. West you're newly married, you should be with your wife. It's not right that you have been separated by a twist of fate. I want you to got to her and be with her always. I wish to spare you the guilt and grief I have had in my life. If something did happen to Willow, how do you think you would feel? I can answer that and I never want you to be able to say the same." He said to West. West looked at him and realized his dad was right. "You are right dad." West said. "West, one of the pleasures of having you as a son has been that you always look at so well. You never seem to let things get to you, but now you have Willow and trust me she will make you so angry, so mad, so glad and so happy." Zack laughed. "Go to her and remember don't let her go."

West finished eating and got his pack together. He would travel light to make time. He was getting the insight on what it might be like to be a runner. West was soon on his way and everything his dad had said was starting to hit home. He loved Willow and didn't want her to go, but standing up to his mom was not easy. Willow would have to find her voice in life and she was sure she would. West also knew that helping the new people was important too. These would be the folks that would bring in the new beginnings of life. His mom was right there. West wasted no time, not being weighed down with a heavy pack. It was a new experience; he ran a lot and could see clearly now the runner' point of view and he liked it. He was at the settlement by early afternoon. He headed to the common house and at a hot vegetable stew.

He was on the trail again and always scanned the woods with a keen eye. Late afternoon he started looking for a place to camp for the night. He kept moving, 2 days to the fort and he was hoping to make it in a little over one day. His thoughts as always were on Willow and how surprised she would be to see him. His mom might not be so glad. She would be worried about Zack. He wondered if they were almost at the fort. They should be getting close. He thought of Carry and knew they were safe; he would take care of them. The trip would be a long one for the runners; they would be used to travelling faster. West realized just how fast they could cover the distance now. He found a spot to make a shelter and had a lean to made as night fell. He fell back and watched the stars. He saw the satellites pass as he poked the fire for a bit more to stir up the coals. He was tired; all the travelling was catching up on him.

"Carry! How big is the fort?" Willow asked, now feeling more comfortable in the present company. "Oh I would say twice, if not three times as big as the settlement you are from." Carry told her. "We have nearly 600 people now. They have been working on the valley south to move some folks there." He said. "What was the reasoning to go south Carry?" Jo asked. "The older folks say they might get a longer growing season. With so many to feed it's worth the effort." Carry told her. Jo looked to Perry "You have not spoken three words this whole trip." Perry the other runner just smiled. "I don't have much to say Maam." He replied. "Where do your folks live?" Jo asked. "They passed a long time ago. The smithy has cared for me as long as I can remember. I am thankful they took me in." Perry told her. "I'm surprised you aren't learning the trade. He's a good smith." "I guess I like being a runner. It keeps me busy and I feel like I am in the hub of what's going on." He smiled. It was Willow that spoke. "You never wanted a family or wife?" "Hey" Perry said "I'm not that old yet" and everyone laughed. Willow blushed. "Don't you fret any" Perry said "I just haven't found her yet" and Perry smiled.

They had made it almost to the fort now and after a brief meal at the last settlement they moved on. Jo didn't mind too much, the place had changed since her and Zack had stayed there the first winter. Her thoughts drifted back to the hours of playing cards and the closeness they shared. He was a good friend and she missed him. When she got home she was going to mention he still owed her for the games he lost. She smiled. Willow was now getting excited; her trip to the fort was her first. She wondered what it would be like to see such a large place and so many people.

They crested the last mountains; down below the valley and all the patchwork land with all the different crops planted. Willow looked at Jo, she had no idea it would looked like that. The fort took up so much land with all the buildings and each had a trail of smoke reaching into the sky from the chimney. She saw the paths heading to the prairie and the rolling hills in the distance. Carry watched her and could see the wonder in her face. To him it always had been home, he never thought of it as anything else much. To see her view it like she did in some way made him proud.

They made their way down to the fort and Carry took them straight to the cook house. His mom had rooms for them and she welcomed them. She sat them in the back room, the cooks used for meals and the boys took their packs to their rooms. Carry told Jo they had to speak with the elders and he would be back. He hugged his mom and said "look after these two, they are friends. Jo, Willow this is my mom Freda. Mom this is Jo and Willow. I gotta get my messages delivered. I will be back when I can." Carry said. "Thank you Carrie." Jo said and was happy to sit in the kitchen. The trip had been long and she was tired. Freda in no time had tea and food on the table. She had water taken upstairs for them to bath. It was about half an hour before Freda sat down for tea with them.

"Well there will be no shortage of work now for the next year." Freda smiled at Jo. "Yes" Jo replied. "You will be one of the busiest here in the cook house." Freda smiled. "I can't believe we have found so many new people. Im sorry it's under such dire circumstances." "Yes, I agree." Jo said. "It will all work out. The council of elders have the men working overtime on things." Freda told them. "It's almost like when the virus broke out. At least this time we have some warning." "Yes" Jo said to her. "I was here when the virus broke out. My husband and I headed West. It was an awful time that's for sure." "Yes I was so thankful when things started falling into some kind of a system. The first years were hard." Freda told Jo. Willow sat and listened to the women talk. She was born after the outbreak and was glad for that. Hard it must have been Willow thought.

"I wonder how sick the people are. If it's hunger we can fix that in no time, but if its flu, colds and all the things that go with them, it might make it much harder. They can pass that on to others here." Jo said. "Yes, that's true, but I think they will be quarantined in the common house until they get well enough to join the main population. I'm sure the elders in the council will fill you in." Freda said. "Now you two go have a bath and get in some fresh clothes. Carry will take you there after you have rested some," With that Freda strolled back into the kitchen and examined her pots steaming on the stove.

Willow look at Jo "This place is amazing." Jo just smiled "Come dear let's get this road dust off. We need to start getting busy; the people will be here before we know." They climbed the stairs to their rooms and soon were both in their tubs.

Willow thoughts were of West and Jo in the next room thought of work about to begin. Willow was done before Jo and tapped on her door. "I'm going to look around a bit, Okay Jo?" "Okay dear, but don't leave the fort." Jo replied. "I won't" Willow said and made her way downstairs and outside.

The fort was amazing. They had gravel roads and walkways to each building. Fruit trees lined the streets, providing not only fruit but shade as well. There were benches along the way and flowers planted around each one. Willow picked one and sat down. She watched all the people coming and going, all of them seemed busy. She watched some children at play in an area made for them and listened to their squeals of pleasure as they played. It was a lovely place. She wished West was here, in some ways she felt like an odd ball sitting here alone. She knew no one, except the runners and Carry's mom and then not really. She sat there for about an hour and decided to return to her room.

She knocked at Jo's door and Jo answered "Come in." Jo was lying down "How did you like you tour?" Jo asked. "Oh it was okay, but I'm out of sorts." Willow said. "I'm going to get some sleep while I can. You might think about doing the same Willow." Jo said. Willow nodded and headed to her room. She washed her few clothes from the trip and after hanging them to dry, she lay down. The bed was so comfortable and she was asleep before she knew it.

West arrived at the fort the next day. He had run most of the way; once he started it was hard to stop. The amount of ground he covered amazed him.

Jo had been to the elders and the common house was being transformed into a large medical house. All the women had been washing all day. Beds were being set up and linens, blankets, etc…were being stock piled. There was a bath house set up and everything that one could think of was being gathered up for the new people. They would arrive in a week and the settlement, both to the south and west were building new cabins. Five cabins in the south and three cabins in the west, along with three more in the valley Jo and Zack lived in. West said he would build one, so that would be a few families well on to being settled. Next year they would build more. They planted extra fields and everyone rationed what they had. Surviving the winter would be their first priority.

Willow had no time to think there was too much work to do. She had spent all day washing and cleaning.

West watched the goings on and he worked his way to the cook house. He found Carry there helping his mom. When Carry saw him he stopped working and went straight to him "West, what on earth are you doing here?" he asked. "I came to help and be with my wife. Where is she, do you know?" "I think they are all at the common house. They are making a temporary medical center." Carry told him. "Come in, come in. I want you to meet my mom. Mom! Mom!" Carry called. She appeared from the kitchen. "Whatever is wrong Carry?" she asked. She saw West and Carry "Mom, this is West, Willow's husband and Miss Jo's son." "How do you do young man?" she said. "You have been spoken of by my son since he has been home" she said "Carry take him to Willow's room so he can clean up. I will get him something to eat." She said and headed back into the kitchen. "So Willow doesn't know you are here then?" Carry asked. "No I couldn't find her out there." West told him. "Come upstairs, I'll show you where."

West followed him upstairs. "How was your journey with the women?" West asked. "Slower than normal, but all in all it was okay. We made good time." Carry told him. "Do you want me to tell Willow that you are here?" Carry asked. "No, I think I would like to surprise her, if you don't mind?" and Carry smiled. "No problem." Carry said. West entered the room and Carry told him he would be up with some water. West thanked him.

West sat down and stripped off his shirt and dug out a clean one from his small pack. He got clean footwear and by then Carry was back with the water. West washed up and then rinsed his shirt and socks. It felt good to clean the trail off. He headed downstairs and sat in the common part of the cook house. Carry's mom brought him some hot food and water to drink. He was hungrier than he thought and made short work of the meal. He thanked Carry's mom for the food and he and Carry sat at a table in the far corner.

West asked where he would be needed most. Carry told him that the carpenters were overflowed with work. After getting some directions from Carry, he headed towards the work shops. West liked working with wood and didn't mind any work that might have to be done.

Jo and Willow ate at the building they had been working at. By the time night fell they were exhausted. They both headed back to their rooms both knowing that tomorrow the work would be just as intense.

When they arrived at the cook house they went straight to their rooms. Willow went into her room and in the dark made her way to bed and fell into it. She was so tired. She dragged herself to sit up and undress. Jo washed up. She lay down and fell asleep. Willow undressed and climbed under the blankets. She too was soon asleep.

West of course worked until late. They wanted to finish cutting the pile of wood for the bed side rails so they would be done for morning. It was past midnight when he finally made his way to their room. He quietly entered and he stood over the bed looking at Willow's shape under the blankets in the moonlight. He didn't want to startle her, so softly he called her name. "Yes West what is it?" she said still asleep. "You should be here with me" she said "I miss you." "I'm here" West said softly. "No you are not, you're far away" she told him. "Willow wake up" he said again. "I'm awake" she told him and rolled over. West smiled "Wake up Willow." West told her. Then all of a sudden she sat up with a start. Willow looked at him "West, West is that you? Really you?" she said. "Yes it's me" he told her "but, I thought, I mean, how did you?" and at that he crawled in beside her and took her into his arms. She held him close feeling the warmth and strength of him near her. He kissed her and after a few brief moments they dissolved into each other and soon had become one. West and Willow now had a bond together no one could shatter. The two slept comfortably. No words could describe how they felt at that moment.

Morning would come soon enough and like most days it did. Willow woke, she was snuggling into West. She could feel his steady breathing and warmth and it pleased her. She got up and went to wash. She now saw his pack and things. Had she not been so tired last night she would have seen them then. She started to dress when West woke. "Good morning, you're up early" he said. "Oh West there is so much to do." She told him. "Come here" he said and she went to him. He pulled her down and held her firmly. He kissed her and told her he loved her. Willow never felt so good. She hugged him close and told him to get up and get dressed. He was up and washing. Willow watched him and each movement he made she noticed. "What?" he said to her. "Oh nothing, I just like how you look" she smiled. "I'll sure to let you watch me whenever you like" he said and smiled. "You are such a brat" Willow told him and he laughed.

After he dressed he asked "Where's mom?" "I imagine she's downstairs by now." West nodded "I have to talk to her. West!" Willow said. He turned towards her, "I love you" she said to him. West went to her and pulled her into his arms "Willow I love you too" and kissed her. Then he headed for the door. "I'll be down in a few minutes" she said "I need to comb my hair yet." West nodded and went downstairs.

Jo was there and at the sight of him he could tell she was wondering what he was doing there. He went to her table and after 15 minutes he relayed the whole story to her. "Well" she said "I can't say I'm sorry you are here, we will need your help here, but Zack is alone and that bothers me." She said. "He'll be okay Sara and Lily will help him and Brad and Gary are there too." "True" Jo said "What's done is done. I am glad to see you and I'm sure Willow is too." West smiled and said "I'll be working in the wood shops if you need me mom." Jo nodded "That's fine, where is Willow we have a lot to do today?" "She said she would be right down" West told her.

Carry and his mom had the food ready and Willow arrived just as it was set on the table. The three ate and after West headed to the wood shop and Jo and West went to the common house. Carry spent a few hours a day in the wood shop, being the cook's right hand kept him busy. He would be making another trip to the settlement in the next day or so and welcomed the break. The food, clothes and furniture kept arriving at the different shops and store houses all day. If they kept up at this pace they would be more than ready for all the new folks.

Any time Willow and West could steal away they did and could often be found sitting on one of the benches under a tree on the main road. Jo was glad to see them finally together and knew they would be fine.

The next week passed uneventfully and the work slowed as so many things were ready. Carry, West and Willow spent many hours together, as did Jo and Carry's mom, Freda. Jo met all the children again they had brought to the fort so many years before. She was so glad to see them, all well and happy.

Jo knew this lull in the activity would soon be over and the new people should be arriving soon. Runners and helpers had been sent to meet them and from what Carry told them, they would soon be at the fort.

It was three days later that the first line of people could be seen on the road. They carried all their possessions they could with them and they moved slow. Fatigue, hunger and not to mention stress showed on them. It was a line of disillusioned people arriving. The ones in best health arrived first. They were bathed; their clothes washed and clean beds to rest on.

It was mid day before the sick, hurt and old started arriving. West and Willow just looked at their hollow faces, sunken cheeks and pale completions; it was awful to see them like that. It could not have been anything but great suffering that marked their faces. For the whole day they came, slowly and not without great effort they arrived at the fort. Many cried, some smiled and others never said anything, moving more now as instinct was driving them. Jo knew some would die, but she had hope for them. The sickness was on the most part lack of food which soon they would have under control. Jo was amazed at the things they brought. The long trip was hard for them bringing their possessions, so many faces and so many sick.

The women all worked together. The very old and the very young were the ones that suffered the most. Broth was first given to most and within a few days they were able to start on more solid foods. The ill were brought on stretchers. They were survivors and now had such a good chance to do just that.

Jo comforted the older folks as she fed them. Willow spent most of her days boiling the soiled sheets and clothes. Others washed the buildings and dishes. After about a week some were well enough to move out of the common house. Different families made them welcome in their homes. Jo had lost only four people and she was concerned about six more. The elders made a point of getting everyone's names and keeping families together.

The men through their labours had three cabins built and three more almost done. Land had been designated for the following spring to each family that would stay at the fort. The families moving south were given supplies to last them the winter. Their journey was not yet done, but this time they had the knowledge they were not alone and help would be near.

Jo felt sorry for the old folks. She spent long hours listening to them tell the stories since the out break. How they had endured the hardships of lost crops, dust storms and of fires. The fires were the worst, they cried when the fields of food burned before them. The losses endured as so many starved to death in winter. Jo would pat their hands and reassure them that they would not be hungry anymore. She would tell them of all the different foods they grew and fruits. Some had not seen apples in years.

Jo found herself reflecting on her own life and realized just how lucky they had been. Coming to the mountains had been a blessing in disguise.

Of the 200 people expected they counted 193 that arrived and 4 passed away here. They were buried and mourned by the ones left behind. Jo heard one woman say they were so to making it and they chose not to live, they gave up, it was just too much for them.

The children were now regaining their colour and with that came the endless exuberance for life. They were taken for fresh air and the park was full. They were watched by the older children to maintain order. The council found work for the adults well enough to work and they worked hard. They all knew if they were to survive all had to pull their weight. The older women were given flax to spin and they were happy to be able to give to the well being of all.

West worked ceaselessly, he and Carry spent every hour they could doing some job to make the next days work easier. The families moving south started gathering their goods together and the young men from the fort all helped. Everything they needed would have to be packed to their new settlement. The people bid their farewells to those left at the fort, but knew that any news would be carried by the runners. It was a comfort to them that word could be sent for what ever reason.

The first 30 people were on the way to the settlement. The new cabins would be full, but they would be fine, Jo thought. The sick now on the mend soon had colour in their complexions and the spark for living in their eyes once again.

Jo found Freda's company a great comfort as did Freda with Jo. They shared many things from recipes to growing techniques.

West and Willow were never far from each other when they were not working. They had Carry as a friend that soon would find something he hadn't counted on.

News arrived from the settlement to the west. They had two cabins done and they were expecting some people. Jo and Freda watched as two more families packed their stuff and with the help of the runners began their journey to the west. The first settlement was well established and Jo knew they would be fine.

Some of the new folks wondered why the people had not started to farm the land just east of the fort. The elders told them they had, but fire had destroyed the crops. The river there was the only thing that stopped it from moving into the valley. People fought any fires that managed to get a grip on this side. It was decided to just keep the grass low on the far side to act as a barrier from further fires.

The new people started to thin out. There still was an extra 100 people at the fort which was more manageable. With their health returning and their labour added to the work force, West, Willow and Jo could soon go home. The harvest would be ready soon and soon after the first snow. With the sick well on the way to good health, it was decided that night at dinner, they would start the journey home. Willow was glad; she did want to go home. Home she thought, a place she had yet to see.

West and Carry shared what tasks still needed to be done between them and Jo gathered her belongings together. She had her few clothes packed and was ready for a good nights sleep. She was glad to be going home as well. She would miss Freda's company, but she would be happy to see Zack and the others at home.

West and Willow packed up for the morning trip. Home was a long ways away. The morning would be spent getting food stores for the next few days. They all slept well that night. Jo was relieved the hardest work was over and West and Willow, now so closely bonded slept enclosed in each others arms.

Morning always came too soon, after washing and packing the last items, they headed downstairs. Freda had all the rations they would need nicely wrapped and ready to go.

After some sad goodbyes they started their journey home. Carry was at the work shop and never got to see them off. West, Jo and Willow started off, as they climbed the trail; they looked back as they crested the hill leading into the next valley. "Do you think they will be okay now?" Willow asked. "Yes they will" Jo replied. "They have found new hope and this is a new beginning for all." Willow asked "Do you think there are others out there?" as she gazed to the east. "Well only time will tell. The east was at one time a place of many great cities with millions of people. What has survived I'm not sure, but if they made it time will bring us together." Jo told her. West never said anything, he thought about Cambry and how nothing was left and the piles of human bones, millions of people he thought most would be just a pile of bones. It sent a chill down his spine. He then thought of the complex and knew he had to look for it.

The women kept up a hardy pace through the woods and they travelled quickly. "Did you see how many paths in the fort were gravel? That's such a good idea" Willow said. "I like it; maybe we can implement something like that at home. There is a lot of gravel near the river" Willow smiled.

"You will have your hands full next year digging your gardens Willow never mind building a road." Jo said. Willow just smiled.

West never spoke much his mind was on home, he to needed to build a cabin for a new family. He was going to talk to Willow about offering it to Carry once they had it built. He had to get the winter wood cut for fire as well, better to have too much then not enough. He agreed with Willow that gravel for paths would be a great improvement and would tell her so later. He wondered how much of the cabins Brad and Gary had done. Those two men worked together so well, what they could accomplish was awesome. West , although deep in thought always scanned the woods. It was more of a habit than a need.

The women finally said "West slow down, you are almost running." He stopped "Sorry about that I was thinking." "What's got you so preoccupied?" Jo asked. "Oh, nothing much, I was just thinking about what I have to do when we get home."

Willow strode up beside him and tucked her arm into his. He held it tight and smiled at her. Jo watched and felt warmness in her heart for the two of them. She could rest easy now, he had someone and she approved of Willow, they made a good pair. It was Jo that decided to stop; she didn't have the energy the young had anymore.

West had the wood gathered in no time and the fire crackling as Jo heated water for tea. West was beside Willow and they were discussing the cabin West had built. She was excited about seeing it. They laughed and kidded each other and Jo watched in silence. West told them; soon he would find a spot for the night. He had been watching the sky and was sure rain was coming. Jo agreed.

"How do you know rain is coming?" Willow asked. "You can feel the chill and the dampness in the air. See those clouds? They are dark grey and full of water." West told her.

It wasn't long before they were on the move again. West soon had a good spot picked and began building a shelter. He just finished when the first of the rain began to fall. "You were right." Willow smiled at him.

It was almost an hour later when they heard someone on the path; it was Perry, a runner. He stopped and said "Hello." Jo offered him tea and he accepted gladly. The rain was sweeping down in waves, harder and lighter. "You are welcome to hold up here until the worst passes. Jo and Perry just smiled. "I'm used to the rain." He thanked them and was soon out of sight.

"How far do you think he will go?" Willow asked. "He will travel until dark." West said "then find shelter. They are trained at the fort. He will be okay." West told her.

Jo laid back and listened to the rain. She could feel the cold in her bones. She was getting older and this trip had brought that clearly to her mind. She wanted to be at home and the only thing she wanted to worry about was how often she and Zack would have the grandchildren. That brought a smile to her face.

West and Willow laid out for sleep and soon night fell into early morning and found them sleeping.

West was first up and he silently swept the area for dry wood. With a fire going Jo woke and smiled at West. "Morning" he said to her. He went over and gently woke up Willow. They warmed up around the small fire, soon tea and porridge was made. "We will be at the settlement tonight." West told them. Jo's first thoughts were of a hot bath. Willow wanted a bed to sleep in. West cleared the area and put out the fire. "Let's get going" he said to them.

They all moved at a slower pace than yesterday. By midmorning the kinks had been worked out and travelling was easier. The day passed quickly and before dusk they could see the settlement in the distance.

The pace was picked up and when they arrived they went to the common house. Jo waste no time in getting the water for a bath, Willow and West had something to eat first.

It wasn't long before they saw Perry. He was deep in a conversation with an elder council member. West thought it must be with new people. Before long he finished and West motioned him over. As Perry sat down he smiled. "Sure has been a lot of commotion with the new folks" he said. "Listen Perry I never got a chance to tell Carry I wanted to talk to him. Would you be so kind as to ask him to come and see me in the spring?" West said to him. "Sure" Perry said "Well, I'm going for a bath." Willow said and got up to leave, West took her hand and told her he wouldn't be long. He and Perry chatted awhile longer.

West took his leave and headed upstairs. When he entered Willow was in the tub. He soon was stripped off and in the tub with her. The water felt great. Willow washed his back and climbed out.

After drying off, she combed out her hair. West soaked for a bit and when he got out he threw the clothes they had been wearing into the water. Willow went to wash them and West told her to comb her hair. He rinsed the clothes and they hung them to dry. They crawled into bed and Willow snuggled to him. The bed felt great, before long they both were asleep.

Jo on the other hand was downstairs enjoying tea and stew. It wasn't often she had the time alone and after watching the comings and goings of the people, she headed to bed.

Tomorrow they would reach the final settlement, then one more day until they were home. Jo was happy, her thoughts drifted to Zack, then the garden. There would be a lot of work to do and Jo knew it.

Chapter 24

*D*ana and Todd arrived at Dirk's dorm for dinner. Carla and Ann had made a lovely meal. Mark had his girlfriend there. Her name was Tracy. After a very pleasant evening about the animals and how it seemed that they all survived the outside. It was a bonus to mankind, the refurbishing the animals to the outside world. As they reproduce here they would let more out. It was important to work with Karen and David as well. The bugs and plant seeds set in the wind would be necessary for many things to live from foxes to canaries.

After dinner dishes had been cleared, Dirk stood and announced that Mark and Tracy would wed soon. Todd and Dana were so happy for them. When the excitement wore down, Dirk then announced that Mark would be taking over the main care of the animals.

Dana was happy for Mark, but had concerns for Dirk. She knew he was aging and hoped that he was well. Mark had many new ideas for the breeding programs and Tracy was a stickler for their care as well.

Carla was happy that a lot of the work had been turned over to the young. She to, had trained 4 younger folks to do her job. She was going to try and not work so hard. For the next years she would just be able to enjoy the complex and the company of her all too hard working husband. "So what has you two wanting to retire?" Dana asked. "Well my dear the young folks need to try their hands at running things, besides I miss my wife." Dana smiled. "It is as it should be" he said. "Carla and I aren't as young anymore and we want to relax a bit now." Dirk patted her hand. Dana knew they were as were Rainie and Elsa. She knew that there would be times in the future that they would not be there for her to council with. She also knew that Todd would be the main source of comfort and understanding.

They visited until late and then Todd and Dana headed home. When they got a ways down the tunnel, Dana said to Todd "I'm worried about Dirk; he doesn't seem to be himself." "Well my sweet he's getting older. He probably has so many aches and pains he keeps to himself. He has after all worked hard since he has been here." Dana knew he was right, she just feared losing him.

Todd had led her in the direction of the communications labs. When she realized that's where they were headed, she hugged Todd. He smiled.

They had arrived to see the monitors blank, after checking all fax machines, nothing, always nothing. They sat and watched the monitors viewing the outside. They watched, but saw little as dusk was falling outside and nothing could be seen in the night. Todd leaned over to her "Maybe tomorrow" he said. She smiled "Yes maybe." He thought how hard it must be, knowing her father may be out there still alive and maybe on his way back. He thanked his lucky stars that his family has always been there. He loved her and he would never leave her. "Come on Dana, let's go home." They got up and went home.

The last of the evening was spent sharing themselves with each other. When sleep finally found them, Dana was snuggled up beside him and Todd listened to her steady breathing, he to then fell asleep.

The next morning it was Todd that woke to the smell of fresh coffee. "Morning love" he called out and Dana appeared at the door. She was dressed and in a soft voice told him to get up. He jumped into the shower and in no time was with her at the table. She had made a light meal and told him she was off to visit Rainie. "Can I meet you for lunch later?" she asked. "Sure" he said "How about our spot?" Dana smiled. "Sounds good to me" she said. Todd watched her leave and decided to go see Andy at library.

Dirk had told him much of the beginnings of the complex. He wanted to read what was available with the animals surviving it would soon be time for some folks to venture out. The prospect frightened him, but excited him at the same time. He wondered what the wind and rain would feel like or snow. He wanted to be the first outside. He never talked to Dana about it and knew he would have to, but first he wanted as much information he could get. He wanted to talk to all the folks left that had lived outside before the virus. It was Andy that would have that information.

He wasted little time in getting there and as always Andy was behind the desk reading. After explaining, Andy agreed to show him the books and the information off the many discs he had.

Dana had ventured to Rainie's studio; she knew that's where she would be. When she arrived she saw Rainie admiring her work. She had a cup of tea before her. When she heard Dana, a smile crossed her face when she looked at her. "So how's my young dear?" Rainie asked her. "Oh, I'm okay" Dana told her as she sat on the couch beside her. "That's your best piece yet." Dana told her. "Ahhh, so you like it? I'm not sure about it. It represents the last of the people that passed with the virus." Rainie told her. Dana asked "Rainie what was it like before the virus, I mean like outside?" Rainie looked at her and after taking a sip of tea she began to tell Dana of the many places and beautiful things she had seen, from the Alps to parks in the great cities. "It was a wondrous place, but it's all gone now." Rainie told her. "All the people I knew and most of my dearest friends are gone. Had Simion not loved me I too would have perished for sure. It was so long ago, this is my home, my future and my end now." Rainie had tears in her eyes. "I'm sorry I did not wish to upset you, I just wanted to know." Dana told her. "It's okay my dear, I have long since come to terms with it. Did I tell you Eric and Gwen are going to have a baby?" Rainie told her. "I'll be a grandmother I can hardly believe it. I have great hopes that the young will be able to breathe fresh and live out under the stars." Rainie sighed. She looked at Dana "You know I'm tired?" she said. "Did you stay up all night to finish this piece?" Dana asked. "No, no, but it has been a tough one." Rainie stood "It's strange it seems to have drained me somehow." She placed her hand on the statue. "Well, I just need some sleep and then I need to think about what my next piece will be." She turned to Dana and smiled. Dana told her "Todd is having lunch today with me and we have chatted all morning. You go have a nap and I will call you later" Dana told her. Rainie smiled "I think I will."

Dana got up and headed for the atrium. She thought about all the things that Rainie had told her. It must have been a wondrous place. Why were they so foolish to have done what they did? What a shame they threw so many things away and what a cost to those left. If indeed there were any left other than the folks here.

She found her and Todd's spot and as she waited she thought about all the things that were never to be again.

Rainie was tired; she lay down on the bed. She knew that was the last piece she would ever carve. She thought about her life and the good things as well as the bad. How she missed Simion, how lonely she had been, even with her son Erik. She thought about her whole life, how selfish and thoughtless she had been when she was young. How she took things for granted. Had Simion not loved her she certainly would have perished in the virus. After all the years in here alone, she wondered if it wouldn't have been better somehow. Rainie closed her eyes and thought of Simion. It was the last thought she had as she passed away. It was a peaceful passing and her work for the complex was finished.

Todd met Dana and he was full of excitement about what he had read and the folks he spoke to. He kissed her and asked how her day had been. "I had a lovely visit with Rainie." She told him. "She told me things about the old world. It must have been a wondrous place." She said to him. "I've been talking to a few people myself" he said. "I have read so much and I think if the animals survive we can too. We could live outside Dana, I'm sure we could." He told her. "I want to go out and see." Dana looked at him "The council has forbid any outside contact Todd, you know that. We aren't even sure the animals have made it." She told him. "They did we saw them on the monitors, you know we have." He stated. "Yes that's true, but will they stay alive that's what's important. Promise me you will wait until we know for sure it's safe, promise me." Dana held onto his arm." He looked at her "Of course Dana, when we go out we go together." She smiled. "Let's go look at the monitors, if we have proof the council will have to agree to it." She smiled and Todd smiled too. They walked to the labs and spent the afternoon watching the monitors.

Dirk and Carla watched as their children did the rounds. They need no supervision; they knew what had to be done. It was a rewarding feeling for both to see them in action. Dirk looked at Carla "We sure did right when we made them." He laughed. "I agree." Carla said equally pleased with them. "So what do you want to do with the rest of our lives?" Dirk asked. "Humm let's see, soak in a hot tub, eat chocolates and spend time sewing and reading." "Really?" Dirk said "and where is it that I fit into that pleasurable thought?" Carla said "You will be beside me in the tub and then feeding me chocolates. After that I will be sewing new clothes for us, as we get fat from eating the chocolates. Then I will read to you at night." She said and they both broke into laughter. Dirk took Carla's arm "Let's see, shall we test out the hot tub? It might be too hot for us." They laughed again. "Old fool let's go home and have a tea" Carla said. "Fine plan" Dirk said. The two left the animal tunnels and made their way home.

Dana and Todd were now home enjoying the evening. They had a plan worked out almost. If the animals made it through the winter, then next spring when they were sure they did indeed make it, then they were going to start pushing at the council. Todd quoted Simion's writings from his diary. "One day people will reclaim the world as they should. This time they will have the lessons of greed and selfishness has taught them. Make it a truly wondrous world and keep it that way for everyone not just the chosen few." Todd looked at Dana "I guess the world before the virus could be a hard place for the less privileged." "Seems so" Dana said. "But we are the future and it's up to us to see everyone gets opportunities. The complex runs by the cooperation of all. I see no reason not to carry that on with us when we live outside." "I agree." Todd said. "We need to talk to Andy; he is a wizard at writing detail papers on things. We will have to pick a couple days then after we get off our work shifts and go talk with him more." Dana agreed. They went to bed and shared themselves with tenderness and simple compassion.

It was a knock at the door that woke them. Todd got up and answered it. Dana could faintly hear Erik in the other room. It wasn't long before Todd came back to the bedroom. He sat on the bed and from the look on his face she knew something was wrong. "Dana, I have some bad news." "Oh my God, Todd, Oh my God' he had to tell her, but he knew it would be painful for her. "It's Rainie, Dana" he said. "Is she okay Todd?" "No she is not. She is not with us anymore." He told her. Dana sat in their bed and cried. Todd sat beside her letting her lean on him. He never said much; just let her get out the emotions. "I just saw her yesterday" Dana said through the tears. "She was talking so strangely. We discussed the last statue she did. Oh Todd, they are all leaving us" Dana cried. "I know dear" he said as he held her. Even though they knew the old would pass it was never pleasant. All the knowledge, understanding, compassion and memories passed with them.

Todd shed his tears silently, he was concerned for Dana. Her steadfast pillars of emotionally stability were going. He thought how would he fill the gap of so many losses for her? "Erik told me they will take her to the tombs tomorrow. He also told me that she passed away and suffered very little." Dana looked at him "She suffered everyday since Simion died and before that with her mother's passing. She has wept silently daily for a long time, that does not strike me as suffering very little." Todd never spoke. With the pain he knew there would be anger and he also knew she had few outlets for this. He was confident enough in her love for him that he let it pass. She cried for a long time and being so emotionally drained, she slept. Todd gently eased her away and had a shower. Arrangements would have to be made.

He went to Elsa, she could stay with Dana. He also had to see Nick. He hated this part of being a stone cutter. Rainie would be followed by more he knew that, but he always hoped that it was many months before time took another of the founders. He soon had Elsa at their dorm. Elsa knew Rainie well and would be able to comfort Dana when she woke.

He stopped to see to see Eric and Gwen. Is there anything special you want for her spot in the tombs?" Todd had to ask after he let the pour out their grief. Erik never said a lot, but he was adamant that she was beside his father, Simion. "Her spot was never questioned there and had been made long ago, Nick saw to that. Her place should note her contributions to the complex." Erik said "Yes, I agree." Todd told him. "I will talk to Nick. I just want to tell you how sorry I am for your loss." Erik thanked him and Gwen nodded, her child would never know Rainie. It was a sadness the whole complex felt. Rainie's passing was just another thing to be added to the long list of history past. Todd shook Erik's hand and made his way to the stone cutters tunnels.

The news has spread through the complex. Nothing is kept under wraps for long. Many of the founders would be present at the service and it would affect them greatly as another of their contemporaries passed. They had lived outside, seen its fall and saved everyone here. Now most had passed without the opportunity to breathe fresh air or feel the sun on their skin. Todd was more determined than ever not to ever give up on opening the complex. Too many had passed missing that. For him and Dana, they like many others never had been outside or were too young to remember. Life seemed to be normal in here, in the complex. He knew it was a reality; they had to stay in, but the outside at every turn called to him.

He didn't need to discuss much with Nick. He had known Rainie for the whole time the complex existed and her having been a sculptor and him providing the stone, they shared much. He was saddened by her passing. She was a talented lady to look into the stone and see a figure, then to free it wasn't easy only the best could do it. He knew the two had discussed many things and he left Nick to do what needed to be done. Todd headed to see Dirk and Carla.

When he got there the news had reached them as well. After a brief visit, Todd made his way to his parents. He knew they would be saddened by her passing as well. They had heard and were concerned for Dana.

Todd's mom made coffee and the conversation was near the same in content as the others had been. He watched them and knew someday they would pass also. He couldn't think of that at the moment. After coffee he told them he was going home. His mother asked him to tell Elsa to meet with them. He nodded and was soon on his way home.

Dana woke up a few times and cried herself back to sleep. Todd knew losing Rainie was hard. Elsa and Carla were the only women left now for her to confide in. He hoped his mother would fill in the niche, but that took time. Dana was strong and after her cry out and the burial she would put things right in her mind and continue living.

Todd thanked Elsa and passed his mother's message on. Elsa left after assuring Todd that Dana would be okay.

Todd made a pot of tea and took it into the bedroom. Dana was awake. He crawled into bed and held her. He soon poured the tea and Dana shared with him her feelings and thoughts. She didn't cry anymore and Todd knew she wouldn't cry anymore. For such a gent soft person, once she had something sorted out that was it.

They spent the rest of the day at home, not in lengthy conversation, but in quiet contemplation. They did not rest easy that night. The next day would be full of sadness.

Erik now held Gwen. His father Simion had built the complex, he was gone and his mother now passed as well. He understood the reason Simion gave the complex to the people and in his mind it was right. He had no problems with it now. He and Gwen carried their genes and memories into the future. Simion saved them for that and now they would have the next generation. Maybe in their lives they could reclaim the world. The world would be different. He would miss his mom and dad. It was too bad she never got to know his child, but the child would know of them. Life was not far from being in the hands of the first generation of the complex.

Elsa joined Dirk and Carla; they all went to the tomb tunnel, there all the founders met, as they did with each passing of one of them.

Andy poured everyone a small brandy. He looked around at all the old faces; how he remembered them all young and working here, the project of the millennia. Space travel was the guise Simion used. The best of the best, now as he looked over the crowd, what had been several hundred were reduced to less than one hundred. It was sad to see them go one by one. He lifted his glass "To Rainie" and they raised their glasses and said "To Rainie!" After a few brief words between them they went back to their homes.

Karen and David walked with Elsa and Andy. It didn't take long for the crowd to disperse. There would not be another gathering until another founder passed.

The next day they added Rainie to the tombs. It was felt by so many. She had left so much beauty there for them and passed on her skills for those that had the talent for them. Gwen and Erik talked of her likes and loves and how she would be missed.

Dana stuck close to Todd. After she was entombed flowers were placed and the people slowly made their way back to their homes.

It was an exhausting day for many and the complex was very quiet for the rest of the day.

Dana and Todd went to the atrium and Dana told him of the things Rainie had told her about the outside world. He listened to her talk. He never spoke much, but was more than ever committed to opening up the complex. They watched the birds and listened to the frogs in the pond. Todd knew why Dana loved this place, because he loved it. He was surprised how the things calmed him and after the last two days he wanted some tranquility again. Dana lounged in his arms and was thankful to have him. The torch was being passed from the old to the next generation, one life at a time. It was a massive responsibility, if they made the wrong choices all the people would pay the price and no one was sure they were not the last.

Dana's days found her working hard in the tailor shop and Todd cutting new tunnels for the masons. They spent any spare time with each other. Todd worked hard with Andy researching everything he could on the virus and its effects. Dana helped him too; she too wanted to see the outside world, but the council was not budging on the subject. They felt the loss to the complex was still too much until the positioned lost to the virus could be filled by the young. They needed to be trained fully before they could consider opening the doors. Todd and Dana spent what time they could with Dirk as well. Any surplus of animals and insects were let go.

Days passed into weeks, Todd and Dana grew closer. They shared many interests and both longed to fulfill Simion's dream of living outside. Erik and Gwen were often in their company and the four of them to get any position filled. Dana watched Gwen and Erik plan the future of their child and often thought how she would be as a parent. Todd had asked her about having children and she shied away from it. With her mother Dee passing away during child birth; she was in no hurry to have one. She consoled herself with, if it happens it happens and although she was afraid she knew that the love she shared with Todd was precious. If they bonded their child from their love everything would be okay.

She thought about many things when she was weaving. The steady gentle thumping of the loom was comforting and she could let her mind wander, that was of course unless the threads got tangled or broke. Her tailoring team made yards of cloth. With so many in the complex, it was always welcomed.

Erik watched the monitors in the labs and everyday Dana asked if there was anything. Erik would look and shake his head. Todd often took her to watch the ones to the outside. They sometimes got glimpses of animals that warmed them both. Todd always surprised her how he always thought of the people in his life.

Sundays they spent with his family and dinner always a fun time. Dana learned much from his mother about cooking and care of children. She no longer was a nurse, but shared her experiences with the students under her. Dana was no exception. Todd had basic medical knowledge right from when he was young. He hoped he would never have to use what he knew, but was glad to help when he had too.

Time passed quickly, one day seemed to run into the next, with no sun to indicate day. The complex found its own method of running. Things seemed to be getting back on track; many stations that had been shut down were starting up again. The children of the founders were growing up and filling the positions. The teachers never lacked for pupils and most of them found the children capable even exceptional in most fields of education. Weather the genes or the parents had the biggest impact or the realization they had to learn or all would perish drove the children not only to learn but to excel in their studies.

Dana and Todd found time to spend at the atrium just to be together and as alone as anyone could be in the complex. "Todd" Dana asked "Do you ever think they will ever agree to let us go outside?" Dana asked. "I hope so" Todd replied. "Let's just work on getting more life out there first. What do you think, we wait three years and see what the council says then?" he said "by then there should be ample animals out there." He added and smiled at her. "Three years seems like a long time and yet it really isn't." she smiled at Todd. He shared her lament, but if they were to continue, the council had to make sure all the, I's were dotted and the T's were crossed. "How about we go see Dirk and Carla later and see what they think?" Todd said to her. Dana smiled "You're a special man Todd and I love you for it." Dana told him. Todd smiled back at Dana and said "You say that to all the men in your life." He kidded her. "I will go and talk with Nick and Andy tomorrow to see what they have to say as well. So what do you want to do after we see Dirk?" Todd asked. "Well let's see how it goes. Sometimes when we visit them an hour leads to four or five hours." Dana said. "Alright are you ready to go?" Todd asked. "Yes dear" and she tucked her arm in his as they headed for the animal tunnels.

It wasn't long before they arrived and as always Dirk and Carla were happy to see them. Todd took up Dirk's time asking about his recycling projects and Dana talked with Carla about the animals. Her detailed records were amazing, every animal; their lineage, date of birth, death or release. It was just as Dana predicted, the hour long visit had turned into hours. It was early in the morning when they finally closed the books and after hugs, good nights, Dana and Todd went home.

"We have so much work yet and so many reports to do before we can present this all to the council." Todd smiled. "One step at a time, we will get them done. We have to start somewhere and I think we made a great start tonight." Dana smiled. "Are you working in the tunnels this week or making pillars slabs?" "The tunnels, we are mining that new ore. The vein in there is a good one. The steel won't go awry, it's always needed." "How about you, are you in the tailor station?" Todd asked. "Yes, but if I can find some time I want to check on the children at school. I want to see how many grads are coming up and if we can place them when they graduate." Dana replied.

Todd led her to the communications labs and they watched the monitors for a while. Erik left a note telling her, nothing, that day. "Let's call it a night." Dana said and they headed to their dorm.

It was Erik that came to them the next day. "Todd, can I talk with you for a moment?" Todd stepped out of the dorm and Erik proceeded to tell him of the tragedy. "Early this morning there was a cave in. I came to ask you to help. Nick and several others are still trapped. They have been digging for about two hours now trying to get to them." "Why didn't someone come and get me earlier, geesh!" Todd sighed. "Let me get my gear. I will be down there shortly." Eric nodded and left.

Todd went back into the dorm and found Dana up, she had tea brewing. "I can't stay Luv I have to go. Nick and some others are trapped in a cave in." Dana looked up. "Oh my God Todd, how did it happen? I thought Nick was always about that and took extra care all the time." "I'm not sure." Todd replied as he dragged on his clothes and soon was grabbing what gear he thought might be needed. "I must go" and he kissed her as he headed for the mining tunnels. Dana dressed quickly and headed for the kitchens. The men would need food and she would be of some help there.

Todd arrived to find order and chaos. The medics were there and the tunnel was being checked to make sure no further cave-ins were apparent. The rubble was just starting to be moved. Todd inquired as he made his way further into the tunnels as to who was unaccounted for and how this could have happened. The younger men didn't have much to say other than they had not followed the safety precautions to the letter in the haste to get to the ore. Nick was about to pull them out to do more stabilizing when it happened.

Todd and the other men dug as quickly as they could. They had to move slower, making it safe was imperative so no one else got hurt, but it made the rescue excavating slow. Todd just couldn't stop the flow the thoughts, he shared with Nick. He just had to be okay. Nick was strong, but even the strong can succumb to shock if injured.

Dana was now in the lichen helping with the food for the workers.

The medical team waited for them to get to the survivors, if there were any. The next few hours passed at a snails pace. Todd knew if they had air they would be okay, but it would be running out soon. He kept digging.

It was late afternoon when they reached the first of the men. The cave-in crushed them and their families would be informed. There were still several missing, Nick was among them. It was late that evening when they finally reached them. They were all alive thank God. From the first account it seemed broken bones and the shock was the worst, by evening that last had been found and the runnel was evacuated. The wounded were whisked away to the med station. As Todd and the others came out of the tunnels cheers from the crowds working a long with them came up.

I was long before Dana found him and after a long hug, they found a nearby bench to sit on. Todd was covered with dust and dirt. He told Dana about the men that had passed and how Nick had survived. He was to work in that tunnel the next day he was at work. It would be shut down now until the ones that passed could have a proper service. Todd was beside himself, there was always danger opening new tunnels. Why had they been so careless? He was tire and emotionally drained, all he wanted to do was go home and go to bed. Dana urged him up from the bench and they slowly walked home. "I must see how Nick is" Todd told Dana. She just nodded. "First I'll make a pot of tea and you shower." He never argued. He wasted no time washing off the dust and dirt from the tunnel.

It felt good to stand under the shower. He was concerned about Nick so the shower was not as long as he would have liked, but he was clean now.

After dressing and having tea, Todd wanted to so see about Nick. Dana walked with him. She knew he needed her support and she worried not only for Nick's well being but for Todd's as well.

They soon were at the med labs and found it still in a buzz. With the few doctors they had it was busy for them. When Todd enquired about Nick, all he got was that he was stable. They sat in the waiting room and the kitchen had trays of cookies, cakes as well as tea and coffee for those waiting to hear about loved ones. The only deaths were those crushed at the beginning of the tunnel. The rest seemed more bruised than broken, at least that was something Todd thought. It was clear after a few hours that the rest would be okay to the relief of the families and friends there. No visitors, just immediate families that night. So Dana and Todd went home.

Todd felt the tension of the day wearing him down and wasted no time in falling asleep. Dana stayed up for a while longer. She thought about what Todd told her. He was to work in that very tunnel the next day. It was a hazard they all lived with all the time. Dana knew cave-ins would happen and it sparked the drive to work harder to get the council to start venturing outside. With Todd they would get those doors open again. She stayed up late working on papers that had all the stations in the complex and who was running them and what was needed to keep them that way.

Todd's sleep was fitful; he woke several times with visions of the cave-in. He had seen three so far. He knew it was just a matter of time before another. Nick was right, in his ridged policy for safety. Todd knew Nick's time as head man would soon be at an end and they would elect the new head man or woman. He had learned a lot from Nick and how having him hurt in the meds station didn't sit well with Todd. He would go see him tomorrow. Then start with the others, the clean up in the tunnel. He gave up trying to sleep; he just lay in bed resting. He thought about his whole life. Every bit of it spent here in the complex. He envied the older folks that got to live outside. How wondrous it must have been. He knew the labs continually worked with samples from the outside, the air, the water and the soil were all monitored. Why was the council so against them venturing out? What were they afraid of? He would find out.

His mind slipped in and out of sleep. When he woke up, he got up. He just wasn't getting the rest he needed. When he ventured out into the living area of their dorm, he found Dana asleep in the big chair with her work papers around her. Todd quietly went to the kitchen area and put on some coffee.

It wasn't long before Dana woke. "Mmmm, that smells good" she told him. She stretched "Did you get any sleep at all last night?" she said. "No not much" Todd told her. "I have to go to the tombs today and make sure the places of rest are ready." Dana knew this always pained him. He did not like this part of his work. Dana tried not to think about the deaths it was always numbing to her. She couldn't cry about them because death stalked everyone. She tried not to feel bad because all the sadness had an avenue to get hold of her. So she said little and offered no opinions. She just let Todd as well as the others that were grieving alone with their own thoughts.

Dana walked over to Todd and hugged him. He knew she felt bad and her was of dealing with it, was what it was. "I'm going to see Nick before I go to work. Would you like to come with me?" Todd asked. "No I think I will go to the kitchens and see if there is anything I can do to help. The funeral will be soon and I think I would be more helpful there. You go get dressed Todd and I will fix the coffee and a bite to eat."

He went into the bedroom and before long emerged dressed and ready to go. They spoke little during this meal. Todd kissed her on the cheek after they finished, "I'll be home late" he told her. She held his arm before he left "Be careful Todd" and by the look on her face he knew she was worried. "I will sweetie, I will" and he headed for the med labs.

His thoughts travelled back over yesterday and what happened, Nick would know, he was there. He wanted to know what caused the cave-ins.

When he got to the med labs he was met by the doctors. Todd was escorted to an office where he was told that Nick passed away. Todd just sat there. "He was alive, I pulled him out myself." Todd said. "His injuries were to extensive. I'm sorry there was nothing we could do to save him." The doctor told him. The doctor told him "I'm sorry" Todd nodded and left the med labs.

He was in shock almost. His steps took him to his mother's home. When she opened the door her first thought was something had happened to Dana. After a brief moment Todd told her he needed to talk with them. Mom put on some tea and his dad was soon there. "I need you to call a council meeting." Todd told them. "Nick is gone. He passed in the cave-in" Todd told them. "We have to start looking to live on the outside." Todd was getting almost angry.

"Now listen to me young man" his mother said. "We are safe in here thanks to Simion and his great foresight. When the viruses were let loose on the world we were safe here. We never knew how many or what the consequences of those were until by a mistake one got in. We lost so many people. It was awful to see friends and family perish unable to do anything. Never knowing who would be next and how awful their deaths would be. We didn't know what else was out there and I for one am in no hurry to find out. You forget yourself my son. You are alive only by precaution and thorough work of so many." His mother looked at him. She saw almost depression. "Look Todd, I know Nick was a big part of your life as he was for many including ours, but we must continue to survive. Going outside before we know for sure it is safe would be stupid and I can not in good faith condone this. I will not vote for a council to convene on this, I'm sorry" she said. Todd knew she was right and although he was miserable inside about it, there was nothing he could do about it, except continue the research with Dana. He finished his tea and went home to his dorm.

He hoped that Dana would be there. This was one time he needed to talk with her. He lay on the couch and thought about everything his mother had said to him. His father agreed and he knew it was the feeling of most if not all of the council members. He had to go to the tunnels to help there. He wanted to collect his thoughts. It would do no good to go and be miserable to the people there.

Dana's day was not faring much better. The parents and wives were suffering. There was nothing she could do but listen. Lives, with so many things that happened were gone now, just memories to sustain the ones left behind. It would be a long time before the people would get back to any kind of normal existence. The services would be over soon and they would then be left to fill the spaces left with their loved ones passing. Dana knew that is a poor compensation.

The morning passed into the afternoon and Dana listened to all the stories of the loved ones lost. She made a mental note that in the future to get them to write them down to keep a history of the complex. She cleaned up as the people filtered out. She heard about Nick and her heart felt sad for Todd. He was very close to Nick and she knew news would not be easy for Todd.

It took a few hours to finish and then she made her way home. Todd was there and after a hug she told him how sorry she was. He never said much but Dana knew he was suffering hurt feelings. She made a light dinner and afterwards they sat on the couch together.

"Dana" Todd said. "Yeah, what's up?" she replied. "I talked to mom and dad today. I don't think we will ever get out of this mountain." He said. "They won't even consider it" he told her. "Did you think they would?" Dana said. "They are afraid, Todd. We may be the only ones left alive. It is up to us to repopulate everything. There is no room for error. They lived through that. If we work hard and do the research, we will make it, I'm sure. I still believe my dad is out there somewhere and if he made it there has to be others. What we need to do is keep this place as safe as we can and work hard to get us all out of here again." She told him. "Dana" he said "I love you." Dana smiled "You just stay safe" she said. They spent the evening in comfortable conversation and both knew as they went to bed the next few days would not be pleasant.

All the council members were at the services. It was a sad time for all involved, the loss of the young men that had been trained to do the work and Nick. His knowledge would be forever missed. The services were not long and the walk to the tomb tunnels would have seemed endless for those that lost a dear one. Todd walked with Dana and they each thought of Nick and the others as the way led to the tombs.

After a few words about each of them they were sealed into the mountain to rest for eternity. The crowed stayed to say prayers and place flowers. Then they slowly started to disperse.

After an hour or two, Andy again was leading the council members to the meeting chambers. As the last members the doors were shut. It was Andy that poured the brandy. When everyone had a small glass, he raised his glass and toasted Nick. They all raised their glasses and repeated, 'To Nick. The conversation was minimal as each knew their time was near. They were getting old and knew if their children were to succeed them, they had to do their very best to teach them anything they had not taught them already.

The members slowly filtered out and then to their homes. Andy remained behind. He missed most that had passed and knew many others would follow; how strange his life had been. The knowledge he knew of the past and the wonder of what might be, all in his mind. He never stopped working on preserving as much as he could for the generations to come. Andy hoped that Todd and Dana would never give up on going back to the outside world. Todd was right, they were never meant to live like this. Andy knew if they moved to quickly, everything gained might be lost. Andy decided to help Todd and Dana. He would help them do what had to be done, find out things that would be needed to be sure of the safety of the outside. It would be a massive undertaking, but like anything, you start at the beginning and see where it takes you. With that thought and the council room clean and empty, Andy closed the doors and headed to his dorm.

The next few days were spent by many just coming to grips with the losses and the stone workers clearing the collapsed tunnel. A team was set up to supervise any new tunnels and the clean up. There would be no room for errors and a procedure was put into place that would be strictly followed. The regular work of pillars and dorm modifications were put on hold. The council was convened and covered many articles, for reopening closed work shops, what new policies would be put into place.

Dana and Todd fell into a routine of work and training younger folks coming of age. The head person of each work shop would present their needs and Dana would see what students would fit the bill.

Todd spent more time working with Andy and finding out more about what evidence would be required to someday move back to the outside. His work often had him with Erik in the science labs.

The air, water and soil samples were tested regularly. The only thing the council agreed upon was if these test remained safe for three years, they would consider the matter. Until that time the outsides were off limits.

Dirk and Carla would still let out surplus animals as well as David with insects. Any animals outside would be watched on the monitors. After a set time they would be studied too. Todd and Dana knew it was hope and hope was all they had at the moment.

The complex seemed to be running smoothly since the cave-in and life was back on track for most.

It was usual that Todd made the morning coffee. He had his shower and was soon off to see Andy. Andy had proven to be a great help. He knew what seemed to be a lot about everything and if he didn't know he would find out. Todd enjoyed his company and found himself looking at the complex through new eyes. He had always felt trapped, but now he thought of it as an adventure. Everything they did was to improve the standard of living inside and once they were back outside setting up a new way to help mankind to never make the mistakes that led to this. He didn't want to miss his time with Andy so he never pushed Dana to wake up.

Soon he was on his way to the library and a note on the table for Dana. Andy had been listing all the needs of the people in the complex and what stations needed to do to keep everyone healthy and happy. They had to start on the list for the animals soon. There was much to consider, Todd kept notes and lists. As each workshop was presented the two men worked on the needs each had. How many workers, what skills were needed and what raw materials, etc...

Dana spent hours working and training new people to fill the stations. Anything she didn't know, how to do, she read up on and laboured until she did. The tailoring facilities were complete after months of study and training. Todd did the same after the tunnel that caved in was cleared. A new policy was written the regulations slowed the work, but it was safe now and would be from there on into the future.

Todd had taken to learn things in the machine shops. He preferred working with stone, but he found metal was a medium he liked. There were many parts and pieces needed to be made and Todd soon mastered the equipment to make them.

Erik worked in the science labs and communications station. He found the work easy and enjoyable. He started a project with the med labs to test the outside. So far there had been no signs of anything harmful. He kept written reports on all his findings.

Karen and David and their daughter Petra worked endlessly in the agro tunnels. Petra was seeing a young man and he seemed to be a good match. His interests tended to carpentry, but that never kept Petra from her interests in plants.

David was training a few young people to take over his job; much to his dismay the idea he would not work was not appealing at all to him. He was pleased just the same with the progress and the fresh ideas the young presented him with. It gave him pleasure to see the interest in something he enjoyed most of his life.

Winter passed indifferently to those in the complex. Spring was here and with it new life.

Dana had found the time to watch the outside monitors and Todd often joined her there. It was coming alive outside and they watched for birds and any animals. The trees budded and soon fresh new leaves appeared. Both watched as the breezes came and the leaves danced on the limbs. It was Todd who saw the first birds. He and Dana watched them fly in amazement, they had survived. It was confirmation of the hard work. They knew that life outside was beginning; they kept notes, dates and times.

Dana and Todd were elated. It was clear that hope was there and it filled them with a sense of well being. "Todd" Dana said. "We have to help Dirk this week. I told him I would." She looked at him "Sure" he said.

"There are enough people working the station now. I'm sure we can go give him a hand" Dana smiled.

They left the communications labs and dropped off their notes at home before venturing to the animal tunnels. They found Dirk and his family well into the work of the new life there. Every animal had to be numbered and vaccinated. Carla, as always kept the records. Dirk had just delivered a calf and as always smiled and felt a great honour at being the steward of any animals born here. Dana and Todd's help would be appreciated. The next week would be the hardest. Most of the animals birthed at this time and then the fall would be hard work again. They worked together and found joy in the new life being brought into the world of the complex.

Each night they ate in the kitchens. After a hot meal and pleasant company of the kitchen staff they returned home. Dana soaked in a hot tub most evenings. Todd preferred showers. After they worked on any papers that needed their attention, they would sit together talking and watching the monitor reruns looking for anything they may have missed. "You know" Todd said "We haven't really had much time to visit anyone or even spend time together." "I know" Dana told him. Todd looked at her as she snuggled closer to him. "Well I think we have to fix that." He said. "How about we say, Sundays are visiting day or time for us day?" Dana smiled "Sounds good to me. We haven't even had dinner with our folks for months or Elsa. She is probably wondering if we are still alive." Todd smiled. "Okay let me plan this Sunday and you plan the next." "Sounds good" he said to her. "It does" Dana replied.

"So what do you think of the new animals this year? I thought they were looking good. Dirk, I believe has an eye for breeding them." Todd told her. "I agree" Dana said. "But don't be fooled; I think Carla has a hand in that one too." Dana smiled and Todd laughed. "Do you think we have enough information to make our first report to give to the council yet?" Todd asked. "I think we should try. It will be the first of many, but we have to get it started." Dana replied. "Oh Todd, do you think we will ever get to go outside?" she asked. "I truly will do what I can" Todd said "All I can do is keep working at it. The council will have to relent sooner or later." Dana laughed.

"I saw Elsa today; I'm worried about her she doesn't look well." Todd just looked at her. "Maybe you should be spending more time with her, after all she did give you a home after your mother passed away." "I know" Dana admitted although she loved Elsa, there never had been that closeness that she had with Warren.

When Warren died in the outbreak, Elsa took charge and Dana was never without, but Elsa's own children took priority. It never bothered Dana that she was not blood and Elsa was kind to her, but they never shared a close bond. Dana knew Elsa loved her, but not like the bond she and Warren shared. Elsa provided well, but Dana drew away from her. "I will go see her tomorrow." Dana told Todd.

"Well" Todd told her "Let's hit the hay, another long day with the animals. If you go see Elsa in the morning we can meet at the tunnels. I'm sure Dirk will keep me out of trouble." He smiled. They went to bed and sleep took them.

Morning always came too soon. Todd and Dana were still tired and neither wanted to get up. Todd rolled over and held Dana "Let's play hooky and stay in bed all day." Dana smiled "Oh I would like that too, but…" Todd smiled "Yes I know, alright." He said and crawled out of bed.

He went to their small kitchen and put the coffee on before heading to the shower. Dana lay in bed and listened to the shower and then the coffee brewing had an aroma she couldn't resist. Dana got up and joined Todd. After about fifteen minutes they ventured into the kitchen for some of the coffee.

Chapter 25

Jo, always the first to rise was downstairs and having tea when West and Willow stumbled downstairs. She smiled at them. Their lives were beginning. Gone was the rat race she grew up in and now a peaceful pleasant existence awaited them. She hoped West would not follow Zack's folly in trying to find the complex. It had caused nothing but great harm to him.

"Morning" West said with a smile and Willow sat beside him at Jo's table. "Good morning you two" Jo replied. "Get some breakfast into you two" she told them. "We have a long walk today." They just smiled. Soon they had eaten and Jo pushed them to get their gear together.

West led the way Willow and Jo followed. The day would be warm and the forest provided some comfort. The trail was well worn and made travel easier. "What do you thing of the fort Willow?" Jo asked. Willow pushed her hair away from her face "There were lots of things I liked" she said "I like the way they had the lanes and the fruit trees along them. I never saw so many people and the farm area was so well planned out. The workshops and everyone seemed to have a job that was important to all. Yes, I think I liked it. It's too bad we had to see it under such dire circumstances. I feel sorry for those people, they have lost everything." Willow said. "Not everything" Jo said. "Now they have hope and with that there is a promise for a future. That will give them peace soon. It won't be easy for the next year or two. Once they all get settled they will find the joy they have longed for." Jo told her.

Willow glanced over to the woods, the sun beams were breaking through any openings above. "They have suffered for so long and no one even knew they were there, just seems so, well unfair." Willow said. Jo looked at her "Life is filled with many trials met with failure, but many with success. It's the later that most find life worth living and striving for tomorrow." Willow smiled.

West never said much, but listened to his mom. She is a wise woman and his father a wise man. He was glad to be their son.

The day passed by with the conversation turning towards their valley and of Zack, Lily, Brad, Gary and the children. West knew Jo wanted to go home and she soon would be there. He was glad to be almost home himself.

They reached the settlement in late afternoon, they had made good time. Jo went to the elders and filled them in. They had messages from the runners and knew three to five families would be coming before winter. The cabins were ready and the whole settlement had worked to turn over garden spots for next spring.

Willow and West spent their evening walking around the small village and talked of what they would do in their valley. "West" Willow said "I'm not sure about sharing our valley with strangers." "Willow what is it?" West asked. "Oh I don't know, it's just that we have always had our family around us." Willow said. He smiled "I was going offer Carry our extra cabin. Is he too much of a stranger to you?" Willow smiled "Oh I do hope he would consider it. His mother, Freda is getting on in years and the work in the kitchen is getting hard for her." "Well then I will ask him" West said. "Oh wouldn't it be lovely if he found someone and they started a family. We could have the valley humming with our families in no time." West smiled. "Let's go find mom."

Jo was in the common house now. She wanted to continue home, but knew travelling at night wasn't a good idea. They enjoyed a nice meal and soon Willow found herself with all her old friends. They talked of many things from the fort, to new found men in their lives. They teased Willow about becoming a mother and Willow laughed saying give me some time, I just got married. Jo sat back and listened to the chatter.

West left the hen party to sit outside. He planned to get on the work that had been delayed. He thought about Willow and how she liked the gravel walkways at the fort. He decided he would load a wagon at least three times a week and see if he could improve his area at the cabin. He wanted to get as much work done before winter. He missed his dad and would enjoy his company again. He could feel the chill coming in the air and knew within a month or so it could turn cold. He knew winter would keep them cabin bound, but with the endless work still it was not a hardship. The produce from the gardens would keep them from being hungry and he had plenty of wood cut to keep the cabin warm.

He wandered over to the elders' house and asked them to send Carry to his valley on his next run. The men told him they would and asked how things were going in the valley beyond. West told them of the progress and they were amazed how much they accomplished. It was getting late and West said his goodbyes and headed back to the common house.

The women had gone. West found Jo and Willow drinking tea at their table. Jo, on West's arrival left and headed to her room for a hot bath. Her old bones needed it badly. It wasn't long before Willow wanted to go to their room for a bath as well. West followed her upstairs.

After closing the door he unpacked fresh clothes as she disrobed and got into her tub. West watched her and without hesitation helped her wash her hair. It was a small tub and after Willow got out; West stood in it and washed off the road dust. He rinsed with fresh water from the nearby buckets and without a thought the clothes soon found their way into the water to be washed out. West never minded rinsing them out and Willow was happy he did them. She had done so much laundry at the fort she didn't want to wash anything for a few days. They crawled into bed and West enclosed her in his arms and were soon sound asleep.

Jo as usual was first up. She knocked at their door until she had them awake. Jo headed for something to eat. She would be home today and none too soon for her. She was tired of travelling and tonight she and Zack would be in their bed. She had so many things to tell him and she knew he would be wondering where they were.

She was pondering the gardens and the winter ahead when West and Willow came downstairs. "Morning mom, did you sleep well?" West asked. "No not really" Jo told him. "I always sleep best at home." She smiled. Willow kissed her on the cheek and sat down. "You look tired Willow, are you feeling okay?" Jo asked. "Yes just tired. I agree it will be good to be home." "Well then" Jo said "Let's eat and get this show on the road."

It wasn't long before they were on their way. The weather held fair for them. The talk was seldom as each pondered their own thoughts. West as always scanned the terrain and Willow looked for mushrooms.

It was Jo who spoke first "Did you find any nut trees in your valley yet?" West answered "No, not yet, but I haven't really looked yet. Willow and I will look it over this fall." "I can't wait to see it" Willow smiled. "Do you think dad enjoyed his time alone?" West asked. "He better not have"

Jo said and they all laughed. "He is a very smart man, I'm sure he wasted little time. He is forever thinking of new things to make our lives easier. I do love him so and I have missed his company." Jo said "Well, just a couple more hours and we will be home." The conversation petered out and they walked in contented silence. Jo passed out fruit strips and trail mix and they pushed on without resting.

It was late afternoon as they crested the last mountains to see the valley below. It was home and all were glad to see it. The new cabins added much to the scenic view, soon families would live there. The little hideaway Jo and the others had come to know was well on its way to becoming a village in its own right.

Before long children spotted them coming down the trail and raced to meet them. They were happy to see them come home. They asked one question after another and soon they were back to the cabins.

Zack was on the porch and before long so was everyone else, Brad, Gary, Sara, Lily and even Willow's mom. There was much talk and food. Jo was glad to be home. West and Willow, now married would stay the night and then they would travel on. The stories of their journey, the fort and the new people dominated the conversation.

After a few hours folks started to go home and Jo and Zack managed to find some time alone. "So dear, how was it really?" Jo proceeded to tell him of the people and how they were. Their faith gone and how despair had such a hold on them when they arrived. She talked of nursing them and the terror some had of fires, how when given fruit, the old cherished it. They had not seen fruit in years. She told him of the deaths and how sad it was when they finally found people; they perished before they could share in the joy. How happy the dying appeared to be fed, warm, clean and cared for. It made Jo cry when she told him of the stories they related before they passed. How she held their hands and told them it was okay now. They were safe and they could let go.

Zack sat and listened to her. Jo was a good woman and she had her share of heart aches in her life as well. He made her tea and heated water brought by the children for her bath. "I'm so glad to be home and I feel good that so many have added to our population. There will be a few hard years ahead of them. With everyone helping them get set, then it will be good for the young to have many more people to choose from for partners. When we stayed at the fort I met Freda, Carry's mother. He is a runner, anyways West is going to offer Carry his extra cabin. I think that will be good. I find it comforting that she will be in the valley with them. I do so hope they will agree to take it. She is such a lovely person, we got on so well. Oh and I met the children we found on the road that day. They have done so well, I am so glad for them. It seems like yesterday and yet it also seems like so long ago." Jo said. "You have listened to my chatter long enough. How about you tell me how you have been?" Jo smiled at Zack.

He talked as he heated the water. "One day is much like the next here. I have been making tiles. I want to do the roof to the work shop. I think it will be an improvement over the shingles. I have finished the pathways to the cabins and the household furniture for the new cabins is well underway. The children have been a great help and I enjoy their company. The lessons are going well and I can say all the children here can read." He said. "Oh that's wonderful" Jo said. She knew he had made great strides there. "Yes I am pleased" he said.

He filled Jo's tub, she unpacked her gear and put it away. "Your tub is ready malady" he said and Jo climbed in.

Zack washed her back and after washed her hair, Zack poured clean water over her head. "I'm so happy to be home" she said. "I'm glad you are home too. Lily and Sara have cooked for me, but it's not your cooking" he smiled. "You might not be so happy about being home when you look and see how much work has to be done in the garden. Everything is near ready to be harvested." He patted her hand. "I will deal with that tomorrow." She said.

Jo's bath was done and it was about time for West and Willow to come in. "Okay you two, the bath is free and I want your travelling clothes." She said. West looked at Willow "Yep, we are home" and they all laughed. Jo and Zack moved onto the porch. She sat in her chair Zack made for her and she gazed out over the yard and onto the gardens. She was glad to be home.

West and Willow bathed and talked of how much work had been done here. West held Willow after they finished bathing "I want you to be happy Willow. I just hope you will be in your new home." "I will be, I will be with you West and that's all I will need. You have been a big part of my life. You always have been kind and considerate to me. Helped me without ridicule and had the patience and understanding I needed so desperately." "Willow I love you. I have from the first time I saw you in the forest." She melted into his arms knowing that she was truly cared for, safe from harm and free to be herself. "West I love you so" she said and they enclosed into each others arms and kissed.

After holding her for a moment longer, West said "Let's get this cleaned up. Night will be upon us and we still have to travel tomorrow." She nodded and after rinsing out their clothes, she joined West with a cup of tea.

On the porch sat Zack, Jo, West and Willow. It was Zack that asked if they were leaving in the morning. "Yes it would best I think. We have a lot of things that must be done before the first snow falls." "Lily and Sara have both gone to the valley and tended your garden" Zack smiled as he told West. "Really, how did they ever find the time?" West said. "I think they enjoyed it, having some time alone for a change." Zack said. "I must thank them before I leave" West said. "No, No it's supposed to be a surprise. A wedding gift so to speak. I just wanted you to know who did it for you before you left." Willow was teary eyed "I sure will miss you so much. You both have made my life so much better." She hugged Jo and Zack. "We love you Willow" Jo said. "You must promise to take care of our West" she smiled. Willow smiled back. She was happy for them and knew they had a good chance at happiness. They had no baggage from the virus. No memories from the old world and the tragedy of it. She was thankful for that.

They sat and watched the sky from the porch and all knew this was the last night they would spend as a family unit here. West and Willow were now adults and soon parents with luck. "It's late" Zack said "I have much to do tomorrow." Jo was gathering up the dishes. "It had been a long day, but I am glad I'm home." They got up and went into the cabin. West and Willow sat on the porch a while longer star gazing and watching the satellites cross the sky. "Well sweetie, let's call it a night" and headed to bed.

Jo woke to the children outside. She had slept in and that was unusual for her. Zack had the tea and breakfast ready. She smiled as she appeared from the bedroom. "Are the children still sleeping?" she asked. "Yes, but with the kids playing outside they will be up soon." Jo sat down and sipped her tea and combed out her hair. She looked up to Zack "What have you planned for your day?" "I'm still working on the tiles. This afternoon I want to finish the chairs for the new cabins and of course the children will be here for their lessons." He smiled as she listened intently. "What great plans have you today?" he asked. "I want to see the gardens and visit Sara and Lily, I'm sure they will fill me in on things." she said. "If harvest is ready I will be busy."

It was soon after this when West and Willow appeared. "Good morning you sleepy heads" Zack said. "Come have some tea and something to eat." There was no argument to that. West was more awake than Willow and sat easily at the table. Zack asked when they were leaving and West replied as soon as they get things together.

"I made a wagon for you and loaded it with a few things" Zack smiled. "Everyone has donated something" he smiled at them. "I want you to come visit before snow flies if you can" Zack said. "We will father. It might be a long winter and one more visit would be nice, but at the moment we must get our home in order." With the trip ahead of them they finished their breakfast and started packing their gear. They soon had their things ready to go.

Willow went to say goodbye to everyone. As soon as they approached her parents house Willow was overcome by how sad a home it was. She worried for her siblings and confided in Jo, She asked Jo to keep an eye out for them. Jo assured her she would and that set Willow at ease. Her father was not there and her mother hugged her. Willow knew that her mom would miss her. Her father had always been a stern person and she knew he would not be there when she went to say goodbye. He almost resented her happiness. Misery loves company and she was escaping him and his surly ways. "Willow my dear, be happy" her mother told her "Find joy within yourself and it will be a comfort to you." The children were up and her mother's work never seems to end. Jo and Willow went back to where West and Zack were waiting.

The wagon Zack made wasn't too large and West could easily pull it. The wheels were large to move over anything that might be on the trail. They hugged them and the two young folks were soon on the trail to their new home and the new life that awaited them.

West didn't seem to have any trouble pulling the wagon. Willow helped when the going got tough along the path. By mid day the rest for something to eat and drink was more than welcome. "West are you happy?" Willow asked. "Of course I am, why do you ask? You are not having misgivings now are you?" he asked. "Oh no" she said "I have never been as contented as I am now. My life is full of promise and it's you that has given it to me." West sat down, his back to a tree and Willow sat beside and leaning on him. She listened to the breeze passing through the limbs of the trees and to West's steady breathing. She felt the warmth of him as his arm draped over her shoulder. "We have some work ahead of us, but we will be just fine" he said to her. "I have some great plans for the place." He told her. She smiled, she too had some plans. The cabin needed a female touch and she looked forward to it. "Well let's go, the trip will not be over if we sit here. I want to get home and get the fire going." He said. Home she thought, she had a home. He home would be filled with love and not anger and resentment like she had for most of her life. West would never know how much he had given her. She kissed him and got up. Soon they were on their way again.

There were a few parts of the trail that needed to be worked on to make passing over it easier, with the wagon. Many things that West planned would make life easier. The forest was cooler than in the sun and it was welcomed as they passed through it. Fall was on its way and some leaves had started to turn the warm colours of autumn. Autumn would soon be here and then snow. White clean and like a blanket covering the ground, protecting everything underneath from the bitterness winter winds brought.

They didn't talk much now, both just wanting to be at the cabin. By late afternoon they crested the last hill and could see the valley below. A bright smile crossed Willow's face. It was a sight that she would never tire of, home.

They soon made it to the cabin and before long West had a fire going. West swept out the dust and opened the door to let in some fresh air. West brought in some water and by night fall they had it warm, ready to settle in for the night. West filled the large basin with warm water so they could wash and Willow had fresh linens on the bed. Tonight would be an early to bed. Tomorrow would be upon them and work with it. After they washed up they went to bed. For the first time since they married they were totally alone and let the passions they shared flow uninhibited. When they were both spent they slept in the comfort of each others arms, warm and secure at peace with each other and the world around them.

It was thunder that woke West up. He slipped out of bed and after pulling on his pants headed out on to the porch. He never liked storms and wanted to watch the sky for any smoke. He watched for about an hour and the rain started. Willow by now was up and had a fire going and soon tea and breakfast. She carried a cup of tea to West, who was sitting back starring into the sky. She sat down beside him. "West, what's the matter?" she asked. "Oh nothing much I just always watch the storms. If they start a fire it could be dangerous, nothing for you to worry about." He said. "Too bad it's raining today" Willow said. "We won't have much done in the wet." West said. "Yes, but another days rest won't kill us either." He smiled. "We can unpack our things and a warm cabin will not go amiss." He said. "West, come in you will catch your death outside." Willow called to him. After she had been in the cabin for a while, he came in, sat at the table and watched her unpack things. "Would you get me some water please?" she asked him. "Sure" he said and pulled on a shirt she had set out for him. He slipped on his footwear and headed for the well. He was glad Zack had made the clay tiles. He had paths to everything and no mud to tramp through. He filled the buckets and returned to the cabin.

Willow had taken over the house. He was of little use and spent his time on his chair whittling. The day passed pleasantly and by suppertime the rain had stopped. Willow had the place looking like a home, West thought. She made something for them to eat and asked West what he was making. He handed her the spoon he had made. "It was a love spoon" he told her. "It's beautiful" she said and soon had its place among her treasures. She kissed him. "How about some popcorn?" he said. "The fire is coals and would be perfect to make some." Willow brought out the clay jar the corn was in and handed it to him. As Willow cleaned up the dishes West popped the corn. Before long both were eating it and talking of the valley. West told her he had found a nice pond with plenty of reeds for weaving. He told her he had seen mushrooms and wild berries. Willow sat listening to him talk. She liked the sound of his voice. She would never tire of it, she thought. West was totally at ease with her and it surprised him how she fit perfectly to him. With night falling and soon no light other than what was given off by the fire, they called it a night and went to bed. The love they shared would carry them to the end of their lives.

Morning came and with it the sun. Today would be a working day and there was plenty of that to do. West, first up went to the well and filled the buckets for the house. Willow was soon up and after washing and dressing; the two discussed the plans for the day. Willow prepared something to eat and West watched her. He talked of burning a few stumps by the other cabin and making sure there was ample wood cut for winter.

Willow's day would be spent in the garden and the porch would serve as a drying area for the herbs that needed to be preserved.

Before long the two had their jobs in hand and by noon a break was well earned. Willow had fried bread and jam with rose hip tea, the all time staple. West always drank plenty of water as well. Willow was surprised at how well the garden was doing and how nice it was that Sara and Lily had come to care for it while she was at the fort. She must thank them when she next saw them. "Looks like you have the area around the cabin cleared out well" Willow said to West. "Yes it's coming along. I still need to clean up the area between here and those fir trees." West told her. "What have you got planned for this afternoon?" he asked. "The flax is ripe I have to harvest that and maybe dig a row of potatoes. I have herbs that need to be picked yet too." Willow told him. He helped clean up from lunch and the headed to the jobs that awaited them.

After a few hours they both tired and took a break. West had taken the wagon to the garden and told Willow after the break he would help load it. She smiled "Thanks West my back is starting to ache." She stood up straight and stretched her back. He had been to the cabin and brought water and fruit strips. They sat under a big tree and looked over the garden and the cabins beyond. "West this is so lovely here." Willow told him. "Yes" he said "I liked it here right away when I came here." He had plans for it here and they were coming together. "Willow after we load up these potatoes let's go for a walk. I want to show you the pond." He said. Willow smiled "I would like that" she told him.

They soon finished eating and West gave Willow his hand to help her up. "Well" she said "Let's get these spuds into the wagon." They began picking them and before long it turned into a race. They were picking them as fast as they could, when the last potato was in the wagon they looked at each other and began laughing. "That was quick." West smiled. Willow's only comment was "I picked more than you." And again they laughed. Both now covered with dirt pulled the wagon to the cabin.

Willow set the bucket down the well and West pulled it up. They washed off the dirt from their hands and faces and then dumped several buckets over the wagon rinsing off the potatoes. "Let's go" West said and grabbed Willow's hand.

They headed into the bush on a small trail West had used several times. Soon they found themselves at a pond. It was lovely there, Willow's eyes lit up when she saw it. "Oh West" she said "It's like out of a dream." There were several spots to sit on stones that surrounded it and the reeds surrounded it. A small stream cascaded into it and poured out the other side. West watched Willow as she walked around it and he could see that she was pleased. "I'm glad that it meets with your approval" he said smiling. She dashed over and hugged him. "It's wonderful" she told him. "It's sp quiet and serene." The sky above beamed into the opening and the sun warmed them. Not much wind blew there, the trees protected it. "We must come here often" she said. West leaned against a tree and watched as she picked some reeds. "Well don't just stand there come over here" she said. West smiled and headed to where she was. He was soon weighted down with reeds and they started home.

Willow's red hair tumbled over her shoulders was soon pull back and tucked under her scarf again. She had never been so happy. On that fact, West too felt his life was full. Before long they had made their way back to the cabins. Willow wasted no time instructing West where the potatoes were to go as well as the reeds. She headed back to the garden and cut a few armfuls of flax. They would have to be worked into strands that could be spun. It was not hard.

After an hour or so, Willow had whipped the bunched reeds over a nailed board. Each time she dragged the bundles over the nails the flax grew silkier. She would let the bundles dry that night and then she could spin it.

West had the potatoes in the root cellar and had taken the wagon down by the river. He filled it to the point of being hard to pull with gravel and headed back to the cabin. He would start the gravel on the trail to the valley beyond. He pulled it up the trail and dumped it. He smoothed it out and thought; one wagon three times a week. That was the first of many to come. By the time he returned to the cabin it was dusk. He checked the fires he had going on the stumps. When he was satisfied they were out he headed home.

Willow had water for a bath waiting for him and fresh clothes. He wasted no time getting into it. He was tired and it was a hot soak he needed. "How did you know I needed a hot soak?" he asked. "You have been working all day and you must be tired." He washed off and Willow continued cooking. She had a bean soup and fried bread ready for him to eat. After he was out, dressed and sitting at the table she started heating the water for her bath. It took no time to empty the water and sitting at the table to eat as well. "Where did you go after you put the potatoes away?" she asked him. "No where, I just checked the fires at the stumps and wandered about looking at the availability for a work shop." He told her, but he didn't want to tell her about the gravel. It was to be a surprise. "Did you see what you needed?" she asked. "Yes there's a stand of pine nearby I can use." "Well that's good" Willow told him. She finished eating and the water she was heating soon found its way into her tub for a bath.

West started clearing the supper dishes and told her to have her bath. She smiled and wasted no time getting into it. After she washed she threw in the work clothes of the day to be rinsed off. West told her to sit by the fire and brushed her hair out so it would dry. He rinsed out the clothes, hung them to dry and emptied the tub. He joined Willow by the fire and they relaxed. "We got a lot done today" Willow said." I just love the pond, it's so lovely there." West smiled. "Yeah I like it there too" he told her. "What have you planned for tomorrow?" Willow asked. "I think I will fall those trees for the workshop. If they set over the winter they will be dry by spring. I was hoping Carry would be through this way soon so I could see if he wants this cabin." "Oh that would be perfect if he did." Willow said. "Do you think he would bring his mom? She is a nice lady. She was so good to us at the fort." "Yes she was" West said. "I'm sure he would not leave his mom that far away." He smiled at her. "What are your plans for tomorrow?" West asked. "I must start drying the herbs and tomatoes. We have lots of corn as well. I will have to make oil from most of it, but there will be enough left over for eating this winter." "With all the work facing us we had best get some rest." Soon they were in bed and asleep.

Dawns first light had West up. He soon dressed and was at the well. Willow, was up not long after him, and dressed while he washed. "I'll call you as soon as I have something ready to eat." She called as West headed out the door.

West's first stop was at the stumps. They burned out nicely and he soon had the ground turned over and smoothed out. Willow called him in and they ate porridge and dried apples. Tea was at every meal and it never took them long to eat. Willow started the clean up and West headed back outside. It didn't take him long to pick out the trees and cut them down. Willow was in the garden and watched the trees fall. It worried her a bit, but West was a capable man and knew what he was doing. She watched him swing the axe and it seemed so effortless for him. He was very fluid in his motions while working and Willow always marvelled at this.

She kept at the garden and soon had another row of potatoes dug. She pulled the wagon close and started picking them up. She stopped about half way down the row to make some lunch. It didn't take her long to make the trip to the well then into the house. As she washed some carrots and lettuce she looked out the window, that West had installed and saw him coming. They had a good lunch, as they were cleaning the dishes Willow asked "Did you get all the trees down?" "Yes I think there are enough. They need to be delimbed and stacked yet." West told her. "How's your day going?" he asked. "It's going slowly, but going. We still have nearly three weeks before frost settles in." She replied. "True enough" West replied. After they finished the dished they both went back to work.

Willow's afternoon found her making several trips to the drying table set up on the porch. She had the potatoes loaded and poured water over them to wash them off. After looking over the tables of drying herbs and tomatoes, she went and cut several bundles of flax. The bundles she had prepared the day before were dry and in the cabin waiting to be spun. She worked hard to turn the flax bundles picked that day into the fine fibres to be spun.

West also made progress, he had the trees limbed, burned out some of the stumps and manoeuvred the logs to the side to stack until next spring. It was late afternoon when he appeared out of the bush and made his way to the cabin.

Willow was still working with the flax when he arrived. He made a trip to the well and went into the cabin. "I'll be done in a few minutes" she called to him "this is my last bundle." "No worries" he called back. He washed and put a few potatoes on the coals. He had fresh carrots that Willow had pulled from the garden, those with some radishes and some corn, their dinner was soon on its way to being cooked.

When Willow came in she knew West had dinner ready. "Oh this is so nice" she said "that last bundle seemed to take forever" she told him. He smiled. Willow washed up and set out the dishes. They shared the food and the evening was spent sitting together. "I'm so tired" Willow told him. "I am as well" West replied. As night fell they crawled into bed and fell fast asleep.

The next few weeks passed and both West and Willow prepared for the coming winter. The garden was harvested and the food stores were tucked safely away in the root cellar. West had an ample wood cut and fell plenty of wood for the workshop and extra for anything else that might be needed. Willow was happy and contented here in the valley with West. She found that she didn't miss the other folks as much as she thought she would. West too found contentment with Willow and was secure now with himself and their home. He knew they would warm and well fed all winter.

With the cold weather approaching, West decided to make a trip to see his mom and dad. He wondered why Carry had not been through yet. His thoughts carried him back to the fort and all the people. He knew Carry was more than likely working on cabins and in the gardens. He hoped he would get a chance to see him before the snow started to fly.

West was burning out the stumps when Willow came out with hot tea and bread. She was a welcomed sight. "Ahhh this great Willow" he said as he sipped the tea. "How would you like to go see mom and dad tomorrow?" he asked her. "I would like that very much" she replied. "We can take the wagon and load the extra food for the new families as well."

Willow told him. "Done then" West said and smiled. He was going to talk with his dad more about the complex. Next spring and into the summer he wanted to hike into the next valley and maybe beyond. He could spare some time now that he had cut enough wood to last a while. He wanted to ask his mom for some paper as well. This area should be mapped and trails marked. The runners had maps of a lot of the areas where people were, but not much elsewhere. He finished his tea and bread and Willow put the cup in the basket. "You have done a grand job of clearing this area West. What do you plan to build here?" "I'm not sure yet Willow, but I will keep it cleared until we decide. I will just clear around these stump fires and we can go start loading that wagon. How does that sound?" West said. Willow smiled "I'll get started" she told him and headed back to the cabin. He watched her go and the cabin ahead of her fit well into the picture. She with her basket and the cabin the distance gave him the feeling he had done well for them.

It didn't take him long to clear up around the stumps before heading to the cabin. Willow had a basin of water ready for him to wash in and it felt good to get the smoke and ash off. It didn't take long to load the small wagon. The rest of the evening was spent talking and wondering how well the harvest was in the valley beyond.

Willow had heated water for a bath and both wasted no time in washing off the days labour. West emptied the tub and Willow combed and then brushed her hair. She sat by the fire and the heat soon her locks dry. With the remaining light, they worked on small projects that they had on the go. West was making utensils for the cabin and Willow was preparing everything to be able to spin flax when they got back home.

The morning found them rested and anxious to go. West packed up the wagon with fresh clothes and small travelling meals that Willow prepared for them. They covered the wagon and they started their walk to the next valley. They pulled the wagon with ease and knew the hardest part was coming up. It didn't take long to reach the gravelled part. Willow looked at West "Oh my goodness" she said "Whenever did you do this?" she asked beaming. "It's wonderful" she told him. West smiled "Oh just a little here and a little there" he said. "I will have the whole trail done someday" he said. "Well I want to help" she told him. "I will make some effort tee" she smiled. West looked at her "The gravel is awful heavy" he said "best let me do it." He watched her face and clearly saw disappointment "Well maybe if you start down by the cabins" he told her. "It wouldn't be so far from the river and if you promise to do just a very little at a time..." "I will, I will" she said "I won't carry anything too heavy or pull in the wagon more than I can handle with ease." She was beaming. "Alright then" he told her. It took two seconds and Willow had him held in her arms. His strong arms enclosed around her and he kissed her. "Let's get this over the hill" and he looked at the wagon. They both smiled.

It was after lunch when they finally reached the midway mark. With the meal Willow brought they found them resting and talking of their road. "You know father will be able to visit us then. The road will make the journey much easier for him." "Yes I thought that too. It will also clearly mark the path in the winter if we need to travel then." Willow had roads built all the way to the fort by the time they were on their way again. The trip down hill was much easier going and by night fall they had reached the valley West had called home for most of his life.

The children were the first to see them arriving. Soon the families were all at Zack and Jo's to visit. The extra hands had the wagon unpacked and the ladies had tea and toasted bread for everyone. Before long everyone slowly made their way back to their homes.

West could see that Willow was somewhat disappointed that her mom and dad never come to see her. She would go see them the next day. Jo was thrilled to see them and it didn't take the two women long to be in their own conversation about things.

Zack sat by the fire and West sat in the chair across from him. They talked of many things from building to some new ideas Zack had to build a smithy in this valley. With the night firmly set in, they called it and made their way to bed.

As normal Jo was the first to rise and Willow not far behind her. The two women shared in the morning tasks of preparing food and talked of how the families were doing. Jo told Willow they were expecting the first family soon and next spring two more. Willow asked about her family and Jo kept it light. She did not wish to alarm Willow that she thought her father had become abusive physically now to her mother and the other children. There was not much they could do if Willow's mother didn't ask for help. She feared that if it didn't stop, someone would really be hurt beyond what they were already.

Gary and Brad did not like it and she feared they would take matters into their own hands. Jo was happy to see Willow and was thankful that she and West had found each other. Willow would be spared and one child of that household would be saved.

Soon the men were up and Willow and Jo had them fed. It was so quiet in the valley and like an alarm clock went off, it came to life, and all the sounds of living clearly filled the air. The children made most of the noise.

Jo, Sara and Lily were still getting the last of the garden cleared and the men were chopping wood.

Willow made her way to her mom and dad, when she got there she found her mother weeping. When her mom looked up and saw her she dried her eyes and went to meet her. "Mom what's the matter?" Willow asked. "Oh Willow I think he is losing his mind, he just doesn't care anymore. He's so angry all the time. Willow felt so awful for her mom. "Where is he?" Willow asked. "He left early this morning. He is not likely to return until dark. I don't know where he goes or what he does." She told Willow. "Who is helping you here?" Willow asked. "The children and I manage" she said. Willow's heart sank. She could see the state of things her mother could not keep up. "Do you have enough food and wood cut for the winter?" Willow asked. "Well let's get some tea going Okay mom?" and Willow went into the house. It was a mess.

After tea Willow soon had the children getting water and helping with the clean up. Willow and her mom did the laundry well into the afternoon. With the line full and house cleaned, Willow looked over the wood pile and then into the root cellar. She knew the food would last, but not the wood. She made her way back to her mother's cabin from the wood shed. She told her mom she was going to find her hubby; he must be wondering what she was doing all day. Willow's mom smiled and hugged her. "Thank you for the help today. I truly needed a hand." Willow knew her mom meant it and smiled "its okay mom. We all have some good days and some bad ones. I'll come back later and have some tea after dinner Okay?" she said. Willow's mom smiled.

Before long Willow was at Zack and Jo's, the men were off in one of the sheds and Jo was sitting on the porch. Willow soon found a chair and Jo had tea done in no time. After a few minutes Willow asked "How long has it been like that?" Jo looked at her "It was right after you left it started. I think your father; well I think it's been coming on for a long while. He's like an animal being eaten up from the inside out. I don't know what to say or do to help him." Willow looked at Jo "He's been mean my whole life. I'm worried about my mom and the children." "You rest easy my dear I'm sure that the men here will not let him step over certain borders. He has not made it easy on anyone and they will not put up with it much longer.

Everyone must pull their own weight for all to survive; your father is no exception. He will be told." Willow knew what Jo was saying and she also knew her father. He was good at putting on a front for everyone to see, but behind closed doors he could be totally different. "I looked to see if they had enough wood for the winter and I'm sure they don't. They have enough food though." Willow said. "We'll as West tomorrow I'm sure he won't mind and the other children can come for lessons. That will give your mom some peace for a bit." Willow smiled. "It will and I will help her clean up the yard some too. Get in a little organization before winter."

"Did you know that we are expecting a family soon? They should be here any day." Jo told her. "Must be a great relief to them to know they have a home now." Willow said. "Yes and we are glad to have them. Do you know how many are in the family?" Willow asked. "From the runner's news it's a mother, father four children and I believe the mother's brother." "Oh my goodness, quite a hoard then?" "Yes, the children will be glad to get settled and have playmates here. The parents with luck will be a nice addition for us." Jo smiled. "Are they going to pick over the cabins or have you picked one out for them?" Willow asked. "We decided to let them choose." Jo told her.

It was then that West and Zack came out of the workshop and headed for the cabin, both talking and laughing. "Looks like they are enjoying themselves" Willow said to Jo. Jo smiled "I wonder what they have been planning?" Jo said. The two women got ip to put on some tea and started dinner.

The evening was spent talking of the valley and the plans both made for them. Willow and Jo traded recipes of new ways of dying yarn and making paper. Pop corn was made and the evening passed quickly.

Jo and Zack headed to bed, Willow and West soon retired as well.

West's old room was comfortable and clean. When they were in bed Willow told West of her visit to her mom and dad's. She shared her worries and West told her he would make sure they had ample wood for the winter. She snuggled to him and drifted to sleep. She knew she was a lucky woman to have him and how he always made her feel safe and secure.

The usual hustle and bustle in the morning soon had West and Zack up. Jo and Willow far ahead of the men had their breakfast ready and had the wash almost done. Today they would make some apple preserves for all to share.

Zack and West now amply fed headed to Willow's mothers. Zack would get the children to help clean the yard and West would chop wood.

Willow's mom had her house things to keep her busy and the garden to clean up after. It was just after lunch when Willow's mom came out and was amazed at how the two men and the children had cleaned up. It was one of the few times that Zack saw her face light up with joy. It was soon gone and she peered over the forest around the cabin. Zack knew she was looking for her husband. West had chopped a lot of wood, but he knew it would not be enough. "We are going to take a break" Zack said to her and she nodded. "We will be back later alright?"

Willow's mom was relieved that the wood was getting done. She had no idea if her husband could have managed it. She was sure he was losing his mind. She was filled with such sadness herself and it was everything she could do to keep things somewhat together. Her mind drifted back to when they were young. How they would go to all their friends and have such good times. The outings to the lakes and the shopping, the movies; all the food you could think of was gone and would never be again. She had resolved herself to it, but her husband never could. The losses were just too great for him. He could not see that they were still alive and had hope. Hope that what they did now would be more for the children and not for the money. Things had new meanings for her. You made what you needed and treasured what you had. Where was he anyways? He had been gone longer than normal if anyone called hiding in the forest normal. She went back into the house and was soon busy getting food ready for the winter.

Willow and Jo had the preserves well on to being done. One more day and they would be finished. As Willow finished them up, Jo started a meal for everyone. The men would be hungry. They soon appeared and after washing up they sat on the porch talking. West was filled in on Willow's dad's behaviour more by Zack. "I think the poor fellow is losing it" Zack told him. "I fear that nothing can be done for him at this point." West nodded. "Poor Willow and her family." Willow was safe, but what would become of the others? West had always been lucky; Jo and Zack never lost their love of life. He had grown up with security and never feared living, but many other folks carried burdens he knew he would never begin to understand. At this point he was sure he didn't want to understand loss like they had.

By nightfall Willow's dad had still not returned. Worry had set in on Willow's mom. Brad and Gary along with West set out to search for him. They found nothing. Zack assured Willow's mother they would find him the next day and for her not to worry. They all returned to their own cabins. After a hot tea and conversation they met the night with rest well earned.

The dawn came and with it the daily living choirs. Willow and Jo had breakfast ready and the men ate appreciatively. Zack soon had the three set to look for Willow's dad.

Willow went to her mom's and found her and the children eating. The air in the house was fresh and it was tidied up. The yard looked great and West had a lot of wood cut. "Mom" Willow asked "Are you going to be Okay?" She looked at Willow "Yes dear I will, but my heart tells me he is gone." "Don't think like that, they will find him" she said. "I don't think so Willow. He is not in his right mind. The man I knew was no longer there. He has not been there for many years." Willow looked at her. "The change happened too fast, he just couldn't accept it. Deep inside him he was angry and lately it showed more and more." Oh mom, please don't say that. He will be home you'll see" Willow told her.

He mom looked at her and then back to the dishes she was washing "Is there anything you need a hand with" Willow asked. "No" she told her "You and West have helped so much already. You must think of your own home and needs now Willow not mine. We are safe here and I have a good garden area. The children are getting to be more help now. Zack has done that." She told Willow. "You finish your tea and start getting your things together, you will be leaving soon to your home." She smiled. Willow did have a lot of things to do "Okay mom, if you are sure you will be alright." Willow said. Her mom just smiled "I'll be just fine" she said. Willow left and was concerned; her mom seemed odd reconciled to her dad not coming back.

It wasn't long after she got to Jo and Zack's. She related the conversation and told Jo her worries. "It's just not like her. She's so weird about it." Willow told her. "Don't fret Willow I will go speak to her later, alright?" Jo said. "Would you? That would be so great. I'm worried about them." Willow thought about her dad. He had always made sure there was food, but never a happy place. He was bitter and everyone felt it around him, but he did provide for them. Her mother always made concessions for his mean words and ways. Willow knew she loved him. Maybe he was losing some fight within himself that had been tearing away at him for years. Maybe he would never come back.

"Willow, Willow, Willow" Jo called and got her attention. "Gee you were lost in thought there" Jo said. "Here is your share of the preserves" Jo told her. "Oh okay" Willow replied. "Put them in last, the wagon we will have a few other things for you two." Willow smiled. Jo had some cloth, dried herbs and a bag of salt. She had seeds from flowers and a few pumpkin seeds brought from the fort. "These are from Freda" Jo told her. "Oh my goodness. How nice of her" Willow said. "Yes" Jo replied. "I have this bag of nuts here too" Jo told her. "Do you have any nut tree stands there?" she asked. "I haven't seen any yet, but we have been so busy, we wanted to get the work done." Jo nodded; she remembered the first few years here.

The day had passed well into the afternoon when the men returned without Willow's father. Brad and Gary went home and West stopped first at Willow's moms. He never stayed long and was soon at the house. "There is no sign of him" West said. "What's the matter with him anyways, taking off like that?" It was Jo that spoke "He's not well West. Take care how you scorn. Be thankful that you don't share his illness." West nodded. It was not like him to be so cruel with words and he knew he had crossed the line. He should feel sorry for him not angry.

Zack put his hand on West's shoulder "We will find him. Let's just hope he makes it home tonight." West nodded. Jo made some tea and they sat on the porch.

When West looked up he saw Carry coming down the trail. He was a welcomed sight. West got up and started out to meet him. Jo went in to get another cup. The two men met with a handshake. "It's good to see you Carry. I was beginning to wonder if you would make it before the snow fell." West told him. "Aye, I almost never got away." Carry said "It's been crazy at the fort, but I believe we have enough for all to last the winter. With all the donations from the settlement it's worked out well. Your family that is to take the cabin is on their way. I passed them 2 days ago." "Good, good" West said. "We are ready for them. Next spring I believe 2 more cabins will be waiting." West told him. "That's great" Carry told him. They had reached the porch and Jo had tea poured "You rest up Carry" she said. "It's so good to see you. How's your mom?" Jo asked. "Well, this last influx of people has been hard on her. She's not 20 years old anymore. She has been training a few women to run the main kitchen. I think she wants to give it" Carry said. "Well now" said West "that brings us to the reason we sent the message." Carry listened intently. "We want to offer you a cabin in our valley" West told him. "I would rather it go to someone I knew" West smiled. "Please saw you will" Willow said with a smile. "That is a kind offer. I know my mom has been wanting to away from the fort. It will be a long haul with all our stuff. I will ask her when I get back." Carry said with a smile. "You are welcome to stay the night" Zack told him. "Oh my goodness dad, I'm sorry, Carry this is my dad and dad, Carry." The two shook hands. "I want to thank you for looking out for my wife while she was at the fort." Zack told Carry. Carry smiled.

It wasn't long before they all were talking of the fort and the people there. "With the new people" Carry told them "we have the road to the first settlement almost all gravel. It has been a great improvement. They are working on the one to the south, but it's just getting started." Jo looked at Zack "roads that's going to help folks a lot." "Oh" Carry said "did I tell you they have built runner stations? There are two now between the settlements and have a young couple in each. It will make for some winter travel now." West smiled "It was a good idea. With so many people it just made sense." He said. "That did it" Carry smiled, "no more nights in the rain. The runners still have to learn to build shelters. It's just good sense." Carry said. "I agree" said Zack. "Well seems we can expect our new arrivals in a couple days. That's good to know." Zack was glad to have more people coming. It was starting to become a nice little village. He then thought of Willow's dad. Where could he be? They should have found him by now.

"Zack would you pop some popcorn and Carry, here are some jam sandwiches for you." "Thank you kindly" he told her and smiled. Zack got up and made his way inside. Carry watched and realized he was almost crippled and knew why he did not journey to the fort with Jo. It was Willow who spoke next "Have you found a partner yet?" Carry smiled "Well…" "Tell us Carry" Willow said. "I was kind of sweet on this young woman that came with the new people. She is alone, her family is gone. She stays with the older women. They watch out for her." What's her name?" Willow asked. "Nimuri" Carry smiled "She's fair haired with green eyes. We have spent a lot of time together. My mom likes her too." "That's a good thing" West said and they laughed. "Are you going to marry her?" Willow asked. "The thought has crossed my mind." "Well get on it" and West slapped his shoulder. They laughed. Night had its hold and after a bit more conversation they all found their beds.

"West" Willow said. "Yes, what's the matter?" West asked. "I feel guilty having a good time when my dad is out there somewhere." She said. West laid there and pulled her closer. "We will look again tomorrow" he said "Don't feel guilty" he said "Your father has issues that have nothing to do with you. From all the folks that I have talk to, the old folks, many have troubles with it. I mean they have lost an entire way of life and many have lost their entire families and friends. He is not alone in that. It must have taken all these years to finally take him beyond reason. I am more worried about how to help him once we find him. You have been a good person all your life and have nothing to feel guilty about." He let her snuggle closer and kissed her fore head. They soon slept knowing tomorrow would be there before they knew it.

West woke to the smell of bread and porridge. He could hear Carry talking with Zack and Willow. It was Jo who rapped at the bedroom door. "Get up West" she said. West pulled on some clothes and washed at the cupboard in their room. When he ventured out into the living area he found everyone sitting at the table. Willow brought him some food and he ate everything. It was Carry that told him that he would speak with his mom and if she agreed, they would take the cabin. West was glad. "I must take my leave." Carry told them. "I have a long journey home" he smiled. They all knew this to be true. Jo had given him some food for travel and a jar of apple preserves for Freda.

West got up and walked up the path a ways with him before he turned to come home. Carry shook his hand and was on his way. West walked to get Gary and Brad. The children had told him that Willow's dad had not come home. Where was he? West thought. If he didn't come home soon, winter would soon send the first snows.

Willow had gone to her moms and Zack had his hands full with all the children. Jo, Sara and Lily were all preparing flax they had harvested.

The three men searched in vain, but they could not find Willow's dad. Again they returned without him.

West knew Willow was concerned, but there wasn't anything he could do about it. After the men returned West told Willow there was no sign. Jo looked at Willow and somewhere inside her she knew he would not return. She never said anything. They needed to sort out things on their own. West told Willow they would soon have to go home. There were things that needed to be done there as well before the snow came. Willow knew he was right. She thought her father may have gone there. It was hope.

They spent what time was left of the day loading the wagon. This was their last night here. When they finished with the wagon all sat on the porch. The conversation was light. Willow mentioned maybe her dad had gone there and they agreed it was a possibility. "I'm going to go and see my mom for a bit" Willow told them. West said "I'll walk you there. I need to see Brad and Gary as well."

The two young folk left and Jo and Zack were left on the porch. "What do you think about this?" he asked Jo. "I think he is lost" she said. "His mind is full of troubled thoughts and he's gone wandering too far. I don't think we will see him again." She told Zack. "Maybe you're right" he said. "Let's hope Brad, Gary or West find him." Jo patted his hand "Let's go in dear" Jo said to him. The two made their way inside. Zack added a few logs to the fire and they went to bed.

Willow was at her mom's door and found it to have some order to it. Her mother seemed to be keeping things together. The house was clean and tide. She was spinning flax when Willow arrived. "Are you okay mom?" Willow asked. "As okay as I can be. He has not returned and in my heart I don't think he will." "Mom, don't say that." Willow told her. "I can't help how I feel Willow. My life has not been an easy one and I will not harbour thoughts fanciful and wonderful." She looked at Willow. "Those" she added "are for the young." Willow knew she had resigned herself to the fact he was gone. "I'll be leaving tomorrow. We need to get things done before the snows come." Willow's mom looked up. "Im sorry your trip had to involve this. We never wanted to interfere in your life." "I know mom, I know." Willow said. "Im off to my husband, he'll be wondering where I am." She told her. Willow's mom stopped spinning "Are you happy Willow with West?" she asked. "Yes I am. He is such a good man. He is always there and is a comfort to me."

Willow's mom started spinning again. "Good, then it is as it should be. I hope the rest of our girls find what you have." She said. "Will you be back in the spring?" she asked. "Yes I believe we will. I'm not sure when, but we will." "Then be off with you" she said. Willow went over and hugged her. She felt sad for her. She got outside and looked back. To be unhappy for so long had to be hard for anyone she thought.

It didn't take her long to reach Jo and Zack's cabin. West was on the porch waiting for her. "How was your mom?" he asked. "It's all so strange. She doesn't seem to be sorry he's gone. Maybe the years of unhappiness have taken their toll on her." West put his arms around Willow "Don't worry, Brad and Gary will find him. Your mom is dealing with it the only way she knows how to." "You are right as always West, whatever would I do without you?" They sat on the porch and watched the sun make its final decent over the horizon and went inside to bed.

West was first up, he had a restless night. Willow's missing father had weighed on him more than he realized. He started the fire and Jo got up. She knew he was troubled. After she had tea ready she sat with him for a while. "Don't worry so West, things will be as they are you are not a superman. He will be found and brought home or he won't be. Either way fretting does nothing. Brad and Gary are good men they will look" West just nodded. "You're right" he said to her. "Let me make you something to eat. I don't get a chance to anymore." She smiled.

Before long everyone was awake and all at the table. Jo had given West a roll of paper and Zack produced a few potted items and carved things for them. Jo had several jars of preserved fruit, small bags of dried tomatoes and herbs. "Next spring I will start some trees for you Willow" Jo told her. Willow smiled. Soon the dishes had been washed and the last of the gear packed.

West and Willow had said all the goodbyes to everyone in the small settlement and started on their way home. When they were on the trail West scanned the forest for any sign of her dad and saw nothing. He was glad to be going home. Willow didn't talk much. The trip had been an odd one filled with sadness and joy. One extreme to the next and both walked and pulled the contemplating everything.

"Well they are on their way" Jo said to Zack. "Yes and we probably won't see them until next spring. When the snow comes it's hard to travel." "What was all that stuff in the wagon?" Jo asked. "It looked fairly weighted down." "Oh he wanted to take the sidewalk tiles I made him and he asked me to make more." Jo smiled at Zack. "I saw the two guys go look again for Willow's father" Zack said. "I hope they find him." Jo nodded. "Yes as do I." "The new family should be arriving today. Maybe I will get the women to get some food together and you go rest." Jo told him. Zack smiled and headed to the porch. "Maybe you could send the children for a while?" Jo nodded.

Soon the children were on their way to see Zack and the women were involved in the preparation of food for the new people.

Lily and Sara wished Willow's mom would come over, but she never did. She pretty much stayed to herself. Jo looked at Sara "Are you okay?" she asked. "Yes quite alright." Sara told her. "Oh my goodness, how far along are you?" Jo asked. Sara looked at her "How do you know that?" she smiled. Jo asked again. "Oh about 2 months now" Sara smiled. The women spent the next couple of hours sharing the work and talking.

It was the children outside that alerted them to the arrival of the people. The women wasted no time in going out to meet them. Zack was walking up the path and was the first to greet them. They looked tired and the men soon had the women on the porch at Jo and Zack's. "How was the journey?" she asked. "I'm Jo and this is Zack." She pointed to Sara and then

Lily. The children were all named and smiled. "You go down to the play area and let the new folks rest. They squealed with joy and ran to play.

"I am Herb and this is my wife Jean, her brother Kalvin and assorted children; June, Rose, Art, Tanner and Sven." "Well, here, sit here and relax."

Food appeared out of no where and soon everyone felt at ease. They all talked and laughed. "We are a small village here. Sara here and her husband Gary, Sara and her husband Brad. The assorted children off there and in the far cabin live our daughter-in-law's parents Duke and Helen and their children. I'm sorry Brad and Gary are not here to greet you, but Duke has been missing for a few days now and they have been out looking for him." "Oh I do hope he is well" Jean said. "I fear he has some troubles. He never seemed to get past the virus outbreak." Jo said. "Oh my dear, there have been many that suffer so. From out on the prairie many suffer such terrible things, but to be locked in the past, how awful. The men are sure to find him." Jean said.

Kalvin listen and then said "I can help look tomorrow. It will give this mob a chance to get settled a bit and me a chance to see the area." "That's good of you Kalvin." Zack said. "I'll tell Brad and Gary when they get back." Zack smiled.

"You have three cabins to pick from; we thought we would let you choose one." Jean's face lit up. "It's like a dream. Everything was such a struggle and all the time you all were here. I am happy to have so much hope for the future." She told them. "My children will now have a future not like before. I am truly a blessed woman." "What are you sitting here for?" Jo said "Come let's go take a look at these cabins." The women got up and headed for them. "Let's give them some time." Herb said. "They will be the ones to decide anyways" and the men laughed. "It's too true, when it comes to a choice like this, best let them decide." Zack said. "We were the first ones here" Zack said "and in the past few years it has grown. It's a good valley. The soil is fertile and with the river there is plenty of water. The weather is fair, so the growing season is good." Kalvin and Herb were glad to here this. "I think you will find Brad and Gary easy to get along with." Zack told them. Kalvin asked "How long has this Duke fellow been gone for?" "He's been missing for over 2 days. Kalvin just nodded. "With the amount of forest out there the chances of finding him now are getting slimmer." "What's in the next valley?" Kalvin asked. "My son West and his wife. That's all at the moment. They have built an extra cabin, but I think they have found some folks for it." "Do you think he went there?"

Kalvin asked. "I don't think so, but one never knows. He's not of his right mind. Who knows where he went. It's his wife Helen and the children I am worried for. West spent the day chopping wood for her, but I'm sure it won't last the winter." "I'll lend a hand there" Kalvin said. "It's good to know your work is not in vain. I think I'll walk about some. You have got this little hamlet running well." "Sure, go ahead" Zack told him. He was going to like Kalvin and Herb.

Jo and Jean returned before too long. Jean was beaming and Herb knew she had picked her new home. It was Herb's turn for the tour to see his home. When he arrived he was surprised at the quality of the cabin. It was fairly large and very well built. The logs had been knocked well and the rooms were large. There was a fire place and 3 rooms up in the loft. Each one of the bed rooms had a bed and the kitchen had a sturdy table with chairs. These folks had gone to great pains for them. There were pots, dishes and hand crafted bed quilts. Herb hugged Jean and said "We have once more a home." She took him outside and showed him the small herb garden. "The private garden and look a root cellar. It can be accessed from the inside as well as the outside. My sweet man we have been given a great gift. God has heard our prayers and seen our suffering and has brought us to find contentment." She hugged her hubby and he felt the joy she had. Life had been so hard on the prairie. There always was the fight to have enough food. The struggle to fight the fires and the losses they had. "Where is Kalvin? I want him to share this." Jean asked Herb. "He went for a stroll. He said he wanted to check out the area." "Well he has always been a loner somewhat. Since he lost his family he has spent many hours alone. I hope he can find some joy." Herb looked at her "We have a new life here as does he and knowing him as I do things will be fine. You will see." He said. "Let's get the wagon and see if we can add our touch to this beautiful home." Herb told her. "When we get settled we will have a gathering and invite everyone to give our heart felt thanks." Jean smiled; she had not felt so happy in such a long time. They set off to get the wagon.

Jo and Zack had Kalvin on the porch drinking tea, when Herb and Jean got there. "Come and have a cup of tea" Jo said. Jean beamed "How can we refuse, you have been more than kind. The cabin is wonderful. I am just… well, I can't tell you." And the tears won over.

Jo patted her hand. Herb sat close. "Now Jean best not let the children see you cry. They will not know they are tears of joy and not of sorrow." Jean wiped her tears and Jo patted her hand again. "We are glad our efforts have made you so happy." And Jean smiled. She took the tea and sipped it.

"When we get settled please come over. I will get the chance to make tea for you all." "We will" Jo assured her "We will."

They soon had the tea done. Kalvin, Herb, Jean and the children pulled the wagon with all their possessions to their new home.

Jo sat with Zack and waited for Brad and Gary. When they came alone fear for Duke's survival was getting slimmer.

Brad walked over to Zack "It's like he vanished. There is no sign at all." "Thank you Brad I will go and tell Helen." Zack got up and made his way to see Helen.

Jo cleared the dishes and knew Zack would tell Helen the news with care and tenderness. When he came home they sat on the porch and watched the sun set. "Life does have its twists and turns" he said to her. "Everyday brings something different to our lives." "Yes it does" Jo answered "Yes it truly does."

Chapter 26

$\mathcal{T}$he days and nights never carried much meaning to the people of the complex. They loved and worked at the hours that felt comfortable for them. Todd found himself in the machine shop more and more. Since Nick passed away the work as a mason did not have the feel to it. He still carved, but now it was a hobby. He was glad Dana was happy to have him working somewhere else. The cave-in gave rise to fear she almost couldn't bear. Elsa her step mother had taken ill and spent her days now resting in the med centre. Dana spent time with her whenever she could.

Dana decided today she would make a lovely meal and have a small get together with her adopted siblings and she wanted Erik, Gwen and Petra to be there. Dirk and Carla were knee deep with animals, so getting Mark and Ann might not be able to happen, but she would try. She spent the day putting everything in order. She wanted everyone to have a good time. The year would soon be over and snow had already been falling on the outside. Soon Christmas would be here and Dana still had so many gifts to finish.

The young were not young anymore almost the age of their parents when the complex was being built; many of them had passed now. The council still consisted of only them, but that would change and with it the opportunity to open the doors to the outside. That dream never left Dana and Todd. With Andy's help they had amassed a great deal of information and Dana had worked endlessly as did Todd. She was waiting patiently for him to arrive at their dorm. She picked up her handiwork and relaxed the best she could.

It was then that Todd arrived home. She was glad to see him. He always gave her heart a pitter patter. "Hi sweetie" Todd said to her and wasted little time getting to her and wrapping his arms about her. He was glad to be home. It had been a long day today. As hard as he worked he still didn't get done what he wanted. The work shop would need the parts he was working on. "So has everyone agreed to come to our get together?" Todd asked. "Indeed they have." She replied. "Well I best get into the shower then before they start arriving." He kissed her forehead and headed to the shower.

Dana felt better now. How could one person change your outlook so fast in life she thought and he did do that to her. Something she was ever grateful for.

It was Gwen and Erik that arrived first. Todd was still changing in the bedroom when he heard them arrive. Erik brought the daily reports from the labs and communications room. Dana put them in the makeshift office that was overflowing with the complex information.

Jake and Fern arrived next. Dana hugged her and asked about Elsa. "She is still not getting better. Hetti is staying with her tonight." Not long after Carl and Rose appeared. They looked well and Dana wondered why they had not started their family yet. Although she had grown up with Jake and Carl she never truly felt like their sister.

Tea and coffee were set up for everyone to help themselves. She had platters of snacks for them to enjoy. Soon Petra arrived, bringing reports from the agro domes. The crowd was getting bigger. Todd by now was in their midst and the conversations varied. To their surprise Ann and Reg arrived, with them the reports from the animal tunnels. Drew from the kitchens and Julia and Stewart from the tailoring station arrived soon after them. Tyler, Dawn, Toni and Jaylene brought things that Andy had sent. Jaylene brought the news from the masons. Drew was the last to arrive and with him a lovely platter from the kitchens. He too had a report from there.

The complex was together. This crowd would someday form the council and all had wanted to return to the outside.

It was Todd who spoke next. "First I want to thank you for all coming. You might think this is a work effort, but not tonight. We want you to relax and enjoy yourselves. You have worked so hard and I think we deserve some off time." And with that they all cheered.

It didn't take long for the conversations to begin, each shared thoughts and ideas. News of the families shared and plans they dreamed of were talked about. The work ethics was high and most took it seriously. They had to, their lives depended on it.

Tonight was a time to relax and soon they did. Dana stood back and watched. She had known these people all her life and it was a comfort to her to see them enjoy themselves.

The even was a pleasant one and around 10 they all started to depart. Work had to be done by the next day and all knew that, by 11:30 they were all gone.

Todd and Dana sat on the couch, they were tired. The evening had gone well and the crowd would be meeting a lot more in the future. It was the team of the future and it would be through them that the complex would be run. "Well dear, what do you think?" Todd asked. "Do you think this mob is ready to be leaders?" he asked again. "I think so, we all know what has to be done and it will be our generation that opens the doors. Time will tell." Todd said. "Yes" Dana replied. "So what do you think?" she asked him. "I think I don't want to think, come here." He said to her and when she did he wrapped his arms around her. "Todd" she said. "Yes Dana, what is it?" "How about tomorrow we spend the day in the atrium. It's been too long since I listened to the birds sing." He smiled "sounds like a plan. I too miss your company. We have been working non stop too long. A break would be nice." They sat for a while and soon the dishes and clean up called to them. It was well after midnight before they went to bed. They shared themselves and after rested comfortably before sleep found them.

With a basket packed and a good night's sleep under their belts they headed to the atrium. The work was left at home and the day was spent enjoying each others company. Todd picked a few flowers and Dana wandered about. She was pleased when he gave her the flowers. They lazed the morning away and at noon lunch was served. "Todd" she asked "Do you think they will agree this time, I mean to open the doors?" "They might." He said. "Well I just feel, well closed in. I have never been outside and I can't believe we were meant to be here forever. It is starting to drive me crazy. It's the same thing every day, day in, day out. I think I know every inch of this place and that's crazy." She said to him. Todd looked at her "I know what you mean. We have to dig new tunnels so often I wish we would just break through to the outside. Part of the reason was Nick's passing. I stopped doing that work. Another was I can't get passed how many others died trapped in the prison of rock." He told her. "That's what this place is to me" she told him "a prison." "Oh we have everything and want for nothing, but there is no real freedom. If you and I feel this way, what about others? Do you think they do too?" Dana asked. "Oh more than likely, but I know my mom and dad fear the outside. I have always seen it in their faces every time we talk about it." Todd said. "I know what you mean, Elsa is like that now, afraid the complex has no use for her now and begging the doctors to let her stay. It's awful really." Dana said. "Andy is partial I think he would vote yes. I have no idea about Carla, Nick, Karen or David. Do you think people might never want to leave Todd?" Dana asked. "Well the children of the founders and the others of the families have never been out. Can you really miss something you have never known?" Todd asked. "I don't know, but I do." She told him. "That's probably because your dad might be out there. You had reason to think about it. I wonder if very many think about it?" Todd replied. "Never think it, they must" she said. "Not everyone believes we should. Talk to them; ask the children if they have any or if their families have ever talked about it. The terror the parents feel about it has been passed down. Outside is taboo. It was for everyone's safety." Todd told her. "Oh sometimes I could just cry" she said to him. "Dana what ever will I do with you?" Todd said. "We stick to the game plan and prove the outside is safe. Squash the fears and provide concrete evidence its okay. Don't give up, we keep at it." Todd told her.

They were both lying on the blanket watching the birds and butterflies. The birds, so tame now came close and often would permit Dana or those who frequented the atrium to hold them. Dana drifted off to sleep and soon found herself in a great forest. The trees so tall they shaded out most of the sun. The ground was covered with pine needles. Years of them growing as such prevent much undergrowth. She wandered aimlessly among them, marvelling at their size. Then she felt afraid and the fear was becoming overwhelming. Out of no where there was this huge bison. It snorted at her and stomped the ground and before she knew it the thing was after her. Dana didn't know what to do. Running, she couldn't escape. She clung to one of the massive trees and realized she could climb it. The bark was gnarly and she could just get enough to climb. The great beast of a bison roared passed underneath her. Fear drove her to climb higher. The bison snorted as if to wonder where she went. It wandered around the nearby trees and bellowed.

"Dana, Dana!" Todd called her out of the dream. "Are you okay?" he asked. It took Dana a few moments to gather her wits about her. "Yes Todd I am. I just had a bad dream." "It must have been a dilly. You were not looking like it was a good one." He smiled at her. "No it wasn't" she said.

"Do you want to talk about it?" he asked her. "No it was just a dream. How long have I been sleeping?" "A couple hours, I let you rest. You must have needed it." He smiled. "Let's go Todd I want to go home." The dream had startled her more than she was letting on. "Sure" Todd told her. Soon they had their belongings picked up and left the area as they found it.

The walk back to their dorm didn't take long and Dana drew a hot bath once inside. Todd knew she was troubled and when she was ready she would tell him. He made hot chocolate and took some into her. "I think I'll head to talk with Andy. I have been thinking about what you said about some never wanting to leave." "Thank you for the hot chocolate Todd. I won't stay in here long" she told him. "You relax" he told her, on that he kissed her forehead and headed out. Dana laid there in the tub. She would have to talk to one of the doctors. If this kept up, she thought she would go crazy.

After a bit of a soak she got dressed. She wandered around the dorm and found herself at the desk with all the new reports. She towel dried her hair and as she brushed out her hair she was drawn back to the reports. Before long she was reading them. Each report was becoming the same. There was nothing to hurt them outside, it had been a year and still nothing. Dana thought about what Todd had said about some not caring about the outside. If it never was how could they miss it? Those words rang in her ears and mind. That's the big problem she thought being in here made the old safe and in turn made the outside unsafe for the children they had. At first this was the case, but not now.

Todd had come home and they sat and talked till early morning, Dana with her ideas and Todd with his information from Andy. "Dana let's call it a night we have been at this for hours." She set down the reports and smiled, she had a plan and now just how to work out the details. She got up and made her way to bed. Todd was there and they cuddled to each other and slept.

Todd was up and at work early, he let Dana sleep. She woke late and after a brief shower made her way to the medical labs.

When she got there she almost had second thoughts about going, but was soon ushered into an office to talk with a doctor. He was an older man and wore glasses on the tip of his nose. His hair was salt and pepper grey. Dana knew he was one of the founders.

"Dana isn't it?" he asked. Dana replied "Yes." "What brings you here? I can say I have not seen much of you." He asked. "A few things" Dana replied "I'm really not sure where to start." She said. He looked up and said "How about at the beginning" he said and smiled. "Alright" she said "First off I just want to know, did you ever live outside?" she asked him. He sat back and put his hands behind his head. "Yes I did' he answered. "Do you ever miss it, I mean the outside?" Dana inquired. "Yes often, but it does no good to dwell on it. The door will not open until it is safe out there." He told her. "With all the research I have done it seems it is safe to go out." He looked at her "Did you know it wasn't one virus that killed the entire world?" he told her. "No I didn't. All the reports never said anything like that, it shows only one virus." She answered. "Well it is now, but when it was set upon the world it was actually three different ones. They got it all wrong the viruses mutated together and in a sense merged as one. It was that combination that was what killed everything." He told her. "How come that wasn't in any of the reports?" she asked. "It didn't seem relevant after the fact. Im sure you realize it may run into another virus and mutate again." He told her. "No one is sure how many countries let go their biological weapons and what form it will finally mutate to." He told her. "Oh my God!" Dana said. "Yes I agree" he said. "Mind the reports" he told her. "I have seen it to be stable at the moment. If it stays as such for another year or so, I'm sure the complex will start venturing out of here." "That's what brings me to my visit." She said. "I'm feeling well closed in. We work and sleep and try to entertain ourselves with what's here, but I feel constricted like I'm in a prison." She said. "Well, you and more than half the folks feel it too. The others have become, in a word institutionalized. They are completely content and have great fear of the outside. They would be able to stay here their whole life and never think twice. You are not alone Dana." "What is there that can be done about it? Sometimes I feel so trapped in here." "There is not mot much I can prescribe. Some relax therapy, but it has to be put right inside you or it will not go away." The doctor told her. "What would happen if the door would open to those that have no wish to go out?" Dana asked. "Not much, I think they would just stay in" the doctor replied.

"I wanted to ask you about my mother too" Dana said. "Ahhh Dee, a delightful woman as I remember. Smart, talented, quick witted, you knew where you stood with her." He replied. "What exactly happened to her, why did she die?" Dana asked. "It was a combination of things really" he told her. "The virus outbreak, the loss of Zack and she had some trouble in her birthing. There was a loss of blood, she gave up. There were too many losses for her to handle in her state. I always believed you knew this Dana." He said. "I just wanted to make sure. I am married now and have been for some time. I just… never mind" she said and got up. "Thank you very much for your time." Dana told him.

Dana wandered into the main living area and watched the collection of people; the children swimming, the mothers doting after them, their squeals of pleasure as they enjoyed the water. The younger folks were playing tennis and basketball. The older were sitting together on the benches watching all as she did.

She glanced at all the statues Rainie had carved and the meaning each held. The vast walkways to the kitchens, library and schools always seemed to have people travelling them. Dana pondered what the doctor had said that a lot of people never even thought of a life outside. They lived contently here and she could understand why. Todd's statement how could they miss something they never knew rang its tone in her head. They were safe and if the virus did mature again who would suffer.

She looked at the children with their mothers and fathers. Her glance passed over the old folks. What if they had another great passage of folks into death, who of all these left would be able to sustain the complex? It had taken years to fill the stations left by the first onslaught of it.

It seems things were getting so clear. Had she and Todd been pursuing a folly that should be left to the next generations? The weight of these thoughts was heavy.

Dana got up and wandered to the communications labs. She sat watching the monitors. Erik stopped in several times and soon he came with some papers for her to read. "Dana I thought you might like to read these." He said. "What are they?" she asked. "They are logs to the monitors. We have been noting some interesting things." He set the papers in front of her and with a smiled said "I hope you find them as interesting as we did." She thanked Erik and proceeded to read.

In the past month we have noted the following animals to be alive and well outside. The list included deer, squirrels, birds, moths, mice, fox, and snakes. It was impressive, if these had survived then it was safer outside. She kept reading, the squirrels are travelling in small groups as are the birds in flocks. They are reproducing, how wonderful. The experimental valley was enclosed with the mountains, all around many animals would never venture that high up or over. The birds may fly, but seemed to be hovering near the complex.

This was indeed great news and she gathered up the papers and went in search of Erik. "Erik!" she called to him as he headed down the hallway. He stopped and waited for her. By the smile on her face he could tell she was glad of the news. "Mind if I take this to show Dirk? I'm sure he would want to know how his animals are indeed surviving." Dana asked. "Sure go ahead it will be in the next report anyways. I am waiting to see if they survive the winter." He smiled.

Dana was soon on her way to see Dirk. It was good news' she knew Dirk would be happy. He felt animals should be in their own habitats, but he knew his grand nursery might be the last vestiges of the world's population of them.

Dana arrived at the animal tunnels and found Dirk busy as usual with the sheep. The sheering had been done and he was giving them the look over to see all was well. "My goodness if it isn't my Dana" he said with a smile. "I'll be finished here in a moment. Go inside and get Carla to brew some tea would you?"

Dana nodded and headed to their office dorm. Carla was happy to see her and had tea on in no time. Dana sat at the table and before long Dirk was there. "I brought some reports I thought you might like to read." She smiled. Carla and Dirk both read and smiled while reading. "It seems our work has not been in vain." Dirk smiled. "Well it's a grand promise that's for sure. There is still winter and then we will see how sturdy our stock is." He smiled.

The next hour or so was spent in conversation. Dirk teased Dana that she should be with child. Carl scorned him for involving himself in her private affairs. Dana never minded "Well" she finally said "I must go home Todd will be there and I have much to share with him." Dirk and Carla remained seated and Dana half hurriedly headed home.

Todd, still in the work shop had been making parts for the new saw. The carpenters had worked the old one passed redemption. It wasn't a complicated machine to make, but had many parts that worked together to make it run. He sat looking at the diagrams of the parts and felt sure he could have them done the next day. When he glanced at the clock he knew he had worked enough for one day and set his work table to be ready for the completion tomorrow. He cleaned up a bit and headed for their dorm.

Dana was there when he arrived and it didn't take long before she had him sitting the table indulging in a meal. "So what's up?" he asked knowing Dana as he did. He knew she had something to say. "Well I went to see the doctor today to ask about things" she said "I found that I'm not the only one that feels closed in here, lots do, but then there are lots that don't, just like you" she said. "I did find out that the virus is not just one; it was three that mutated into one that devastated everything."

"That's interesting" Todd said. "Why is that not in the reports?" he asked. "It seems that just the founders knew about it. It could explain why they are so adamant about not opening the doors." Dana told him. "After that I headed to the communications labs and Erik gave me some good news." She told him. "Which was?" Todd asked. "Most of the animals we let out are doing just fine and have reproduced." She smiled. "I went to see Dirk and Carla and told them as well. It was such good news." She said. "It is good news." Todd replied. "Oh and I went for a walk after I came out of the doctors. I think I'm a bit more resolved, well maybe not in such a rush now to get the gates open. There is such a great deal at risk, things I should have paid more attention too." Dana told him. "It's been a really remarkable day for you then." He said. "All I did was work on making a new saw for the work shop." Then he winked at her.

After she cleaned up the dishes they sat and cuddled on the couch. "Dana" Todd asked "Do you want to have children?" He said to her. She looked at him "I think I do, I'm kinda scared, but with you here I think all will be well. If it happens it does." Todd smiled. "I hope we have a girl when we do. I think I would like a little Dana running around." They laughed.

Life had taken a turn for Dana and something gave her peace within herself. Having Todd, the responsibility of caring for all who lived in the complex and the closeness of her dear friends changed something within her. She knew the next step to getting to the outside world would be slow and life in the complex was not all that bad.

Todd picked her up and carried her to bed. They shared a loving night with tenderness and thoughtfulness, both resting comfortably afterwards before sleep took over.

The morning found Dana in bed alone and Todd long since gone to work. She laid there feeling warm and secure. Her mind wandered over things in her life and her thoughts drifted to Rainie. Rainie was never resolved to living in the complex. She did what she had to, but her heart was never there. Dana could see that even though most could not. There was unhappiness there inside Rainie and Dana never wanted that for herself. She counted her blessings and thought of all the future could bring for her. At the conclusion of her thoughts she felt comfort at the fact she was alive, loved and cared for by many. She got up and showered.

She was off to see Andy and see what his views were of the complex. Then she was going to all the founders. Not knowing if the views they held were through fear and stubbornness, but care and concern. She wanted to get a bigger picture of life in general.

Todd working in the machine shop had been busy the entire morning. He was making the last piece to the saw and his mind drifted to Dana. He wanted her to want children and it seems she had crossed the threshold of fear holding her back. Todd wondered how many children they would have. He thought four was a good number. Then he smiled. He had completed the piece he was working on and set it with the others. He glanced over all the parts and decided to rebuild it in the wood craft area. The parts would be easier to move there.

His thoughts moved back to Dana. He was a lucky man to have her. She was thoughtful, kind, loving and dedicated. Maybe she was right about things. He didn't want her to lose hope about getting outside. From reading Simion's papers he knew people needed the fresh air and sunlight. This temporary shelter had turned into a permanent residence for many.

It wasn't long until he had all the parts wrapped and on their way. She was certainly right about the monotony of the complex. He felt it too. The question was how you consign yourself to never going outside or even wanting too. All the history he ever read placed mankind as adventurers and explorers. He now had the parts on their way. He washed up and decided to go to the science labs. He had an idea that might do some good.

He wasted no time getting to the labs. "Erik, my good man." "Hey there Todd" Erik replied. "Sit, sit" Erik told him. "How's the family?" Todd asked. "Growing fast, too fast" Erik smiled. "What brings you here?" he asked. "I was wondering do the robotic cars still do the sampling outside." Todd asked. "Yes they do." Erik replied. "They're marvellous, we just sit here and they go where we can't." "How long do you think it will be with all clear before we might test the water, so to speak?" "5 to 10 years I would think" Erik replied. "It's still a long wait then?" Todd said. "It's just been a few years since the virus went through here. If it stays clear for a decade we should be able to open up. So when are you starting your family?" Erik asked. "When it happens I guess." The two smiled. "Well thanks Erik, take care my friend." Todd left and Erik headed home.

He was going to start a wish list, all the things that Dana and himself would do when they opened the doors. Before long he was home and found it empty. Dana was not home yet. He showered and got fresh clothes on.

Dana was in the library with Andy and she really noticed how old he was getting. He was a man of knowledge that's for sure and his helpers always kept on their toes with learning new things every day. They spent a lovely afternoon discussing everything from the present, years in the past and to years in the future. He had told her not to give up her quest to once again be outside. She was right in what she thought all the founders agreed, but to take care not to without checking everything they could first. The survival of mankind may depend on it. She thanked Andy for his time and ventured towards home. She knew it would be years before her dream would be fulfilled. Just what was she supposed to do to fill her time?

News spread out through the complex that the masons had broken through to an open cavern. Todd was one of the first to hear. He was home relaxing. He was about to go find Dana when she appeared at their doorway. She too heard already. "Todd did you hear?" she asked as she hugged him. "Yes I did I was about to go in search of you." He told her. "How long before we will be able to see it? I wonder." Todd told her. "I don't know. It will have to be deemed safe first, but I imagine not too long." Todd told her. "So just where have you been all day?" Todd asked. "I went to see Andy. He is a wonderful man." Dana told him. "We had a grand chat, he's really an intelligent person." She smiled. "So how did your day go?" Dana asked. "Oh I suppose well, I got the saw finished." He told her. She had a nice meal on the go and then asked Todd "Do you think we can go later and have a look at the cavern, just a sneak peek? The last one found was when they built this place. I kinda want to see it before it's like the rest of the place." She said. "What do you mean?" Todd asked. "Well in its natural form, not like everything else made to suit us." Todd looked at her. He knew the cavern was most likely safe it had been there since the mountain itself and he could tell it sparked some excitement in her. "Alright I will talk to some of the masons." He told her. She smiled and giggled "I feel like a bad little kid" Then laughed aloud.

The next day found Todd and Dana talking with the masons. They had granted them access because Todd spent many years working with them. They had been over the cavern all night and felt it was safe.

Todd and Dana dawned hard hats with lights and safety gear. They soon found themselves lowered down to the new tunnel floor. It was a massive cavern. The talk of the masons was to leave it as it was and just build a new platform above. Dana was a little scared and stuck close to Todd. He sensed her fear and took his time making sure foot holds and hand holds were good for her. Dana couldn't believe what she was seeing. It was so ancient in there. There were huge stalagmites and stalactites, some strange rock formations that she could have dreamed of.

"Look here" Todd said. "It's a crawl space. Want to go have a look?" he said. "Sure" she told him. Her nerves made her tremble some. Todd squeezed through and called back "Come sit here with me" and she did. He held her hand and said "Turn off your light." He turned off his light and kept holding her hand. She too turned hers off. It was total darkness. "Oh my goodness I can't see you right beside me." She told him. "Yeah kinda eerie isn't it?" and turned his light back on. Dana followed suit. "It's almost cold in here" she said. "Not almost, it is cold. Put on the extra shirt I got you to bring." He smiled at her. "I was wondering about that" she said. It didn't take them long to add the extra clothing they brought. Todd had been looking over the cavern they were now in. The rocks he was standing on gave way, he never fell, but they revealed another small space. "Hmmm" he said. "Are you okay?" Dana asked. "Yeah, but check this out. It looks like they missed this." He pointed to an opening. "Let's go see" Dana said. Todd, all to familiar with cave-ins was reluctant to go further. "I really don't think we should. It might not be safe" he told her. "We can look a bit please" she asked. "It's our discovery" she said. "I feel like a great explorer." Todd looked at her "You have spent too much time with Andy." He said with a smile. "Okay I'll go have a look. If it's iffy we leave. Understand?" he said to her. "Got it" she said.

Todd moved a few more rocks to make the passage a bit larger. He manoeuvred his way in and to his surprise there was another room larger than the one they had just came from. He took his time looking it over. He wasn't bringing Dana in here until he was sure within himself it was okay. After 15 minutes Dana called to him. "You okay in there?" she asked. "Yeah" he called back. "Just a second" and called back for her to join him. "Mark the way" and Dana sprayed a heart shape at the entrance. She soon found herself with Todd and the two stared in awe at the cavern. "I wonder how far this thing goes?" she said. "It might go for miles." Todd told her. "Might be this one ends too."

They sat there together and talked of how old it might and where it might lead. "We should go back" Todd told her. "Todd" Dana said "Can we keep this place as our secret place? It's nice to have somewhere where no one has been before." Todd looked at her "They will no doubt find it soon you know?" he replied. "Not if we cover up the entrance." "Dana!" Todd said. She looked at him "Who would ever know?" she said. She was serious Todd knew that. "Okay, okay" he finally relented, "but stay away from here." He told her. "I will not come here without you. It's our place, alright?" she said. "Promise me that Dana and I mean promise me."

Todd said. She knew by his tone that he meant business. "I promise" she said. Todd had never had reason to doubt her word and the two formed a pact.

They made their way out and they concealed the entrance. They climbed out and traversed the ropes to the top. Both covered in dirt, but of good cheer. The masons asked Dana how she liked it and she smiled. "It's wonderful; I hope you leave it the way it is. It's really quite remarkable." She looked at Todd. He was seeing a side of Dana he never dreamed he would see. She was devious it was a surprise to him. He didn't think revealing their little cave was too detrimental and it gave Dana such a thrill. In a ways he too like the fact they had a place no one had been to. It made their place private and concealed.

They made their way home and wasted no time showering off the dirt. They sat at the table long after eating and talked of the small cavern they found. Todd finally said "We need to map it so we always know where any tunnels are, if there are any" he told her. "How are you going to have our comings and goings not look too obvious?" she asked. "Just how often are we going there?" he smiled. "Oh, I'm so excited, an adventure, our adventure. I can't believe it. We are going where no one here had been, maybe no one ever. It's scary and thrilling" she said. "So our adventure begins then" Todd said. Then Todd added "Not until weeks end. I have work to do and I might add that you have not been at work for some time." Dana smiled. "Well tomorrow knows not where I will be" and she added "most likely at the tailor shop." They laughed.

The following day found them both at work. Todd building the new saw and Dana in the tailor shop. Dana was busy with the newly harvested cotton. The process wasn't to long and soon she and the others had it all cleaned and ready to start spinning. Work went by quickly the day seemed short. Dana found pleasure in her day. She thought often of the cave.

Todd was not having such a good day; he rebuilding of the new saw was proving to be a pain. By days end he had it together and was glad of it. He headed home and he was tired

When he arrived, Dana had a nice meal started "Hi there handsome. How did your day go?" she asked. "Long, it was a long frustrating day." She looked at him. He did look tired. "I can finish the dinner, you go have a shower." She said. He made his way to the show. It did feel good. Soon his frustrations went down the drain with the soap suds. When he ventured out Dana had a lovely table set. "Looks good Dana" he said. "Thanks, after dinner do you want to go for a walk?" she asked. "Sure" Todd told her.

"Where is it you want to walk to?" he asked. "Oh lets wander and see where it takes us. How about we start at the library?" Todd raised an eyebrow. Just what is she up too? He thought. "Sounds good" he answered.

In no time she cleaned up and they headed to the library. "So just what are you looking for in the library?" "I want to see the plans of this place" she said. "Right from the beginning when they discovered the first cavern. I want to know how these form and what there is about them." Todd had to agree with learning about them, but he wasn't sure she wasn't going overboard on it. He wanted her to have a distraction, but maybe this was way too much.

They reached the library. It didn't take Dana long to have a pile of records for them to start looking over. Andy came over and inquired as to what they were looking for. Dana wasted no time in telling him about the new cavern. She went on telling him one cavern was a discovery and two, well there might be more. "Andy do you know what causes them to form in the first place?"

Andy pulled up a chair "Well" he said. "From what I read, all these mountains were pushed up when 2 plates of land met. The land here was once, way back when, covered by an inland sea. They were formed by water. As sea levels went down and land went up underground rivers were formed. The water carved its way through the softer rock through time." Dana looked at him. "There's water with the first cavern Dirk adapted it into the fish farms, is that water coming from the outside then?" "At first we thought that" Andy told them, "But it seemed to be an underground river fed by a glacier. There is no great threat posted by it." "That's great to know." "I have had a long day. You enjoy your research" Andy said and got up. "Thank you Andy. You know so much" Dana said. He smiled and left them alone to study the paperwork in front of them. "Dana just what are you up too anyways?" Todd asked. She looked at him "Up too?" she asked. "Nothing, I just want to know more about the caverns. They are so strange. Here look at this." She showed him the papers. "According to this the caverns are east to west. Todd I haven't been this excited about anything in my whole life with the exception of you." She smiled. Todd soon was enjoying himself and the two cooked many things to give them call to be in the caverns. Science first would be the agreed reason the two would adventure into the cavern.

Two weeks past in much the same routine, when they finally got the chance to go back they were a bit better prepared. They entered their secret cave and had lamps set to give off more light. It was a beautiful place in many areas the rocks shimmered with the flickering of the light. Dana brought a drop sheet made thick to give them a more comfortable place to sit. They had dried food and water. They spent hours looking over the spacious cavern. There was no water here like in the first cavern so it must be higher. The two relaxed and found the quiet soothing. "I never realized just how noisy the complex is." Todd told her. "I know" Dana said. "It's so nice. I like it you can think here. Be at peace in your mind." She said to him. "I agree, let's get some samples to take back for the labs. When they finish with it they can send it to the school. It will give the teachers something new to teach with." Todd said. Before long he had hammered a few pieces of rock to take back. The blanket, food and lights were left behind and the extra ropes. No sense in packing it back up just to bring it down again.

They brought the samples to the science labs. The masons had not found any useable ore so it was agreed a viewing stand would be built and the cavern left basically they way it was.

The lab checked the samples and they soon made their way to the schools for the children to see. The cotton had been spun and the weaving was next. The tailors would be happy for the new supply of cloth.

Todd's work never seemed to end. New machinery was starting to become an all the time thing. Even with the care that had been taken with them they were starting to wear out. He was thankful the masons had found the vein of ore, it had been a great help. The wood on the other hand had got down and the trees in the tunnels had not reached the age to cut. For a place that was self sufficient it still had its troubles.

Dana had been working hard and the cavern had provided just the distraction she needed. Her renewed energy had brought many benefits to the complex. She had all the cotton done and the tailors were very busy making anything needed from the cloth. They found some time to work on the papers piling up in their dorm. Dana worked on them more than Todd.

At weeks end Todd found Dana preparing another trip to the cavern. Armed with mapping tools and extra food, she rushed him to hurry up. Todd hurried and soon they were being lowered into the cavern. After checking there was no one around them, they uncovered the entrance to their little cave and went in, Todd always taking the lead.

Once inside Dana started measuring the small cavern. Todd helped, he didn't have much of a choice, but he cooperated with a smile. To see her happy made it all worth while. After marking everything they saw on the blanket Dana had brought on a previous trip there. Dana sat beside Todd who was leaning against the wall. She was eating an apple when she saw her hair move as if Todd was blowing on it. "Stop that please." She said. "Stop what?" he asked wondering what she was talking about. "Stop blowing on me" she said again. "I'm not blowing on you." He said. "It must be your imagination." He told her. Dana sat there not moving "Yeah maybe you are right" she said. Then she felt it again. She stood up quickly. "There's a draft in here" she told him. "Dana please don't let you imagination get away on you. Down in the tunnels men and women think they heard things or felt things."

Dana knew she felt it. She saw the bangs of her hair move. "Todd I'm telling you there's a draft." He got up and went to where she was sitting. After a moment or two he said "See, nothing. It's your imagination." She looked at him and then sat beside him. "I guess you are right" she said and then it happened again. This time Todd saw it. "Oh, my God! There is a draft, but where is it coming from?" They looked at each other and started examining the walls. They found a crack behind a protruding rock and after about an hour, they chipped away enough of the area for Todd to squeeze through. It was a small tunnel, not too small so you would feel trapped, but not big enough to do anything other than crawl. Todd went about 50 feet and the tunnel started to descend. Rather than go any further he headed back.

Dana couldn't really see down the tunnel and was relieved to see Toad come back. "What's up there?" she asked. "Not much. The tunnel starts to descend after about 50 feet. I didn't want to go that far. I'm not geared right."

Dana helped him back into their cave and Todd secured a line to the floor. He had on a belt he guided the rope through and donned a hard hat that had a new light on it. He squeezed back into the tunnel and followed it. The descent was not too bad and would be an easy climb back up. After about 100 yards the tunnel opened into another cavern. This was the reason for the cave-ins he thought. The place was riddled with small caves. When he shone the light around him, he could see quartz crystals everywhere. It looked like something out of a fairy tale. Dana had to see this he said. As he looked around he saw another opening. He edged his way over and found it to go down quite a ways. I will have to look there next time he thought.

He called for Dana to come down the tunnel. She attached a rope and entered where Todd had. It was easier for her as she was smaller. As she made her way to him she felt so weird. What was this place and where would it take them? She edged down the decline and found herself in total awe. The crystals shone like glass. The citron was amber coloured and glistened. She had never seen anything like it. "It's beautiful" she said to Todd. "Yes it is" he replied. "Don't go over there. It continues on, but it's quite steep." She nodded.

She touched the quarts crystals and marvelled. "How could anything this beautiful be way in here?" she said. Todd smiled. He too could see the endless beauty they held. "Well this is where the draft is coming from. There must be a river causing it." Todd told her. "I can't hear any water, can you?" she asked. "No not at all, but it's probably near. Okay you did bring the writing tablets and pens? We need to map this out. Where's that compass?" he asked. She handed it to him. After standing and checking the compass he mad a drawing of a tunnel. "Do you think we should take some of these back" Dana asked. "We can, but how are we going to explain where they came from? We would have to reveal our cave. Do you want to do that?" he asked. "No I don't, but can we take a piece of each for our bedroom?" she asked. "Sure, why not" he said "not likely they will ever be seen there." She almost jumped for joy, but the ceiling prevented that act. Todd went over with a hammer and chipped a piece from each and handed them to her. She gingerly wrapped them and stowed them in her pockets. "It looks like we have a real adventure here." He said. "We have to bring some different gear the next time. A rope ladder might be a good idea too, but I will have to see how far down it goes first." Dana smiled. Todd knew the tunnels and how to explore them. She was thankful for it. She would never have adventured in had he not been sure it was safe. His bravery and knowledge was a great comfort to her

After spending another hour in the cave they made their way back. Before long they were sitting in their cave. Both were in quiet contemplation of what they had found and the impression it left was immense. It didn't take long to clear the area around the opening and move out to the main cavern. They concealed the entrance and climbed the way up. "A ladder here would make this easier" Dana said. "I agree. I will talk with the masons about it" Todd said to her. She smiled.

At this point she wanted a shower and a closer look at the rocks they had found. After a few words with the masons, Todd soon joined her again. "Well we are back to the land of the living" Todd said. "Yes I know what you mean" Dana said. They walked arm in arm and talked of their discovery.

Soon they raced to see who would get the shower first. Dana won first dibs. Todd washed his hands and face while he waited on Dana, he filled the coffee machine. The coffee was almost done when Dana finished her shower. She got out and with a kiss on her forehead, he got in. "The coffee is almost done" he told her and turned on the water. Dana dug the rocks from her pockets and went into the kitchen area. She set them on the counter. She would wash them after Todd finished his shower. She poured a coffee and sat at the table. After a few sips she went to the rocks. Treasures she thought and the stories of the explorers; of pirates she had read about when she was young. It was amazing how these beautiful things could be in some dark underground cave. They would still be there had they not stumbled across them, their beauty unknown still.

Todd soon finished his shower and she turned on the water. Soon the dirt was off and the rocks were more brilliant than Dana could have imagined. "Some nice little memoirs you will be able to tell our children of our adventures." Todd said and smiled. "Oh don't worry they will know." Dana said. "They! So we are having more than one." Todd kidded her. "I wish I would get pregnant soon. I'm beginning to think something is wrong." Dana said. Todd was standing close and reached over and lifted her chin. He kissed her forehead and then her cheek "Don't worry it will happen when it does. In the mean time we can enjoy ourselves" he said to her. "I know, but every woman should have one or more children. We have to keep the lines going" Dana told him. Todd looked at her "I don't want you to have children out of responsibility or some line must be continued." He said. "I know" she told him. "I do have other commitments other than our love." She said. "That didn't come out right" she looked down at her feet. "I am the only thing left of my mother and father. For them not to be lost I have to have a child. It keeps them alive in some way." Dana said. Todd looked at her "Dana!" he said. "Just let it go and stop worrying. I'm sure it will happen when it is supposed to."

He smiled and picked her up and carried to bed. He lay to rest any fears she ever had with tenderness and consideration for her. Todd loved her and she loved him. Both slept comfortably.

Morning found them rested and relaxed. "Good morning there" Todd said to her. "Morning" Dana replied. "How about some coffee?" he told her. "Oh that would be lovely" Dana told her. He kissed her and rolled out of bed. He put the coffee on and washed up. By the time the coffee was ready he was dressed and ready to go. He brought Dana a cup of coffee. "I'm off" he told her "I have to get some things done at the shop." She sat up and sipped the coffee. "You work too much" she said. "Somebody has to around here" he said and smiled. "What are you going to do today?" he asked her. "Oh I thought I would go see Dirk." "Alright I will catch up with you later" he kissed her and was on his way. Dana lay there and drank her coffee. She showered and dressed after she finished.

She walked to the animal tunnels and all the while she thought of the cavern. The beauty still stuck profoundly in her mind. The faint breeze she felt was natural not from an air filter fan. It was raw nature and something inside her felt free somehow.

Dana arrived at the animal tunnel and went in search for Dirk. She found him in the stables. He was tending some horses. They were magnificent creatures and Dirk cared so well for them. "Hey there little one" Dirk said to her. "Long time no see" he said. "Hi Dirk" Dana said and went over and hugged him. "I've been kinda busy studying the new cavern." She told him. "How do you fare? Anything interesting?" Dirk asked. "As a matter of fact I did come here to talk to you about them." Dirk looked at her over the horse he was brushing. "It seems strange to find another cavern." "The one you converted to the fish farm has a big pool in it and the other one doesn't. I just wondered why, if the water created them in the first place, why the second cavern not have any water now." "It must be higher in elevation." Dirk said. "The water in the first is fed by an underground river that starts at the glacier in the mountains." "Do you think we might find more caverns in the future?" She asked. "It's possible. I guess it depends on the rock. Sandstone is a soft rock and water over time is washed away" he said. "Here let me show you" he set the brush down and they both went to the fish farm. "See here?" and he broke a piece of sandstone from the edge of the pool. "This is sandstone, but all the walls and ceiling are granite. The pockets of sandstone have almost completely been washed away over the eons it took to create this." "Do you think we will find more caves?" she asked. "It's a possibility, but what is the question?" he asked her. "Are they joined, I meant this one and the new one?" she asked. "They most likely are, the water was there first then here. The river may be making new caverns as we speak" he said. "Where does the water go?" she asked. "They looked at that when we found this place. It connects to a river and joins underground. It never comes to the surface" he told her. "You know it just amazes me how many things I find out about this place still" she said. "Yes it is a wondrous place that's for sure. It took a long time to get it to what it is." He smiled.

"Now come, let us go find something to eat. Carla will have some food ready by now." He was right Carla had sandwiches ready. She smiled when she saw them coming. "Dana dear it's been so long since your last visit." Carla said to her. Dana smiled "I have missed you too. How's the family?" Dana asked. "Busy, too busy with the animals." "I don't know how you do it." Dana said. "Years of practice, years of practice." They enjoyed lunch and after Dana headed to the communications lab.

She found her chair and watched the monitors for a while. Snow was falling and Dana couldn't imagine what it would be like to be out in the snow. Well enough of this she thought and decided to go to the tailor station.

When she arrived the tailors were busy with all the new material. Dana sat at the sewing machine and began to do some piece work.

Todd had not gone to work he had gone to the masons. He had a ladder made and took the supplies he needed down to the cavern floor. A breeze coming in could mean only one thing. Air was getting in from the outside. Since the cavern was open to the complex anything that would have happened would have happened by now. He got the rigging set up. Todd was not going to tell Dana. He was going to see where the caves went to. He would not cave traverse alone, but getting everything ready for when Dana next went there and that would be soon.

It was late afternoon before he felt he had everything they needed. He leaned against the wall and thought about everything. Air from the outside was coming in; they had jeopardized the whole complex. If anyone got sick it would be on them, but two weeks had passed and no one showed anything, Maybe this thing should be called off. He should go and talk to someone, but who he thought? They would be punished, ostracized if anyone got sick. Andy came clear in his mind. He would talk to him.

He made his way to the library. Andy was there like a pillar in time. Andy was likely the man that knew the most about the complex now. When Todd approached Andy looked up from his papers and smiled. "Well young man what brings you here again?" "Andy, I need to talk to you. Can we go into your office?" Todd asked him. "Hmmm this sounds serious" Andy said as he motioned for him to go into his office. Todd went in and the door closed behind them. "Coffee Todd?" Andy asked now pouring one for himself. "No thanks" Todd replied. "Sit down and tell me what seems to have you so troubled" Andy told him. "I hardly know where to begin" Todd said. "Well how about at the beginning" Andy smiled. "I think we have started something that may cause harm to the whole complex." Andy looked at him. "How is it that you think the complex is in danger?" "Well I don't think it matters now, it might already be too late" Todd said. "Listen my boy, you aren't making sense. What's happened?" Andy asked. "Okay, okay. You know the new caverns they found?" Todd asked. "Of course Todd." Andy said. "Well Dana and I have been exploring it and it was Dana that noticed a draft." Andy's eyebrow went up "A draft you say?" "Yes it was a faint, hardly noticeable, but I can confirm a draft." Andy just sat there for a moment. "Well you are right it could be a danger, but the cavern has been open for some time and as of now there have been no ill effects. With the cavern being the size it is there are probably many places air could be getting in. Other than sealing it off there is not much we can do. All the caverns are connected it could seep through else where." "Well let me think on this for a bit. You may want to keep this under wraps until I look over all alternatives Todd." "Thank you again Andy. I'm glad I told you." "Does Dana know the air might be from outside?" "No I don't think so. I never wanted to panic her." "It would create a panic that's for sure." "You go get a pot of tea and bring it back. By then I will have some thought on this." Todd left Andy.

Andy picked up all the reports he had on the virus. It didn't take long before he came to the conclusion that the air could not be stopped now. If it had any damaging microbes they would have done any damage that they were going to do by now. To tell the founders would have them seal things so tight.

Andy's thoughts drifted to Simion and the talks they shared, how fear would rule out over common sense. Dana, Todd, Erik, Gwen, and Petra all the young people need to have hope. The older folks held too much fear.

Tap, Tap "It's me Andy" and Todd appeared with a tray. "Sit down here will you Todd. I am going to relate to you a conversation I had many years ago." Todd sat and listened. Andy began telling him of his close relationship with Simion. "We often talked of the future for all concerned. After the outbreak we had several conversations about exactly things like this. Simion knew that the fear of death would be so frightening for them that they would not be able to look beyond. He was right, most just existed here. They don't think about the outside or not very often. The world is a wondrous place. It has many beauties beyond our comprehension. Simion also knew that some would never be happy here. They would be the minority. Simion also confided in me that the virus had done its worst and time would not change it. It works on DNA, nothing could cure it. If you had a particular code you would live. Now you know I have always been for opening of the place" Andy looked at Todd "It is my opinion that this conversation never goes anywhere. It stays here. The animals have survived as will we, but fear will cause panic, etc...Do you understand this Todd?" Andy asked.

Todd was astounded, he knew that Andy was the one to talk to, but he never expected him to say what he did. "I understand" Todd told him. Andy looked at him and said "and so it begins" and smiled. "I don't understand" Todd told him. "It's okay my boy you aren't supposed to." "Well, I must go meet Dana." Todd told Andy. "Alright you go; fill me in on anything else you might find will you?" Andy said. "Thanks Andy, you have lifted a great weight from me." Todd said and Andy just nodded. Todd left to meet Dana.

Andy sat back in his chair. He took out a bottle and a glass and headed to the tombs. After finding Simion's tomb he sat by Simion's marker and filled his glass. He lifted his glass in a toast t Simion and said "So it begins Simion. You were right; your intuition always amazed me. The need of us all to adventure and explore would drive them to find a way out." Andy sipped the drink and sat there for some time thinking about everything that was and things that would be. He smiled and said "We made it my dear and we owe it to you." Andy finished his drink and headed back to the library.

Dana and Todd planned their next trip into the tunnel. Dana as was her nature was excited to be venturing further in. Todd was more at ease now that Andy knew what he did now. The planning had paid off on our next journey into the caves. The rope ladders made the descent and ascent of the cavern much easier. They mapped about a quarter of a mile. Todd mounted hangers for lights. He put up motion lights so it would be easier to see their way. Most of the passages they found gave them room to stand and walk. Only a few places were there a call to crouch. The walls and floor were smooth as well. The water must have flowed for eons to make this and other passages yet unfound.

Dana and Todd called it a day and headed back. They rested in the last cavern to the complex. "Todd where do you think they will lead to?" Dana asked. "Oh I don't know, most likely to the river. It's all been formed by water. Why, where were you hoping they went to?" Todd asked. He knew her answer before she spoke. "I guess I had a fanciful idea it might lead outside." She told him. He looked at her and smiled. "One never knows now do we?" and with that he saw the spark light up in her eyes again. "Let's go home and get cleaned up." They once again concealed the entrance to the new cavern and climbed back up to the hub bub of the complex.

When they reached their dorm both found the shower a pleasure. After a light meal they settled down to research the maps and tried to understand the complexity of the tunnels. "Of course you realize it's all just random. The tunnels could go anywhere." Todd said. "Yes I know" Dana replied. "This has to be the biggest discovery ever made here" she said. "After we map it as far as we can should we present it to the council?" she asked. "Let's get it mapped first" Todd smiled. "So are you working tomorrow?" Dana asked. "Yes, I have to complete a couple motors I'm working on" Todd answered. "What about you?" he asked. "Yeah me too, I have to get caught up as well. There is always the work that needs to be done." She had been making him a new outfit for Christmas and that with her other obligations would put further adventures into the tunnels on hold until next week. "We had best call it a night then." And they retired to the sanctuary of their bedroom. Both slept deeply, tired from their adventures they had in the day.

Todd, always the first to wake was up and showered before Dana stirred. He as always brought her a coffee. The morning small take was a ritual. Todd was soon gone to the shop and Dana slower to rise found her way to the tailor station later. They both worked and in the privacy of their dorm shared the day's news.

It was mid week when Erik appeared at the work shop where Todd was. Todd looked up and by the look on Erik's face he knew something was amiss. Todd stopped work and went to see him. Erik took Todd aside. "It's Dana Todd; she is in the med labs. I was sent to see you." Erik told him. Todd just looked at him. His fear that the air had brought something in seemed to be confirmed now. "What happened? Is she hurt? Erik, tell me please." "I don't know the particulars Todd just they want you to go there."

Todd hastily washed and thanked Erik for bring the message. It's all my fault I should have told the council about the air. I should have…he thought. He wasted no time getting to the med labs. His fear was preying on him the whole time. When he arrived the doctor called him into an office. The look on Todd's face must have revealed volumes and the doctor assured him Dana was fine. "What's wrong then?" Todd asked. "She fainted at the tailor shop and after a few tests I am glad to say you two will soon be three." Todd sat down, he had prepared himself for the worst and she was okay, more than okay; she was going to have a baby. Their baby he thought. "Can I see her?" Todd asked. "Of course you can" the doctor said. "Just a few words first. Because her mother had such a hard time and the result was her passing. I want to monitor Dana a bit more, but other than that, I think with some rest and light duties for the duration things should be just fine. Now go see your wife, she's a little upset about being here." Todd smiled "Yes I know she likes home best."

As Todd made the walk to her room, his mind flitted from one thought to the next. The main thought was Dana was going to have a baby, his baby, her baby. A new life was being added to the world and it was up to them to nurture the child. To make sure they impressed the importance the child was to them and the world it was being brought into. Todd soon was at Dana's bedside. She never was so happy anyone as she was to see Todd. He held her as he sat on the side of her bed and they shed tears of joy. Todd brushed her hair away from her face "Boy you gave me a fright" he said. "I can assure you it's not been a picnic for me either" and they both smiled. "I want to go home, but they won't let me." Dana wept softly. "Don't worry I will stay here with you until you can. I just want to clean up first. Now my sweet darling, a baby; I can hardly wait." Todd smiled. "You are happy then?" she asked. "Happy! I'm in love and I have the dearest most wonderful wife and now she is going to have a child." He stopped. He said nothing and looked at her "If I could sing I would" and they hugged. "Dana I gotta go clean up. You rest here and I'll be back in less than an hour. Do you want anything from home?" Dana told him what to bring her and he walked swiftly, but light on his feet, to their dorm.

He showered and gathered a few things she asked for and hurried back. He couldn't believe Dana was going to have a child. He had a permanent grin on his face. When Erik first came in, the dread he felt was so overpowering. He stopped in mid stride, what if the air wasn't good Dana had been exposed. What about the baby? Andy felt confident that all was okay. His parents needed to be told and their friends as well. This is one of the few times in life should be celebrated, but first it's back to Dana. My poor Dana he thought this was something they both desperately wanted but feared. He would make it wonderful for her and calm her fears. He needed to talk to his mom, all of a sudden there seemed to be so many things to do.

He was almost running he was walking so fast lost in his thoughts, blindly making his way back to the med labs. He found Dana in bed with a dinner tray. She was beautiful; she glanced up and saw him. She smiled and he went in and sat beside her. "You look lovely" he said and Dana made

a face at him. "I don't feel lovely. I'm sick to my stomach and I look pale."
"They will give you something to ease your upset stomach and you look
just fine." He smiled at her. "Are you okay with this Dana? I mean are you
happy?" She looked at him "Yes I am, but I'm scared to death." He hugged
her. "Everything will be fine you'll see." He told her. "Now get some of
that food into you. The sooner you eat and start feeling better, the sooner
we can go home. Then my sweet cherry I will be at your beckon call." He
smiled. Dana smiled too.

She ate her toast and drank her tea. When she was done she lay back
and was soon sleeping. Todd sat for a while and watched her breath. His
thoughts carried him back to when he met her and all the events that had
brought them to this point. He thought of the future, the future of the
child, what life would be like here and would it be a life worth living if they
didn't get the doors open. The child would be a prisoner here too.

A nurse came in and Todd made arrangements to stay with Dana. His
father and mother arrived and asked about Dana. When the news was
told hugs were in no short supply. From mom and dad the news travelled
quickly in the complex.

Dana woke the next day to Todd sleeping in the chair beside her bed
and several bouquets of flowers. The nurse had just come in and after a few
tests went out again. It was Dana that watched Todd sleep this time. She
did feel better now and going home was top on her list.

As Todd did, Dana's thoughts carried her life over in her mind. She
remembered Rainie; how she felt about the complex and everyone in it,
her art and how she created beauty to give the place something more. She
thought of Dirk and Carla, she thought of the animals that had been so
much in her life and how lonely she had been until she met Todd, then
how the world seemed so different. She closed her eyes and thought of
the child growing inside her. What kind of a person would this child be?
Whether it would be a contented child or restless like her? She felt strange
like all her old hurts were fading away and it was a pleasant feeling. She
drifted off to sleep. The nurse came in and saw them both sleeping and
left them get rest.

Dirk and Carla had heard the news and were happy for Todd and
Dana. Pf course Carla would have to see Todd's mother about a baby
shower. All the women would be making things she would need for the
baby. This was a joyous time for them and Dana would have the comfort
of the women more so since her own mother and step-mother wouldn't be
able to be that for her. Carla smiled and remembered when she carried her

children. How the virus had them locked in here and how she worried if they would get sick. Then worried about what kind of life they would have in the complex. Dirk could see she was lost in thought and reached out and held her hand. With his touch she smiled and then hugged him. Things had been good, they lost some children, but life had prevailed and now they had children. "Would you like some tea?" she asked Dirk. "Always" he told her and she headed to the kitchenette. Dirk watched her go and knew she was having private thoughts and never pried.

He wandered into the stables and waited for her to call when tea was ready. Dirk smiled; Todd and Dana were now on a new journey that would give them a fulfilment beyond their comprehension and he was truly happy for them.

Erik, Gwen, Petra, Hetti, Carla, Mark, Ann and all of their peers were happy for them. Most had children and now Dana and Todd would add to them all. The children always gave all renewed hope for the future.

It was the doctor's arrival that woke Todd. Dana was awake and she did look better. After a few minutes the doctor finished his exam and asked "So how about you go home and rest there?" Dana smiled "Oh please yes." "You mind me I mean rest." The doctor looked at her then at Todd. "You make sure she does light duties only." Todd smiled "I will" he said. "No more work for her for a while." The doctor looked at them "I want you back here next wee, alright?" Dana nodded and Todd assured him he would have her back. "Alright then, I'll let you get ready to go." He looked once more at Dana. "You just relax and enjoy yourself. You work too hard all the time." Dana smiled. It didn't take her long to get dressed and gather up the few things she had there.

Todd carried them and they walked to their dorm. He was going to make sure she did just what the doctor said. Dana didn't mind she still felt tired or drained, well just not herself.

When they arrived at home Todd had her seated and tea on in no time. Soon he was sitting beside her and they spent the day lounging around. Todd never revealed to Dana that the air was coming in from the outside. He didn't want to alarm her or get her going on the drive to open the doors. All he wanted now is for her to enjoy having the baby and to rest so there would be no complications. Todd never brought up the cavern and hoped Dana would not want to go now that she was with child.

The next few weeks were spent roaming the complex and enjoying the things it had to offer. Dana was sick most mornings and Todd catered to her. It was nearly a month later when Dana mentioned the cavern. Todd skipped around the subject, but Dana not being dissuaded wanted to go back. Todd was firm in his opinion that there would be no adventuring until after the baby was born. Dana knew he was right if she fell or hurt herself now the loss would be too great. So she contented herself with working on the reports, visiting everyone and spending a great deal of time with Dirk and the animals.

Todd was happy that no effects had been noticed throughout the complex and he often talked with Andy. The terrible guilt he had felt was fading into the past.

Andy smiled after each meeting and thought it wouldn't be long before they would be opening the place up. The concern was for those that would have to come to grips that they were the last survivors being tucked away safe in the complex. The children had no idea really just how big the earth was. The joy of rejoining with it would be compounded with the fright of it. What an exciting time it would be. Andy knew he would not be there to see it. He was getting old as were all the founders. Soon the young would be making the decisions and he felt confident in them. He knew Todd would be a leader as would Dana of all the young. Their sense of adventure and willingness to learn reminded him of himself in his younger days. He had seen much of the world and always the written word called him back to study. The library became a second home and at age 40 found him spending more and more in with the books, searching and reading. The more he learned the more he needed too. Each string of information led him to another. Ah well he thought, those days were gone now. He had the young people discovering the things he so long ago found out. They would learn the path had been laid and it was up to them to break their own trails.

Andy headed to the med labs to visit Elsa. She had deteriorated so much and would pass soon. The vibrant young woman he knew was but a whisper of a woman now. He arrived to find the nurse tidying her bed covers. Elsa was starring off into nothingness; she never seemed to know anyone was there, but then again maybe somewhere deep inside she might. Andy sat down and patted her hand. "Well Elsa my dear" he said to her "where are you?" he spoke to her. It would not be long before she passed he thought. Then he pondered the fact that most passed in the spring or later winter maybe to make room for the new life coming into the world. He looked at her and then with a start she looked back at him and said "Andy don't let them put me outside" with that she closed her eyes and died. Andy held her and then gently laid her back on her bed. "Don't worry dear no one will put you outside." He patted her hand one more time then went in search of a nurse. After so many months in almost a coma her last months were dreaded fear of the outside. She climbed out of the abyss she was in to beg him. Andy shed a tear and knew he would fulfil her wish.

He went to tell her children of her passing, each was almost relieved that her nightmares were over. The last stop was Dana. He did not wish to upset her, but she must be told.

He tapped the dorm door and it was Todd that greeted him. "Andy, it's good to see you" and Todd invited him inside. He saw Dana spreading patterns on material hand thought how beautiful she looked. She was swelling with child and had such contentment about her. "Would you like some coffee or tea?" she asked. Then they both realized that something was wrong. "What is it Andy?" Todd asked. Andy told them of Elsa's passing and the three spoke little. All knew that each held her close in their own way and had to let her go themselves. The visit was not one of joy and Andy having told the children got up to leave. "I have things to attend to" he said and left Dana in Todd's capable hands.

It wasn't long before the last of the council met at the tombs. Andy poured each glass and in the ritual toast said "To Elsa". The small band replied "Here, here to Elsa". They drank the drink and made their way to their own homes. Andy went to his dorm and soon found he was tired, Sleep was the escape he needed.

Dana found Elsa's death almost a blessing in disguise. To watch her wither away from being a woman Warren loved and mother to his children was so sad. Dana rubbed her rounded belly. Elsa was always good to her, but was not her mother. Dana felt for them. They would be glad it was over; sad the woman that loved and cared for them was gone and now they were alone as she had been all her life. The children of Warren and Elsa were her peers and friends. She wept for Elsa; another founder gone. Soon all of them would pass and they would have to take everything they had learned to secure the future for all the people left in the complex.

Dana went to bed and covered up. Somehow being in bed and covered with warm blankets felt better. Soon Todd joined her and they lay together. "Are you okay Dana?" Todd asked. "Yes I will be alright" she told him. "I'm glad her suffering is over, but I'm not glad she is gone. Sometimes I worry for us Todd. Will we be like her? Will the stress of the complex break our minds like it did to her?" "Dana! I don't think that will happen. We will live long happy lives; our children will watch the sun rise, feel the snow and know what a soft breeze feels like" he told her. "I hope so Todd,

I really do." She answered. They soon found the comfort of each other and the warm bed drew them into sleep.

Todd's mom and dad; Carla and Dirk, Karen and David and Andy were all feeling their age. It seemed after Elsa's passing they could be found together more often with other council members. Todd was concerned that they were going to pass the reigns of power and he did not wish them too. For a lot it was such a big part of their lives. If they gave it up what would become of them? He did not want to lose anymore of the ones he held near and dear to him. They needed all of them. The funeral was held for Elsa and she was entombed next to Warren. Andy thought "you're safe now dear Elsa you are with the one you loved." After the service the people slowly ventured back to their own homes.

It was several days before Dirk and Carla had the company of Dana and Todd. Dana wanted to see the new animals being born in the complex. Todd always enjoyed Dirk's company and seeing the joy in Dana after the funeral was worth the trip. He watched Dana with some of the new born sheep. She was so at ease with them. He was warmed by the knowledge that she would be a good mother. The tenderness that she showed the animals would just bloom when she had her own child.

The time was passing so fast for Dana was already five months along. By late summer, early fall he would be a father and she a mother. "Oh Todd come see this little one." Dana called to him. He made his way over and she plopped the lamb in his lap as she picked up another. "They are lovely" he said and smiled. They had a wonderful time with the animals. Dana always seemed to have such a way with them. As she held them in her lap they would lie against her belly and sleep soundly. Dirk noticed that she had a way with them as well.

The evening found Todd and Dana at his parents for dinner. His mom and dad were pleased for them and hoped that their grandchild would be healthy. Todd's mother had made a lovely dinner despite the small burn she got from the hot pan she removed from the microwave. After the meal Dana and Todd enjoyed tea and cake. They were sitting and Todd's mother told tales of Todd as a young boy which drew much laughter. "Oh the baby is moving" Dana said and put Todd's hand to her belly. He smiled at the sensation. Dana called Todd's mom to feel and she did without hesitation.

She laid a hand on Dana's belly, it was like a dream. The life she felt moving inside was like it was part of her. She drew her hand away. It had been many years since she felt that. Dana smiled and Todd's mom sat back down. Dana feeling more tired than usual asked to go home. Soon Todd had their things together and arm in arm they departed for home.

Todd's mom and dad cleared the rest of the dishes and sat for one last cup of tea, "It won't be long now" Todd's mom said to his dad. "It's been a busy day and I need to rest" she said. She was almost in bed when she said "Oh dear I must put on a fresh bandage." She went into the bathroom to change her dressing on her burn. To her amazement the burn was gone. She must be tired. She called to her husband "take a look at this" she told him. She showed him her hand and he said "Look at what" "The burn" she said. He looked at her hand and then at her "There is no burn there Hun." She looked back and said "There was, but it's gone now. I think I will go see the doctor tomorrow, to heal that fast is too weird." She looked at her hand again. "Nothing, not a mark; very strange indeed." She made her way back to bed. For some reason she felt more tired than usual. "Must be getting old" she thought and was soon sleeping. Todd's dad had not trouble sleeping and they both slept contently.

Dana and Todd arrived home. Dana was soon in bed and in slumber land before Todd made it to bed. His mind soon no longer thought as he too fell asleep.

The next day found Todd off to work and Dana with ample time on her hands. She decided to head for the community center. She had taken to going and watching the mothers with all the children. To her surprise Carl and Rose were there. Carl was kissing Rose who like her was with child. "I must go Rose, Erik will be wondering where I am." Dana couldn't help over hearing. "Alright" Rose said "I will find something to do." Carl turned to see Dana. "Dana" he said. Good to see you out and about>" He smiled and Rose smiled too. "Seems I'm to be alone again all day, your brother has to work." "Well I'm off" Carl said and he was on his way. "He's awfully work oriented" Rose said almost pouting. Dana smiled "Looks like both our men are off working and left us to our own devices." Rose smiled. "Are you thirsty? Maybe we could have some tea?" she said to Dana. "Sounds good to me" Dana said. "I haven't been able to eat or drink too much in the mornings since..." as she looked at her swollen belly. Rose laughed "I know exactly what you mean" as she looked at hers.

They got some tea and sat at a table in the open area. Dana was nervous she never spent much time with Carl, Rose, Jake or Hetti for that fact. She was a loner and spent as much time away from them as she could. Not that it was she disliked them; she did it to cause less friction. Elsa's children were just that, Elsa's and Dana was not. "Carl has told me a lot about you?"

Dana asked. "Not much of any tales, but he did say that you were kind and considerate and that he always thought you spent too much time alone. He said you have a mind of your own and sought your enjoyment in places most children never went. While he, Jake and Hetti fought over nothing, you were exploring and enjoying the wonders of the complex something he wished he had spent more time doing." Dana was surprised to hear that Carl had such an opinion of her. It did make her feel good. It was a terrible thing that happened to your mom. She suffered so. The older folks in my family passed a few years back. They went quickly not like Elsa, she lingered for so long. "Carl never said but I think she was relieved when she went. He told me once that he was not going to do to our child what Elsa did. She was not very enjoyable to have around. She seemed so stern. Did you know that I was terrified of her for a long time?"

Rose chatted for a few hours. Dana could hardly believe one person had so much to say and so much of it was of no consequence, but she enjoyed her company. She was not vicious or mean, just a chatter box. She was seeing a side of Carl she never knew. She had spent so much time away from them she not seen the changes that time had made. It made her think of Jake and Fern. She wondered if they had changed as much. "Dana, do you want to go for a walk?" Rose asked her. "Sure" Dana said "Where should we walk to?" Rose asked. "We should go to the atrium it's very nice there." Dana said. "Well, it's the atrium it is then."

Rose and Dana walked and talked and before long they had arrived at the atrium. Dana had gone here so much that the birds flew near and as always looked for handouts. Dana went to the feeding stations and got a handful of seeds and went back to sit with Rose. Soon the birds flew to her and ate seeds from her hands. Rose's eyes lit up and she smiled. "How do you get them to do that?" Rose asked. "It's not a trick really, just spend more time here and they will get used to you." Dana said and smiled. Dana felt good to be able to show Rose the wonder and joy of the birds. It dawned on her it would be another avenue to pursue in getting more people the drive to leave the complex. "Rose" Dana asked "Are you happy here in the complex?" "Yes I am" Rose told her. "Haven't you ever wondered about the outside world?" Dana asked. "No not really. All that's out there is death and a great reminder how stupid mankind has been. In here we are a new society. There is not the wonton greed or lust for dominion over our fellow man; the prejudices that were before." Rose told her. "Don't you think you would ever like to see it outside?" Dana asked. "No not really, my father talked of the old world and of the weather and things. How the winter was so cold people would freeze and the summer was so hot old people died from it. I have no interest in that. Here we have everything. No one is hungry, besides it will never be okay to go out again. Why do you trouble your thoughts with such fantasies anyways? It is a fruitless venture." Rose said. Dana was stunned. How could she be so small minded? How could she wish to condemn mankind to living in a mountain? Never to breath fresh air or walk in open fields.

She was about to say something when Rose promptly spoke. "Dana you must get your head out of the clouds so to speak and realize how fortunate we are. The world has taken its revenge on mankind for his insolence. They polluted, destroyed everything they touched and finally completed that by killing themselves off. There is no one, we are the remnants of them and I pray we don't make the mistakes that led us to nearly the death of mankind. Be happy you are safe and don't have to fear what they may have left behind." Dana sat there and listened then she had something to say. "Well it might be interesting to you to know my father survived the virus. He had communications with the complex after the outbreak. There may be still people out there." Rose calmly sat and looked at Dana. "How could he survive? The virus killed everything. There are no animals, insects, etc… How could he eat or find food? I know you want him to be out there, but the chances are slim. It's been too many years." Dana knew she was most likely right. "Dana you have us here." Rose said. "Life might not be what we want but we have life and we are not in danger of losing it due to starvation or exposure to the elements. Be happy and maybe someday we may again live in the outside world, but until that time seek things that warm your heart and soul here. It will do no good to dwell on things that may be." The truth in her words stung Dana, but she would never give up hope. "Maybe you are right Rose." Dana said. "Good" Rose said "maybe now you will find things here not so bad."

The two women never talked of the outside for the rest of their time together. Rose because it was not a priority and Dana because she knew Rose was not interested in the least. They spent a few hours more looking at the plants and watching the birds. Rose chatted about the people in the complex, but always with kindness. It was Dana that broke up the company with her feigning tiredness.

The two walked towards the dorms. Rose told Dana to rest and that she hoped they would spend more time together. Dana assured her they would. She liked her and thought it would be good to have friends her own age. Rose left Dana at her dorm and continued on her way.

Once Dana was inside she sat and relaxed. So many thoughts filled her, a lot centered on the child she seemed so calm about everything. Being with child had surrounded her inner being with a softness and with more contentment than she ever felt before. Her drive to leave the complex didn't seem as big an issue for her. She got up and soon found herself looking over the last reports. They were all good. "I guess we should finish these up my little one" she said as she placed a hand on her belly. "Maybe everyone is right, maybe I should be thinking about making sure everyone here stays well and let Mother Nature clean up the outside." She worked for a few more hours compiling the information.

Todd arrived home and gathered her into his arms. "So did you have a good day?" he asked. "Yes it was pleasant" she told him. "I spent the day with Rose. I enjoyed her company surprisingly enough." Dana said. "Why does that surprise you? She's just a young woman, married, expecting a child much like you" he smiled. "I know" Dana said. "I just never realized, well it doesn't matter." "You need a shower" she smiled. "How was your day?" She asked. "Hard today" he said. "We are working on building new drive shafts for the water wheels." "Sounds like not much fun" Dan said. "No, but it's interesting." Todd replied. "So how are you feeling all in all?" Todd asked. "Better" she said. "Good, let me shower" he said. Dana smiled and agreed.

Todd showered and dressed. They were soon sharing salad and cheese with tea in the open area. Todd did notice that Dana didn't talk about the cave much and in his heart he was glad. "How would you like to go see Dirk later? The young animals should all be born and I thought we could watch as they get them all tagged." "No I think I would like to stay home tonight." Dana said. "I think just being with you tonight is more what I need." Dana smiled. Todd was tired and staying home was just as good if not a better plan.

After they ate they made their way to their dorm. "Are you feeling okay Dana"" Todd asked. "Yes just a little tired is all."

When they got home Todd made another tea for them. He was working on a cradle for the baby. It was made of wood and he was carving the headboard. Dana sat contently and picked up some sewing. "Todd, are you happy here in the complex? I mean really happy?" Dana asked. He looked at her "What seems to be the trouble Dana?" Todd asked. "Well just my day with Rose. She is so contented here. For so long I have thought about, my father and getting out of here. I have spent years alone, my brothers and sister have grown up and are having children. You know I hardly know them. My life has been torn with longing to find my father and leave this place. My heart felt as if it had a great sadness in it and I always believed it was because I was here." "It seems your day with Rose has upset you." Todd said. "No not upset me" she answered "just shed a different light on things. I have you and now a child coming. I have friends and family here and for some reason I don't think I appreciated them as much as I should have. The struggle to live is not yours and mine alone, everyone is in the same boat. I have to ask myself would leaving the complex really give me fulfilment. It's like I can't see the forest because too many trees are in the way. Then I can't see the trees because the forest blocks the view. For so long I have had that weighing on me and now I don't know. It makes me think I have been selfish in a way." Todd got up and sat near her. "You are not selfish nor have I ever known you to be. Just because things in life change some it doesn't mean things that were important to you and don't seem so much so, won't be so later on and doesn't make them wrong. You are just seeing a different perspective on them. People living outside are the ultimate goal for everyone here even if some don't see that yet. The old have lost everything they knew and most of what their lives were are gone. For them it will never be the same. For us it is different because we never knew the outside. It doesn't mean we never should. I pray that out there, there are some that have survived not just for their sake but for all of us as well. We would need them as much as they need us. What ever our lives have in store for us is what it is. The test is how we deal and live with it. I believe all will one day be well and in out lifetime the doors will open. For our children the rediscovery of the world will be theirs." "Todd, how do you always manage to make me feel at peace with things?" Dana said. "What would I do without you?" she smiled. "Well you two are stuck with me." He smiled. He went back to his carving and she continued sewing. Life had taken a turn for her and him as well.

The daily routine fell back into place. It was a few weeks later when Dana brought up the cave. She had been looking at the maps and thought the two of them should continue mapping after the baby was born. Todd's mind whisked back to his conversation with Andy. The outside air had been coming in all the time with no ill effects that could be detected. "Do you think its wise t leave our child while we adventure?" Dana smiled. "We wouldn't have to spend a lot of time there just daily trips after all" she said. "Who knows what wonders still await us?" Todd nodded "That's true, but let's just wait and see." Dana smiled. "You know we need something new here. The life for most is well, boring." Todd laughed. "You my dear always have to have something going. That pleases me, you know?" Dana smiled. "Maybe you should have a vote. Get everyone's opinion; set up a ballet box and see what others say. Their ideas might surprise you and maybe you could set up something for a majority vote." "You know Todd that is a good idea." Dana said to him. "Now before you get all Gung Ho on this you remember to take it easy." He smiled. "I will I haven't long to go and I can feel the tiredness the weight gives me. Besides it's just an idea I'm after." "Well my dear I am off, that new equipment I have been slaving over is still there. I want to get things set up for tomorrow. Do you have something to keep you busy today?" Todd asked. "Not really" she answered. "I thought I might go visit Petra and see how things were going in the tunnels. I haven't been in such a long time." Todd smiled, hugged her and was off.

Dana was in the mood to smell flowers today and a perfect place for that was in Karen's gardens. The morning sickness had passed and Dana was on her way to see Karen.

With new found serenity she walked down the tunnels. Karen was testing the soil when she arrived and soon Karen was explaining what nutrients were best for each type of plant she was going to grow in the empty areas. Dana listened carefully. She enjoyed learning about how to grow things.

It wasn't long before David appeared. "Dana!" he said. "It's good to see you. Karen I need the excess plant material you set aside for me." Karen looked at him the called Petra. Petra appeared from around the corner. She had been planting and was covered in dirt. "What is it mom?" she asked. "Take dad to the bins with his stuff in them would you please?" Petra smiled "Dad, come with me?" And before she turned away she said hello to Dana. David followed his daughter and the two were gone in a few minutes.

Karen motioned Dana to sit down. "I never did ask what has brought you here." Karen said to her. "I have been trying to think of different things for people to get involved with here. Life for most of us can get well, boring. The same thing day in and day out" Dana said. "Oh I never noticed that too much" Karen said to her. "I don't think you would have noticed as you have such a great love for gardens. What goes on out here probably does little to sway you." Dana said. "Most of the people have so much less in their lives. You know Karen, in some ways I envy you. Seems that the gardens and you were matched up and both depend on the other, you on them and the gardens on you." Karen smiled. "It is true" she said. "I admit,

I derive great joy from the plants, but to me they are much more than just plants. Look what they provide. The food we eat the air we breathe, the clothes we wear and well the list is endless. They ask for nothing in return and one of my favourite things is when they bloom and send off their aromas. It just makes me feel like I have accomplished so much." Karen smiled. "You have." Dana told her. "You also feed the animals and provide them with bedding. That alone is no small feat. I would hate to think of what would happen in the complex had we not had your expertise." "I didn't do it all alone." Karen said. "I have had help from many. Petra has taken up the slack, even when she was small I could depend on her. I have been growing some new flowers. Would you like to see them?" Karen asked. "Oh yes" Dana said. "I would, I just love the flowers." "Well then come let me show you my new triumphs."

The two women walked to Karen's special place. It was a little Eden among all the tunnels of food and product plants. Karen showed Dana her new plantings and Dana soaked it all in like a big sponge. It was David who broke the bliss on the moment.

"Karen, Dirk wants me to get together my surplus insects to be ready to be set free. I could use a hand." Karen looked at Dana. Without having to explain Dana told her she had to head home anyways she was feeling tired. "I'm glad you came to see me." Karen said. "So am I, it's been a visit long overdue." Dana told her smiling. Karen and David headed to his work area and Dana went home.

As she walked she thought how many had worked so hard to bring beauty to the complex, her mother, Rainie and Karen.

Dirk brought the wonders of animals and even Todd with his sculpting, we the list went on. Her mind drifted toward the time soon at hand. Her baby would soon be born. She was a bit fearful yet, but nothing like she had been. She was surprised at herself. She never realized how much she wanted this baby. It was strange how she had such a good feeling about it. How she knew things would be okay. Then she thought of Todd and how happy he was, how much she loved him. She was almost home and it was a good thing as she was weary. She went inside and made tea. Todd would be home soon and she would start making something to eat, but she decided to have a bit of a lay down first.

It was a few hours later when she woke to Todd's cooking aromas. She got up and went to see him. "Hey there sleepy head" he said when he saw her. "Did you have a good rest?" he asked her. "Yes I did" she told him. "I was going to start dinner but decided to lay down for a minute." He smiled. "It's okay it's my treat tonight." He told her. Dana went to wash up. It didn't take Todd long to have everything ready. They sat and ate and talked of the days events. Dana had a lot to say about her visit with Karen and Todd filled her in on his work day. "I miss going to work" she told him. Todd smiled. "You will have your hand full before long enjoy the pampering while you can." Dana smiled.

She took up some needle work and soon found herself totally involved with it. Todd put the finishing touches on the cradle. He had a surprise for her when the child was born. He had worked on it for a while now. It was past midnight when Dana finally gave into tiredness. She wished the baby would come soon she had been so uncomfortable for what seemed forever. They went to bed and Dana was asleep right away. Todd lay close to her and could feel the child moving inside her. He marvelled at just how much it did move. He also enjoyed immensely the feeling of it. His mind went to the fact the outside air was coming in and prayed everything would be okay. The cave and tunnel seemed to have been forgotten by Dana. He thought just as well too. He did not like the fact the two of them have exposed the complex to the outside and no one knew except Andy. The air coming in never left Todd's thoughts for very long. He worried it would be a danger. Several times he thought about sealing it up, even though nothing had happened didn't mean it couldn't. He thought about what their lives would be like after the baby came. He worried about Dana and hoped she would whether this all with no problems. Finally sleep took him.

Dana was up first and she made coffee and started breakfast. Todd woke to the sounds for her in the kitchen. He was a lucky man to have her. He didn't think anyone was as lucky as him. He got up and showered. He had finished as Dana served out their meal. "You going to work today?" she asked. He nodded yes. "I have a few things I have to finish, but then I will stay home for a few days." Dana was glad to hear that. She was feeling odd today. "What do you have planned?" he asked. "I was going to watch the animals being set free. Its spring and time to let out the surplus again." She told him. "Promise me that you will only be a spectator." He said and Dana laughed. "So what do you think I could do in my condition?" He smiled. "I'm off, you just take it easy. I won't be putting in a full day today. Maybe we can go for a walk after." Todd said. "Sounds good, if I'm not home I will be watching the monitors, alright?" He kissed her and told her he would see her later.

Dana smiled and watched him leave. He wasn't gone very long when she started having pains. She knew the baby was coming, but she also knew it would be sometime before the child would be born. She walked about the dorm and tried hard to relax. A few hours had passed and the labour was becoming intense. Dana decided to go to the med labs.

She slowly made her way there and what seemed a buzz of activity she found herself in the labour room with a child being born. Todd was sent for, but the child was not waiting.

After what seemed a very short time the baby had arrived and a new person was in the world. The doctors checked him out and found him to be healthy and then turned their attentions to Dana. She had come through it just fine. No problems and a short labour.

The doctor let the nurses clean them up and he went to see if the father had arrived yet. He found Todd at the reception desk. "Well young man" the doctor said "You have a perfect healthy son and your wife is just fine." Todd looked at him "She's had the baby this fast? I just got the word." The doctor smiled "She came through with no problems. Both are well and you can see them in a few minutes."

The nurses laid the child beside Dana and gently caressed his head. He's perfect, just perfect she thought. She softly touched his hands and then his feet. "How tiny you are my young son." Dana surprisingly felt no pain now, just joy. She had the baby and all was well. Dana held his hand again and a feeling of warmth spread through her, contentment was what she felt. Some how this small child had taken away her uneasiness and made her feel one with her and him. The world was abetter place now and the three of them were safe.

She put the child to her breast and he took to it like a duck to water. As he fed Dana thought of her mother. How happy she would have been to see her child. Zack also filled her mind; he too would be filled with comfort knowing this little fellow was here and well. Dana understood so many things now that she just couldn't before. The baby and his future were hers and Todd's. Responsibility and care must be taken to insure there was a future for them.

It was then that Todd came through the door. She looked up and saw him. When she smiled it seemed to provide him with a comfort he needed. He came over and sat beside her on the bed. He too caressed the little fellow's head and softly touched his hands. Todd leaned to Dana and kissed her. "Just couldn't wait for me, huh" he kidded her. Dana just smiled. "This little guy made the decision not me" she told him and Todd kissed her again. Dana let him take his fill and after a burp or two she handed him to Todd. Todd took him with no hesitation. Dana watched as Todd stared down at him. "I think he looks like me, but he has your eyes" he said. Dana lay back, "What will we call him? Have you picked his name?" she asked. "Let me look at him a few more minutes." Todd said. Todd looked at his tiny son and said "I name you Dern. You will grow strong and kind Dern. You will always have your mother and me to lean on in times of struggle and in your times of joy have us to share it with you."

Todd looked up at Dana. "We did well. He is a wonderful young man." He handed Dern back to Dana. Dana lay back with Dern resting on her chest and held Todd's hands. It was a few hours before Todd got up to leave. "I must go tell mom and dad." He leaned over and kissed her then Dern. "I will come back soon." She smiled. Todd left and Dana listened to the tiny breaths Dern made soon she was drifting to sleep. The nurse came in and took Dern to his own bed beside Dana. Dana relaxed and slipped in to slumber.

Todd's steps were light and wasted no time getting to his mom and dad's dorm. He knocked on the door and his mom called "enter." Where's dad?" he asked. "He is in his study" she told him. Todd went to the study and asked them to join him for a cup of tea. Todd went to the kitchen and put the water on. "So what brings you here today Todd?" his mom asked. "I have some good news" he said. He looked to see his dad coming to join them. "Well" Todd said. "Dana had a baby. It's a boy and both are doing just fine." Todd's mom hugged him. "Oh my goodness, thank the Good Lord" she said and hugged him again. His dad shook his hand and the hugged him as well. "That is good news." Todd smiled and said "He is a handsome little guy." "What did you name him? His father asked. "We called him Dern." "Well that's a good name" his father said. His mom had finished the tea. "So your sleepless nights begin." She said and his dad smiled. "I don't mind losing some sleep, I can deal with that." Todd said. "I'm so grateful to have them both safe and sound" he said. "True" his father replied. "That is great news" his mom said. "A new generation begins" she patted Larz's hand. "We are getting old my love" she smiled. Larz just smiled and said "Not old, just not young anymore." She smiled "We are so happy for you and Dana" she said. "Mom" Todd said. "You will give her a hand, I mean help her. She doesn't have a mother; well you know what I mean." "Todd I interfere, but yes I will help her. There are many tricks to the trade of motherhood, but Dana must be the one in control. She is the mother and Dern maybe ours by blood, but he is hers first." She patted his hand. "Drink your tea son and relax. It may be one of the last times we are here like this now that Dern has arrived. I think you will find him to be a lot more work than you expected" and then she smiled. Todd was happy and it pleased her so and Larz was proud of his son. They had done well with him. He is a good man.

After tea he bid them goodbye and went home. He showered and then brought the cradle into the bedroom.

Then he made his way to the shop to get Dana her gift. It took some time with everyone congratulating him on the arrival of the child. Todd took the gift home and hoped that Dana would like it. He picked up some personal stuff to take and went back to the med labs.

On his arrival the doctor met him. Todd asked if everything was okay and the doctor did say yes, but he wanted Dana to sleep and Todd nodded. "I won't disturb her" he said and the doctor smiled. "Good, I just want her rest, no repeats of what happened to her mother." Todd nodded again. He quietly went into her room and sat in an easy chair. He watched her sleep and it seemed to caress him into a slumber as well.

Dern had made his arrival and as with any new life the complex sent gifts and well wishes. Dana and Todd fell into family life like most, with lots of trials and errors, but mostly sleepless nights.

Rose had her baby and she and Carl were going through the same as Todd and Dana. It brought Dana closer to Rose and drew Todd and Carl together. Having family changes your ideas about things and Dana was no exception. All the things she thought were so important didn't compare to Dern and what was going to be in his life. Dern was sleeping through the night and none too soon. Dana had a routine down that gave her sometime to herself. She had watched Dern sleep when she noticed the citron and quarts on her bed dresser. She went over and picked them up. The water was heated in the microwave and Dana was soon sitting with a cup of tea looking at her crystals. Her mind wandered to the tunnels and how driven she had been to get outside. It was still important, but Dern was now the issue. His care was a full time job. She glanced to the reports on the desk and knew she would have to put them together for the council.

She sipped her tea and it occurred to her that time was slipping by so quickly. Dern now over a month old and it seemed just like a day or two ago her and Todd were exploring the caves. She picked up the map they were making and Dana smiled. Funny she thought, all her life getting out of here was just a big element, now her Dern was to be considered. She had grown up and now things were being seen through new eyes. The prison was becoming a home and that was not as frightening as she thought it was. Todd had seen the changes in her as well. He was happy that she was becoming more settled within herself. The contentment suited her he thought.

He had returned to work and found it now had so much more worth because everything he did he knew his son would benefit from it. "Well what's going through that mind of yours?" Todd asked her. "Oh, nothing much" Dana answered. "I was just thinking about the caves" she told him. Todd tried not to think of them "What's got you thinking about them?" he asked. "I was just looking at the crystals. We should finish mapping what we can" she said. "I know your mom and dad would take Dern for the day" Dana said "The break might be what we need." Todd smiled. He had no desire to go into the caves. "We will have to see" he said. "Maybe in a week, I have some things at work that need my attention at the moment." Dana smiled "I need to get after these reports as well. Maybe in a week we can go."

It was Dern that broke up the conversation. "Maybe not too" Dana said "Dern is still a lot of work." She smiled and went and got him. She sat in the rocking chair that Todd made for her. It was a perfect gift and it was used faithfully. Todd looked at his wife and child and felt proud. His mind went to the caves; maybe they should follow them to the source and seal it up. The danger was much too high in spite of what Andy had told him.

It was during the next week that Todd went back to the caves alone. He knew he should have let someone know where he was going, but he couldn't tell anyone. Going alone into them was asking for trouble. He made his way down to the tunnel and everything was as they left it. He decided to rope the passages. Any places that were cramped he would open then up. He had brought a change of clothes and enough water to wash with before he went back up. He laboured for hours to open the first cramped opening. The limestone chipped easily and he had the passage to the next cavern passable before he left. He washed and changed before he climbed up.

He headed home and found the dorm empty. A note on the table informed him Dern was making his first visit to Dirk and Carla. Todd smiled. His shower was swift and then made his way to the animal tunnels.

When he arrived he found Carla holding Dern and Dirk tickling his cheek with a feather. "Look there's my dear he's smiling." Dirk said to Carla. She just looked at him "He more likely has gas" and put Dern over her shoulder and patted his back. Amidst the laughter at Dirk, Dana looked at Todd "Come have some tea" Carla told him and Todd joined them. Dana asked how work was going and he told her it was going. He didn't like lying to her but he had to seal off that air pocket before they suffered for it.

After lunch the conversation ranged from children to animals Dana and Todd got ready to go. Dirk and Carla watched them walk up the tunnel to home and it was Dirk that said to Carla "It's good my dear. I will rest easy now to know all my children are happy." Carla rubbed his arm. She knew Dana was like his child and she said "Yes dear, we both can."

Todd carried Dern and was amazed how such a short time he had grown so much. "What have you been feeding him Dana?" he teased her "He's growing like a bad weed." Dana just smiled. "Want to go home or for a walk first?" "I think home, Dern should be in his bed." What shall we do tonight then?" he asked. Dana just smiled again.

When Dern was settled in his cradle, Dana put on some tea. Todd sat at the table and when Dana sat down she looked at him. "Where were you today and don't tell me work. I was there" she said. Todd's face dropped. "Oh Dana I'm sorry, I wanted to tell you, but I can't I gave my word." "Todd this is me, your wife; the mother of your child. I'm your best friend and confidant. Tell me where you were." Todd knew she had the right to know. "Dana what I'm going to tell you must be kept quiet. You are to tell no one. In telling you I'm breaking my word and promise to Andy" he said to her. Before he went any further, Dana looked across at him. "I don't want you to break my word. Don't tell me, but next time you secret away let me know. They spent the rest of the evening talking of their child and Rose's baby. They made plans for Dern's future and what method of care he would receive. They soon found their bed and both slept.

Todd worked the next day and found that it was slow. Most of the machinery was running fine and now other than making spare parts it was a pleasure to be there. He had been troubled within himself. He needed to talk to Andy and tell him how he felt.

He left the shop and went to the library. He found Andy sitting at his desk behind what seemed to be a mountain of papers. Andy looked up and smiled. "Todd good to see you' he said. "How's the baby and Dana?" he asked. "Oh they are just fine" Todd said. "I have to talk to you." Andy looked at him and told him to close the door. Todd closed the door and sat down. "Andy, it's not right, I mean about the air coming in" Todd said. "We are putting the whole complex in danger. I can't do it anymore. They should be told" Todd said. Andy looked at him "I think the council should know" Todd said. Andy sat back "I can understand your concern Todd, but I disagree. Bear with me." Andy said. "I want you to come see me tomorrow I have some things I would like you to read. If after you read it and you feel the same. I will tell the council." Andy told him. Todd reluctantly agreed. "Alright then tomorrow morning" Andy said. "Give Dana a hug for me and bring that boy by so I can see him sometime." Todd smiled and left.

Todd walked home and found Dana doing some needle work while Dern slept. "Your home early" Dana said. "Yeah, I had to see Andy. I will be busy with him tomorrow." Todd told her. By now she put down the needlework and was up and hugged him. He hugged back "Let me have my shower." "How was your day?" he asked. "It's good. Dern has been good. He's such a good baby" she said. Todd smiled and headed for the shower. He let the water run over him for a long time. His life was getting complicated and he didn't like it. "Dinner's ready!" Dana called to him. He dried off, dressed and hurried to the table. Dana just finished her diner when Dern's quiet cries beckoned to her. "I'll get him" she said and got up. He soon was quieted and contented with his meal. Dana rocked him in her arms and Todd sat looking at them. He never ate all his meal. When Dern was fed Todd took him. He held him and softly talked to him. It wasn't long before Dern was asleep and Todd returned him to his bed. Dana knew that something was bothering Todd, but also knew he would tell her in his own time.

Todd slept with uneasiness; tossing and turning all night. When he finally woke up he gave up trying to sleep. It would be a few hours before Dana and Dern woke up, so he dressed and went to the atrium.

As he sat there, the many trips he and Dana had taken there flooded his mind. Too soon the thoughts of Andy and what he was going to show him came front and centre to his thoughts. What was it that made Andy so confident that the air was okay and that it should be kept quiet" Why did that sly old fellow know that escaped everyone else? He sat and listened to the birds singing and finally made his way to see Andy.

Andy was waiting for him and the two sat in his office. Todd knew he was at the beginning of something, but what? "Well my boy" Andy said. I must remind you that what you read here today is not common knowledge yet although in my lifetime it will be. My life is coming to its close as is all the founders." Todd looked at him again. Andy continued "We all knew one day we would have to re-enter the world, but of course we thought we would find a cure for the virus. It was never supposed to get in here. Not to say that possibility had been taken into account. Simion spent his life trying to protect mankind from himself. Long before the world let loose the virus he could see that people had become consumed with control and the lust for greed. In our past, world wars had been fought as one country lusted for what the others had. It was Simion that financed this place and everything in it. He knew man would destroy everything if given the chance and I am ashamed to say that the people of my time did just that. It was our time that locked you all in here. We did everything to solve the mystery of the virus. It was Simion that realized it was not one virus, but three that mutated together to the one that killed most everything outside. He discovered it was not curable. It attacked your DNA, if you had a certain strain you survived, if not you died. Once the virus attached itself to the DNA it could actually change man." "What do you mean?" Todd asked. "Change man?" "I will get to that" Andy told him. "Have you had any breakfast yet?" Andy asked. "No I didn't" Todd answered.

Andy got up and went to the door. He called his assistant and sent him to the kitchen for some food for them. He was dumbfounded how could Andy be so calm? Change man, what did he mean? Andy closed the office door.

"Where was I?" he said. "Oh yes the virus, Simion discovered the virus not only killed, but it enhanced the normal abilities of man. Let me see, here is an example. Did you ever read anything about telekinesis or faith healing?" Andy asked. "Some, but most were not able and considered charlatans." Todd answered. "Yes that is true" Andy said. "But there were some could do these things and folks called them miracles. In deed miraculous abilities most never used or knew they had, women more than men could use their abilities unwittingly. They called it woman's intuition. Finding lost children or knowing a child or loved one was hurt or in danger. I think it was something to do with the internal bond shared with being pregnant; two separate people living as one." Andy said.

There was a knock at the door. Andy opened it and received the tray of food and drinks. He informed his assistant that they were not to be disturbed. He closed the door and told Todd to come and get something to eat. "Andy, how can you be so calm? You just told me the virus is changing us?" Todd asked. "All in good time, all in good time" Andy said. "Eat something, we just begun." Andy smiled. Todd just couldn't wrap his mind around all this. As they ate Andy continued. "Where was I, oh yes, the maternal bond; woman's intuition. Well Simion believed that once the virus attached itself to the cells it would be a normal action like eating, drinking or walking." Andy told him. "I have followed medical reports and I believe it had already started." Andy said. Todd's mouth dropped open and he dropped a piece of toast he had been eating. Andy looked at him "Do close your mouth and pick up your toast." Andy said. Todd fumbled around and after retrieving the toast sat back down. "What do you mean already started?" Todd asked afraid of what Andy would tell him. "I'm not sure, but there was a case of a burn disappearing. It was there then gone. I am confident it was a case of healing." Andy said. Todd just starred at him. "Todd, Todd wake up young fella!" Andy said and Todd's attention was his again. "Am I moving too fast for you lad?" Andy said. "No" Todd replied. "I just can't believe what I'm hearing is all." Andy laughed "You have heard nothing yet." Andy said. "You best eat some more and drink your coffee" he said.

Todd followed his advice. After they both finished eating, they sat back. "Andy I always knew you were a man of great knowledge, but this is too much." Todd said. Andy just smiled at him. "As I said before there is much more yet to tell you and I'm trying to simplify it for you some. Now where was I? Oh yes" and he continued "Simion was also sure there would be people that would survive outside, Zack, Dana's father for one did. He was a wonderful man I have missed him more than once in my life. Of course out there life will be tough, but knowing Zack he would survive. The ones left would have to find each other and help one another. It would be their only way to make it. Food and shelter, just the common illnesses would have to be overcome. Yes a hard time they will have." Todd was again given a blow. "You mean there are people out there?" his voice rising. "Calm down Todd." Andy said. "Yes I believe there are people alive out there." "We need to help them. We need to open this place up and find them" Todd said. He thought of Dana and her finding Zack. Who knows what others? Andy sat quietly and could see Todd's mind racing. "Sit down Todd" Andy said. Todd sat. "Now listen to me" Andy told him. "This complex is many, many miles from anything out there. If and I say if they survived, the lives they lead are simple lives, Gathering just enough food to sustain them through the winter. It would be a tough go. You want to just run out there and if you find them, everything in here would be long gone out there. No electricity, just think of that and what would your life be without it?" Todd sat and listened. "Most of the people would be your age and they most likely never seen a smidgen of what you take for granted. If ever we find people they would have to be eased into what's here. Do you understand Todd?" Andy asked him. "Yes I think I do." Todd replied. He had believed they were the last of mankind. All the people here were the last and now the fact that more than likely there were others. Todd just sat there. "Now where was I?" Andy said "Oh yes. Simion, we had so many decisions on what to do in the future. Simion knew the next generation born in the complex would become condition, no institutionalized. The home here would fall into the daily living and most would not question going outside. Their parents lived through the outbreak and the destruction it caused would instil a fear in them. As we the founders passed, the younger your children would be so accustomed to life in the complex that leaving would not be an issue. There would be some, a few which would realize there we were to live outside not in some constructed fortress. We sat many hours figuring how long it would take the virus to take to start its transformation on those with certain strands in their DNA. With the experiments to excel the mutations we also found out it's dormant at the moment and soon will change again. This is important Todd. You and Dana must have more children. There is going to be a time when the women will be unable to get pregnant, only the children born in the next five years or so years will be able to have more. We will lose almost a whole generation. When your son's time comes to have children the virus will be a threat no longer. He will be free as all the people born after. The world will belong to them."

Todd couldn't believe this. How could they have known this so long ago? "Do you know what the people will do when no children are born? "They will think we all are going to die. Even with everything we teach everything that is known, I'm afraid of the panic and despair this will cause. When the virus came through it was everything the founders could do to keep folks on the right track. I believe there are many that still seek retribution. Man has not changed in some ways. Always have been those that seek to blame others when ones they love pass. Simion knew this too. He told me that he feared those that wouldn't be able to get over the depression it caused. Elsa never did and from reports I have read there are many yet. Todd do you know why Simion chose this mountain and why he picked the people he did to work here?" Todd could only reply "No." "Let me show you something"

Andy got up and went to the book cases that had maps rolled up in them. He pulled out the map of the mountain ranges that made up the areas around the complex. He laid it out and pointed out the mountains that enclosed the valley outside. "Here is where we could let the animals go" and he pointed to the circular valley that the monitors watched. "It's like a protected glen. It was Simion's idea it would be better to keep the animals here. The fact that the mountains around here were so extensive and the range the highest kept them in. They would not be able to cross over the top. The birds being the exception, with that in mind he knew without their food they would perish if they were left in the valley. Simion knew even the insects did not survive the virus. Seed eaters were the exception to be able to live outside the valley. If they flew over the mountains they would fly south and stay there, if they found enough to feed on while going.

Now David for years has been letting insects go, but his surplus is not nearly enough to repopulate anything other than our valley. Dirks animals have depended upon the pollination done by them to provide them with food they need. It's all a chain of life, but I am getting sidetracked here. I want you to read these." And Andy plopped down several of Simion's journals.

Todd was stunned. He picked up the first journal and started reading. It told of the complex; its construction, the fact that Simion was aware of the caverns and that there was a vast chain of them in and about the complex. He read of his concerns that the complex would not be completed before the disaster he called would happen.

Andy now sat down and was now reading reports. Todd had started the second journal when Andy got up and told him to stop for a moment. "Todd I fear this is going to take sometime, it's already early afternoon. Would you like to send word to Dana where you are?" Andy asked. "Early afternoon!" Todd was surprised how much time had passed and agreed to have word sent to Dana.

Andy opened the door and instructed his assistant to send word to Dana and get more food brought to them. When they tapped at the door with the food Andy instructed his assistant his assistant they were again not to be disturbed.

It was nearly dinner time when Todd finished reading the journals. He sat back and tried and tried to put into words what he was thinking. "How could Simion have known all this?" Todd asked. "He was a man with a vision is all I can say." Andy replied. "Simion knew one day someone like you would come across the caverns. He knew the air was getting in long ago. The virus was an inevitable fate we all would have to endure. It came sooner than he would have hoped, but it arrived. Since then we have in many ways been preparing for the future. Most have no idea that's what they have been doing." "Are all the founders aware of everything you have told me?" Todd asked. "No they all take care of each unit they were hired for. Some read reports from other units, but most are not aware. Most of the people here have what I call tunnel knowledge. In their field of expertise they have no match, but that's it. Give them something to contemplate and most, not all have little or no comprehension. Let me give you an example. The doctors here can heal most anything given to them, but put them in the agro tunnels and they would be lost as would the growers be in the operating rooms. Do you understand?" he asked Todd. "Yes I do." "What do you think of Simion's version of re-entering the outside world?" Andy asked. "I think opening the outside doors and short trips out then back in are the right idea." Todd answered. "I think the isolation of the people at first is really not necessary." Todd continued. "I thought about that too" Andy replied "But now you have to remember that by the time, we the founders will be gone and it's another of his safety mechanisms to help the people here adjust. Not really a must, but it would give the feeling of security to those so long enclosed in this mountain." "I think I understand." Todd said. "So here we are. You have discovered that the air is coming in, but you are not to blame. Long ago it was known that the day would come to pass when we would be exposed to the outside. Of all the things Simion had the foresight to see, he missed that. He saved us all, had it been a nuclear war we would have died later, inevitably like the others." "How did he keep the animals alive when most died outside?" Todd asked. "He had picked top breeds and the best lines. I'm not really sure what he looked for. I asked the same thing." Andy said. "Simion told me that some animals would survive outside, but any domestic animals that depended on human care would most likely die in the first winter. Then with the lack of food the people would most likely kill off some and finally the disease from the masses of dead would take more, with the animal population so low finding mates would be slim." "The insects surely would have made a better fight." Todd said. "That's a good point." Andy said. "Insects through out time had always been the survivors, but again with the virus working on DNA rather than just attacking cells, they suffered the worst. The cross breeding that David had been doing seemed to save the insects. He has the genius to have bred them with the qualities of several different strands of DNA. He managed to save many. Of course I don't think he realized that, it was his persistence in breeding; in trying to improve them to save them. On the outside they would not have bred with other species of the same lines." "How many people do you think made it? I mean survived?" Todd asked. "That's hard to estimate, but I don't think there are many. If the country has one hundred thousand people, I would be surprised." Andy told him.

Todd had just spent the day learning things he could never have imagined. To try to even explain any of this to Dana would never happen. He must let her discover things in her own time. He no longer felt guilty about the air. It was a process that had been going on for a long time. "Todd" Andy said breaking him away from his own thoughts. "Do you understand why I told you all this and why you must keep it all to yourself?" Andy asked. "I understand why I must keep it to myself, but why did you tell me?" Todd asked. Andy sat back in his chair "When you came to me and told me about the air coming in and the story of how you discovered this, I had to tell you. Letting you go and watch the guilt build inside you was not right. I believe you to be old enough to handle the facts and wise enough to follow Simion's advice. In many ways I envy you." Andy told him. "Envy me?" Todd said. "Why, you are much more aware of things than I could ever be." Todd was surprised at the comment. "I envy you because you will be one of the first in so many years to venture out; to feel free in what will be a pristine world again. You will see the world with freshness, the excitement and thrill of discovery. Yes, I do envy you that, but I also am delighted for you as well. Your life with Dana and Dern is just beginning and mine is coming to its close. Enjoy it and treasure what you have and dream of what will be. It has been worked hard for and is a great gift." Andy told him.

Todd got up "Thank you Andy for telling me everything. I feel good knowing I am at no fault and have not put anyone in danger. It's a great relief to me." Todd told him. "I will have a great many more questions and I know where to come to seek the answers." Todd shook Andy's hand and both shared an understanding. Todd left for home.

His mid wandered to what Andy had told him and how Simion knew what would happen. It was a relief to know the he was not responsible for the air getting in. He thought about the fact that Dana had always believed Zack was alive out there and Andy had just confirmed that it was possible. He too Andy's challenge and tried to image life without the conveniences they had and he couldn't. His mind drifted to the fact the virus was changing them, their children would be enhanced. How he wished he could tell Dana. He would tell her someday he told himself.

When he arrived at home he found Dana rocking Dern here things were calm and peaceful for him. Dana looked up when he came in and then took Dern to his cradle. Todd made some coffee and was sitting down when Dana returned to their small kitchen.

"So how did your talk with Andy go?" Dana asked. "It was definitely interesting. He has given me a few things to think about that's for sure." Todd sipped his coffee. "How did your day go?" Todd asked. "Oh, it went. Dern fills my days. He's still taking a lot of my time" she answered. "Well it won't be forever and I have a feeling as he grows you will wish you had another" Todd said to her. Dana smiled "You think that because you don't have him all day. There's a lot of work caring for him. It's so worth it though. It's a labour of love." "You, my dear are a good woman" Todd told her. "You know we haven't done anything together for a while. How about we take him to see Dirk and Carla? I think he likes the animals" Todd smiled at Dana. "Yes I think I would like that" Dana replied. "I like the animals too" she said. Todd relaxed for the first time in a long while. The knowledge that he was not putting the complex at risk was a great burden lifted from him. He could enjoy himself with a clear mind.

The rest of the evening was spent in quiet company for them both. Love was a beautiful thing and sharing it with the person that was truly your friend and companion was even better. It seemed no two people could have made more suited to each other as Todd and Dana, but then all couples that love each other feel that very way.

Todd slept well and woke to Dana talking to Dern. She adored the child and it was pleasing to Todd to see it. How afraid she had been and now it seemed so long ago. "Good morning sleepy head" she said to Todd. "You slept soundly last night, first time you have in a long while" she said. She had Dern dressed and the diaper bag was being filled with everything but the kitchen sink, Todd thought as he watched her. "Looks like I am the one holding things up" he said as he went in for a shower. Dana was happy the three of them were going somewhere today. It wasn't long before they were fed and on their way to visit Dirk.

Life had settled into a routine for Dana. She had become a mother and the world changed for her. She was seeing the complex as a secure place to give Dern the best chances. Her mind drifted to Rose and she remembered Rose telling her life here had many things for them and she agreed. Dana still wanted to get the people out, but now with Dern to think of, she wanted to make sure it was safe. "You are awfully quiet Dana" Todd said. "Oh I was just thinking about something Rose had said to me a while ago and I think she may have been right" Dana told him. "We must visit them soon. We have not seen much of them" Dana told him.

They had arrived at the animal tunnels. Dirk and Carla were always pleased to see them. Dirk picked up Dern and before Dana and Todd knew it, he and Carla were headed toward the corral. "You must see our latest baby" Carla said. "He's the first to be born in several years to an old couple here." They all followed Dirk and he led them to a section that was not open to everyone. When they arrived at the pen Todd and Dana were amazed to see a pair of large work horses and their foal. "He's lovely" Carla said "and we nearly lost him. The pair is old and there are only five mating pairs. He was quite a surprise because we didn't think she could foal anymore." Dirk kneeled over and Dern patted the foal gently. "Easy Dern he's not well" Dirk said to him, not that Dern would have understood. Todd and Dana watched as Dirk sat Dern beside the foal resting on the hay. Dirk looked over the animals and then at Carla. "I don't know my dear, he's not good yet. It's such a shame, there are so few left. He would have been a good stud. The bloodline he carries is all but gone now."

No one paid much attention when Dern leaned on the foal and patted gently. He almost seemed to hug the foal. "He may make it. He's not getting worse and that's a good sign" Dirk said. They got up and picked up Dern. Dana and Todd looked around some and were amazed at the large animals kept in those tunnels.

Carla now had Dern and was heading back to the front tunnels that the public had access to. "You have some interesting stock in there" Todd said to him. "Yes I agree" said Dirk. "Someday they will be the beginning for so many lines for the outside. We have had low birth rates with them though. It might be the cross breeding we had to do. They might make it if we can keep them alive." Todd was beginning to grasp what Andy had told him how frantically they worked to create breeds that were immune to the virus. "How many animals did you lose in the outbreak?" Todd asked. "We lost the purebreds, the cross breeds faired better. It's a good thing that we were breeding them to the others. We were trying to get as much diversity as we could for future breeding and it turned out they were the survivors." Dirk looked at Carla "It was that old girl's idea too. I believe she was the one that saved everything you see in here." Todd smiled at Dirk. "Did you know she has records on every animal here and their bloodlines?" Dirk said. "She takes on too much I think sometimes." Dirk told him. Todd watched the two women talking and was amazed how well the got on.

The rest of the day was spent visiting and Dern was the centre of attention. By the time they left Dern was asleep and he could see Dana was weary as well.

When they got home Todd put Dern to bed and then Dana. He lay down beside her and was soon asleep.

Todd was up early for work before Dana stirred. He came in and kissed her and Dern before he left. He walked lightly and left quickly.

He was soon at the machine shop. He had left the plans and orders for the others. It seemed they had everything done.

Todd made his way to the communications labs. Erik greeted him when he went in. Todd asked how Katrina was doing. Erik beamed "She's getting big now and walking." "And how is Gwen?" Todd asked. "She is doing well. She's been doing work in the kitchens. Since Katrina was born she has been food conscious. It's good to see her take an interest" Erik smiled. "I understand completely, Dana is the same. Motherhood becomes them" Todd said and they both laughed. "I just came to watch the monitors a bit" Todd told Erik. "No problem, I will be working on the reports for the council." With that Erik returned to his office and Todd found a chair and began watching the monitors. He noted the wind blowing, but nothing in the way of wild life. He watched the monitor and it was like a dream to him. He thought about Zack. His life out there, witness to the virus outbreak on man and if he had survived what was he going through? Todd thought about the caves and decided he would continue looking for the air coming in. I wonder how long Andy knew the air was coming in. He thought about Dirk and Carla thinking it was the release of the animals that let the virus in. He felt bad for them to be left believing that to be so. His mind wandered to Simion's journals hand him using his influence to get Dirk, Carla and David to breed the different breeds of insects and animals to build a stronger stock. What a shame he got the virus and his death soon followed. He saved us and lost his own life to the very thing he saved them from. Zack could be alive and others as well. How many Todd wondered. Would they ever find their way back? He looked at the monitors and with more questions than answers he got up and went home.

He found Dana and Dern and smiled at them. After hugs all around, he sat on the couch. He knew someday he would have to tell Dana everything Andy had told him. Dana gave him Dern and as he held his small son and looked into his small face he felt his heart warm. "Dern, your life will be good and you will feel the wind in your face and feel the rain on you skin.

I promise this." Dana was in the kitchen and called to him. "You have been your old self almost. Are you okay?" she asked. "Yes Dana. I am and I am in a good cheer. Our future looks brighter" he said. Dana looked at him and smiled. She had been concerned for him, but he seemed to be his old self again. The evening was spent in quiet company, both enjoying each other and playing with Dern.

Tomorrow was another day and the future could just get better.

Chapter 27

West and Willow pushed and pulled the wagon back home to their valley. Willow kept hope that her father would be at their cabin. West knew that there was no great love that Willow had for her father she harboured no hatred for him, more pity than anything else. She was concerned for her mother and other siblings.

The trip seemed longer than normal with the added tension. By the time they reached the last hill over looking the valley all seemed still and quiet. Willow knew in her heart that her father was not there. West put his arm on her shoulder "He's probably at home as we speak" he said to her. Willow nodded "Brad and Gary would not give up the search and they will find him." With that some tension settled. "Well let's get this wagon home and get a warm fire going." The two had the wagon at the cabin before long and West told Willow to go in that he would unload it.

Soon the fire was going and West had the treasure from the wagon inside. He retrieved water and they soon had tea and started sorting the good they had brought home. Willow looked at the material and all the goods. "They have been so good to us again" she said. "Look at all these things. I have never been so cared for. Zack is getting to be an excellent potter. The bowls and pitcher are lovely" West agreed. "He did a great job on the tiles as well. We will have a nice place here. I'm glad we asked Carrie to take the other cabin" West told her. "Me too, if Freda comes it will be grand. She was so good to us. What do you think this new girl is like? The one her met, Nimuri was her name" Willow asked. "If she makes him happy that's all I care about" West smiled.

The cabin was warming up and they had plenty of things to keep them busy. They spent the rest of the day putting away the things they brought home. When they finally go organized Willow made tea and West cooked something light to eat. The two sat at the table, Willow asked West "Do you think they will find my father? I don't think he thinks right. There's been something wrong with him for a long time." Willow knew he was losing his mind. "They will find him" West told her with confidence. "He may yet show up here." West knew chances were getting slim that they would ever recover him. With illness in his mind he could be lost in the woods until he died of starvation or exposure. The nights were getting far cooler now. He knew the snow would soon be flying. That did not mark well for anyone lost in the woods. "Well seems we have some time before it gets too cold want to help on the path tomorrow?" West asked her. Some hard work would keep her mind off her father. "Yes, I think I would like that. It sure would be nice to have some nice paths in the spring. I'm not looking forward to all the muddy trails." "Then it's settled we will start with the trails around here now that it's not a secret anymore." West winked at her. Willow had to smile in spite of herself. "You were sneaky to do that trail up the hill. I had no idea. It was such a nice surprise" she told him. "In the morning we will see how nice you think it is" and they both laughed. The sun had set and the little light they had was gone. The fire flickered and sparked as they watched it. "Let's go to bed" West said "It's been a long day." Willow too was tired and after washing, the fresh bed was comfortable and inviting. West loved Willow and she never ceased to be amazed at his tenderness. He was a considerate lover and in her mind she knew he would always be hers. West too found Willow to be everything he dreamed of and loving her was easy for him. He just seemed to know or feel his way to pleasure her. They held each other close and they slipped into dreams none of which they would remember the next day.

West opened his eyes to Willow's empty spot on the bed. She was up and busy in the kitchen. He lay there and listened to her sounds. He liked her sounds, they made him feel secure. He thought about how she would feel when hope was given up on her father. It was getting to that. He was gone too long and with no signs of him in the forest.

West got up, dressed and joined Willow in the kitchen. It didn't take them long to finish the porridge and fried bread. "It looks to be a good day to move gravel" West told her. Willow smiled. She thought of the fort and how they all had all the trails gravelled and trees growing down each lane. "I have plans for it here you know?" she told him. "I want to make an open area for the children to play in and a kinda courtyard shaded in for us to sit and watch them. I want flowers and a table or two, with chairs. Yes I think it will be a nice place to relax." West raised an eyebrow "but we don't have any children yet" he said. "Well we will, I'm sure and besides there will be Carry here and Nimuri. You never know maybe another family in the future" she said with a matter of fact, West smiled. "Well then we best get at the paths between the cabins first."

The two went to the workshop, gathered up the shovels and a wagon. West set out for the river and Willow went back into the cabin. She had a basket packed with food and a jug of water. It didn't take her long to catch up with West. He took the jug and basket and put them in the wagon. "It seems to me that first a path to the river might be the place to start. It would be easier to pull the wagon over gravel then a dirt trail." Willow agreed. So they set to work, West shovelled and Willow pulled the wagon to each spot further down the trail to dump it. It didn't take long to have the trail to the cabin done.

By mid afternoon they had enough. Both were happy that the path to the river was done. Tomorrow they would start the paths between the cabins and work sheds.

Willow wasted no time in starting the fire in the cabin and West fetched the water. They washed and made dinner of steamed vegetables with bread. West filled the big tub with warm water. Willow, tired was soon in it and soaking. West sat back and watched her enjoy her bath. It was worth the effort of filling the tub. Soon he was over washing her back and hair. Willow had a way of getting him to do what she wanted him to do. The worst part was he didn't mind at all. He picked up a jug of rain water to rinse her hair. Jo, his mom always rinsed her with rain water, seems to make it softer. West never thought much about it, but after many years of habit with his mom it just flowed over to Willow.

When she had her soak he took his turn. Willow sat by the fire and brushed her hair. "You know" Willow said to him as he washed "I don't think they will find my father. I think he is gone, lost forever to the forest." "Willow, don't give up hope. He may be found yet." "Maybe it's a good thing" she said. "He was not happy and I think the life he had before the virus was where he still wanted to be. I heard him and mother often on how they wished they to had passed in the outbreak. How much they disliked the world now. Maybe mom will find something worth caring about and going on for now that he is gone. He always made her, well, unhappy with it all." West knew her home life was not that good, but to hear her talk about her dad like that made him feel sadness for her. "I can't imagine that Willow. My father was always so positive and mom too" West said. "I know" she answered. "They helped me see so much beauty and I found the woods often very soothing. Guess that's why I always collected mushrooms. Not so much for the bounty of them, but the tranquility of finding them. You are lucky your mom and dad are so nice. I wish we will be half as positive as them. Our children will be happy and always safe and secure. Will you get out of the tub? I want to empty it before night falls and its dark out."

West hurried and soon dressed. West emptied the tub and she made tea. After they settled down they both could feel the day's labour catch up to them. "So how do you like road building?" West asked and smiled at her. "Just fine, I can't wait until we get started on the road" she replied. "Well that might be in a few days yet."

The following days they worked on the paths and watched the leaves start falling. Willow had found a stand of maples, now they would have syrup.

They took a day off to roam the woods. Both were now sure that hope was gone for finding her dad. Willow was sad, but at the same time a relief washed over her. No more bitterness, bad tempers and rages he would have taken out on them. She had been freed when she married West, now her mom and siblings were free too. She felt such pity for him.

Fleeting thoughts of Carry and his mom coming came up in the conversations. They had the cabin ready and waiting for them to come.

Snow was covering the tops of the mountains and crispness could be felt in the air. Not just the mornings but well into the day. No word from Zack and Jo about Willow's father. West now felt the search was fruitless labour. He was gone and most likely passed away.

The calm serenity of the valley was broken by the sound of people. Willow looked out of the cabin to see West helping Carry and his mother Freda. The most anticipated arrival for Willow was Nimuri. She put on a pot of water and joined them on the path.

"Carry, Freda it's good to see you" Willow said and hugged them both. Carry beamed and introduced Nimuri. "This is my wife." Willow took her hands and told her welcome. The two women smiled and from that moment on a bond was formed. "Freda, come into the cabin where it's warm and I'll get you some water to wash off the trail dust." Nimuri and Willow helped Freda down.

"So this is the home I'm to have?" Freda said. "I think I will like it here. I have always envied the peace the folks outside the fort had."

The women were soon inside the house and West and Carry were left outside with the wagon. West looked at Carry "Do you get the distinct feeling that we get to unload the wagon at out cabin?" They both laughed. "We best get after it they will want to be sorting out all this stuff out before bed no doubt." Again a knowing look passed between the two young men. "It's good to have you here my friend." West said to Carry. "It's good to be here" Carry told him. "I was getting tired of the fort and the people. Nimuri and I want our own lives away from all that. Mom wanted to get away for a long time. The work was getting hard for her life. I will be happy to see her have time for herself for a change. Come on let's unload the wagon. I have much to tell and there's much I want to learn of the valley." Carry noted there was plenty of wood stacked outside and thanked West. "You have to tell me all your plans for the area. Oh yes, Zack wanted me to tell you that they did not find Willow's dad. The search has been called off." West looked at him "Thank you for the message and please don't say anything to Willow. I will tell her." Carry nodded. The two men unloaded the wagon and before heading to West's cabin, they started a fire in the cabin to get it warm for their later return.

With all that done they headed to the other cabin. They could smell the food cooking and picked up the pace. When they arrived Willow and Nimuri had things well in hand. Nimuri presented them with a pan of warm water to wash up. The two looked at each other and smiled. They knew that the women owned the day and if they wanted to eat they both better wash. Willow had a pan of water for Freda to soak her feet in.

Soon the table was set and they all sat to eat. "I'm surprised to see you started a road. I can tell you it made travel much easier" Carry told them. They have the road down to the settlements, both sides from the fort done now. Travel has become much easier" he added. "Is there still a lot of folks at the fort?" West asked. "Too many if you ask me" Freda added in. "They need to get them out and on a piece of land they can work if you ask me." "It takes time to build cabins mom, they will have more made next year and that will help." "Anything new that might be a help?" West asked. "No not really, but once the folks get more settled things will be made to help in daily living."

Willow was making sure everyone had enough to eat also took note that they were not telling her that her father had been found. She knew he had not. Nimuri and Willow washed up. West and Carry teased his mom about her sore feet. She took it all in stride and all the time kept an eye on Willow.

When the dishes were done it was Freda that told West to take Carry and Nimuri to their new cabin. "She needs to see her new home" Freda insisted.

When they all left Willow asked Freda if she wanted more tea. "No thank you, but I would have you come and sit with me a moment." Willow went over and sat beside her. Freda looked straight into her eyes "They have not found him and they are not likely to. The search has been called off." Willow sat there not moving. Then she said "Well it's done then. He's gone. I will not pretend that I am broken, I am not. I feel sad for my mom. She will suffer the most. He was with her most of her life. I wish I felt sad, but I feel more pity and almost relief for them." Freda watched her and was satisfied she spoke the truth. "Willow some never could get past the outbreak and what it destroyed for them. I was lucky I lived at the fort, but the stories I heard and the sadness of the people. It was heartbreaking, So much so, but life has crossed another bridge in time and it will again. You have shown great strength and wisdom not to follow in his footsteps. It's easy to wallow in denial and self pity. It is much harder to pick up the pieces of your life and carry on. If his mind was gone as I was told he would not even be aware of his own passing. That can be a blessing too."

Willow looked at Freda "I am glad you're here" then hugged her. Willow nodded. "Alright then, would you walk this old woman home?" Willow smiled and the two women were on the way to the cabin. Freda held Willow's arm and told her to come see her often.

When they arrived at the cabin, Willow and Carry couldn't believe how nice the cabin was and the furniture and linens, even the dishes from Zack. West took Willow and Freda strolled about the cabin. "After all the years in the fort it seems strange to be in a real home" she said. "It's going to be nice here." She found a chair and sat down. "Well" West said. "We will leave you to get settled. I want to hear all the news from your journey after" he said. "We have a root cellar well stocked so no worry about food. Tomorrow then" West said and he and Willow walked home.

West held Willow close when they got outside. "I'm sorry I have some bad news for you" he said. Willow interrupted him "Freda has told me West. It's okay I will put it right soon. I just can't believe he is gone. To just vanish the way he did" she said to him. "Willow, he just went so far into his own mind he couldn't find his way out again or he didn't want to." "I know "Willow said. "All hope is not lost yet in finding him, to bring him back to us from the depths of his own mind is something else altogether. I will not give up on him until they find him alive or passed. He's out there somewhere." West just hugged her, he was at a loss as to what to do at this point as well. "Let's go home" she said and they walked to their cabin.

It would be different to share the valley with Carry, Nimuri and Freda, but this winter the company would be a great comfort. Sleep came quickly for West and Willow. It had been a strange day with the sad news about Willow's father and the grand arrival of Carry and his family.

Carry and Nimuri loved the cabin. "I can't believe he built this cabin for us" Nimuri said. "Life is good. I have never been this happy" she said to Carry. "Look at all the wonderful things they have made for us." Nimuri wandered around the cabin looking at everything; the furniture, the dishes, the blankets, everything. Freda watched her and was filled with joy for her. Truth be known Freda was as happy as Nimuri. She to, had a home now, a real home. She had lived at the fort for so many years even before the outbreak. Her parents had lived there too. She had grown up learning the old ways and it seemed it was a good thing after all. She was so comfortable in her rocking chair West had made. Carry and Nimuri were making up the beds and unpacking the things they brought from the fort. Freda had enjoyed the visit with Zack and Jo. She liked Brad, Sara, Gary and Lily, Helen was a strange person, but from what Jo told her when Duke went missing she changed. Duke had not been easy to live with as he had such troubles, then the new family; Herb and his wife Jean and her brother Kalvin. The population was spreading out; soon the people would be living everywhere again. Freda was sure that there were people that had not been found yet, but they would be just like the folks on the prairie.

"Mom, your room is done for tonight" Nimuri called. "Thank you my dear." Carry and Nimuri's room was at the other end of the cabin.

Freda got up and gathered a few of her things she brought and headed to her room. It was a lovely room she thought. She was tired and it didn't take long for her to fall asleep. Tomorrow their lives were to take a new turn. For some it would be another turn in many trials life always seems to place in front of you.

With morning came the organizing of the things Carry and his family brought. The cabin had everything they needed. West and Willow worked hard to see they had the things they would need. Carry had a few things for them as well. He would give them to them later.

Willow was surprised when she woke to the sounds in the kitchen. West was up early she thought. She welcomed the tea he gave her. "You're up early West" Willow said. "I was thinking I might take a quick trip to see Zack. Did you want to come with me?" he asked. Willow wanted to go, but with Freda, Nimuri and Carry she decided to stay, besides seeing her mother would be too upsetting. She just put it all in order in her mind so she could accept his passing. To go and have it all in an upheaval would do them no good. "No I think I will stay" she told him. "I really don't mind now, Carry and his family are here. Besides they will need someone to help them get acquainted with the area." West smiled. "I will go see them before I go, but for the moment eat your porridge" he told her. She was hungry now that she was a bit more awake. "What are you going back for?" she asked. "I asked dad to make more tiles and I want them before the snow flies. Then I would like to get more trails done in gravel. I will get Carry to help me." "It might be an idea to get him to go with you. He will just be under foot until Freda and Nimuri get the cabin in order" she said. "I think I might at that" he replied. "The breakfast was lovely, thank you" Willow told him. "Would you like me to pack anything for you?" she asked. "No I have a bag together" he said. "It won't be a lonely home for you. Carry and I will have to build another cabin. Maybe we can do it in the spring while you women are in the garden" he told her. He went over and hugged her. "I want to have a look for your dad. I need to put it to rest in my mind that he is really gone." "West I love you and will wait for your return and word of my father." He had his pack full and headed out. He told Willow he would ask Carry to keep an eye while he was gone.

He stopped at Carry's cabin and told them he would be gone for a few days. Carry was more than happy to keep and eye out for Willow. With her safely at home he headed to the river.

He decided to follow it for a while thirst would have driven Willow's father to it, West thought. He walked the bush line looking for any sign he had been there. It was midday when he stopped at the river to fill his canteen. West eyes were keen and he was always surveying the area he was in. He filled his jug and continued on around the bend. He saw a log jam and as he got closer he realized it was more than just a log jam. It didn't take long to see it was Duke in and amongst the logs. West had no doubt he was gone. He was not sure what to do. He knew he had to get him out of the river and jam. West was startled by the appearance of Duke; at closer inspection there was no doubt that he had been in the water for some time. He really wasn't prepared for what he was seeing. Poor man he thought.

West made his way back over the jam to the shore. He would need something to carry him out of the woods. He cut down some saplings and made a cot of sorts. He made some rope from bark strips and hoped they would be strong enough hold the weight. He had two blankets with him; one he used to cover the makeshift cot and the other to wrap him in. West knew he would have to break up the jam to free him. It was getting into early evening and West had to make a fire and shelter for himself. He knew he was about half a day from his parent's valley. The mountain was steep and as he sat drinking his hot tea he decided maybe floating him down on the river was a better plan than trying to take him over the mountain.

West sat there and the knowledge that Duke was just off shore gave him an uncomfortable feeling. He had never seen many dead people other than the bones of them, but Duke was there and the water had disfigured him so much. He had the urge to run out there and pull him free, but he knew by the skin floating in the water separate from his body it was not a good idea to try that. West fed his fire more; think about Duke was making him colder than normal. He would start to break up the jam in the morning.

With that thought West knew he would need something to pry with and knew he would need a sturdy log pole to help him with the job ahead of him.

He lay back against a tree and stared into the night's sky. The familiar satellites passed over and he thought about the world that Duke and his parents came from. How different things were now. Duke was one of so many that never could accept things as they were. West never having known anything else, had a hard time understanding why. This life was good; he always had the things he needed. He thought about Willow, now she would be able to find peace knowing her father's body would be laid to rest. She would be able to put it behind her instead of maybe, just maybe he was alive out there somewhere.

Helen, Willow's mother would suffer as she loved him and such a big part of her life would be gone now and it was fact now that West had found him. Sleep was evading him; he could not turn off his mind. This was the first grave in his home valley, he thought and although he knew that would be a fact of life he dreaded the day his parents passed. Again his mind wandered to Willow passed the thought of her passing and he stopped almost as fast as that thought entered his mind. Tears welled in is eyes and he knew he would not handle that well when that time came.

West fed the fire more. He had to settle down and get some rest, tomorrow would be a long and sorrowful day. He could see his breath in the night air, winter was coming. He knew the work that he and Willow had done all summer would sustain them and Carry's family through the winter. Next spring there was much to be done and with Carry to help it would make the work much easier. Maybe they would be able to start a flax field this year. With his mind on more pleasant things West soon found sleep.

It was the last pops in the fire that woke him. He was stiff with the cold and he fed the fire more to get it going. With daylight, the log jam loomed off shore. He was tired this morning. He got some tea going and ate some of the food he packed, saving some for lunch. If he had not freed Duke by then he would go get help.

After an hour or so he had warmed and searched for more fire wood and a sturdy pole. He found what he had been looking for. West started out for the log jam and once on it looked for the easiest log to break free. He watched as the ones he got loose floated away down the river. He tried not to look at Duke, the sight of the body almost made West sick to his stomach. It was hard work freeing the logs.

After a few hours the log he was working on finally came free. The whole jam he was standing on began to move. West lost his footing and plunged into the water. He held onto a log and with a great creaking and an almost moaning the jam started to break up. West was not prepared for that although he should have been. The thought of the jam shifting and completely breaking up had not occurred to him. He watched the logs float passed him. The water was cold.

West looked over to see if Duke's body was still there and it was gone. West couldn't believe his eyes, where had he gone? He knew he had to get out of the water or he would share Duke's fate. He swam towards the shore, his limbs growing colder faster. He saw a log moving towards him and he knew he had to get out of its way, with no where to evade it. He dove underwater to swim under it, when he tried to surface he was blocked by another log. He swam further under the water, his breath was running out. He had to get some air. Almost in a panic he thrust upwards with all this strength he crested the surface and gulped in the air. He turned to see what was holding him under to find Duke's decomposing head and shoulders sticking slightly below the surface. West grabbed at Duke's shirt and dragged the corpse with him to the shore. West was freezing now and knew he had to get warm; Duke now free of the jam was still in the water. West pulled him to the shallows. He stopped when great chunks of skin started falling away. West, although freezing and tired turned and wretched.

They had come down river some and West knew that Duke would not float away from where he was. He made his way back to his make shift camp. He stripped off his clothes and wrapped in a blanket. "Oh I can't believe I got more wood before I started this" he thought. Soon he had the fire going and it did take long to stop the shivering. He put on dry socks and the shirt he brought. He had to dry his pants and other clothes. He ate the food that was left and with no tea a cup of warm water helped. The thought of Duke almost made him sick again. He had to wrap him up. It would save West from looking at him and would help keep him together. It seemed to take forever for his clothes to dry. West took the blanket and the ropes to the cot and knew the job at hand would not be a pleasant one. He walked back to Duke's body. He took off his footwear to keep them dry. He covered Duke's body with the blanket and rolled him up in it. Then he tied the blanket around him. He was glad he didn't have to look at the corpse anymore. With the wrappings done he pulled the body onto dry land. The floating him down river plan was out. West no longer wanted anything more to do with the river for that day.

He put back on his foot wear and went back to his camp. He packed up what was left of his gear and dragged the cot to Duke. With the other blanket on the cot and the ropes long enough to strap around his shoulders, he loaded him on. He lifted up the one end and started to pull him along. He was thankful Duke was passed, had he been injured the trip would have been awful for him. The bumping and jerking as West pulled one end of the cot and the other dragging on the ground. It seemed to take all his effort to get him up the hills to the crests and then down the other sides always worrying that he would tumble away. By suppertime West was exhausted, but the sight of the valley below was welcomed. He had made it to his father's.

He sat and rested at the top of the hill looking down into the small valley. The streams of smoke were dancing out of the chimneys of the cabins. He could see the children playing and see someone chopping wood at Willow's mother's house. He looked over to Duke's body "Well you are home now Sir. Sorry it took so long, but I have done my best" West left the body there and went in search of his father.

The children were the first to see him and by the time he was at his parents they knew he was coming. Zack was sitting on the porch and Jo walked up the path to meet him. She took one look at him and knew something was amiss. "What's wrong West?" she asked as she got closer. "Hi mom" and he hugged her. "Let's sit on the porch" he said.

The two joined Zack on the porch and West told them of his last efforts to find Duke before the snow came. It was a mission to set his mind free and Willow's as well. He told how he followed the river reasoning that thirst would draw him there, right mind or not. Zack and Jo listened quietly. West told them of the log jam and what happened there. He never went into graphic details to save his mother's feelings. Jo sat and when West said he had recovered Duke's body and as his strength waned he left it at the top of the trail on the hill.

Jo looked at the two of them "I'll go tell Helen she must know." She headed there and met Brad and Gary on the way. She told them to see West and Zack on their cabins porch.

While his mother was gone West told Zack of the condition of the body. Zack knew it would not be pleasant sight. He would tell Jo and when they told Helen it would be her decision to look at him or not.

Brad and Gary were coming to the porch and after a greeting the news was told to them. Brad and Gary knew they would have to look at him to be sure it was Duke. It was a matter they both would rather forego. "Where are we going to bury him?" was the next question. Zack told them it would be a place Jo had long ago picked out for the ones that passed. She would tell them where. With the body so decomposed the decision to leave him where he was until morning was made.

Jo now with Helen told her the news. Helen had known for some time he was gone and it was more relief than a shock at this point to her. She would now lay him to rest and morn him. Jo didn't want to leave her alone, but she knew Helen was a private person. "Do you want me to stay for a while?" Jo asked her. "No, I will be alright. I am quite reconciled with the fact that he is gone. There is really nothing you can do at this point, but I do thank you for the concern. I will be okay, really. There is much I want to tell you when we have some time, but now we have to bury him." "Are you sure you are okay Helen?" Jo asked. "Yes I have done my crying for him. I can not weep in my soul anymore than I have. I will tell the children, they will have to know." Jo was worried about her. "I need to go see West, but I will come back" Jo said to her. Helen nodded.

She watched Jo leave and went and sat in her chair. She cried. The tears were not of great sorrow more tears of ending of a life that had been twisted, a relief in some ways. How they had so much enjoyed everything when they were young. Then after the virus, she thought how he had become so angry, an anger that could never be curbed. How such sadness it gave her to watch it eat him up inside and unable to do anything about his frustration. It was over, she thought, in many ways a blessing in disguise. Helen watched the children; they were understandably upset at her crying. She gathered them all to sit with her on the couch. They didn't seem to miss him; he had not been kind to them. To him they were just bodies to do work he didn't want to do. He never let them go hungry of cold, but the past had left him cold and unloving. He told her once that "I can't love them much because if they die I could not take it." She had watched the children be children since his disappearance. Helen sat with them. She told them, their father had been found, there was just quiet. John and Sam looked at her "Mom is he coming back here?" "Yes and No" Helen told them. Dawn never spoke. "Your father has passed away. We will bury him here where they will bury us when we pass away." Dawn spoke then "He has died mother?" "Yes" she told them. Dawn spoke again "We will be better now mom. I will help you" and the two boys agreed they would help. She knew Dawn was right, they would be better now. She was filled with pity for Duke. He missed life; being so bent on the past and not seeing the future.

By now Jo was home again. Brad and Gary went with West to Duke's remains. When they confirmed without a doubt it was indeed Duke they returned to Zack and Jo. Brad said "It's Duke, no doubt, but I would not let Helen of the children see him in his condition. Gary and I will make a box for him tonight." Gary asked Jo if she had an area set aside for burials.

Jo knew one day there would be folks that passed and directed them to a smaller area up the valley, it almost overlooked the valley. She always thought it would be a place for the ones that had gone before them. Being a bit out of the way it would not be passed in everyday living. Some could not cope with that she thought.

Zack told Jo he would make a headstone and to ask Helen if there was anything special she would like written on it. Jo nodded. She took out a sheet of paper and a measuring rope. After a few minutes she had what she needed and sent West to the workshop for several stakes she could use as markers. Duke being the first to pass away, Jo until then has no reason or mark the area for graves. It would have to be done now. The evening was closing in and she wanted it done so they could bury him the next day.

She took the items and headed out to the lot of land she planned for the graveyard. It was not a pleasant job, but one that needed to be done. Each plot had to be marked. It would eliminate a lot of unnecessary grief to dig a grave and have it part of a past grave.

As she walked up the small hilled area, she thought of Zack's parents and how they had been buried. How Zack buried the farmer they had found on their journey here. How different their lives were from when they started out. Jo was a quick and efficient worker and soon had the plan drawn on the paper. She took out the marking stakes and marked off where to bury Duke. She thought she would bring some flowers to plant over him that would grow each year. Jo, now on her way home had a few other ideas too about the graveyard. She would ask Zack's opinion and see if he agreed with them.

When she arrived home she found West in the tub, tea for her and Zack on the porch. "Did you get it marked off?" Zack asked her. "Yes I did" and she showed the plans on the paper. After a few minutes Zack agreed that she had planned the best way to use the space. "Zack I thought we could take a wagon load of rocks up there and as a gesture of kindness for Helen and the children, everyone in the valley could place a rock around the grave. I was thinking it would be nice to plant some flowers there that would bloom over him every year as well." "You never cease to amaze me Jo. It's a lovely thought and as always you help others to find comfort in the trials of their lives. Now I'm going to tell you something fairly unpleasant" Zack told her. "West had quite a time of things, I told him to bath and I would like you to boil his clothes tomorrow. He can use some of mine. As you know Duke was in the water for sometime and West had a hard time of it to get him out. I don't want to have to worry about any diseases, etc…he's bathing now and the water he is using I will get him to dump in a hole later. We will have to pour boiling water over the whole tub, alright?" Jo agreed. "I must go back and see Helen I want to make sure she is alright." Zack nodded. "Stay as long as you wish I will wait up for you. With West here I will have company." Jo left and made her way to see Helen.

When Jo arrived at Helen's she found her in the company of Kalvin. He had been very kind to her and the children since Duke's disappearance. He had chopped wood endlessly and with the children and yard. He did what repairs to the house that had arisen and to it the children minded her. Unlike Duke, there was a kindness of heart in him and the children were always eager to please him. Jo liked Kalvin and was happy when his sister and husband took the extra cabin. He had lost his own family so Helen and he had someone each other could understand how they felt. She had noticed that they spent many an afternoon together on the porch. Jo also knew that Kalvin never overstepped the bounds of her marriage vows. It made Jo think even more highly of him to never take advantage of Helen while she was travelling through a low time in her life.

When Jo came up the path Kalvin got up and offered his chair to her. Helen looked okay as far as Jo could see. Kalvin turned to Helen "I'll come tomorrow and help with the children. It's going to be a long day for you and I don't mind." Kalvin smiled and nodded at Jo as he left.

Jo sat down and Helen offered tea. "Well Helen how are you?" Jo asked. "Better now" she said. "I had a bit of a cry and I'm sure there will be more. I just can't help feeling he is in a better place now. He was so unhappy Jo and it spread out to us all. Jean, Kalvin's sister sent her condolences; she's a good person like you Jo" Helen said. "I could never tell you that before, Duke would never allow it. I never realized how much control he had over us and so much of it was not good. I did love him, but it was not an easy life with him." Jo knew that, living with anyone that was troubled in the mind would not have been easy. "Zack wants to know if you have anything special you want on the gravestone." Helen sat for a moment "Let me have some time to think on that" Helene said to her. Jo patted her hand "You take your time Helen."

The two women sat and talked for sometime. Dusk had passed and it was getting dark. Jo felt that Helen was going to be alright and after they talked Jo knew that Helen had accepted what had happened. She found his passing almost a relief for her and the children. They were going to be fine. Tomorrow would be a hard day and then the road to rebuilding a life for them would begin. With the people here life had promise and that made Jo feel better. She bid Helen good night and told her to try and rest.

Jo walked back home and found Brad and Gary there. They had finished their work on Duke's coffin. They also dug the hole to pour the tub water in. Zack had boiling water ready. West and the other men carried the tub to be rinsed in the boiling water. With that done they brought back the tub and West filled in the hole. Although he had bathed the sweat from the work did not feel like the seat of death he had from Duke. He felt clean now and it was more comforting. West had no trouble sleeping this night. He was in his old room; his mom and dad were in the house made him feel like old times. His thoughts had been so mixed and soon he just slept.

Zack and Jo stayed up and talked more. "How is Helen?" Zack asked. "She's going to be alright" Jo answered. "I think life with Duke was harder than we knew and I know his death has lifted a great burden from her. Kalvin was there and he is a good man. I think she will be fine" Jo told him. "Did she have anything special for the stone?" Zack asked. "Oh yes she wanted some time to think on that. I told her there was no rush." Zack nodded. "How's our by, he looked exhausted?" Jo asked Zack. "I'm sure he was" Zack said. "He had a shock himself finding Duke and it was not an easy time for him to retrieve him from the water. He told me he was stuck in a log jam." "Oh my goodness" Jo said. "How did he ever find him?" "He's got keen sight that young fella. He will help tomorrow, but wants to get back, Willow still doesn't know and the snow will soon be falling." "Oh dear Willow" Jo said. "I'm glad that Freda is there. She gives me such comfort. I know they are in good hands. She will help Willow to learn to deal with his passing as will West and Carry." "Well young lady we best go to bed" and Jo smiled at him. "Young lady" she laughed "Old woman more like" and Zack smiled. "You will always be my young lady."

The sun rose to find Jo in the kitchen. West woke to his mom "West get up, I need your help today." West rolled out of bed and washed. Jo had breakfast ready and West ate even though he was not that hungry.

When he finished eating, Jo took him up to the graveyard. He dug Duke's grave, it was almost noon by the time he finished. "Thank you West" Jo said to him. "You wash up when you get back" West just nodded.

Jo left him at the cabin and walked to see Kalvin. She had him take the children to gather some stones to put around the grave. While he was gone grabbed Brad and Gary to go get Duke and have him in his coffin before they brought him to the settlement. With the two men off to do what had to be done she stopped to see Helen.

She found her tiding her house. "Helen, it's me" she said as she entered her cabin. Helen looked up and nodded to Jo. "We are going to bury him soon. How are you holding up?" Jo asked. "I'll be okay" Helen said and she headed into the kitchen area. Helen sat down and let Jo make the tea. She could feel the finality of it. Her life would be so different now. She was a bit frightened of being alone, but knew the alone feeling would pass. Her plan at the moment was to keep busy. Everyday that passed would make things easier to deal with. "Have decided about the headstone yet?" Jo asked. "No not yet, I've been finding it hard to concentrate. After we get him buried I think I will find a routine and then be more clear minded." Jo agreed. Helen didn't question not seeing him. She knew to see him like that would be in her mind forever. She wanted to try and remember the good things about him.

The two women had tea and Jo told her she would be back when everything was ready. Helen thanked her. "Death is never easy. We always live and enjoy life; we teach our children everything about living, but most often we teach them nothing about dying. I don't fear death" Jo told her. "Nor should you. It's the completion of one's life. Be thankful he had life and take all the good things it will make your life all the better and easier in the future." Helen looked at her "I will try. He wasn't a bad man. His mind was gone." "I know" Helen said. "You have had a deal with so much. I would like to tell you, if ever you need to talk my door is always open and the tea pot is always on. I must go see Sara and Lily. Would you like me to come back later?" Helen told her no "I'll be ready before supper. We can bury him and put him to rest. He never had much rest, his mind never let him." Jo patted her hand and she left.

She met Kalvin on the way home. He and the children had collected enough stones. She asked if he would take them to the graveyard and he did with no objections. She saw Sara and Lily and then went to see Herb and Jean.

Brad and Gary brought Duke to the village.

Jo arrived at home and found West and Zack talking of the complex. After she had cleaned up they started to Sara and Lily's, then to Jean's and finally to Helen's. Everyone walked up to the graveyard. The men brought Duke. This was his final journey. No one talked much.

It was Zack that spoke the words over him. He asked everyone to remember his good points and to remember that he fought a terrible war within himself. He asked God to take him and then they buried him. Zack asked each person take a stone and with a good thought place it around the grave. Then he said a prayer for Duke and for all of them. With that the folks ventured back to the village.

Jean asked everyone to come for supper that she had plenty for all. They did and as the evening fell they each found their way to their own homes. Jo helped Jean clean up while West and Zack visited with Herb.

By night fall everyone was in their cabins and reflecting on the day that just passed. West was first to go to bed. He was going home in the morning. The weather had turned cold and poor Willow knew nothing of what had happened, Zack reminded him to save her feelings and not tell her of his condition when he found him, but tell her of the burial and the regrets of all the people. West was relieved it was over. Sleep found him after a while and tomorrow always came too soon.

Zack and Jo slept easier as well. They had seen so much grief in their time and now it seemed for some then end came before it should have. It was so sad that Duke lost his mind. He was too young to go, but as Zack reminded Jo. Maybe it was for the better as he was so tortured within himself. Life will prevail as it always does, but the cost could be too high in some cases.

The night was cold and they woke to a thick frost on everything. Winter had its grips on the village and it was only going to get colder.

Jo was up and had the fire going. It didn't take long before the cabin was warm. Jo had made West some food for journey home. She had some extra socks and added them to his travelling pack. She started breakfast and the two men were soon up. West ate and soon had his gear packed. He said his goodbyes and was on his way.

The walk home would be a long one. He hated to tell Willow. He was thankful that Carry and Freda were there. He knew Nimuri would be a comfort to Willow; she was of the same age. Now he was alone; he thrashed all the events of the last few days over in his mind. He was glad Duke had been found, but not on how it had come about or the state he was in which he was when West found him. Well he is home now and all the things that haunted him are gone forever. Soon the older folks would be gone and the world would be left to the young. West thought this might be good and bad. Good because of the memory of all the things past would be gone and the longing for it gone too. Bad because the knowledge they possessed and never passed on would also be gone. Time moved ever forward taking all on their short journeys. Then leaving them behind to gather new life and start them on their journeys. He thought about Zack and the complex. He wondered how they were closed up in their mountain. Zack would never see them again. West wonder how often he thought about them.

He made it nearly half way home before he stopped t eat. He made a small fire to keep the cold at bay and in the quiet he tried to think of a way to tell Willow about her dad. She would be okay after the immediate sorrow of it. West knew she would be alright. She loved her father, but the respect had long passed and she just pitied him now. He drank his tea and put out the fire. Best get on his way, the sooner he made it home the soon they could put all this behind them.

Willow had spent the days with Freda and Nimuri, she enjoyed their company. The women sewed and cooked. Freda showed her some new ways of making some things.

The last few nights had been long and lonely for her. She wished West would come home. She had her needle work and sat by the fire at night, that's how West found her when he got home. Willow was so glad to see him.

After he got in and cleaned up, West told her of her father. "It's okay West I guess I knew he was gone, but I am glad he at last been found. Now mother and all of us can get on without worry for him.

The evening was quietly spent. Carry had been over and left soon after he found out West was home. The news was told to Freda and Nimuri. Willow never spoke much that evening and they both went to bed early. West held her tight and Willow was content to feel the safety and security of being close to him.

The life of Duke was over and that was it, both knew that and did not dwell on it any further.

Willow slept and West found sleep easier now that he was home.

The next day they both stayed in bed. It was comfortable and warm. It was West that finally got up and lit the fire. When the cabin was warm Willow got up and made some food for the both of them.

West looked at Willow "Are you okay?" he asked. "Yes I will, but let's not talk of it alright?" West agreed.

Winter now had its grip on the land and soon the snow would come. Winter was the time to weave and sew. West had marked out the garden area on paper from Jo and they planned out the garden for the following spring.

Days drifted into a few weeks, the daily routines of each didn't waver much. Between West and Carry they spent a lot of time in the work shop. They had cut lumber for the out buildings they would need in the spring. That and any household items that could be made were made. The two men worked hard and West always found much to talk about. Both seemed to work for the things in their houses with pride.

Freda kept Nimuri and Willow busy; it was amazing at the amount of cloth they made. Willow and Nimuri spun flax and Freda weaved. They would all have new clothes in the spring. It was Freda that suggested dyeing some with onion skins. The result was a lovely yellow cloth. Food was still to scarce for dye, but the skins from the onions wouldn't have been eaten anyway. The three women talked of many things and children were often the topic.

With winter firmly imbedded in their valley the snow piled up. West and Carry kept the paths cleared. They all got on with the business of living and found each other company most welcomed. Willow never talked of her father and maybe it was just as well. West often talked of returning to search for the complex when they were alone. Willow was excited about the adventure that awaited the, but for now they just let the days slip into each other in the wait for spring.

Willow's mother kept busy all the time. Her home had taken on a new look, she had cleaned it up and order was established. She had the children go to Zack and learn how to read and write. She started to visit with more people there. Sara, Lily, Jean and Jo welcomed her. She had spent too much time alone when Duke was alive. He did not like her to have friends or to have anyone but him. Helen often thought now how the illness had kept her away from everyone. Kalvin visited her often and did any repairs that needed to be done. Often he would come with gifts that he had made, for the children and household things for her. It was so strange how in the last few months her life changed so much and changed for the better.

Kalvin arrived one day with a lunch packed and a sleigh in tow. He gathered them all and they spent the day sliding down a small hill. The children laughed and the ensuing snowball fight left them all tired and happy. The lunch he brought was filled with many goodies Jean had made. Helen found herself happy, a feeling she had not had in many years. Kalvin was a good man and had a kind heart. He knew of her suffering, the loss of his family made him even more thoughtful towards her. The attention he paid on her did not go unnoticed by the others. They gave them room to have the friendship they both needed.

Jo was weaving when Helen came to visit. "Hi Jo, is the tea pot on? I would really like to talk with you if the offer is still open." Jo stopped weaving and set down her shuttle "Come in Helen and yes the tea pot is always on."

Zack took the que and grabbed his coat "I will be in the work shop. I have some plans here I want Gary and Brad to have a look at." He gathered up the papers on the table and headed out the door. "Oh wait Zack" Jo said and picked up her shuttle "Could you ask Herb if he could carve me another when you're out" and Zack took the shuttle with him.

Jo put on some fresh tea and took Helen's coat. The two sat down. Jo not wanting to push Helen into a conversation asked how the children were. "You know Jo I don't think I have seen them so happy. I've been watching them and they play now. I have Kalvin to thank for that. He's a good man." Helen looked at Jo. "That's what I came to talk to you about."

Jo poured the tea and offered some jam and bread. "Helen" Jo said "Are you happy, I mean in his company?" "Yes I am" Helen told her "I have not been happy for so long it's startling to me." "Helen you have had a rough time of it. I know what our generation lost and what we have had to endure. I was lucky to have Zack, but after the outbreak it was not easy. Not only did you lose the way of life, you had to live with Duke's illness. Don't deprive yourself of some happiness because of some misplaced guilt. Any joy that can be found in life should be cherished. We know only too well how quickly it can be gone." Helen looked at Jo "How did you become so wise? You look at things with such clear thought" Jo smiled. "I never think of it like that I just think of life. It's a gift and everything happens for a reason. Kalvin came from the prairie. He must have watched many awful things go on around him that he could do nothing to stop. He travels here and after many months at the fort finds a new home here in the valley. He lives with his sister and her family and now you and your family have given him reason to find joy in himself. In doing that he has given you back the joy. I can't see this as anything but good. You find solace with him and I'm sure he does with you as well. The tragedy that you both went through has given you a bond that I for one would never object to or criticise." "Do you think, so soon after Duke's passing that I should feel so much for another man?" Helen asked her. Jo sipped her tea and said "Helen, Duke passed away not you. You're here and life is going on. Don't pass up something that might never be again over one that is no longer here. Think of him, but don't let his memory rule over you. You have many years yet to live and you have children too. If Kalvin feels the same way for you as you do for him then I think you both are lucky" Jo told her. Helene finished her tea and got up "You have made me feel right with the world Jo and I will always be thankful to you for it. You are truly a good person and my life is better for knowing you." "Thank you Helen" Jo said "But I never did anything. I just told you what I thought." Helen got her coat and as Jo was at the door with her, Helen hugged her. "You are a good person, thank you."

Jo watched her leave and knew Helen was a new person. Life had dealt her some nasty blows and she gathered up the pieces. With Kalvin's help the two were putting them together and forming a new life. It warmed Jo's heart to see it. She closed the door and returned to her weaving. Her mind drifted to West and Willow; she planned a trip to see them when the snow melted enough to get over the pass.

Chapter 28

"Dana! Dana!" Todd called "Are you just about ready?" "Yes, yes, just give me a second." She was putting the last of Dern's things in a bag. He was spending the weekend with his grandma and grandpa. It was the first break she was to have since he was born. Time seemed to have flown by, he was almost walking; well almost she thought. Dern was crawling and into everything. It was a constant battle making sure he didn't get into something he shouldn't be in. Todd had the weekend planned and she was looking forward to it. "Gee with all this stuff you would think he was going for months" Todd said. Dana just frowned. "Oh come on" Todd said "I'm just teasing you" and they both smiled.

It didn't take long to deposit Dern at Todd's mom and dad. He left strict instructions unless Dern was at death's door not to come look for them. Dana needed a break and Todd was going to see she got it. Todd's mom just raised an eyebrow at him. "You my son forget this is not new to us, we did have you remember" and they laughed.

Dern wasted no time in venturing forward to see what was new and exciting at Grandma's and Grandpa's. It was Todd that slipped his hand over Dana's and whispered "Let's get going while the going is good." She smiled.

They walked back to their dorm. Dana was surprised to find Todd had some packs ready to go. She knew immediately they were going to the cave. She looked at him and smiled. "It's been a long time since we have been and it's the only place that I could think of that's ours and private" Todd told her. Dana had no objections.

They gathered the packs and Todd had them in the cave in no time. The mason knew they were going down into the cavern again. With the books and the packs the masons knew they would be down there doing who knows what kind of research. Todd had been coming to the cave often unbeknown to Dana.

They got to the spot to enter the hidden cave, when Todd pushed the wall and a door opened. Dana looked at him. He had a hidden door. She lit up with a smile and told him it was perfect. Once inside she couldn't believe her eyes. He had carved the stone for a bed and a place to sit. He had lights and blankets here and even a vase with flowers in it. He thought of everything. Her eyes were huge at the sight of everything and Todd smiled. He was pleased with her reaction and with himself.

They set down their packs and Todd dug out the food he brought. To her surprise he even had a bottle of wine. With the food and drink out, Todd proceeded to tell her of the times he came to fix it up here. Dana was shocked that he had done all this and she had no idea. They shared the food and drink. Dana was finally relaxing. It seemed far too long since she had Todd to herself. With Dern there was always something that had to be done for him. She enjoyed her short freedom from him and relished the undivided time with Todd. With the meal done Todd told her "There's more I want to show you. I have something I want you to read later too, alright?" Dana nodded.

Todd took her hand and they started for the tunnel leading to the cavern where she found the crystals. She was so surprised to be able to walk there. He had carved the passageways big enough to walk in and stairs at the end. She recalled how they squeezed through the path before. "Todd, my goodness you have worked so hard, it's wonderful." He had lanterns set at different spots and turned them on as they walked by. When they reached the far side and looked back all the crystals shimmered in the light cast by the lamps. "It's beautiful!" she said to him. He smiled "Come I want to show you more."

Todd took her hand and led her further. He had carved a bench right into the wall. Along the way there were little spots in the walls for lamps, which he turned on as they went. As they sat there Dana could feel a breeze and she told Todd. "Yes I know the breeze is getting stronger the further we ho." They sat on the bench and let breeze flow over them. "Todd I can't believe you have done all this work here. Its wonderful thank you" she told him. "Have you found the water yet? I would like to see where the air is coming in." Todd smiled, he wanted to tell her the breeze was air from the outside, but decided to let her find out for herself. He had mapped this tunnel and knew they were very close to the outside.

"Dana" Todd said as they sat close together "I have been talking to Andy and he seems to think there is a good possibility that people did survive on the outside after the outbreak." "Yes I know" she said "My father contacted the complex after the virus did its damage, but then there was nothing. I often hoped he was still alive, but after a long while I wondered if that was good. You see they might not have food and starving to death would be a terrible way to die. The struggle for food might cause many to kill for what food there might be. If he did survive I fear he would never find his way back here. So I try not to think of it anymore." Todd's heart sank at the thought of her words. It was true. "I'm sorry he never made it back for you" Dana smiled. "It's okay Todd I have you and Dern now. I am happy. We will continue working here and testing what we can outside. Maybe, just maybe Dern will be able to venture out there. That gives me much hope." Dana held his hand just a bit tighter. "It will be as it is and when we finally get out; there is much work to be done just to get the animals into the land again."

Todd admired her determination. He also knew that getting outside might be a lot sooner than she knew. "So is this to be a working holiday or are we secreted away down here?" she asked. "That my dear is up to you" he said. "I didn't bring you here to work> I brought you here to have you all to myself" he smiled. "You said that you had something for me to read, what is it?" she asked. "It's a report I want to submit to the council, but no rush. Let's head back a ways."

They started back; Dana was still in awe of what he had done in here and was surprised how little she thought of it since Dern's arrival. He was growing so fast and before long he would be walking. It was when they were back at the first cavern that Todd started to tell her what Andy said. She was comfortable on the makeshift bed he carved into the stone and listening intently.

Todd told her what Andy said about the virus mutating and how some would develop abilities. Dana wondered how many generations would pass before they would realize they had these abilities. "You know" she said to Todd "It's strange how the virus took so much from people and now it seems like it was setting the environment and the people for new things. I mean can you imagine what it will be like if our future children had gifts? If thought could be passed without words or things moved by brain power alone" she said. "We are the new race almost." Todd never thought of it like that, but it did seem to be the case. He never told her that Andy believed that already there are children with gifts as she put it. "I wonder "Todd said "That if those with gifts might get abusive to those without the ability to stop them. What I mean is I'm not sure I would like it if someone read my mind and now my thoughts without me ever knowing they could. That is a bit scary to me" he said to her. "True" Dana said "But if people's thoughts could be read by others then those with the gifts would be in the same boat as you. This is all hypothetical and may never come to pass.

I was up to see Karen and David not long ago. Not to change the subject and I don't think David is all that well. We should make some time for him." Todd agreed. He poured the last glasses of wine and gave her one. "The founders are getting old now. I can see it in Andy and mom and dad as well. I can tell you we have a hard road ahead when they are gone. It's always seemed safe and secure with their guidance. When our generation is moved into power I hope we can follow in their foot steps with even half the integrity they have had and hold this place together as wisely as them."

Dana looked at him "If we have men and women that can see a smidgen of what has to be done we will fair well. Erik is now head of communications and he had his feet planted firmly on the ground. Petra has the agro tunnels down pat. Dirk and Carla's children run the animal tunnels to the sane standard as them. I think we are fine. I am more concerned with our own children. We still have connections to those that lived outside, when we pass all that will be just words on reports. Will they find the drive to seek the outside or be like Rose, content to stay here in the complex?" "Andy told me something similar to that. He said there will always be a few that will want something more, like the first explorers seeking out the world. He said it will be no different for all of us in here. I hope he was right and there are some that want more" he said to her. "This is such serious talk. I brought you here to be alone and spend the time with you. I feel like we should be in a council meeting" and they both laughed.

Todd lay down beside her and soon they were no longer in or out, just them and the pleasure they shared. Todd indulged her completely and Dana him. It was hours later when they both woke and realized the quiet of the cave let them sleep peacefully.

Todd got up and took the thermos of coffee. It was a long time since Dana had enjoyed a coffee so much. Todd kissed her forehead and asked her if she slept well. "Yes and I might add that it has been to long since I felt so good we have to have these getaways more often." Todd smiled and agreed.

Todd leaned back against her knees "Well do you want to see if we can go further along the cave and maybe map a few more feet?" "Sure and now I know you were down here working we should have tried to come more often. I didn't think that Dern took so much of my time, but he has. I love him so, but I think I better not forget me in there somewhere" she said. "It's pretty hard not to spend so much time when they are small" Todd told her. "They are so small and depend on us for everything, but he's starting to get around now and I don't want you to lose things you have done in the past. You have so many talents and you should be able to have time to pursue them." Dana told Todd. "How many women can say they have a truly kind husband as I do?" "Never mind the mushy stuff and get up" he said to her. "There's water there for washing" he pointed to the water jugs. "I'm going to turn on the lamps" as she settled with the coffee he started down the small walkway.

Dana sat up and drank more of her coffee. She felt wonderful and now she would be on an adventure, she smiled. She wondered how long it would be before Dern could be brought here? He would have to understand that was not to be talked of or come to, unless they were all together. Dana was older for her age so she could have been shown this place when she was twelve, but more children did not have her temperament. With that she got up and washed. Someday, but that was in the future, until then this was hers and Todd's place and that suited her just fine.

Todd was back and he retrieved his notebooks from his packs. He gave Dana her things. After she dressed and studied what he had mapped so far. He had a map of the mountains and on it he had marked how far he had gone. Dana stared at them and looked up at him "According to these the outside of the mountains is not that far away. Are you sure you have marked right?" Todd looked down at the maps "I thought the same thing that's why I'm glad you're here to double check my work. I do believe them to be correct though." Dana was almost shocked; if his calculations were right the outside world was no more than 500 to 700 yards away. "Of course these tunnels can twist and turn, we may be at the closest point right now" Todd said. Dana had to agree with him. "Let's see if they are right" she said and with the compass and tape measure they started checking his map. It took the better part 3 hours to complete the task. His accuracy was right on. Dana could feel her heart throbbing in her chest with excitement. "Just think that way" she pointed as she looked at the compass in her hand "is the outside world." She went over and touched the wall. "Someday we will be out there" she said. Something stirred in Dana at that moment. It was like almost reaching out to her father. She took her hand from the wall.

Todd never noticed he was looking over his maps. He stood up and looked into the tunnel. "Well" he said "looks like it takes a sharp right. Of course we will have to go in to see for sure. I think we can fit." Dana was now at his side looking in the tunnel. "Well, let's go." Todd got a rope and a spray marker for Dana. He pounded an axe into the wall and fastened the rope to it. After he set up the ties between them they entered the tunnels.

After squeezing through the opening, to the right the tunnel headed east. From what Todd see it was a tight fit. The tunnel twisted and turned more. They finally stopped after an hour and realized that the tunnel was going down. "Let's go back" Todd said "and get cleaned up. We can mark the map and just see where we are going in here. The rock is still limestone and I should be able to open this up for better movement in here." Dana knew there was a lot of work to do that. "What have you been doing with all the scrap you get from here?" Dana asked. "O I just carry it out and put it with the scrap heap in the mason's tunnel. What's a backpack of extra to them they never notice." "Smart" she said. "But that's a lot of dirt and rock to move" she said to him as they made their way back. "Yeah, but it was worth it. The look on your face made it well worth the effort" Todd smiled at her. "Are we going to start opening it?" she asked. "Not this trip. It's pretty dirty work. I'll work on it when I can" Todd told her.

They made their way out now and after they brushed off the loose dirt, they headed back to the first cave. They sat at his table and looked over the map. Dana got up and got them a coffee and they started to mark where the tunnel went. It was going down and now by the looks of things they had been almost where they started except about 20 feet below. Todd was right the tunnel did turn in and they were no closer to the outside than before. Todd could see the disappointment in Dana's face "Hey sweetie, don't look so glum. We have nothing but time on our side and I know we will find the way out" Dana smiled. She had poured out a basin of water and they both washed off the dirt. Todd brought out some food and said "Our last supper here for a while." Dana knew they had to go back. It had been a lovely break, but she was missing Dern. Now that he was getting bigger there would be more visits to grandma's and grandpas. They shared a lovely meal and then they cleaned up the cave. Todd had a bag to put the blankets in to bring home at a different time to be washed. He turned the lamps off and it seemed the trip was over far too soon.

They opened the hidden door and with packs full of things that had to be washed they climbed up and made their way home. They showered and went to get Dern.

When they arrived at Todd's mom and dad's they found Dern sleeping on grandpa's chest and grandma sleeping as well. Todd's mom led them into the kitchen area for some coffee. Dana smiled at the two of them sleeping in the chair. "I don't want to wake them they look so comfortable." "You know your dad Todd, he likes to think he is 20 years old, but he's not and Dern tired him out. I have been worried about him. The doctors say his heart is weak. Too many years of hard work is my guess. So how did you make out? Did you manage to spend some time together?" Todd smiled "Yes mom we did. It was long overdue too." "Well you can bring Dern anytime. He's such a lovely child. He just makes you feel good when you are around him" she said and smiled.

Dana was pleased they had a good weekend together. The one on one she had with Todd was lovely and she planned to repeat it when she could. They finished their coffee and Todd's mom went and got Dern. He never woke up as she lifted him up and put him in his father's arms. Todd looked down at his son and it warmed his heart to see the small sleeping face.

They had him home and in his cradle before long and Dana put his things away. It was good to be home, but she did miss adventuring. She often used to sit in the atrium and imagine the outside, what would it be like? Sometimes she was consumed by it, that was back then and this is now. She thought about Todd's mom and dad and she was glad they had a good time together.

She had just put Dern's things in for a wash when Erik knocked at the door. Todd answered and Erik came in. Todd knew there was something amiss. "Hi Todd, I do seem to be the bearer of bad news. Its David he's not well. The doctor's can't help him. I'm afraid he won't be with us for long. I just thought you might like to know." Dana sat down. "David, Oh my goodness. What's wrong Erik?" Dana asked. "He had a vein in his head burst. They don't think he will last long. I'm sorry Dana I know you spent a lot of time with him and Karen." "Karen, Oh my goodness, how is she and Petra? They are peas of the same pod." "I never spoke to Karen. She has not left his side. I wish I could say he will be alright, but I can not." "Thank you for the message Erik. I will go see Karen later and see if there is anything we can do." Erik nodded and left. She knew Karen and David were very close. This would not be easy for her. "I will go and see if she needs anything "Todd told her. Dana was glad he would go.

Todd was soon at the hospital. Karen and Petra met him in the waiting room. "Karen" he said "is there anything we can do?" he felt it was such an inadequate thing to say. Karen looked at him "He's gone Todd, but thank you. His work will be taken over by his students so no help needed there. I have Petra staying with me. She's been such a help. No I don't think we need anything, but thank you for the offer." Karen turned to Petra "Let's go home I need to rest for a while" and Todd watched them go. He felt helpless to do for Karen. Todd knew he would be buried soon and they lost a good man in David.

On his way home his mind wandered over things. There were few founders left and in time there would be none, all their knowledge gone with them. It was sad for him. Time moved on and where it would stop for each of them was unknown. In past times, the complex hummed with all the fresh new minds. Now in his time life was closing its hands over the lives that they led. It had found so many already and just continued to click by. Todd shock his thoughts free, time all in time. He scared himself when he thought like that. He knew he would have to tell Dana. First he needed to talk with Andy.

He stopped at the library and found Andy in his office. "Come in, come in Todd" Andy told him. Andy never betrayed how he felt with his conversation. "I just wanted to tell you that David has passed away." Andy looked up "Yes my lad I know. He was brilliant with his work on insects. I imagine his students will take over now. How's Karen holding up? Do you know?" he asked. "She seems to be okay, her daughter Petra is with her" Todd told him. "Good, good that will be a comfort to her. You do know those two made life possible, her for growing all for our needs and him for providing pollinators. What a wonderful match. Karen is a strong woman she will weather this storm."

Todd just looked at him. He seemed so business like, cold almost. Andy said "Spit it out lad, what's troubling you?" "You seem to be so cavalier about his passing. I find that, well unnerving." Andy sat back "Todd do you think you can stop death, well you can't. Death stalks us all and we will lose; it will find us, me, you, Dana and even little Dern. Everything has its place in life and in death. I will miss David and who he was, but I know I will most likely join him and all the others before you. You are young and should cling to your and I am old. Maybe that's why I have a different view than you. I have lived a long and wonderful life. I have seen things that you can't begin to imagine and have forgotten more than most will ever know. David will be missed, but the well being of those still here must take priority over those gone. There is nothing more we can do for them. I will talk with Karen soon and thank you Todd for coming to tell me." Todd knew that he had just been dismissed. It almost angered him that Andy didn't seem to care. He headed home; he had to tell Dana the bad news.

After Todd closed the door, Andy sat back. He opened his desk drawer and took out a bottle and a glass. As he poured a drink, his mind wandered over David's life. He remembered how he came to the complex with Karen; an odd couple. They never socialized much and both were brilliant, unlike any others in their fields of expertise. They had a work ethic almost a strict regiment. Andy remembered how once on a visit, David was working on a project of taking one aspect of ants and trying to cross breed it with ants of the same family tree. He worked for months and finally after his efforts almost seemed in vain the pupa hatched. The new breed or species had what he had project they would. He was like a child that just found the mother lode of candy. Yes, he was more interested in bugs than people, how he ever met Karen. She was the same as David; devoted to her crops and the two equally devoted to each other. They lost children in the outbreak and Andy knew it was a pain held deep inside both of them. They knew their work here was for everyone and must come above anything else. Karen would be hurt by this more than most would realize. He poured a drink and in the privacy of his office toasted David and wished him a quick and safe journey to the beyond.

Todd reached home and when he came in Dana knew that David was gone. She cried and Todd held her. "David was such a gentleman" she told Todd. "Oh my goodness, Karen will take this so hard. David was her other world, her crops one and David the other. I will miss him so." Dana wept for sometime. Todd told her go and lay down; he would tend to Dern if he woke. Dana did go and lay down and was soon asleep.

Todd found himself to be alone with his thoughts. He wasn't prepared for Andy's reaction. He wasn't going to dwell on it. Some people had different was of dealing with things. He had to let Andy deal with it in his way. He knew Erik would have told his mom and dad as well as all the other founders. Poor Erik he always had to bring the news good or bad. He seemed to take it in stride. Erik just fit into the place and his job suited him.

Todd finished putting the gear away from the cave and caught up with Dern's laundry. He checked on him and Dana and was glad to have them safe at home. Dana would be okay and her hurt feelings would mend. Dern was lucky; he was too little to know what was going on. Todd went to bed late, tomorrow was going to be a hard day. David would be taken to the tombs and all the people would have a chance to say goodbye. He was glad he was not a mason anymore. The tombs bothered him somehow and he hoped that his remains would be buried outside. Sleep found him and his mind found peace for a bit.

Dern woke them with his cries for food and dry clothes. Todd got up and got him. He changed his clothes and took him to Dana. Todd went to the kitchen put on the coffee and made the little fella some food. Dana did not nurse him anymore and when Todd went to retrieve the little guy he was more than happy to be fed. Todd always enjoyed feeding Dern and while he did Dana got up and showered. For her it was nice to have that for herself. She appeared, showered and Todd handed her a cup of coffee. The three sat at the table and David was not mentioned. Dana washed Dern up and started cleaning the small kitchen area. Todd had his showered then. When he dressed it was Dana that started the conversation about David. They would go to his burial and then come home. Todd nodded. It was a sad day and there was no way around it.

By noon they decided to go to the tombs. All burials were at 2: o'clock. It gave time for the masons to ready the tombs and all to gather. When they got there it was surprising to see all the people. David had always been a private person, but he seemed to have touched many lives. The speech in his name was not long and he was placed in the tomb. Karen and the other founders waited until all had left and then went to the conference room.

Andy had trays of drinks and each founder took one. Andy raised his glass as did the others. Andy spoke in a clear voice "To David." They all drank and dispersed back to their homes or work places.

Petra spent time with her mother and Karen found solace in the agro tunnels.

Todd and Dana took Dern home and there they passed the day. A death in the complex was a humbling thing. For many the complex was the only home they had ever known or ever would know. For some it was a sanctuary, for others it was like a liveable prison, but it still was home and losing anyone affected them all. David would be missed not only by Dana, but by Karen and Petra.

The next week things fell back into a normal routine. Dana decided to go see Karen. Todd had gone to work and Dana decided that she needed to see Karen.

She found Karen in the agro tunnels and it was Petra that was gathering samples for Karen. Karen was at her tables with various plant segments in front of her. Karen didn't seem to see her coming. It was Petra that saw her and welcomed her. "How's your mom?" Dana asked. "She's not doing as well as I would like. She has been deluging me with information this week. It's her way of coping I think" Petra told her.

When Dana approached the table Karen looked up. "What brings you to the inner garden today Dana?" she asked. "Actually I came to see you" Dana told her. Karen sat down and her attention was on Dern that was fussing a little now. Dana picked him up and it was Petra that asked if she could take him for a stroll. Dana agreed. Karen offer Dana a drink and the two women sat looking at the table with all the samples on it. "What have you been doing here?" Dana asked. "It's for Petra; I want her to see the genetic changes that happen over a few years. She has to understand it completely; there is no room for error. The lives here all depend on it. I'm running out of time Dana, David's passing has impressed that fact deeply in my heart and soul. We knew our passing would come and knew its part of living, but Petra our only child left and I fear for her. She still has many years to live and it's imperative that she knows this place like the back of her hand. David had several students that excelled in his field; the only one that I feel has the feel for a plant is Petra. She must learn everything I can teach her before my time comes."

Dana was almost stunned by what she heard. "Karen if you push her too hard it won't help. She won't be able to absorb it all. She has watched you her entire life and I for one have seen the love for you she shares with you for growing. She needs you now not to driver her intellect to the breaking point."

Karen lean over to Dana "I'm surprised that David passed first. He was always such a strong man. We had talked of him caring for Petra and leading her to the studies I had laid out for her. To help her progress to the next stages she would need to learn.

Dana interrupted Karen "You sound like you are not going to be around. I'm sure David thought the same thing. Life is not as predictable as you seem to want it to be." Karen looked at Dana. "Dana' she said "I'm dieing and I have known for quite some time. I managed to pin point where in my life I was exposed to the agent that had given me cancer. I know that soon my health will make me unable to work. So you see the urgency of what I'm doing?" Dana was stunned by what Karen had just said. "Does Petra know?" Dana asked. "Yes she does Dana, I told her before David's passing. I'm asking you to keep this to yourself. I don't want the folks to worry. Petra is good at her work and the complex will be in good hands." Dana asked "How can you be so calm about everything?" Karen looked over to her "Dana, my life is coming to its close there is nothing that can change that. I have never doubted that this time would come. I'm not afraid nor should you when your time comes. We are born, live and die, those actions come with little effort. It's what we do and how your actions affect those around us that count. I have always accepted that. What you did yesterday is gone never to be again, what you do tomorrow is where your thoughts should lie." Dana never thought of Karen as fearless, now she saw a side of her she never knew was there. "Now young lady" Karen said "Let's go find my daughter and your son."

Dana still amazed and slightly stunned went with Karen. They found them, Petra kneeling beside Dern who was looking directly into a giant sunflower head. It was a finny sight, the flower was so big and he was so small. What ever was transpiring the two of them were enjoying it immensely.

The four of them strolled around the flowers and it had a calming effect on them all. Karen and Petra showed Dana a species Petra had propagated, it was beautiful. Before long Dern let Dana know it was time to go, he was hungry and it was time for his nap. Karen and Petra walked back to the entrance with them and saw them off.

Dana couldn't get over what she had just experienced. Karen had stunned her. How could she be so calm about everything? As she walked she tried to really understand Karen. She finally came to the conclusion that many ways Karen was right. Things that happened yesterday were gone and the things you did today and tomorrow were the things that mattered.

Dana found herself at home. She turned her attentions to Dern and soon he was fed, changed and ready for his nap. She sat in the rocking chair and rocked. Dern always settled down and today was no different. Dana let her mind wander as she rocked, she thought about Karen being so resolute about her own passing. She was right there would be nothing one could do. It made Dana think that Karen was so brave, but if she faced her passing, would she break under the pressure of look at it as Karen did? Dern was sleeping now and Dana carried him into the bedroom.

When she returned to the living area her eye caught the desk now loaded with reports she had to get done. She made a cup of tea and settled down in front of them. She was studying them when Todd came home. He had been working long hours today.

They had finally decided to make a viewing balcony in the cavern and Todd had the job of making all the hand rails for it. He had been at the computer making the patterns and had been down to the smelting room to take all the scrap iron for smelting. The workshop looked remarkably better now all the scraps had been cleaned up.

He was glad to see Dana working on the reports. He had no desire to do them himself. "Hi sweetie how was your day?" he asked. "It's been a strange day" she replied. "Go have your shower and I'll tell you about it." Todd never hesitated, a shower would be good. He was covered in metal dust.

It didn't take long to shower and soon was with Dana in the living area of their dorm. Dana had coffee and a plate of leftovers heated for him. She wasn't all that hungry and munched on some fruit and nuts.

"I had the strangest conversation with Karen today" she told him. "How is she holding out?" Todd asked. "I'd say good under the circumstances. She has no fear of death or her dying, almost an unreal thing." "Really" Todd looked up "not much point in being afraid of something that will happen to us all" he said. "Todd, are you afraid of death?" she asked. "I think dying is a bit scary. I mean I don't want to linger for a long time or be in great pain, but after that I'm sure there is nothing to fear." Dana looked at him; he was right just like Karen. It amazed her that she had never had to face these things. Warren and Rainie's passing totally upset her. They were cornerstones in her life and when they were gone she crumbled inside. Now when she was reminded of them she thought of the love for life they had; for life's beauty and complexity." "So, what's in those reports that has you so quiet tonight?" Todd asked. "Oh nothing, just sorting out some things is all" she answered.

Todd finished eating and laid down on the couch, he was tired tonight. "You know there are not many of the founders left Dana. I will be sad to see them gone" Todd said. "I know what you mean; they have also been such rocks for us all to look up to. From these reports I'm reading I think we will be okay. We are going to be alright they have taught us well." Todd drifted on and out of sleep and Dana finally told him to go to bed. She spent a few more hours reading and she joined him when she was finished.

Dern woke them and the morning ritual of feeding and changing him went on. Todd headed for work and Dana sat and watched Dern play with his toys. He was a happy child and it warmed her to see him content. She decided to take him to the main living area in the complex. He liked other children. It wasn't long and the two were off.

Before long they were at the play area and Dern wasted no time finding others his size. The mothers sat on the benches and watched. Dana sipped a cold drink and she watched Dern with another child. The child was trying to walk and tumbled down. The cry was one of pain and Dern to her surprise crawled quickly to the little girl. She had skinned her knee. Dana and the little girl's mom wasted no time getting to her. Dern of course was there first and he did the strangest thing. He touched the skinned knees and almost immediately the child stopped crying. When Dana looked at her knees the scraps were gone. The mother looked at Dana then Dern and picked up her baby. Dana picked up Dern. The both women saw what had happened and neither could say anything. It wasn't possible. Not sure what to say Dana told her she hoped the child was alright and she held Dern close. The woman looked at Dana and said "I think she is thank you." It was too unreal for Dana and she took Dern to his carriage to go home. She had never seen anything like this before.

When she got home she let Dern play with his toys and her mind tried to grasp what had happened. She must talk to someone, but whom? If she didn't approach this right they would think she had fallen off her rocker, literally. She watched Dern play and he was content like any other child. Todd would be home soon she would have to tell him too. He would probably think she was this mother that thought her child was so wonderful and gifted. It almost sounded sappy, but it was true Dern healed that little girl's wounds. She saw it and so did the mother of the other child. Maybe Dirk and Carla might have some answers or Andy. Maybe she should take him to the doctors. Dern had given up on his toys and stretched out for a nap. Dana let him sleep.

She went to the kitchen and started making Todd's dinner. Todd was home before she finished. His day had been a hard one. The railing for the observation point in the cavern was on the way, but it did take time. "So how are my two favourite people today?" Todd asked. Dana looked at him "It was a strange day. I will tell you about it after you shower" he smiled and headed for the shower. She sat Dern in his high chair and prepared his food. She got about half done feeding him when Todd made it to the table. Dana let him fill his plate while she continued feeding Dern. "Okay so tell me why your day was so strange." "First promise me you won't say I'm seeing things or that I didn't see what I saw, okay?" His curiosity was getting the better of him now. Dana finished feeding Dern and sipped her water.

"We were at the main living area and Dern was with the other children. One of the children fell and skinned her knee. Dern was right there Todd. He did the most amazing thing I ever saw. He reached over and put his hand on her scrape and I'm telling you the scrape vanished. Now don't say I didn't see it, the other child's mother saw it too." Todd couldn't say anything, his mind flashed back to the conversation he had with Andy about some children having gifts. "Todd, Todd! Did you hear what I said?" "Yes, yes" he said to her. "Well, what do you think? Should I take him to see the doctor or maybe Dirk and Carla?" "No, no!" Todd said. He stood up. "I have to go see someone. You stay here with Dern I'll be back in a while."

Todd left his dinner; as he was almost at the door; Dana shouted "Did you hear anything I said to you?" Todd stopped in his tracks and looked at her "Dana I heard every word and I believe you, but I must talk to someone right away. I'll be back as soon as I can. Now relax until I get back." He kissed her forehead and went out the door. Dana was startled by Todd's reaction. How could he just leave? She had to do something.

Now alone with Dern, she decided to take him to the doctor tomorrow. She would find out what was happening to him. She sat in her rocking chair to wait for Todd. She knew what ever was so important would have to play seconded fiddle to Dern. Dern was their future and Todd was going to be reminded of that.

Todd was on his way to see Andy. He was almost worried about what he would say to him. It still amazed him how they knew so long ago the things that would unfold in the complex. How did Simion ever manage to learn so much and then manage the people so they would ease into the discoveries without even realizing it.

He reached the library and headed straight for Andy's office. Andy of course was there behind the stacks of papers. He looked over his glasses when Todd came in. "Well come in Todd" he said. Todd found himself sitting down and looking at Andy. He thought he looked like the old oracle of the complex.

"So what brings you here at this time?" Andy said. "Do you remember telling me of the virus and how it would mutate so some would have the ability to well do things most could not?" Todd asked. "Yes I do. Did you find something of interest?" Andy asked. "Would you think it would be possible for someone to be able to heal another?" Todd asked. "Yes I believe that will happen. Simion knew it would happen and I have no reason to doubt what he has foretold. So you do you think has this ability Todd?" "I think my son Dern has the gift of healing. What can we do to know for sure? Can he be tested to make sure there is no doubt?" "Yes, but it must come from him. No one can force him to do anything. If indeed he does have the gift." Andy said. "Bring him to the med labs tomorrow. Just try to keep it quiet for his sake. Tell me what makes you think he has this gift?" Andy asked. "Dana saw him heal another child in the play area. She was not the only one to see him do it." "Well then he must be tested." Andy told him. "I will see you there in the morning, alright?" Andy said to him. "I have to tell Dana some of what you told me. She must know what happened." Todd said. "Yes I agree" Andy said. "I will come with you and explain to her" Andy told him. Todd was somewhat relieved to know Andy would tell her. Having been told some much and then not being able to say anything had always weighed on him. It didn't take long for Andy to clear of his desk of things he wished to remain for his eyes only and they went to see Dana and Dern.

When they arrived Dana had put Dern to bed. She was still annoyed at Todd for his apparent lack of interest in what she had been saying to him. She was surprised to see Andy. The three sat at the table, with the coffee on Andy was the first to start the conversation. "My dear, Todd has confided in me about what you had told him earlier." Dana was a bit shocked that he was listening to her, but why did he go to Andy with what she told him. "Now" Andy said "I want you to tell me just what happened." "Well I took Dern to the main living area to play with the other children. While we were there a little girl stumbled and scrapped her knee. She immediately cried and it was a cry of pain. Dern was very close to her and placed his hand on her knee. She stopped crying and when the child's mother and I got there the wound was gone and the child was fine. Andy, do you know this could have happened? How did he help the child? How did he know how too?" Dana asked.

"First I must relay some things I have known for quite some time and then maybe we can answer some of your questions. When the complex was being built by Simion we all believed we were building a station that would replicate a craft that one day would fly into space. Simion knew through his world wide contacts that there was going to be another world war. He never told us this whole project was to protect us from anything they might do out there. When they let loose the viruses no one knew the three would join and in the process wipe out most of the living creatures on the planet. Simion was always under the impression that it would be a radioactive war. Needless to say he closed the doors and we on the inside watched as the outside world died. It was then the research began everything that could be found out about the viruses were looked into. Simion soon discovered that it was a virus that attacked us using our own DNA. If you had a mutated segment it couldn't penetrate to kill you; if you didn't have it your passing was inevitable. Through further study Simion discovered that breeding the pure lines with as many others as possible would this mutation in the DNA. So he set Dirk, Karen and David and anyone we had here to start this process of his work. When the virus found its way in here we had done enough breeding that most animals survived as did the plants and insects. Unfortunately the people did not share the luck, as you know many passed away Simion as well. Before he died he told me of the many things and gave me the research he had done. We knew that if we survived then there must be those on the outside as well, but no contact had yet to this day been confirmed. Anyways, back to the complex; In Simion's research he discovered that children in the future would gain extra abilities. The virus you see mutated through time and things that seem unreal or impossible would be breathing or walking to them. Not all would be able to just those born with certain codes and this now mutated again, the virus would activate new strands and this would give them new abilities. Now with all that you and Todd have told me, Dern may be one of the newly gifted. My advice is to take him, have him tested and see just what he can do. So tomorrow I thought we could all go to the med labs and get a start on the tests." Dana sat looking at Andy. "Why has this not been told to the populace here? It's not right it has been kept a secret. The parents of the children must be beside themselves with worry thinking there is something wrong with them and not knowing what might be the problem."

Andy and Todd never thought Dana would be so upset at this. Andy leaned back a bit at Dana's outburst. "I never thought about it in those terms, but I can see that it might be or present a problem for many. I will consider your idea about letting the complex families know of the possibility." Dan felt that she had administered a blow for the rights of everyday folks that live in their world.

"Might I suggest that we still focus on Dern for the moment and see if the young man is indeed a gifted child?" Dana relented and agreed that

Dern should be tested. With the coffee pot empty and the evening late, Andy bid them goodnight and he would see them tomorrow.

After he left Dana looked at Todd "How long have you known all this?" she asked. "Not long, I'm really still in the dark about a lot of things when it comes to Andy. I'm sorry I left in such a rush, but I still can't believe our child would be a gifted child like Andy says and when you told me and I know if you said it happened then it did happen. He just seemed to be the one to know what to do." "Well it does put my mind somewhat at ease, but I still worry about Dern" Dana said "All my life I grew up being different it was always there; there is the orphan the little girl who's parents are gone, poor child. It made me feel so alone. I don't want for Dern. I want him to grow up being Dern with parents that love him." Todd looked at her "Dana, if he has a gift then he is fortunate beyond our imagination, if and I mean if the there will be others. He won't be alone. I love you Dana and I love Dern we can make sure he is taken care of" Todd told her. "I just want him to be normal" Dana said. "From what Andy said about his gift, if he has it, it will be normal for him" Todd said. "I'm still worried Todd." "I know" he replied. "Everything will turn out okay you'll see." And he hugged her. "Tomorrow always comes."

And for Todd and Dana it brought the morning ritual of feeding and changing Dern. Dana knew that Dern was to be tested and she was on edge. Todd was not as anxious as Dana. He wanted Dern to have the gift. It was a miracle in his mind and they should be thankful.

Andy was waiting at the med labs when they arrived. He had briefed the medical staff and they had set up a series of tests. These tests were to check his brain waves and they felt confident they would be able to tell what happened if and when he used his gift. Todd and Dana know that the other children would soon come to be tested too. The news of Dern's gift would have the mothers of the other children afraid to say anything or bring their children to be tested as well.

The day was long and Dern was no worse for wear by the tests. By mid afternoon he was getting cranky and Dana had enough. She took her baby and headed home.

Dern was over tired and was soon was sleeping as Dana rocked him in the rocking chair. After he fell asleep she put him to bed. Todd was hoping that Dern did have a gift, how wonderful for him and the people of the complex. He thought about Dana and wondered why she was not so keen on Dern being gifted.

"Dana what exactly has got you on edge about Dern?' "I just want him to have a good life" she said "To fit in where I never really did. If he has this gift I will be happy for him and worried at the same time. Todd what if he is the only one? What if there are no others?" Dana said. "From what Andy has said, there is no doubt there will be others. It's the virus that's changing them. Just be happy for him, the gift of heal is really a wonderful thing. Think of how the little girl felt hurt and crying; our little Dern gave her back her happiness." "You're right I never thought of it like that" she told him. Todd hugged her "It will be okay you'll see. It comforts me to know that he might be able to do something like healing. When we are gone his gift might be a great value in his life." Dan agreed maybe she was worried for nothing. "I will make a concerted effort to think of the good of this." "We have to" Todd told her. "He will need our love and support." "Well tomorrow will tell if he is gifted." Dana didn't have to wait for the doctors she knew he was gifted. Todd knew Dana was worried. He thought about taking a few days and have some one on one with her. Dern could stay with his parents again. With that thought in his mind he would seek to have the next few days off from work.

The next day found Todd and Dana at the med labs. Andy was there and he was more than interested in what they had to say about Dern. The doctors first assured them that Dern was fine and the only thing they could find was a larger than normal penal gland in his brain. This gland is usually smaller and almost never used by many. It was what was believed to be the reason Dern had his gift. How it worked they didn't know, most peoples were like an appendix; there but not used. They believed it had something to do with foresight, but no one knew for sure what the function of the gland was. The doctors asked Dana and Todd to keep a record of anything he might do in the gifted sense, other than that to take him home and enjoy his youth. Dana was relieved to know Dern was okay. Andy knowing the things he did was thrilled about the fact he could heal. They didn't know to what extent yet, but his opinion it was an honour to know Dern and his parents. Andy wondered just hoe many would have gifts and to what degree. Todd never let it upset him, it was what it was and he would love Dana and Dern regardless.

After the meeting with the doctors and Andy, Todd suggested they go visit his mom and dad. Dana agreed, she always felt safe when they all were together. "Todd, don't tell them about Dern please, not yet okay?" she asked. "Sure" he replied "We don't need to advertise this and I think just let things take a normal course it would probably be better for all." "Hey" he said. "How would you like to get away for a few days?" Todd asked her. "Dern is fine and my parents always enjoy him. I think some work on the tunnel might be interesting too." Dana smiled "Yes I think it would be fun and a break would do me good as well."

It was not long after they agreed that they reached his mom and dad's. As always they were more than happy to see them. The rest of the day was spent in good cheer. They agreed to keep Dern for the next few days. Todd and Dana smiled at one another knowing that their secret place would soon be the hub bub of their joint efforts.

When they arrived at home it didn't take them long to pack up what they would need and a bag was packed for Todd's parents for Dern. Todd returned to his parents with Dern's things.

When Todd got back to their dorm, Dana was making sure everything they needed was packed. Todd was right it was what she needed, keep her mind busy. They confirmed the list and went to bed feeling things were right again in their world.

By 9:00 the next day they were in the tunnel unloading gear and eating. They looked over the maps and soon were on the way to digging out the camped areas. By noon they had cleared most of the area they had mapped and the afternoon was spent piling the rubble for Todd to dispose of later. While they ate their dinner both looked over the maps. They decided the following morning they would start venturing further. Todd was thankful not much dust was kicked up and stone broke easily. Dana's mind wandered as she imagined what new wonders the tunnel might uncover.

They shared ideas of what they might find and laughed at the silliness of some of them. Dana was happy again. Todd was right about getting away; it gave her a fresh outlook on things. He always made her feel renewed. Todd was self assured and was glad to see his wife smile again. They slept well that night secreted away from the others in the complex.

Todd was the first one up and not long after Dana joined him. They both worked together to make sure they had what they needed to map the tunnels ahead. After a few additions to the small bag of items, they were on their way, Todd taking the lead and Dana not far behind.

The passages opened up and were far easier to travel. They had reached where they had left of in no time. Dana agreed the passages seemed bigger now and they made good time through them. Todd always made sure the paths were marked and lighted. Dana was studious in marking their progress on the map they were making. They knew they were close to the river that was inside the mountain.

Todd laboured tirelessly and that afternoon, with Dana not far behind the tunnel opened into a cavern. When they crawled through they were startled to see the river. It came up from the ground and flowed to an opening not fifty feet away. They could see the light coming from the opening. Todd was not sure what to do or say; Dana never said a word. They slowly made their way there and just before they looked out at the light, Dana grabbed Todd's arm, "Its okay, its okay, let's look" Todd said.

They followed the light and crawled through the opening to find the valley below them. A soft breeze blew; Dana felt it caress her skin and flow over her hair. Todd stood outside and marvelled at the sound of the river as it flowed out then back into a hole just below. He too felt the wind blow and they felt the sun on their skin. Dana was almost afraid; she had wanted to be outside for so long and now she wanted to go back into the caves. She was shivering with some fear and the reality they were the first in decades to breathe fresh air. "Todd what have we done?" Dana said. "We have exposed the whole complex to what's out there." Dana was almost in a panic "What will we do? We can't go back there. Oh, my God, Todd, Dern, we can't jeopardize his life." Dana sat down and broke into tears. She would not see Dern again, how could she? "Dana! Dana! Listen to me" Todd grabbed her shoulders. She looked at him through teary eyes. "I'm going to tell you something and you must promise never to reveal it." Dana couldn't really grasp what he was saying. "Todd you don't understand we can't g back to the complex. We have exposed them far too much." "Dana! Listen to me." Todd was almost yelling now. "We have been breathing the outside air for a decade or more, the whole complex has, just they don't know it" he told her. Dana stood up. "What! How can this be?" She now was yelling. Todd looked at her; this was getting out of hand. "Dana! Sit down." Still angry she unceremoniously sat down. "You better explain this" she said to him curbing her anger. "What do you mean we have been breathing the air from the outsides for decades or more?"

Todd sat beside her. "Alright now, don't say anything until I have explained, agreed?" he said to her. "Alright" she said. "No one knows but three or four of us now. There was a breach in the tunnels many years ago. Simion knew and he told Andy. The breach was never revealed to the people because of the damage the virus did. Simion told Andy not to reveal it because he was concern of the mass panic that could ensue. To survive everyone had to stick together and get the complex back to stable running conditions. With so many people gone, the complex was on the verge of failing. From what I understand any life that survived would be sheer luck. The complex is the storehouse fore the future, almost like a huge nursery for many animals, etc...What do you think most would have done had they known they were still exposed to what killed so many of their families? Simion knew long before he succumbed to the virus after the initial deaths he knew the rest would be alright. He wrote everything down in his research. It still startles me when I think of the genius of the man. Anyways, he had an agenda laid out for us to follow. He even knew the children would be able to do things that most are not capable of. He wrote of gifts and how some certain DNA would have them and some wouldn't."

Dana was stunned, she looked over the valley, but she didn't really see it. Her mind raced at the implications at what he was telling her.

Todd continued to tell her that Simion believed that the complex would be a new beginning for all mankind. He had to keep order and structure for those left, so they would have security. "He told no one but Andy." "How long have you known all this?" she asked. "Not long, Andy told me a few months ago." "I can't believe you never told me Todd. You just let me work on all these reports and dreamed about outside." It was then Dana realized they were really outside. "Oh my God, Todd we are outside" she said to him like she really hadn't realized it before.

She stood there overlooking the valley; she definitely was seeing it this time; the flawless blue sky, the lush green grass rolling its way to the small emerald green trees. The wind had been blowing lightly the whole time and she trembled as she pushed her hair behind her ears to keep it from flying in her face. Todd reached out and held her hand as she looked at the same vista with awe. "We did it, we made it outside" and smiled at her.

They ventured no further, it was frighteningly beautiful and they were unprepared for the onslaught of feelings they were feeling. It was Dana that noticed the wall below and that view was not of the valley that had the monitors on. "What should we do Todd, I'm afraid to think? What if the choices we make are the wrong ones?" she asked him. "We'll take a good look Dana" he said. "We will be back here soon, but for now let's go back in. I need to get my head on straight before I do anything and I simply can't go out here it takes my breath away" he said. "I know what you mean Todd" she told him and with a glance they headed back into the opening of the cave.

They crawled into the opening and once inside they sat together. Dana looked over to Todd "You said Andy knew this all along, crafty old fellow." Todd just sat for a few moments. "Does Andy know about the tunnel Todd?" Dana asked. "No, I have never told anyone" Todd told her. "Dana do you realize we are really outside?" he said. "I know" she said. "I have always wanted this and know I'm wracked with doubt and misgivings; fear almost. I want to go out there, but tremble at the thought of it. Yet every time I have worked and strove for it, it is a mere 20 feet away and I can't get my being to accept it. Part of me wants out there and keep going and the other part wants me to crawl back into the tunnel and seal it behind me."

Todd sat for a few moments. "Well" he said "We made it, we fulfilled a dream and everything tells me that it's meant to be. I think this must stay between us. Dana, we can come and go at will our life in the complex will never be the same as it was. I do think the work we have been doing on the projects to open the doors needs to be continued now more than ever. Did you feel the wind and sun? It was glorious. We were meant to be out there not in this mountain. One day it will be open for everyone to come and go as they please. We must ensure this happens." "I agree" Dana told him. "It's almost unreal out there Todd" she told him.

They sat and gathered their wits about them. When they felt relaxed as they could be under the circumstances, they decided to look one more time.

They crawled out the opening and stood looking over the valley. The sun was now setting; the hues of the pink and the orange lit the sky. The wind had died down and Todd pointed out they had to return to the inside. They crawled back into the opening and made their way back down the tunnel they had travelled.

Soon they were at the section they widened. The glowing lights helped them to see their way back to where their gear was and they collapsed on the makeshift bed.

"Todd" Dana said "I feel like I'm in a dream. Did you ever see anything like that?" "I know what you mean" he said. "The complex will never be the same. It's going to be one of the hardest I have ever done to willing stay here now, knowing that just through this tunnel I could be free." "How do you think we should handle this?" Dana asked. "Maybe we should keep a journal and leave it here" Dana said. "Well that's an idea. We should finish the map as well." Todd replied. "I don't want to move. I don't want to wake from this dream" she said. Todd just stayed beside her.

After some time passed she got up and dragged his body with her. "Let's do this." She poured out some water in a basin and they washed off the dirt from the tunnel. With a change of clothes and a light meal they sat and filled in the map. They discussed how to open the passages. They were still to small to freely walk through them. They decided a door near the exit was the best idea. With winter coming, keeping the cold out was a good idea. They knew that if they revealed the truth of what they found before the people in the complex were ready it would cause chaos. They also knew they would eventually need to tell them, but for the next while they would strive to keep the reports moving and continue the efforts to open the doors for everyone. It was very late when they rolled up the map and went to bed. Tomorrow would be their last day on this trip, but knew nothing could keep them away for long.

It seemed all too soon when they woke. They were tired and sore from travelling through the caves. Dana's thoughts renewed her drive to get things in order. She felt like it was up to Todd and her to really make the council understand about opening the doors to all.

Although both wanted to go back out they decided to approach this with care and first things first. The rubble had to be cleaned out and the last part of the tunnel opened for easier travel. They had to go back inside. To be gone so long would arouse suspicions, besides she missed Dern. "Todd, are you sure it's safe to go back in? We really aren't putting anyone at risk." Todd looked up from his packing "It's fine Dana" he said "Don't worry."

Dana more confident continued to pack up their things and soon they were done. Anything that was connected to what they found in the tunnels was left behind. "Are you ready to begin our new life?" Dana smiled as she brushed herself off and said "To our new life." "After you" Todd said and with a half bow she stretched her arms across the hallway and they started on the way to their dorm.

The walk there held little conversation; they were lost in their thoughts. It was Todd that broke their silence. "Want me to get Dern or would you like to visit with mom and dad?" "I think I would like to visit with mom and dad a bit. They always make me feel better." Todd smiled.

After depositing the gear on the floor they headed for the showers. It felt good to wash off the dust and dirt. Revived, they set to work putting the gear away and cleaning up before going for Dern. It surprised Dana that it was evening already. The day had moved swiftly. With everything so fresh in their minds they were finding it hard to completely relax. They sat at the table drinking tea. Dana and Todd had been outside and now had to keep it low profile. "Do you think we should tell Andy?" Dana asked. "No I don't. We tell no one like we agreed, it's safer that way" Todd said to her. "Let's get Dern, mom and dad are probably wondering where we are." "I don't think I can act normally now" Dana said. "I'm afraid I'll slip up somehow and let it escape from me that we have bee outside." "You'll be fine, try not to think about it" he told her. "Well that's not easy." And they both smiled. With the tea gone they headed out to get Dern.

They arrived to him sleeping on Todd's dad as he rocked him. It was Todd's mom that told them the pair had spent most of the visit like that, "What a pair" she said. "You would think they never slept before." Todd's mom put on the coffee and asked how they enjoyed their free time. They looked at each other and Todd told her it was inspiring. Dana almost shocked, laughed. Todd's mom missed the sarcasm and was happy to see the young couple in love.

She had worried for Todd when he was young; he seemed to be so alone. Since he had grown into an accomplished man, he had a family and life for them was beginning. She thought as she poured the coffee what life would be for him. Although they were closed in this mountain they were safe and alive.

She brought the coffee and they sat, in quiet conversation. Todd's mom told them how Dern and grandpa were always together. "They seemed to nap a lot" she said.

With the coffee done Todd went over and got Dern. Neither of them stirred as he lifted Dern. Todd put him in his stroller; Dana and his mom gathered his things together. Todd asked if she might mind Dern again soon and she smiled "We love having him, he is a good child." With that and a hug they left.

"Inspiring?" Dana said "never thought of us together" and they laughed "and I was worried I might slip" as she looked at Todd. "I know" he said "I will have to be more careful of my choice of words." The three headed home, life was changing and the beginning was before them.

Chapter 29

It was the steady drip of water from the icicles that was the first beginnings of spring that Willow noticed. She thought of the maple syrup that soon would be cooking on their fires and how all the children looked forward to the big event of gathering the sap. She thought about Jo and how she had always seemed to make work fun. Freda had the same ability.

West and Carry managed to make a sleigh and plenty of buckets for them to take to gather the sap in. This would be Nimuri's first time to go. They did the same at the fort but she had never gone with the hordes of children that gathered the sap. West was already gathering things together for the trip to the small grove they had found.

West mentioned going to see his folks in the valley after the spring planting. She wanted to see her mom and siblings. They had made yards of cloth this winter and with Freda's help some was a beautiful yellow.

Willow had packed some food and was waiting for Freda and Nimuri. West and Carry appeared with the sleigh, buckets, spouts and anything else that might be needed. It was about then that Freda and Nimuri appeared down the path carrying blankets and a basket as well. The troop was ready.

Nimuri, new to collecting sap was quiet and watchful. It didn't take long for them to reach the stand of maple trees. West wasted no time in pounding in spouts and hanging buckets to collect the sap. Carry started the fire and the women sat near it watching West and now Carry as they walked past each tree hanging a bucket.

Nimuri watched and was amazed at how easy it seemed. She like the syrup from the maples. Freda and Willow talked of the garden and

Nimuri them she had a surprise for them this year if everything went right. After much needling and teasing would not reveal anything, so Freda and Willow were left to anticipate the forth coming surprise.

The men finished hanging the buckets and soon found themselves warming by the fire. "It seems to me we could open a new field this year" Carry said. "Some extra oats and flax would not hurt to have." West agreed. Freda mentioned the extra food for the new comers would be helpful still. It was Willow that asked if another cabin was to be built.

West and Carry looked at her "Willow's right" West said. "But to have another family here would mean a lot of extra work for us all. We have to prepare new fields and build a cabin. Next year would be the soonest anyone could come" West said. "Well the population is growing and the fort can only sustain so many" Freda added. "We can try for the coming fall. One less family at the fort and a home for them is such a blessing after all they have been through." Nimuri never said much. "I think we should try. If it's not done till next year then so be it" West said. They all agreed.

"I was thinking of a visit to my mom and dad's and Willow's mom before we start the fields. Would everyone like to go?" Again all agreed. "It will be good to see them again" Freda said. "Maybe we should take some material I'm sure Jo would like to have some" Nimuri added. "Then it's settled a visit on a grand scale" and everyone laughed.

The lunch that had been packed was soon gone and the first sap poured into a tub. The buckets were hung back up and the first load of sap was pulled back to the cabins.

Willow, Nimuri and Freda got to get to work rendering it down. West and Carry stayed to collect the next batch. "Carry" West asked. "How many more cabins do you think this valley can sustain?" Carry looked around and in his opinion three or four more. "Have you hiked the next valley beyond?" Carry asked him. "Some, not a lot I have had my hands full just getting this area in order" West said. "We will have to take a good look when we can" Carry told him. "Yes I think so too. I would like to have a cabin in a few valleys" West said. "Why is that?" Carry asked. "Oh I don't know" West told him. "It's more of a safety net than anything else. You never know what might happen and it never hurts to have a safe place to be" Carry had to agree. "I wonder how much road to the new settlement to the south is gone" Carry said. "I don't know. With the extra people they might have it well on its way. Do you think they will find more people West?" Carry asked. "I don't know Carry, but if they do I'm sure all will pull together to get them settled. I'm amazed they found those on the prairie. There might be small pockets of people all over. Then there might not be too."

The two men talked of the cabin yet to be built and of clearing a new field. By early evening the trees had given them plenty of sap and buckets were hung one last time. Tomorrow would be the last gathering of this season; the trees would need time to heal.

The women slowly evaporated the water from the sap and soon were pouring syrup into clay jars. With the evening, friends departed for home.

Willow was tired, but satisfied with the work they had done. She made tea for her and West. "So did you and Carry decide where the new cabin would be built?" she asked. "No not yet, but I'm sure that we will sort it out. Do you have any idea about where to put it?" he asked. "Well we built these two cabins closer to the semi-cliff here so we could look out. It might be nice to keep going" she said. "You know" he said. "I like that. I will draw up some plans and see what you think." "What do you think Nimuri's surprise will be?" Willow asked. "I couldn't hazard a guess, Nimuri keeps to herself" West said. "I am happy for Carry though, she has brought him much joy." "I know what you mean" Willow said. "I am glad she gets on well with Freda too. She is not exactly a spring flower anymore and Nimuri cares for her. It makes me miss my mom. I hope she has been well over the winter."

West hugged Willow and as always his love for her made her feel safe. "She has had many people to help her there and she is a strong woman" West said. "Well let's go to bed. I want to get the last sap in and then we can plan the garden layout" West said. With the fire burning down the two slept. The next day promised to be fair and springs work would be soon underway.

It was Willow up first. She added wood to the fire and soon had the water boiling. West joined her and after breakfast was off to collect the last sap. Willow sat at the window and watched him go.

With the warmth of the cabin the snow was melting from the roof and the dripping noises filled her ears. She had been knitting socks for West.

Spring was such a busy time. The cabin would have to be cleaned and the garden planted. The paths still needed more gravel and the road might get done. It would be nice for West to have Zack able to visit.

Willow wanted to talk with Jo and her mom. West and her had been together now for sometime and she was not with child yet. Maybe something was wrong with her. Willow always wanted her own children, West never said anything about it. With him being an only child he told her it would happen when it did and not a moment before, then he would smile. Willow smiled at that thought, how lucky she was to have him. She always thought that and knew she always would.

Willow got up and went to their store room. She had to decide what they would take for food for Jo and Zack as well for the new people. The extra blankets and kitchen things would be helpful as well. It didn't take Willow long to sort what would be taken with them. She went back to her chair and started knitting again.

West was the one that broke the quiet when he returned with the sap. He took Freda 4 of the 8 pails full and brought the rest to Willow. Willow had the water boiled to clean everything before West stored it. So while she rendered the sap West washed the buckets.

Carry was outside chopping wood and it wasn't long before the two men disappeared into the work shop.

Willow cam across some pressed flowers. She decided to make a picture and have West frame it for her. She had a small table with flowers spread all over it. She picked the ones she wanted. She had paper and soon arranged the flowers to her liking and with dabs of pine tree sap glued the flowers to the paper. With it done to her satisfaction she started lunch, West would be hungry.

Soon West came in and she was right he was hungry. He sat at the table and while eating they talked of many things. After they finished West cleared the table and helped her with the dishes. West took out some paper and started a drawing of the valley and cabins. "I think we should ask Carry what ideas he might have before I get too far on this map" he told her. Willow nodded and added "Freda might as well." "That's true" West said. "She has many good ideas. "How long before you are done with the sap?" he asked. Willow went over to check "A couple hours yet" she said. "Alright I'll go and ask them to come over after supper" West said. Willow nodded. "After we get the fields in I want to see what's in the next valley. Would you like to come exploring with me when I go look?" West asked. "Oh I would love that. Every valley from here to the fort is so different. We might find something grand you never know." West raised and eyebrow "Grand?" he said teasing her. Willow smiled "Yes like a stand of nut trees or an old bee hive. We could use the wax or a new mushroom patch." "Okay, okay" West said "I get it" and they laughed.

The afternoon passed quickly and when the sap was syrup Willow poured it into the clay jars. West helped her and when they were done Willow made dinner. West and Willow found things they could do all the time. They were comfortable in each others company.

West was at the table drawing out the valley and Willow was finishing her knitting. By the time night arrived they finished their projects and prepared for the following day.

"West" Willow asked as she lay beside him in bed. "Yes" he answered. "I'm a little concerned about not being with child yet" she told him. West gathered her in his arms and softly told her "No worries okay, I have always believed that things don't happen until they are supposed to." West kissed her forehead and soon followed her into dream land.

The days warmed and spring was on its way. Although the mornings still held fast to the crispness of winter, the afternoons warmed and soon the snow was almost gone.

West and Carry decided on the new cabin spot and clearing the area and getting the lumber ready would be enough work for them, the new fields had been marked off and anticipation grew as it got warmer. The trip to the next valley was finally given a day and they prepared for it.

West and Carry filled the days with minor repairs needing done after the winter storms.

The women all wondered what news they would here. Willow wanted to see her mom and Freda looked forward to see Jo and the other women. Nimuri, still feeling a bit like an outsider could see the joy the trip was bringing and couldn't help feeling some of the excitement. The wagon was loaded and the weather was cooperating. If the next day was sunny they would make the journey. They all would not rest easy that night with the trip first thing in the morning.

Willow had a hot bath and when West got in she had one ready for him. While he soaked Willow made tea. West soaked and eased his aching bones. "You know" Willow said. "You work to hard. You will be an old man before your time." West laughed "Not yet my dear Willow and not for a long while yet." Willow smiled. "Want me to pop some corn. We haven't had any in such a long time." Willow asked. "Sure" West told her. He now dressed and emptied the tub as Willow popped the corn. "Do you think all is well in the home valley?" Willow asked. "I'm sure a runner would have brought news if things were not as they should be" West told her. "Are you looking forward to the trip?" Willow asked. "Yes it will be good to see everyone again" he replied. "I'm curious to see what new ideas dad has put into motion. He always seems to have something he's planned" West told her.

The corn popped into large white puffs. They ate and talked of the trip. The day's light vanished and night crept in leaving only the light from the fire. West and Willow long finished with the pop corn headed for bed. West listened to her soft breathing and knowing she was sleeping followed her into slumber.

Morning came and with it the sun, bright and warm. The trail would be harder to travel now with the heat turning much of it into mud. Carry and West managed the wagon while the three women carried what they could to ease the load.

As they made their way up the path West was glad it was gravel, but knew all to soon it would be mud. Carry made the suggestion that the road should receive much more attention in the future as he and West struggled to pull the wagon through a mud hole. Both laughed.

The sun warmed the air so their breaths could not be seen as in the morning. By lunch the two men were tired and thirsty and welcomed the lunch that was brought. Although West worked hard with the wagon he always scanned the forest. He noticed the snow was still piled high in spots and the sun filtered through the evergreen bows. A new year was beginning and he was glad of it. Being snow bound to the cabin for so long was frustrating. He was at home more in the woods.

Carry put out the fire and said to West that this would be a good spot to build a small hut, even just for dry fire wood. West nodded in agreement. There was never any end to the work needing to be done.

Willow and Nimuri carried more than Freda and helped her when stumbled or faltered. She was getting old and Carry never missed her starting to show it.

The trip all in all went smoothly and by mid afternoon they crested the hill to see the cabins below. Carry and West were surprised to see the path here was gravelled which made pulling the wagon easier again.

As always the children playing outside saw them first and before long most everyone was there to welcome them. Jo, Zack, Brad, Lily, Gary, Sara, Herb, Jean and to her surprise mother and standing beside her, Kalvin.

Everyone walked to Jo and Zack's and before long food and hot drinks appeared. There was much laughter and teasing each other. Willow's mom was a big part in the circle of women. The men talked of farming and building; the women talked of cooking and children. After an hour or two the people started drifting back to their own homes. Willow couldn't believe her mother was laughing and sharing in the efforts of all the other women, such a change had come over her.

When, most had left Helen wanted to talk with Willow. She could see the bewilderment in her daughter and knew it was time the two talked. "Willow" Helen said "Come walk with me." Willow got up and the two walked arm in arm up the path to a small bluff that overlooked the valley. As they walked Helen spoke of Duke; how their life was before the outbreak and then after. They soon reached the small area where the grave yard was. Helen picked up a stone and told the story of the service then handed Willow the stone. "Think of something good about him Willow and add your thoughts with the others." Willow remembered how when the harvest was done and father would smile at Helen. He would say "We won't go hungry this winter." Of all the things he did or did not do, he always made sure they did not hunger. With that thought Willow placed her stone with the others and after a moment her mom said "Come away now."

Helen took her arm and they sat on the bench nearby. "After your father passed Willow I did not know what I was going to do. Jo, Zack and all the others have given me new hope and a new view on the world. Over the winter I have come to fully understand what was will never be again and to live in the past I was losing my future, the future of my children, everything. So I have chosen to live for now and tomorrow." Willow was almost in shock. Helen turned to Willow "I have not done right by you and I know I can not change the past or heal the hurt that was the result of others anger and self pity. I do want to be your friend and help you if ever I can." Willow started to cry "Mom you will always be my mom; I love you and always have, but father, well it does no good to dwell on it. He is gone and the demons that chased him are gone with him." Helen hugged Willow and let her have her cry.

The sun was starting to set when Helen and Willow started back down the trail to the valley. "I'll take you home and make you some tea," she patted Willow's hand.

As they approached the cabin Willow was astonished. It now had a porch and plenty of wood. When they went in Willow found order and beauty from dried flowers, to the curtains and hand made doilies. It was clean and warm. Willow looked at her mom "It's a bit different isn't it Willow?" Willow just sat down her mouth open. "Close your mouth Willow, what would West say?" and she laughed. Helen made tea and sat at the table. "Where are the children, mom?" "Oh I imagine Kalvin has them to give us time to talk. He has been such a comfort to me. Did you know he lost his entire family in a prairie fire? How awful it must have been for him." Willow was astonished still at the change in her mother. "Kalvin has done so much work to the cabin. He is so different from Duke. He lives life; finds joy and the children adore him. They are doing well and Zack has them learning so much and Kalvin teaches them to do so many things too." "Mother" Willow said "You are happy aren't you?" "Yes Willow, for the first time in so many years I am happy." "From listening to you I would say Kalvin has something to do with this transformation." "Willow, try to understand, Kalvin and I have much in common and he knows how I feel. He sees things the same as I do and I am comfortable in his company." "What are you trying to tell me mom?" Willow said. "I guess I'm trying to say that if he asked me I would spend the rest of my life with him." "Well if that's the case I hope he asks you soon." Helen smiled. Willow understood. If nothing else in the world ever comes to anything, Willow had made it to a sensible, caring person. "Oh Willow, you're not angry then about Kalvin?" Helen said to her. "Angry! Don't be silly mom. All winter I have been worried about you. How you would get on and all the time you have been courted by some gallant man." At that they both laughed. Willow finished her tea and told her mom she must find West he would be wondering where she was. "Of course dear" her mom told her.

As Willow was leaving Helen took her hand "I love you." Willow hugged her "I'll see you tomorrow" and walked down the path to Jo and Zack's. As she walked she thought about everything that had transpired.

As she walked up the porch, Jo opened the door, took her coat and told her tea was on the table. West and Zack were talking. West stopped when he saw her. "I was beginning to think you got lost" then smiled. "How's your mom?" "Oh she seems okay" Willow said. "Willow come sit with me at the table." "Where are Freda and Nimuri?" Willow asked. "Seems Herb and Jean have stolen them for tonight. Carry wanted to see what new things Herb was working on." Jo poured the tea and gave her some bread and jam. "Did you have a good visit with your mom?" Jo asked. "It was interesting and yes a good visit all in all. Jo, tell me is Kalvin a good man?" "He is the best of the men Willow. He has a heart of gold and has been truly a God send for your mother." "Yes it would seem so" Willow said. "Willow it took a long time to get your mom to open up to us. It never would have happened, but for Kalvin. Did you know she loves him and he loves her?" Jo said to Willow. "She won't let herself be totally happy yet" Jo said. "Why not?" asked Willow. "She needs your approval" Jo said. "My approval whatever for?" Willow said. "I guess she is worried, she can't face anymore loss for a while. Helen has just started reclaiming some happiness that had been so long overdue." "If she loves Kalvin and he loves her, then what's the problem? I would never deny her anything that would give her joy." Willow said. "I know dear, but it's at a stage of her coming back to us all. She needs your approval Willow. Enough said, let's see what the two have been cooking up in our absence."

Willow and Jo joined Zack and West by the fire in the living area. "What great schemes have you two cooked up?" Jo asked. "Dad was just showing me some plans for the new cabin they want to build and the garden area yet to be cleared. Here, look at this" West said. "It's the plans for a smithing house and this" West said "These are plans for a pump that would make getting water a lot easier" he smiled at them. Zack said "Making things is not the problem, getting the raw materials is." "Well enough, how about some cards? We havent played in so long?" Zack said. Jo found the cards and Willow and West popped some corn. The evening was quiet, but the company was wonderful.

The next day was filled with visiting everyone. Willow managed to get Jo to discuss her not being with child. Jo of course told her not to fret. It took her a few years before she carried West after her and Zack got together. Willow thanked Jo for helping her mother. Jo pointed out that it was Kalvin more than her. "Did you get out looking for any nut stands in your valley yet?" Jo asked. "No we have been busy. This year promises to be easier. We have planned to adventure some" Willow told her. "Well I must go visit with mom. I'll be back later" Willow said. Jo smiled and picked up her knitting.

Willow walked down the path and was happy to see fruit trees planted in abundance. The place she called home was changing. Things were moving on and in some ways she was sad to see the things she remembered gone. She was glad to see new things that made peoples lives easier.

When she got to her mother's house she found her outside marking off a garden plot. Kalvin was there and Willow was a bit uneasy. When they saw her they stopped and joined her on the walkway. Kalvin felt her uneasiness and let Helen talk and he stood in the back ground. It didn't take long for them to go inside and Kalvin made tea for them. Kalvin said "I think I will go and see if the children have done their chores" and he smiled and went out.

With a kind of strained silence it was Helen who spoke first "He's a good man really. Give him a chance" she said. "Oh it's not that, I just don't know what to say to him" Willow told her. "I want you to be happy and I can see you are. Dawn, John and Sam seem to like him. I am happy for you all." "Willow, talk to him. If you don't like him, well to tell you the truth we want to get married, but if there is any question I won't. It's important to me that all the children are happy. The years with Duke caused too much…well I won't live that ever again."

"Mom it's not up to me to decide who will make you happy or not. I have a life of my own now. What I think is of no importance either way" Willow said to her. "I know that Willow, but I just can't be with someone if it pains my children, any of them."

"Well" Willow said "I didn't come here to stir up the pot. I came to visit. I have upset you and I'm sorry for it" Willow told her. "No child, it's my own sensitivity" Helen said. "Let's start again. I am happy you are here. I have missed you" Helen said. Willow smiled and told her many times over the winter she had thought of her and how they were. "Now" Willow said "I can have comfort knowing that you are alright." "Now that we are talking of more pleasant things, how come you are not with child yet?" Helen asked. It struck a cord with Willow "Oh I don't know, I guess it will be when it will be." She forced a smile.

The visit between them turned out to be a strained one. Willow wanted to be so much closer to her mom, but knew it would take time. "Well mom I think I will just take a walk about." "Well enjoy your walk" Helen said. She knew the visit was anew beginning and let Willow have the room to set things right with her.

Willow walked down the paths and found herself walking towards a small bluff where her father lay. The sun was warm but you could still feel the cold in the air. She watched her siblings and noticed they had made attachments to Herb and Jean's children. How clean and happy they seemed.

Willow now found herself at the bluffs where her father's grave was and Kalvin was there. He was pulling the weeds that were on the grave. When he noticed her he stood and told her he would leave so she could sit there undisturbed. Willow, a bit stunned at his polite comment asked him to stay. "Thank you for tending his resting place" Willow said to him. "I find it almost an honour to do so" Kalvin said. Willow wondered why. With all the times their home was filled with harshness, Kalvin continued "You see my wife and children passed in a prairie fire. I thought my life was over. Everything that meant anything to me was gone swallowed up by fire. By the time it passed there was very little left. I buried what I could find of them as did the others, but life changed for me. Jean and Herb have been so good to me, but I felt like nothing mattered much after that. Then we came here. Jo, Zack, Gary, Lily, Sara and all have been so wonderful. Jean has not been so happy in years. Herb, the good man, has his confidence back. I met your mother then. With your dad missing and winter coming, helping her made me feel like my work amounted to something, I was useful again.

When West found your father I felt your mother's pain was my own resurfaced. I was so torn, I knew how she felt. The loss of someone you shared most of your life with. I know Duke had his troubles that just made it harder for her. There were all the "I should have, if only I had done this or that. My intention was an honest one. I just wanted to ease her pain. I guess in some way it helped to ease mine. Your mother is a lovely woman. I must admit it wasn't hard to feel love for her. I come here often and talk to your father. Im sure he is comforted in knowing Helen and the children are looked after. I don't believe he was evil. He was hurt down in his soul and it blocked his way to the future. Things will be what they will be, but now my future has hope as does your mother's. That is something to be happy for and I am and I believe her to be as well."

"Will you listen to me talking your ear off." "I don't mind really I have enjoyed our time together. I am sorry about your family" Willow said to him "But I'm glad you were here to help them. It will ease my thoughts to know that you will be here for them."

Willow patted his hand. Kalvin's heart was lifted maybe Willow's mother would take him as her spouse? His life would be full again. "Well" he said. "If you like I could leave and you could spend some time alone here?" "No" Willow said "My mind is easy now knowing he is not ill anymore or lost. Let's go down" Willow said to him.

They talked of more pleasant things and Willow knew her mom and siblings were going to be okay. He was a good man and it occurred to her that they were both lost and now were found. They would be happy together.

"It has been nice to talk with you Kalvin and I am happy to know my mother will be safe in your hands, but I must find West. He will be wondering what has happened to me." Kalvin smiled and turned to walk to Herb and Jean's.

Willow continued on to Jo and Zack's. She arrived to find Freda and Nimuri there and to her relief tea was made. "Come join us Willow" Jo said and in no time she was involved in the conversation.

That night Willow shared much of her day with West. He listened to her and knew she been troubled all winter. He hoped that now she would be more at ease with things. West didn't like the fact there wasn't anything he could do to help her other than love her and let things find a way to settle on their own.

When Willow finally slept West knew the future would only get better. One never knew, maybe he would find the complex as well.

His thoughts travelled to the complex and the wonders that would be there. Finally sleep found his mind and morning would soon be upon them.

The next few days they all spent visiting and Willow assured her mother that a relationship with Kalvin would not upset her.

The children were all growing and soon would wed and need homes. West's idea about a cabin in between villages was a plan soon to be out into the making. Life seemed to be getting a foothold again.

By weeks end West, Willow, Carry, Nimuri and Freda knew they had to get back to their own valley. It was warming up and things had to be done. With potted apple trees and blueberry bushes, along with gifts from all, the wagon was loaded and the five headed back to their homes.

The conversation floated from the antics of the children to the funny stories each told. The sun was warm and the snow was gone, spring was here. The time before planting would be used to turn sod and prepare the new fields. There still could be a late snow fall, but West didn't think there would be one.

At noon they stopped for lunch and the fire pit made from the past trips was a welcomed sight for weary travelers. "Why does it always seem like we have more coming home than going" West said. Freda laughed "Probably because we do" and they all laughed.

It didn't take West and Carry to get the fire going. The women soon had the tea made, and bread and jam along with some trail mix for them to eat.

"This is where we need to build a shelter and have it stocked for our trips" Carry said. "I agree" West said. The two men talked of bringing some axes up here to clear some of the area. Freda said "If they want more work let them" and they all laughed.

It was late in the afternoon when they made it to the gravelled part of the road. The valley below looked wonderful to Willow "Home" she said. West smiled, but he felt it too, He knew he had to take care of things here before he could look for the complex.

They made their way down the hill and all tired from the journey went home. West and Carry unloaded the wagon and the women got the home fires burning.

By dark the wagon was unloaded and West and Willow found the peace of being alone, nice after all the visiting. She made a small dinner and the two now warm and comfortable, talked. "Willow, where do you think the complex is from here? Dad thought it was not far" West said to her. "I fear it will be like finding a needle in a hay stack. It could be anywhere West" she replied. "That's true, just think of it and the wonders inside. I sure would like to see it" West told her. "What if you never find it?" she asked. "Then I will set our children on the path for it like my father did." Willow frowned. "Dad told me they have animals there. I would love to see some kind of creature" Willow smiled at him. "We don't know if we will ever find it, but I will tell you after the garden is in. We can take a week maybe two and look for it. Carry and Nimuri will keep an eye on things here." West was happy that Willow wanted to help him look.

Willow had enough water for a bath done and West always let her bath first. When she was done he took his bath. Willow put fresh blankets on the bed and when West was done his bath, the two loved each other, West tender and considerate and Willow soft and obliging. It was dark when they were both spent. Willow, tightly held by West soon found sleep.

Willow was up first and soon had the cabin warm with fresh wood on the fire. Spring had made its firm hold on the land and the trees would soon be in full bud. West got up, after porridge and bread was off to cut trees. Willow kept to the cabin and did an inventory of her seeds for the garden. With the plans her and West made over the winter it would be a grand garden. She still did not know what Nimuri's surprise was. She couldn't needle it out of her no way. She thought about gathering mushrooms with some luck she might find some strawberries. Jo had sent some apple trees, however it would be a few years before they repeated a harvest from them, but it was a start. She had her inside work done and decided to haul some gravel. The ground still hard to dig would be ready before they knew it.

She put on a light jacket and headed to the tool shack. West and Carry had chopped down several trees now and it really opened up the area where they were going to build another cabin. She found the small wagon and headed to the river for gravel.

The next day fell into the same routine for them and their work was beginning to show. Willow hauling gravel made a big improvement to the road. West and Carry were burning stumps now. Nimuri had been clearing bush with them and helping Willow as well. Freda kept everyone fed. The buds on the plants were beginning to open and that was a sign to start digging the garden.

Most of the work came to a stand still as the four dug the garden. When the vegetable part was turned over and worked some with the spades West and Carry dragged a weighted rake over it to further soften it up. Willow and Nimuri followed them with a small isle digger to make rows to plant. It was tiring hard work for them.

West and Carry stayed in the fields till dark, Willow and Nimuri stayed till dinner. They returned to the cabins to bath and get things in order for the next day. When the men got in, hot baths, food and drink awaited them.

Willow and Nimuri would start the planting the next day. West and Carry would dig the oats and flax fields. It was then that Nimuri revealed her surprised. She opened a small bag to reveal wheat. Freda reached her hand into the seeds "I haven't seen wheat in a long time Nimuri, how wonderful. Corn and oats are good, but wheat is something different all together." Nimuri opened a few more bags "This is Nasturtium, it's a flower, but you can eat the leaves and the flower too. They are hot too the taste, it would be better to plant these by the cabins." She had one more small bag "These are squash; acorn squash and they are really good too." Where did you get these Nimuri?" Willow asked. "The old women brought them from the prairie when I moved here; last year they gave them to me" she smiled "Now I share them with you." Freda and Willow smiled. "This is going to be a grand garden" and it renewed their energy with joy. They had the first part of the garden done. If it grew they would be able to share with others. What a wonderful gif Nimuri had given them.

By night the women headed home to again prepare for the next day. Freda being older would not work the hours in the garden. She did the laundry with the water Willow and Nimuri hauled while the men finished digging the flax field.

By months end they had the garden in. The flax field was at least a third bigger as was the oat field. A small field was dug for the wheat and two mornings before they went to the fields, the women planted the Nasturtiums. The work was done just in time as the rain was beginning to fall. It would be wet on and off for the next while and the rest was needed by all.

With the planting done West focused on burning out the stumps in the newly cleared area, with the rain it was a tough job. Carry delimbed the fallen trees and Willow and Nimuri hauled gravel. The rain held on for a week and to everyone's relief the sun broke though the clouds bringing the warmth with it. It didn't take long for thing to start to dry out.

It was West that put into planning a week's adventure to look for the complex. He had taken a day and carried food and bedding into the next valley. It would give them extra food and ease the weight they would have to pack. Willow knew that home would be cared for by Nimuri and Freda. She was excited to see what lay beyond their safe haven.

The day chosen to start had finally come. West carefully packed what he knew they would need. Willow watched as he methodically placed things in his pack. She knew he was miles ahead already in his mind. "West do you think you will find the complex this time?" she asked. He looked up and smiled "Let's hope" he told her. He started going over his check list and when he was satisfied he closed his packs.

"Well are you ready my red headed beauty?" he smiled and Willow was glad to see him happy. "You bet I am" she said. With that statement they dawned their packs and started out. Carry and Nimuri waved from the clearing and Freda from the porch of the cabin.

West kept a slow pace. Willow found she had no trouble keeping up. It was fairly hard travelling with no trails They had to pick their paths carefully to avoid accidents, West obviously scanned the area to find the easiest way to go.

When they stopped for lunch West had dry fire wood waiting for them. Willow was still amazed at how he could make a clearing comfortable and with the basic things needed in no time at all. Willow so admired his talents and abilities. "What exactly are we supposed to be looking for out here?" she asked. "Well from what dad says, a long wall attached to a mountain. He said if we saw it there would be no doubt what we were seeing. He told me that the mountains around it were snow covered. The wall was a good 20 feet high and 100 feet long. When they were building the complex helicopters would land on the platform above. That's about it" West told her. "It's been 25 years since he was last there so it may be covered with growth." Willow could feel the excitement he held for it. "Well we aren't going to find it sitting here" Willow said and smiled.

She set about cleaning up a bit and West stowed everything into the makeshift shelter. He reinforced it as Willow gathered their belongings. "Are we going to be back here tonight?" Willow asked. "No I don't think so. We can carry enough to last us a day or two, then we will head back here." Willow unpacked what was not of urgent need and stuck to carrying food and water. West took the blanket and axe; his tinder box and ropes. "I think if we head toward the river the walk might be easier" West told her. Willow just smiled and said "Lead on great explorer" and they laughed.

It took a few hours to reach the river. Willow was surprised to see how high it was. The spring runoff was starting and the river was swollen with it and recent rain. West was right, travelling the river was easier. As they walked, the conversation went from their parents and friends to the valley they called home, even the prospect of finding the complex. "West it's hard to believe that one day people will fill all these valleys" Willow said. "There does seem to be more people now then when we were young. All the children have grown and will be starting their lives together" West replied. "I can see our own valley soon too full and this one the next place people will live. From the runners it seems they have roads right from the fort. They say many people are going to the south" Willow told him. "Willow, do you think you would like to live in a place like the fort?" "No I don't think so, there are too many people" she said.

They kept to the river and soon found they had to start climbing up. When they heard the falls they thought it was closer than it was. By the time they reached it the noise was intense. The water thundering over the rocks was impressive without the runoff, but as it was now. "We better start looking for a place to camp" West told her. "I think the top ground would be better." Willow agreed.

West, always in the lead secured the way for Willow. When they reached the top they were stunned to see an almost open area. Everywhere they looked they saw burned and weathered tree stumps. The lush undergrowth was obscuring any paths, but the openness of the hillside would make travel easier. The foliage just forming anew, painted the area in many different colours of green. "This is breathtaking" Willow said. ""I've never seen anything like it." West looked around "Let's just hope we never do. This is where a fire went through." Willow's mind flashed back to Kalvin telling her of the fires on the prairie and the loss of his family. "We should head to the tree line, it will provide more shelter" West told her.

Soon Willow had a small fire going. As they sat and ate Willow talked of the prairie fires Kalvin told her of. West listened intently "I've always feared a forest fire" he told her. "One good thing the river is not far away. It's the only hope we have if a fire ever was upon us." Willow had never thought much about a forest fire, but now that it had been brought to her attention it certainly would be a frightening thing to see. She glanced over the open area and could see that not much was left of the forest that once stood there.

They sat by the fire as dusk approached and West tried to mark on his map what he could see. Willow watched him and pointed out to the ranges they could see wondering which might be the ones that held the path to the complex. Night quickly engulfed them and West laid out the bed rolls. They watched the satellites cross overhead. Sleep came easily after their day of hiking.

Willow did not sleep, she was troubled by the thoughts of the fire and the vivid images she now had of the great fire that had passed this way. The moon, high in the sky gave some light, but on the most part the only light came from the small fire. The flames licked at the wood and consumed it. Willow put a few more small branches on it and rolled over to warm the other side. Sleep finally found her when the small fire was almost out.

They woke to rain. It didn't pour, just a steady drizzle. West was glad they were in the trees, it did provide some protection. The fire crackles and hissed. Willow made some porridge as West looked over the open meadow deciding which way to go. He took out his compass and told Willow west was the direction. They ate and soon had their gear packed again. The rain had stopped to West's delight. The day might turn out alright after all he thought. Willow just followed him. She could see that he was headed to a ridge to get a better view.

They crossed the area made by the fire and by the time they crested the ridge they were soaking wet. It was a better place to see the area around them. The hills and the mountains stretched as far as one could see. "Oh West, how will you ever find it? Look at all those mountains" Willow said to him. West looked at the view and knew she was right. Like finding a needle in a haystack would be easier. "Well dad" said West "so west we look, but first let's build a fire and dry out some." West soon had dry wood and a fire going. They sat and drank tea and had trail mix that made a nice lunch.

They waited until their footwear was dry before they packed to leave. West always made sure his fire was out before they moved on. The hike was hard and tedious. Breaking a trail through it took time and he thought that however far they got today would be as far as they could go before turning back. Although they had not covered and extensive amount of ground is did give a clearer picture of what was out here.

When they made camp West made an effort to clear the area around it better. "What are you doing?" Willow asked. "I want to clear this area well; it will be a good spot to store stuff. Like a base camp in the future." "Come eat and sit with me" Willow said. "I'll help more tomorrow, tonight I want you to myself." West soon found himself beside her. The food was good; he was hungrier than he realized. With the fire to keep the nip of coolness from them, they laid back and watched the stars. "I hope we find the complex West. It would be so wonderful to see it really and how happy Zack would be." "Yes I think he would be happy. I wonder how far he would have gone had he not have broken his legs?" West replied. "Well there's a down side to that you know. Had he not hurt himself I never would have had you" Willow said. West smiled "Things don't always work out the way you think they will" he said to her. "True, but that gave his life meaning after Jo" Willow said. "That might be true, but mom never wavered in her love for him. I often wonder what would become of them when one died. They are peas of the same pod. They just fit together well." Willow looked at West "I think that they will always be bound together somehow and I find comfort in that." West pulled Willow close to him "Like us, bound together" he said.

West kissed her and she returned his affection willingly. They loved each other far and away from the world they were comfortable in. It was as if they were the only ones left in the world out there in the forest. Their lovemaking was the only sound for the trees to overhear. By the time the fire was out they were asleep and quiet was all that was left.

West woke first and soon got the fire going. Willow didn't sleep long and was glad he had the tea ready. The sun was out and the mist rose from the ground as the heat warmed it. Willow made porridge with corn bread with syrup. They started the day.

They worked clearing the bush from the area. Willow's thoughts soon found in some ways how she missed having the valley to themselves. This is how it was when they first went there. She was glad for Nimuri and Freda's company, but it was nice when they had it to themselves.

West cut down smaller trees and stood them against a log. They would be good firewood the next time they came. They would have to start back clearing a path best they could. A few more trips here and the path would be a lot cleaner and easier to travel. They cleaned up around the fire pit and made sure it was out before they left.

They headed back down the ridge above the meadow near the forest fire. They worked to clear a better path. By late afternoon they found the area they camped at and did the same work. By nightfall they were tired. They managed to make a rough trail, but still had 2 more days of the same before they had to go back.

As they sipped tea and ate West told her each trip would be easier. She smiled; it was true the more they cleared this time the less they would have to do the next time. "How many more trips do you think we will get this year?" Willow asked. "I'm hoping for five, but we will see. Carry and I have to finish the cabin and did more garden area. I would like to get the cabin built between our valley and mom and dad's. Maybe he could make the trip then to come and see us." West smiled. "That would be nice for you West." He just smiled at her. "You sure have done a lot to the road. I am impressed. It will soon go all the way to mom and dads." Willow smiled "Yep and one day maybe to here." "Nimuri has helped a lot, I am glad she came here."

"You know Willow, when I was younger I travelled to the city of the dead. Cambry my father told me at one time held thousands of people. Although time had eroded the buildings I could see the city in my minds eye. It was huge and the buildings were everywhere. I know someday we will again live in places like that. People will spread out through these mountains and the human race will renew itself." Willow just smiled she wished she could add a human or two to that. Well she thought it does no good to dwell on it, just please let it happen someday. West added some wood to the fire and they slept close to it for warmth. As they lay there Willow thought about having a cabin out here. It would be fun, but it would be an awful amount of work. She watched the sky with West sleep finally claimed them.

After clearing the path more the next two days found them at the camp they made first. "Well Willow we will be home tomorrow, are you glad you came?" West asked. She smiled "I am and I'm looking forward to our next trip. I do think it would be an idea to get Carry to go the next time, two men could get more done than we did" Willow said. "I'll bring him, but I much prefer your company to anyone's" West told him. Willow hugged him. "Don't be a silly man. Carry and you could build a small cabin in now time. I think the only issue would be water. We will have to find a spot with a stream nearby. If it is to be a base camp then water would be a must" West just smiled at her.

"I wonder if the garden is up?" she told him. "Might be, but I think it will be a week yet before we will see any sprouts" West replied. "With the new cabin, do you have any suggestions as to who lives there? I thought we could asked Brad and Gary" West said. "The kids aren't little anymore they should have first dib" he added. "Yes I think that's a good idea. We might talk to Herb and Jean. If they don't want it maybe they have some folks that might want it" Willow told him. "Well until we get it built the valley will still be ours" West told her.

West added more wood to the fire. Willow fixed the last of the food and they ate quietly. West was sitting with his back to a log and Willow sat beside him. Willow yawned and West soon followed "Why is it when you yawn I always have too?" West said and they laughed. The last week had been an exciting journey for them and now it had come nearly to its close. They found their bedrolls and with the warmth of the fire they slept.

The following day was warm and Willow knew that with rain days before mushrooms would soon be out. The work now would be to sustain them. As they reached the last leg of their journey they looked down into the valley and knew by the smoke winding its way out of the chimney below they were home.

West notice Carry working in the clearing and was glad to see he had burned out many of the stumps. The logs were there and almost enough for the new cabin. They walked down the path and with greetings from Carry and Nimuri; they carried their gear into their cabin.

West wasted no time getting the water and Willow started the fire. They needed a bath. Willow made some tea and soon the gear had been unpacked and put away. West had his maps out and studied them while Willow had the first bath. It felt so good to wash after being in the woods for a week. West never said much as he intently looked at his maps. The ones his father gave him were starting to look vaguely familiar. "You know, I think we are heading the right way Willow" West told her. Willow couldn't see what he did, but was content to believe he knew what he was talking about.

The fresh water was ready and West didn't hesitate to bath. The hot water felt good on his aching muscles. Willow dried her hair by the fire and West watched her as he bathed. It wasn't long before life seemed to pick up its normal pace.

They had been home for a while and work was starting to show everywhere. The garden was up and most of the days for the women were spent there weeding it. The men also worked hard the walls of the new cabin were up and the place had taken on a new look.

Willow and Nimuri took at least one load of gravel for the road. They were satisfied that they had it all the way to the top of the ridge.

Freda cooked a lot of meals. Nimuri and Willow always felt she was a God send after working hard all day they didn't have to cook. The wheat and squash had come up; the nasturtiums were just starting to show. It was a pleasure to watch the food they so depended on start to grow.

Willow took the odd morning to look for mushrooms and did often bring home strawberry plants to grow nearer the cabin. The reeds were well on the go at the pond; hats, baskets and mats were always needed. Willow would try her hand at making paper this year and start a record of the people here. Her thoughts drifted to Jo and Zack and how they kept records of the births, deaths and who lived where, etc…It occurred to her that the valley they called home should have a name. It struck her as odd that people didn't that people didn't name the places like they had in times gone by. She decided to bring it up at dinner and see what the others had to say. Willow spent the time as she looked for mushrooms to think of a name for their valley.

When she arrived back at the cabin to her surprise a runner was there. He had a letter for her and West and Freda as well. He stayed for lunch and after headed back. Freda was the only one to send a letter back with him.

Willow, never having received a letter before opened it carefully. As she read the lines, a smile crossed her face. West, Carry, Nimuri and Freda all received the same. Willow's mom and Kalvin were to be married after harvest and this was an invitation to come for the celebrations. Her mind raced to think of something she could give her mom and Kalvin. The others were happy for her and her mom. "Can you believe it, they are to marry?" she said. "I am so glad, mom needs Kalvin and he needs her." "Life can be so good at times and well I'm glad." Willow just smiled. She carefully folded the letter and took it into the cabin. She placed it into her box of treasures.

West and Carry now finished the frame work on the roof of the new cabin and started to make the shingles. The new cedar trees were used for only the best things and the shingles were made from the ends of the logs not suitable for furniture.

At dinner Willow asked the others about naming the valley and all thought it was a good idea. Each wrote names on scraps of paper and everyone would discuss at the dinner meal which they liked the best. By weeks end Cliffside was the winner as all of the cabins were built on the cliff side.

"Well we are officially the village of Cliffside" West said. "Here! Here!" was the comment from the rest and they drank their tea. "Well what are we going to make for mom and Kalvin?" Willow asked. Freda spoke "If it's something from the heart it will suffice." "I know" Willow said "But, I want to make something special, both have lost so much and now they have found each other. Well, we have until harvest so let's put our minds together and I'm sure we will come up with something.' Willow and West finished dinner and walked home.

"Well fellow of mine, how do you like the well gravelled roads in Cliffside? The towns' folk have worked ever so hard to present such a beautiful place for you to visit" Willow said to him. He smiled "Well thank you, I'm sure I'll enjoy my stay here. Does the cabin have a maid service" he asked her. They looked at each other and laughed "Well it is a good name just the same" Willow said. "I like it, Cliffside, our home" she smiled.

West picked her up with ease and carried her into the cabin. "West put me down" she said "put me down." West would brook no reprove and carried her into the bedroom. There they loved each other, neither holding anything back. They were one together and one in the universe.

The cabin had grown cooler with not wood added to the fire when they returned. West got up and banked the fire. He put water on and returned to bed.

Willow was warm and comfortable, she snuggled to him on his return and they talked of children. West told her he would add more to the cabin when the time came and he would have a fireplace in it to keep it warm.

"I shall weave a bassinette for our baby" Willow smiled "and she or he will wear the best I can make for them. What a wonder, our love combined to make a person, another human being. Oh West! It will be wonderful." West held her close "You forget the dirty nappies, the crying in the night, the do this and don't do that." West smiled. "Oh yeah" she said "Well you can handle a few nappies and of course with your leadership they won't go astray too badly" she teased him back. Then they laughed.

West got up again and made tea. When he came back they drank the tea and stayed warm in bed.

The next two weeks were spent with work on the cabin and the garden.

Faithfully every night Willow would haul a load of gravel. Nimuri declined to go this time as Freda wanted to help.

West was on the roof putting the last of the shingles on and he watched her dragging the wagon of gravel up the road. He smiled thinking she was a hard worker and the road was so important to her. She wanted Jo and Zack to visit and the road was the answer for Zack to be able too. Tomorrow he thought he would go help her. He climbed down from the roof and Carry and he went inside the new cabin.

"It's done well" said Carry. "We have done a good job my friend." West smiled "you're the reason it turned out so well. I never could have this good without you" West told him. "Thanks" Carry said. They headed to Carry's cabin for dinner.

Freda always had a hot meal waiting for them. Nimuri and Freda sat with them and the talk was pleasant of what still needed to be done. West finished his meal and wondered what was keeping Willow. She should have been back by now. In a matter of a moment a great dread washed over him and he got up and went outside. He looked up the gravelled road, but could not see her. "Willow!" he called and no answer. "Willow!" he called again and no answer.

Carry and Nimuri were at the door now. "What's the matter West?" they asked. "Willow is not answering. She should have been back by now." "I'll run to the river" Carry said and was on his way calling to her as he ran.

West started up the path "Willow" he called and still no response. His pace quickened, as he walked and half ran he saw the wagon and Willow laying there. Now he was running, when he got to her the sight of her laying sent waves of almost pain through him. He reached down and to his relief she was breathing. He could see no injury except some blood on her face coming from a wound on his head.

He called to Nimuri and Freda. "She's here I found her. I need your help." He yelled to them not knowing if they heard. With Freda starting up the path West knew she had heard. He was on his knees beside Willow and was afraid to touch her for fear she might be hurt more. He felt the tears well in his eyes "Willow don't leave me, I love you, I need you" he spoke softly to her.

It seemed like forever before Freda arrived. She got down and began to check her limbs for broken bones. West watched and as he watched everything his mom Jo taught him came flooding back. He panicked when he saw her and was afraid to hurt her further. It didn't take Freda long to assure herself and West she could be moved.

Carry and Nimuri now there showed concern "What could have happened? She hasn't been sick" Nimuri said. "I'm concerned it is her heart. She never should have been hauling that load alone" Freda said.

West, Carry and Nimuri all felt shame wash over them. "Freda, No one is to blame I just want her safe and well."

West picked her up and carried her home. Freda undressed her to look for any hidden injuries and gave West the order for water to be boiled. Nimuri got tea going. After Freda finished washing her she sent Nimuri for the sewing kit she had for injuries. Nimuri quickly retrieved it. Freda called West in and pointed out the wound on her head. "It must be sewn. Better to do it now while she is unaware." West agreed with Freda. "Get me more hot water the needle needs to be boiled." West moved, but his mind was in a panic. Nimuri saw this and told him to sit with Carry.

The two women stitched Willow's head and sat with her. Carry sat with West "She will be alright she is young and strong" Carry said to him. West got more wood and put it on the fire.

Night was closing in and Freda decided to spend the night with Willow. After a bit Carry told West that he was going for the wagon and Nimuri went with him.

West sat there alone with his thoughts. He looked around the cabin and noticed Willow's touch was everywhere. She had made the cabin their home. She had made his life complete. As he paced back and forth he thought Willow just had to be okay, she just had to be.

Freda appeared out of the bedroom "West get some rest, I fear this will be a long night for you." "She's okay right Freda, tell me she's okay" he said to her. "West I will not lie to you. Her breathing is steady and her heart beats strongly. The wound in her head is bad, but I think the bone is in tact, if she bleeds inside I'm not sure. What caused this I don't know either. Did you see anyone in the woods? I would hate to think it was an injury inflicted upon her." West was stunned by what she said. He never heard or noticed anything, but he was not looking for anything. "Thank you Freda for helping so much."

Freda had been making tea "You drink this and get some rest. I will sit with Willow tonight and with luck she will wake up. You will have to care for her tomorrow so get some rest. You will be no good for her if you can not keep your eyes open." West nodded and sat in the big chair by the fire. Freda was right.

He sat there and thoughts of Willow filled his mind. How happy she was and how hard she worked all the time. She was so happy their valley had a name Cliffside. He thought of her and the ways she had; the softness of her touch and the tenderness she had in her heart. West held his head in his hands and wept. How could this have happened? What could he do to help her? "Think man, think" he said to himself.

Freda had been with Willow for most of the night. She came out and found West was finally asleep. She picked up a blanket from the chair near to him and covered him up. Freda opened the door and filled her lungs with fresh air. She was surprised that Willow had still not come around. This was not good. Freda rubbed the back of her neck it was stiff from sitting. She decided to send Carry for Jo, if Willow didn't wake by morning. She went back in and closed the door. She quietly boiled some water. After making a tea she went to Willow with a bowl of warm water to freshen the compresses on her head.

Morning came and the sun shining in the window did not wake West, he was emotionally drained and his sleep was deep now. Freda was still up and rose to stretch her legs. She opened the door and saw Nimuri on her way there. Freda closed the door and asked Nimuri to fetch Carry.

Before long Carry was there, "I need you to go get Jo as fast as you can." "Mom is Willow going to be okay?" he asked. "I don't know Carry she should have woken by now, I'm getting worried. You two promise me not a word to West. I will tell him if and when the time comes." Both nodded. "Nimuri come in with me. Carry you get a move on" Freda said.

With that Carry wasted no time, he was back to the cabin, grabbed a canteen of water, some trail mix, a light jacket and was off.

Nimuri had listened to Freda's instructions and took her place in the chair beside the bed. Freda went home to get some rest; it had been a long night and the longer Willow stayed unconscious the great the chance of a coma.

Carry moved like the wind. He ran as fast as he could, when he couldn't run anymore he walked as fast as he could. West and Willow had given them a home, worked by their sides and always treated him and his family as equals. West is a good man and Willow is a good woman, the thought that this should happen to her was terribly sad. She would be alright his mom and Jo would bring her around. Carry thought how happy they had been since they moved there, Cliffside it was a good name for the place. He thought how much better his mom had been, how he and Nimuri had become so at ease. It was Willow's friendship that had done it. She had made Nimuri feel welcome and important. Not the outcast she had been at the fort.

Nimuri wiped Willow's brow and spoke quietly to her. "Come on Willow wake up, everyone is worried about you, me included. Poor West is beside himself he needs you so, we all do. Freda is getting old, without your help we simple can't do. You have been a true and dear friend to me. Did I tell you about when we went to the fort from the prairie and how I never felt so alone? When I met Carry he scared me to death, funny huh? He was so good to me, his mom too. She loves me I think, I know I love her. We knew the work at the fort was too much for her. When you offered us this cabin I was overwhelmed. They both thought so highly of you. I was terrified to come here. I knew I would follow Carry to the ends of the earth, but to live here, well it was frightening. Now I don't know what I would do without you and West. You have given me more than you would ever know." Nimuri continued to talk with her in soft tones. She did not want to wake West.

West did wake in the early afternoon. He stretch and realized why he was on the chair. He got up to find Nimuri sitting with Willow. He asked "Any change?" Nimuri shook her head. "Would you like to sit with her? I need to walk around a bit" she told him. Nimuri told him to keep the compresses on her head and not to worry she would come around.

West sat beside Willow and did what he was told to do. He held her hand and told her how much she loved her. He asked what had happened and of course she never answered. Nimuri appeared at the bedroom door with tea, bread and jam. She set it beside him and told him she was going to check on Freda.

When Nimuri went home she found Freda asleep in the chair beside the fire. The cabin was warm and Nimuri put some more wood on the fire. She made herself something to eat. She did not want to leave West alone too long. Her thoughts passed on to Carry. He should be there by now. She hoped that Jo would know what to do. Nimuri covered Freda up and went back to Willow and West' place.

West never stopped talking to Willow, "Please wake up Willow" he said as he changed the compress. Tears now streamed down his face again. Nimuri again appeared at the bedroom door. "West go get some air" she told him "I'll sit with her, go stretch your legs."

West got up and wiped his face. Nimuri took the cloth, pan and followed him. He went out and she went to the kitchen to get fresh water. West looked up the gravel road and decided to look and see if there was anyone up there. When he reached the area, he looked around and there as nothing, no broken branches; no footprints. Whatever happened, it wasn't the fault of anyone else. He glanced down and saw blood on the path. He walked over and kicked some gravel to remove the stain. He looked down over the valley and everything seemed so peaceful. The wind blew the trees and the new leaves rustled as it passed over them. The brown garden had some green rows on it. The cabins nestled against the cliff looked quiet and calm. West knew without Willow he would find no more joy here in Cliffside. He walked down the path back to the cabins.

Carry was winded when he reached Jo and Zack's. After telling them what had happened Jo wasted no time in getting a bag together. Zack gave Carry a drink and some bread and jam. Jo was ready to go before Carry finished eating. He picked up the bread to take it with him.

Jo was older now, but surprise Carry how she set a pace and kept up with him. Carry carried her pack and that made it easier for her. Jo asked many questions Carry could not answer. "I did not see much of her" Carry said. "Well" Jo said "The journey will take sometime. I hope we make it before it gets too late" Jo said. "We will" Carry said and smiled.

"Brad and Gary have done a good job on the trail. It's much easier to travel now" he said. "It's been Kalvin that's been working on the trail. He told me he would like to gravel it soon. The visits between us have been to few and he wants Helen and the children to make more trips." Jo smiled. "He's worked hard since he's been here." He told Jo about the idea to name the valley and all agreed it was to be called Cliffside. Jo looked at him "Willow is a good woman. I have been blessed to know her and have her as part of my family." Carry looked down at the ground "You don't know how much Freda, Nimuri and I think of her. I have never been as happy as I am now. We have a home and mom is doing well. Nimuri has come out of her shell. Willow has been a good friend to her and mother. West is like a brother to me. I can't imagine how he is feeling now. I'm worried for everyone concerned" Carry told her.

Jo put a hand on his shoulder "I'll do what I can" Jo told him. "I fear her brain is bleeding and she is in a coma" Jo said. Carry stopped in his tracks "Oh my God!" he said. "Will you be able to help her?" Carry asked. "I'm not sure, but I will do what I can. Willow is young and strong; until I see her I just don't know."

By dinner time they were at the halfway camp. Carry got a fire going and Jo sat by the fire. Carry was tired although he tried not to show it. Jo could see it when he sat down his weariness could not be hidden. "You must eat and have something to drink." Jo handed some bread and a canteen, Carry smiled and took them. "West and I were going to build a cabin here, just a small one for when we travel; it's near the half way mark. Dry wood, food and a rain barrel for water, West says there's a creek near for water as well. I think if we clear it a bit around here it could provide a small garden area."

Jo let him ramble on; it kept her mind from worry. "How's your mom? I have missed her company" Jo said. "She seems fine. I know she misses you and Zack." Jo smiled. When they finished the soup made by Jo from the dried veggies she brought, Jo suggested they get going.

Carry dragged himself up. He shouldn't have sat so long. Jo gathered up their things and Carry stretched as he put out the fire.

They headed out and it was Jo that set the pace. It was faster than before it seemed to Carry. "Has Zack been well?" Carry asked. "His legs have been bothering him a lot more, but he doesn't complain" Jo replied. "Is everyone been doing well?" Carry asked. "Yes the valley has been good to us and the people have benefited from its bounty. We are all healthy and happy." Jo knew the conversation was to help pass the time. "How are you holding out Carry? I know you are getting tired" Jo said. "I am, but don't worry. I can rest when we get to Cliffside" Carry replied. Jo smiled and walked faster. Night was falling when the reached the gravel path to Cliffside.

As they approached West's cabin Jo saw West sitting on the steps. It pained her to see him there. She knew if he was there then Willow had not come around yet. West was lost in his thoughts and never saw his mom approach. "West" she said and he looked up. "Mom, mom!" he said as he stood. She hugged him "Take me to her West."

West took her inside. Freda was there and the two women hugged. "West, make some tea will you?" Jo asked. "Nimuri take that man of yours home and put him in a hot bath." West went out with Carry and Nimuri.

"Thanks for getting here" West said to him. "No worries" he told him. "I just hope she can help" Carry said. Nimuri and Carry walked home.

West got a bucket of water, when he got back in Freda was leaving. She stopped and hugged West "She will be okay West" she told him. West added more wood to the fire and put the water on to boil. He walked over to see Jo sitting beside Willow. "She's not in a coma West, but if she doesn't wake up by morning she will start to get dehydrated" Jo told him. "How do you know she's not in a coma?" he asked. "She is responsive to pain" she said. "You hurt her?" he asked. "No not really, but a little yes" his mom told him. She could tell by the look on his face he was letting his temper get away from him. "I pricked her finger and toe. If she was in a coma her reflexes would not have reacted. Her heart is sound and with movement in her hands and feet her spine is fine. She has a small concussion. The area around the wound is a bit soft to the touch. It is not swollen with blood so she is not bleeding inside her skull. Now young man is the tea ready?" West knew he had been foolish and he looked at her "Sorry mom, I'm just worried about her." "I know West make the tea and we will talk, alright?" Jo told him. West, feeling like a jerk left and made tea.

When he returned he set the tea beside her and his gaze went to Willow. "Don't fret so" Jo told him. "She has good colour too. She will be fine." "How's dad?" he asked. "He's doing okay. His legs have been bothering him this winter, but with the warmth he is getting around better." "Well that's something" West said. "How's everyone else?" West asked. "All are well" Jo replied. "I'm glad you are here mom." West looked at her. Jo never said anything. "I want you to get some rest West. I will need to rest tomorrow and I want you alert." West just nodded, he would rest better knowing his mom was here. "Is there anything you need mom?" he asked her. "I want enough water to have a good wash" she told him.

He drank the last of his tea and went and got water for his mom. He lay down in the biggest chair and was soon asleep.

Jo sat with Willow while West slept. She had a good wash. She let her feet soak as she sat there. It had been a long walk and her feet were sore. She checked Willow every half hour. Just before dawn Willow rolled onto her side. Jo knew that she would soon wake up. It was a relief. She now felt comfortable enough to dose a bit.

When the sun was up Freda appeared. "I'll take over Jo. Go to our cabin and sleep. I have changed the bed linens so you will be comfortable" Freda told her. "Thank you Freda." Jo told her that she felt Willow would wake up soon and for her to come and get her when she did. Jo turned the chair over to Freda and went to get some sleep. Freda had brought water and would soon have tea.

The young people never stirred much this early, but Freda knew Nimuri would soon be up. Jo walked quietly to the cabin. It didn't take much convincing to go to bed.. She was tired. With the worry lessening she slept easily.

Nimuri got up and started breakfast. Carry joined her in the kitchen. He was soon fed and Nimuri sent him for West and Freda. Carry didn't mind he wanted to see how Willow was anyway.

When Carry went in West was still sleeping. He took the food to Freda. Carry never spoke and Freda smiled. Carry could see Willow and she looked fine laying there. She had good colour.

He turned to leave and was soon on the path home. He was so stiff from his run to get Jo. Funny, he was a runner for a long time and now his legs pained him. As he walked along the path the idea hit him. He turned and headed to the workshop.

Nimuri now finished tidying in the cabin decided to see how Willow was and then work in the garden. As she walked up the path she heard someone in the workshop. She stopped in to see who was there. Carry looked up from the cedar plank he was working on. "What are you making?" Nimuri asked as she moved closer. "Well I wanted to do something for Willow" he told her. "It crossed my mind that she was so happy when we named the valley and how she worked on the road. It meant a lot to her" Carry told her. "That's true" Nimuri said. "So what's this then?" she asked. "Well it's a sign. I want to mount it on the road at the crest of the ridge. Cliffside, so anyone and everyone will see the pride and love we feel for our valley and the folks here." Nimuri hugged him "It's a lovely idea." She left him to work and went to check in on Willow.

When she arrived Freda was in the kitchen and West now awake was with Willow. "Nimuri fetch Jo will you? Willow has come around." Nimuri wasted no time in getting Jo.

West now sitting with Willow was holding her hand "So you have come back to me" he said to her. "I never left you" she told him. "Well you gave me a fright. I have been beside myself with worry" he told her and kissed her forehead. "What happened?" he asked. "I'm not really sure. I was just going to empty the wagon and now I'm here" she said. Jo was here now and asked West to wait in the other room.

West kissed her again and went into the living area. He added some wood to the fire and headed to the wash basin to clean up. Willow was awake and she was going to be okay, he thought as he washed.

Jo tentatively looked Willow over and helped her drink some tea. "Well young lady tell me what happened." Willow related the same thing she said to West. Jo just looked at her. Willow tried to get up and Jo helped ease her into a more comfortable position. "Oh my head aches" Willow said. "You took a nasty blow to it when you fainted" Jo told her. "Fainted!" Willow said. "Yes" Jo told her. "I have never fainted in my whole life" Willow said. "Hmmm" Jo said. "I'm going to make you some broth. You, young lady are to stay in bed until I tell you different."

Nimuri and Freda along with West waited in the living area. When Jo came out she told them she felt Willow would be okay now, but she was to rest. Freda had started to make tea and Jo heated some water to make some broth. "Freda" Jo said "I think Willow may be with child." A smile crossed Freda's face "Of course" she said. "I must be getting old to have not thought of that."

The two women passed the all knowing glances between them. "I didn't want to say anything until I'm sure" Jo said to her. Freda knew what she meant. Soon the broth was done and then Jo sent West to find something to do, while she helped Willow to eat.

West, now feeling his soul renewed sat on the porch and enjoyed the feeling of the sun shining on him. Willow was going to be okay, he thought and sighed. He watched Nimuri in the garden and listened to Carry in the workshop. He glanced up at the road and the guilt came over him. He should have been hauling the gravel not willow. He was ashamed of himself. It was work for a man. He started it and now knew it would be him that finished it

Freda appeared out of the house. "I am happy Willow will be okay" she said to West. "Freda, I don't know what I would have done without you. Thank you" he said to her. Freda smiled and put her hand on his shoulder for a moment. "Well a new day is here" she said "and I have work to do" she smiled and walk towards home. West got up and headed to the workshop. Freda was right there was work to be done.

Carry was intent on his project and West asked him what he was making. Carry smiled "Nothing much. So Willow is going to be okay, that's great" he said to him. "Yes" West replied "she gave me a scare. I have been torment by thoughts of being without her and I can tell you that it's not been a pleasant prospect." "I don't even want to think about being without Nimuri" Carry told him. "The day is half gone and I have done nothing" West said. "Don't worry" Carry told him "Just be handy for Willow." West smiled and went back home.

Jo was coming out of the bedroom and told West to go in to her for a few minutes. "Then I want you to find yourself something to do she needs to rest. I will stay with her." He knew his mom well enough not to argue. West sat with Willow until she fell asleep. It was not long before Jo appeared at the door. He was glad she was going to be okay. Jo took up the chair beside her and West took the hint and went outside.

With the roof done West decided to work on the road. It didn't take long before he was headed up the road with gravel. I felt good to work he thought. He had been so worried about Willow the peace in him had been thrown into chaos. West worked harder and found he was peaceful again.

Carry put aside the sigh when he realized West was hauling gravel and joined him. By dinner time they added a good 20 feet more to the road.

Freda and Nimuri food cooked and they washed before they ate. West took a tray to Jo and Willow. Jo was glad to see him and after a look at him she told him to take a bath. West's mom never minced words.

He started heating the water for his bath. When he finished his bath he heated more water for his mom. After he filled the tub again he went into the bedroom and found the two women chatting. "I drew a bath for you mom" West told her. She smiled and patted Willow's hand. West sat beside Willow and told her of the road.

The next few weeks followed a routine similar to the past few days. Willow was moving from bed to chair on the porch. Her stitches were removed and other than feeling peeked in the mornings, she was well. Jo had been there almost a month and needed to go home. Carry would travel with her so West could stay with Willow.

Jo said her goodbyes and West and Willow watched as she and Carry walked up the road. It was then that Willow told West she was with child. West looked at her. She looked wonderful to him. He smiled and said "I best get busy and add on an extra room." Then he smiled and hugged her. Willow was under orders, no heavy work. She didn't mind, but she did want to do her fair share.

Chapter 30

Dana and Todd fell into a routine of going to the tunnel and sneaking outside at every opportunity. Dern had not shown any more healing to Dana's relief. It wasn't until they went to pick him up from Todd's mom and dad's that his gift was brought fully to their attention.

It was Todd's dad that was the recipient Dern's gift. When they told Dana and Todd of the improvement in his dad's heart condition they just looked at each other. "The doctors just can't explain it. What the cause of this repair was unknown."

The joy on Todd's mom's face was unmistakable "Dern and grandpa always seem to be together." He loves Dern and it was clear Dern loved him.

After a coffee they gathered up Dern's things and started for home. Dana was the one that spoke first "Do you think it was Dern?" she asked Todd. Todd never said much just a plain "Yes I do. Dana he has healed my father. He has given him years more life. His gift is strong in him" Todd told her. When Dana looked at Dern all she saw was a happy little boy. "Please don't say anything Todd" Dana begged him "Let Dern have as much time as he can to be a little boy." Todd just nodded. He was proud and happy. He just wished Dana would look at the bigger picture.

When they arrived at their dorm and got Dern settled Dana told Todd she was going to the atrium. Todd didn't mind as it would give him time to work on the maps of the tunnels and begin to plan their next trip.

Dana was soon in the company of her birds and butterflies. "Well Dern was a healer and that was that" she thought. They had been outside several times now. The world she had known was changing quickly. She thought about the other children and wondered what gifts they might have. Then she thought about her father. How many survived out there she thought and could he have been one of them.

She watched as a honey bee landed on a flower close to her. How hard life would have been for them with everything dead. What joy she had watching the birds. It struck her then like a light coming on in her head.

She was off to go to the agro tunnel. She found Petra there. "Petra answer something for me would you?" Petra looked at her "Sure if I can." "I was thinking this whole place is like the nursery of the future. If you were to start outside what would be the first thing you would do?" Dana asked. "It seems to me there are plenty of plants still alive. I would think first get the pollinators out there to stabilize what's already there and in crease them." "Anything else?" Dana asked. "Well insects are the basic food for many creatures. I guess I would start there. What's this all about Dana?" Petra asked her.

Dana knowing she must be careful "I was thinking about writing a plan for the future is all. With Dern with us now I have been putting thought into his life one never knows they mat deem it safe in his lifetime to open the doors. I think we spend so much time checking to see if it is safe, but nothing after it is deemed safe." Dana smiled and thanked Petra before making her way to where the insects were.

When Dana arrived she found David's students hard at work. After she posed the same questions to them; each had their own insect to release from ants to maths. Each explained why, some for pollination, some for food sources for others and some to keep growth under control. Dana listened to each and when they were done she thanked them all for their time.

The last stop was at Dirk's. Carla made her feel at home. Dirk was happy to see her. "I thought you had forgotten about us. It's been ages since you have been here." Dana could hear the disappointment in his voice. "We have been very busy. Dern takes up so much time and work is always there. I am sorry Dirk I will make a point of making sure we come and visit more often." Dirk smiled. "Oh for heaven sake Dirk let Dana relax and enjoy her drink" Carla said. With that they all laughed.

Dana posed the same scenario to Dirk and Carla. He suggested finches, squirrels, deer and mountain goats. The list went on. "We have been letting animals go for years now" Dirk said. "True, but they have been confined to our valley. What about the rest of the valleys?" "Well dear let's see how they do in our valley before we get too beyond ourselves. Speaking of animals"

Dirk said. "That little colt is doing just fine after you left he perked right up. Never seen anything like it" Dirk said. Carla agreed it was wonderful to see it get over its sickness so quickly. Dana just looked at them "Oh!" she said "I'm glad he got better. Well" Dana said "I must get home to Todd will be wondering what happened to me." "Don't wait so long to visit next time" Dirk said and Carla saw her to the door.

Dana walked home and Todd was glad to see her. "Where have you been?" he asked. "Oh here and there" she teased him. "Sit down Todd I need to talk to you about two things that have been troubling me. I think I have found some avenues to make me feel better about things." "Alright" he said "I'll make us a drink."

They sat in the living room. "First I want to tell you how much I have thought about the world outside. I know that my father may not be alive, but if there have been survivors after all this time I think they need any help we can give them." "Dana I don't understand what you mean" Todd said. "How can I help them?" "I'm getting to that" Dana said. "Okay with all the animals and insects gone, food would be a priority right?" Todd nodded his head. "Well with no insects unless you have wind pollination the only other was to pollinate is to do it yourself, one blossom at a time." "Okay" Todd said as he leaned back in his chair. "We have been letting insects and animals go for years now" Todd told her. "Yes I know, but only into an enclosed valley. They are surviving out there. We need to let them go into the other side of the range" Dana told him. "Dana even if we did it would take years before any insects would be seen. It's a big world out there" Todd said to her. "I know, but at least it's something, a try. If people have survived we don't know how if they are close or far away. I just think that even if it takes years then so be it. Eventually we will be going out and with this start it would benefit us in the long run."

"Okay what do you want to do?" Todd asked. "I want to let go a few queens and some drones through the tunnel" Dana told him. He sat for a moment and then said "You may be right Dana." Todd, who was now was rolling this around in his head, said "We would have to let them go in early spring. I think they would have the best chance then." "I agree" Dana said "I think we should add some ants, butterflies and finches to the list as well." "How do you suppose to do that?" Todd asked. "All the animals have been numbered and counted." Dana sat for a moment "Well the atrium is only counted after the birds fly. We could sneak a few from there, same as butterflies. The bees might be more difficult, but all you need to make a queen is royal jelly." "My God, Dana I never believed you to be so sneaky"

Todd said and smiled. "Okay this will take time, but we have lots of time in here" Todd told her. "What was the other thing troubling you?" "I was getting to that. It's about Dern. I have spent many hours thinking about him and his gift. Did Andy not say that other children would be born with Gifts?" Dana said. "Yes he did" Todd answered. "Well I think we should find out more. Dern should be around them so he will not grow up thinking he is different, gifted yes, but still just a member of the society in the complex. Do you think Andy would tell you who they are?" she asked. "He might" Todd told her.

"I went to see Dirk. Do you remember that sick colt we saw when we were there? Well Dern healed it." Todd looked at her "Tomorrow I think I need to talk to Andy again. He wanted to be informed as to any healing Dern did." Todd finished his drink "You really get things going when your own devices" he told her. They both laughed.

"We have excited the complex, found a way to help anyone out there and our future. We found a plan of action to help our son to grow up as normal as possible. Think you can handle a little one on one with your husband now?" Todd asked her. Dana just smiled "Oh I think I could fit you into my schedule somewhere." Dana teased him. Todd carried her to the bedroom.

Todd and Dana found Andy as usual behind his desk. It had been a few days since Dana decided they were going to set a few things go outside the confines of the enclosed valley. Andy did not look good. His age seemed to be showing. "Well what brings you here today?" he asked and smiled.

Todd spoke first "You asked to inform you if and when Dern did any healing, well he has" Todd said. Andy sat back in his chair. "Who and what ailment?" Andy asked. "He has healed my dad's poor heart" Todd said and smiled. Andy coughed "You are a very lucky couple" Andy told them. "I was wondering if any other gifted children have been found" Dana asked him. "Not as yet" Andy told her. "But those already born may not show signs for a few years yet. Dern's gift is more noticeable then let's say the gift of thought." Andy clearly saw the disappointment on her face. "We have been scanning all the children born in the last 3 years and I can tell that 5 children show the larger pineal gland so they may develop gifts" Andy told her. Dana smiled and said "5 children, so 4 others may have gifts. That gives me some relief" Dana said. "Thank you Andy you have lifted my spirits" Dana told him. "I'm off to take Dern to the atrium." "I'll join you soon Dana" Todd said. "I want to talk to Andy a bit longer." Dana smiled and Dern and she were soon on their way.

"Andy you don't look well. Have you been sick?" Todd asked him. Andy looked up and had a good chuckle "No Todd I am not well. I am dieing. It happens to most people my age" Andy smiled. "I have lived a long life. Did you know that there are but 10 members left of the council now and I know their health fails them as well?" Todd looked at him "Maybe Dern could help?" he asked. Andy looked at him again "Dern can't change the passage of time nor should he try to breathe life into such an old carcass such as mine." Andy smiled. "It is as it should be. I just wish I could have seen the outside one more time" Andy told him. "But that was not meant to be. I envy you Todd, one day you will live outside as we all did and should." Todd looked at him "Andy" he said "I have found something you might find interesting. I'll come get you first thing in the morning, alright?" Todd said. "Well now" Andy said "That's an interesting proposition." "Trust me it's something I need your opinion on. Can you trust me Andy?" Todd said. "Alright I will be waiting" Andy said to him. "Tomorrow then" Todd said as he got up to leave. Andy nodded and went back to his papers.

Todd went to talk to Dana. He found her at the atrium. She was right Dern was enjoying the birds and butterflies. "There you two are" he said as he approached. Dana smiled "So what was so important that you stayed to see Andy?" Dana asked. Todd looked away from her "He's dieing, did you know that?" Todd told her. Dana looked down "No" she said. "Dana" Todd said "I want to show him. I think he deserves that. He wouldn't tell I know he wouldn't" Todd said. "I don't know Todd, he's a founder" she answered. "Well what of it if he speaks out then we start living on the outside. Isn't that what we have worked for all these years?" Todd said. Dana looked at him "What of the others? Andy knows things that others don't. If he speaks out, what about them and the fear that dwells within most of them. The virus killed everything and almost everyone. Do you think they will welcome the news? I fear they will close off the tunnel." Dana paused for a moment. "Dana he knew about the air and he never told. He knew about the children and he never told. He knew that the people would eventually find their way out." Dana looked at him "Alright, we will take him." Todd smiled and hugged her. "First we need to take Dern to mom and dads."

It didn't take them long to make their way there. Todd's mom greeted them with a big smile. Dern squealed with glee as Todd's dad appeared next. "Well little man has come to visit me again" and Todd's dad scooped him up. "Come in, come in" Todd's mom told them. "Mom, can't stay we just came to ask you to mind Dern tonight and tomorrow. Andy needs our help" Todd told her. Todd's mom looked at him "Andy always has something he's working on. I guess we could help him" she said. "Of course we can" Todd's dad said with a smile. "Well" Todd said. "Andy has some experiments for his students in the caverns, so we will have to go home and pack some gear. I'll pack a bag for Dern and bring it back, alright mom?" "Sure son" she smiled at Todd. Dana and Todd left.

They turned a few more corners and they were at their dorm. It didn't take them long to pack what Dern needed and Todd hurried them to his mom and dads. Dana finished the pack for the tunnel. It was easier now they had most of everything they needed already there. Soon Todd was home again. With the prospect of taking Andy to their private get-a-way it wasn't easy for them to sleep.

As morning came around it was Andy that appeared at their dorm. The three of them headed to the new cavern. The masons had the view point done and Andy was intrigued to see what Todd and Dana had the sparked such interest. Todd looking like he had a study underway let the ladder down. He let Dana do first and let down the clipboard and gear. Andy went next and Todd followed.

"Well it looks like the same as the other caverns" Andy told them. Todd just smiled "Not quite the same" he said as he pushed the wall revealing a room behind it. Andy's eyebrows rose "Now this is interesting" he said with a smile.

After they all went in Todd closed the door. He turned on his light and after they deposited their bags, Todd turned on the lights in the tunnel. "My God Todd" Andy said. "You and Dana have done all this? It's amazing!" he added.

Todd kept moving and they entered the cavern with the quartz and citron crystals. The cave flickered and Andy just stared at it. He followed Todd and Dana and picked up the read. "It was a lot of work through here; we had a lot of rubble to move" Todd told him.

They soon reached the open cavern with the water. "This is amazing" Andy said. "I had no idea the tunnels were so extensive." Todd reached what looked like the end of the tunnel. He had built another door to keep out the weather. "Andy" Todd said "This is for you" and he pushed the wall. It slowly opened and a small breeze blew in. It was hardly noticeable with the bright light of the sun. They slowly walked out. Andy never said a word. He found a spot to sit and he stared out over the valley.

The sun warmed his skin and the wind blew his grey hair into his face. They all sat there not saying a word. When Dana looked at Andy, his face streamed with tears. She sat closer to him and put a hand on his shoulder. Todd stood and looked over the terrain and he too never spoke.

Andy wiped his face and took a deep breath, Dana faintly heard him say "And so it begins."

It was an hour or two they sat there speaking little just soaking in the sun light and listening to the wind. It was Andy that spoke up "How long have you two been coming here?" he asked. "For some time" Todd said. "It's hard to stay in knowing that through a few doors we are out. It's still a bit frightening I find" Dana said. Andy smiled at her "I can understand that, but for me, well it's like having my life back again. You may never know the gift you have given me" he told them. "I thought I would die never feeling a soft breeze or the heat of the sun. It brings back so many memories; my childhood and so many things in my life I experienced out there" and Andy motioned to the valley beyond. "There is such great wonders and beauty out there. I am so excited for you. The world awaits you and a journey far beyond what you could imagine is beginning."

Todd looked at him "When do we tell the others?" he asked. "WE don't" Andy said. Dana spoke next "Why not? They have the right to know Andy." "I agree" said Todd. Andy took a deep breath "Let me try to explain something to you. Look out over those valleys" he told them. "How far can you see, do you think?" "Miles" Dana told him and Todd agreed. "Well that's true, but the reality is about 30 miles the human eye can see and what do you think is out there now?" They looked at him "What do you mean?" Todd said. "Before the viruses were let loose the land you look at teamed with life, there were amazing amounts of creatures. Some were benevolent and some were just another food source for others. The skies held birds and insects; the water was full of fish, but no more. It's empty out there now. I have prayed for your entire life that some people survived or animals. I knew our society then was based on an abundance of animals for food, not to mention everything that was made from them. The human race was not like it is in the complex. We put faith in gold, oil and the rich took advantage of the poor. Material items were worth more to some than lives of their fellow man. There were nearly 7 billion people on the planet and we have watched monitors for all these years and nothing. No sigh that man survived. We are vestiges of what is left. Dirk, Carla, Karen and David had their hands full. Through their efforts we have animals alive waiting one day to be free like us, waiting. We must prepare all this to be capable to sustain us again. There past few years of letting out our excess animals have barely scratched the surface of giving back to the world what was lost. I will never see it. You may never see it, but Dern may. By then maybe life will have reproduced enough for people to leave the complex and start to live once again in the world. There is much work to be done yet."

Todd and Dana listened to Andy. "In the scramble to get out they failed to grasp the meaning of it. Get out of what? They and the others were bound to the complex like a tree is bound to the soil, for its every need. It wasn't that they couldn't let the animals go; they didn't have them in quantity enough to make living outside a possibility yet."

"Andy how long do you think we will be just letting out into the enclosed valley?" Dana asked. Andy thought for sometime and then he told her "At least 5 more years. Then we can leak the fact outside air has got into the complex. Then after a few more years then we can open up and let animals go else where. It has to be done carefully. The original founders will be gone by then, but the new council will have to proceed cautiously. People are not all like you and Todd. Most find safety in groups. They cling to each other for safety. If you take that away they will perceive it as a threat and it causes distress. People under duress or perceived threats will do things they never do otherwise."

Todd motioned they should head back inside. They had been gone for sometime now. They helped Andy up and as they headed for the door back in, Andy looked over his shoulder. He stopped and gazed over the mountains one more time. He knew in his heart it would be his last time he would see the world he had known for the most part of his life.

They walked back through the tunnels to the first caver. Andy had to rest. Todd showed him the maps they had made and Andy rested as he studied them.

It was another hour before they left to climb back up the ladder to the complex. Andy asked them to come to his office he had something to show them.

The day had taken its toll on Andy and it showed. By the time he was back in the library and in his chair Todd and Dana could see that it was hard on him. Andy told them more of the things they should know about the founders and the losses most suffered. He talked about how many in the complex died and how they needed to come to the library for a list of things he wanted them to hide in the cave.

By the time they left him for the evening they felt tired mentally and physically. Andy knew his time was getting shorter. His death was approaching. He had chosen Todd and Dana to care for the knowledge he held, secrets and knowledge to be released to the people of the complex at the right time. He felt sorry for them to have the burden he had carried for so many years. They were the future and the beginning of the complex's journey back into the world they had been so securely hidden and protected from. With other young people of the complex, he had planted the information they needed to eventually be aids to Dana and Todd. The gifts were starting to appear in the new born children.

Andy smiled, the world he knew and so many knew were gone as they would be. The new children would make the world anew as did the viruses. Andy thought of being outside and how good it felt to be free again even if it was for only a little time. "Well old man" he said under his breath "go to bed" he shut his books and went to his dorm.

Todd and Dana felt at ease about their secret tunnel. Andy told them many things. They were like children who had not taken things into consideration. "Todd" Dana said "How naïve we have been. There are so many things I didn't know or even thought of. I feel foolish" Todd looked at her "If Andy thought we were foolish do you think he would have confided in us? He is leaving a legacy to us and is depending on us to see the rest of the people here to live to see the outside world and prosper in it. He has given us a great honour." Dana looked at him "With great honour comes a great sacrifice. I hope his faith has not been misplaced. I am worried about it all." Todd hugged her "Worry when you have to, not before" he smiled. "Now let's get cleaned up and get that boy of ours." Dana smiled.

When they arrived to pick up Dern, he was sleeping. They didn't stay long at his mom and dad's and made haste in going home. The day had been long for them. With Dern in his bed they too followed suit.

The following day passed quickly for them. They had been neglecting their work and now had to make up for lost time. Dana had the harvest of cotton to deal with and Todd's job demanded his attention to set up the machine for making parts. The evenings were spent with Dern and Todd found himself transporting things to tunnels for safe keeping for Andy.

With Karen's passing it left few of the founders alive. There were but 10 left now. Andy was sicker with each day and Todd and Dana found losing him slowly was worse than if he passed quickly. He had everything arranged for his leaving this world for the next. It was like sands passing through an hour glass waiting for his end. It was Andy that arranged a meeting of the young people picked to fill the positions the founders left open as they passed. This was after a vote of the majority of the people still living there. Most of the people were the children of the founders and the workers. Although many were content to let these few hold the positions, it was open to all that excelled in any given field of study. Society in the complex was efficient and many just wanted to work and care for their families. It was harmonious there. With no money to create greed and the basic needs of living fulfilled the people fell into routines and were content.

When they were all assembled, Andy watched and listened to the latest of the state of the complex. What he found a bit troublesome was no one talked of preparing to go outside, fear still held them back. Here was the think tank of the future and not one talked of preparations to leave.

It was halfway through the meeting when Andy spoke up to them. "How many here will have thought about what would be needed to live outside again?" Petra spoke up first "I know that for me and my work I don't believe it would take much to get a garden growing outside. Each time I brought this to my mother's attention she told me that plants would be the easiest of tasks to accomplish to reunite with the outside world. Pollination might be the biggest problem to solve, but with my father's work well in the hands of more capable people I feel secure to think when that time comes it will be taken care of."

Mark and Ann told the meeting that animals were surviving on the outside, but it was still too soon to tell if they were reproducing. Just how well they were doing, without their recapture and tests done it would be impossible to tell as yet.

Erik added his voice and said "According to all research done, the virus was at the moment stable, but that like any virus it would adapt to the world. If it mutated again or joined another virus it could again jeopardize the people here." It was opinion that the doors remain shut and any ideas of exodus be in written reports. Andy thanked him for his comments.

Hetti, Carl and Jake thought that if we were planning to leave the haven that a reliable plan was worked out for the benefit of all, it would not be a wise decision to attempt it at present or in the near future. Drew never said much, he felt moving outside would be the best for all, but not without due care, attention and at a slow progression. Steve and Toni added that any materials for building would be in abundance when they were needed. Julia agreed that work clothes and protective gear would have to be stock piled before and that would take time.

"Well" Andy said to the gathering "I need you all to submit your ideas and lists of what each of the needs were for each work station. I believe the virus has done its worst and we need to get a workable program set up for the future." "How soon do you believe we can think about going out?" Petra asked. "I am unable to give a time frame, but I d know the first thing would be food. So until that could be put into place the rest was on hold" Andy said. "Petra I would like to talk to the people in charge of your father's work to get some kind of idea." Andy said to her. "So I want you all to contemplate this and give me a report on what you would need to do. We have been hiding in here too long; we need to rejoin the world." There was an eerie silence in the room.

Andy concluded the meeting and after an hour or so the group started breaking up. Todd and Dana stayed behind to talk with Andy about everything.

It took about 10 to 15 minutes to reach the library where Andy spent most of his time. "Are you going to tell them Andy?" Todd asked. Andy smiled "Not yet" as he sat down "All those at the meeting tonight are the future. I have no doubt they will make up the new council. Most of the original founders are all gone. The virus killed a lot but I'm afraid old age is claiming the others."

"Oh Andy what will we do without your guidance and understanding" Dana asked as she stood beside him with a hand on his shoulder. Andy patted her hand. "You will be fine my dear. Over there, those books you must hide them in the tunnels. Don't bring them back until the doors have been opened and if you find yourself in a situation where guidance is needed, talk with Dirk." Todd looked at him "Does he know everything?" "No, but he is a wise man and he knows more than most. We have some interesting things to talk about." Andy smiled "Yes, he is your man. Be cautious with what you tell him when others are present. The others at the meeting are, well let's say controversial. Erik and Petra are the ones you need to trust the most with anything. Now let me rest and Oh yes, I think Erik's child might be a good playmate for Dern" and Andy smiled. "Now off with you two."

Dana and Todd knew that Andy had concluded this meeting. Dana kissed his cheek and her and Todd went home. They had the books Andy gave them. They were Simion's journals. Todd knew they held important information most were not ready for.

They spent the night together and as mornings do, it came early. Dana went to get Dern, as always he was happy to see her. Dana thanked them for minding Dern and was on her way home when she decided to go to the living area for a cold drink.

Todd was on his way to drop the books off and then to work. The weekend would be when he and Dana would read Simion's journals. He thought about Erik, Petra and Erik's child. A good playmate for Dern, is what Andy said? He wondered if Katrina had a gift. After the ensuring the books were safely in the tunnel, Todd made his way to work.

Dana had taken Dern to the weaving dorms with her. He had been in the childcare area and Dana sat at her station and began the weaving machine. Her mind wandered over all the things that happened in the past few years, and then she skipped to the next years ahead. Andy was right; there still was an enormous amount of work to do.

At days end Dana and Todd found themselves at home. Dana had just finished washing up with Todd's help when Erik knocked at their door. They both knew it was not good news; Erik always was the same when he brought bad news. "I came to tell you that Andy is no longer with us. Arrangements have been made for a service tomorrow. After which I think we need to talk" with that Erik took his leave.

Dana and Todd both shed tears for Andy. His loss would be felt throughout the complex.

Sleep did not come easy for either of them this night. By morning they had all the sleep they were going to get which wasn't much.

Todd went to the masons to see if he could help and Dana to the kitchens. It was a helpless feeling knowing that the founders would soon be gone.

The service for Andy was attended my many. Petra had an abundance of flowers set up for the tomb area. Dirk was the master of ceremony and after the crowds left, the last remaining founders met in the conference room. Dirk poured out a drink for all and with a raised glass "To Andy" he said and they all drank. With so few founders left it didn't take long for them to depart.

Dirk cleaned up the conference room and all the while thought about what Andy had told him. Dirk and Carla always felt responsible for the virus getting in, but from what Andy had told him it was not the case. He knew the people lost so many loved ones and that any action to go out would be met with fierce opposition. The world they had grown up in relatively care free was now a feared and empty place. Dirk wondered just how long the air had been getting in and just what people would do when they found out. Andy had each station preparing reports of what would be needed when they started the move outside. Well he felt good that the grand start with the animals had been made. Todd and Dana had pushed that. Andy was adamant about Todd and Dana being keys to the future and Dern. Dern was a gifted child. He had no idea that so much was going on and that he had been blind to it. At one point Dirk would never have missed anything, but the animals and his own family kept very busy. He knew he would change now. By the time Dirk was home his mind was full and the sorrow of loosing Andy was mixed among them.

Todd and Dana, now at home talked much of Andy as they held in their tears. "I'm so glad we showed him" Dana said. "I am too" Todd replied "But you know he was right. We have to start letting things go out there, but how are we going to get them?" Todd said. "I agree" said Dana. "Some we can get from the atrium, but I think bees would be a big help. Maybe if we tell Dirk he could help us?" Dana said. "Andy was very strict about us not telling anyone" Todd told her. "I want to read Simion's journals. I'm sure that the answers too many things will be there. I wonder what gift Erik's child has. Andy said she would be a playmate for Dern. It seems life is getting complicated again" Todd said. "Just when we thought things were settled a little a whole new set of circumstances present themselves" Todd told her. "I know what you mean" Dana said. "Andy's children will run the library. I hope they will be as reliable as Andy was. I will miss him terribly Todd" Dana said. "I will too" said Todd.

The next few weeks passed as normal. Todd and Dana fell into their normal routines. They read the journals and were amazed at how many things that had come to pass that Simion wrote about. They wondered more about him now and how in tune he was to human nature.

The younger council held meetings with the last of the founders. It seemed that objection was the rule to opening the doors. The biggest argument that held them tight shut was the fear of the virus mutating again to cause havoc. It was believed by many that if they were the seeds of the future human race no mistake could be made. Todd and Dana knowing that the outside air was getting in barely could contain themselves at the meetings. Dirk knew it was a good thing to keep them in until the environment was once again filled with life. Animals were resilient with plenty of food; he knew they were doing well.

The following spring Dana was there when the animals were to be released. She helped carry many creatures to the tunnel to be released.

When she went to get the insects she carefully placed a queen honey bee and its drones along with 20 or so workers in her back pack. When she loaded the others into the tunnel she watched as they closed the door before opening the outside one. The monitors showed mainly the large animals re-entering the world and once they were free she headed home.

Dana got changed and went into the tunnels. She almost felt like a thief in the night, but was determined to do what she wanted to do for so long. Todd never wanted them to travel alone here in case of an accident. She would not have to explain he would never know.

When she reached the final door she pushed it open and was first blinded a bit by the light. It took a few minutes for her to climb down to the heli platform. She sat on the edge and starred out over the land, nothing but the sound of the wind in the trees could be heard.

She opened her pack and took out the container holding the bees. She opened it and stood back. It only took a few moments for the bees to take flight. They flew over the side of the mountain and down into the valley below.

Dana stood there listening to the sound of the wind and then spoke aloud "My gift to you father if you're still alive." Then there was just the wind.

Dana climbed back up and just before she went in she looked back one more time. "I hope you made it dad, I miss you" and then she went in.

Todd was home when she got there. Soon they talked of the day they each had. It seemed in some senses the complex was the same as before. The next few years would be spent trying to get them to open the doors.

Chapter 31

The garden was in, Freda and Nimuri doted on Willow. She spent her days sitting on the porch. She did do some work, but she wanted to help more than anything. West and Carry had the road well into the forest and the sigh of Cliffside was hung, Willow watched everyone working and it made her restless. She often walked to the river and listened to the water flow by.

West and Carry had the logs cut for the addition of the extra room for the baby. Freda had walked down to where Willow was. "How are you today?" she asked and Willow smiled. "Restless I can see" Freda said. "Yes I feel like I'm not pulling my weight." "Well I wouldn't worry too much you will have your hands full when it's Nimuri's turn. So things all work out." Freda smiled. "I brought a basket, I think we should see if any mushrooms are about and I was thinking some cattail roots might be nice for a change."

Willow got up and the two women walked into the forest. "When I was a young woman the forest was full of animals; birds, squirrels, deer and to go alone was not a good idea. There were bears and wolves you never could imagine the noise the forest held if you listened, but I'm afraid all there is now is the wind." Freda told her. "Do you think any animals made it Freda?" Willow asked. "Well it seems some people did, so I believe some maybe. The earth is a huge place and they would take an awfully long time to fill it up again, if they did indeed survive. Let's just hope that they had survived like us." With that Freda smiled.

It didn't take long for them to gather the roots; however the mushrooms failed to make a good showing. They had a few, but maybe in the coming weeks they would be more plentiful.

When they walked back to the cabins, Nimuri had dinner well under control. The garden looked great. West and Carry were talking of hiking to where Willow and West had hiked before. West wanted to cut a stack of wood for the cabin to be built there. Willow was a bit hurt when she listened. She had felt it was their project and now just because she was with child she couldn't go. After listening for a bit longer it occurred to her she was being silly. Cutting down trees for a cabin was mans work and with a cabin built and stocked up she would be able to travel there with West and their child. That brightened her mood a lot.

That evening a runner came. Kalvin and Helen had gotten married and would bring the children for a visit. The news set the women to talking of where they would all sleep, what meals would be made, etc...

West and Carry spent the evening talking with the runner catching up on the news. Seems Jo had liked the naming of their valley so much they named theirs as well. The name that won out was Green Meadow. "Well" the runner said "It will make it easier for us with towns rather than names. Letters will be easier to sort."

West had the trees down. He and Carry burned the scrap. The runner set his tent near the fire and as night settled in so did everyone else.

In the quiet of the night Willow and West talked of the baby and what projects he wanted to get going. Willow was excited about everyone coming. It was late when they finally fell asleep.

When Willow woke, the sun just broke over the mountain tops. As with most mornings she was not well. She would be happy when this passed. It didn't take her long to get the fire going and heat water. She washed up and it helped a lot to making her feel better. Then with breakfast, waves of unwell washed over her again as she made West something to eat. He was up by now and could see she was struggling with making the food. She put his food on the table and took some dry bread to eat while she sat on the porch. All in all she thought it might be a good day as she nibbled on the bread.

It wasn't long before West joined her to talk. He sat close and waited for her to talk. "Looks like the runner left early" she said looking to where he had slept. "He has a long ways to go back to the fort." Willow smiled "Seems I've started something by naming our valley. To think we are from Greenmeadow and now residing in Cliffside." West smiled. "Want to go for a walk?" West asked. "Sure I have been awful restless" Willow told him. "I thought you might like to see how far we have the road now" West told her. "Oh yes I would. I can't wait until it's done then Zack can come visit us. It will be good to see something new and different I think" she said to him. "It would be grand to see him be able to travel here" West said. "From what the runner has told us, roads are being made from here to the fort." Willow was glad. "It will make travel so much easier. They are going south as well." "How many people do you think there are now West?" Willow asked him. "My guess would be 2000 maybe more. The runner also said they have the lumber cut and are building 5 more cabins to the south. The land is cleared and with the extra space food will be grown so all will not go hungry."

They reached the top of the hill and stopped for a rest. Willow looked down over the valley and leaned on West. "How do you feel about more cabins here?" West asked her. "Gary and Brad's children are grown and soon will take homes of their own." "West I guess that was bound to happen. I did like it when it was just us though. In some ways I miss that" she told him.

They continued their walk and Willow was surprised how far they did have the road built. "I thought you were going to build a cabin at the half way mark for the runners?" "I was cutting the lumber for the cabin the other way first. Then we can come and do this one. There always something needs to be done" he smiled "but I guess being busy is being happy. Our child will benefit from our work and the children born in the future. I doubt the world will be like before and I think that is a better thing, a new beginning for all of us. In 200 years from now I wonder how things will be like." "Well if we keep going as we are I imagine the world will be a good place for our children because we made it that way for them." Willow tucked her arm in his "Let's go back" she said.

Jo was busy putting things together for West and Willow. With Helen and Kalvin travelling to see them it was a good opportunity to send some things along. She had started several apple trees and was sending half to them. Zack had made some pottery; Sara and Lily made some extra material for baby clothes. Jean and Herb were sending some wooden bowls. Helen, Willow's mother had toys and clothes for the baby and she made a picture of dried flowers. The children were excited to be going somewhere and it didn't take them long for the group to be on their way. The well wishes from everyone went with them.

The road Kalvin and the children worked endlessly on was proving its worth as they pulled the wagon along. The children's boisterousness soon waned as the trek became harder. At the end of the road Kalvin and Helen kept their spirits with tales of animals that once lived in the woods. Kalvin pointed out trees, plants and the children named them as they travelled along.

It was a relief when they reached the half way mark. A fire pit was there and a lunch was made ready. The sounds of the children filled the nearby woods. They had made good time and Kalvin was sure they would make Cliffside by evening.

Helen was excited, she had not been this happy in such a long time. Kalvin was a man's man and life was good. She wondered how Willow was and how she was feeling. Kalvin seemed to sense her worry and as always made her feel better.

By mid day they could see the road coming from Cliffside and with the children tiring it was a welcomed sight. Once on the gravel the children knew they were getting close and excitement filled them again.

When they crested the ridge of the valley the family looked down and Helen felt good at the sight of the cabins nestled against the cliff. She could see why Willow liked it here. The gardens were all growing and it was a pleasant sight to see cabins after the day of just seeing forest.

Willow was sitting on the porch when she noticed them and called to West. Soon Carry and West had the wagon down the hill and everyone was at their house for tea and dinner.

Helen was with Willow. West and Carry soon had Kalvin talking of plans for the future. Helen and Willow watched the children and Willow noticed that Sawn, her sister was aloof from them. It was surprising to see her maturing into a fine young woman. Willow called her over and Dawn looked relieved to be away from the others.

Helen and Kalvin were to stay at West and Willows' Dawn sat on the edge of her seat until Willow asked her to stay with them as well. John and Sam were to stay with Nimuri and Carry. Now with the sleeping arrangements made Helen and Kalvin could unpack.

Great O's and Awes were shared when the items were given to Willow and West. How different things were with Kalvin. He had taken the gloom and despair from Willow's family. It had been replaced with joy and hope. Willow was happy; her life was good not just for her, but everyone around her. Dawn told Willow that they had been working on the road from their side and now it headed into the forest. How many things were changing thought Willow.

Helen settled into the chair by the fire. Her bones ached from the long trek. Kalvin sat near her. Willow and West sat opposite them. Dawn sat on the floor by the fire. Night had closed in quickly. With the only light coming from the fire they talked of family, friends and any news from the other settlements.

Willow got Dawn to pop some corn and the evening slipped happily by.

The boys at Carry and Nimuri's listened to Carry's tales of being a runner and the old stories of the world before from Freda. It didn't take long for all to sleep.

The next day brought a storm. The thunder crashed and lightning lit up the sky. West as always in a storm spent much time on the porch. He and Kalvin spent time talking. Helen, Dawn and Willow kept the cabin warm and made lovely vegetable stew for everyone to eat. She had panned fried corn bread and strawberry jam. Tea was brewed most of the day. The storm as well hung on most of the day and West continually scanned the sky around the valley.

By late afternoon everyone was there and the cabin was full of cheer. West had come in, but he never took his mind totally off the storm. Kalvin was to help the next day with the extra room. Then when they went home Carry and West would fall the trees at the halfway point for the cabin there.

Willow had time with Dawn and Helen with Freda. The boys followed Kalvin like puppies. He never scolded and found things they could help with. "Dawn you have grown so much" Willow said to her. "You have been gone for so long Willow" Dawn replied. "I guess I have at that" Willow smiled. "Are you still having lessons with Zack?" Willow asked. "Yes, but he thinks I'm almost finished" Dawn told her. "Then you are almost ready to make your own life" Willow said to her. "I would be, but I can't get Chad to see me as a woman yet. He just sees me as a girl." Willow looked almost shocked that Dawn had let her secret out. "Chad is it?" Willow smiled. "Yes I do like him. He's so smart Willow and hard working. I like his temperament, but he never looks at me." Dawn looked down. "Did you ever think he might be shy or maybe he's just not ready yet?" Willow told her. "Are you sure he's interested in you that way?" "He is always the first to help me when I ask and I see him watching me when he thinks I don't notice. When he is close to me he never says much" Dawn replied. "Give it some time and after a bit if he doesn't come to you, maybe you better tell him how you feel. Then you will know one way or the other." Dawn seemed satisfied with that and they cleaned up the cabin.

The next few days were filled with work and comforting happiness that they were together. The room had been added and the roof was up. The cabin was bigger then Willow expected. They had to make her and West's room bigger too. The outside wall had been removed and made the full length of the outer walls. It was a great improvement.

By weeks end the work had been finished and it was time for Helen, Kalvin and the kids to go home. The wagon was much lighter going home and there were no complaints heard at that point.

West and Carry followed them to the halfway point. As Helen, Kalvin and the kids continued on, West and Carry cleared out the trees. Just after dinner they headed back home. One afternoon was not going to be enough to get the job done.

West and Carry had become good friends. They both knew that if needed they could depend on each other. With the world as it was the help from all was needed to survive. They had a hard life, but it was a good one. There would be enough food this winter for them and for the new people. A few more cabins to build and life could get back to a less urgent state.

When they reached Cliffside Freda and Nimuri were planting the apple trees. Willow stood there and watched. West knew his life now had bounds. His responsibility lay with Willow and his child on the way. He had his life before him and his family came first. The hunting for the complex tugged at him. If he could find it their lives would be easier, but for now the well being of those still alive must be first.

Willow turned to see them coming. She waved and smiled. Tonight in the comfort of their cabin West and Willow would begin to fix the room for their baby. The visit had been a good one and life seemed to be happy again.

Over the next months Willow's morning sickness passed and she helped more in the garden. It would soon be harvest. The weather had cooperated and it was to be a bountiful one this year.

West and Carry had the cabin at the half way point done and cut ample trees for wood to keep it warm for the coming winter.

The runner had sent word to ask if an older couple from the fort might occupy the cabin. West had no problem with that nor did Carry. With the harvest they would have extra and stock the root cellar.

Kalvin and the children worked the road from their end, but it was slow going. West, now finding he had some time asked Willow if she wanted to make a trip to the cabin to the west. He and Carry had made a few trips there and it was up. West wanted to start the clean up and get the wood pile going. It would be a slow trip because of Willow's condition, but the break would be worth it.

They packed food and a change of clothes it was all they would need. Carry and West had carried most of the heavy things already. Willow was excited about the trip. It broke the tedium of daily living at home. With all the things at home taken care of West and Willow planned to start out in the morning.

The sun came up and a fresh breeze blew up the valley. Willow had been up for a while she had a hard time sleeping last night with the journey at hand. West rolled out of bed and with the porridge and tea on the table he knew Willow was ready. He washed and ate his meal. Willow sat on the porch and waited for him to appear. "Willow" he called "did you pack extra socks?" Willow smile "Yes" she answered. How he hates to have wet feet she thought. With not much more a due they soon were on their way.

The trail Willow had first been on with West was now more worn with the two men having been there several times. They followed a path near the river and were soon at the falls. It was here they rested. West made sure Willow did not over due it.

The path to the top was much easier to traverse now. It didn't take long for Willow to open the packages with the sandwiches. They sat watching the water fall over the edge of the cliff and the sun's warmth it was a wonderful spot. "You know Willow, my dad says as do most of the older folks that the land was alive with animals. I've always that it was lonely now. Sometimes when the wind blows it sounds like its crying the way it howls through the trees" West told her. "I've never thought of it like that West" Willow replied. "I guess I always thought that some animals did survive like the people, but they too have to struggle to survive. It's a terribly large world out there and maybe we just havent found them yet. Kinda like the people from the prairie" Willow told him. "Maybe you are right Willow" West said.

"When I went to the city of the dead, there were so many bones of people everywhere. I couldn't believe that many people could live in one spot and dad said it was a small place, that there were bigger towns with more people. I wonder how many survived and when if ever we will find them?"

West stood by the water scanning the terrain as normal. "Hon, are you ready to go on?" he asked. Willow got up and picked up her bag. West carried the heavy pack.

They soon reached the meadow left after the fire. West stopped and looked around. "This must have been a terrible fire. You know I worry about that in storms" West told her. Willow looked around as if seeing it for the first time. He was right a fire this big was terrifying. She thought about Kalvin and his story of the prairie fires and the awful losses they endured. "West are we safe in our valley from fire?" "With the river at one end and the cliff at the other I think so. Fire needs fuel to burn and there are no big trees there anymore. This area might help as a break as well if ever one came our way. I have never heard of a fire in my whole life so far so I think we are safe enough."

They reached the small cabin late that afternoon. West got water from the creek not far off and Willow aired out the cabin. It was good to be alone out there, just her and West. It reminded her of when they first went to Cliffside. It didn't take long before the fire was going and they settled down to the approaching night. After a few hours of star watching Willow called it a night and went to bed. West put out the fire and followed her. Tomorrow would be a work day and that in it's self was enough to make anyone tired.

West moved methodically as he stacked the wood. Willow had a rake and soon the area around the cabin took shape. The stumps were burned and the brush Willow raked was consumed. It was a small cabin, but as West said "A pit stop on journeys further into the mountains." "West, when you find the complex, how will they know you are outside it?" Willow asked. "I'm glad you have such confidence in me" he laughed. "Dad said they have machines that will let them know, monitors I believe they call them." "I wonder what animals they have. I think I would like to see a creature. The pictures in the book at mom and dad's seem real to me" Willow told him. "If you had a choice, what animal would you like to see?" she asked. "Oh I don't know, I think a bear or wolf, maybe an owl anything really" he told her. "How about we take a break, we have got a lot done and I don't want you to over due it Willow" she smiled at him.

They sat in the sun and had cool water from the creek and trail mix. West leaned over and patted her belly. "I wonder how much different the baby's life will be to ours?" West said. "Oh I think it will be close to ours.

The big changes have happened. Mom and dad's life was in the time of huge change, but now it's a lot different" Willow said. "Do you wish you lived a different time West?" Willow asked. "No I'm in the right time for me. When I was younger, before we were married I thought the world before was so awesome until I saw the city of the dead. It was so sorrowful for so many to have had so much that nothing meant anything to them. They destroyed it all including themselves. This is the time for me with you and the world as it is, peaceful and folks that care about each other. This is better." He smiled. Willow had to agree, this is better.

West got up "Well sweetie, I have to fall a couple trees and I would like you a ways away. I never looked to see what was growing in the meadow. How about you take a small walk and see if there is anything good." Willow knew he was insuring she didn't over work and it pleased her. There might be something good there if nothing else some wild flowers for the cabin would be nice.

He helped her up and with his axe in hand he headed for the trees. She watched him for a minute then turned and walked into the meadow. She soon had a lovely bouquet. She found some wild berries and to her total joy hazelnut trees. She had not gone far before the sound of the tree crashing to the ground filled her ears. She headed back to the cabin.

After putting the flowers in some water and watching West delimb a tree she took up her rake. The days passed and they had enough by mid-afternoon.

West after working hard was sweaty and dirty. Willow was not much better off. West went into the cabin and retrieved a change of clothes for them. When he came out he took Willow by the hand and they headed to the river. She showed him the hazelnut trees and if they made a trip this fall the nuts would be collected for her.

When they reached the river, they wasted no time in going in. West, the better swimmer teased her. The water was refreshing. Willow was happy to be clean again. They soon had dried off and West washed out the clothes they had been wearing. Willow combed out her hair and they carried the wet clothes back to the cabin.

West hung a line and the wet clothes were hung to dry. The stumps they burned out were now ash. West poured water on to make sure they were out. Willow had dried veggies and made panned fried bread. They sat outside to eat. "I had a wonderful day West" Willow said to him. "I needed to spend time with you alone. Thank you" she said. "I know what you mean. I needed to get away too. I couldn't think of a nicer place to be than here with my wife." He leaned over and kissed her. By the time they finished eating and cleaning the dishes night was encroaching in.

They sat on the steps of the cabin and watched as the stars began to appear. Summer was the time for shooting stars and with the night clear they got a spectacular show. The small fire in the cabin was almost out when they climbed into bed. The first stepping stone to the journey inland to find the complex was almost done.

West pulled Willow into his arms and with her close he listened to her breathing and as it slipped into a rhythm of sleep, he joined her.

West woke first and got up to let Willow rest. He went and got water to make tea. He washed and when Willow got up the fire was going. The water was ready for her to wash and tea was made. He sat on the steps and was whittling. He had watched the sun crest the mountains not long before. Willow joined him with some porridge. "What are you carving?" she asked. "Something for you" he replied. He set it down as he ate and when he finished he started carving again. It didn't take long before she could see it was a comb for her to keep her hair out of her eyes. With a few more shavings on the ground he handed it to her. Willow smiled. West never ceased to amaze her at the things he could do. She kissed him and pulled back her hair and set the comb in it to hold it back. "Thank you" she said. West smiled "Well I think 3 or 4 more trees down and I think that will be ample wood here. I want to burn these two stumps there and those over there today." Willow had cleared most of the area around the cabin and decided fresh straw in that bed would be an improvement.

She took the bowls in the cabin and after washing up she told West that she was going for fresh straw. She liked it there, it was a lot different than Cliffside, but it had a beauty all of its own. The huge meadow made from the fire long ago; the forests close, the green land and the river. Yes it was a lovely area.

After she had enough straw she went back to the cabin and made a new mattress. The old straw she took out went to the fire and was burned. She brought in the dry clothes and folded them.

West had two trees down and was almost finished delimbing them when she joined him outside. She gathered up the scraps and put them on the fire. The day slipped by and when the afternoon arrived West called it quits.

They took food to the river and after a swim and fresh clothes, they ate the food. West again washed out the clothes. "We'll go back tomorrow alright? We have done what we needed to do here." West told her. "Carry and I will be back before fall and pack up here. Anything we don't need leave it here" Willow nodded.

It had been a wonderful few days, but work needed to be done at home as well. West walked with Willow over the meadow and they knew the trip was near its end. When they got back to the cabin they hung their wet clothes. The fires were watched until they were embers. West put them and they retired to bed. The fresh straw was a vast improvement and sleep found them quickly.

They slept in this day as the work was done and they just were going to be travelling. West ensured the cabin was ready to leave and Willow waited for him to finish.

The trip back seemed shorter than when they went, but going home always seemed to take less time. They arrived in Cliffside tired and hungry. Freda had dinner ready and they shared the news of work, the nut trees and the shooting stars. Cliffside changed little over the last few days. Carry spent his time in the workshop. Freda and Nimuri enjoyed the peacefulness of having a few days of leisure.

After they ate West and Willow headed home. The fire was started and water heated for a bath. Willow enjoyed bathing in the warm water and West took his turn after Willow.

Tomorrow the gardens needed to be tended and life would be back to normal. Harvest would soon be upon them and work that could be done before was done. Herbs to be dried and all the mushrooms Willow had collected.

Willow worked on the bassinette often. It was near completion. On her walks to collect mushrooms she gathered the fluff from the poplar trees. She had a good basket full now. She wanted to make a mattress for the baby from it.

The flax would soon be ready and there was work to turn it into fibre to spin. Nimuri had woven large almost flat discs to separate the wheat from the chaff. Willow was interested in how all this was going to be done. The tomatoes had been dried and the preserves finished, Nuts soon would be dropping and those too would be stowed away. Beans were done and the corn would be ready soon. Harvest was a good time with lots to eat and plenty for winter stores. The work was worth it.

Willow had enjoyed the hot peppery taste of the nasturtiums. Nimuri worked hard and Willow thought she was over doing it. She stopped often.

West and Carry helped with all the heavy work. When areas in the garden were cleared they added the compost and turned it in.

The workshop was the haunt for the men. Willow was never surprised by the work they could do. There were buckets and barrels made to catch the water at the cabin at the halfway mark. There was a creek not far into the woods from there, but any water that could be obtained, was.

Willow thought about the older couple coming to live there. She was happy to see more people; yes she did like it when she and West first came to Cliffside. She thought about how different her baby's life would be. Things were once again becoming more secure.

"Willow!" Nimuri was calling her from not far away in the garden. "Come see this" she said to her. Willow stopped picking the potatoes and went to see. Nimuri was at the edge of the wheat field. When she got there Nimuri placed crowns of wheat in her hand. "We can harvest this soon." The wheat was turning a golden colour. "Just wait until you taste the flour" Nimuri said smiling.

The two women sat down. "Do you miss the prairie Nimuri?" Willow asked. "No not much it was awful there. Here, there is so much and I feel safe here. Carry has been a dream come true." They both smiled. "I have learned much from you Willow and Freda too." "Well we are a team and always will if we stick together. We have a good foot hold here now and it will just get better" Willow said to her. "You know its funny Willow. I always thought about how things would be and I never thought I would be so happy" Nimuri told her.

They sat for a while when Willow said "If we keep this up I'll never get the potatoes in." They both laughed. "I have been weeding the squash and corn. It's nearly done. I'll come and help" Nimuri said. With that they got up and headed back to the potatoes. They called it quits when both wagons were full "Leave those for the men. Nimuri agreed that the men could pull them back to the cabins. "I'm going back to check on things I have drying" Willow said.

Nimuri walked with her to the path. "Tomorrow we can start the flax" Nimuri said and Willow nodded.

When she arrived at the cabin she washed up. Digging potatoes was always a grubby job. She knew Freda would be cooking dinner so she looked over the dried things and put what was dried into containers.

West appeared out of the work shop and Willow sent him for the potatoes. Night would soon be upon them. With the wagons close to the root cellar it was easy to unload them.

Freda made a lovely dinner. The cornbread was hot and the beans were thick with tomatoes and other veggies. With the meal done, Freda started the clean up.

West and Willow headed home. A bath tonight would not go amiss and before long with the lights waning, West and Willow found comfort in the warmth of bed and each other.

The day was started much like any other day. After eating, Carry and West went into the workshop and the women headed to the garden. With the potatoes dug, they started on the corn. Oil had to be extracted and some dried and it was a favourite picked fresh to eat. The squash was picked as well.

The day wore on and by late afternoon Nimuri and Willow called it a day. It wasn't dinner time yet so Willow decided a bath was in order. She brought in water to be heated and it wasn't long before she was in the tub. Fresh clean clothes awaited her. She sat by the fire combing her hair. West washed up as well. It was then that Carry knocked "You two best come see." West looked at Willow and they went out to the porch.

West could hardly believe his eyes, up the road was his mom Jo, Kalvin, Chad and his dad. West smiled and ran up the road to meet them.

After a hug and a hand shake, they soon arrived at the cabin. West helped his dad to the porch and Zack gladly took a chair. "Well my boy" he said "Looks like you are doing just fine here." He glanced about and smiled. The women were soon at Freda's and Willow could hardly contain her joy at seeing Zack here.

With the extra mouths for dinner sandwiches were added to the meal. Kalvin and Chad unloaded the wagon.

West was glad to see his dad. Zack was just glad the trip was over. He loved West and could see he and Carry had done an immense amount of work. He too was happy to see West and to have travelled some. Before long everyone was there. The conversation was happy and all had a few laughs.

Jo had brought some blankets for Zack. She was worried, but he seemed to have made the journey without too much pain.

The dinner was done and the women cleaned up the mess. The men all talked of news from the fort and what was planned for the future. It seems that the food shortage was not as bad as feared, so the extra was sent to the fort. The nearer communities kept their extra food. How things managed to fall into place so quickly showed everyone that together they would be able to keep going. The completion of the road to Cliffside was going to make travel easier and future visits from Zack would be possible.

When everyone was settled for the evening, the serenest of the valley started to take hold as the star began to shine.

Zack spent a hard night and Jo had willow bark to add to his tea in the morning. She worried all the time about him. He saved her life all those years ago, how far they had come. How each other had brought highs and lows of quiet comfort they shared with each other. Yes she loved him and always would. With Zack on the porch, Jo brought out a blanket and his tea.

West and Willow soon joined Jo in the kitchen. She had breakfast ready for them. They took their tea to share with Zack.

Kalvin was up at Carry's before Chad got up. Chad finally joined the others.

The day was warm and although there were people here the harvest must be done. Kalvin joined Willow in the garden and before long Chad was there as well.

By weeks end the flax would be done and the wheat ready to start. Kalvin having come from the prairie was more familiar with the wheat harvest. He told Nimuri he would cut and stook for her. Nimuri was happy to hear that. To have Kalvin here for the wheat harvest was a blessing.

Carry, West and Kalvin brought in the oats. Freda and Jo cooked for everyone. Zack worked on the plans for a wheat bin and a windmill stone grinder. The flax had to be worked to turn the flocks into fibres for weaving. Seed stores for the next year were soon ample.

It was then the wheat harvest began. Kalvin took the lead and before long he was cutting and stoking it. West and Carry followed; soon they had the technique down. Nimuri and Willow gathered the stooks. Freda helped break the wheat from the stocks and it was then Willow watched as Nimuri placed it on the big woven discs. She flipped the grain into the air and the wind carried away the debris. What were left on the discs were wheat kernels. Nimuri smiled as she and Willow spent the day working on it.

Jo tried her had at the task and found it easy to do. One bag of wheat turned into nearly twenty. Nimuri gave two to Jo for Greenmeadow; put three away for seed and the rest would be ground into flower.

The beginning of the week had found the harvest in and the men turning the gardens and adding the compost. When it was done the waiting for the winter began. The women started the spinning of flax. The past week had given everyone the chance to visit and Willow was happy. Jo passed any information she could to Willow about having a baby. It was due soon.

Zack spent a lot of time watching everyone from the porch. Freda brought him his meals and tea while Jo helped in the garden. "Ah thank you Freda" Zack said "Won't you sit with me a while?" Zack asked her. Freda sat down. "I do believe I'm getting old" she said. "I can still see the spark in your eyes yet" Zack told her "And I have noticed that you still carry yourself with ease." "You're an old brat" Freda said "If you were there when I soak my feet at night, the ease you speak of would soon reveal its true colours." They both laughed. "I must say life can certainly throw one some twists and turns" Zack said. "Yes it's true" Freda added. "I must tell you though; last year in Cliffside has been one of the best in many years." Zack smiled. "I never did ask you how you came to be at the fort" Zack said. "Oh not much of a story really, when Carry's dad left me for anther I went to work there. It seemed to fill the need I had for a simpler life. It seemed that the choice turned out to be a better one than I could have ever imagined" Zack nodded. "It was about then that Jo and Willow arrived."

"Well" Jo said "Seems we can go home soon my dear." Willow smiled "I'm so happy you came and now you can come again with the road done" she smiled at Zack. "I think dinner tonight will be a grand one the garden is in and winter will be upon us" Freda said.

Kalvin and Chad arrived next "Let's set up a table or two at Freda's and we all can eat there."

Willow had been the cabin heating water. Nimuri had gone home as well and a tub was waiting for Carry there. With West and Willow bathed they filled the tub for Jo. Carry and Nimuri did the same for Chad and Kalvin.

With everyone washed supper was put out. Everyone shared good cheer and ate well. The squash was excellent and the bread made from the wheat was relished by all.

As the night closed in on the valley everyone slowly made their way to the beds that awaited them.

With the morning sun shining on the cabins it didn't take long for Cliffside to come to life. By midmorning the wagon was loaded and they headed up the road to Greenmeadow. Zack chose to walk as long as he could.

"Well Willow we wait for winter" and West patted her belly. She smiled, the baby would come soon. West and Willow walked to their cabin. Willow found she tired easily now and West did what he could for her.

A breeze blew and with it the touch of winter could be felt on it.

Freda, Nimuri and Willow prepared the flax to be spun. It was then that Nimuri told them she to was waiting for the arrival of her and Carry's first born. Willow could not contain her joy. Freda smiled the knowing smile only the older women had.

West soon heard the news from Carry which put both men to work on smaller furniture. The task was met with joy from both men.

When the flax was all prepared for spinning Willow took a bundle home. West had the fire going and the cabin was warm. Cold hung in the air in the valley, snow would soon fall and the long winter would keep them bound there until spring.

"Willow I want to make a trip to the cabin in the valley beyond for no more than 3 or 4 days." Willow wanted to go, but she knew she was better off where she was. She knew West would be restless all winter if he did not go. "I'll be fine here with Nimuri and Freda" she said to him and smiled.

That evening Willow spun by the fire and West looked over the map he had been working on. She watched him as he studied it and hoped he did find the complex Zack had told them of. She was contented and hoped that West would find the same contentment, but she knew that until he had looked for the complex to the best of his ability, he would not be totally content. She finished her spinning and made tea for her and West. He folded up his map and when the tea was done they found comfort in each other.

West was up before Willow, he had a fire going and water heated before she stirred. He was packing a bag to take and Carry soon joined him. Before he left he kissed Willow and told her to seek comfort with Nimuri and Freda if she got lonely. The two men were soon on their way.

Willow now alone went back to bed. She did not have that pleasure often, the weight of the child made her more tired than normal. She napped for a few hours and got up to a quiet home. Soon the child would be here and this solitude would be gone. She made a light lunch and went to get more flax.

West and Carry free from the daily routine of daily work hiked quickly through the forest. They always competed with each other and it was an enjoyment they both shared.

Once they made it to the cabin and unloaded their packs West brought out his maps. Carry looked out over the meadow created by the fire and marvelled how quickly things had already started growing. "So West you want to travel which way to add to the maps?" Carry asked him. West pointed to the map and Carry nodded. "What is it you are looking for?" Carry asked him. West stared at him for a moment "Why do you think I'm looking for something?" West asked him. "I've seen you, you always look to the west and the talks you have with your dad. He's no ordinary man, his ideas are unique. Are you going to tell me what's up or keep me guessing?" Carry was wise West thought, but he had given his word not to tell. "Well I am sure there is a larger more fertile valley out there. If people are to survive then it's up to adventurers like us to break the trail for them. I kinda hope we find more survivors yet." He knew Carry didn't buy it completely but let the matter rest. "West it is then?" Carry said.

They started a fire and the cabin started to warm. West grabbed a bag and gave one to Carry. "Come on" West said. He took him to the hazelnut trees and they had the bags filled in no time. By dusk they had settled in for the night. The following days adventures would be tough going and rest would be slim pickings as they broke trail to the next valley.

When the star shone bright West watched for and pointed out the satellites his dad had shown him. He told stories of the people before the virus. Carry never believed a lot of them, but listened anyways. "If they were so advanced and had all these things, why did they destroy it all?" Carry asked him. "That my friend is the saddest of all. They did it for greed and power over others. They tried to kill each other for things that really meant nothing, like gold, money, power" West told him. "It seems to me that maybe its better they are gone then. We have good lives now. People we love and who love us, we have enough to eat and clothes to wear. No one is hungry or cold in the winter." West smiled at Carry. "It's true they didn't realize what was important until it was gone.

Did you ever go to the City of the dead Carry?" "No, I never felt the need" Carry told him. "It's gone the bones they say are there and should be a good reminder of what is not to happen again" Carry told him. "I went" West said "I saw things there that amazed me. The buildings alone" West stopped "In the future I can see places like that again" Carry looked at him. "They all died there are you sure we should think of building and living as they did again? It was their undoing." West never realized Carry didn't think much of progress. "You mean if we stay as we are forever you would be content with it Carry?" West asked. "Well put it this way. Tomorrow will come whether I want it or not. There will be work to do just the same as always. We will have children; watch them grow and one day die. I am happy I have people I care about and they care about me. My life is simple but full. It seems to me all the things they had before didn't add to their life. It gave them too much free time to become jealous and selfish. Too much time to worry about what someone else had instead of caring if they could help those with less. No not any kind of world at all and seems it was the cause of the destruction of theirs."

West like Carry's matter of fact attitude. He couldn't disagree with what he said either, but West knew that of the bad in the world there was good too, his mom and dad were proof of that. "Well it seems that all the said and done we are here and we will make the best of it" West said to him. Both slept, the adventure tomorrow would bring was awaiting them.

Willow arrived to Nimuri and Freda spinning. She brought the ball of flax yarn and gathered another bundle to take home. The women shared tea and talked of Jo's visit. Willow told them of Dawn's interest in Chad. They talked of babies on the way and Freda told them they would need so many diapers and night gowns. It was a pleasant visit. Freda prepared a light meal for them and with the meal much laughter occurred.

Late afternoon found Willow on her way home with the bundle of flax fibre. Nimuri had save many stalks from the wheat. After the wheat heads had been broken off she had stacked a good pile in the corner on the porch.

Willow, now at home added more wood to the fire. She sat at her spinning wheel and spun for the best part of the evening. When she stopped she made tea and sat on the porch under a blanket. She sipped her tea and watched the sky. She thought about Zack and all the things she had learned from him. Then she thought of Jo and her mother. Her mind wondered over many of the things that happened in her life. When she decided to go to bed, she concluded that she was happy and lucky to have a cabin, a husband that loved her and friends and family. She got up and went inside. She added more wood to the fire, washed up and soon was in bed trying to get in a comfortable position.

West and Carry started out early. There were no trails to follow so travelling was slow. Clearing as they went it was well into the afternoon before they stopped. They shared the trail mix and drank some water. "I was hoping to get to the ridge today" West said. "I want to see what's on the other side. I might be able to see any other valleys and how the ranges are situated." "And you say you aren't looking for anything." Carry laughed. West looked at him "So what do you think might be out there that would have me so intrigues?" West asked. "I have no idea, but I'm sure one day you will tell me." Carry smiled and West just looked at his map.

"Well old man, are you ready to reach the top?" Carry said with a smile. It didn't take them long to gather up their gear. The push was on and the top was their goal. They laboured hard, but the coolness of the air helped them keep up the pace. As they approached the crest West was filled with anticipation as to what would be found over the rise. Carry although he never said was filled with the same curiosity.

When they reached the top the wind blew gently and the break in the trees revealed a huge valley with much of it meadow. There was more land there then in the valley by the fort. Both stood and marvelled at the vastness. There was no sign of human habitation which they found disappointing, but the size and fertileness was inspiring. Tired from their hike they sat. "Now there's a valley for the future. There's enough room there to grow and feed at least one hundred people" Carry said. "I agree" West told him. "There's a beauty in the land, untouched for so long" West said. "It's new and old at the same time. This is a place for the future, for our children" Carry said. "That may well be, but for now it's ours" and they sat and stared at it for a while. "Well, let's get a shelter built, it's going to be cold tonight" West said. "True enough" Carry answered.

It took the two experienced woodsman about an hour to have a suitable lean-to made and a fire going. Rest was the remedy for the moment and with night falling they settled down. The sounds of the wind in the trees, the motion of them gently swaying was a rhythmic toon played for untold ages. The fire crackled and West poked it to stir the embers. "Do you think you would ever consider moving here?" West asked him. Carry looked at him "Not for a while, my mom is happy in Cliffside. She is happier than I have seen her in years. With Nimuri with child, no not for a while, but the valley below would be a good future that's for sure." Carry laid back. "I know what you mean. Now mom and dad can visit I wouldn't consider leaving, after they pass maybe. Willow will not be easy to convince with the surplus of food this year she'll hold fast to Cliffside, but in 5 or 6 years who knows." West followed Carry in lying down. He watched the stars always looking for the satellites. He thought about his dad; about the children he left behind in the complex and the wife. He had to try and find the complex for him, for Jo, for everyone.

The adventure the next day would be it until after the winter. West would want to mark his map with the discovery.

Willow's day started out without much difference from any other day. She ate, rested, and spun flax she got the day before. As always she gathered up the scrape fibres to make paper. The fire kept the cabin warm and comfortable. Willow found the baby move a lot now. Each time it stretched a hand or foot out she softly felt the lump and smiled. She made the mattress finish now. She also had made 2 dozen diapers, several night shirts and clothes she pounded to soften them. To dry the baby after a bath she made a blanket from all the scraps of material.

They were ready. Was she ready she asked herself? A little soul made from love between her and West, innocent and completely dependent on them. The momentary fear left and the baby moved. A feeling of warm filled her. She had spent the day alone and now found she wanted the company of Nimuri and Freda. She covered herself with a shawl and walked to their cabin.

When she arrived she found Freda making broth for Nimuri who was resting. Willow knew all to well the sickness she suffered from that only time would cure. "Come sit Willow" Freda said to her. "Nimuri is resting and I think she should" Freda told her. Willow made tea when Freda took in the broth for Nimuri.

Before long the two women sat and spun, Willow watched. It wasn't long before Freda and her tales of the people had Willow laughing. Freda stopped periodically to add dried veggies to the broth. The three women would have a lovely soup for dinner.

Nimuri got up and to Freda and Willow's relief she was feeling better. A few hours of spinning and talking and the soup was ready. With bread made the table was set. Willow enjoyed the company. With West gone Cliffside felt empty to her somehow.

Freda and Willow wound the yarn into balls. The spindles were emptied for the next session of spinning. Willow gathered the scraps and when the spinning was done she would make paper. Freda had saved onion skins for dye. Things were getting back to normal.

It was dark when Willow went home. The moon was up and it gave ample light to see the path home. Willow shivered, snow was coming and it would be cold this year. When she arrived at the cabin she added wood to the fire and soon the sounds of the wood burning made her feel safe.

She had a bundle of flax to spin for the next day. When she sat by the fire she thought about the past year. It had been a good year, with all the cabins almost made for the newcomers and the grand harvest going hungry was no longer a threat. Life was going to make it, the hardest struggles were over. She smiled and went to bed.

Chapter 32

*I*t was Dern that woke Dana and Todd. He was quite capable of climbing out of his bed and into theirs with ease. He would not take no for an answer for them to wake up. After a few tickles and laughter Dana took him into the shower with her. Todd lay in bed and thought about the day ahead.

The last few years had been hectic. Many of the founders had passed. His parents, Dirk and two or three others were all that was left of the old guard. The younger people in the positions to make decisions had been pushing to open the doors. The old guard stood fast and to most of their surprise over half of the population voted against it. With that it seemed the doors were to remain closed.

Todd sat up and ran his finger through his hair. What was it going to take to convince them it was safe out there?

"Your turn" Dana said as she and Dern walked into the bedroom. She soon had Dern's clothes out and Todd was in the shower. As she dressed Dern she planned her morning. She set him down with his toys while she dressed.

Before long the bed was made and Dana was making breakfast. Todd made it to the table as she was serving. "Well what have you planned for today?" Dana asked him as she fed Dern. "I guess I will head to the workshops. I can't believe so many people still afraid to open the doors" he said to her. "Be patient Todd we have made great progress. We will convince them. They are still afraid; their parents' whole world was destroyed. They have grown up being told the outside world is dangerously deadly and out of bounds. If they go there they too will share the fate of the world before.

That will not be erased to easily from them. You and I are lucky we know my father didn't die in the outbreak. The possibility that he may still be alive gives me and you hope. He's the only one Todd, all the rest are gone, no communications everything gone to them." Dana lifted Dern from his chair and set him down. He wasted no time in finding his toys.

Todd looked at her "You're right, it's so frustrating to know what we know and not be at liberty to tell others. I think Erik is aware as are others, but we must persist. I want Dern to go outside to play; to breathe the air; to feel the sun and the wind" Todd said. "He will Todd, I know he will, if not through the complex then through us. I will not deny him his right to freedom."

Todd was glad he had Dana. He thought about being with someone else that had no desire to leave the complex. They were educated and still the desire for freedom somehow evaded them. The daily living one day to the next consumed them. With that thought he got up and went to Dana, kissed her and Dern. "I will be back before dinner" Dana smiled and Todd left.

Dana would have to take Dern to the atrium today. She was to meet Carl and Rose. Her son Dean was showing signs of a gift. Jake and Fern's child June also had shown signs. Being the children of Warren, her siblings she wanted to assure them it was nothing to fear. Dern's gift amazed her, but he never seemed to have it unless he was in contact with someone in need.

She arrived at the atrium to find Carl, Rose, Dean, Jake and Fern with June. It didn't take long to figure out that they could communicate without words. Dern talked and they talked that is as much as a 2 and 3 years olds could, but Dean and June spoke to each other without words.

After the greeting Rose set out a lunch and they talked of gifts. "I can see that it may be unusual, but they seem to play with Dern fine. The communication they share has not hindered the normal growth of speech with others" Dana said. "The blind in the old world used dots to read and the deaf sign language. I see this as different, but much the same." "That's right" Fern said. But Rose was not of the same opinion. "I think it was totally careless on Dirk's part to have let the virus get in and my child to suffer the results of it." Dana glared at her. "Rose your baby is not ill, he's gifted, and he's special." "It's not normal for children to talk without speaking" Rose said. "It's normal for them and I for one am happy they are gifted." "Well I'm not" Rose said.

Dana could see that Rose did not care for Dern. Oh what a dreadful thought, Dana said to herself. Carl spoke to Rose "It will be fine Rose. He is happy and playing." "He is abnormal." Rose almost hissed at him. "I'm not having anymore children. I won't bring any more freaks into this world." Carl was beside himself "I'm sorry" he said. "We had better do. Come on Dern." And Dean looked at his dad as a big smile crossed his face. He touched June and she smiled. It took about 2 seconds before Carl had him in his arms.

When they left Jake and Fern spoke. "I don't know what the matter is with her" Fern said. "She won't accept this and poor Carl and Dean." Dana sat there trying to absorb what she had just witnessed. "Why does Rose resent Dean's gift so much?" Dana asked.

Jake sat quiet for a moment "I think it's because it's something she can't control. Rose is or has been very domineering in Carl's life. She rules the roost; they come and go at her will. Carl follows along like a sick cow, it's pathetic." "Jake, Warren would beside himself if he heard you talk like this" Dana said. Jake looked at her "Maybe so, but it's true." "Well" Dana said "If Dern is to have any kind of life we will have to talk to Carl."

Fern spoke then "I have no doubt that he has great love for Dean. I think he should sort this out on his own with her. Carl is not this sick cow. He loves her and forcing her to accept this might cause her to reject him all the more. She has to put it into terms she can deal with." "Well that might be true" Dana said "But she will have to accept it. The longer she takes the harder it will be."

Just then Carl returned "Jake, Dana come quickly Rose has fallen down the stairs and she won't get up." Carl was frantic. He had Dean under his arm and Fern took him. Dana and Jake ran to where Rose was. "Carl she needs medical help" Dana said. Jake volunteered; he got up and ran to the med labs.

In the commotion Dern was down the stairs now. He knew something was wrong. He went to Rose and before anyone realized he held her foot. Whatever was his gift, how he did what he did, no one knew, but after a few moments Rose opened her eyes. She looked right at Dern and said "Thank you."

Dern let her foot go and climbed into Dana's lap. He was almost instantly asleep. Rose looked at Carl and cried. "Are you okay Rose?" he asked. She looked at Dern "I am now" and she cried more.

By now the med team had arrived to find Rose was fine, but drifted in and out of sleep. Dana was worried because Dern did not want to wake up.

They were both taken to the med labs. Dana and Carl sat in the waiting room. It seemed like forever until Todd came in. "Dana is he okay?" "We are waiting to hear." Dana had fought back the tears and if she didn't soon hear that Dern was okay the tears would win. Carl paced the floor, he was deep in thought.

When the doctor came in, smiled and announced "They are fine" he said. A sigh from all filled the room. "Rose broke her back, had Dern not been there she most likely would never have walked again; she is a very lucky lady. Dern is resting, seems his gift exhausts him. I'm sure he will be fine after he rests." "Can we see them?" Dana asked. "Of course" the doctor said "But let them sleep if they drift off." He left the room.

Dana looked at Carl, when his gaze met hers, he sat and cried. "Dana, I don't know what to say." She sat beside him "its okay Carl they are fine that's what's important now" Dana said. "Let's go see them."

When Dana got to Dern, he looked so small to her in his bed. She cupped her hand over his and held fast to a couple fingers. He stirred a little, but Dana was not moving from there until he was responsive. Todd rubbed his back and stroked his hair. He knew he was going to be okay. "I better go tell Jake and Fern" Todd said. He kissed them both and was off to bring the news to them.

Dana sat with Dern for hours. After several hours Dern started to stir. He opened his eyes and rubbed them before he sat up and crawled into her lap. Dana held him close, her treasure, and her heart of her heart. She sat there rocking him while he woke up.

After a while he got down and as if he had a tracking beacon on, went straight to Rose's room. He walked over with such a matter of fact air and climbed up on her bed. She opened her eyes and Dana watched as Dern lay down beside her and Rose put an arm over him. Dana never went in she stood at the door amazed at this small child being held by a woman that yesterday considered him a freak of nature. Dana knew that Rose was going to be different to the children now.

Todd was there now and she left him to get Dern when the time came. She was going home to sleep. Now she knew both were well.

She passed Carl on his way to see Rose and said to him "Things will be okay now Carl." Carl looked at her "I hope so it's be hard to see her so hateful towards the children" he said. "I think that has changed now"

Dana smiled. "How can you be so sure?" Carl asked. "You will see" Dana told him as she held his hand and patted it. "I am going home to rest. It's been a long night" and Dana left.

Carl, not sure what to think went to his wife. He was amazed to see Dern snuggled beside her and her caressing his head. When Carl approached Dern sat up and smiled at him. He hugged Rose and when he saw Todd standing there he wasted no time in climbing into his arms. Todd left and looked for the doctor to see if he could take Dern home.

Carl was literally stunned by what he just saw. Rose looked at him and all she could say was "How could I have been so blind that I could not see the gifts as gifts and not hindrances. I am ashamed of myself. Oh Carl, can you ever forgive me?" Rose started to cry. Carl always loved Rose and went directly to her side. He sat on the bed beside her and let her cry. "It will okay now, it will be okay." What ever Dern did or how he did it Carl would never know, but he did know this small child had saved Rose from a life of being a cripple and maybe even her life. He was truly gifted and now he was proud his son was gifted as well. If Dern could help like that what did the future hold for Dern and June.

Todd now with the doctor as if he knew just what Dern did. The doctor showed him Rose's x-ray. The spine showed; the break newly healed and the spinal cord was healed as well. Then he showed the brain haemorrhage. "She would have died had he not been there. She is a very lucky lady and Dern a very special little fellow. In that boy is a wealth of medical knowledge beyond what's in our texts and he uses it without study or training. He just does it, I envy him" the doctor said. "My life has been devoted to helping people; repairing or easing things that medicine has made it possible to do. Fixing ailments that injure or bad genes that heredity hands people and Dern with one touch can do things that I can only dream possible. He is blessed."

Dern now hugged the doctor and was now back in Todd's arms. "Why was he so listless afterwards?" Todd asked. "I'm not sure, but it must be like running a marathon the energy used. I think it's because of his age the less he does in the healing department the better until he is older. I can hardly wait to see what he will be able to do." "Well" said Todd "Can I take him home?" The doctor smiled "Yes, he is good to go Todd just let him relax for a few days. Then bring him back I want to make sure there are no residual effects from this." The doctor told him. "Will do" and Todd headed home.

Dana was ready sleeping when they got there. Todd spent the day reading and playing with him and his toys. Dern took a few short naps leaning against Todd. Todd felt he was the luckiest man alive with a wonderful wife and son.

Rose, now awake tried to explain to Carl and the doctor what it was like. "I was in dreadful pain; then it turned warm, almost hot and I could feel the pain leaving. It washed over me, over and over, I knew it was Dern. I wasn't afraid; there was no fear. I felt safe and warm. I could feel his heart beating; it was in time with mine. Then it was soft and tender and then it was gone. I opened my eyes, and the pain was gone, but I was so tired. When he let go I was empty again, not with him. This sounds crazy doesn't it?" she said. "It wasn't empty just the warmth was gone. I can't explain it really" Rose told them. "No worries" the doctor said "It's not really important. I don't think it really matters how it felt just that what he does appears to not hurt you." "On the contrary" Rose immediately to Dern's defence "How he made the crushing oppressive pain disappear, well I can tell you the relief I felt." Rose stopped and thought "It was like he took the pain." Then she said "You're sure he's okay, that he will be fine?" "Yes he's gone home already. I want to make sure that your mended areas are not disturbed too much, so strict bed rest for you for the next few days." The doctor said to Rose.

Carl dried his tears "It's alright Rose, things will be alright." She soon drifted back to sleep. Carl didn't want to leave, but he had to tend to Dean. Jake and Fern had been so good to watch him.

Before long he was at their dorm and over tea he related what had happened. Jake and Fern sat back in their chairs. "Well it seems all it took to bring us back together was the touch of a small boy" Jake said. Fern said "Go lie down on the couch" Fern told him. "The children are having a good time together." Carl got up and lay on the couch. He closed his eyes and thought the last day had been so exhausting. Something in Rose had changed. He knew that Dern and the other gifted children would no longer be seen as misfits in her world, but the children of the future. He drifted off to sleep with the laughter of the children lingering in his ears.

Dirk was amazed at the reports when he read them. Andy was right. Dirk took the reports with him and walked to the living area. He sat at a table gazing at the statues Rainie had carved. He had a coffee and reread the reports. When he knew of the virus and what the prediction was for the future with the mutation was yet to unfold.

Dirk watched the people, the children playing most had never known anything but the complex nor did they want too. This was their world; what would they do and think when the virus changed again, if it did. What was predicted was the complex would be in jeopardy again. How many would suffer for it? How many would blame him more? Dirk never felt sorry for himself, but he did for those that lost so much because of him. He knew letting the animals out had to be done. It was for the future, their future even if they couldn't accept the fact that one day the doors would be opened and his work was vital to that.

He had been there since the beginning, it seemed a lifetime ago. He remembered the arrival of the animals and of Simion's overseeing everything. It was glorious back then, the project of a magnitude never undertaken before. Simion worked for all those years to protect them.

He sipped his coffee. Tears came to his eyes when he remembered watching the monitors and the chaos, then as it went to static as the world died outside. The fierce determination of Simion pulling all together to begin the struggle to survive; the hours and years of cross breeding; the animals and the virus getting back in. Dirk would never forgive himself that all those people were gone because of an error on his part. Dirk looked around and finished his coffee. He left the living area and went to see Dana and Todd.

It didn't take long to go anywhere in the complex, even with the opening of the new tunnels it was still small compared to the outside. Dirk thought of the cave-ins and the protocols now followed so it would never happen again. He stood at his dorm door for a minute and pulled his thoughts together.

He knocked and Todd answered. "Dirk, my goodness come in it's good to see you" Todd said. "I'm glad to see you out for a stroll" he continued. They sat on the couch and started to talk. Todd held Dirk in the highest respect. "I've received so reports from the med labs and came to check on my kids" Dirk smiled. "It was amazing I never saw anything like it" Todd said. He related the events to Dirk and he listened amazed to hear. "Well it seems our Dern has turned out to be a remarkable fella." "You say Carl and Jake's children are gifted too? It will be interesting to see what avenues their gifts will take them and us too" Dirk said. "Have you heard of any other children yet?" Todd asked him. "No one showing signs, there are some with the same physical aspect with large glands, but no signs as yet that they use them." Todd nodded.

Dana heard Dirk and got up. After she washed she came out of the bedroom. "Hey there sleepy head" Todd said to her. Dirk smiled and Dana hugged him. She looked over to Dern and Todd saw her glance "He's fine, he's had a few naps, but other than that he is okay. Sit down sweetie I will get you a coffee." "It's good to see you Dirk" Dana said. "You rarely come to visit." She smiled at him.

"I've been reading the report from the med labs seems it was an exciting day for Dern." Dana looked at him "He seems to be no worse for wear" Dana said. "How marvellous it is that we have been given Dern as a gift" Dirk said. Dana smiled "So how have you been Dirk"" Dana said. "I'm fine I have just been thinking about things. How my mistake of letting the virus in and everything that has been the result of it. I must say that after all the guilt I've harboured over it, Dern has lifted the weight somewhat, but I will carry most until I pass. Let us talk of more pleasant things" Dirk said with a smile.

When Dana heard Dirk refer to letting in the virus her heart sank. Poor Dirk to have carried that burden all this time and to have others think ill of him; she felt so sad. "Tell me" Dana said "How are the animals doing this year? Will there be many for the spring turn out?" "Yes I must say there will be. The wool will be sheared soon and that's always a big event" he smiled. "How are Mark and Ann?" Dana asked. "Busy" Dirk said "Mark has animal husbandry in his blood and cares for them so well. Ann is much like Carla. She has not faltered on the records; she is a thorough as her mom." "I miss Carla so much" Dana said. "Aye" Dirk said "Her passing changed my life and left it wanting in so many ways." Dirk harboured so many memories of Carla and their life together. "Well" Dirk said "I must go. I have to go to the library yet. I'm glad you all are well."

Dirk got up and started for the door. Dana walked with him and hugged him and promised him that she and Todd would come and visit him before the sheep were sheered.

As she watched Dirk head to the library, Dana said to Todd "It breaks my heart that he feels guilty about the virus getting in. We will have to tell him one day." Todd agreed, but when, that would have to be decided later.

The day before them was pleasant, Rose was fine and Dern was as well. It would be an at home day today with rest and relaxation.

Dern seemed to be back to his normal self by weeks end and Rose was up and about. Carl was amazed at Rose's transformation. Whatever happened during the healing had completely changed her attitude towards the children.

Dana and Dern went to the animal tunnels to watch the sheep being sheered. It was a sight to see and it was pleasing to her to take the raw wool and follow its production to yarn. The cotton would soon be ready and Dana often had a hard time deciding which she liked better, cotton or wool.

Dern squealed with pleasure at the sight of the animals. They never feared him. Dana often wondered if they knew he was gifted somehow.

The fall reports would be ready soon and again they would be presented to the council. The council would then vote on the results. It was frustrating beyond belief for Dana and Todd as they waited for the results. Each time hoping the doors would be opened and resignation when it was turned down.

It was Mark that called to Dana and broke her chain of thought. "Dana!" he called again. "Yes Mark" she answered. "Come I want to show you something" he said to her. She picked up Dern and followed Mark. They came up to the stalls with the horses. Dern squirmed to be let down. When Dana relented and put him down, the colt he had healed came right to him. It was a fair sized horse now and it gently nuzzled Dern. He was so small compared to the horse. Mark smiled "I think those two will be friends forever" he said. "How fast the horse has grown. It's been nearly three years since it was born" Dana said. "Yes they change a lot in that time" Mark told her. "Ann has told me that he's strong and thinks he will be a great addition to our breeding stock. One day they will run free" Mark said. "We provide a good environment here, but horses should be able to run." He smiled at Dana. "I'm glad you still work to open the doors. I think the same as you. If the animals survive then we can too. One day we will" he told her. "I know" Dana said. "But convincing the frightened and stubborn is another thing." "Don't give up Dana" Mark told her. "Ann and our other halves are with you." Dana picked up Dern. "Thanks Mark" Dana said "I must go and get the tailors ready for the wool." Mark looked over to and nodded "I'll get the wool delivered later" he said. "Tomorrow would be better; it takes a while to get set up." Mark nodded "Tomorrow it is then." "Thanks for letting Dern see the horse." Mark just smiled and tussled Dern's hair as he walked by.

Dana walked to the tailor station. She put Dern in the children's area. There were too many machines in here to let children run free. She made the arrangements for the machines to be set up for the wool that was on the way. She sat back at her desk and filled out the requisitions for each machine; what they would be set at and who would run them. When she was done she gathered up Dern and headed home.

Todd had been to see Erik. They had been in the communications station all day. Erik being around the monitors all the time watched with envy at the animals that were periodically caught on camera. "They look perfectly fine to me" Erik told Todd. "My dad knew we were to live out there, not in here" Erik told him. "You know, I watched Dana and you fight the present system for years to get the doors open. We have to have the facts; cold hard facts and the numbers of people will change I'm sure" he told him. "You might not think so, but Dana and I have come across many here that have no interest in leaving. They were born here and like it. Everything is provided for them and they are safe. I can understand that. After the virus got in and the deaths well not only that, the fear has been drummed into them by their parents that outside is death" Todd said. "Then we have to change that" Erik replied. "We have to start teaching them more of the outside world. Dad said that this day would come and he was right."

"Erik can I ask you a personal question?" Todd asked. Erik stopped "Sure if I can answer I will, but be prepared to hear something you may or may not like" Erik told him. "I have read some things that Andy gave me." "Andy?" Erik said. "Yes" Todd replied. "Sorry to have interrupted" Erik said "Go on." "Well there are many things that most don't know and I was wondering how much you know and what you would be willing to tell me" Todd said. Erik smiled "I can tell you I agree with you and Dana that the outside world is where we should think about going. I believe it to be safe and that the virus has done its worst. I believe we need to educate everyone and I mean young and old about what it is, what it did and how long with what to expect it to be done in the future. My father actually predicted this conversation and I must admit I am glad it was with you Todd. I can tell you a few things that must not be spoken to others including Dana.

First, the gifted are not as plentiful as some might think. In time it may change, but at the moment I know of only four. I will say the outside is closer than any of the complex knows. I will tell you to also look out for Dern. There are those that would do him harm" Erik said. Todd looked at him "What do you mean? Is Dern in danger? Erik, my God tell me Erik. Is he or not?" "Fear makes people do things they normally would not do. They fear what they don't understand. Urge Dana to have another child" Erik told him. "Andy told me the same thing. Why Erik, tell me why?"

"The virus is changing again and it will affect the ability of women to have children" Erik told him. "Oh my God, do you know how long before this will happen? Will all the women and men be sterile forever?" "I'm not sure just how it will work, but its coming" Erik told him. "That's why I have not pushed so hard to educate the people. They had just suffered great losses and the complex was in jeopardy. When things calm down I couldn't tell them more hurt and despair was on its way."

Erik sat down and Todd paced a bit. "Seems we wait, keep working on getting people aware that there is an outside and that that's where we should be starting to look instead of more tunnels." Erik looked at Todd. "That is true, but if the virus can change again would that be it or is it going to be a problem for us for eternity?" Todd said. "I wish I could give you a better time frame. All I know is that it will happen. If we get them to open the doors when it does they will run back in here. I feel sorry for us here in our man made home."

Erik knew far more than he did, Todd was sure of that. He was his father's son. Todd was in no doubt of Erik's intelligence "Just how do you think we should proceed then?" Todd asked. Erik sat down "We need to start with the children, get them learning more about the outside and the animals. Then it will filter into the homes. Most of the old council is gone, there are very few that can truly remember the outside world and to the death they saw. Well I don't need to tell." Eric looked at him "Once they are gone then the negative force will be gone. It will be easier to persuade the generations left, if there is no one pounding into them outside is bad, death, etc…" "You're right, I'm sure Dana can get the teachers set up for that." "Good" Erik said. "Oh I meant to ask how Rose was" Erik said. "She is going to be okay. Whatever Dern did seems to have a good effect on her" Todd smiled. "You should go talk to Petra as well; she is no less brilliant than her parents. She might be able to help with the teachers as well. Talk to Mark and Ann as too, they have great potential to sway people through the animals."

The two men were now in the monitor room. Erik checked them all as Todd watched. Before long Todd said "I have to get home, Dana will be wondering where I am." Erik smiled and continued with the papers he was looking over.

Todd headed for home. He thought about everything Erik had told him. Erik knew far more than he was letting on. He knew Dana would want to hear what had transpired.

Chapter 33

West and Carry made it back home. As they told of the valley they had discovered the women spun flax and listened intently. "How wonderful to know it's there" Willow said. "Who knows maybe our children will claim it as their home" Nimuri smiled. Life for Cliffside was good. They had passed the crisis of the food shortage and shelter problems. It was a time of easy carefree living. The worst hurdles had been closed now they could live and not fear starvation or homelessness.

Willow wanted to see the valley West and Carry discovered. She couldn't imagine a valley so large and beautiful. She pictured it in her mind and knew that next year she would see it. In the mean time winter had its chores. Although not as intense as spring and summer it still had to be done.

Over the next few weeks the flax all had been spun and Freda was kept busy weaving it into cloth.

The snow had come and Willow watched it through her window as it gently fell. The quiet that came with it always marvelled her. It muffled and wind or outside noise. The baby would come soon she knew that. She would be glad to be relieved of the weight she carried.

West worked on his maps and watched her. He knew the child was due as well. He never really cared if it was a boy or girl just that it be healthy. He hated to see Willow struggle now with things that had seemed so easy for her to do before.

"West would you get me some water? I want to make some paper. It will clean up all these scraps around here. The baby will be here soon and I might not want to do it after the child is born" she told him.

West soon had the water in and helped her soak and break up the flax in the water until it was like a thick soup. The screen she used to dip the fibrous contents from the vat took her a long time to make, but the paper was worth it. Soon they had a good pile; each layered between the cloths that were only for making paper. West placed a board on top of the pile and weighed it down with several flat rocks.

They cleaned up the work things and Willow sat down satisfied. "That should be enough for us for some time" Willow said and West smiled. "Want some tea Willow? I think you have worked too hard today" West said. "Sure tea would be wonderful" she replied. She had beans soaking and soon they would be put on to cook.

"West, tell me about the valley again. I can't wait to see it next year" she told him. West set the tea down and pulled out the map from under the things on the table. "Okay this is where we are, Cliffside and here is Greenmeadow." He pointed to the map and described the area in between for Willow. "It's a good valley and from the ridge I could see the mountains beyond." Just then she could see the disappointment cross his face. He smiled then said "Well I never saw the range my father spoke of but there are many mountains. I'm sure its there." Willow looked at him "You'll find it West, its just going to take time." "Carry is wise to me. I think I underestimated him. He knows I'm looking for something" West told her. Willow laughed "He's your dearest friend West. If he didn't have brains I doubt you two would get on as well as you do. Are you going to tell him?" Willow asked. "No" West almost snapped at her. He saw the hurt in her face "I'm sorry Willow that was uncalled for. No, dad said tell no one and I can't betray my promise to him." He kissed her forehead.

West glanced at a few more books his mom had given him. He walked over and picked one out. He sat with Willow at the table and looked through the book together. "The complex dad says has many animals and wonders. Finding it is one thing; getting them to know we are outside and then to get them to let us in is another story all together." Willow glanced at the page "It must have been a wondrous world once. I am still in awe of just the beauty that is here now, but to think it was full of things, all kinds of things. It would be nice if one day the animals that survived actually were seen" Willow said. "You still believe some survived then?" West asked her. "They had to have, we did" Willow said. "You'll see I'm sure some made it. They had to. I'm positive" she said with a smile. "I love you" West told her.

The evening was spent eating a lovely meal; talking of the new valley, the baby and what would be the first animal they would see. West thought they would see bugs and Willow said birds.

They slept comfortably in the cabin, warm from the winter that now had its first covering on the ground.

Carry, Nimuri and Freda talked of adding to their cabin in the spring. Freda kept busy weaving as Nimuri and Carry planned out what they would need for extra space. Freda loved them. They never resented her for being there with them and treated her with the utmost respect. Nimuri was the part of Carry that for many years was missing, but now he was complete. She watched them talk, laugh and work together. When she leaves this world her mind and heart will be at ease knowing they had each other and now a child.

Her mind wandered back to when Carry was a baby. How hard it had been when his father left them. She had gone to be with her mom and dad at the fort. She remembered standing at the gate staring at the sign, Welcome to Fort Reed; Carry in her arms and three suit cases. She had run back home to her mom and dad. How disappointed she was in herself and the world. It didn't take long to find solace in her work there. Getting back to the basics in life renewed her in so many ways. She never had another man, the pain she felt to have her heart broken, to be used and tossed away as if it was nothing. Never again she thought. Carry grew up there and she watched as he turned into a fine man. So much had happened, the world she knew was gone. The world now had in many ways been reborn; new, fresh and maybe better than before in many ways.

"Mom, mom" Carry said and she looked at him. "Wow you were miles away" he said. "Want tea?" he asked. Freda got up from her loom "Yes that would be lovely" she told him. "Are you okay mom?" Nimuri asked. "Yes, yes I'm fine. I was just involved with my weaving" she said to them. ""Here, sit yourself here and take a look at the drawings of the cabin and the addition I want to put on." Freda could see it was a large addition, room for her and the baby. Carry smiled "You like it then?" "Yes, I do but it will be a lot of work" she said. "Aw pfft" he said. "It will be worth it. After all this is our family. West will help and Brad and Gary. It will be an excuse for Jo and Zack to visit as well" he smiled.

Yes, Freda thought she had done something right in her life and having Carry was it.

The day was coming to a close and night found them ready for bed. Soon sleep would have them in its grip.

Greenmeadow was celebrating. The harvest was excellent and folks were happy. Zack and Jo were the first to know, Brad and Sara were having another child. It was good news. The families all got together and wished them well.

The first snow had the children in a buzz. Snow men and forts were the agenda for them.

The flax spinning and weaving would keep the women busy. The men were making furniture for the cabin the old couple were occupy in the spring.

Jo watched everyone and for the first time in a long time she was comforted by the fact that life was making it and they would too.

Zack almost sensing her thoughts patted her hand. His legs were always the worse in the cold weather, but he never complained. It was as if the day he decided to go on living and have Jo as his wife was just that, he would go in living. She loved him and she knew he loved her. It seemed funny to her that as they approached the eve of their lives things that seemed so important, didn't really matter. She watched the children playing. Life was so different yet so much the same. She sipped her tea.

Sara's new baby was the sign of hope and man's tenacity for life, any life was strong.

The winter ahead hopefully would not be a long one. Jo smiled; she remembered West and how he changed her. Yes, West and Willow would be different but it was as it should be.

The meal they had that night was good. It had been the work of everyone that made it so good.

Jo took Zack home early and she heated water for his bath. The two went to bed and Zack told her "After all these years I think I love you more."

The winter brought large snow flacks and kept West and Carry busy keeping the paths clear. Willow was glad the new apple trees were protected from the freezing air. She went to the fire and added more wood. The cabin was warm, but she had shivers through her today. She checked the paper they had made and it was dry. Willow had dyed some cloth yellow and it had been hung near the fire. She examined it to see if it was the colour she wanted. Maybe she should dye it again she thought. She was restless today.

After making some tea she sat and opened one of the books Jo had given her. She glanced at the words but it was the pictures that intrigue her. It brought back the conversation she had with West about the animals.

Willow had thought it over so many times, some must have survived somewhere.

As she sat there lost in her thoughts the baby decided it was time to start its arrival. It startled Willow at first, but she realized what it was. From what Jo had told her she had time and she paced the cabin. Willow had water heating and wished West was here. West came in from the workshop as always. When he came in it didn't take him long to realized something was wrong with her.

"Willow what's the matter" he asked. "I'm not ill West" she told him. "Would you go and ask Freda to come please?" she said.

West wasted no time in filling her request. Freda was not sure it was the baby. She asked West to stay with Carry and after they ate dinner to send Nimuri over.

With West and Carry taken care of Freda made her way over to West and Willow's cabin.

Willow paced the floor and Freda let her. They talked some and soon Nimuri was there. The water boiled and by midnight the child was born.

Freda and Nimuri cleaned up and when they had finished, Freda held the child first then handed it to Nimuri. Nimuri rocked it beside Willow's bed. Willow slept and Freda went to get West.

When she got to the cabin West looked at her "Is everything alright? Is Willow okay?" he asked. Freda smiled "They are fine" she said "Go to them" she told him.

West wasted no time in getting home. When Nimuri heard him come in she placed the baby in his arms "You have a son." West looked in at his small face. How small he is he thought. He looked at Nimuri and Willow; Nimuri said "She is fine, tired but fine. She will have to feed him soon so let her sleep until then." Nimuri gathered up her wrap and went home.

West held the baby and watched Willow sleep. At that moment he could have wept had the baby not started to fuss. West took him near the fire and held him close. "Well young man what should we call you?" West smiled. The baby tired from the ordeal of being born slept as West held him. The fire cracked and hissed with the fresh wood on it. West found he had trouble laying the small child down as he added the wood.

Finally Willow woke and called to him. He placed the baby beside her and sat down. "He's lovely just like his mother." West kissed her and held the baby's face with one hand. "Have you thought of a name for him? What do you think?" she asked. "I would like to name him Daniel." "Then Daniel it is" she smiled. "You rest now dear, our Daniel will keep you busy for many years." West smiled and Willow did too. She had fed him and he slept. West changed him and put him in the bassinette beside their bed.

He left them to sleep and found comfort in the chair by the fire. His life was now changed again. The freedom he had known for most of his life was gone. He thought about his dad and how he had always been there for him. Zack taught him so much and now he must pass it on to his son. His mind wandered to the complex. How was he ever to find it now, he couldn't just go when he got time. Well, he would cross that when the time came. He had a son, West smiled. Mom and dad would be thrilled he thought. He wished now they were in Cliffside and not in Greenmeadow. He would take them to see mom and dad when spring came, after the winter the trip would do them all good. The warmth of the fire soon had West too comfortable to stay awake.

It would be three weeks before Daniel would sleep through the night. West never hauled so much water as he did now and the diapers seemed to never end. Nimuri and Freda were of great help the first two weeks; Willow now up still didn't have the strength she did before. West had to take up the slack. He didn't mind but it amazed him how much change a small baby caused in one household. He grew to love Daniel more each day and it surprised him how he could become more fond of him with each passing day.

When Willow had afternoon naps West carried Daniel everywhere with him. Willow scolded him and said the child would expect it always if he didn't stop. West would just smile.

The winter had a firm hold on the outside world still. Nimuri often braved the cold to come visit them. When she did West took the opportunity to get out and clear the paths and head to the workshop to visit with Carry. Carry teased him about having soggy hands from washing diapers. West just laughed and replied; your turn is coming or have you forgotten that Nimuri will have your child in late summer. That usually stopped the teasing.

The winter always slowed things to a stop for most everyone and spring was the thing they all looked forward too.

Chapter 34

*T*odd sat at the table, he couldn't believe it. He always thought his dad would pass before his mom, but it seems his father would out live her. "Todd, are you alright? We must go." Todd moved slowly, he had done his crying in the wee hours of the night. Now he must walk with his dad and put his mom with the others that had gone before. Dern was holding his hand and it was a comfort to him. Dana walked on the other side of him. She felt so awful for him. There was not a thing she could say to bring solace to him. There was no solace in the passing of loved ones. Getting through this day and the ones ahead almost seemed like a subtle torture.

The service was short and they watched as they laid Todd's mom to rest. Dana had Dern; Todd and his father stood and waited until the tomb was sealed. Todd's father wept silently, his life would never be the same again. It would pain him each and every passing moment. Todd with him to the council room and Dana took Dern home.

In the council chamber Dirk had poured out a drink for everyone. He raised his glass and said "To Andrea" and they all their glasses, repeated the toast and drank. Slowly they all left.

Dirk put his hand on Larz's shoulder "If you want old man you know where to find me." Larz looked at Dirk, he knew he had lost Carla not long ago "Thanks Dirk" he said. Dirk just nodded. He knew only too well how he felt.

Todd walked with his dad to his dorm. "Dad, I want you to stay with us for a while" he told his dad. "No my boy this is my home, besides what would your mother say if I felt I couldn't come home. I'll be alright and I want some time to gather my thoughts." "Dad, are you sure?" Todd said.

"Yes I am sure." They went in and his dad sat in the big chair. "You go home son Dana will be worried about you and I will be fine." Todd wasn't sure he wanted to leave his dad there alone, but there wasn't much he could do about it. "Well if you are sure dad. You know where we are" Todd said and his dad nodded.

Dana had food out when Todd arrived. She was surprised his dad was not with him. "Where's dad?" she asked. "He wanted to go home" Todd told her. "He shouldn't be alone there" Dana said. "I know" Todd told her "But, he wanted to be there." Dana told him to eat something, he didn't and went and lay down on the bed.

Dana fed Dern and set him with his toys. Dana went to see Todd "I'm so sorry" she said to him. "I'll be okay. I just miss her already."

Dana left him to his own thoughts. He needed time and that was the only thing that would help him learn to live each day without knowing his mom wasn't there.

As Todd lay there, the memories of her flashed through his head. She had been in the med labs until the virus came. It affected her so badly watching her friends and coworkers pass and being unable to help them in any way. It changed her; she never went back after that. She was opposed to any contact with the outside world. Todd wished he had taken her out so she could see it was safe. The world she had known most of her life was gone to her. It tormented him that he could not speak of the tunnel. The whole thing was making him angry. People were not meant to be closed in, locked up. Now they could go out. They were so conditioned; it was a concept of living so many didn't want. He thought about those that let the virus go in the world; what greed and selfishness to kill the world because they couldn't dominate it, forever. Did they not think about what would happen? Did they care? Todd sat on the bed. She had lived a long life and did find her happiness eventually. He must be thankful for that. He thought about Dana and how sad it was she never knew her mom and dad. He wept.

Dana let him have his time. She knew to let him alone until he had it right in his mind. She watched Dern playing and thought of Andrea; she was a good woman. She loved so many things and Todd needed to remember that too. It was not easy to lose a close friend and family member. The life that was shared with them was over and that was it, over. Filling in the areas that they filled in your life was the hard part and would take time.

By dinner time Todd still had not come out of the bedroom. Dana sat at the table and fed Dern. He knew something was wrong and did not misbehave. Todd joined them just as Dern was finished. When Dana set him down he went to Todd and hugged his leg. Todd tussled his hair and Dern headed for his toys.

Dana poured Todd a coffee and never sought conversation. Todd looked at Dana and said "I loved her so much." Dana's only reply was "I know you did." "I'm going to miss her a lot" Todd said. "Yes, yes you will" Dana answered. Todd knew that Dana knew all to well what he felt. The rest of the evening was spent at home quietly. Todd thought about going to see his dad, but he knew he had to sort out how he felt too.

By bedtime Todd found himself exhausted, the emotional strain had taken its toll, tomorrow, always tomorrow.

He slept fitfully and Dana knew he had to pass through the grief in his mind before life would get back to any kind of normal routine. She would be there waiting for him to make it past that point. "It's terribly hard to accept the things you can not change or do anything about" she had told him. Todd knew she was right. He had to get over feeling sorry for himself, if the world for Dern was to be a better place and not the feared realm his mother left it as.

The next month was the hardest for Todd and his father, but life does go on and it is as it should be.

Winter was always a long time. The stillness and emptiness they watched on the screens made it seem longer somehow. The only blessing was the shortness of the days which helped a little in the passing of the time.

The animals getting ready for birth occupied much of Dana and Dern's time. This year Dana planned to let out through the tunnels a few things, the trouble was getting them before they were counted and put into the record books.

Todd had many visits with Erik in that last month and decided not to tell him of the tunnel. Dirk on the other hand could be an ally in smuggling out animals. He still remembered what Andy had told him not to tell anyone.

The reports of what each station would do to start the journey were starting to come in. It was soon clear that insects and birds were first to be introduced. Todd and Dana followed the reports as were submitted.

Todd was with Dern now that Dana worked in the tailor stations. The wool and the cotton were in and now the work was on the way to be finished. Todd's workshop had a few repairs that had to have parts made for, but nothing he had to oversee.

Soon Dern would be going to preschool. That thought had Todd starting to look at what they were teaching the children. Instead of never talking of the outside, he sometimes heard the children at the play centre in the great living area tell their parents of things that once lived outside. It was starting, Todd thought. When spring came Todd knew that after being stuck in this mountain for so long he and Dana would venture outside again. The complex was an enduring, monotonous existence and although they were alive they didn't live.

Todd had taken Dern for his medical. While there he asked several questions as to the effects of the complex on the people that lived there. The doctor explained for the young it never affected them much because they had never known anything different. The older folk to have to live with being institutionalized was another thing, but with so few left now it was not representing too many problems. "What kind of problem did they have?" Todd asked. "Some get claustrophobic, some acrophobic; everything from sleep disorders, nervous tension to panic attacks. Unfortunate the children of those affected developed some problems as well, not all just some. Now that time has passed we see fewer cases of it."

Dern's health was given the stamp of approval and Todd thanked the doctor for his time. He knew that if there was not a light at the end of this tunnel he would leave the complex on his own and live outside. He was getting tired of fighting them all the time to open the doors. He was tired of living in the complex the way it was.

He soon reached their dorm and started dinner for Dana.

Dana was tired when she got home. It had been a long day for her in the tailor station and she worried about Todd. He had not been himself since his mom died. They ate a quiet dinner and played with Dern afterwards. Todd never said much his mind was not there, he was deep in thought.

By the time Dern was in bed, Todd began reading the reports. "You know Dana the only way they will open the doors is if someone goes out and proves to them it's safe." "You might be right, but what if they decide to not let them back in again?" "They would have to Dana that's the beauty of it" Todd told her. "Well it's an idea that's for sure" Dana told him. "Any ideas as to who should be the ones to go out?" Dana asked. "Yes as a matter of fact I do, but I need to work on a viable plan first if the council is going to accept the idea." Dana was glad Todd was this way. Whatever the plan was she would help him. It was the old Todd back.

"Well, I'll leave you to it then, I have to get some rest. I'll help you tomorrow." Todd looked at her "I'm sorry I havent been myself. It must be hard on you. Of all the people I know you know how I feel."

She got up and hugged him "I'm just glad you are back." Todd let her go to bed. He wanted to get on this. He thought, it's so simple why didn't he think of it before? He had to talk to Dirk and Erik. His father would be a good person to talk too. Eli from the kitchen and Thomas from the tailoring station, that just about covered the old guard and they would know what to expect on the outside.

It was the wee hours in the morning before Todd went to bed. Tomorrow he would talk to Erik first. He would let him know if he had a chance and then Dirk. First he must rest. Todd closed his eyes and slept. It was the first night in a long time he slept.

Dana was up with Dern. She had him dressed and fed before Todd got up. After a shower and coffee, he started to tell Dana what his idea entailed. She listened and was impressed. "You know" she said "All the animals could be checked and the plant life etc. I think you're onto something here" Dana said. "First I want to run it past Erik and see what he thinks" Todd told her. "First eat" Dana said and Todd smiled at her. She made him some breakfast and before long they were off to see Erik.

They arrived at Erik's dorm and Gwen let them in. Dern and Katrina often played together; this gave Gwen a chance to listen to Todd's plan. The coffee pot was filled a few times by the time before Todd finished laying out the plan to Erik. "Well Todd I think you have something there. It would be an awful lot of work to do just to prepare for an extensive stay out there. It would provide us with information that would be first hand. Yes, I think it might be worth considering. What do you think Gwen?" Erik told her. "The idea is a good one, but who would go? Who ever it was not only would have to go out, but then to come back in. They would have to go into isolation until they were thoroughly checked out. It might take 3 to 6 months maybe a year t run the tests. Well it's not just go out we have to think of the fact they might be carriers of something. I fear the isolation might be longer" Gwen said.

Dana spoke next "If that sacrifice was proved to be safe outside, then would it be worth it?" Gwen looked at Erik "It won't be you dear, there's no way." Erik smiled "The old guard knows much more about the outside than we do. I think you should run it by Dirk and see what he thinks." Todd smiled "Thanks Erik and you too Gwen. We may get out there yet"

Todd said with a smiled. "Its time for lunch, how about we dine in the living area today Dana? I think it would be a nice change."

Dana smiled and gathered up Dern. He wanted to walk not be carried. Dana held one of his hands. As they walked to the living area Dana smiled. She had everything right now, everything to make up for the past. She had a future and she was happy. Todd told her after they ate they would go see Dirk. Dana didn't mind and Dern would not object.

The lunch was light, salad and tea. Todd wondered how much lumber would be needed for a house outside and what equipment would have to be taken to do the science to prove the outside was safe. The lunch was good and they headed for Dirk's dorm.

"You know Dana this idea might give my father something to work at too" Todd told her. "He had had not done well since mom passed, I hope it will help" Dana said. She was right Todd thought, he had watched his father grow more distant and saw the loss in him take its toll in more ways then one. "I'll stop in and see him after we see Dirk."

Dirk opened his door and a wide smile crossed his face. "Come in, come in" he said as he led them to the table. He went to the book shelf and got down some book to look at and then put on the tea. "What brings you here on this winter's day?" Dirk asked. Todd told hi of his idea as Dirk listened intently. When Todd concluded, Dirk sat back. "It could work. The people that are afraid would be given the security they need, living proof. Have you thought about who would go? It would be a tough journey, then the quarantine to get back in. It would have to be extensive, and then the science labs would have to test whoever for everything they can think of. It would not be pleasant, but it would open the doors if the test came back negative. Well you have come up with something Todd. It will take time to organize this I know. Let me think of this and get back to you" Dirk told him and smiled.

Dana, Todd and Dern walked towards home. Todd stopped to visit his dad and Dana took Dern home. He had been a good boy all day and Dana smiled at him. She made his dinner and bathed him. He was in bed before Todd got home.

When Todd went to see his dad, he saw a man lost in a world all of his own. He talked to him and noted he was not the man he was before his mom passed. It left a hole in his soul and he had not made attempts to fill the void. He listened to Todd, but did not hear what he said really. Todd couldn't find anything to draw his interest. Dern could not heal a broken heart. "Well dad I just thought I would tell you" Todd said. His dad told him "the outside is a grand place, but held no interest for him anymore, nothing really did. If he was bound to go, be sure the choices he made did not hurt those he loved the most. It was them, not where you live that mattered. I think I'm going to go lay down, I feel tired" he told Todd. "Alright dad you rest easy" Todd said "I will visit you soon" he said as he left.

Todd thought about what his dad had said, it was true it didn't matter where you lived, but that you took care of those you loved the most where ever it was. Todd almost felt ashamed of himself it didn't matter where you live just that you loved and cared for those close to you. That's how they endured the years inside. It didn't matter, they were alive and that was the most important thing of all.

When Todd got home Dana had a meal waiting for him. A smile graced her face and Todd at the moment loved her more than he could have imagined. He hugged and kissed her. "Gee I think I will make you go see your father every night before you come home if this is the outcome." She smiled. "Your dinner is getting cold" she told him.

Todd sat at the table. "Want me to fill the tub for you or are you going to shower?" Todd smiled at her. "Neither" he said "I need to work on the plans then go to bed." Dana smiled "Well I'm tired and I need my beauty sleep." She told him and kissed him on the cheek. "I have to work in the tailor shop again tomorrow. The cotton has been woven and we have to make up the used supplies" she told him. "Okay" he said "I won't be up too late then." He told her before she went to bed.

Todd sat there and it was like a like had come on. He knew his fathers words would be with him always. It was for the love of Dern he continued with his plan. His life would be the best he could give him and the wisdom from his father Todd would pass to Dern to make his journey on this planet easier. Todd went to bed his day would be full caring for Dern. It was a full time job.

Todd was up first and had the coffee on when Dana got up. Dern followed and soon all sat at the table. "So what plans do you have today?" Todd asked Dana. She smiled "As little as possible." "Well I have paper work to do. I have a plan what will be needed to build a shelter. We could do tents, but I think a more permanent building would be better" Todd told her. Dana set Dern down with his toys. "You might be right. There are many times I watched the monitors and see it raining heavily and the wind blowing. A tent would not be enough protection" Dana said.

Todd now started filling the table with papers and maps. Dana cleared what dishes were there and sat with him drinking her coffee. "Okay" Todd said "I think this would be easier" he said. Dana said "Easier?" He looked at her "Do you think Erik and Gwen would mind Dern for the day?" he asked her. "I'll go see" Dana asked "What do you have planned?" Todd smiled "You'll see."

Dana walked to Erik and Gwen's to see if they would take Dern for the day. When she got there Gwen was with Katrina and she had the day planned. Dana thought about dad, but wanted to check with Todd first.

Todd had a pack with things he felt would be needed for the day. Dana knew he was going outside and told him that she would have to stay with Dern. Todd didn't really want to go alone, but knew he would have to. "I think I would get a better idea if I looked out and thought of things that would be needed." "Todd it's winter, it's not a good idea. You are taking unnecessary chances." "It will be alright Dana I'll be back before dinner." "Todd I don't like it" Dana told him. "Don't worry so much I'll be fine" he said.

Dana watched him pack his gear. It wasn't much and Dana still didn't like it. He smiled at her "See you soon" he said and left. Dana knew her day would be one of worry until he walked back in that door.

She glanced over the papers and stacked them up. She moved then to the desk and decided that she may be over reacting. Todd wasn't going to make any judgements that would endanger him. She decided to take Dern to the atrium. After all this time she always found solace there.

Todd had to go to the library first. He wanted to read up on the climate patterns. It would be a good idea to know just how cold or how warm it did get outside. His mind totally absorbed in what he was doing that he didn't see Dirk and nearly knocked him down. The contents of his pack spilled out when it hit the floor. Dirk helped pick up the items and Todd red faced never said a word. Dirk could see the things packed were not the regular things one would be walking around the complex with. Dirk handed the things he picked up and said "Todd we need to talk."

Dirk walked with him to the library and into Andy's old office. Todd sat down and Dirk crossed his arms and with one hand he rubbed his chin. "Are you going to tell me what a person would be doing with a compass, maps and well do I need to go on?" Dirk said. Todd just stared at him. "Let me put it this way. You're not leaving here until I'm satisfied with the answer you give me." Todd still never said anything. "Andy told me that you and I were going to have a talk, man to man, one day and that I would be pleasantly surprised and a bit aggravated at the conversation. He also told me that I was to help you and Dana as well as Erik. Now all this cryptic talk and no real idea as to what all this pertains to." Dirk went to the door and asked one of his assistants to bring coffee.

Todd wanted to tell Dirk, but he could seal off the cave and that Todd would not let happen.

The coffee arrived and Dirk told the young man they were not to be disturbed. He sat down at the desk "Alright Todd let me tell you a few things you may or may not know. Do you know Simion's plan was a great undertaking and he failed?" Todd almost jumped to defend. Dirk held up his hand "Hear me out. The complex was built to keep us in and safe from what was out there, but he failed. The outside got in and killed, well did you know it wasn't through the animals? Simion asked me on his death bed to take that burden to save the ones left." Todd couldn't believe what Dirk had just said. "You knew all the time, you knew." Todd blurted out. "Yes I knew and I know a lot more too. Not all the founders were told. It was to keep some kind of security in here. I also know that the virus will change again and when that comes I will again be resented by many. It makes no never mind to me; it's a burden I gladly carry. Now your turn Todd, I want to know what had your thoughts so absorbed you nearly knocked me down and what you need those items for."

Dirk emptied Todd's pack. Todd a grown man had been reduced to a child being scolded; he did not find it very pleasant.

Todd took his pack and started to replace the items "What I do is really none of your concern Dirk." "Todd I'm not asking you t tell me what you are doing, but it appears to me that you may be getting in over your head. Andy told me when the time came you would have some interesting things I might like to know." Todd looked at him "How do you know that if I had anything to say that you would not keep it between us? At this point I just want more than this, more for Dana and Dern, if it comes down to it more for everyone. Do you have any extra clothes?" Todd asked him. "Yes" Dirk told him. "Then get them and meet me at my dorm." Todd got up "I want to talk to Dana. Be ready with your change of clothes."

Todd went to the construction section in the library and pulled out 2 books. He took them to the desk and then headed out the door.

Dirk wasted no time in getting his change of clothes. He just had a bag to put them in but it was good enough.

Todd now was back home and told Dana what had happened. Dana looked relieved almost. "Todd I trust Dirk is not one that would go back on his word. If Simion trusted him and Andy, then I think we can too" she smiled. Todd paced the floor "Do you have a warmer coat that Dirk could use and gloves?" Dana had knitted things for Todd in the spare time she had. She went to the closet and retrieved them. She was glad he wasn't going alone but another would know of the passage.

"You know if Dirk keeps this quiet, he could help us" Todd said. Dana thought that and yes with his help letting the animals go out of the enclosed valley would be easier.

There was a knock at the door, Dirk was there. Dana looked at the back and soon had a pack for him. Dirk looked at Todd "Does Dana know what's going on?" Todd looked at Dana "Yes" Dana said "I think you are in for an interesting day Dirk" she said. "Okay we're ready Dirk please keep an open mind" was all Todd would say.

They headed for the cavern and when Dirk saw the ladder he knew this was not the first time that Todd had been there. It didn't take long for them to reach the false door. Todd held his breath and pushed it open. Dirk's eyes widened.

They went in and Todd closed the door. The blackness was soon brightened with Todd's flashlight and he had the wall lights soon on.

Dirk looked around "My God" he said. "This must have taken you months to do." Todd sat at the table and took out the contents "It's soft stone it didn't take that long" Todd said. "Here, put these in your pack." He handed him gloves and a sweater. "Come on" Todd said and the journey through the tunnels began. Dirk never said much he just followed Todd.

When they reached the river he kept close to Todd. Todd stopped and pushed the wall and as it opened to the outside world, Dirk just stared. He opened his eyes and the blast of cold gripped them both. The air was crisp and the sky was blue and clear.

Dirk took several steps and when he cleared the doorway scooped up snow in his hand. His breath fogged in front of him. He looked at Todd. Todd stood there watching him remembering how he and Dana felt when they stood there like Dirk did now. "I didn't think it would be this cold" Todd said. Dirk's eyes had just adjusted to the light. He didn't feel the cold. He just stared out over the forest and valley now covered with snow.

"Dirk we have to go back, it's too cold out here." Todd was now shivering. "Yes, yes" Dirk said and returned inside with Todd. Todd closed the door and they put on the extra clothes. "It wasn't cold it was freezing out there."

Neither spoke as they made their way back to the little area Todd had excavated out. Todd dropped his pack and took out the thermos with the coffee in it. He handed one to Dirk and they sat there.

Dirk's mind raced over what he had just seen "Did Andy know?" he asked Todd. "Yes" Todd replied. "What did he say?" Dirk asked. "He said so it begins and we were to tell no one. Then he cried." Dirked raised an eyebrow at that. "He must have known he was dying then" Dirk said. Todd nodded. Dirk could see that Todd was still very uncomfortable "This place is best kept quiet" Dirk said. Todd sighed with relief. "How long have you been going out?" Dirk asked him. "A few years now" Todd said. "Andy never said anything about it" Dirk said. "I think we are supposed to start getting people to live outside again" Todd said. "The only trouble is they are not interested. They like it in the complex." "Aye" Dirk said. "They are afraid. Most have never seen it." "What frustrates me the most is they don't even want to see it" Todd said. "There is nothing left for them anymore out there Todd, everything is in here. They were born here, live here and most have families and friends buried here. Erik says we have to start pushing the outside to them. Get them interested in what's out there" he said. "The children were the beginning; get them to realize there is a world out there." Todd told him. "He's right; the children will be the first to question things. What's out there for them when they have everything they need in here?" Dirk said. "We are not meant to live in here" Todd said to him. "This is true, but not everyone thinks as you do. Most people just live, they don't worry about things. Here they know what needs to be done to survive and do it, beyond that they live simple lives; Family, friend and routine keeps them happy. So very few look for more. To see; to know and to do you are one and so is Dana. There are others, but very few. They are leaders that seek change."

Todd brought out the sandwiches. "Andy was right. You know when he said so it begins, he meant the journey of the people here back to the outside world again. It was never a question of if, but when. He knew it would happen" Dirk said. "Why did you not plan for it?" Todd asked. "Everything else was planned. I can't believe that the progression would not have been considered" Todd said. "It might have been, but Simion died and we lost so many. The future f those left had to be the first priority. Once we got things running again most just wanted to live and not worry about death. The trials they had been through, then there were you and Dana stirring things making most remember all too clearly what they lost. What had happened seemed to weld up inside and they didn't want to deal with it. The rush to go out was a threat; they just wanted to enjoy what life they had left. It's sad really to be afraid of where you came from and who you are in the scope of living things. We won the battle with the virus, but to what ends? The people here are in all likelihood the only people left."

Todd sat there, "Well I think they survived out there" Todd said. "Zack didn't die in the virus outbreak we know that. He is a very smart man. He would have known what to do." Dirk looked at him "Maybe, but without animals food would not be easy to come by. It would have been very difficult to survive alone." "Then there must be others" Todd said. "That might be, but at the moment what are you going to do about this and where do we begin to sort out that herd out into a coral of understanding?"

They laughed, "Now what are we going to do about all this?" Dirk said as he looked around. He looked straight at Todd "Young man, we will say nothing of this" Dirk said and smiled. Todd's face must have shown his relief. "I must admit to you that it was wondrous to feel snow again. The air was so crisp and fresh. I had almost forgotten what it was like. Thank you my boy." Dirk smiled. "Of course you do realise this will not be the last time I come here. There is a young man hiding inside these old mans clothes. Let's get back before I'm missed."

They packed up what they needed to go back and soon had climbed up the ladder. Dirk followed Todd home. When they arrived Dana was there with Dern.

"I don't know what I am to do with you two" he smiled. "He knows Dana" Todd told her. She looked at Dirk "Todd, I think Erik is right about the children, but I think you have a good plan in going out and I want to be one of the ones going. I know the animals and the testing that would have to be done on them." "I want to go too" said Todd "But the quarantine after would be too long." "Let me think on it" Dirk said "I think I could find a few willing to go. After all it would be one of the biggest things to happen in the complex in many years. Work on the plans for that as a mission. When you have them done bring them to me."

Chapter 35

The winter passed slowly. Willow was glad to see the icicles dripping on the cabin. It was time to get the sap from the maples and the outing was looked forward to by Willow and Nimuri. She was over the sickness now and her little belly was starting to show. Daniel was getting big and Freda agreed to watch him while they collected the sap.

West and Carry pulled the sleigh with the buckets and pots. Willow had packed food and dry wood for a small fire.

When they arrived at the maple stand West and Carry took the buckets and spouts to the trees. Willow and Nimuri cleared a small area for a fire. Soon the fire was warming them and water for a hot drink.

They spent the best part of the day collecting sap and when night started to arrive they headed back to the cabins. The day was a good one. They had plenty of sap to render down. They would start in the morning. It was brought into the cabin to prevent freezing. With Daniel fed and sleeping West and Willow soon followed.

Spring was coming and it was exciting to Willow in many ways, the garden, being able to travel. Being cooped up all winter always gave them cabin fever. West looked forward to exploring more, but the reality of the garden, cutting wood must come first.

Willow was up early and had washed many pots to put the syrup in. She had the fire going and the syrup was thickening nicely. Daniel was content in his bassinette by the fire. She had a paper on the table ready for her and West to start planning the garden

When West finally rolled out of bed Willow had most of the morning chores done. "Did you sleep well?" she asked. "Why did you let me sleep so long?" he asked. "Enjoy it while you can, before long you will be working hard." She smiled at him. "Your breakfast is on the table." West washed and sat at the table. As he ate he watched her stir the syrup; she had already marked in the cabins. "You want to do the map at Carry's then we all have a say?" he asked her. "Sure, but with this going on I can't leave it for a while."

West finished his porridge and searched for last year's garden map. The plants will all be rotated and part left as fallow. With the wheat he wanted to ask Freda and Nimuri, how long before they could use that field for wheat again. When he found the map he sat at the table.

Daniel started to fuss and West went and got him. The two sat at the table and soon were playing. The maps were forgotten for the time being. It warmed Willow to see West enjoy Daniel so much.

The morning was gone and Daniel made no secret that he was hungry. West took over the syrup stirring and Willow fed him. She set him in the bassinette and started a late lunch for them.

The sun was out and the path was peeking through the snow that had covered it all winter. "It's going to be a good season for the garden, spring will be here before long. I can feel the air getting warmer" Willow told West. Tea, bread, jam, dried fruit and nuts were the lunch and between eating and stirring the syrup was ready to be poured into the jars. West did that as Willow tied cloths over the openings and set them to cool. With that done the rest of the afternoon could be spent planning the garden.

Soon Daniel was bundled up and West and Willow headed to the other cabin. They were met with good cheer and Daniel was still the center of attention.

They planned the garden and for dinner they had cornbread and a vegetable soup. Daniel kept the women busy and at dusk West and Willow headed home.

Willow always washed diapers at night and West got the water. When she finished hanging them up the fire was the only source of light. She fed Daniel and by the time she finished bed was a welcomed sight.

The next weeks passed much the same. The snow had melted and the days were getting longer. Willow watched the apple trees hoping soon to see the buds start to open. It was a sure sign that spring was here.

West had been out with Carry cutting trees. He had slowly enlarged the valley. He cut the trees above the cabins. Carry asked why, he told him just a safety precaution. Not only could a storm blow them down, it was a fire break as well. Carry had to agree after seeing the old fire burn in the next valley. The two men preferred to cut trees in the early spring as it was cooler and the work was hard. Carry had shown the plans for the cabin and they picked the trees for that.

In a week or two they would visit Greenmeadow. Gary and Brad and maybe even Kalvin would come back with them to help to add to Carry's cabin.

Willow was already getting things together for the trip.

The old couple would take the cabin at the half way point this spring.

Willow had noticed the buds on the trees had started to open. They all had survived the winter and it pleased her so much.

The wagon was loaded and the next morning they would be off. Freda would walk slowly, she was getting old but that never bothered anyone. The wagon would be hard to pull with the furniture on it so it all worked out. The extra time would give them time to enjoy the woods along the way. This was Daniels first of many trips that would be made to Greenmeadow. Willow had him tied to her back and he seemed to enjoy the trip.

By the time they reached the cabin they needed the break. Nimuri and Willow got a fire going. Freda and Daniel sat by the fire for warmth. West and Carry unloaded the furniture and Nimuri got the lunch out. Willow picked up Daniel and fed him while she ate. The trip now would be easier going; Freda would ride and hold Daniel. With the furniture off loaded the wagon was easier to pull. The fire was put out and Carry noted that more firewood would not go amiss.

By early afternoon they reached the ridge that overlooked Greenmeadow. It didn't take the children long to see them. Before they made it down the path everyone was out to see them. They all went to Zack and Jo's cabin. Before like magic all kinds of food was there and tea all around.

Daniel stole the show. Jo had him first then Zack. He never made strange to them and he sat with Zack, all the children came to see him. Daniel giggled and giggled and all patted his head or held his hand.

Soon all the women were bunched together and the men made their way to the workshop. Even Zack handed Daniel to Helen and joined the men. It was a good time for the men to discuss anything that needed to be done and the women to catch up on all that happened over the winter. The children never made any mind after the arrival and Willow soon saw them happily playing in their park. As she watched them play she realized how much they had grown. Willow was happy and it felt good to be around people.

Then she heard it, a sweet melody like whistling only more melodic. She followed the sound and when she saw Chad blowing on a stick and Dawn too. Jo touched her shoulder "Aw you have seen our musicians then?" Willow smiled. "How are they making that melody?" she asked. "It's a long story, but Herb made the flutes. Those two took to them like they had always played. They always play them." Jo smiled. "Well are you going to tell me the story?" "They were here studying and Herb brought me some new spoons. We had been discussing birds and how I missed their chirp and song. A few days later Herb arrived with flutes for all the children. Those two just loved them and as you see they play them well. Chad and Dawn are always together I wouldn't be surprised if they stay together for a long time" Jo said and Willow smiled. "All the children have grown so much." "Yes children have a way of doing that" Jo said and put her hand on Willow's shoulder. "Let's have more tea."

When they returned to the inside the women were all talking at once. They teased Sara and Nimuri about the babies they carried and when Willow and Jo sat down, it was Helen that spoke. "I have good news" she said "Kalvin and I would like you all to know that we are too expecting a child." The room erupted into well wishes and now teasing included Helen.

Willow was happy for her mom and Kalvin. How wonderful for them. Kalvin would have his own child to add to the tribe she called her siblings.

With the meals to make and the regular chores that needed to be done the women started to go home. Helen stayed on to talk to Willow and Jo.

"I'm worried" Helen said "It's been a long time since I had a child and I'm not a spring chicken anymore." "You'll be fine Helen" Jo told her "Just make sure you don't over do it." "Oh Willow, Dawn wanted to know if she could go back with you for a while? She is getting to old to always be with children." Willow smiled "Sure she can come." Helen hugged Willow. Willow was so happy; this year will be a good one.

Daniel started fussing and Willow knew he was hungry. As she fed him Helen and Jo talked of the old couple coming. "They should be here soon. What are their names?" Willow asked. "Doug and Angie" Jo told her "They lost everything in a prairie fire. I'm glad they will have a home they can call their own. They had no trouble housing any runners that go through. I am interested with any news from the fort. It's been a long time since we have heard much."

Willow finished feeding Daniel and put him in the bassinette by the fire. Supper was started for everyone; soon the people of Greenmeadow had a variety of things for everyone to eat.

Dawn had Daniel now and Zack sat with them. West was busy getting wood and water for later.

Everyone settled in as the night closed in the valley; Daniel was put to bed. When the diapers had been washed and hung, West and Willow went to bed. The day had been filled with laughter and good company, but after the days travel it was good to finally rest.

The dawn brought the sunshine and before long the valley of Greenmeadow started to wake.

Willow was up to tend to Daniel and Jo had breakfast on early. The men soon joined them and after the morning chores were done, West packed water for a bath. Zack sat on the porch with a blanket over his legs. Jo joined him with willow bark tea she had made to help ease his pain.

It didn't take Willow and West to bathe and wash their travelling clothes. With Daniel napping West and Willow join them on the porch.

West soon in conversation with Zack, Willow took the opportunity to visit her mom and Kalvin.

The children all headed to the play yard as soon as they could. Willow found contentment talking with her mom.

The next few days were spent much the same, soon the gardens would have to be done and they would have to head home. The furniture finished the cabin off. What they needed now were blankets, utensils, pottery all to make the cabin more like home. Food would have to wait till after the harvest. They would be comfortable there in a home they yet had to see.

It was always sad when it was time to go. They all knew it would be a few months before they would see each other again. Dawn was excited about going. Chad was invited too. Kalvin and Gary were coming to help with the cabin. Herb and Brad stayed home to start the gardens. The week had gone by fast and with the wagon ready to go they set off for home.

Willow noticed that in just a week that past the buds on the trees were opening and the grass had gone from yellow to green. With all the extra people along the journey seemed to take no time to the halfway cabin.

Daniel was demanding Willows attention so Nimuri started the fire. Freda rested in a chair by the fire and the men unloaded the furniture that came from Greenmeadow. The linens and dishes were left on the table when they continued on to Cliffside.

The wagon, now relieved of most of its weight was much easier to pull, Freda now road in it. Willow and Nimuri talked of the new addition to the cabin. Chad and Dawn talked together in their own conversation. The men talked of the valley Carry and West had found.

It was late afternoon when they made it home. The extra room was given to Dawn. Chad, Kalvin and Gary slept on longer benches and in chairs. The fire soon had the cabin warm. Dawn kept Daniel amused while Willow helped make food for everyone.

The follow day would have the men working hard. The walls, roof and floor would have to be done quickly, even if it was spring it was still cool. Everyone slept knowing the next day would be a long and hard one.

As the day passed Willow watched as they took apart the walls and added new ones to Nimuri's cabin. Kalvin and Gary were not strangers to hard work and they were on the roof by late afternoon. West and Carry had the floor almost done when the last shingle went on.

The next day was not a good one, a spring storm moved in and travelling back to Greenmeadow was put on hold. "Seems we got the roof on just in time" Kalvin said. Gary laughed "A few days off never went amiss either." "What do you think about this valley they found Kalvin?" Gary asked. "Never hurts to have farmland, but its to far away at present to do much good." "True, but it does give hope for the future" and Kalvin looked at Chad and Dawn "That might be true" he said and smiled again.

Willow had helped get some organization back to Nimuri's home. Willow found the brooms made from wheat stalks worked wonders. Gary and West had Freda's new room back in order. Now they had the extra one for the baby that was due.

Dinner was made and after everyone ate the dishes were cleaned. Soon it was dark and sleep was welcomed by all.

The sun shone with the dawn and Gary along with Kalvin had to head back. Chad and Willow's sister were to stay on for a while.

After the two men were fed they were on their way back to Greenmeadow. West liked it after a rainstorm, the air smelled so nice. It was good that rain did come then. It would make the soil in the garden easier to work.

Carry and West were working around the cabin stacking up all the wood scraps and just general cleanup done. Once the garden work started it would be a good month of hard labour. Chad worked along side them and he was eager to lean anything they passed on.

Dawn helped Willow with Daniel so she could have a few moments through the day to herself. She had washed clothes and a never ending line hung with diapers starred back at her when she was done. "Willow, do you like being married?" Dawn asked her. "Yes very much" she said. "I think I will too, but mom says I'm too young yet." Willow smiled. "I think she wants you to have a little freedom first. When you marry, Dawn your freedom will be a few moments stolen where it can be stolen from. It's a lot of work and hard work" Willow told her. "I'm not afraid of hard work" Dawn said. "I can't see it being different from what I do now except I would be doing it with Chad and no one else." Willow looked at her "The more help you have the less arduous it is. Look how fast they fixed the cabin. One day; if West and Carry had to do it alone it might have taken a week or more." "I know" said Dawn "That's not what I meant I just want to do what you and West did. Have my own things, my own home." Willow laughed. "What's so funny?" Dawn looked at her. "Seems mom wants to keep you a little girl, but you are not. Did you want me to talk with her Dawn?" Willow asked. "No I have to do it" Dawn replied. "Have you made any plans as to where you want to live?" "Chad said he wanted to see the valley south of the fort. It's too far away, besides all the people from the prairie will be moving there. Cliffside is close, but it's still not right. I don't know I think Chad will have to see what's open for land." "Well Dawn you have lots of time to decide. You and Chad should make a trip to the fort and see what's out there before deciding" Willow told her. "Thanks for treating me like a young woman Willow. Most treat me like a child."

Dawn went to Daniel and picked him up. "Come on sweet Danny let's get some air" and Dawn went and sat on the porch. Willow watched her and knew it wouldn't be long before Chad and her married and started their life's journey.

The spring was here and with it all the work it entailed. Dawn and Chad stayed until the planting was done. They headed back to Greenmeadow happy and the melodies of the flutes went with them.

The old folks had occupied the cabin so there was a stop along the way to rest. Daniel was growing and Nimuri was due soon. West and Carry ventured off to explore more of what was beyond Cliffside and the women enjoyed the peace and tranquility if summer. Willow always worried about West when he was adventuring, but she also knew he was a good woodsman, with Carry the two would handle themselves.

The lovely afternoons hard turned dark and Freda knew rain was coming. They soon had gone home to avoid the downpour they could see was coming. Willow watched the storm from her window and Daniel cried at the claps of thunder. Summer storms were always the worst. The needed rain came in buckets only the garden suffered if there was hail. Willow watched as she made Daniel and her something to eat. West would be getting wet and she smiled knowing how much he like wet feet.

Her day passed much the same as always. Daniel would soon be walking and she doted on him. He was West all over, she saw similarities in him all the time.

The storm lasted two days and when the sun broke through the clouds Willow was glad. After a good rain it was time to collect mushrooms. She took Daniel to Nimuri's and was off into the woods to see what she could find. As luck would have it she soon found plenty.

She was on her way home when West and Carry appeared in the distance. It always warmed her heart to see him return home safely from his journeys. Willow was soon with them and the last walk to the cabin was with good cheer.

Daniel was glad to see West and was soon in his arms. With his pack and Daniel West still moved with ease. Willow was glad to have him home. She set her mushrooms out to dry as West filled a tub. Daniel was quiet watching his dad. West made sure he paid mind to him as he came and went with the water.

As West bathed he told Willow of the valley and how much land there was for farming. Willow knew he wanted to go there more often and the only thing holding him back was his mom and dad. "You know Chad and Dawn will probably marry soon" Willow told him. "What about the cabin you built in the area that was burned? Think you might offer that if they get married?" "They are free to it. The area would be easy to clear for farming" he said. Willow smiled. West was the best man she had ever known.

Daniel was with West like a shadow. West never pushed him away he just picked him up. When he went to the workshop was the only time Daniel was not welcome to be with him. It was not for the lack of love, but because of it. Daniel could get hurt to easily there.

The trips away were put on hold and the valley fell into a routine of garden and getting things started for the coming winter. Wood was a never ending job for the men. The fires consumed so much and everything made needed it.

As the spring melted into summer and Nimuri soon showed the signs of strain. She was getting large with her child and tired easily. Willow did extra to help her. Daniel, now walking had to have extra eyes on him. Freda never wavered from that when Willow and Nimuri worked in the garden. Carry worried for Nimuri he knew their child would soon be with them. Freda patted his hand as she passed him and often told him to stop fretting.

The harvest would soon be on them. The forest had been generous with mushrooms this year. The apple trees never bloomed, maybe next year thought Willow. Life was good; the work never ended but they wanted for little.

Willow watched West and Carry pull wagon loads of gravel to start the road to the valley beyond theirs. Since she had mentioned it for Dawn, West put effort into the trail. She stood up straight and looked over to Nimuri. She would have the baby within days now. As much as she wanted her to rest now she also knew that work was good therapy for her. The last week or so were the worst when expecting.

"Nimuri you go get a cold drink" Willow said to her. Nimuri stood up "Yes, I think I will. Do you want one?" she asked. "Sure" Willow said. Willow watched her go and then went back to work. The potatoes were ready as were the carrots. The tomatoes were dried as they ripened so they would keep. She put her hoe against the tree she was now at and Nimuri came with the cold drinks. They sat in the shade quietly. Willow watched the breeze blow over the flax and wheat. The flax harvest would be the first then the wheat.

"Willow" Nimuri said. Willow looked over to her. "I'm not feeling that great I think I will go to the cabin' she said. "You have worked hard today. You need to rest more" Willow told her. "Want me to walk with you?" Willow asked. "No I will be alright" Nimuri told her. Willow watched her go and she sat a bit longer enjoying the quiet under the tree. Daniel was sleeping in the shade in the fenced off area. Willow decided that she had worked enough for today.

She walked back to the cabin and brought out the tub. She packed water keeping an eye on Daniel. When the tub was full he went and got him. The tub was great even if Daniel was woken to join her in the tub. He never minded much. Freda would have supper ready and after dressing herself, then Daniel they started over to the cabin.

West and Carry were already at the table eating when she and Daniel arrived. "There you are" West said. "We were just talking about the valley and how long it would take us to make a road to it. I think it would make a nice addition to our world. We have been at the end of the road for too long" West said. Willow smiled and started meal. Daniel had his own chair and wasted no time in feeding himself. The talk at the table soon turned to the harvest and West told Willow that he and Carry would dig the potatoes. Willow, happy at that knew she could start the flax. Nimuri never spoke much and Freda told her that she would watch Daniel.

The meal over, Willow helped clean up. West took Daniel and headed home. Willow soon joined them. The evening was spent on the porch. West hauled water to bathe and Willow entertained Daniel. When West joined her on the porch he rocked Daniel. "After the harvest I want to make another trip before the snow falls" West told her. "I was thinking about taking Chad" he said. "Oh he would like that it would give him a chance to see the cabin as well. I do want to visit Greenmeadow before winter" she said and West smiled. They had a few letters from family over the spring and summer, but a visit was always looked forward to. This year was no exception.

Chapter 36

*T*odd called a meeting of all the young leaders. Soon he had them all working on their own ideas of the outside world. The school was pushing towards teaching of the world beyond their caverns. The trips to the animal tunnels and the agro tunnels were routine outings for them.

Erik and Todd used the maps to work out shelters. First it would be ventures to explore the valley and get an inventory of what animals had survived and how they were doing.

Dirk had volunteered to be the first to go out. He would go in the spring and stay out until late summer. He would stay in the outer tunnel that they had let the animals out through, with two chambers of closed doors between him and the complex. The medical labs set up an isolation ward to be able to examine him when he came back in.

Todd and Dana were never so happy; the journey to reclaim life outside was beginning. Dirk knew after this adventure people would again start to live where they should and his animals would be going to be free once more. There were still those against the idea, but they had been out voted.

The complex was buzzing with everything. Todd caught up with Dana in the atrium. He had been looking for her and knew it was the most likely place to find her. Dern had a way with the animals and they showed no fear of him. Dana watched as he found interest in everything around him.

She thought it had been over a year since they showed Dirk the outside. The progress never slowed in working to that end. Dern now starting to talk never seemed to stop for long. He was a real gentleman. Dana wondered if his gift had something to do with the fact he seemed like such an older soul.

"Ah there you are" Todd said and Dana turned to face him. Dern's face lit up with a big smile. Todd sat down on the blanket with them, after a hug or two Dern went back to exploring everything.

"I went to see your dad today" she said. "You should visit him Todd. He seems so much further away." "I will I'm afraid I will lose him before long. There are so few older folks left now." "I know what you mean. I have been thinking about Dirk, he's an old man and he has such a job ahead of him." Todd patted her hand "There are going to be two others going as well. From the talk they are very capable young people, I want to go Dana" Todd told her. "Well" Dana said "We all can go next year. Can you believe it? One more year and the doors will open." "I know" Todd said. "It's exciting and frightening at the same time. I have thought a lot about it" Todd told her. "It will be a few years before any attempts can be made to look for survivors." "Yes" Dana said "I have thought about that as well. You know Todd; I know he is still alive. I can almost feel it, it's crazy huh?" Todd looked at her "No, it's not crazy Dana" and he smiled. "Let's go to dinner. We can stop and get your father along the way" Dana said and Todd smiled.

They made their way to his father's dorm only to find he was not there. He often went to the library or went and sat in the open pavilion to watch the people. They continued to the open area and soon had a table there. They ate and watched Dern play in the playground.

Before long they went home. Dern was bathed. After his day of exploring he needed one. Dana soaked in the tub after Dern was sleeping. Todd and Dana spent the remainder of the evening talking of all the wonders they may get to see.

The complex seemed to fall into a smooth machine once the decision was made to send someone out. They all pitched in to make it happen. The committee was set up to handle all the questions and it was kept busy handling all the incoming ideas.

Dirk had his work cut out for him. The animals would have to be counted and have health checks. He had a computer set up and ready to take out with them. The plant life also had to be catalogued. Staying in the end of the tunnel would save a lot of work. They wouldn't need to build shelters. Erik had the monitors to the outside valley set to view anything they needed to communicate with the inside. New scanning models of the cameras would be set up. The operation work for going outside was moving quickly.

Todd made an effort to keep his dad informed about what was happening with the work, He saw his father slipping away from him more all the time. It saddened him to see it. He decided to invite him for dinner.

He arrived at his dorm to find him gone. Todd went to the open living area, the library, but couldn't find him. His heart started pounding, where was he? He checked everywhere he could think. Soon he had Erik looking and Dana joined in.

The men started in the machine tunnels. Dana thought where would he go? She knew, she knew where he was. Dana found him in the tombs. He was sitting in a chair beside Todd's mom's grave. He never stirred when she came over to him. Dana put a hand on his shoulder and he slumped over. Dana felt his pulse and knew his time on this earth was over. She sat down and spoke softly to him "Thank you for Todd I'll look after him the best I can. I know you loved him and me." Tears weld in her eyes.

He had some paper in his lap. Dana picked them up. There she found drawings of a small house and notes to his wife about the things she had wanted. He had been working on what looked like a house they once had wanted when they lived outside. Dana gathered them up and put them on the bench. She had to get him to the med labs and find Todd and tell him.

It was not a pleasant journey for her to the med labs. She watched as they carefully and tenderly placed him on a gurney to be wheeled back. She picked up the paper; now that Frank was in the proper care she started out to find Todd.

It didn't take long to find them. Dern seemed to know and was quiet and never fussed. She told Todd that his father was at the med labs. Erik left them to go see him. When Erik was gone she told Todd. He walked to the med labs saying little.

He went into the room where his dad was and Dana stayed out, giving him time to be alone with his father. He walked over to the bed. His father had always been a kind man. Todd knew that with out him his life would have been so different. He taught him so many things. Given him directions; taught him respect and nurtured kindness. He had loved his father. Todd held his dad's hand and "I love you" he said "I am going to miss you so much." Todd stood and left the room.

He joined Dana and Dern. The doctors told him he had passed quickly and Todd was comforted to hear that. After thanking the doctors they went home.

Dana never spoke, but had her arm tucked in his the whole way. Dern walked holding his pant leg. Dana felt so bad for him and herself. The pillars of strength they had always counted on were diminishing. The funeral would have to be done and that was never a pleasant thing for anyone. So many thoughts flooded both their minds. They talked little that night. What could be said really and both new he was nearing the end of his life. Learning how to live without him would be hard for them both. Dana never showed him the papers; she would wait until some time passed.

The funeral was held and the procession took Todd's father to the tombs. He was laid to rest beside his wife. Todd waited until they sealed him in.

The luncheon was held in the reception hall. Todd was surprised to see how many lives his dad had touched. When the people slowly out and to their own homes, Dirk took the last of the founders to the conference room. He filled their glasses and raised his "To Frank" he said. They all raised their glasses and said "To Frank."

The founders left at a slow rate, each sharing the same knowledge their era would soon be gone. Dirk stayed and cleaned up. His mind wandered as he thought about the generations that would be left behind when he passed. The world that he and the few others left was gone forever. The new children must never let what happened to destroy the world happen again. So much had been lost. It was a new beginning and Dirk hoped close to the heart that they would cherish the world and once again thrive in it.

Todd and Dana stayed after all the people left. Todd was now as alone as Dana had been most of her life and she felt awful for him. She watched as he arranged the flowers and wished there was something she could do. She knew that was wishful thinking. Todd had no regrets, his father loved him and he loved his father. He had lived a long life and had much happiness; the loss of his wife was too much for him at the end. Through all the bad she had been beside him, but when she passed his will to go on was not there. It was a crying shame that they both passed just before the doors were to be opened again. Todd's mind flashed to Dirk and the other founders. He wondered how many would get to go out again other than Dirk.

The touch of Dana's hand on his shoulder reminded him it was time to go home. He picked up Dern and started for their dorm. "I'm going to miss him so much Dana" Todd said. "Yes you will Todd. He would not like to see you mourn him too long. He wanted you to do so many things. Keep that in your heart now too, alright?" Dana said to him. "I will miss him a lot myself, but I know he is no longer suffering or in pain. He's with your mom and happy again" Dana said, "That may be" Todd said "but it still is no compensation for me not to have him around in our lives." Dana patted his back. It was true, but there was nothing they or anyone else could do about it.

When they got home Dana put Dern to bed for a nap and she made tea for Todd. She never pushed him to talk. She knew that talk just might make it all the more painful.

The next week they stayed home. Todd was often lost in thought. She knew he had to sort it all out in his own mind and she never pushed anything on him. It was Dirk's arrival to their dorm that brought him down to home base again.

"Todd we need your help with the last pieces of equipment. Can you make these items for me? They would be a great help." Dirk handed him the drawings. Todd took them and looked them over "They shouldn't be hard to manufacture." "Good" Dirk said "I'm sorry your dad didn't get to see all this. He was quite an outdoorsman at one time, but that was many years ago now. I am glad that you and the ones coming in the future will once again live as we should." Dirk smiled and said his goodbyes.

"Todd" Dana said. "What is it?" Todd asked. "I have been meaning to show you these. Your dad had them with him when I found him." She handed him the plans. Todd took them and as he looked Dana could see the amazement come across his face. "Do you know what this is?" Todd asked her. "It's the plans for a house or cabin" Dana answered. "Yes it is" Todd said. "It's for the outside. He has it all planned out. Look here, even notes of things my mom wanted. They must have wanted to build this before the outbreak." "Well I think" Dana said "It might be a good tribute to them if one day it was built." Todd looked at her and a smile crossed his face. "Yes you're right it would be. We could build it. You're wonderful." It was as if new life had been put into him. He grabbed the plans and the ones from Dirk and headed to the manufacturing tier. Dana was happy to see him with something good on his mind again.

The complex was ready to send out Dirk and his two helpers. They all knew what had to be done and that they would be isolated for months when they came back in. The last tools from Todd were the only equipment left to add to the stores in the tunnel to be opened. The people in the complex were apprehensive and excited. If this excursion failed they all knew it would be years before another attempt would be made. The few that knew that the air had been coming in for a long time kept hope that nothing went wrong.

The night before they were to go out, there was a gathering of people. They had a fine meal and plenty of gaiety.

Dana knew Todd would not be over his loss anytime soon, but with work to be done and the work after they went out, it would give him an avenue t work through some of his hurt feelings. She thought about all the time it had taken to get to this point, the hours of work and the frustration. Dern and the others' lives were about to become so much bigger. In some ways it was frightening. It was an immense world and if they were the last survivors it would not be easy. Todd, lost in his thoughts was pained that his father had not made it to see this. The old guard was gone. They saved them all and now they would never know that their young were almost back into the world.

The crowd gathered in the morning to watch the three go into the tunnel. The doors closed behind them and then the outside doors opened. The sun shone into the tunnel and lit it up. They shielded their eyes and the voice contact was kept open. The work started. They prepared the cameras and Dirk stood looking out into the enclosed valley. They did it, they finally did it, and some of them were finally free.

Todd and Dana watched them, when Todd picked up Dern to see he smiled and pointed to Dirk. "Uncle Dirk" clear as a bell came out of him. Dana held his hand "Yes baby it is and one day we will all go there."

The work was now left to those in the communication and science labs. Todd and Dana went home. The big moment was over. Soon they would have time in the sun. They felt good at what they had accomplished; it took years to get there. Satisfied and happy they opened the world for Dern and all those that come after. Dana knew the shadow was over Todd, but knew he would come out of it. Losing someone is never easy. Time would find him filling the void with anything it could. She felt his sadness and it pained her as well.

Todd never seemed to stop amazing her. He came home from work and grabbed her in his arms. "Dana I have thought over many things. First my mom and dad are gone, but they will always be with me. I just have to look at Dern and see my dad looking into myself and feel and see my mom. I will not let their work and sacrifice go. We are going to build that house for them and live in it too. Dern will be one of many to come to live, work and thrive out there where we belong." Dana looked at him and just hugged him "Yes we will."

The days following Todd took Dana and Dern to the communication lab to watch Dirk and the others work. It seemed so anticlimactic for them. They had been out and all this show for the insecure in the complex. Todd thought they were a pampered lot. How were they going to live without the complex? He thought about the times gone by before his mom and dad, when everyone had lived outside. Just the battle with the weather would have been a major obstacle. They had so much to learn and the only satisfaction was it had begun, that was something.

"Todd, Todd!" Dana said. He looked over to her "Yes, what is it?" "You are miles away Todd" He got up and put a hand on her shoulder. "I'll be okay" he smiled. "Let's go home. There is not much here for use to do anyways. It's up to Dirk and his crew to get things done they need to do," He picked up Dern and Dana tucked her arm in his. "It's just the beginning Todd it's started and that's what's important." Todd nodded and they walked towards home.

Dirk had his hands full. The outings in the valley proved fruitful. He was concern about setting up the food chains needed for the captive critters they so long cared for. He was like a child in a candy shop. What should he do first? What insects would be needed to start the whole thing going? He had consulted his partners on the outside about it and they were all in agreement that earthworms would be the first. The bees had already made the adjustment and Dirk had let out a colony of flies, grasshoppers, water bugs, aphids would be followed next spring with lady bugs.

As the crew sat and ate their evening meal they all knew that the world was going to be alive once again. Next year would be a great year, fish and amphibians could be considered maybe some birds whose diet was seeds or bugs. The mice if they survived would allow a set or two of birds of prey maybe a coyote or two. The work to count the numbers progressed continually. Butterflies and moths once they had established, they could consider even more.

Dirks mind wandered to Todd and Dana. They had done it, opened the world again and Dirk could not have been more proud of them. So mush work had been done to get to this point, how more wondrous for all the children now here and to come in the future. They had given life back to them. Next year they would be able to come out, work with the animals would be a bigger part.

The morning arrived and watching the sun rise brought tears to Dirk's eyes. How long it had been to see this and how precious it is. He stared at his partners and watched as they watched also. They were children of the complex, some of the first to witness what almost had been forgotten to most. A simple sunrise such beauty set awe in their hearts and minds.

The mapping of the valley proceeded. Dirk watched his companions marvel at the few clouds that drifted by and point as the birds flew among them. The plant life was doing well the bees had been busy. The sound of the wind passing over the trees always made them look. Dirk was startled at how many of the simplest natural things he had forgotten. Things that many in the complex never even knew existed. Dirk sighed and got back to work. It was work done with pleasure and pride.

By summers end they had completed most of their work. The next few weeks would be spent cataloguing as mush of the flora as they could. It would give the agro tunnels a better idea of what was growing and what could be gown there. Dirk had no desire to return to the locked up complex, but knew he had to. During the quarantine he could study all the data they had collected. Next year they would open the doors. Dirk continued his work and was content with the progress they were making.

Todd found himself frustrated with all of it all. He went to the masons and watched as they worked on the new tunnels and thought, they still didn't get it. Next year the outlook would be to start moving into the outside world. He never spoke as he stood there watching them. The frustration grew and he decided to go to the library. Maybe Simion had written something that might help.

Dana worried for Todd, he was not himself. It had been many months since his father passed and he had been brooding ever since. Dern was walking, talking and never missed anything. He might be able to heal wounds of the body, but the wounds of the soul that was another story. Dern had turned into a thoughtful soul. He managed to intervene in arguments at the right times and the people arguing seemed to see how foolish they were being. The other gifted children blended into society and found they were accepted even if they possessed gifts.

Dana sat in her rocking chair watching Dern play and her mind wandered over all that had happened. She was getting older and although she was relieved they were finally going to get out of the complex the hard work would be up to the young. Dern's life would be the adventure now more than hers and Todd's. They would finish what she, Todd and the others had started. Soon she would be too old to carry the torch. Then she laughed to herself that wouldn't be for sometime yet. She might be in her midlife, but that was that. She smiled. Now where is Todd she thought? Then she wondered how Dirk was, they would be coming in soon for their confinement. She pitied and envied Dirk. He was outside only to return in here. He must have seen many things in his life having been a founder and lived everywhere before outside, to be locked up for over thirty five years now. To have freedom tickling his senses, but not yet almost a torture she thought.

"Hi sweetie, I was just wondering where you had gone to" Dana said. "I've been in the library. Well first I was watching them dig a new tunnel." He made his way to Dern who like always reached to be picked up, Todd obliged. Dana sat in her chair and watched them. "I wanted to find out if Simion had anything to say on things and as usual, he did." "Oh really" Dana said. "Let me make some coffee and you can tell me all about it." Todd nodded.

By the time coffee was ready Todd was bursting at the seams to talk. "Dana I must have been so awful to live with this past while." Dana smiled "I love you Todd. I can't force you to come to terms with things in your heart and mind. I can only be there and give you the room to sort it out for yourself." Todd put his hands over hers. "While I was watching them dig that tunnel I could have screamed why you persist in all this. I decided to see what Simion might have to say on it. Seems he knew a lot about human nature. Anyways he wrote of people in general. How work was good therapy and if it seems futile to some, to those doing the work it gave them purpose. I sat thinking about it and he was right. What are all these people going to do when the doors open? I always thought that it might be a great migration out, but now I'm not so sure. What was it Rose said? They have everything they need here and she was right, they do. It will be Dern and his generation that will begin the journeys. They will be the ones to brave the world again." Well" Dana said "I hope that doesn't include us. I want to see what's out there." She stood looking at him. Todd smiled. "Well you won't be alone and beside we have a cabin to build." Dana smiled Todd was back, he was himself again.

Todd spent many hours in the workshop designing and putting together the plans to build the cabin. The secret outings through the tunnel had him venturing further and further down the mountains into the woods below. Dana spent most of her time with Dern, but she too accompanied him on some trips.

Fall had come and with it the cold. Dirk and the others were to come in and slowly they filled the tunnel with everything they had. Dirk was insistent that the outside remain as it was when they found it. The last few days were spent cleaning up the area. Other than a few cameras they had installed, the area was to be left as pristine as possible. Dirk was satisfied that he had started enough food chains for the next release of larger animals. He smiled to himself; life would come back to the outside. They valley was so enclosed and the mountains were so high other than a horrific hurricane, everything that was there would stay. The birds may not, but so be it that was their nature.

With the closing of the outside door Dirk and the others sighed at the thought of their confinement. It didn't take long for all the medical tests to be done. They waited to find out that nothing had changed. There would be tests conducted weekly to make sure they had not been affected by anything outside.

During the time they spent there the information gathered was studied. The information was then sent to each tunnel and anything that could be helpful to them. The visitors came and many asked what it was like outside. Dirk listened to his companions try to explain the awe they felt. He smiled to himself knowing before long they would see for themselves. Although they were in confinement and enclosed in a Plexiglas room, the people of the complex came often. Dirk note it was the young and children the most. The middle aged and the older never came. He was old now and knew it was beginning curiosity would drive them to seek out the world that had been so maliciously taken away in the first place. His mind felt at ease he could leave the world now and feel like he had done something for the generations to come.

Todd, Dana, Dern and Dirks children came to see him everyday. The understanding with Todd and Dana of how things really were, were never pressed upon. Todd kept things light in the conversations while they both knew the true reality. Dana patiently stood by the two men. Her thoughts were often about Dern and how his life would be. She marvelled at the plans Todd had drawn of his father and mother's dream cabin. Todd was beginning to be happy again, this pleased her.

It was several months before the three came out of their confinement. When the time came it was with some fan fare. A lot of people came and when they had been cleared of all the effects that might be outside the doors to the confinement were opened. The vacuum seal was broken and they were free. Dirk was happy and went to the animal tunnels with his children. The others sought out their homes too. They were glad to be back in the fold of the only people they had known all their lives.

It didn't take long for a council meeting to be called. It was not to be the old meeting, but a public meeting. With the outside now available to all, it was decided that all should have votes. Meetings continued for weeks. The fears of the people seemed to be smoothed with the research provided.

Winter had set in and no one had any plans or desires to brave the outside during the cold and snow. Dirk raised his concerns about too many going out until the food chains had been firmly established. They would not find the world a place of wonder until the animals could be established.

Todd was frustrated with Dirk, but in his heart he knew he was right. "We are so close now" Dana said "Just think this year, maybe next we can freely walk out those doors and start a whole new journey" he told her. He put his arm over her shoulder and they walked home.

Dern was well aware of what was going on and was now in school learning more. His mind was like a big sponge absorbing everything. Although he never talked much at school he out did himself with Dirk and any other adult he could talk with. Dern was wise beyond his years. Dana often wondered if it had something to do with his gift.

It was just before spring that Dern arrived at home from school. He was full of questions about other gifted children. "Mom, how come the gifts are different?" he asked. "Which one is the better gift and how come not all the kids have them?" Finally he said "I'm not sure I want to be different. I think I want to be the same as everyone else."

Dana stared at him for a moment. "Come sit with me Dern." The two sat together on the couch. "First off, we don't know why any of you got the gifts, but you did. It has something to do with DNA, the very thing that makes us who we are. Each DNA is different that's what makes us boys and some girls. It's more involved then that. Your DNA is half mine and half your dad's, in that mix you became. Now as far as your gift goes, it's just that, a gift. Not all have it and it's precious. It should not be taken lightly. Do you remember when Rose was hurt and you helped her?" Dern nodded. "Had you not had your gift Rose most likely would have died. It was the fact that you were there and had your gift that Rose is with us today." "I guess that's good. I like Rose she's so nice" Dern said. "Now, the different gifts, I'm not sure why they are different or what all the gifts are. Since not all the children have them we simple don't know. You're not different from the other children you just have an extra ability like some children can draw more clearly then others or sing sweeter or swim better. It's the same. Does that help at all my little man?"

Dern sat for a moment his brow furrowed then he smiled and said "I think you are right" and he got up from the couch. "I want to go see Dirk. Can I mom?" Dana looked at him and nodded. "You be back soon. Dirk is getting on in years and doesn't need the 50 million question drill, Okay?" Dern wasted no time in leaving. Dana often wondered how he saw himself. The picture was beginning to take form.

Todd arrived home from the construction tunnel. He was full of dust and dirt and headed straight for the shower.

Dana had a nice dinner ready and before Todd was finished in the shower Dern too was back. "You weren't gone long" Dana said to him. "Dirk was tired, he's resting they said." Dana was sure he would be. Todd now showered ate like a starving man. They had their dinner gone in no time. Dern cleared the table. For a man of 6 years old he seemed so much older.

The three relaxed and found comfort in their own company.

When Dern was asleep Todd told Dana that he had been looking at the cabin. He thought it might be a lot of work to build, just the lumber alone that had to be cut. He wondered if maybe he had bitten off more than he could chew.

"Well we won't be building much for some time yet. Dirk is right about setting up some food chains first. Until the animals can survive on their own it doesn't make sense to go and damage their chances. We need to think beyond our valley if we want to go back into the world. Once things are surviving well there we can set more things free through our door." Dana smiled. "You know Dana I can taste the freedom, catching small pieces of it through the back door isn't enough anymore" Todd told her. "I know what you mean Todd, but we are so close now.

"So often I have thought about sneaking out for a week or more, but someone would miss us if we were gone that long." Todd knew she was right. "I have dreams I want to realize and they are out there" Todd told her. "Well" Dana said "I have a few you well know, but I would endanger the chance now. It's too close to becoming a reality. If he's out there I want to give it my best shot in looking for him."

Todd had always kept hope for her, but it was fading as each founder passed away. If they didn't find him soon chances were against ever finding him. After all this time he should have been able to make it back. Everything he read or heard from the founders told him that he was a resourceful man. Zack would have found his way here, time was against them. Todd kept his thoughts to himself, but knew Dana must have thought the same thing.

Sleep found them, but it was not an easy peaceful sleep. Both knew and felt they were on the verge of new beginnings not only for themselves but for everyone in the complex.

The winter passed slowly. The anticipation for all that they might venture out was on everyone's mind. Some saw themselves as explorers, others wanted to study everything. There were even conversations about the stars and a telescope was dug out of deep storage. Several council meetings had been called. Dirk still adamant about animal release and making sure they were well established before too much human occupation took place. It had been decided that the valley would be kept as close to pristine as possible not just for the animals but for security as well. If there were still people out there they may be hostile, not by nature but by the need to survive. The existence of the complex must remain a secret. Of course this would limit any excursions outside by the masses until scouts had searched the valley and beyond t ensure their safety.

Dirk had been working all winter and the release of many more animals was on the agenda. Each set of things setting up the chain for the larger animals above them. He had spent many hours with scientist working on the insects. There were many more that needed to be released. He decided on turtles, mice, snakes, spiders, damsel flies and grasshoppers. Frogs would have to wait until the bugs were more plentiful. It was an ominous undertaking as Dirk sat at his desk surrounded by all his paperwork. How he missed Carla and her efficiency at keeping things in order. He missed her and was getting tired of being without her. He sat all night putting things in proper order.

When morning came Mark and Ann came to see if their dad was coming into the animal tunnels with them. Dirk never stirred at his desk when they approached. When they reached him they knew he was no longer with them. He was the last founder; the few others had gone this past winter before him.

Mark and Ann saw to him and knew how much they would miss him. Within the day everyone knew of Dirk's passing. It was felt by all, the last founder was gone. All the leadership and guidance now fell on the shoulders of the children. The era of their lives were beginning as he passed on. There was no one alive now that had seen the world as it had been before. It was thought by some to be a great tragedy and by some; the ones that had confined them to the complex were gone. Dirk had carried their blame for letting the virus in to give peace to them all. Some remembered but most were born after.

Dirk's service was long and ceremonial. It was straining for Mark and Ann. Todd and Dana stayed while the masons sealed him into the tomb beside Carla.

When they finally made it home afterwards it was so hard not to cry. They would miss Dirk and each had many reasons why. Dern had been there and Dana was worried about how it would affect him. She knew she could not withhold the truth from him. Passing was part of life, most hoped and prayed it came later rather than sooner.

Dana felt more alone again, but was thankful for Todd and Dern. Todd felt the same had he not had them his life would have been much different.

Mark and Ann had been given time to mourn, but then the council was called. There was much debate on the recommendations Dirk had left, would they be followed? If not out of respect for him or it was a viable plan or until a better on could be found. Small scouting parties were to go out in the spring and the completion of the food chains were to be done, for most of it was not upsetting the environment. The outside world was not going anywhere, but for a few the longer it took the less chance Dana and Todd would have to try and find out if her father was still out there.

That night at home Dana rocked in her chair. She was lost in thought about her father. Todd entertained Dern and she found comfort in the companionship they shared. She wondered why she never had more children. Things worked out the way they do she thought, having Dern was a great gift and she was satisfied. She imagined Zack, her father there enjoying the moment as she was. Then she thought of Dirk and tears weld in her eyes. They are all gone she thought and probably her father as well. What a shame she never got to know her parents.

She got up from her chair deciding it did no good to dwell on it and made hot chocolate for them all. Once Dern was in bed they spent the evening conversing. Todd always her friend decided to work out a plan to search for the others when the doors were opened. Until then they would have to be satisfied with the small escapes they could make through the secret tunnel.

The idea of letting more bugs into the valley beyond was one way of letting Zack know he had to be coming closer to the complex. He would follow the concentration and it was another small hope.

The spring came and went as did the winter. It was several passing of the seasons before the council was called to open the doors. There was great fanfare and the doors were opened.

"Finally" Todd said and Dana smiled. They had made plans to go and spend some time outside as did many others. Many people that ventured out the doors and the sun shone on them for the first time in their lives. Its brightness made them shield their eyes and the warmth was felt on their creamy white skin. Most did not like the brightness and many didn't like the openness. The wind when it blew took their breath away. For lots, the outside was not where they wanted to be, but that was a personal choice each was free to make for them self.

Todd and Dana took Dern out to stay out and camp for a week. With packs loaded they ventured into the valley. Dern followed closely behind them. It was his first experience with them beyond the tunnels. At first he found himself completely startled and anxious. Soon he was delighted with the plants and fresh air. When he discovered bugs and birds living free he was thrilled.

They had hiked for a few hours when they decided to make camp. It was fun trying to set up the tent and the day slipped into evening. They started a small fire and ate the food they brought. When the night was well upon them they lay on their backs looking into the heavens. They counted shooting stars and watched for passing satellites. Dern as always had questions about everything. Todd and Dana answered what they could and let him ponder the others. The fresh air was sweet and Dern soon found the day had caught up to him and he slept.

Todd and Dana lay together for a long time staring into the vastness of space. It occurred to Dana how small they really were and how big the world was. It would be some time before they would be ready to travel anywhere in the wilderness.

"We did it Todd. The doors are open. No more sneaking and hiding" Dana said. "Yes too bad my father and Dirk missed it, but we are free. Do you know that, really free." They smiled at each other, yes they were free. The world awaited them and although they were not young it made no difference. They would have it to explore, discover and reclaim what had been taken away from them all.

The following day found them enjoying the valley. Many wonders caught them. Dern was in awe of everything. He was more comfortable now. The sound of the wind in the trees almost made music Dana thought. The sounds were so different sometimes the leaves rustled or and through the pines or washed against the grasses that whispered softly. Then cracks of wood sticks being broken as the deer walked over them. Todd watched the clouds drift by and was comforted by the warmth of the sun. The tunnels were still home, but he could get used to this out here he thought.

Dern watched his mom and dad and wondered at their ease. They showed no fear of the outside like some of the others. Dana sketched pictures and Todd looked at the timber growing. The complex was getting short of wood and now they could harvest some. Everything was going to be okay now and they were happy for it.

The cabin was still in the back of Todd's mind, but to his dismay he had not found a site here in the valley yet.

The next day it rained and yet they were not alarmed, everything drank the moisture in. The ground sucked it in like it had never drunk before. The air was warm and Todd had to get Dana to come into the tent. She wandered about letting herself get soaked with it. After she dried off she smiled. "It's wondrous I shall never forget these days, ever" she said to her two men. Todd looked at her and frowned. Dern smiled. "Seems to me all you did was get soaking wet" Todd said. "Maybe so, but it was glorious and I think you should get as you put it soaking wet to" Dana replied and Dern smiled.

They all broke into laughter and the rest of the day was spent watching and listening to the rain.

"Well I can see why the cabin was so important to your mom and dad. I fear that to live in the elements could challenge anyone" Dana said. "Did grandpa live out here mom?" Dern asked. "Yes long ago before the viruses were let go, everyone did." "I have learned a lot about things, but I always thought it was long before grandpa" Dern said. "I have lived my whole life in the complex" Dana told him "We worked many years to be able to once again live out here" she smiled at him. "What was wrong with the complex? Dern said. "There's nothing wrong with it, but we are not meant to live there forever. It was built to be a haven until it was safe to come back into the world" Dana replied. "Why did they kill everything?" Dern asked. "Did they want everyone to die?" Dana looked at Todd "I don't think it was like that Dern" Todd told him. "Let's see if I can explain it to you. The outside world had billions of people living in it and with all those people things became unimportant to them. Not all things, but they took a lot for granted. The outside world was forgotten as their home, it became things that could be bought or sold. It created greed in them. Some wanted more and more, taking from those that could not defend themselves. Finally some decided if they killed the people that had things they wanted they could take the things. In their foolishness they created a virus to aide them in killing. What they did not realize was others did the same. The viruses joined together and almost killed all of them, the ones that wanted to take and the ones that were being taken from. Everyone lost, every living thing almost died. Simion built a haven to protect those he could, the animals too. Now almost half a century later we can start to rebuild what was lost. Although it will never be what it was we can make the world our home once again."

Dern looked at him "The teacher told us that some survived. Do you know where they are?" "No we don't and if they did they would not have all we did in the Haven. We have to learn how to live out here again. Just like now and soon we want to start looking to see if we can find them." Todd smiled. "Your life will be so different from ours and in many ways I envy you that." He looked at Dern and smiled again. It was a lot for someone so young to understand, but hiding the truth would not help him.

The rain stopped and the sun soon had dried up the moisture. They spent the afternoon exploring and the evening talking of all they saw around the fire.

The week was over and they headed back to the haven, full of stories about what they saw. Going back wasn't as awful for Todd and Dana. They knew they would be venturing out again very soon. They left the area as they found it and nature would reclaim the small area they had disturb before long.

When they arrived at the complex it was buzzing with all the new news from those that had ventured out. Each had a story and those that wish to hear did so enthusiastically.

There were regular council meetings now; everything was discussed about the two worlds becoming one. Until the members of the Haven were completely sure of no survivors outside, no permanent structures were permitted. Todd was not pleased. He was of the opinion the council was holding them to the complex. Although strangers could pose a threat it was not yet apparent. He and Dana, the older members now of the complex joined with the many others working on the repopulation of varied species outside. They still had the work for the complex to do as well.

All fell into a rhythm and during the next passing years they had released many different animals. It was Todd and Dirk's children that pressed to start the release program beyond their enclosed valley. The council finally relented and as in the beginning the insects were first.

Dern now a teenager had become very familiar with their valley and wanted to join training for a scout team position. With his gift he would be an asset. Children with gifts that applied were trained for first encounters. The ones with the gift of thought some had the ability to tell if one spoke the truth or not. Dern's ability was as a healer. They would be the elite teams and the council made no objections to them being search teams. Dern took the training very seriously. He knew that if an accident happened his team members depended on him. He relished the responsibility and although he knew his gift was important the gift of thought maybe the earliest warning. Being able to sense others thoughts was a definite asset. The ones that had this gift could not read ones thoughts just sense others around them. Two gifted could share bonding, but only if both had the gift.

Dern had met a young girl that like him could heal. They found many things to talk about and learn from each other. Dern liked her, but he was more interested in scouting and learning how to use his gift to the best of his ability.

Tamara was 2 years younger than Dern and looked up to him. It was Dern that helped her heal a young woman with child that had fainted and fractured her skull in the fall. The two shared a bond that at the moment was unique. It would soon grow into something neither would have expected. It was Dern that discovered an alarming fact during his studies. There were less and less children being born. The medical staff had been aware of the falling birth rates, but the entire tests showed nothing.

It was over dinner that Dern told Todd and Dana what he had discovered. He was surprised to see it was not a total shock to them. They seemed to be aware of it. The medical labs had now been in contact with the science labs. All that could be discovered was that the virus was mutating again. "Did you know about this?" Dern asked. "Yes we have been aware of this possibility for many years now" Dana told him. "Well" Dern said "Are we doomed to extinction after all?" He looked directly at his mom and dad. "We don't know. We have managed to overcome many obstacles; this is just another hurdle along the way." Dern was not unaware of what no children being born meant. They just had to wait and see what would happen.

"When the virus first got into the complex we lost a lot of people. It was a hard time, many children had to work and learn what was needed to be done in order for all of us to survive. It was not easy" Dana told him. "Dern" Dana asked "When you heal women can you tell if, well, have children?" Dana asked him. "It doesn't work like that. I just follow the flow of life and untangle the disturbances in it. I can't explain it" Dern said. "Don't worry I'm just looking for all possibilities is all" Dana said. "Mom, do you think we are the last?" Dern asked.

It was Todd that spoke "Life has many ways of changing to meet all challenges. Don't worry son it will prevail again." Dern found comfort in his words and relaxed more.

Council meetings had brought up the facts and once again fear set upon the people of the complex. Some blamed the opening of the doors; it was soon put to rest by the council. Whether the doors were opened or not the virus still would have mutated. Again time was against them.

Tamara and Dern found themselves thrown together more and more. It didn't take forever for them to find that they enjoyed each others company. Todd and Dana liked Tamara and knew Dern loved her even if he didn't know it.

Time passed slowly and although the outside world was coming alive, the world within the complex had a doomed aura that hung over it.

Dern and Tamara worked outside a lot and Dern marvelled at her lust for life. He was amazed at the tenderness she showed for everything alive. It gave Dern a far more powerful insight into human compassion then most. It was during a scouting expedition that she had come across a squirrel that had fallen from a tree. Tamara had no trouble healing the poor little creature and he watched her set it free. "Tam what do you think about the future?" Dern asked her. "I try to just live and do my best" she said. "It's all you really can do" she added. Dern took in her words as he watched her. Tamara was not a beautiful woman, but not plain either. She had her hair cropped short and had brown eyes. Her hands were small and so were her feet. She was not as tall as Dern and had a slim figure. She moved with an easy grace through the woods and Dern was becoming more and more attracted to her. She was a good solid person not given to silly fanciful things most young women her age were. It probably had something to do with her gift and no one knew more than she did about how it felt or worked.

"Tam" he said again "Have you ever thought about the fact we might be the last of our species?" Dern said to her. "Dern" she said "Life is to be lived. If we are the last then we are. Look around you life is everywhere around us. I can't believe any idea that it's coming to an end" she said. "What's troubling you Dern" Tam asked him. "I just never though about it all ending, with no children being born it is just futile in some ways. Take us for instance, before all this I wished, well wanted us to be together. Now without the promise of the future it doesn't seem right" Dern said to her.

Tamara stopped in her tracks and turned and looked at him. She sat down right where she was and Dern looked at her. "What are you doing?" Dern asked. "I'm not going on, what's the point? I might as well sit here until death finds me." Dern's eyes opened wide. "Point taken" Dern said and sat down beside her. "Tam I want to tell you something. You are the only woman I have ever known that I think understands me. Maybe it has something to do with our gifts, but that's the truth. Many times I have wanted to ask you, well to be my other half." Tam looked at him "I think I'm in love with you." He said "You think" she replied. Dern looked at her. "We have been close friends for so long Dern. I have wanted you to be so much more and you finally say something and it's I think. Well let me tell you I know and until you do this conversation is over." Tamara got up and brushed herself off.

Dern was up and grabbed her hand "Tam I know" and he pulled her to him and kissed her. That was it they would not be separate beings again. It didn't take long for them to tell their parents. It brought joy to more than one home in the complex.

The work continued for those running the complex. The scientist and the med labs were working to find the reason no children were born, but for all their efforts they found nothing. The women all seemed fine and the men functional. It was a problem that had to be resolved if life was to continue.

Dern and Tamara had often been pressed upon t heal people but there was nothing they could do. The repopulation of the next valley with insects and small animals continued. The scouting teams had travelled for weeks around their valley and found nothing to indicate anyone was out there. No sign what so ever. Each expedition came back with the same news. Dana was always there waiting to hear.

Todd and she went to watch the monitors still. It had been done for so long it was part of their daily lives. Dern was missed immensely by her until he was back. She always harboured a sickly fear he would not return one day. Todd had not given up the dream of building the cabin, but it seemed to become more distant with the passage of time.

When Dern was away scouting Todd and Dana spent the days they were not working enjoying the outside. It was a victory and sweet for them both. Often they would picnic and just enjoy the days outside together. They had found a lovely spot near a grove of trees by the stream. Dana often chose this spot. She watched the birds and butterflies and listened to the frogs.

Dana had finished her day early in the tailor shop. She hurried home hoping to find Dern had made it back. He hadn't come home yet. Todd arrived later and Dana had a lovely dinner. After he showered and changed he sat at the table with her. It was the first time he say the grey hairs on her head. "Dana I have to admit I do so love you." Dana looked at him "So what has you so sweet tonight?" "Oh I have just had a good day; come to think of it I have had a good life with you" he told her. "Well don't make it sound like it's almost over" she smiled at him.

They ate their dinner and Todd helped her clear the dishes away. Dana made tea and they sat in their chairs. "Dana have you had the life you wanted with me?" Todd asked her. She smiled "Never could have been better off" she answered him. "It's been an interesting one at that. Look at all the things we have accomplished" she said. Todd nodded "Not to mention the secrets we have had" they thought mostly of the tunnel and smiled. "I guess Dern will want to marry Tamara" Todd said. "Yes I don't doubt it. The match is a good one they suit each other" Dana replied. "I must admit they do at that" Todd answered. "I wish I could have found your father for you" Todd told her. Dana smiled "Todd no one could have done more or worked as hard as you to that aim for me. I fear he has left this world and I have always known that is the most likely course that life could have taken. I am not unhappy I think even though most of our life we had to be locked in this mountain it has been a sanctuary as well." Todd smiled. Dern's life will be different and I think that's a blessing. I just hope that whatever is stopping the young from bearing children will right itself. There have been no children for nearly three years now and that has been a concern to me" Dana said. "Dana I just can't believe this life long struggle for the lives of all have been in vain" Todd told her.

"I'm tired tonight think I will soak in a hot tub." Todd watched her walk into the bedroom and sighed. He leaned back into his chair and was soon asleep.

Dana had filled the tub, her gaze caught sight of the stones they had brought out of the cave. She wondered if she should tell Dern. There were so many things she wanted to talk to him about. She took off her ring. It was the same ring her mother Dee wore when she wed Zack. She climbed into the tub and remembered Rainie saying how much she loved her bubble baths. Where was Dern she thought? Dana, stop worrying she thought. She soaked for an hour or so and got out. She didn't feel tired and decided to go watch the monitors.

After she dressed she found Todd asleep in his chair and decided to let him sleep. He always worked so hard.

She walked through the complex and watched the people. The playground had children, but it was not the same without the babies and toddlers. Dana walked around the living area and stared at the founders statues. She said a small prayer at the end and wished they had been alive to see the doors open again.

She headed to the communications lab. Erik was there "Hey there Dana" he said. Dana smiled "Anything Erik?" she asked. "No nothing I must admit the new camera gives a better look at the valley" he said. "Are you glad the doors are open Erik?" "Yes and No, yes because it would have happened sooner or later and it has given hope and joy in more than one family. I'm sure the world will be a better place" Erik told her. "Okay that's the yes why the no?" Dana asked. "Paperwork, paperwork, paperwork and more paperwork" Erik said and frowned and the both laughed. "How are Gwen and Katrina?" Dana asked. "Gwen is good; she says she's getting old. She has some trouble getting going in the mornings. I think she should go to the med labs, but she won't. Katrina and Robert have been trying for a child, but with no luck as yet. How is Dern?" Erik asked. "And Todd" he asked. "Dern is fine. He's grown into such a nice young man" Dana told him. "Todd is having a nap at home. He is getting to be more like his dad all the time." Erik smiled. "You two have been a bright light for the complex all these years and I am happy I have had the good fortune to know you" Erik said. "How do you see the world now?" he asked Dana. "With the doors open so many possibilities have been opened" Erik added. "If children are not born soon we may have less time then we want" Dana said. "Well" Erick said "I'm on my way home. Hope tonight is your night on the monitors" Erik told her and left.

Dana watched them, all static. Maybe she should give it up. There were no founders left and her father would not have had the life they did here. She got up and went home.

Todd was still sleeping in his chair and she quietly crawled back into bed. She found sleep and with it emotional peace.

Dern and his companions had travelled further than on normal missions. They travelled well through the forest, each stepped where the ones before had. "Nothing there, there was nothing; we had better start heading back" Dern spoke to them all. "I agree" Tamara said. "They'll be worried about us, we should have reported in yesterday." "We'll never find people if we don't look" Dern replied. "So what would you do if you found someone Dern?" Tam teased him. Dern just looked at her "Nothing, probably just watch them then return my findings to the complex" he said. Tam smiled "Quick escape" she taunted. "That's enough you two" Mike said. Both turned quiet. Dern was ticked off by Tam. "Why did she torment him so?"

When they stopped to rest Tam went to him. "I'm sorry Dern. I don't mean to tease you I'm just covering up for my own fear." Dern smiled "You afraid, I doubt that." "No it's true really. When you're out here sometimes I feel so alone. There is nothing, no birds or animals just wind. It whispers its remorse for the world in its branches." Dern had no doubt now she was freaked out about being to far away from the complex. "Tam you have to think of it different. No as a sad thing but more rejoice. The wind is not sorrowful, but welcoming the rustling of the leaves calling the creatures it senses to them. Opening its great arms to hold them tight for they have been gone too long." "You like it out there don't you?" she said. "Yes I guess I do. I want to see as much of it as I can; go everywhere, learn every valley and each grove of trees. I want to breathe the fresh air; smell the sweet grass in the meadows; everything feels so alive not like the cold stone of the complex."

They were on the move again. They followed the stream, it was slow moving and Dern stopped to throw stones into it. "We will be home soon" Dern told her "Just over the ridge, over the mountains; four days at the most." "I'll be glad to be back, hot water and soft bed. Clean clothes too" Tam said. Dern smiled, he knew she was feeling better. Mike took too many samples he knew his mom would be very disappointed if he didn't. Petra stayed in the tunnels when they opened the doors. She ventured out, but found it too alarming to her tastes. Even though Mike's father Ian had been lost in the cave-in Petra still clung to her plants in the agro tunnels. She always took his samples into the labs away from her own gardens. She had a few plots of growing things outside, but nothing of real consequence yet. Mike was married to Lilith and no children yet. Mike could always tell if you were being truthful. He was very matter of fact. Dern always believed it was because of his gift.

The three of them stopped for lunch. The trek from here on in would be hard so they needed to eat before they continued" If there are people it's not likely they are close. We have been all over these valleys and nothing, no sign at all" Mike told them. "I always thought they would have stayed near the cities" Dern said. "I don't think so" Mike said. "With all the death they would have congregated elsewhere. Food would be a major issue. If they survived the first few years it's possible they are out there somewhere now." Dern looked at Tam "How days travel to the nearest old time town do you think?" Tam studied the maps of the old territory "On foot I would say at least a month or two that's being lucky. The worlds a big place out there, we havent even searched 2 miles around our valley and we have searched for a month now, I have noticed some insects; bees more than others, but they are migrating into the valleys and that's a positive." Tam smiled. They finished eating and Mike made sure no sign of them stopping was apparent.

Dern watched as Tamara's spirits got brighter as they got closer to home. He would ask her to marry him when they got back.

Mike continued to gather samples and Dern put the lay of the land to his memory. He would be an adventurer; he would learn all this area. When they reached the rise to the valley is was getting dark. They knew that climbing in the dark was foolish and made a camp.

There was still a chill in the air. Tam sat close and slept close to Dern. He could smell her softness he thought. She was warm and he didn't mind her there at all.

Dawn came with its orange pink hues. It was beautiful, but it was also a sign that poor weather was on the way. With still a days travel ahead the thought of being soaking wet was not on the top of the list for any of them.

After a meal they cleared the area they had slept in and wee on the move. Mike had noticed more insects although not in great numbers they were there. When they reached the meadow before the final climb to the complex valley it was profuse with flowers. Tam was stunned at its beauty and the fragrance. It would have been more brilliant if the sun had shown, but the sky was overcast. Humidity was high and in the distance flashes of lightning were seen. Dern liked it. It was frightening yet thrilling at the same time. He took a deep breath and thought how much his mom and dad would like it here. They had worked so hard to open the doors.

Now he understood why. What amazed him the most is that they never had been outside and yet they had the insight to know it was where they should be.

When he was a child he would listen to them talk of the founders and how they saved them from the virus. He missed Dirk. He was the only founder he knew and it was not for long enough. "Dern" Tam said to him! "What Tam, sorry I was lost in thought." He glanced over to her. "I was just saying do you think it will be long before we live outside. I mean everyone in the complex?" "I'm not sure it might be years yet. We are not sure if people survived and if they did what are they like?" he told her.

Then mike said "I can not see many wanting to leave the safety of the complex Tam. We still have to conceal the fact we are there. What if the people have turned to killing each other for what the want or need? We really don't want a war on our hands." "Well" Tam said "I think if they survived they would have to have had to work together. Killing what might the few left doesn't sound smart. If you think about it they would have to depend on each other. I think the council might be wrong there, but that's my opinion" Tam said. "You might be right" Dern said. "But don't you want to be sure before we let them know we are there?" Mike looked at both of them "I don't think they survived. We have scouted all summer and I have yet to see anything. They probably all starved. I have seen no smoke in the sky, no human element anywhere as of yet." Tam and Dern looked at him. They knew he was close to the truth. All they could do was hope someday they would find them.

When they arrived at the complex many were relieved. They were a week overdue. Dana was waiting for Dern when he got out of the briefing. When he saw her he smiled. Dana knew he was fine. It was to be the last scouting party sent out this year. The doors were closed to the people for the winter, but plans and studies still were to be done this winter.

"Well" Dana said "find anything?" she inquired. "Nothing mom, not a sign anywhere; we hiked far beyond our given area too" Dern told her. Dana nodded. "So how are things going with Tam?" she asked. Dern smiled. "She's fine mom. I don't know about her. She can make me so angry at her" Dern told her. This time Dana smiled. "Where's dad?" Dern asked. "He's still in the machine shop." "Is he still working on grandpa's cabin?" Dern looked at Dana. "They won't let him build it you know. They don't want any sign of us out there" Dern told her. "Yes I know, but it won't always be that way and his plans will be viable for the future" Dana told him. "I don't know mom from what I have seen we are all that's left. I can't see many moving to the outside when everything they need is here." "They will Dern this has been a home and sanctuary for many years, but we are meant to be out there. Once we are more assured of it folks will go."

They reached home and Dern went for a shower and Dan started dinner. She was glad to have Dern back it worried her when he was scouting. "Did Mike get many samples for Petra'" she asked when he appeared from the shower. "Yeah they have lots of things to do this winter. The insects are moving too. I think next spring reptiles and a few others can start being released out there. I am surprised the birds have not gone further" Dern told her. "They have just started to be released Dern. They will need time to discover their food sources. With the insects moving it will help." "It's quiet out there at times. Other than the wind blowing, all I can hear was my own breathing and my heart pounding. I wonder what it will be like in a hundred years from now." Dern said. "Noisy" Dana answered and they both laughed.

Todd arrived not too long after and his face widened with a smile when he saw Dern home. "Well son it's good to see you back" Todd said. Dern smiled "Good to be back." "Well anything?" Todd asked. Dern shook his head "No, nothing not a sign anywhere." "Let's keep our hopes up. We'll find someone someday." Todd looked over to Dana, he could see her sadness. Although he long thought the search futile he tried to keep her dream alive." "How are you and Tam getting on?" Todd asked him. "I'm not sure. She can make me so angry one minute and the next I want to hold her forever" Dern told him. Todd smiled "Sounds like most women" he said. Dana looked at him. "Really" she said and they laughed.

There was a knock at the door; it was Dana's step brother Carl and his wife Rose. After the hugs and welcomes they sat for tea.

"What's up?" Dana asked. It was Rose that let out the news. "Well" she said. "Dean and Nedera have been trying to have a child for sometime and finally they are" Rose smiled. "Oh my goodness" Dana said. "This is good news. This will be the first child in years, how wonderful." "Yes we are so excited. They didn't want to say anything. I think they were afraid something will go wrong" Rose said. "If they are with child then they are the first in a long time" Dana said. "It will be fine, no others have even become with child" Dana added. Rose looked at her "Dear and Nedera said something to me that I thought was odd. They said they can dream with him. They know it's a male child and they talk to him in a dream. I don't understand their gifts at all." If they said they can communicate with the child then it's true. They can communicate with the child, it has the gift of thought" Dana said to her.

"Well I think it's great" Dern said "It solves a problem of mine as well." Dana and Rose looked at him. "I can ask Tam to marry me now. I would not have asked her had I believed we were the last, but now this has brought great hope." "This is great news" Todd said. "Seems we are in for a celebration soon; a wedding and a birth."

The rest of the evening they spent talking of the future. It seemed once again life prevailed and there would be one.

It didn't take Dern long to find Tam. She was in the library researching the fauna that at one time lived outside in the area they had been travelling. She was very interested in repopulating the world of animals.

When Dern caught up with her she was very involved in the intricate food chains, how every animal depended on the other. She was surprised at how many insects they had to let go to sustain the higher forms. Dern watched and soon Tam had him interested. They spent the best part of the day before hunger drove Dern to drag her away from the books and monitors to go eat. Dern knowing it was going to be possible now with luck to have children had a new prospective on living and now the outside became a far more wondrous place.

When they reached the living area they sat at a table nearer to the statues of the founders. "You are being very mysterious" Tama said to him. "Let me get some dinner for us and I'll explain" he told her with a wink. Soon he returned with a tray of food. "Okay tell me what's up" Tam looked at him. "First" Dern said "I want to ask you a few things.

Would you ever consider living away from the complex in the outside world?" Tam was almost stunned by the question. "I have never thought too much about it" she replied. "How far away did you mean?" she asked. "Far enough that the complex would not have to fear us living out there" Dern said. "Well that's a tall order Dern" Tam told him. "Tam I would like you to marry me and I want to build a cabin outside far enough so the complex would not be affected. It would be a great place for researching" Dern told her. Tam looked at Dern "Did you just ask me to marry you?" she said. "Yes Tam I did. I love you and have for some time. Would be so generous as to become my bride?" Tams eyes welled with tears. "Why did you wait so long to ask me Dern? Of course I will."

She up and they embraced in a hug, soft and loving. Dern held her face and kissed her. "There's news I must tell you. Dean and Nedera are going to have a child." Tam looked at him. "They didn't want to say anything so we have to keep this to ourselves" Dern told her. "Dern there will be children again this is wonderful news" Tam said. "It's why I never asked you sooner to marry me. If we were to be the last alive I just couldn't with that lingering hope that maybe, you could have children" Dern kissed her. "You should have still asked me you know. What if I don't want to have babies? I still would have wanted to share my life with you." "You are a special person Tam, I think I would have sooner or later, but with the new hope for the future it just made things right again." "Let's go tell your mom and dad Dern then mine. I'm busting to share the news." Dern tucked her hand into his and they headed out to share the fact they were to be married. The dinner was forgotten for the moment.

Chapter 37

The nights were coming sooner as fall slowly slipped away.

West and Willow found the warmth of the cabin comforting as the chill set in. They put Daniel to bed and had no sooner got into bed themselves when Carry was at the door. "Nimuri is having the baby. Freda sent me to get Willow" he told her. "You stay here tonight with West" Willow said. "She'll not likely have the child until morning." West could see his friend was beside himself with worry. Willow dressed and was soon on her way to the other cabin.

West put on some water for tea and assured Carry all would be fine.

When Willow arrived she soon realized that something was wrong. Freda took her aside "The baby is not positioned right. It will have to be turned." Willow nodded. "What do you want me to do?" she asked. "I'm getting old Willow. I will tell you how to turn the child."

Willow washed in very hot water. With Freda's guidance she felt the child and turned into the right position. For Nimuri it was a great suffering, but with the child now right it was born quickly.

The cord was wrapped tightly around its neck and the two women tried in vain to get it to breath. It was then that Freda tried one more thing. With a basin of cold water and another of hot water she started dipping the child from one to the other. Like music the child wailed out loud. "What ever made you think to do that?" Willow asked. "Something my mother told me when I was a young girl. I don't know how I remembered it" Freda told her.

With the baby now breathing and bawling they tended to Nimuri. She was exhausted and in pain. The bleeding kept up for too long before it stopped, leaving Nimuri in a bad way. Willow had made tea and heated broth before they let her sleep she finished both.

The sun was creeping over the mountains when Willow and Freda sat for a well deserved tea. "She will have to rest" Willow said and Freda nodded. "I can bring in the flax. West and Carry can help with the wheat. You get some rest Freda. I will get the water going to wash things." She knew Carry would be waiting for news and once Freda was lying down she wasted no time in going to tell him of the arrival of his child.

The three men were enjoying their breakfast when Willow came in. Carry stood "Is everything alright?" he said. "Yes" Willow said "She had a hard time, but all is well. You have a son. I need to wash up yet and just came to tell, you can see her now. Don't wake your mom, okay" Willow said to him. Carry nodded. He got up from the table and headed home.

"You look tired Willow" West said. "I am, we almost lost the child. Had it not been for Freda he would have passed on." West poured her tea and rubbed her shoulders. "I will help you heat the water and do the wash" he told her and Willow sighed. "Thanks West. I will have to make Nimuri more broth and change her linens again. I want Freda to rest today. Tomorrow the flax will need to be started as well. With both of them laid up you two will have to help." West smiled "No worries and now we have a population of seven at Cliffside" he smiled at her. She made some porridge for herself and West hauled the water for her. Carry doted on Nimuri and before days end named the baby Seth.

Willow not having slept fell into bed and was sleeping soundly. Freda now revived took over the duties of cooking. When the laundry was near dry she brought it in to hang over racks inside to finish drying. The moisture in the air would be good for both mother and child. Carry had the water for the next laundry in the buckets on the deck. He spent the evening holding Seth and telling him of his mother, grandmother, friends and the valley which was hone.

Daniel liked the baby and looked at the small face peering through the blankets. When West picked him up to go home Daniel blew the little Seth a kiss and it brought warmth to all.

The next weeks passed slowly. The last of the harvest was hard and slow. The last of the wheat was finally in and it brought joy to all. The talk was to go to Greenmeadow before the snow came, but Nimuri was not fit to travel. The new baby was a lot of work. So at the dinner table all talked of a spring trip.

West being tied to the valley wanted to get away. Willow knew it gave him time to think and find any solution to anything he might be working out in his mind. She was never happy for him to travel for long periods of time, but also had the sense to give him room. He worked extremely hard all the time and these small adventures were almost a reward for it. Carry opted to stay in Cliffside. He was not eager to leave Nimuri and Seth yet.

When they left to go home West carried Daniel and Willow tucked her arm in his. "How long will you be gone?" she asked. "Not too long. I'm interested in the valley beyond the cabin we built. It's big Willow and soon you and Danny will be making the journey there with me. I know you will see the beauty there." He squeezed his arm. "I'll be back in a week or so." Willow smiled.

Although the harvest was in there was still much work. The flax all needed to be spun and paper needed to be made. Carry would be making brooms and with Nim's new baby lots more laundry.

They spent what was left of the evening preparing things for West to take. With Daniel asleep and the fire now embers they crawled into bed and into each others arms. West never let Willow feel unloved and not cherished. He was the best man she had ever known. They slept and dawn came so early.

West checked his packs and after he ate he kissed Willow and Daniel. "Hold the fort for me" he said as he loaded on his pack he kissed her one more time and started up the new road.

Watching him go always gave Willow pangs in her heart, but then Daniel would tug at the material of her trousers and she knew her day was beginning. It was much the same as many; hauling water to wash and wash she did. The cabin needed to be vented and everything was scrubbed down. Fall cleaning.

She spent the afternoon clearing and cleaning her herb plots. She planned on spinning that evening if she didn't go to bed early. Carry had been chopping wood. He would be at it for the next while. Winter might be long and being cold was not on the list.

By dinner time Willow had already worked hard. Freda as always did the dinner. Willow and Daniel enjoyed spending time there at dinner. Willow was happy to see Nimuri regaining strength. Freda had bundles of laundry ready for washing the next day and Willow knew that would take up most of the day. She wondered how West was.

When she walked home holding Daniel's hand she gazed over the gardens and paths. How Cliffside had changed since they first came here. She was happy and knew the others had found the same security there she had.

West hike rhythmically and as always scanned everywhere. He was pleased they had the road as far as they did. At the end of the gravel the path was harder to travel, but by late afternoon he had made it to the cabin. With night soon on him he unloaded the things he would not need on the further trek ahead. They had been stocking the cabin and it was well equipped.

Soon the fire in the cabin had it warm and comfortable. West sat on the porch and listened to the world. He stared into the sky and the familiar satellite sped across it. He listened to the soft breeze blow through the trees as the last of the sunlight passed over the ridge of the mountains and blackness of night took over. West went to bed. He would have to make an early day of it in the morning. The night left West to his thoughts. He had found nothing man made so far. He could survey the valley beyond from up above. If he found nothing he knew, he would follow the ridges and have access to two more valleys. Now with a plan he fell asleep.

West woke with the dawn and smiled when he found Willow had packed extra socks and trail mix. He made simple porridge and took the dried fruit and nuts for the journey he was making this day. He made sure the fire was out and the water bags were full before he ventured out.

It was slow going now with new trail making to be made. It was when he stopped for lunch that the quiet brought a sound to his ears. West scanned everything and could see nothing. He sat to eat and heard the sound again, but louder and then it was right in front of him. He hit it with a branch and he watched it struggle for life before it died. West was astonished. Willow was right something had survived and now right before him on the ground was a something. West picked it up and wrapped it in cloth. He put it gingerly into his pocket. He didn't know if he should look for more or take it back and show it to his dad. West decided his dad should know about this.

He back tracked and headed home to Cliffside. He kept his eyes and ears open for any sound or sights. He reached the cabin sat down and took the cloth from his pocket. He opened it again and really had a look at it. It had to be a bee he had seen the pictures dad had drawn. If this was a bee then it must have a colony and if that was so which it obviously was; there would have to be a hive with wax and honey. West just sat looking at the little insect in the cloth, then he wrapped it up and put it back in his pocket again. He packed up his gear and headed home to Cliffside.

His pace was quick and the weight of his packs didn't feel as heavy. West wondered what his mom and dad would make of his discovery? How had this little bee survived? Where did it come from? Had others found any? All these questions ran through his head. News like this would have travelled quickly with the runners. The wax would make all the women happy and the honey. He had never had honey, but his mom and dad talked of the old days honey was spoken of like candy and medicine. He kept his eyes and ears open for more bees but he saw none or heard anything.

It was evening when he headed down the gravel path home. He dropped his gear off at home and headed to Carry's cabin. Everyone would be there eating.

When he opened the door he gave everyone a start. Willow was up and at his side in an instant. "Are you alright? Is everything okay West?" he looked at her "Yes fine." "How come you're home so early?" she said. Then she smiled. "Just couldn't stay away from us huh?" she teased him. West smiled "Well how about some of that stew I'm hungry." "Geesh" Willow said "Food won over" she smiled and got him a bowl. West joined them at the table. Daniel bubbled with joy to see his dad had not gone. West ruffled his hair and put his face down for Daniel to pat.

Carry asked him what made him come home so soon. West never said too much, but told him that he had thought of some things he wanted to talk to Zack about that couldn't wait till after winter. The subject was dropped and they well into an easy conversation.

Willow cleaned up the dishes and West headed home to have a bath. Freda tended the children and Carry doted on Nimuri. It didn't take West long to stoke the fire and get the water going. He had unpacked his gear when Willow and Daniel arrived home. Willow knew West had more on his mind, but he would tell her in his own time.

When West was in the tub Willow handed Daniel to him and soon both men were fresh and clean. When Willow went to put his shirt in the water after they got out West took it from her and removed the cloth from the pocket. West never said anything as Willow emptied the water and hung his now washed clothes up. He had Daniel dressed and the two sat together near the fire. Dusk always brought with it the end of daily tasks. With no light other than from the fire it was just as well they slept. With Daniel's last nursing Willow put him to bed.

West had retrieved the small piece of cloth and was sitting by the fire again. "Willow I want to show you something" he said to her. Willow joined him by the fire and he revealed the tiny creature. "What is it?" she asked. "I think it's a bee. It was buzzing around me and I swatted it." West said. "It startled me, had I thought quicker I would have tried to follow it." Willow looked at him. "Do you think there are more and is this something we should be careful of?" she asked. "My dad will know more. I have never seen one before. I'm not even sure it's a bee." "Freda would know" Willow said. "I don't want to say anything until I talk to dad." Willow nodded and found it hard to take her eyes off the little creature. "Do you realize that this has survived maybe other things as well?" Willow smiled "It appears so." "And with that comes many questions. Just what has survived?" West said to her. "From what I remember mom and dad talked of many creatures and some could be dangerous. That's why I want to ask them. I'll be leaving in the morning" West said. With that he wrapped up the bee and out it in a small clay jar. "West this is important" Willow said. "Yes it is" he answered. "I want to go with you. The harvest is in and there is nothing that can't be put on hold for a few days." West hugged her. "We will leave shortly after dawn. We will travel light and quick." Willow smiled. She knew the morning would come quickly so after setting out a few things for the morning they went to bed.

With morning came the chore of getting some light packs together. Willow went to Freda and told her they would be gone for a few days. Freda knew something was up, but Willow assured her all would be well. Carry showing concern something was wrong was eased by Willow's happiness at going to Greenmeadow. Soon they were on their way.

The weather was cool, but not cold yet made the trip easier. They had decided on a small wagon to pull rather than carry Daniel. He was getting bigger and heavier. The wagon allowed him to sleep if he needed to as well. They talked over the discovery and wondered what Zack and Jo would have to say. Each new thing that could make their lives easier was a treasure, the bee would be a help.

They reached midway cabin. The old couple made hot drinks and offered them lunch. It was good to see them happy and content in the cabin. The news from the fort was promising. It seemed the young had been going to the city of the dead and salvaging what they could. Many new things were available to everyone. West learned the forge had produced an abundance of tools more than they ever had. Life was looking like it was going to keep its hold again. Willow listened intently on the finds of things for women, sewing needles and kitchen implements.

They enjoyed the break in the walk and after an hour or so were on their way again. Daniel soon slept; the motion of the wagon helped him drift off. West was happy to be on his way to see his mom and dad even if it was only for a short time. He had grown up in these hills and soon many familiar spots appeared along the way. Willow too found solace in the area as they got closer to Greenmeadow.

It was the children that always saw anyone on the trail first and today was no exception. Willow and West astonished to see that the place was getting bigger. Kalvin had opened new fields with Herb and another cabin was being built. Soon everyone knew they were there all congregated at Zack and Jo's. With hugs, greetings and hot drinks the families met them. They all talked for a few hours before they went to their own abodes to start the evening meals.

Willow wanted to see her mom and after she heard what Zack and Jo had to say she would go to see her.

Jo took Daniel and he was content to be on her knee. West and Willow along with Zack and Jo sat at the table. "I found something dad and I need to know what you think" West told him. He opened the small clay jar and pulled open the folded piece of cloth. When he opened it Zack and Jo both smiled. "Well now my dear" Zack said to Jo "What do you think of that?" he smiled.

Jo picked it up "This is one of the prettiest things I have seen in many years. Where did you find it West?" she asked. "In the valley about 2 days hike from Cliffside. It just buzzed around me, instinct took over and I swatted it before I realized it might be a bee. Well, is it a bee?" he asked. "Yes it is indeed a bee and there is never just one. It has a colony somewhere" and Jo's face lit up again "with it honey and wax." "Oh what we could do with wax" she said. "It appears the animal world have its survivors as well" Jo said. Zack looked at her "I'm sure about that. It's been many years, too many and now out of the blue a bee. The complex could be releasing things" Zack said. "It would be feasible to think that they did have the animals and now with the danger passed they could be releasing things" Zack said. "You could be right" Jo answered. "I am afraid to say it must be miles away if only now have the firs signs." Zack picked up the cloth and smiled. "Well my little friend you have just made more work for us" he said.

"West I want to go where you found him next spring and try to find the hive. When do you, I want to come get Jo and show her where it is." West nodded "And be careful these can sting you. It's a painful sting, but unless you get swarmed you won't suffer much. If they are letting out bees then there may be more things to come in the future."

Although Willow wanted to stay and talk she also wanted to visit her mom. With time short on the visit she soon left Zack to go to her mom. She knew it was better not to say anything at present Zack and Jo would tell Greenmeadow folks.

West and Daniel stayed at his parent's cabin. Willow had no trouble in finding her way to her mom's. She looked around and many memories of her young life came back. It was all so much the same here yet so different. She was surprised at how much her siblings had grown over the spring and summer. They all could read and write as Zack was still teaching.

Kalvin had turned the cabin into a home for them and it was a happy place now. Willow talked of Nimuri's child Seth and knew soon her mom would have the child that bulged in front of her. Willow's mom was not young anymore and she worried for her after what Nimuri had been through. She never told her of the trouble Nimuri had, no sense in upsetting her.

Kalvin doted on her and Dawn had worked hard to keep things up for her mom. Dawn would marry next spring and Willow wanted her to take the cabin beyond Cliffside, but it was their decision to make. Chad was a good man and Willow knew that whatever path they took they would be fine.

Before long, Willow left to go back to Jo and Zack's. Her mom tired easily and rest was good for her. It was a strange trip. Willow was not sure what to expect, but it was as if a new chapter was about to begin for them all.

When she got back to Jo's they had been talking of the complex. West was always sure he would find it some day. Zack was never that sure, but he kept that fact well hidden. It was a form of hope for West and the future.

The bee had been put back into its little clay jar and Zack told West to show it to Freda. Since the bees would soon be in Cliffside they should know about them. Zack smiled "Watch her face when she realizes what it is. Keep watch for other things like birds or other insects. If it is the complex releasing things your world is about to change into something wonderful." West smiled. He felt proud of himself. He had found a connection to the complex and it felt good after all these years.

The next day passed quickly with just enough time for visiting. West and Zack talked of new tools being made and Chad had been elected to go get some for them all. Kalvin was going and Dawn as well. They would have their chance to see more of their world and then decide to move south or west of Cliffside. Runners were still not plentiful, but letters did get through. They were excited about their trip and so they should be. Kalvin would see what things would be useful for their settlement. Some furniture had been made for them and pottery, extra cloth and now even extra wheat to take.

Willow enjoyed the soft melodies the children played on the flutes and mentioned maybe one could be made for Daniel and Seth for Christmas.

West and Willow did find time for themselves. They spent an hour or two walking the river and a visit to show respect to Willow's father a well.

It was when they had gone on their walk that Jo reprimanded Zack "You should not worry them about your frailness. I don't want to leave you all, but I will not live on false hope. You know my legs are almost gone now. They cause me much sorrow and pain. My mind is able, but my body is letting me down." Jo looked at him. "Well I will do what I can to ease things for you, but even that is limited" she smiled and handed him a piece of bark to chew on and rose hip tea.

She left him at the table with his wrapped up creature. Zack opened the cloth and smiled. "Here is a new beginning for the future. If it was the complex letting out them out, all those here were in for some surprises." He smiled to himself and thought about his young life at the farm. How wonderful things were then and how now he realized how much he had taken for granted. He could almost see the animals on the farm and all the meals his mother made. Meals like roasts, fried chicken and ham. Oh how good some roast turkey would be with a hot cup of real tea and pie with whipped cream. He gazed down to the bee "well little fellow you are a blessing yes indeed you are." He sipped his tea and the willow bark did little for his pain.

West and Willow soon arrived at the cabin. They would be leaving in the morning. The visit had been short but it renewed Willow. She wished her mom's baby was born but it would leave something to celebrate later. Daniel was happy to see them. West had him on his lap in no time and they talked of the world and what it might be in their future. Daniel was the first to fall asleep and Zack not long after.

Jo made tea for them she knew that West was worried. "Don't let worry you he gets contrite when his legs are bothering him. The cold coming always sets in his bones and it pains him." West knew there was more to it, but chose not to pursue the subject." "Signs outside point to a milder winter this year" he said and Jo smiled. "How is the work going in Cliffside?" she asked. "I know you have been clearing a lot of trees" she said. "Yeah, I want some space between the forest and the cabins. Any good storm and the trees might blow over on to them" he told her. "I see what you mean" Jo said. "When are you two going to have another child?" Jo asked. "I guess when it happens" Willow smiled. "Don't wait too long Daniel will soon be too old to bother much with a sibling. He needs a brother or sister" Jo smiled. "How's Nimuri's baby getting on?" Jo asked. "He's doing fine" Willow told her. "Nimuri is getting stranger now too" she added. "By spring things will be back to normal" Jo said. "You are coming in spring again? I would like you to" Jo looked at West. "Most likely" he said. "Before the garden if the weather's good if not then after it's in. I'm curious to see what news Kalvin will bring back from the fort" West added. "Things have been good this year we have some extra again" Jo added. "Seems life has taken hold and the future holds great promise." "Hard work more like it" West said. "But we are blessed that we made it this far and you're right it is getting easier. Do you ever miss it the way it was mom?" West asked. "Yes and No" she said. "Some things were good and some not so good. I am happy and have been for a long time so I guess it doesn't matter what you have. It's how you live and how you treat and care for others that count, besides there's no going back. Well if you two young folk want to stay up all night you can, but this old woman needs rest" she smiled. "Yes tomorrow will be a long day" Willow said. "And bed sounds good to me." Soon all retired to sleep. The dawn would bring with it the day and that still meant work for most and travel for others.

Jo was up first and had tea and breakfast made when Willow got up. Daniel, wide awake enjoyed the porridge Jo had made. West got up and soon after Zack.

The morning seemed to be passing quickly. West hurried to pack up the wagon while Willow said her goodbyes to the women and her mom. By midmorning they were on their way home. Kalvin, Dawn and Chad were still packing and would get a later start.

West pulled the wagon with ease and Daniel sat in it looking at everything everywhere. Willow walked and was glad it was still too warm to see their breath. "Next spring I want to find the hive we could use the wax and I really want to taste honey. Mom and dad made it sound like food from heaven" West told her. Willow smiled. She could make many preserves and trade the extra for many things. "I wonder if it was from the complex and if it is what other things will we see. Zack was sure it was them you know. Maybe we are closer than we think to it, this complex I mean." "Maybe" was all West could say. "Maybe its still months away in the bush, I have travelled a fair distance and found nothing man made. It might be a survivor of the virus too" he added. "Well the wax alone will not go wanting" Willow smiled. They kept the pace and made good distance by noon.

Kalvin, Dawn and Chad had a bit more trouble. They had worked on the road but carrying the packs slowed them down. It would be 3 or 4 days to the fort if all went well and then a day or two there. Chad wanted to go to the south settlement to have a look; no doubt Dawn would go with him. Kalvin didn't mind he knew many if not all the people that came from the prairie.

He didn't want to leave Helen since the baby was due, but everyone knew if they did not travel now it would be spring before they could go. The news of the new tools was the draw. Anything that would make working in the fields easier would be a benefit to all.

Zack sat at the table and called Jo over to him "Get me some paper Dear I want to talk to you about the bees" he said. "Me, what do I know of bees. It's been almost 40 years since we have even seen one until the past few days" Jo answered. "Put on the tea pot and I will tell you what I know and how it will make a difference" Zack said.

Jo always liked it when he had some plan for something; it took his mind off his pain. He had made his mind work on other things "Once I get this all worked out you will have to get this letter to West before he goes looking for them" Zack told her. "On the farm we had bees. We had several hives for the farm pollination. Dad showed me a thing or two about them. Let me show you on this paper." Zack drew out some plans for a hive and Jo soon say it take form. He explained how the bees built the cones for honey and the next brood. He explained that catching a wild hive would not be easy. They had to get the queen and drones to stick by her until they finished the new hive with them. He explained that smoke calmed them and it would make them docile so they could be moved from the wild into the new man made homes. Once there they would work for the queen. It would then be possible to harvest some of the wax and honey. The following spring they would need a few, royal jelly while in the pupa state and the new queens would leave to make new colonies. Jo was totally enjoying seeing Zack working on something new. It was her Zack back.

She watched him work on his drawings and her mind wandered over what he had told her. He was sure the complex had released these bees. Maybe they did and maybe they released other creatures and she smiled. How nice it would be to see squirrels or birds; hear frogs, ducks or geese. She stopped thinking about it, to wish for things of the old world was not always a good thing. It made the present harder to endure. Those things were better in the past.

Zack continued his drawings and Jo left him to his work to go see Helen.

"West?" Willow said "What is it?" he replied. "I was just thinking about you telling your mom about cutting the trees around the cabins. There were none that could have reached the cabin. Is it because of fire?" she asked. West looked at her "Yes" he answered. She thought about the burned out valley beyond Cliffside. "It's funny, you hear people say lightning never strikes the same place twice, but I think whatever drew it to the spot it hit might draw it there again" he told her. "If ever there is a fire, get to the river and stay there." He looked at her and she nodded.

They reached the midway cabin and the older couple made them tea. Daniel as usual captivated them. He was happy to be out of the wagon and burning off that endless energy children always seemed to have.

It seemed too soon before they were on their way again. West never spoke much on the last stretch to home and Willow never pushed him to talk. Daniel soon settled into a sleep from the motion of the wagon and Willow enjoyed seeing the different scenery from home.

Kalvin, Dawn and Chad made good progress. They reached the first settlement later that afternoon. Kalvin spent much time talking with the elder folk while Chad and Dawn found old time friends to visit. Dawn was excited this would be the first trip to the fort and she was happy to be going. They had a long way to go the next day. An early night was called as they found their way to the common house for the night.

When West and Willow reached Cliffside the smoke was streaming up from Carry's cabin and it was a welcoming site. Carry had been chopping wood when he saw them. He hollered to Nimuri to "put on the tea the long lost travellers were home."

They put the wagon in the shop and Willow took Daniel who was still sleeping into the cabin with them all. The sounds of them talking woke him and Freda soon had his attention.

It was then West revealed is small clay jar and its contents. Freda looked and a smile drew across her face. "You know what this is then?" West asked her. "The question should be do you know what it is" she replied. "Okay" Carry said "What is it?" Freda smiled "It's a honey bee and where there is one there are more" she answered. "Where ever did you find it?" Freda asked. "About 2 days walk from here" West told her. "Dad said you would know what it was" West smiled. "You didn't have to walk for a day to find out I could have told you"

West looked at the gathering around the table. "I have long held my thoughts to myself. I consider you all my family and I want tell you some very interesting things, but if I do you must never talk of it or tell others." They all looked at him. "You all know my father" and they all nodded. "Well long before, in the old world he worked for a very rich old man. This man knew something wrong was going on in the world. With his wealth and power he built a place somewhere here in these mountains. Dad called it the complex. There they worked for years to save themselves and the animals from what was coming. Dad always said this man thought it would be a war with bombs, but it wasn't, it was a virus. Dad and mom started their journey to this place when dad had his accident. He had told me many things to look for to find them. He also thinks the bees are from there. Now he told me, bees travel about 5 miles from their hive and if they have reached us the complex may be close. He also told me we should expect other creatures. Dad says they will be trying to set up new food chains. If this is true we can expect many new creatures."

They said nothing as he talked. "I believe my dad is nearing the end of his life and I need help to find the complex. If you decide not to help that's your right, but I must continue, I have other family there. Think on this tonight and let me know in the morning if you want to help, but please no one must know." West got up and he, Daniel and Willow went home. Giving them time to think about what he had told him.

"West do you really think we did the right thing in telling them about the complex?" Willow asked.

West reached over and pulled her close to him "Carry, Nimuri and Freda are more than friends. They have the right to know it's out there somewhere. We have lived side by side with them most of our entire adult life and no truer friends could one have. If they choose not to look with me it's up to them" West just held her. "West do you think you will ever find it? You are always drawn away from us. I don't mean that you don't care for us or provide, but you are drawn out there. I miss you when you go, as does Daniel" Willow told him. "It's because of you and Daniel that I continue to look, for my father, for everyone. He told me of the wonders held there, things that are unbelievable. So many people and things that would make our lives so much easier" West replied. "Well it seems to me that if they are so wonderful how come they have never been seen or heard of? How come they have not come to look for us? Maybe the virus killed them too and you are chasing a dead mausoleum?" Willow was trying so hard to understand his reasons. "Look Willow, think about it, the old world. How it was with all the people and everything they had; things that flew in the sky and things that travelled easily on the ground and all the animals. Then you see it all go; disappear not in months or years but in days, a world full of nothing. They are there I know they are. Would you not have a great responsibility to make the world out there a viable place again? When I found the bee a lot of things became clearer to me. They are trying to make the world back to its natural state again." "Well I don't think it's all that terrible now. We have enough to eat and we are warm in winter. We have family and our life is full" Willow said. West looked at her he knew she just didn't understand, but she would one day. He wanted to be there when it became clear for her. They went to bed.

Dawn creped into the valley too soon as it always seemed. Mornings were much the same as they always were. By the time Carry, Nimuri and Freda arrived Daniel was ready for his nap.

Willow made tea and they sat at the table. It was Freda that spoke first "West if what you say is true and I have no doubt it is because I remember the old world then your complex could be anywhere. The fact that you found the bee could be a good sign they are out there. It might just be a survivor like us as well. I am too old to be travelling through rugged terrain, but I have told Carry if he wishes to pursue this he has my blessing" Nimuri looked at Carry "If you want to look I think you should. Had we not looked for others we would still be on the prairie or dead by now."

Carry looked at West "I always knew there was more to our trips into the bush. I'm game to look but I wish you would have told me ages ago." Willow looked at them "I guess you need to look for this place West. All I can say is I worry every time you go. What happened to your dad could happen to you too. Then where would be? I am torn between preserving things I have and letting you seek things that improve our lives. I guess it's no different then Kalvin, Dawn and Chad going to the fort. Kalvin is looking for tools to improve our lives; Chad and Dawn are looking for a place they will call home. Just you remember where home is" Willow smiled.

West was happy he didn't have to keep so many things to himself anymore, it was a relief really.

Soon the women were off home and Willow sat spinning flax. West and Carry decided to make maps of the cleared areas, clear paths and build small shelters at set points. Any shelters had to be stocked with food, water and the closer to water the better. Willow tended to Daniel when he woke up.

The follow weeks passed much the same. Winter was coming and Willow watched out her little window for a runner to bring news of her mom's baby and the trip to the fort by Chad and Dawn.

It was after the first snow that the runner came and with him the news of her new sister, her name was Lisel; both were fine and doing well. Chad and Dawn had returned to Greenmeadow and decided to move to the southern village past the fort. Willow smiled when she read that. Dawn would like the fort with the entire goings on. The runner did not stay he headed back to the midway cabin.

When West came in from the shop she shared the letter at the evening meal. The news was told to all and life seemed to slip into the winter routines. The snow was heavy this year and kept West and Carry busy clearing the paths. There was ample wood and plenty of food. They were secure in Cliffside as were the people spread over the land they called home. The population was growing and next spring there would be another move by people seeking out their own piece of land.

Willow watched the snow fall and knew all too well West would be off searching as soon as he could for the complex. She thought maybe the fact that she didn't go with him was the trouble, but it wasn't that. She looked at Daniel and he returned her glance with a huge smile. Willow couldn't resist hugging him for that. He was a contented child. He found amusement in simple things for long periods of time. West never failed to spend time with him and Willow finally decided she was a lucky woman. If he wanted to tramps through the bush looking for a mysterious place then let him go without putting guilt on his shoulders. It occurred to her she was being selfish. With that conclusion met in her mid the winter seemed to pass quicker.

The days ran together in winter, maybe that was what cabin fever was. One day never seemed much different from the next. Willow's favourite spot looking out the window was where she was when she realized the icicles were melting. Spring was on the way. Daniel was walking well and even started to talk. West had spent many hours reading to him, telling him of the complex and grandpa and grandma. He listened intently to West repeat an oral history of the new world.

Willow had planned the garden area, with West leaving some fields were left fallow. She wondered when they would make the trip to Greenmeadow. Seth had grown so much over the winter and Nimuri was back to her fit self. Willow noticed that Freda was not herself and Willow knew it was her age. Nimuri had taken over the cooking which gave Freda more time to rest. The flax had been spun and Freda spent time at the loom everyday. The clack, clack, clack was somehow comforting. When Willow visited the two women had decided they would take turns during spring planting as Freda was not just up to it.

"Willow, Willow" West said to her. Willow turned to look at him. "Wow you are far away today" he said. "Yeah, just day dreaming" she answered. "If the weather stays warm we will be on our way to Greenmeadow" he said. Willow smiled "I have some gifts for Dawn and Chad as well as mom. Lisel should be getting big now." West could see that the long winter was taking its toll on Willow, the daily repetition of everything. "After we come back from Greenmeadow I want you to come with me to look for the bees Willow." "Oh West I can't burden Freda with Daniel she just isn't up to it." "Maybe you won't have to if I can convince mom to come back. I have given Freda's health a lot of thought. You see I do notice more than you think" he smiled "anyways it would do her good to see mom. I want to bring dad back too. His knowledge with mom's and Freda's I think will be needed if we find them." He could see the idea brightened her mood. "West you never cease to amaze me." Willow smiled at him.' "Then start planning what you are taking" he smiled at her.

West picked up Daniel and promptly told her that they were going to the workshop. Willow just smiled.

Things in Greenmeadow were busy with Chad and Dawn. They had put it to the council for some land in the south and had received word that a plot of land had been set aside for them. There was good news from the fort. With the influx of people from the prairie and the abundant crops since that young men had been making trips to Cambry for forging missions. Windows and metal were being brought into the fort throughout the summer. The forges worked overtime smelting new tools and all the things one could think of from hinges to nails. They had managed to drag a railway track in but it was hard to smelt.

Kalvin had brought back axes and saw blades. Chad carried spades. The quality of life was improving and the idea of home and wax ran through more than one mind. Zack had 3 or 4 hives made and they waiting for the bees to arrive. He had become a very skilled potter and had made about 50 small clay pots for the honey when it finally came to pass.

Zack waited in anticipation for spring as well. The extra work for the coming of the honey makers had given him something to keep his mind busy and less time to think about the pain.

Jo was glad to see him working with something that gave him so much pleasure. She had been to see Helen. She was doing well, Lisel the baby was growing in leaps and bounds. She watched Kalvin and Helen both had life renewed for them.

Sara and Brad had settled into life here; her children now almost grown and gone from their cabin to their own.

Lily and Gary were busy with Chad getting things together for the new home.

Herb and Jean were the finest people Jo could have wished to come to Greenmeadow, with their children all grown they too have just settled into just living.

Art had taken over the teaching of the children, but they still came to Zack on some problem or another. Jo looked out her window and realized that they were such a village. With helping each other they had worked life to Greenmeadow. She thought about the bees then her mind took her to when she was young and the flock of geese flying and the hummingbirds. How wondrous it would be to have birds again. Maybe Zack was right, maybe the complex was releasing the animals. Jo got back to work it did no good to dwell on things that may never be again.

Spring was well on its way the heavy snowfalls were melting. The gravel pathways through out Cliffside made so much less work for the women. No mud to be cleaning up all the time. Willow had been putting things together for the trip to Greenmeadow. They would go soon and this time they would stay for at least a week. It would be good to see everyone. Chad and Dawn would be married now and this might be the last time for a long time she would see her sister. It was along journey to the fort and they were moving beyond that. Not many wanted to move west they all wanted to live south. Dawn would like it there she was still young and full of enthusiasm.

West came in from the workshop. They had the job of making the dresser and trunk for the newly weds. He looked at the growing pile of things that would fill the wagon. It would be a slow trip with everything that was going in the wagon. West never minded he knew that the world as they knew it was getting bigger and that was good.

Daniel could walk some too he was good on his feet now. Soon he would be helping with many things, West was happy with that. He was going to be a good man. "Is Daniel up from his nap yet Willow?" West asked. "No he is still snoozing. He is almost grown too much for mid morning naps. We will have to start teaching him to read and write. Dad was very adamant about that." "I know but I have no where near the experience your dad does" Willow said. "When we go see them I will ask him about it. We might have to build another cabin and get ourselves a teacher. I have asked Chad to keep an eye open for a teacher there. There might be someone in Greenmeadow" West said. "I do hope so, but most likely from the fort. That would be good too there are many things going on there that are new. I'm not sure what's being pulled out of Cambry after all this time. Did you hear they have been burying the bones? Think they said it would be months before that was done as there are so many. They have readings for them before they bury the bones. The elders have given instructions with this." "Not a job I would want that's for sure" West told her.

The weeks passed and before they knew it spring was there. The trip was planned for a long time and today was the day. Willow wasted no time bringing the things to West that she wanted loaded on the wagon. West and Carry shared what chores needed to be done before they left.

Daniel was walking well now and with his hand in Willows they set off for Greenmeadow. Willow pushed the wagon going up hills which helped. They stopped often to rest. The wagon was always heavy with things first trip in the spring.

They reached the midway cabin just before lunch. The older couple made them a tea. Daniel, who not long before, woke from a nap and entertained them. Willow took comfort in the joy he provided them. It was all too soon before they were on the road again.

By the time they reached Greenmeadow West was tired of pulling the wagon. Willow too was having a time with Daniel, he did not want to walk anymore and he was cranky.

It was a sight when the small hamlet came into sight. It had grown so much. Every time they arrived over the last ridge to see it below they noticed new things. The crop fields expanded so much. They had taken West's idea to clear a fire break around the whole place.

Their arrival did not go unnoticed long and wagon was taken over by the young men. West was glad to be free of pulling it. He picked up Daniel and that made him happy. They all met at Zack and Jo's.

Soon there would was more food and company then they had seen in some time. Helen and Kalvin beamed over Lisel. Sara and Lily were showing their age as were Brad and Gary. Herb and Jean still had that glow for each other. The young children were starting to grow up. Dawn was a married woman now. Soon she would be far away.

Willow was happy for her but pangs of sadness went with it not to be able to see her much now.

Daniel was not the center of attention it was Lisel that was stealing the show. He didn't much mind; he sat on Jo's lap and seemed content.

Life had made a passage Willow knew that things were going to change even more in the next year or two. Well this year she would be going with West hiking and map making. With a tad of good luck they would find the bee hive and change many hours in the fields pollinating and the wax. They would have candles for light not dull corn oil lamps. Wax for making more preserves. Maybe they would find another species that would change things for all again.

"Willow, come see all the things everyone has made. It will take weeks to get it home. I have things for you all, but you will have to give us some time get set up."

Kalvin had more windows and hinges on the porch to be sent. Zack made more pottery; Brad, Gary, Herb and Kalvin made furniture and chairs.

Dawn was beaming, Chad was young but he did have his work cut out for him. The first trip there would be to work the fields. There would be a trip back to Greenmeadow to retrieve the furniture all had made for them.

Willow, Jo and West made a trip to the graveyard to care for her father's place of rest. The river could be seen from there and it had not gone unnoticed that it was running high and fast. There had not been much rain but the air was warming quickly.

Gary, Brad, Kalvin, Herb and the young men spent most days turning over the ground. The apple trees had started budding as did many of the trees here. The wild lilies that had been brought from the prairie were peeking through the ground.

The week passed so quickly and with the agreement of Jo to come to Cliffside it didn't take long for Zack to convince them he too was fit for the trip. It would be a grand trip home. Dawn and Willow spent much time talking of things Dawn needed to know and expect being a wife. Lisel was a beautiful child.

Willow saw her mother change from a depressed sad sorry woman into a loving wife and mother full of hope for the future. Part of it was in her arms that very moment.

They would be going the next morning. "Dawn you must promise to write me" Willow said. Dawn smiled "I will don't worry." She left Dawn to enjoy Chad's company. Willow hugged her mom and Kalvin and then softly kissed Lisel on the forehead before she left the cabin to go back to Zack and Jo's.

She arrived in time for tea on the porch. West had the wagon ready to go. Jo had been gathering her herbal medicine for Zack.

West and Zack spoke of many things and West carefully examined the drawings Zack had made. West leaned back "Seems we will have to find the hive, but I'm sure Willow will be a great help there" Willow smiled. Daniel had long been asleep. All the new people and the older children wore him out in the park, helped tire him.

They went to bed not long after dark. The morning would arrive too soon as it usually seemed to do.

Morning came and with it the commotion of packing and any last minute things that needed to be tended too. Sara set Jo's mind at ease about keeping the herb garden and flower beds watered. Jo was concerned over Zack; the trip would be hard on him. Daniel was a blessing there, he would ride with Zack and that would keep his mind busy.

By the time they were ready to go the sun was out and it was almost hot. Zack was sitting with Daniel beside him and West pulled the shoulder straps on and started them off. The uphill places Willow and Jo pushed to help and soon Greenmeadow was far behind them.

Willow looked over the woods hoping to catch a glimpse of something other than trees and bush. Jo lost in her own thoughts walked quietly beside the wagon. Zack pointed out trees to Daniel and got him to say their names. West just pulled; he would be glad to be at the half way cabin.

The old couple there were pleased to be hosts for so many. They talked of many things between themselves and Zack, Jo and Daniel kept Willow busy. West watched his family and was just happy they were all there.

When they left the cabin West was glad to be closer to Cliffside. Soon Daniel was sleeping and the quiet of the afternoon was settling in, the sounds of the wagon and the breeze in the trees. It was funny to Willow how far they could travel without talking. There was no need really the quiet was almost a relief after the noise of the past few days. How Dawn liked the constant racket Willow thought. She would be happy near the fort. Just wait till she got honey and wax in her next gift box.

Willow smiled and Jo looked at her "What has sparked such a lovely smile" she asked. "I was just thinking about how surprised Dawn would be when we send her wax and honey." "Oh I see" said Jo. "Let's first see if we can catch them first." Willow smiled again. "We will" she said. They continued on with the sound of the wagon against the gravel.

Late afternoon found them on the last hill home. It was hot today and West felt it the most. He had pulled the wagon all day. Daniel was walking with Willow now and Zack was relieved the trip would soon be over.

Jo looked over the valley and was astounded how much work West and Carry had done. She could see the swollen river at the end of the valley and soon her gaze looked to the buildings below.

Nimuri saw them and soon Carry was there to help West. When they reached the cabin West was happy. Carry helped Zack get down and they all went to Carry's cabin. Freda was overwhelmed to see Jo and Zack. "How did you ever make the trip?" she said to Jo. "I just can't walk that far anymore" Freda smiled. "It's so good to see you my friends." Freda was happy.

Nimuri had tea before long and Willow took some to West. He had a fire going and had been hauling water to bathe. "Don't you ever tire West?" He smiled "I want to get this road dust off and mom and dad will probably as well." She smiled and went to the wagon to unload the things they brought from Greenmeadow. She had made Daniel's room ready for them before they left. She was glad she had now. When she finished putting the things away West was already finished bathing.

He had emptied the water and was putting more on for her. Willow washed quickly and emptied her water. She was dressed and had more water heating when West returned with Daniel. She bathed him in a smaller basin and sat down while he had his last feeding for the night.

West had returned to Carry's while she sat there. He stopped to put the wagon away and refill the wood box. Nimuri had made something for all to eat and drink. West was happy to see Carry had found a good woman. He listened to Freda, Zack and Jo talk of the bees. They had many things they wanted to do. Carry, Nimuri and he listened to them. He was so interested in tasting this honey.

He made a small plate of food for Willow and said his good nights to Freda, Carry and Nimuri. Zack went home with West. He needed his help after the trip. When they arrived Willow was just putting Daniel to bed. Zack smiled at the tub and hot water. Soon Jo arrived home too. She wasted no time heating water for tea. She added willow bark and gave Zack some to chew as well. She filled the tub for him.

Willow ate her dinner it was good she thought. How old Zack was getting passed over her as well. Jo was attentive to him as ever. By the time the tub was filled West and Willow had gone to bed.

Jo added more wood to the fire the heat was good for Zack. She heated some corn oil and massaged his legs before he went to bed. It was at this time that Jo had time to herself. She bathed and washed out the clothes from the trip. She had tea and wondered if it would taste any better with honey. It was quite late by the time she went to bed. Zack was sleeping and Jo soon followed.

By the time the morning work was done West and Zack had the hives up and ready for the new occupants. Freda and Jo drank tea and talked of wax and honey. Willow and Nimuri glanced over the garden plans. Carry sat back and watched everything; content as life was pleasant and secure.

Zack gave West instructions on how to calm the hive with smoke and gave him a box with tiny holes to hold the queen if they were lucky enough to find her. Willow was soon packing up travelling gear and the others fell into the daily routines of Cliffside.

Willow was excited to be going with West. It had been such a long time since they trekked anywhere together.

West showed Zack on his maps where he had found the bee and they discussed the area where to look for the hive. "You know West, this early in the spring they may swarm that would be grand. If you manage to find the hive bring some combs with larva and honey. The workers may make a queen if you don't get her" Zack told him. West looked at his father and realized this man was a fountain of knowledge. It would be a sad day when his passing came.

By mid day with their packs loaded the two were off in search of the bees. As they drifted out of sight it was Freda that mentioned to Jo that some kind of bee caretaking gear should be attempted.

The two women headed to Carry's house. Nimuri had the children with her; Carry and Zack copied plans for hives so many would be needed as well as wanted for the other settlements.

West and Willow settled into a quiet rhythm of walking, both listened and watched for any signs of the bees. The trail was clear and in good shape to the cabin where the fire had gone through. West could see how fast the trees were reclaiming the open meadow. Willow was glad unload most of the heavy gear. They would travel light from this cabin. "Wow Carry has really worked at the paths here, he's hauled a lot of gravel" West told her. "Yes he has, he's been a grand friend to us as well. We certainly made the right choice asking him to move here" Willow replied. "I wonder how Chad and Dawn are. They should be at the fort by now" she said. "Yes they will do well Chad has good work ethics and Dawn too" West said. "I wonder how long before more people move this way. It's inevitable they will spread out" West said.

Willow had a meal ready and they ate. West brought out his map and they decided to stick together for the search. If one lost sight the other might pick it up. Willow loved how West could just take control and come up with a plan. He had always been like that. She truly was a lucky woman.

West hauled water to the cabin for their needs and the wood pile was over flowing. "I think we can start the search tomorrow. Today I just want you to myself" he told her. Willow never argued and found she had missed just being with him. They spent the afternoon enjoying each others company and rekindling their affections.

West tucked Willows arm in his and they walked through the meadow. It wasn't long before they noticed the buzz and saw a few bees at the flowers. "Look here" Willow said. She was thrilled to see them. They both watched intently as the busy creature flew from flower to flower. West pointed out the pollen sacks on their legs. "They have come closer than last year" West told her. In the short walk they saw at least 5 bees. They sat on an old burned log and watched them. West tried to see in what direction they were going. "If we wait till dusk we might get a better idea where their hive is, what direction at least" West said. Willow didn't mind at all watching, it was fascinating to her. "They are amazing don't you think West?" she asked. "I hope it is the complex that has set them free. From what dad said they have so many things there" he said.

West watched intently over the bees and they seemed to be going westward. "Come on Willow let's go I need to wash and I'm starving." Willow looked at him and smiled. "You're always hungry, Daniel is too. He must get that from you." He smiled as they walked back to the cabin stopping only to watch the bees at their work. They heated water and soon dusk turned to night and they went to bed. Tomorrow would be a long day, but with luck maybe not.

With morning came a cloudy rainy day. They decide that today would be spent in the cabin. "Did you know we will be able to make candle from the extra wax?" Willow said. "It will give us so much more light at night. We can wax paper for more preservation with herbs and the jams. It is going to be so much help." West smiled as she talked on about the wax and the future. His mind was wandering over what else the complex might have released. Life was coming back to the world in a way most could not imagine.

He got up and put more wood on the fire. Willow had him string some lines so she could hang up the wet clothes she had rinsed out. "Do you think Daniel is giving them much trouble?" Willow asked him. "I don't think he will be much trouble for mom, Freda and Nimuri" he smiled. "Yes you're right" she said and smiled back. She missed him; how silly she thought, gone one day and already she was missing him.

West made dinner and let Willow enjoy her time. She looked over the maps and talked of things that Zack had told them to look for in finding the beehive. West made some poles from green wood and tied moss to them tightly at one end. "This should work to provide smoke" he said to her.

They sat looking out the door of the cabin at the rain. Tomorrow they would find the hive, both felt sure of it.

The day passed quickly and just before night fall the sky cleared. They watched the moon brighten the area around them. West looked into the sky and looked for the passing satellites. He pointed them out to Willow and they watched as the tiny lights crossed the sky. "Let's go to bed morning will be here before we know it" Willow said.

With morning came the sun and its warmth renewed them. It was still early spring and mornings could hold coldness even yet. They ate and were soon out in the meadow searching for the quarry that still was new to them.

It was Willow that spotted the first bee and they followed it closely. By noon they not only found the hive but had everything ready to capture them. The sound of the buzzing was very intense. West was astonished to hear so many bees. It was as if the hive was humming.

He followed his father's directions and soon had combs of honey and larva in the box. He had such a swarm of bees with it there was no way of knowing if the queen was in there or not. He prayed it was. When he felt assured, the box was tightly secured. West and Willow took one more comb from the hive this they would have for themselves.

It didn't take long to get back to the cabin. Willow watched West in anticipation as he set down the box of bees then gave her a piece of the honey filled comb. They each ate it and both could not be more pleased at its taste. It was so sweet and thick, never had they had anything that could compare. Willow said "Maple syrup was close but honey was something else all together."

After cleaning up the sticky fingers and then the cabin; the trip home was to be fast. They left a lot of the things they brought at the cabin. The food, ropes and the extra cloths would be things they would not have to bring the next trip. The box almost vibrating from the bees was hung from a pole West carried over his shoulder. West carried the packs with ease and Cliffside was the next time. How happy they would all be when they returned with the hive. The slow pace that brought them to the cabin was now hastened to get back as soon as they could. The trip was short, but they had what they came for and now they must concentrate on the garden at home.

With the coming of the late afternoon West and Willow found themselves walking into Cliffside. It didn't take long before they were seen by Nimuri and Carry. It was not long before everyone gathered at West and Willows to see the bees.

Zack had the hive ready. They made them so the queen if she was there would not be able to get out. They needed to become acquainted with the hive and Zack was sure his hive would be accepted fully.

While the men took care of the bees Willow brought out what was left of the comb they had taken to eat. She shared it with them all. Zack, Jo and Freda revelled the taste and Daniel smiled with sticky lips when he tasted it. Nimuri's face grew into a pleasant smile as she tasted her piece. "How lovely" she said "This is like nothing I have ever had" she told them. It didn't take her long to be gone to the workshop with some for Carry.

With the afternoon being late and dusk closing in tomorrow would be the day of tending the hive. Freda and Jo provide the new outfits, veiled masks and thick gloves. Zack had approved them, West and Carry would be the first bee keepers in almost 50 years since the virus breakout.

Jo and Freda searched their memories for all the things honey could be used for. Nimuri and Willow listened and wrote down the things they spoke of. With night fall stealing the light they gathered their things together and made ready for the dawn. Sleep was welcomed by them all. The future was about to become much more secure.

Zack talked to Jo "West's life is about to change and I hope it is for the betterment of all" Zack said. Jo listened to him "The last time man shared his life with other living things he never considered them and the past years have been a lesson needed, but a painful one." Jo snuggled closer to Zack. "The world is not the same anymore Zack" she told him. "Having lost so much and having to work so hard for what we have now. I think that people will put a greater value on things. The bees will be a blessing and will be seen as that now. It's too bad it took such a terrible thing to make most realize what they had and had almost lost forever." With that the two soon took comfort in the sleep that pursued them.

West took Zack and Jo home the next day and spring work kept them all busy.

West hauled gravel to finish the path to the cabin beyond Cliffside. Carry cut down more trees and chopped wood. News of the bees and wax stayed in Cliffside until they had a few more hives producing; there was no point in raising hopes.

By mid summer the bees had worked hard the garden was over loaded with vegetables. They had nearly twenty pots of honey and there was at least a pound of wax. West had two more hives made and was looking out for another wild one.

Willow always missed him when he was gone, she was thankful for Daniel. Willow wanted another child, but it just didn't seem to be happening. Nimuri felt as she did, but it was the same for her.

Freda's age really showed this summer. She seemed to have no energy for anything anymore. Willow didn't like to think about how frail she was becoming.

Daniel was down for a nap and Willow sat on the porch. She was happy at how big the apple trees were growing. They were absolutely loaded with small apples. Willow was sure it was due to the bees. She smiled and thought about when she and West first saw the bees working in the meadow. She glanced over the garden and then went in to start the wash.

West had returned, but was unable to find another wild hive. He wasn't worried this fall the hive they had would decrease its population for winter and the following spring they would swarm. He was confident he could get another hive going. Zack was adamant about being sure to leave the bees plenty for the winter. He had cleared a path at the cabin into the meadow. He wanted to get into the next valley the following year, maybe start a cabin there too. With the population growing he knew they would soon be moving this way.

Summer seemed to pass by and before they knew it harvest was upon them. This was a time of work. They had to fill all the bins and barrels for the coming winter. The abundance of food brought joy to them al. This winter there would be plenty for all. With the harvest almost done West knew if he and Carry were to get any work done on the path beyond the cabin in the valley next to them it would have to be done before the snow came.

Freda had been weaving when the flax was all brought in. Nimuri told her to take it easy they had all winter to weave it. The wheat was the last crop to be done. Nimuri and Willow made new discs for separating the wheat from the shaft. New brooms were made from the straw and the extra was put over the herb beds and then the flower beds.

It was time for West and Carry to take a week to go do the work in the valley beyond. As they packed up their gear for the week Willow started missing him already. She watched him go and Daniel cried because he wanted to go too. West waved and before long the two men were gone from sight. Willow picked up Daniel and went to Nimuri's.

The three women soon had the flax work underway. They had more to spin and weave this year than ever before. Although it was a lot of work the cloth and knitting yarn never went wanting. They sorted out all needs, foods and spices. The extra which was a lot could be shared with Greenmeadow. The old couple in the cabin would need whatever supplies they could get as well. Willow wondered if the bees had travelled there yet and how surprised they would be to get the few pots of honey set aside for them.

Next spring Greenmeadow would have a hive of their own. Willow looked at Daniel and Seth how different their lives are going to be. The memory of the old world would soon be gone when their folks passed on. No one would be able to remember it then. The children would have to make the world a better place this time. She got back to work. She was spinning a bit thicker cord. Freda was going to show them how to make candles. The wax over the summer had been plenty that enough was being sent to Jo and her mother. They could not waste much for candles but Freda wanted to be sure they did indeed know how to make them. She made rolled ones and dripped ones. They each had about 10 and that was all the wax that would be used for candles until the supply became larger.

Not much change over the summer and the familiar cold wind brought winter to Cliffside. West and Willow passed the days with chores and Daniel's care. West had already started teaching him his letters. Willow like the winter because it kept them together and the hard work of the summer was gone. They used the candles sparingly for light. Next year more would be made and a new colony of bees would make its way to Greenmeadow.

Freda was not well this winter. She was old and it was taking its toll now. She had worked so hard all her life. Willow wondered if she would see another winter. Carry catered to her. Seth provided her with so much joy and he loved his grandma.

Daniel followed West everywhere now and West often had him in the workshop. He was growing. Willow still had not heard from Dawn and it bothered her. There was little news from Greenmeadow. One runner before the snow and that was it. With winter had its hold on Cliffside all waited for spring to release the cold winter had enclosed them in.

Willow sat watching out her window. She always knitted in winter. With three people now in need of socks, gloves, hats, scarves and sweaters she was kept busy. The familiar clicking of the knitting needles Willow used was the only sound in the cabin. Daniel long gone to bed and West looking over the maps added with the adventures of the fall. He ran over his dad's description of the circular valley that the complex was built into. There was nothing that looked round, no ranges that looked even close. The map was so faded now after all these years and was not the best map. Willow watched him as she knit and could see him get more frustrated with the time passing. She put down her knitting and added more wood to the fire. The water pot had enough for tea. She made West some and refilled the pot with water. She sat by the fire again and started her knitting once again.

"West" she said to him "Freda is not well her time draws near I think. I doubt very much if she will be with us come summer." "Yes I have noticed her decline" he told her. "I know you want to look for the complex in spring. I am just worried she will pass and you will feel sad you never spent more time with her before she is gone." West knew she was right, but it reminded him how frail his father was too. All his life he wanted to be the one to find the complex and finish the journey Zack had so long ago began. He found he was disappointed that he would not be able to comfort his father in his last days with the location of the complex. For all his searching he had not found anything. West had sibling there that he may never know.

He looked at Willow he had done a fine job providing for her and Daniel. He felt proud that they would be fine in the future with the work he had done. Daniel would soon be able to travel with him when he searched. He was a good child. He already knew his alphabet and teaching him to write would be next. Herb had made him a flute and it was a favourite of his.

Winter was always a time for of thoughts and dreams this year was no exception. West drank his tea and then rolled up his maps. "Let's go to bed Willow. Tomorrow is another day" he said to her and smiled. Willow put down her knitting and they went to bed.

Spring was still far off, but the days flowed into each quickly. The snow melt started and spring brought the long awaiting trip for maple sap. With the sleigh loaded with buckets West, Carry, Willow and the two boys made their way to the maple grove.

When they arrived Willow set about building a fire. The men and the boys trudged through the snow to each tree. The spouts were pounded in and buckets were hung waiting for the sap to start to flow.

Willow had the fire going and hot drinks and soup for them when they hung the last bucket. The fire kept them warm and the present company enjoyed the children and their antics. Willow had the sleigh loaded and they started the collection. When they emptied all the buckets they would be home soon.

Nimuri stayed with Freda she did not want to leave her alone. Willow smiled; the boys will sleep well tonight as they had burned of loads of energy. The collection was done and homeward bound they were.

Daniel and Seth now riding in the sleigh were rosy cheeked and happy. With their arrival at the cabins the children were off to see Nimuri and Freda. West helped Carry and Willow carry in the sap. "West I can manage now would you go and help Nimuri with the boys" she said. West headed towards Carry's cabin.

Willow pulled up her sleeves and started the sap boiling. She hauled water to wash the pots and after a few hours all that was left to do was wait for the sap to thicken more. It was almost dark when she finished.

With the sap all done she headed to Carry's cabin. She could hear the laughter as she got closer. Nimuri had supper almost done and Freda was telling stories of what her life was like when Carry was young. Willow was glad the work with the sap was done as she sat at the table Nimuri served a lovely supper to everyone. After the meal West and Carry cleaned up the dishes. Nimuri and Willow sat with Freda, Daniel climbed up on her knee and Seth soon found comfort on Freda's lap. When the dishes were done Freda told West to take Daniel home to bed, she had a few things she wanted to talk to the women about. Carry was invited to West's cabin as well. Nimuri put Seth to bed and Willow made tea.

When all three women were alone Freda began. "Girls as you probably can see my health is failing me" Nimuri said "Nonsense." Willow said "You just have had a long day." She patted Freda's hand. "Willow you can not change what is to be. My life is coming to a close. I have known for some time now." Nimuri said "Freda don't talk such." Freda smiled "I want you both to know a few things while I can still tell you. First I have some cook books in my trunk. One is all about herbal remedies and the other a cook book. With the bees making a stand in the world again there may be other animals as well. The cook book will tell you everything you need to know. The herbal book I want you both to learn inside and out. You are the only ones here that can care for our men and any others that may become hurt or ill. Although since the virus outbreak sickness seems to be long lost thing just pray it stays that way. It will tell you how to treat things like broken bones, burns, cuts, etc...I would like you to do me a favour, both of you. Plant flowers on my grave that will bloom every year. Take care of Carry, Nimuri I have loved him so and Seth too. Willow, be patient with West he's a determined man and very loyal. He had given his word to his father to look for the complex, let him. They are the nursery of the future it must be found. Don't push Daniel into the search; it's something he must choose on his own."

Willow's eyes were tearing now as were Nimuri's. "Freda please don't talk so. I can't bear for you to leave us" Willow said. Freda smiled "Willow you must be strong for I am sure my passing will be followed by Zack and Jo's too. It is as it should be. The world belongs to the young. They will make it into the new world. As I pass and those that remember the old world it will be a new beginning for all. We take with us the memories of the way it was and leave you young to discover and make the world your place not a remnant of ours." Willow understood what she meant. "It's up to you and Nimuri to hold Cliffside together. You both have lovely homes and your future is secure as will be Daniels and Seth. Care for the land it will be bountiful if you treat it with respect. Oh yes I have made sewing patterns as well they are in the trunk. Keep a history of family both of you.

It is important to know who you are. Don't let the boys marry anyone in the near family, try to see they find a separate family to wed into. I want you both to take a trip to the fort after my passing. I know many things are changing and new ideas are sometimes good. Now I believe I have told you what I wanted you to know. I am dreadfully tired and want to go to bed now."

Willow and Nimuri helped her to bed and when they closed the door the understanding of what she said passed between them. Willow gathered her wrap and headed home.

Carry and West were planning out the gardens for spring. When she got settled by the fire Carry took his leave. West rolled up the plans and sat near her by the fire. "You okay Willow?" he said. "Yes and no" she answered. "Freda is dying and she sorted out some things. I will miss her so much" Willow said. "My parents I fear are not long for this world too. I have known for some time that the lives of our elder family members draw near their end. I don't know how we ever could manage without their guidance. Now it's up to us to be the elders." Willow looked at him. Once again his strength was there. "Let's go to bed" she said "I am exhausted tonight." West banked the fire and they retired both lost in their own thoughts about how the next few years would unfold.

Freda passed away in late spring and they followed her instructions. Willow and Nimuri planted flowers inside the rings of stones that surrounded her grave that would grow and bloom each year. West and Carry built a stone bench to sit on and remember her. Willow decided to copy out both books so she and Nimuri both would have one of each. She studied the herbal book every night.

The garden was planted and life in Cliffside fell into its normal pace. West and Carry searched for the complex as well as wild hives.

Daniel and Seth passed the days trying to help but were more hindrance then help.

A runner came with news from Dawn. Willow was so happy it had been far too long since there was word. Willow poured over the words they were well and had a cabin. Dawn seemed to be happy. Chad worked at the fort on the weekends and Dawn worked spinning for many people. It was a different life there. Everyone worked for everyone, a co-operative. Willow knew Dawn would be happier among more people. Dawn told her of the new books that had been found at the city of the dead. They were being copied out and put in schools there. She told her from the talk it would still be years before all the bones were buried. Fort Reed had new fields for wheat across the river and a new settlement had been started there. It was called Newsprings for the spring water that was found there. The south settlement was still voting for its name and Dawn promised to write when it was finally decided. Willow was glad to hear things were going well for Dawn. She would tell West when he got home.

The rain didn't seem to come much this spring. Willow and Nimuri found they had to haul water for the garden. When West and Carry made it back from their adventure Willow was happy to see they had a new hive. With the new one and the borrowed larva from the two at Cliffside, Greenmeadow was about to get bees.

Still no complex but West did manage to fill in more of his map. Preparations were made to go to Greenmeadow with the bees. Nimuri and Carry would look after Cliffside while they took them the new hives. Daniel didn't want to go he wanted to stay with Seth. With that West and Willow agreed it was to be a quick trip to be sure the bees arrived safely. It didn't take them long to be on their way.

The two of them with light packs made good time, by early afternoon they crested the hills above Greenmeadow. Every time she came Willow could see the changes. This time was no exception. The children all seemed to be much older.

By the time they reached Zack and Jo's the news of the bees had reached each house. Herb, Gary and Brad wasted not time in getting them into the new hive. Everyone would wait to see if they would stay and find favour in their new home in Greenmeadow.

Zack sat of the porch with Jo at his side. Willow saw the same look on his face that Freda had not too long before she passed. She could see that Jo knew too his time was almost done in this world.

As usual the food and drinks arrived along with everyone. Helen brought Lisel and she was so big. Willow couldn't believe how much she had grown. With all the commotion over the bees it was hard to talk long to any one. The women all talked of the wax and honey; the men on the care of the hives.

Willow went and sat next to Zack. "How are you, father?" she asked him. "I'm doing as well as expected I guess my dear. You two have created quite a ruckus here with the bees" he said and she smiled. Willow sat back and found comfort just being in Zack's company. It was a few hours before the party broke up and all went to their own cabins.

"I hope they find Greenmeadow to their tastes" Willow said. "I think you will be pleasantly surprised at the bounty they will provide you all"

Jo smiled. "The young will find it hard not to use all the wax for candles. They like to stay up at night. We soon will have to build more cabins. Sara and Lily's children would soon marry Herb and Jean's as well. We have a good life here in Greenmeadow I hope they will too. The bees will be so much help. West, give me a hand will you" Jo said and West went into the cabin with her. Zack looked at Willow "She is such an old fuss pot. She'll be heating water for my bath. I don't know what I would have done without her all these years" Zack said. Willow smiled. "West looked again this spring dad and saw nothing. He spends hours at the maps trying to decide where to look next" Willow told him.

Zack out a hand over hers "He may never find it, but I hope he does for your sake. I wanted to go back there so bad and now I can't imagine life any better then it has been with Jo. She's a wonderful woman." Willow just smiled. "Come on dad" West said "your tub is full." Zack looked at Willow and winked "See I told you so." They both laughed.

West came and helped his dad up and before to long had him in bed. The tub was filled again for West and Willow. They would be going back the next day. The gardens would have to be watered if the rains didn't come soon.

Without too much ado they headed home. The bees were safely in their new home and Greenmeadow all looking forward to honey. It was hot for spring and the trip home was quick. West never spoke much going home. His eyes watched the forest. Willow moved with the same grace as West on the path home. "If this weather holds up we are in for some bad storms" West said to her. "It's been warm this spring" Willow answered and West never commented further.

They arrived in Cliffside to see Carry and Nimuri packing water for the gardens. Daniel and Seth were in the play area. It wasn't long before they spotted West and Willow and they went over and picked up the boys. Willow nodded to Nimuri and then took their packs into the cabin.

Willow wasted no time in putting away the contents of their packs and went to the garden to help water. West was already there. It was hours later that they finished. "We need some rain" Carry said. "I don't think I can ever remember it being this warm this early in the year" West agreed. "Tomorrow I think we should clear the bush out some around Cliffside" West said. Sometimes Willow wondered why he was so driven.

West and Willow went home after they ate and West had a tub full before she knew it. She handed him Daniel and before long both were fresh and clean. Willow washed out all the clothes and West refilled the tub for her. Willow soaked for a long time. She watched West trying to teach Daniel how to write letters. He was growing up so fast, everything was changing again. She finished her bath and sat by the fire and dried her hair. Daniel was getting cranky and Willow told West it was enough for one night. West picked him up and after a hug and kiss from Willow put him to bed. West emptied the tub and they soon found the comfort of their bed hard to resist.

The heat continued for weeks. The days were hard and arduous. The gardens had to be watered. Late in the afternoon the distant sounds of thunder could be heard. West watched the sky continuously and by midnight the rain came, with it thunder and lightning. West stood on the porch watching the storm. It really didn't rain that much and the dry ground soaked it in quickly. The lightning continued through the night. West came to bed in the wee hours of the morning. Willow knew he was troubled by what he didn't say.

Morning came too soon and although it had rained the ground was still dry. They would have to haul water again today. Daniel and Seth stayed in the play area as West, Willow Carry and Nimuri all packed water from the river for the garden.

It was about noon when West became aware of the clouds over the ridge. He knew that moment they might be in big trouble. He called Carry and the women over. He told them to get blankets from the cabins. Nimuri and Willow soon returned with them. West had Daniel and Carry has Seth; they walked towards the river. Willow was still not sure what was going on.

When they were at the river bank the first wave of wind hit them. The air was hot and smelled of smoke. Those were not cloud but smoke. The forest was on fire and Willow now understood what was going on. "West, West" she cried out. He turned and looked at her "Soak these blankets and you and Daniel cover up." He looked at the dark smoke coming closer. "If it gets too hot get into the river. Do you understand me Willow?" she nodded. There was nothing they could do they just stood there.

The clouds of smoke carried by the wind were getting thicker. How could this be happening Willow thought? She looked at Cliffside their home. The cliffs straight up behind them and the edges of forest above. The wind was now hot and then they could hear the roar of the fire. It was a sound that Willow would never forget. It raged on and Willow could see it consuming the trees above the cliffs. It was then the air began to clear. The wind had shifted and was pushing the fire back onto the area already burned. With no fresh fuel the roar began to die down. Then like a miracle the skies opened up and it started raining. It was a down pour not light rain.

They all stood in the river and watched the fire die down. The hissing of the rain hitting the hot embers soon put out the fire. The firebreak West and Carry made was what saved Cliffside.

The garden escaped the intense heat as did the cabins. Willow knew now why West always watched the storms. They had been saved by hard work and a lot of luck. Had the wind not have changed course Cliffside may not have been saved. The cold of the water drove them onto the bank and slowly they made their way back to the cabins.

West and Carry went to see the remnants of the forest and to see if it truly was safe to stay in Cliffside.

When West reached the ridge he was astounded at the sight; what was once a majestic forest was reduced to pillars of charcoal, the ground was ash and smoke and dust. The fire was out, but the forest was gone. He could see for many miles. As he gazed over the mountain ranges he could see more ranges in the distance. He was overwhelmed by the vastness of the land. Something inside told him the complex was out there beyond the distant peaks. The fire had laid waste to several valleys. West could see the lay of the land so well now. He stared at the river that now ran through this great scarred land.

Carry now beside him stared out over the vast black ash forest. "Wow, this was a nasty fire" Carry said. "I understand now why you wanted the firebreak. How did you know West?" Carry asked. "I just thought if a fire went through before it might again. If a lightning strike started it, it might again. I just wanted our families to be as safe as possible. How's Nimuri?" West asked. "She's okay. She said it was not a prairie fire at all. Those come like walls of flame and smoke. For miles you can see them coming. She'll be okay our homes are safe and the gardens escaped the heat."

Carry starred out realizing the vastness of the land that was before them. "Come on" Wes said "Let's go home the fire is out and now with the forest gone and the threat is gone for many years. We will be safe at Cliffside."

West and Carry climbed down the cliff to the small valley below. West was right they would be safe for many years there now.

Willow and Nimuri walked about the gardens there was little damage. How lucky they had been. She held Daniel's hand and still felt scared. She went into the cabin and waited for West to return.

Soon West was home to find Willow just sitting holding Daniel. "Willow are you okay?" he asked her. Willow looked at him "We live for such a fleeting moment in time" she said. West sat beside her "Yes we do" he said. "I don't think I have ever really been afraid before, but when I watched all the flames devouring the trees like a hungry monster and the smoke." "Willow we all are afraid. How many times have I wondered what I was here for in this time on the earth? Why now? What is my life supposed to mean? What if I get hurt like my dad? Who would look after you and Daniel? What if all the crops fail or sickness comes back to us. It makes me afraid. You just do the best you can and work hard for yourself and those around you. Find peace in yourself, your family and friends and the world will fall into place again. The fire worried me too. I have thought often about the danger. That's why I cut all the trees to make the fire break."

West patted her hand and Willow looked at him. "That's what I mean. You had the foresight to know that and do something about it. I'm not like you, I just muddle day to day. Had you not been here we surely would have perished." West looked at her "Don't underestimate yourself Willow. I saw you at the fort. When the folks came from the prairie you just did what had to be done. When we came here to Cliffside you knew what was needed. We have not gone hungry or cold. You have been wonderful and I would not know what to do without you. I have watched you work for hours and I could not do what you do."

West took Daniel to bed. He got the fire going to heat water. Willow soaked in the tub of warm water and felt so much more at ease, West too bathed. They sat by the fire and the warmth felt good. "You know Willow when I stood up there with Carry today, I could see for miles. I still can not see anything that resembled the mountains or valley dad talked of." "You'll find it West" Willow said. "If it's out there you'll find it." "I want to go see tomorrow. Let's see what we can see." Willow smiled at him. "Yes we can take a look" West said, but knew she was right. The fire would have swept it up in its fury. "I'll pack some packs for us in the morning, first let's get some rest." West and Willow went to bed for a much needed rest. Life in Cliffside was going to change soon and it would be the beginning of another new era for them all.

Zack saw the glow over the mountain ridge and had everyone down to the river. When he realized what it was panic almost took over, West was out there and Willow. The thought of losing them was almost too much for him. Then sense came back to his mind West and Carry knew what to do. He had to get Greenmeadow people to safety. Kalvin, Brad, Gary and along with all the other young men had clear cut the trees back to make a firebreak. West's idea had paid off now. With most of the people at the river they waited for the red glow approaching them to hit. The smoke came first then the heat, but just when it looked like it was going to burst over the mountain the glow started to dim. With sighs of relief the people of Greenmeadow knew luck was on their side.

The winds soon cleared away the smoke and the danger was over. They all made their way back to their homes each knowing how close they came to disaster. The garden was checked as they passed by going home want there was little or no damage.

Brad and Gary told Zack and Jo that they would go to Cliffside the following morning and check on them. It was a relief to know someone was going, but until they return Zack and Jo would not rest easy.

There was the old couple halfway that Zack worried for as well. The only consolation was that with the burned area was no fire would burn there for a long time.

Zack and Jo didn't sleep much that night and with the coming of day they waited for Brad and Gary to leave and then return.

Willow was up before West. She had not seen the fires devastation yet. She packed a lunch and at mid morning the set out. It didn't take more than an to reach the ridge where they could look over the valleys and see the hills beyond. Willow couldn't get her mind around all the black stumps that were once great trees. Everything had been turned to ash and cinder. They could still see smouldering areas. "My God West" she said. "The whole forest is gone." She almost cried. West looked at her and then over the open space. He followed the ridges of the mountains and tried t see beyond them. "It will grow back Willow" he told her. "Nature has a way of reclaiming its own. It will be but a year or two and all this will be full of flowers and bushes." He smiled and put his arm on her shoulder. "Let's go home."

They headed down the cliffs to the valley below. The lunch that Willow packed was eaten on the porch. "I should go check on the folks at the runner's cabin" West told her as he ate the last of his sandwich. "West maybe go to Greenmeadow and tell them we are all okay. I'll tend the garden with Nimuri" Willow said.

The bees never seemed to skip a beat over the fire. They buzzed and worked as if nothing had happened at all.

West nodded and picked up his day pack. He was halfway up the trail from Cliffside when he met Brad and Gary. After a hug and a handshake the three walked back down the trail to Cliffside.

Brad told West that the fire never reached the runner's cabin to their relief and Greenmeadow was unscathed. Willow was surprised to see Brad and Gary, but glad just the same. She made them something to eat and gave them tea. Brad and Gary were glad that Cliffside had weathered the fire. West was a smart man to have clear cut the trees around them.

They walked up to the top of the cliffs after they ate to see the devastation. When they got up there they almost shivered at the thought of all the area engulfed in flame, West pointed out the new ranges to them now they were more visible. He would add that he would add what he could to his maps. They were stunned at how far they could see and how vast the wilderness really was.

They didn't stay up top for long. They had to take the news all were fine back to Greenmeadow. They climbed back down and Brad and Gary headed home.

The following week was hot then the rains came. West was tired of smelling the soot and ash in the air. The rains wee a welcome event.

Zack and Jo were comforted by the knowledge West and Willow were safe. Greenmeadow fell into the rhythms of work and the seasons passed.

It was Daniel that called to West and Willow at the sight of the runner. Willow took the letter from him and offered him some lunch. He smiled and told them he had already eaten. "Some tea?" he said. Willow smiled and went to get him some.

Willow now had the letter and was reading it when she returned to the porch with the runner's tea. Daniel looked at West "What does it say dad?" he asked. Daniel was growing fast and for his young age worked hard with West and Willow at everything he could. West looked up and then gave the letter to Willow to read. She could tell by the look on his face that the news was not good. As Willow read tears began to well in her eyes. "You must go West" she said. "Daniel will help me here." West looked at her "We all need to go. I'll ask Carry to hold the fort while we are gone. If we are gone for too long you and Daniel can come back."

The runner looked at them. "I'm sorry if I was the bearer of bad tidings." "No, no" West said "We have been expecting this news for some time now."

The runner thanked them for the tea and headed to the next valley. After the fire two families came up from the fort to work the land. West didn't mind, with the land cleared by the fire it was a good opportunity for it.

Willow put her hand on West's shoulder. Not much could be said. Zack was passing his suffering was nearly over. She was concerned for Jo. She was always a rock, but where Zack was concerned it was a different story. Daniel was not being left behind. He knew something was amiss, but just what he was not sure. Grandpa is sick mom?" he asked. "Yes dear he is" she answered him.

By the following evening they were in Greenmeadow. Jo was sitting on the porch sewing when they arrived. As always people came and there was plenty to eat and drink. Wax was far easier to come by and an abundance of candles made night time visits more common.

West went in to see Zack right away and Willow stayed with Jo and the others. Daniel had his spot on grandma's knee and was not about to be budged.

Zack and Wets talked and Zack told him to take the books home he had been working on. They were self explanatory Zack told him. "West I am dieing" Zack said "I have to tell you a few things before I go. Take care of your mother. She is a good woman and I love her. Teach Daniel everything in the books he will need to know what's in them. Take care of Willow she loves you son. Now I want to sleep. Go sit with your mom for a bit." Zack weakly patted West's hand. West smiled and left the room.

Zack was now free he passed the legacy to West, everything was in the books. He closed his eyes and visions of Jo as a young woman flowed through his thoughts; his mom and dad and Dee. He thought about the world as it was in his day and how he lived on the farm. Zack passed away his life was over. It had been a good life. He had worked and saved segments of mankind. Those on the outside and built the complex to preserve those on the inside.

It was with the evening meal that Jo discovered Zack's passing. She went in and sat beside him. She cried as she drank her tea. He had given her life so much meaning. He was the one that gave her the courage to face the world as it had become. With his resolve and knowledge he helped people build a new life. He taught the children and made sure they had the tools necessary to survive. She was glad he was no longer in pain, but the pain she felt was overwhelming. What use would she be now? Zack had always needed her. West had his own family now as did the others in

Greenmeadow. "What am I going to do now my dear?" she spoke softly to him. "Life without you just doesn't seem like life" she said. Jo pulled the blanket neatly over him. He would be buried the next day. Jo held his hand then kissed his cheek. "I'm going to miss you so" she said and wept silently.

West and Willow put Daniel to bed and went to visit her mom and Kalvin. They knew that Zack's passing was near and tried to keep the conversation light. Before it got to dark they made their way back to West's mom and dad's. Along the way Willow asked West "Are you okay?" "Yes I'll be alright" he answered. "He has a lot of books for me. He told me to make sure I read them all. He has been an anchor to me Willow. I would be half the man I am today had it not been for his patience and understanding. He is an extremely knowledgeable man. I remember when I was really young he would tell me of all the things in the old world. I can't imagine what life was like for them" West told her. "You're lucky there my parents fought a lot about the old world. My father resented everything that was lost. I could understand, but I found there were many things still here and why couldn't he see that? Maybe the loss of everything he knew just couldn't be replaced in his mind. Mom was different she always had hope. It must have been the children that gave her that. She is so changed with Kalvin and I am happy for that." They arrived at the cabin and went to bed to give Zack and Jo some time to be together.

Morning came with the solemn knowledge that Zack passed in the night. The men went to the graveyard and dug the grave. Then back to the workshop to make the coffin. The women did what they could for Jo. Her life was changed now, for what remained of it. Willow never left her side. West found no solace in anything. His father was gone and he was all that was left of Zack. He had Daniel with him and knew that the lineage of his father continued with him. He was at a loss. He never knew Zack like anyone else; grandpa was grandpa. He told stories and always had things Daniel could play with. Living in Cliffside did not give him enough time with him. Daniel could see the pain of his dad's face and Willow's. It was Sara and Jean that put him to work bringing in wood from the shed to the cabins. Soon the other children had his attention. West relieved him of the job and told him to go play.

Jo had prepared Zack. When the coffin was brought in she made sure he was placed so and put mementos in with him.

Late that afternoon Herb read over Zack and pointed out how many things that he could about his life. They carried him to the yard and buried him next to Willow's father. Each person carried a rock from the river and with a memory they spoke aloud then placed it around his grave. Jo, West, Willow and Daniel remained at the yard quietly spoke and remembered Zack.

By nightfall they were at the cabin again; it was done. Jo put on some water "Mom come live with us in Cliffside" West said. She looked at him "I'm not leaving; Zack and I worked years to get this place where it is. I'm not just going to walk away from it all." It occurred to her that was almost what Zack told her his mother had said about leaving the farm. "West I'm too old and Greenmeadow has been my life. I'll not leave, my friends are here and I will be buried up there with Zack when my time comes." West knew she was not going to leave there. "I'm worried for you mom." She looked at him "West I'll be okay. I've known for some time his passing was near. He was in such pain for so long. I can visit him when I choose. Your life is not here nor would I ask you to give up Cliffside to come here. Besides folks around here need me" she smiled.

West knew she was smiling but the hurt was near the surface. She was right though her life was here in Greenmeadow.

They stayed on a few more days before they headed back home. Life continued on but it was changed. West had to bring the wagon home. Zack had left many things for him and his family.

Daniel never spoke much on the trip home. Seeing the end of life for Zack had put his young mind working. As they neared home, Daniel began his questions. West and Willow answered them the best they could, but like in many things in life they didn't have all the answers. He was concerned that they would pass soon and with reassurance they told him that it was not likely they thought that would happen soon. He shifted the conversation to grandma and was none to pleased that her time was near.

West was reserved since Zack's passing. He never read the books his father left him. He worked on the harvest and anything that kept his mind busy. He had made a few trips to the valleys beyond.

Willow shared her concerns with Nimuri. Nimuri just said to give him time and he would be okay. Willow never understood West sometimes. He had a reserve about him and he thought about things that she never contemplated.

By the time winter set in West had returned to his old self again. Willow now had to do the work that summer harvest had take place of.

With the flax spun, weaving would be done, candle making, wax paper and with the advice from Jo the turnips were washed, dried and dipped.

Bees had made the trip to the fort now and wax was plentiful. Willow made paper and knitted. West sat at the table with Daniel. He had grown Willow thought as she gazed at them from her chair by the fire. West had a book and it was his family history as best as Zack could remember it. He talked of life and his parents and grand parents. What life was like for him as a young man and how he had trained at school to become an architect. West read aloud to Daniel and he listened intently, often stopping West to ask questions. Willow listened to the story of Zack's life and was glad that Jo had made mention of keeping a journal to Willow for the future generations. Willow had asked her mom about many things in her life. Willow wrote what could be remembered by her mom down. Listening to Zack's story made her realize even more the amount of knowledge he held in his life. Willow was almost glad that West had finally decided to read the things his father had left to him.

It was near the middle of winter when West had called her from her sewing to come see the book he was reading. Willow went to the table and looked at the drawings. Some never made sense to her but many did. "My goodness West, he has drawn things I never even thought could exist" Willow smiled. West smiled "I know what they are Willow and understand the use of many of them. Look here is a windmill. The wind turns the sails here and in turn all these cogs and wheels. This could be used to grind wheat. Look here this is a pipe system to bring water to the house from a running source. These designs for cabins and boats and plans for pottery houses, smith houses and carpenter shop. He has water wheels here and look here barns for animals. Seems he thought we would have them one day." "He had faith in you West. He really believed the complex was going to be found" Willow said to him and smiled. "I don't know Willow. I have found nothing, not trace or sign. I have searched my whole life and found nothing." "Don't fret West you'll find it" Willow smiled again.

Daniel had come in. He and Seth had become good friends and the two were nearly inseparable. "Wash up Dan" Willow said and went to make something to eat. West remained at the table looking over the maps and the books. Daniel washed and sat with him at the table. "Why do you think this place is out there dad? How will you know if you find it anyways?" Daniel asked. "Well it's out there the world wasn't always like it is now you know" West told him. "I know I know it used to be full of people and creatures" Daniel said.

It was Willow that reacted first "Look here young man you are getting a bit above yourself. Don't you talk like that" she scolded him. Daniel could feel the heat of embarrassment rise in his face. "Yes mom I'm sorry" Daniel said. Daniel couldn't understand them. His dad was gone so much looking for some place and they talked of all these things that would be there and the tales of the world before. "Before" he thought, this was the only world he knew and it was a good place as far as he knew. Willow looked at him "You know Dan I don't remember the old world, but I have seen things that were left by the people of the great passing. One day you will make the trip to the fort and see for yourself. Your aunt I'm sure would be happy for a visit someday." Willow could see that had brightened his mood some.

How different Daniel was from West, Willow thought. He did have good work ethics, but he was far more content to stay home. Maybe he would get the wanderlust as he grew.

Winter carried on and before they knew it spring was hinting. It was time to think about the gardens.

While Nimuri and Willow planned the gardens Carry and West made new tools to use. They were trying out some designs of Zack's.

Seth and Daniel spent most of their time playing. The sight of the runner was not as unfamiliar as before with the new folks in the valley beyond. Willow wondered how long it would be before more families moved there.

The runner did not pass through but brought a letter for Willow. She offered tea to him and then sat by the fire to read her letter. Daniel had questions by the dozen for the runner. He was happy to answer his questions and waited to see if a reply would be given by Willow.

Willow couldn't believe what she was reading. Her mother had passed away suddenly. "Oh my God, what will Kalvin and Lisel do?" Willow told Daniel "Go get dad Daniel and hurry." Willow took the chair.

West appeared at the door. After reading the letter West jotted down a note for the runner to return to Greenmeadow. He assured him that Willow would be okay. The runner left and Willow wept.

"They buried her already, why did they not write sooner?" and she wept. "Willow the paths are just starting to clear we will go in the next few days if you would like." Willow held West from her chair and cried. West put his arm over her and stoked her hair. He knew all too well how she felt.

Daniel never said a word and West told him to get more fire wood. Daniel didn't like it when his mom cried; she often did when West went away. He filled the wood box outside first and then loaded up his arms to go in. Willow now drinking tea West had made her seemed to have recovered her composer. Daniel filled the box by the door. "Daniel, come here" she said "Sit by me." Daniel sat beside her "What's the matter mom?" "My mother has passed away this winter. She has left us all and I'm filled with sadness at her passing. There are too many things left unsaid between us. I want to go to Greenmeadow and I want you to come with me. Then I want to take the news to Dawn at the fort."

West looked at her "The gardens need to be done soon Willow both of us can't go." "Daniel will be with me and I'm sure someone from Greenmeadow will travel to the fort with us to see Chad and Dawn." West knew she was right and he also knew that her mind was made up. "Then you go do what you have to I will go to Greenmeadow with you."

The rest of the day was not a very pleasant one. Willow prepared things to go. Daniel did not want to go to Greenmeadow or the fort he just wanted to stay home. He knew Cliffside, his best friend Seth was here and Carry and Nimuri. Why did he have to go to the fort? It held no interest for him at all. When the people passing through Cliffside to the valleys beyond he watched the strange faces pass by and wanted to hide from their stare. Who were they and why did they have to live beyond Cliffside. He thought about the fort and all the people there. He was sure he did not want to go.

It just took Willow a few days to have things ready for the trip. Daniel was reluctant to go, but he knew he had no choice.

West took him aside before they left and placed a large responsibility on his shoulders. "Daniel you care of your mother her feelings are hurt. Losing her mother when they finally made a bond between them is not easy for her. I am depending on you to make sure she rests and takes care of herself." "But dad you should do this not me." Daniel protested. "Daniel I have to plow the fields and plant with Carry and Nimuri. If we don't plant we will go hungry. I can't go. I must remain here." Daniel nodded at West "I'll take care of mom, dad" he said. West tussled his hair and went to talk to Willow.

Willow had the small wagon packed. She and Daniel should be able to pull it with ease. West pulled her to him "Be careful Willow, don't let your grief lead your way" West said to her. Willow hugged him and told him she would let common sense lead her.

Satisfied West walked them up the path to the forest's edge. He watched them go and turned to go home. He knew they would be fine and with the gardens a few days away from being plowed, West found solace in preparing the paths and adding to the roads.

He read his father's books and was astounded at the plans for bridges and the maps of the world. Soon the garden work took over his time and once again the books were set aside for later when the work was less.

Willow and Daniel made their way to Greenmeadow. Most of the trip was made in silence. Daniel knew his mom was lost in her own thoughts.

When they reached Greenmeadow Daniel was relieved. They went to Jo's cabin and Willow was happy to see she had Lisel there with her. Kalvin had to work the fields and Jo and the other women cared in turn for Lisel. Willow was hurt to discover that Jean had too passed in the winter. Herb and Kalvin spent as much time as possible working to ease the pain.

Willow, after unpacking went to the grave yard. She took with her two stones for the graves. She sat on the bench there and looked at the growing grave yard. She placed one stone on her mother's grave and one on Jean's, each bearing the fond memory she had for each. How fleeting life was she thought; time slipped by so quickly. She remembered her mom and dad; how sad most of their life had been. Then when her mom met Kalvin and how happy she was, so changed. She would always have respect for Kalvin for that. He gave her life back to her and her siblings. How sad she was for Lisel; how would she be not having her mom there for her. They were passing all of them. Zack was here and her parents, Jean too. Jo was getting older; Sara and Lily were showing their age as well.

She sat on the bench and looked out over Greenmeadow. The memories of her childhood flooded in. She thought about when she moved here and how they struggled then just to keep the gardens going. The bees had made things so much easier. She followed the trends of thought to her mushroom picking and how much she loved the solitude it gave her. She remembered the day West watched her. He is a good man and her life is so much better with him in it.

It was the sound of someone coming up the path that brought her back to the present. It was Jo. She walked with a walking stick now. Willow got up and lent her an arm to hang onto. The two women sat in silence on the bench for a long while before Jo spoke. "She spoke of you often Willow, did you know that? She was extremely proud of you" Jo said. "I want you to know that she didn't suffer. She passed quickly. I believe she suffered with a heart problem." "It's no wonder" Willow said. "My father was not a good thing for her. I am happy she had so much joy in the later part of her life. Kalvin is such a good man." "Yes they were lucky to find each other" Jo said. "I have seen many folks suffer many emotional terrors from the outbreak. It changed things so much; our way of life was gone. It's a hard thing to start over. So many times I didn't think we would survive. It's the young people's world now" Jo told her. "Zack, rest his soul and I tried to teach you the things you would need to survive" Jo told her. Willow patted her hand "Now I must teach Daniel. Is the world so much different?" Willow asked her.

Jo looked out over the valley "Yes Willow it is. It's a barren world almost now. I miss the animals and the bird songs; music in general. When Herb made the flutes for the children it was a sad happiness. It's sad because the sound of the bird song was gone, but happy because music was back. Tell me Willow does Daniel play his flute much?" "No he is very reserved. In some ways I worry for him. He almost has distain for strangers. He has no desire for adventure. He is so different from West. West is always looking over the next ridge to see what's there. Daniel could care less. He is contented where we are. I'm worried about him" Willow told her. "Don't worry, Daniel is not West, he can't be expected to be a mini West. That was something about Zack I never understood. Why he was almost obsessed in finding the complex, that's how he hurt himself, he fell down a cliff. I thought he was going to die. It took so long for him to regain his health. That day ended his search. I wish he never instilled that in West." "Do you think it's out there?" Willow asked her. "Oh I have no doubt, but it's like finding a needle in a haystack" Jo told her. "Even if it is found would they let us in?" "They would be afraid we would contaminate them. No Willow I have no desire to find it. They are the old world. Everything that brought the demise of things I once knew existed there. Maybe they too understand how fragile the world is now and have been working to help us." "Like the bees?" Willow said. "I don't know Willow" Jo said. "The world is a very place natural selection let us survive it has to be the same for the animals, but like I said the world is a very large place."

"Now we have been with the souls of our loved ones long enough. Lets go back and be with the ones that can still talk to and get replies." Jo smiled at Willow and the two women went to Jo's cabin.

Soon Daniel was back from the park. He had enjoyed himself "Mom can I stay here with grandma I don't want to go to the fort" he said unceremoniously. It was Jo that spoke "Daniel, you must go to look after your mom. She needs your strength. It's a long way to the fort I don't want her to go alone." Daniel looked at her; maybe grandma was right mom wasn't herself since she lost her mom. "Okay mom I'll go" he said. Willow and Jo looked at each other and the knowing smile passed between them.

Kalvin came later that evening and brought all the children. Willow was happy to see them all and that Kalvin cared so well for them. She was glad he had Lisel she was the only thing of her mom and him he had left. He did not favour her over the others which was a good thing. Willow relaxed knowing they were in good hands. They stayed another day before they started the trek to the fort.

The day was wet and Jo tried to get Willow to postpone travelling until it was warm and dry, but Willow wanted to get going. They would be at the next settlement by nightfall.

With the small wagon emptied of the heavy things the trip would be easier. They wore oiled cloth capes to keep the wet out. It was Willow that told Daniel how West dreaded travelling in the rain and how much he hated wet feet, she laughed. Daniel smiled "I don't mind being wet" he said "I just don't like being cold." Willow felt the same. "You know I was born in the next village and when I was about your age we moved to Greenmeadow" she told him" she told him. "When I was to marry your father people had been found on the prairie. They were in such a bad way. Grandma Jo and I travelled to the fort to help them. Did you know that Nimuri was from the prairie?" Willow asked him. Daniel smiled "Why did it take so long to find them?" he asked. "From what my mother told me, after the great passing the people that were left sought safety at the fort. It took many years to get the cabins built and to grow enough food for everyone. We had no bees to help with pollination then, it was all done by hand. It was the runners that had gone to the city of the dead that finally found them." "The city of the Dead?" he asked. "Yes, a place of great gathering of people. They lived almost everywhere in the old world, but come now Daniel you have been taught all this." Willow smiled at him. "Yes, but I would like you to tell me that story" he said to her.

"Well, the city of the dead was just that. So many people died; too many to bury and so they fled to the fort those left alive. Those that had passed away were abandoned, left where they lay. People feared sickness. I believe that now they started to bury the bones of those lost back then. There's not much left of the city now. Dawn writes me and most everything that could be savaged has been. The fires and the storms over the years past must have wiped away what was left of it. That's what happened to the prairie people" Willow told him. "Kalvin, Nimuri and Herb are some that survived the fires and famine. You will meet many at the fort and nearby settlements that we helped regain their health and lives. The first years were so hard any extra food had to go to feed all the people. Now they have homes and we all have food." "Mom, do you believe all the stuff grandpa Zack talked about?" Daniel asked her. "Yes I do Daniel, but I don't think your dad will ever find where they are. I will tell you this; if does find them it will change our lives again." "I'm not sure I want him to find them? Daniel said. "What's wrong with our lives now? Dad is always gone when he gets a chance. I wish he would stay home with us." Daniel said to her. "I do too" Willow said. "But he is determined to find them."

They had walked most of the way and Willow decided to stop and eat. The rain had stopped and Daniel was starving. "Daniel, why didn't you tell me you were so hungry?" Willow asked. He just looked at her and smiled. "I knew you would stop and besides" he said "I was listening to your stories." "We will be at the settlement soon" she told him. "I want to get to bed soon and we still have a long ways to go."

They started out again and by nightfall they had reached the settlement. Willow was received by many and soon the common house was full of old friends.

Daniel sat beside his mom and spoke little as he met them all. The common house had hot water for them and after visiting Willow bathes, Daniel did too after Willow and sleep soon found them.

Willow was up first and had everything ready to go when Daniel finally woke up. They ate downstairs and after some goodbyes to old friends and a letter to take to the fort they followed the road again.

"There were a few new faces" Willow told him. "And it had grown since I was last there." You sure know a lot of people mom" Daniel said. "There aren't that many people Daniel, in time you will know many. We live fairly far out, but most people live where we are going. There's always been the hope that more people will be found, but so far none have been."

They reached the river and now a raft had been built to ferry people across. The old trolley car was long gone. Daniel enjoyed the ride. Willow shared her stories with Daniel and after a few breaks they reached the midway valley. Willow was astounded at how many cabins were there. People had been moving out from the fort area.

They again stayed in the common house Daniel and Willow talked with a few folks. The fort, the last time she had been there it was over crowded. She was happy to see they had found homes and land to farm. The central road had fruit trees and a large play area. There was a school house and a public house for meetings and gatherings. It didn't take long for people to bring letters to be taken to the fort. Willow dropped off the ones for here at the meeting hall. They were on their last leg of the journey, the next was the fort. It had been so long since she had seen Dawn and Chad.

The road to the fort had been almost all forest and now had many clearings. When they finally reached the last crest before descending into the fort valley Willow looked out over the open expanse. She was shocked to see how much it had changed. Almost double the cleared farming area and so many more buildings. Daniel just looked. He never knew so many people lived there. His journey to the fort had made him aware of how small his world in Cliffside had been. It was a startling revelation for him.

When they arrived at the common house in the fort it wasn't long before many people knew Willow was there. Most of the people she helped nurse back to health had come to say hello. They had a lovely dinner and hot tea after was shared by many that stopped to see her. Tomorrow they would be at Dawn and Chad's. Willow was sad to be the bearer of such bad news.

With the night approaching sleep was welcomed by both.

The noise of the fort had them up early; after washing and eating Willow and Daniel were again on the trail.

Daniel watched the men going to work with those already in the fields. He listened to the sounds fade from the smithy and work shops as they made their way to Dawn's. By lunch they had arrived. Dawn saw them first and called to Chad in the field to come see them.

After a hot meal and the treasures from Cliffside unloaded, they sat outside in the sun. Dawn knew that Willow had something to tell her. "What is it Willow?" Dawn asked. "It's mom she has passed" Dawn looked at her "When?" she asked. "In the winter. Her heart gave up; at least that's what Jo thinks happen." Dawn never said anything. Willow patted her hand "Time moves on for all of us." Dawn said "I will miss her. The old guard will soon be gone and the memory of the old world with them. Mom's life until she met Kalvin was not a happy one. At least we can take comfort that she had some happiness in her last years. How is Kalvin?" Dawn added. "He's got Lisel and the others. He will be okay."

Dawn's eyes filled with tears and she wiped them away. "I feel tired" she said to Willow and went into the cabin and went to her bedroom. Willow knew she was crying and made no effort to disturb her. She knew Dawn would have her cry and rejoin her.

Willow watched Daniel and Chad in the field. Her mind wandered to West and all the work that needed to be done at home. Work, work, work she thought sometimes it felt like life was one big survival job. When you did finally get a chance to rest winter was there and with it all the torments it brought, the cold and snow. Willow got up and went in; she put on tea and before long Dawn appeared from her bedroom and joined her.

The next few days were spent crying and remembering their mother. They would talk well into the nights. Daniel and Chad spent most of their time in the fields. Willow knew they would have to go back to Cliffside and the next day they would have to start back. The wagon was staying and Dawn was thrilled with the gifts Willow brought; the wax, syrup, cloth and other things.

With the pack ready the last night was spent talking of the future.

Sleep was welcomed by all and the next morning came too soon as it usually did. Dawn walked them to the fort. With hugs and tears the journey home for Daniel and Willow began. The pace was a lot quicker without the wagon to slow them down.

The following days were relatively uneventful as they made their way home. Daniel did talk about the fort some and the people, but admitted he was happy to be going home.

When they finally reached Cliffside, the journey had been a long one. West, Carry and Nimuri were all happy to see them.

Willow had plenty of time to think over the week and Dawn's words still rang in her head; soon the old guard would be gone and the memory of the old world with them. Life had held on and now the new generation would make their own mark on the world.

The following weeks had been hard work. The gardens were planted and life once again had renewed it's self. In the valley the lime green leaves on the trees were turning a rich forest green. The familiar sounds of them rustling as the wind blew through them brought Willow comfort. West was gone adventuring again now the gardens were in. Daniel passed the days with Seth. Nimuri and Willow never seemed to be at a loss for things to do. Carry had gone with West, the two men enjoyed their time away.

The weather was hot to Daniel, Seth and the women had to carry water to the garden.

West and Carry decided to venture passed the valleys they had mapped. The people that moved into the burned area turned it into a green area again. The crops were growing well there and this year they were starting to expand the road.

Willow could see that Cliffside was going to stay small and the people would soon fill the valley beyond theirs. They had called the settlement Blackrock. It seemed Daniel's future was going to be secure. The people were having children and they were spreading out. With the new people found on the prairie the genetic diversity was preserved. Willow wondered if they would ever find more people.

The evenings found her sitting on the porch watching the sky and still watching the satellites as they crossed overhead. Morning would come too soon and Willow knew she must go to bed.

The following few years passed quickly. Life for the people was getting better. The bees provided so much pollination that crops were abundant. No fire or adverse weather had hindered the growing seasons. West still had not found any signs of the complex. His loyalty to his father was unwavering. He never would give up searching.

Daniel, now in his teens had developed a real love of the land. He spent hours in the gardens. Although he never wanted to go anywhere he did go to Greenmeadow to stay with Jo.

The increase in population had brought many new faces to Blackrock. West told Willow they were starting to populate the valleys beyond.

Daniel found blueberry bushes and cranberry plants in the few trips he had made with West. Kalvin had given him some plant clippings from some grape vines that had been found at one of the farms near the city of the dead.

Daniel had raspberries and wild strawberries growing too. Often he sat with Willow on the porch and he would whittle as Willow sewed. He had made tea and as they sat there he would ask Willow about young women. Willow smiled and tried to tell him what she could.

"Do you have some lucky lady that you are fond of?" she asked him. "No, no not yet, but I have noticed some." He continued to whittle the piece of wood he had "I want a solid woman like you and grandma. One that works hard and has a good head on her shoulders" he told her. "I want her to like to farm. I wouldn't be happy if she was like dad always wanting to go adventuring." "Don't be hard on your father Daniel he is a good man. He adventures because he promised his own father he would search for the complex." "I understand that mom, but every chance he gets he goes.

I wish he would just see how much we have here" Daniel told her. "I do believe he knows Daniel." "I know it bothers you that he goes all the time mom why don't you say something to him?"

Willow looked him "Your father works terribly hard for us and all winter he works and makes things for people. He never has not done his duty for his family or our community. I knew when I married him that he would search for it and was under no illusions about that fact. I would not say anything to him. He has to deal with it on his own terms. Now that's something for you to know when you find the person you decide will be your life's partner. Make sure you are honest about what you want and where you think your life is headed. Not being truthful to yourself or to your partner will only cause unhappiness." Daniel nodded he knew his mom was right. "So when are you going to Greenmeadow again?" she asked. "Not until the gardens are weeded again. Then I will feel unhurried for my visit" he told her.

It was about then Seth appeared. "Hey Dan" he said. "Want to come help dad, mom and me? Mom wants dad to build a few hives for the new folks in Blackrock." Daniel smiled "Sure" he said.

Willow found herself alone on the porch. She listened to wind rustle the leaves on the trees and gazed out over Cliffside. How different it was now compared to when she and West first came. She was happy but Daniel was right about one thing she did miss West when he was gone. Her thoughts drifted to Daniel and smiled; he had started to notice and she knew before too many years passed he would be wanting his own cabin somewhere. Then she realized with Daniel gone the lonely hours without West would not be as bearable. She had her work and that kept her going. Maybe West would give up looking someday.

With her sewing done she went into the cabin and decided to read some of Zack's books. She enjoyed them so much. He had been such a prolific writer. She always found something in them that opened her mind to new ideas and how he explained so many things in their world. She had been keeping a journal and a special book for the family tree. It was brought fully to her thoughts as she read Zack's family tree. She knew West's drive to find the complex might have much to do with the fact he might have family there. Zack never talked much about it. Willow was sure it gave him great pain to think of it. Jo never spoke of it much either.

Daniel would be going to visit Jo soon. She smiled; it was one place Daniel always liked to go. He had been going to Blackrock too. He was helping them build a storage house and a small school house. They had turned the burned valley into a green haven with the evidence of the fire disappearing more with each passing year the name Blackrock was almost out of place. There were several families living there now and they had the road finished. Willow had given them apple and wild plum trees. They would be soon producing well for them.

She closed the books and returned them to their spot on the shelf. She could stop her mind from wandering. The rest of the day was spent puttering with her flowers and herbs.

Daniel came in late for dinner and West still didn't make it home. Daniel true to his word spent the next two days weeding the gardens.

When he was satisfied he packed his pack to go to Greenmeadow. Willow had written letters to go with him and by the time he was off he had letters for nearly everyone.

Carry had built a kiln for Seth from Zack's plans. With Daniel gone for the next while Seth spent his time making pottery. Carry and Nimuri tried to keep Willow from being lonely, but West was the missing item that they weren't. He should have been back by now he had been gone nearly 2 weeks.

Willow cleaned out the cabin and spent hours on the loom. The familiar clack, clack of the loom reminder her of Freda.

That evening was spent on the porch and as dusk fell she watched the stars come out. She watched the satellites cross the sky and thought about what Zack said in his books. They made it possible for people to talk to and transfer information all over the world. How interesting it would be if they could do that now. With the coolness of the night Willow went in and added a few logs to the fire. She didn't burn the candles long, there was enough work to do the next day and she was tired. She went to bed and was soon asleep.

Daniel had arrived at Greenmeadow and wasted no time to get to Jo's. She was happy to see him. Although Jo was getting old her mind was fine. She never stopped working she always had something on the go. Daniel filled her wood boxes and after a nice meal they sat at the table. Daniel had passed out the letters soon after his arrival and was now free to just visit.

"So tell me my young man what new things for the garden this year?" Jo asked him. "Nothing new" Daniel told her "But the grapes are getting bigger and the plum trees as well." He smiled. "We should go pick some mushrooms tomorrow morning" Jo told him. "I'd like that grandma" Daniel replied. "How are mom and dad doing? Have they lots of work in the gardens" "Mom is good, she works too hard. Dad is gone again. He's always gone looking. I don't know why he wastes his time grandma. What good would it do really even if he did find it?" Jo looked at him "I wished Zack had never implanted that into West. All it ever did was be the near death of him. Your father gave his word to Zack to keep looking for the complex" she told him. "Well I think he should think more of mom. She does all the work when he's gone. I don't think it's right" Daniel told her. "Well my boy that's really between them and they will have to sort it out themselves." "Grandma" Daniel said. "Yes what is it dear?" Jo replied. "You lived in the old world. Was it better than now?" he asked. Jo paused for a moment "I was not much older than you and it was a long time ago. I don't know; things were easier, but I think the people now have far more compassion then they did then. It's different now. I miss some things, but only for a moment. I have a good life. I have loved and been loved. I have your dad and mom and you as well as many good friends. I miss grandpa, but that's part of life as well." She patted his hand "Is something bothering you Daniel?" "Not really" he told her.

Jo looked at him and knew he would tell her in his own time. He was unlike West in many ways. He liked to be at home and saw little need in travelling everywhere. West on the other hand had wonder lust in him. West had made a trip to the city of the dead at about Daniel's age, but Daniel had no such desires, in many ways that pleased Jo. She always feared that West would share Zack's fate to get hurt in his travels and be unable to care for his family.

"Daniel you don't have to look for the complex you know. It's entirely up to you" Jo told him. She could see the relief wash over his face. "I just want to grow food and build a home. Maybe find new foods to grow. I have been messing with grandpa's old pottery wheel and I can see why he liked it so well" Daniel told her. "Have you read grandpa's books yet?" Jo asked. "Some of them" he replied. "Most of them are more of dad's interest. I was hoping to look at your books." Jo smiled "Sure" she told him. She had collected a lot of information about herbal cures and the processing and storage of the food they grew. Daniel smiled "Thanks grandma" he said.

The evening was passed with the discussions of gardens and medicines. It was Jo that made the move to shut down the evening and go to bed. Daniel slept in West's old room. Jo cleared up the cabin some and after she was done she sat for a while by the fire. Tiredness soon enveloped her and she retired to bed.

Morning found Jo in the kitchen preparing a light meal to take with them. "Come on Lazy bones. The earlier we get there the better the mushrooms will be" she called to him. Daniel was up and washed by the time she had the food packed. He gulped down his tea and ate the warm bread and jam Jo made for him.

The air was crisp and cool. They both carried something; Jo a basket and Daniel their lunch. They walked in the bush and as they sought the mushrooms neither spoke much. It was like they were feeling where the mushrooms were growing. Jo's mind wandered as she listened to the wind blowing through the trees. How silent the world was without the birds and animals. She remembered how each spring she would wait for the first born to appear. All the songs were gone. Well, she thought, the bees are here maybe more insects will eventually appear. Daniel called "We have enough let's go home."

Daniel helped lay out their harvest to be dried. Jo had a reed screen hung high near the fire that dried them quickly. "Grandma, would you mind too much if I took one of your books to copy home with me?" Jo smiled and thought now there is a down to earth young man. "What plans have you been working over in that mind of yours?" she asked him. "I've been thinking every home should have basic medical herbs labelled in small pots what it is and what it's for. Maybe the same for herbs for cooking" he told her. "I think you might be right Daniel. It would be a good project for you" she said. "I have a few ideas that I think will help everyone" he said.

The rest of the day Jo listened to his plans and ideas. By the time evening rolled around she was sure this was no idle young man. His mind worked continuously and his ideas made sense. He had no plans to search for the complex. As far as he was concerned it was futile to waste the time when so many improvements needed to be done for the people here. Deep in Jo's heart she was glad he thought the way he did.

The next day Jo tended her herb garden with Daniel watching and helping. He had chosen the book he wanted to copy and spent the afternoon reading it and asking Jo about things he was not clear on. The next day he would be going home. Daniel always enjoyed time with Jo. She had so much he could learn. His mom took more interest in things like knitting, weaving and sewing. Jo like him found tranquility in the garden.

After a nice meal the last evening was spent in pleasant conversation. He would go home in the morning so they didn't stay up late.

Jo had breakfast ready when Daniel got up. They ate and Jo watched him gather his things together. He reminded her of West, but he was his own man.

Daniel kissed her cheek and with letters for the folks at Cliffside he started out. Jo asked him to stop at the halfway cabin and ask the couple there if they needed anything. He smiled and assured her that he would. He waved as he headed up the road and for a moment Jo wondered if it would be the last time she would see him.

Jo knew her life was coming to its close. She had written down what she wanted done with her belongings and the cabin. She made a cup of tea and headed to Zack's resting place to have her usual talk with him.

Daniel was well on his way too. He had been putting together an idea for a shop for drying herbs, mushrooms and whatever. If the grapevines produced he would try to dry some of them. He gazed out at the forest as he walked; it was so quiet with no wind blowing. He stopped to listen; not much sound other than the odd breeze and a few bees, it was quiet.

Daniel didn't stop long and was soon on the path again. He watched the woods as he walked thinking about what he would make once he was home. He knew his mom would be there working hard as usual, but he didn't think his dad would be. Daniel and West were not alike in many ways. West made sure they were always okay, but Daniel had his own ideas about things.

He arrived at Cliffside to find his mom alone again. She never complained, but Daniel knew it saddened her. Sometimes she went with him, but she did really prefer to stay home.

Daniel's days fell into the rhythms of spring and by summer he had copied Jo's book and started building the small herb shop.

The harvest was always a good time. Folks worked for their bounty and felt grateful that winter would not find them hungry or cold. The snows came early and heavy. They would almost be bound to Cliffside now until spring.

West could feel the distance grow between him and Daniel. He tried many avenues to get the distance closed, but Daniel was having no part in it. He loved West but his ideas and the never ending search for a place that might not even exist made Daniel angry.

One evening as Daniel looked through Zack's books he spoke aloud "Look at all these things of no use at all; pieces and parts we can not make and this oil and gas fuel. What are they?" he spouted. West looked at him and then at Willow "For someone so young you have much to learn" West said. "These things would be a great help to us. We as the people left have to discover ways of making them work" West said. "Then bring back the old world and do just like them? I don't want to be like them. They nearly killed us all. I work for now. I try to use the things we have and improve them; grow better and different foods not try to bring back something gone for fifty years or more." Daniel wanted to tell his father for a long time. "You have always made sure we have had food and shelter dad, but every chance you get you look for the complex. You leave us alone and we do your work. I don't think its right."

West stared at him. "You need more respect Daniel. You have never been in need, understand nor have you learned despair or depression. Your life has not been easy or hard. Each generation reaps the harvest of the ones before. There are so few of the old ones left and most that are were young when the virus happened. I would never have liked to what they did but some like my father spent hours upon hours writing down things that are meant to help us not remake ourselves into what they were. I search for the complex not just to find it, but if and I say if they have survived I have family there. I won't stop looking just as if you were missing. Would I stop looking for you?" Daniel could feel his cheeks redden with embarrassment. "As far as you doing my work; who do you think built all this here? I have never made my searching off limits to you or your mother. The option to come with me was always been there." West looked at Willow and then Daniel and got up. He put on his coat and headed for the workshop.

The tension between them never left. Willow spent a lot of time trying to get them to talk and both refused. One supper near spring West told Willow "It might be a good idea for Daniel to think about finding his own home." Willow was stunned with that comment. "West how could you say that? This is his home." Willow almost cried. West looked at her "It's time the boy had a few hardships. He is a man now and needs to temper his thoughts. I'm not saying this from anger or because I want harm to come to him. He needs to learn the ways of the world and the sooner the better." "Where will he go? Who will help him build his cabin" Willow asked. "He will be fine. I built our cabin. He can build one for himself" West replied. Willow still did not like it. How could West be so cold to his own son? How was she going to tell Daniel?

When she retired for the evening she wrote in her journal that this winter was the worst one in her life. West would not budge on his decision about Daniel leaving. It broke her heart as she wrote and the tears dripped on her pages only to smudge some of her writing.

Daniel was headstrong and he knew he could not live with them much longer. He would find a good place to live, but where. He had not ventured that far from Cliffside his whole life. He would miss his mom and dad even if he didn't agree with the way his dad always left his mom. The complex had become a wedge between them. His world was now not some old world that nearly killed everyone and everything off.

The snow kept coming everyone remarked how it was the most they had ever seen. The passages to each settlement were closed and it seemed would be for some time. Daniel talked with Seth and he told him to make up with his father, but Daniel couldn't. To him it was a matter of right and wrong. West going and searching for the founders of all their misfortune was wrong. West rarely visited his own mom because he was always searching for the complex. Daniel felt this too was wrong. He would not find anything out there; Daniel felt it with all his heart. He was wasting his time on a pipe dream. Daniel made his mind up come spring he would look for land in Blackrock or maybe in the next valley if it had water. Seth didn't want Daniel to leave Cliffside.

Often West and Willow talked in the evening after dinner more than once. The conversation would lead to Daniel and his attitude only to stop and have Willow at odds with West. Willow was beside herself; never had she met such stubborn men. They would cut their noses off to spite their faces rather than bend. How could two people who claim to love her cause her so much grief?

No runners had been through, the heavy snow had all the valleys closed up. Willow wished spring would come, the bickering between West and Daniel was reaching a breaking point. She sat looking out her window hoping for the snow to start melting. How had things come to this, her loving family slowly being ripped apart? Why couldn't West understand Daniel and Daniel, West? Carry and Nimuri stayed neutral. They would not choose sides which was completely right. Willow rubbed her forehead. She still sat looking out the window. The snow was deep this year. She had never seen this much snow.

West and Daniel found different things to do each day; West in the workshop and Daniel pouring over the books in the house. He had been reading some of Zack's books and looked over the designs for cabins. He did find the windmill for grinding corn interesting and the plumbing for the house. He pondered making the tubing required from pottery, but then dismissed the idea. He had been working on the plans for gardens he wanted and what building would be needed. Willow often glanced over them and offered her opinions. West looked too but never said anything. The evenings came and went. West and Daniel grew farther apart. The silence between them spoke volumes.

It was when the warmer weather came that the two started warring. West as usual would make his spring journey when the snow melted some and Daniel planned his trip to Blackrock. Willow with Nimuri and Carry as well as Seth looked forward to the syrup harvest.

Spring was approaching and the work of the new year with it. With the syrup in Willow took walks in the gardens to plan out what was to be planted where. Nimuri and her had always done this each spring. It was Nimuri that pointed out how high the river was. Willow had noticed, but it wasn't until Nimuri pointed it out that she became concerned. West was gone and Daniel had just come home. The weather had been surprisingly warm and the river now was concerting to them all. If it got any higher it would inundate the gardens. Daniel and Willow talked little and argued more.

That evening in the cabin Willow and Daniel sat in silence. It was the clap of thunder that broke the silence. Willow watched the flashes through the window and Daniel continued his drawings at the table. "So are you moving to Blackrock then?" Willow asked him. "Yeah I cant see the point staying here anymore" he replied. "Daniel!" Willow said "How can you say that? You're my only child and we are your parents" she told him. "Mom, mom don't start, I'm going. I can't stay here anymore. Dad and I just don't see things the same way. Besides time I made my own way; time I found a wife and started my own family." He could see the hurt in Willow's face. It was a look that was not often there. "Don't worry mom I will just be in the next valley." He smiled hoping it would be some consolation he wouldn't be that far away.

Willow sat down near the fire and started knitting. The rain was coming down outside in buckets and being snug in the cabin was reassuring. They talked little for the remaining night and went to bed when the light failed outside.

Daniel didn't sleep well, the thunder rumbled most of the night and the rain never eased it seemed. It was when she looked out the window she knew they were in trouble. The water from the river was lapping near the cabin.

The rain continued to fall and it didn't take roust Daniel and send him to Carry's to see if they were aware of the situation. Daniel trudged through the water to Carry's and soon they were all at Willow's cabin.

The rain never ceased and by mid-morning the river was rising again. "We will have to go to Blackrock if it gets higher" Carry said. Willow's mind was on West, where was he? Was he alright? What about Greenmeadow and the fort? Her mind was full of everyone. She knew she had to pull herself together.

Carry, Daniel and Seth soon had things packed and ready for their journey if they had to go.

The water kept rising and the rain went from a steady drizzle to a series of downpours. The water was up to the walkways now and Carry decided they had better go or they might get trapped in. For Carry, having been a runner a few tents on high ground would have sufficed, but with Nimuri and Willow, Blackrock was a better place.

Willow's mind was full of thoughts of West; where was he? Why wasn't he back yet? Maybe he too was trapped somewhere.

"Mom, mom!" Daniel shouted. Willow looked over at him. "Let's get going" he said. She gathered up the things she was to carry.

They started up the path to Blackrock. They had a community house there. Carry, Nimuri and Willow talked of Greenmeadow. It was lower to the river than Cliffside. How were they doing? Were they all safe?

By noon they were in Blackrock with the news of the flood. Blackrock was much higher and didn't see the effects of the flood, but the creek running down to it flowed much more rapidly than normal.

Willow thought about West and when they moved to Cliffside. He had built the cabin upon the hill and hoped it was high enough to escape a flood. All the buildings had been built on a kind of platform above the garden area. Where was West? Why didn't he come home?

Daniel got Willow settled into a room and started hauling water for her to bathe. He went to the kitchens and amongst all the chaos there he managed to get Willow some hot water for a tub to wash. Carry was doing the same for Nimuri. Seth was in the kitchen and the young women were having fun teasing and feeding him.

Daniel sat alone on the stairs after everyone was settled in. He wondered where his father was and how his grandmother was. He lamented over all the work in the gardens, now under water. He thought of the shortage of food there would be if the flood lasted too long.

"Don't worry" the young woman said to him. Daniel looked up to see a plain young woman standing there. Her hair was tied back and she had a broom she was busying herself with. "April, April! When you finish out there clean in here will you. I'm going home to get the kids to bed" and with that the door in the back closed and the older woman was gone. April just kept sweeping. Daniel watched her. She saw him and smiled. Soon she was in the back and Daniel could hear her washing dishes.

The common house was all but empty now; the girls that had been teasing Seth had gone and Seth was upstairs. Daniel knew he had to go back to Cliffside to help with the clean up. This was to be his year. He had hopes of building his cabin but now those things would have to be put on hold. His mind lingered over having his own place and what he wanted it to be like. He drank the last of his tea and took the dishes in front of him to the back.

April had an apron on and Daniel was surprised to see the stack of dishes she had yet to wash. "You could have left them. I would have gotten them when I had my tea" April told him. "You always work here?" he asked her. "No this is my week" April told him. "Most of the time I help at home. Mom and dad are getting older and things are not easy for them." "Do you like it? I mean working here" he asked her. "It's okay" she replied "One day I will have my own place and then I will give this place up to one of the younger girls. It's actually good to get some experience away from home."

As they conversed Daniel found she had him drying the dishes and he didn't mind. He got elected to carryout the compost and carry in wood.

April had tea ready for a break. "Well" she said "Just the floor and I am done. Thank you" she said to him. "You have made the time pass quickly.

The sun was starting to rise and it was light outside. Although Daniel had been up all night he didn't feel tired. They drank the tea and April chatted on about life in Blackrock. It was nearly an hour later she had the floor done. Daniel offered to walk her home, but April declined. "I must wait until the cook arrives." She went and added wood to the fires. Daniel was beginning to feel the tiredness and said his goodnights or good mornings to her.

Daniel made his way upstairs to his room. In the midst of the flood and the devastation it is causing; his father not home, grandma in danger, Daniel felt good. This was crazy he thought. I must need sleep more than he thought. When he go to his room he went to bed.

It was Willow that woke him. "Daniel, Daniel wake up" she said. He woke to see his mom standing there. "Are you alright? You have slept the morning away. I was getting worried" she said to him. "I'm okay mom. I just didn't get to sleep till late." "I'll get something to eat for you" she said.

Daniel rubbed his face and pushed his black hair over his head. He would have to get it cut soon. He dragged on his clothes and then washed.

He found his mom and Nimuri with Seth in the common room. They had already eaten. Seth of course was soon talking his ears off about the girls and Daniel smiled.

Nimuri, Carry and Willow discussed Cliffside; how much damage there would be and how long to clean it up. If they could get crops this year, etc…

By late afternoon the only consolation Daniel could find for their dilemma was the rain had stopped and the snow was all gone. He waited to see if April would be there again. He didn't seem to be able to stop thinking about her. She was a hard worker and was of a kind nature. He sat listening to his mom and Nimuri talk and wondered how long the flood would stay and then how long it would be before they had it cleaned up. He thought about Jo and hoped they too made it to safety.

It was dark when West walked into the common house. Willow wasted no time in making herself to his side. "West I was worried sick" she said to him. "I had to find a safe crossing over the river. I've been to Cliffside the fields are still under water, but the cabins and buildings are safe. I think the flood has peeked" he told her. "I want to go see how mom is as well."

West and Willow picked up his gear and headed upstairs. West stopped when he saw Daniel. "Thanks for taking care of your mom" he told him. Daniel nodded his head and West and Willow continued to the stairwell. Nimuri and Carry headed upstairs as well.

Set sat with Daniel. He talked endlessly of his shenanigans with the girls he met while here. Daniel listened to him talk, but his mind wandered. He watched all the people coming and going. He was waiting for April.

"Daniel! Hey pal, are you miles away? Did you hear anything I said?" Seth asked him. "Sorry Seth I have a lot on my mind" Daniel said. "Are you still going to move this summer?" Seth asked. "I can hardly leave with the flood" Daniel replied. "I'll have to help clean up. I just can't walk away now" Daniel continued. Seth knew that Daniel was troubled "Why don't you just make up with your dad Daniel? He is a good man you know." Daniel looked at him "Good man. He leaves at every opportunity he gets. Mom and me have to do his work and for what? He looks for the old world. He seems to think the ones responsible for all the loss and death are so important. My grandpa looked too and he died a cripple; a life of hardship for grandma. It that what's in store for my mom? Well it's not right and I will never change my mind. The old world is gone and any remnants will be gone in time as well and I say good riddance." Seth had heard this conversation before, it was not new. Seth didn't know why Daniel had such vehemence for the old world and risked losing his dad over it. "You know Daniel we are remnants of the old world" Seth said. "Our great grand parents lived then. Maybe your dad is right if there are people out there they should be found." Daniel looked at Seth "Let it go Seth" he said.

Daniel got up and left Seth sitting there. He walked down the paths of Blackrock and found a bench by a play area. Why did they all cling so tightly to the old? It was their fault the world was almost destroyed. How could they forgive them so easily? He thought about Zack's journals, how he talked of the animals and birds and the things they had. They stole it all from us; made our lives one big struggle. It was chance that those alive today were alive. Seth's own mother nearly died of starvation until the runners found them. Of all the people you would think he would understand, but he doesn't.

"Hey, what are you doing here all alone?" the familiar voice said to him. He looked up to see April. "Just thinking" he said. April sat down beside him. "Well you look like you have the weight of the world on your shoulders" she said and Daniel smiled. "No quite" he told her. "Are you off to work?" he asked her. "Yeah everyone takes turns, but I told you that" she said. "Let me walk you there" Daniel said. April smiled. "So where do you live in Blackrock?" Daniel asked. "My family has a piece of land just over there" and she pointed to the east. "How do you like Blackrock?" he asked her. "It's okay I guess, but I don not wish to live with my parents forever. I love them dearly, but I want my own home and family someday. What about you?" she asked Daniel.

"Well I live in Cliffside with my parents, but I too want my own land. I'm just not sure where yet. There is no land available in Cliffside now so I will have to find some somewhere else. The question is where to look west or south. South means more people and west means new land. It will take me a few more years to get in any kind of order, but I have a future planned and I am going to work until I see it" Daniel told her.

"Sounds impressive" April said. "Mom and dad aren't very adventurous and they had too many children to look after. I'm not going that way. I mean not that I don't want children, but there are many other things I want as well. Mom said it's up to the woman to make sure there will be a strong next generation. I have no interest in being a baby machine. I want my children to have enough and some extra not to live in a struggle all the time for food and clothing." April saw Daniel looking at her. "I suppose you think that's pretty selfish on my part?" she told him. "Actually I don't. What's the point of having children if each day will be a struggle?

It's better to have a bit of extra then not have enough. Save for a rainy day so to speak. No, I think you have a good head on your shoulders." They reached the common house "Well I have to get to work. I'll see you later for tea" she said and went in.

Daniel sat on the porch. The sun felt good on his skin. It's funny how heat from the sun feels better than heat from a fire. It was then when West came out and sat near Daniel. "I suppose it will take some time to clean up the gardens. Your mom is worried about the fruit trees and bees." Daniel never said anything. "Daniel I have decided not to look for the complex anymore. I guess if there are people there they will reveal themselves when they do." Daniel looked at his dad. "This flood is not a good thing. I should have been at home. Willow and you are my life and I have been putting you on the side lines to look for something I know now that I will never find. Its defeated me Daniel." West just sat there and looked into the sky.

Daniel didn't know what to say or do. He never expected this from his dad. "It will be alright. We will clean up the lands. Mom will be glad to have you around underfoot as she says" he told him. West smiled "Yeah, she's such a good woman. Did you know she helped me build almost everything in Cliffside? Well I'm sure you know your mom."

The door opened and Willow stood there. "Come and have some tea you two." Then she went back in. "Looks like we have been told" West said to Daniel." The two men stood and the understanding between them began.

Daniel spent the next week in almost only April's company. Seth flirted and carried on with the other girls.

Nimuri and Carry patiently waited for the water to recede so they could go home.

West and Willow spent a lot of time together. Willow knew that West felt defeated and that he felt he had failed his father. At Willow's urging West was bound for Greenmeadow after they got home.

The runners were making it through now and the news was the same for all the settlements to the fort. The water was receding, but it looked like the crops would still go in.

By weeks end they were packed and ready to go home.

Daniel and April's relationship had become more involved. Willow was happy that West and Daniel seemed to be getting along again.

The journey home was filled with anticipation as to what they would find. To the relief of all when they arrived back was that the gardens, other than a layer of silt had survived the flood.

After ensuring that Willow was settled in West headed to Greenmeadow to see how they were.

Daniel renewed at the state of the gardens spent time reading Zack's books.

The rhythms of Cliffside were almost back to normal. West returned in a few days with the news all were well.

The men starting the ploughing of the fields. Daniel was surprised the grape vines had survived and the fruit trees were almost in bloom.

With the cleanup done and the gardens well established Daniel took to looking for a piece of land of his own. He sent letters to all the settlements and had already received some replies. He also kept in touch with April. The two of them had much in common as to what they wanted for themselves in the future. He had been getting along with his dad much better. He felt sorry for him. The change in him Daniel had no doubt that West had lost part of himself when he finally decided to give up looking for the complex. His mom never said anything, but she could see it as well. Daniel had to decide where to live and get the trees cut for the buildings. Next spring would be his start on his own land. He could hardly wait.

Seth didn't want Daniel to leave Cliffside, but he knew he would. The last few months had driven a wedge between them somehow. The two friends were on separate paths.

The only trips made that summer were to see Jo in Greenmeadow and then to the valley beyond Blackrock for Daniel to claim his piece of land. West and Carry were to help Daniel cut the wood after the harvest.

It was sad for Willow in some ways; she got West back full time, but now was going to lose her son. She also found the change in West was unsettling. He spent many hours in the workshops and he sat on the porch thinking as he put it. Willow was worried. Daniel spent more time with West in the workshops and he had started potting things for his own place.

On the occasions that it rained West and Daniel spent the evenings discussing his cabin plans and where he wanted his land. West made maps and talked of the land in the valleys beyond what was there, etc…He was surprised the maps his dad had were so exact. West had travelled much further and had a good idea what was there. Carry joined them often as did Seth. The journey in the fall was becoming an adventure for them all.

For Willow and Nimuri it was a breather from cooking for them; time to do other work or take time to smell the roses. Willow would be glad to have them home just the same.

It was a runner that brought a letter from Dawn. She claimed there was a child there at the fort that could heal people. She talked of a man that had cut his foot while chopping wood and the child placed his hands on the wound and healed him.

That evening after supper Willow, West, and Daniel sat at Carry's house and the letter was read aloud. "I'm not sure what to think about this" Willow said. "Do you think it would be true and if it is how could a child do this?" she said to them. "When you go cut the wood for Daniel's cabin I want to go visit Jo" Willow said. "She might know of this and how it could be. She did live in the old world" Willow said. West agreed, although he wasn't sure it was possible. "I have no reason to believe she would not be telling the truth West. Why would she make it up?" Willow knew the letter held truth and also knew that Jo might have an answer for it.

Until she could go her days slipped into rhymes of quiet work. Willow and Nimuri wove hats, baskets and mats. The men worked in the shops and gardens. West had plenty of jars and dishes made.

More news filtered in from the fort all summer of the child that healed. Willow finally had a break and decided to take the time to go to Greenmeadow. Daniel stayed home to work on things for his cabin. Willow took Seth with her. He was happy to get away from Cliffside and the work. He carried the packs with ease. Willow was grateful for his help.

They arrived in Greenmeadow to find Jo sitting on the porch. Work had carried on here the damage from the flood was more extensive than in Cliffside. Jo was happy to see them. She had bread and honey ready with tea in no time. Seth, seeing her wood piles depleted found ample work for the time they would be there. Willow could see the age creeping into Jo's face and into her movements. The last 10 years really seemed to show on her.

The first evening was spent with talk of family and friends. Jo told Seth stories from where she and Zack first travelled the mountains. He enjoyed the tales, but knew Jo was tiring out so he claimed he was tired from the trip and went to haul water to wash.

Willow helped clean up and the two women found comfort in the warmth of the fire and each others company. Seth didn't have much trouble sleeping, he was tired. He knew that for the next few days he would be hard at work chopping wood for Jo. The women didn't stay up too late morning would be there before they knew it and with it all the chores to be done.

Seth was up long before Willow and had the water hauled for Jo and wood packed in. She had him bring up the wooden tub and he knew she was going to have him haul water to fill it. He didn't mind.

When Willow got up Jo had Seth fed and already working on restocking her wood pile. She made Willow a bowl of boiled oats and bread with Jam.

It was while Willow ate she broached the subject of the healing child with Jo. Jo didn't seem too surprised by it. "When I was young I worked in a library, a house full of books. There had been many accounts of healers in the world. Many things that people could do like sense the future or the past, people could heal, people could sense what others were thinking. I don't see why this could not be so as well" Jo said to her. "I think I might feel sorry for the child. To have this gift brings with it great expectations from others. The child will always be at the mercy of those around him" Willow looked at Jo. "I'm not sure what to think really. In some ways I think it's a great thing to have the ability to heal, but then it's like you say the people around this child will decide the future." With Willow done her breakfast Jo handed her a basket and grabbed her walking stick. The two women walked slowly into the nearby woods to look for mushrooms.

Seth left behind, soon had the company of the younger men helping him stock up Jo's wood piles. He ventured into the work shops and watched Brad and Gary make furniture. He enjoyed watching them and it made the break from his own work more pleasant.

Jo and Willow talked of Daniel and West. Willow told Jo of April and Daniel's plans for his cabin. "I will miss him when he moves away" Willow told Jo. "It is as it should be Willow. He is a healthy man and needs to make his own way now. You have raised him well and should take pride in that. With so few people still he needs to start a family" Jo replied. "Do you think we will get through this?" Willow asked. "Through what?" Jo looked at her. "I guess I meant do you think mankind would make it through this?" Willow replied.

Jo sat on a stump and held tight to her walking stick. "When the virus broke out and so few of us were left. I had a great fear we wouldn't make it. The gene pool was not big enough. Then we found the people from the prairie. It doubled the population and brought a better diversity into the lives of those here. If the women had 2 or 3 children I'm sure there will be enough children to start again. You never know it's quite possible that there are others that survived as well. The world is a very large place, not only that there does not seem to be any sickness. I remember when the children all had to be immunized against many things. Now there does not seem to be the need. What ever kept us alive seems to have picked a hardy strain of people." This might be the reason for the healing child's gift. I wonder if more children might have gifts that we don't know about yet." "It is possible" Jo said to Willow. "I didn't think things such as this could be possible much less children with other abilities." Jo got up and patted Willow's hand "Don't fret" she said "Everything will be as it is. We just have to learn how to grow." Willow smiled back at Jo. There in the forest with the sun shining down behind her Jo looked almost magical standing there with Zack's carved walking stick. The two women headed back to the cabins.

Willow spoke more of April and Jo listened to her describe the young woman. "Willow, Daniel too must learn how to grow. Don't worry so much about him leaving home. He needs to find out about himself and he can't do that under yours and West's feet" Jo said. "I know" Willow replied. "I have been concerned about West. He has given up looking for the complex. I don't know if this is a good thing or bad" Willow told her. "Well for my own reasons I'm happy to hear that. I always feared he would share Zack's fate and get hurt. If he has decided to give up it's just as well." "Jo" Willow said. "Do you think there is a complex?" Willow asked her. "Yes I do I never doubted Zack about that.. I don't think it will be found for a long time. From what Zack told me Simion hid it very well to save the ones inside from discovery. He thought the surviving mobs on the outside would try to break in and take what was there. I hope they survived, but after all this time I tend to think they did not."

After arriving at the cabins they set out the mushrooms to dry. Seth had a pile of wood growing high now. Jo made lunch and the three talked of the flood and the work needed to be done yet.

It was not long after lunch that Willow and Seth prepared to go home. The visit was short, but the work at home needed to be done. Jo gave Willow some more books Zack had written and some of her own for Daniel. Kalvin was there to see them off and Willow's heart was lighter.

With Seth in tow and the day settling into afternoon the two made haste in getting back. The summer days kept it light out until quite late and this was good because when they arrived back in Cliffside it was getting dark. Willow was glad to see the valley and their cabin nestled into the side of the mountain. The visit with Jo had made her spirit lighter and set her mind at ease.

When she arrived at the cabin West and Daniel both hugged her. Seth waved and headed home. What have you two been up to while I was gone?" "Work" they both said in unison and laughed. Willow noticed West's maps on the table and a few areas marked off. "How is mom?" West asked her. "She is showing her age, but her mind is bright. She wanted you two to have these." And Willow pulled out a few books for them. "We went and picked mushrooms. It was good to be out with her again" Willow said. She held the books Jo had tucked inside her bag for her. It was filled with patterns and designs for woven hats and baskets along with patterns for clothes, knitting and weaving for rugs. Jo must have spent hours putting them down on paper.

She looked up and then sat at the table. Her gaze was on the map. When Daniel sat down and started talking of places he was going to look for land and felt that April being closer to home might be bad too. He would look and when he decided he would ask April to marry him. Willow smiled "She would be a daft woman if she refused you Daniel" Willow told him. He smiled. West continued to tell him what was in the valleys beyond Blackrock. Willow was astonished how well he knew them, but then he wandered in them for years now.

Night had closed in and the candles burned half way before they all found their beds. Willow lay beside West and listened to his steady breathing. She wondered how Daniel and April would be. She thought about what Jo had told her that with so few people yet they needed to have children. Her thoughts drifted to the fort. They had Daniel and Carry and Nimuri had Seth. They just never had another child. Sleep soon took over her troubled thoughts.

When morning came and its new light filled the valley, Willow was awake. She had breakfast ready for her men and already decided it was laundry day.

West, Daniel and Seth had Cliffside almost back to normal. The flood debris had been all but cleaned up. As Willow hung out the clothes she watched West and Carry burn the last of the dead wood the water had brought in. She wondered if Seth would move away too or stay here in Cliffside. She smiled to herself when she thought of April and Daniel with children.

She finished hanging the clothes and went in. It was Daniel first in for lunch. "Mom" he said "Tomorrow dad and I are going to get my land. I have a few places I want to look at before I choose." Willow looked at him. She knew he had to go, but she also knew she would miss him a lot. "I hope it's not too far away. Then we can visit some" she said and managed a small smile. Daniel smiled back. "I hope just to get land in Blackrock and with luck it will be there" he told her. Willow took some consolation in that. West soon joined them for lunch and they talked of Daniel's cabin and that soon he would ask April to marry him. Willow could see that he was happy.

With lunch done the men left to spend the afternoon on furniture for Daniel's cabin. The workshop would now be the place they would be until harvest began.

Willow packed some food for their trip the next day and by night fall things were ready for their journey. They looked over the maps at the table until quite late. Willow was happy to see them together on something. It had been a terrible last few years for her when they couldn't find any common ground. She watched West tell him of the area he was interested in. Daniel wanted land across the river away from Blackrock a bit, but close enough to be sociable. West pointed out an area a little higher than the river and after the flood it was looking like a better plot to have.

Carry had agreed that after the harvest he would come help cut down trees for his cabin. By next spring they would be dry enough to saw into planks. Daniel was happier now than he had been in a very long time. He would soon have his own home and wife. The prospects pleased him.

Willow finally called it "Time for bed, morning will be here before we know it." She lay in bed wondering where the time had gone. It seemed like yesterday and it was West and her building a new cabin. Life was easier now then it was then. With the salvage crews there were so many more tools to help with the work. She thought about her mom and dad and Kalvin of the prairie and Carry's mom Freda. She remembered Zack and how kind he and Jo had always been. Life had been hard and good; each year having its own kind of struggle. Jo must be so lonesome now that Zack was gone. She never said much in her letters, but she had been writing for some time now. She had shown Willow the book of family and on her passing it would be up to Willow to keep it up to date. Jo kept records of weather and the plants life. The more she wrote the more things she thought would have to be saved for the future. Willow knew she was right in that. Her mind carried on with thoughts for some time before sleep found her.

Dawn brought the never ending work with it. The following weeks they all started to prepare for the harvest. The flood had saturated the fields with nutrients and the harvest was proving to be a good one. The flax was the most work for the women. It all had to be prepared to be spun and woven.

The men dug potatoes and turnips, tomatoes and mushrooms along with herbs were dried; onions baked in the sun and then were woven into long braided ropes. Carrots all were packed sand in the root cellar; turnips were washed and dipped in wax. The wheat was thrashed from the stems and Nimuri and Willow separated the chaff with large woven discs. The oats were rolled. The nuts were collected after most of the gardens were done. Rose hips and garlic's were dried as were apples and grapes. The corn was hung and dried as well. This was the time of plenty; the last hard work before the almost slumber of winter.

West and Carry cut the trees back near the cabins to keep the fire break. Seth and Daniel had the job of cutting what was fire wood and what could be used to make many needed items each household could use.

April had been to Cliffside several times and the few weekends Daniel could get away he did. He had his parcel of land and the two of them made trips there to decide what would go where. At the back of Daniel's land was a large lake, one could barely see across it on a clear day; he liked the idea of it being there.

April was indeed a good choice for Daniel. She was hard working and had a mind of her own. Willow was happy that he had found some one to fill the void in his life. Seth was too interested in all the girls to settle for one.

When the harvest was finally in and the ground turned over to rest for the winter; the men packed up what gear they needed and started out for Daniel's land. The saws from the fort had been such a blessing. They were sent to Cliffside and Greenmeadow by Dawn. The salvage crews had diminished whatever was left out there on the prairies. What was left seems would now stay there. The few crews left had scrounged what they could from what was left of Cambry. In a generation or two it would be more of a story than an actual place.

Nimuri and Willow spent the last of the days spinning the flax. With all the men gone it was a pleasant time for the two women. They talked of life and the future. Both could see the age of each other and the toll all the hard work had taken on them. Willow had urged Nimuri to keep a family history going and she had been. Both women had grown up under such hard conditions, their childhood all but lost. The years they spent in Cliffside had been the best years of their lives. Nimuri rarely talked of the prairies; the deaths from starvation, the fires and tornadoes. She seemed to have blocked away the memories.

For Willow the animosity at home with her mom and dad, the bitterness that twisted her dad and devastated her mom were best forgotten as well. What the two women had now was good. Seth and Daniel had grown up with love; enough to eat and relatively times.

The weather had turned, it was cold and frost was on the ground in the morning. Willow knew the men would be home soon. They had been gone almost two weeks. The days warmed some; in the afternoon Willow would sit on the porch and knit. She was right; the men were sighted on the road. They seemed full of cheer so the work must be done. With hugs from them and the tools put away; the family gathered to talk of all that had happened.

They had indeed cut enough wood for the cabin; Daniel was pleased as punch. Next spring after the gardens were in he would build his home. Marrying April was now high on the list. They would winter there if all went well and hopefully hw could burn out enough stumps to start their garden. The first two or three years would be the hardest. Getting the gardens big enough to grow what they needed to survive. This winter they would make what furniture he needed. There was always something to do and it was never ending at times.

The next couple of days Willow spent washing clothes and checking on the stored foods. She wanted to make paper from the scraps of flax and was filling the vat with warm water when a runner came. He was looking for West and Willow directed him to the workshop.

Willow watched the runner leave and then West came to the cabin. The look on his face told volumes. Willow knew something awful had happened. She waited at the table for him to come in. West had to read the letter again just to be sure he had not read it wrong. There must be a mistake he thought. Willow sat patiently at the table waiting for him to tell her. Finally she took the letter from him to read it herself. It was from Kalvin and it read as follows:

My dear boy and lovely daughter Willow it breaks my heart to be the one to write to you with such bad news. It's your mother West; Jo has passed away. We found her last night sitting in her usual place up at the graveyard by Zack's grave. She had a very calm look on her face. We believe she passed quickly and with little or no pain. Please come, we will wait a day or two before we commit her remains to the ground beside Zack. I am truly sorry for your loss and grieve for you. He signed it just Kalvin.

Willow looked at West and hugged him. They were elders of the family. "We must go West" Willow said to him. "Yes I know" he replied. "I should have made time to visit her more. Since dad died she has never been the same" he told her. "They are together again" West said. "I want to go for a walk Willow just to clear my thoughts" he told her. Willow knew he needed to sort it out in his own mind. When he left she sat at the table and wept.

West just walked down by the river. He sat on an old log and watched the water slip by. It was like life, no one knows where its going and how many things will change it along the way. He would miss his mom. Tears escaped his eyes and flowed down his cheeks. One less person in the world; one less person, he thought. He sat there for a few hours before he went back to the cabin.

West gathered what things they needed and then Daniel and he put them in the wagon. There would be things to bring back West knew, so they had to take the wagon. Daniel had his moments of tears as well. He missed her. They soon had things ready to go. The morning would be the best time to travel.

That evening went very slow, they all had trouble sleeping. The journey ahead of them was not one of any joy or pleasure.

With the dawn came the frost. Willow was up and had a hot breakfast ready for them. There was little talk that morning. The trip to Greenmeadow was not one any were looking forward too. They soon were on their way, Willow, West and Daniel off to put Jo to rest. The family was getting smaller.

It was later in the afternoon when they arrived in Greenmeadow and were greeted by everyone. The trip seemed long; Sara and Lily had hot stew and tea for them. Kalvin met them and West thanked him for his letter.

They would stay at Jo's cabin and the next day they would bury her. Daniel soon had the fire going and the cabin warm. Jo's body was in the workshop. Sara and Lily had prepared her. Brad and Gary had made a coffin to her request. West took some candles and went to sit with his mom. Willow unpacked fresh clothes and soon had hot water to wash. Daniel sat by the fire and never said anything,

Willow made tea and after giving Daniel one she headed to the workshop to see West and Jo. West was sitting beside her. He noticed just how old she really was. He thought of many things in his life. He had been so fortunate to have had Zack and Jo as parents. He was convinced had they not survived many more would have perished from the virus. He thought about his dad being so adamant about all the children learning to read and write. They were such a pair and the world will be a sadder place now they both were gone.

Willow sat there with West; neither of them spoke. Willow held Jo's hand and brushed a loose strand of hair from her forehead. "Jo I'm going to miss you" Willow told her. She kissed her forehead and left the workshop.

West remained "Well mom, I never did find the complex. I hope dad was not too disappointed. I did try, but my family was slipping away from me because of it. Well mom this is it." He held her hand; he held it to his cheek, then he kissed it and gently put it back. He found a hammer and sealed the coffin. He didn't let Daniel see her like that. He wanted him to remember her as she was. When he was done he went in and washed up.

The night passed even slower than the previous one. When they did finally go to bed sleep was not easily found.

It was the sounds of Willow in the cooking area of the cabin that woke West. It didn't take long for him to realise where he was and what had happened. West got dressed, washed and sat at the table he had sat at since he was a young boy. Willow made some tea. West set his mind wandering over so many childhood memories. He could almost see his mom and dad there.

"West, Kalvin is coming with Brad and Gary" Willow told him. "Okay Willow" he said to her and went to the porch.

The men were soon at the graveyard to dig Jo's grave; by midmorning they had completed their task. Sara, Lily and Willow had their lunch ready for the men when they got back.

Daniel had spent the morning packing things into crates to be taken back with them.

After lunch most of Greenmeadow walked with West, Willow and Daniel as Jo was taken to her resting place; all carried a stone. Jo was placed down and after kind words Willow read a letter she had found that Jo left.

"Goodbye my children and friends, our time together has passed and I am now moving on to a place beyond this world. I have a good life; I have loved and have been loved. Fear not for me my trials are over; carry the softness for your fellow man as you meet your own trials. You are not alone now or ever in the future keep that close to your heart. There is a power greater than all of us in things we see. Our gift was survival lets not make our new world the same as the world that has been swept away. I love you all, as always Jo.

Willow watched as the men covered over the coffin and then each person placed a rock around the grave; each rock a memory of Jo. Willow sat and looked at the graves. Her dad and mom, West's mom and dad and Jean were here as well. Time was slipping by, Jo might be right about the world being made new again. The new beginning she would talk to Kalvin about it later.

West sat on the bench with her and soon all had gone back to their own cabins. Daniel continued to pack crates with books and things that were personal.

"She knew her time was close" she said to West. "She has things almost ready for us to take home." "I'm going to miss her Willow. She was always the rock in the family. Dad was so crippled although he did a lot it was mom that kept things together." Willow patted his hand and they sat there for a few hours just remembering Jo and Zack.

Daniel was surprised that Jo had sorted things. There were crates with his name, Willow's and West's. She knew she was dying he thought. The way she had things done so matter of fact, but that was grandma Jo. She always seemed to see things for what they were.

Daniel stopped packing and sat on the porch. He looked at all the fruit trees she had planted, her herb garden. She had been a truly remarkable woman. One of the survivors of the virus and had seen it all. He watched Willow and West on the way back to the cabin.

They all stayed inside this night. Willow made a light meal and they all talked of Zack and Jo.

It was West that suggested that the cabin go to Brad and Gary, Willow agreed. With Cliffside their home the cabin in Greenmeadow could go to the younger folk coming of age. "Looks like you have nearly everything packed Daniel" West said. The cabin was full of crates many Jo had packed herself. She had put names on them so West knew where they were to go. He would see to the ones in Greenmeadow in the morning. They would have to come a few times to clear things away.

The following morning found West and Daniel on the trail home. Willow had decided to stay until they returned. "Dad I'm sorry she's gone" Daniel said to West. "She lived a long life Daniel and her last few years had been very hard. She was having many troubles with things that happen to the old." Daniel knew what he meant. He noticed that she was having trouble walking. She had left him her walking stick. It had been

Zack's and he had carves lovely entwining branches on it. He had found a wonderful agate that he had fit into the top of it. Daniel loved it and it was theirs, something they both used for years. "She had many things packed dad. Do you think she knew she was passing?" Daniel asked West. "Yes I think she did" he answered.

The two men pulled the wagon home, stopping at the runners cabin for tea. The old couple there had already improved the area. West wondered when another cabin would be built there.

Willow spent the day with Sara and Lily. Kalvin was not left out. Willow was surprised how well he cared for Lisel, with Dawn so far away now and John and Sam living closer to the fort now as well. She was the only family near now. The women shared many recipes with Willow and they discussed everything from weaving to the amount of people in the world as they knew it.

The evenings were spent by Willow in the cabin packing up the rest of the crates. She dug some of the herbs she did not have and after two nights West and Daniel had returned to take the last things home.

With the wagon loaded and the crates for Greenmeadow passed out, West took his last walk around and then joined Daniel and Willow for the trip home. Sara and Lily hugged Willow and Kalvin and Lisel did too.

The three started the journey home. It was a cold trip. The weather had changed and they knew snow would soon be flying.

After reaching Cliffside and unloading the crates West, Willow and Daniel found relief the last week was over. Jo would be missed for the rest of their lives, but the trauma was over.

Carry had helped unload the wagon and to Nimuri's surprise Jo had a crate for her as well. Daniel wasted no time in getting a fire going and Nimuri had a hot stew ready for them. Willow knew that trips to Greenmeadow would be few and far between now with Jo gone and most of her family gone to live by the fort.

Willow heated water to bathe, she needed a hot soak.

Daniel and West headed to the workshop. They often did when she bathed. It had been a hard week and one she wished not to repeat anytime soon.

After an hour or so West and Daniel returned to the cabin. Night had a firm grip on the valley and although they had candles they too wanted to get some rest. West bathed as did Daniel. The clothes they wore West rinsed and hung by the fire. Daniel emptied the wash tub. When they had gone to bed, the quietness took over Cliffside.

The next few weeks passed and each crate was opened and the contents revealed. West found a box with the things he had brought for Zack from the family farm; the pictures of his grandma and grandpa, a watch and a locket, memories of his trip to the city of the dead. The chance meeting with the children, Jo and Zack had saved. He marvelled at the courage those that survived had shown. West replaced the things in the box and opened a book Zack had written.

Daniel had things in his crate and found himself consumed with the plants and animals Jo and Zack had written about. He tried to image birds flying through the air or huge fish or whales that swam in the seas. The monkeys and lions, what a fantastic world this once was he thought. How could they be so careless almost destroying it?

Willow was laying out all the materials Jo had made, the books of information on so many things. Jo had patterns for so many things. She had cook books on herbal remedies.

The winter would be full of things to read and discuss. The snow was well packed by the time the new year arrived. No floods this year seemed the weather was back to normal.

Daniel was consumed with his cabin and hard worked continuously on the plans; how much lumber was needed, what cuts and lengths. Zack had written so many books and left a treasure trove of plans for cabins.

West spent many hours alone in the workshop. Willow never interfered he needed his space. Putting your feeling right after the loss of family would take each of them some time. West was a realist, he knew things were as they should be, but that didn't take away the pain of loneliness he felt for them. He had to put it somewhere and get back to the living again. His mind went over the looking for the complex one more time. Maybe he could find it this time.

He returned to the cabin "Willow" he said "Do you think mom and dad were let down that I never found the complex?" "No U don't think so. I think it was just that you looked and your dad couldn't and your mom I think didn't want it to be found. Come here West and read this" she said. It was Jo's journal.

"Today I sat with Zack for hours and I could almost hear the birds singing. Maybe I shouldn't have been so against the finding of the complex, but the fact he had a wife and child there would have ended my life. We had West and each other Zack saved my life and I saved his. It was not the life we started out believing we would have had, but I have no complaints. This life has been hard, but it's been a good one. Mankind has relearned to be kind and considerate of each other. I hope West to remembers the value in these few things and teaches his family. When Daniel was born my heart leapt, he was such a joy to me. I have watched him grow into a wonderful young man. He has no wanderlust like West and Zack, but that is fine. He will do well. I will miss so many things. Enough I will write again tomorrow if I can."

"I can't believe how much she wrote and Zack too." "There are years of transcripts here" Willow said. "They have left us what they could and now it's up to us to do the same for the future ahead." West said "I wonder what things will happen that will alter our lives into one direction or another."

"What do you mean dad?" Daniel asked. "Well the bees altered the direction we were going. Think about the child healer, what is the effect she will have and if there are anymore and the impact they will have. Everything reacts to everything else."

It appeared Jo's passing had started her family thinking about things that there never seem to be time for before. The work of surviving had consumed them and now new thoughts entered their minds. West and Willow always kept in touch with those aspects of things, but it always was a struggle for survival. Daniel, however never thought about them. His big things were making sure the people alive now would have enough to eat. Daniel didn't mind talking about all these things, but too much change almost frightened him. Most likely it was why he preferred working in the garden and the knowledge of what he did there would keep him alive to do it again the following year. He was angry that his forbearers had taken away so much. Things were going to get better and his work was going to be a part of that.

It was Nimuri, Carry and Seth that broke the conversation. Carry and Nimuri found their places at the table. Daniel and Seth headed to his room.

The conversation at the table returned to the things Jo and Zack left. Nimuri was surprised there were things for her. Gifts Freda had given Jo now found there way back to Nimuri. Carry was thrilled with the designs Zack had left him.

Daniel and Seth had a totally different conversation going. "So you and April are going to marry this spring?" Seth said and smacked Daniel's shoulder. "Oh give over" Daniel said. "Your turn is not far off" Daniel said and Seth just smiled. "Not me, no way" Seth kidded him. Daniel turned to look at him. "So what is it you plan on doing? Everyone has a responsibility to the future" Daniel told him. Seth smiled "Well, I'm not going to have kids so they can have kids and so on. That's not for me. I'm going to be an adventurer; go farther and see more than any runner, anyone for that fact." "Don't be dumb Seth. What is it you think your grandiose adventures will amount too?" "You know Daniel you have a problem you never see past the end of your nose. Not everyone wants a life of work and drudgery. Some people seek the great beyond. Have you never once wondered what's out there? It's was a thriving complex world." Seth was interrupted "That's the key word WAS. It's gone, not there, over, we are what is left." Seth looked at Daniel If we survived then there are others." "We are lucky Seth we had the fort and people like my grandma and grandpa" Daniel said. "I'm just saying Daniel there could be others. It's a big world." "Well Seth, it will be a small hole in the ground for most of us if we don't get down to the basics and do what needs to be done to stay alive through the next winter." "I can't talk to you anymore" Seth said. "You have closed your mind to the world. You just see here" and with that he got up.

As he passed the table he informed Carry and Nimuri he was going home. West, Carry, Nimuri and Willow knew there had been a falling out between them, but they felt they would work it out. Soon Carry and Nimuri left to go home also.

Willow looked in on Daniel. He was absorbed in the papers in front of him. "Daniel get some rest" she said and Daniel nodded. "Are you and Seth okay?" "Ya, fine mom" he told her. He did not wish to discuss it with her. Willow closed the door and West helped clean up. He banked the fire and they headed to bed.

Carry and Nimuri arrived home to Seth making tea. He started talking even before they got their coats off. "What's the matter with him anyways? I have never met anyone so closed minded in my life. He just works in the fields and he is happy to just do that; his dad and grandpa both adventurers with the thirst of the unknown, the quest for discovery."

Nimuri just looked at Carry. "Not everyone is the same Seth. Daniel, unlike you has had parents and grandparents both adventurers as you say and he does not desire that life."

"Well" Seth said "I want to see what's out there. I don't want to farm my entire life away. West did it and they managed." Carry looked at him "Maybe a job being a runner might fill the void of adventure you have." Carry put his hand on his shoulder "It's a good life I was a runner until I met your mom. I remember when once I too wanted more than being a scullery boy at the fort." Seth smiled "Let me talk to Willow, her sister and brother live near the fort I'm sure we can work something out." The three had tea and then retired.

It wasn't until the snow began to melt that Cliffside began to wake up from its long winter nap. Nimuri and Willow went for the maple syrup, the first real outing of the year. Then the men ensured the tools were repaired and ready for the gardens. April had been to Cliffside and Daniel announced that they would marry soon. The two now spent time looking over plans for their cabin. Seth had left Cliffside to go to Willow's sister's south of the fort. Although they had different ideas about what should or should not be in their lives Daniel and Seth would remain friends, but they would follow different paths now.

The syrup was all gathered now. Willow and Nimuri spent the next day boiling it down and jarring it up.

West and Willow were sitting on the porch when they saw Brad and Gary appear on the road.

Soon they had hot tea and the men had their bags packed to head to Daniel's land. "He will be thrilled" Willow said. "He and April are there now burning stumps." "We have given Jo's cabin to Sven, Herb and Jean's oldest; he will marry soon." Willow was glad to hear that Sven was to have the cabin.

With all the young men in Greenmeadow now they can do the garden this year. West was happy to see Brad and Gary. They were older than him, but that never changed the fact they were like older brothers.

"So has the young man picked his cabin design yet?" Gary asked. "I think that's a question you have to ask him. We will make our way there tomorrow, tonight I claim your company for us." West smiled at them.

Carry and Nimuri enjoyed their company as well. The two women fed them well and prepared the packs for them. April would be chief cook at the camp. Willow packed dried veggies, honey syrup, jam, and a sack of flour for her.

The visit seemed short and in a whirlwind of noise and carry on, the men were on their way.

Nimuri and Willow sat on her porch and found Cliffside to be quiet and peaceful. All too soon the hard work would begin. They knit and sewed, drank tea and tried to think of what future held for their children.

The men had their days filled with cutting timber. Daniel was filled with joy when he saw them coming.

April couldn't believe the work they had done in just a few days. Everyday she used a new stump as the beginning of her fire for the day.

She was a good cook and the supplies Willow and Nimuri sent were very welcomed.

By the weeks end most of the lumber was cut. The cabin would now go up quickly. The cabin was twice the size of most.

Daniel had sent many letters to Dawn asking her to get as many pains of glass as she could. He was going to make part of the cabin a greenhouse. Fresh things in the winter were going to be a treat. He discovered the plans in one of Zack's books.

The men had the log walls up and the rafters set. The remaining work would have to be gone by Daniel.

After hand shakes, hugs and many thanks the men left. Daniel had been given 4 saws as a gift from Greenmeadow. He was happier now than he had ever been. He watched them go and then turned his attention to the cabin. It needed its roof before the rains came.

West and Carry dropped off in Cliffside as Brad and Gary headed home to Greenmeadow.

Willow and Nimuri listened to all the chat about Daniel's cabin. "He's got something there" West said. "He's been thinking for sometime about it." "I agree" Carry said. "The two of them will have a good life." "He's a good man West, his life with April will be good. They both work hard and that will show in a few years. He's picked out a nice piece of land. It's up from a lake and it has a creek not too far away. He's shown a lot of interest in Zack's books which kind of surprised me. He always seemed so against anything from the old world" West said. "Maybe April will cure some of that animosity in him. It's surprising what powers a woman has over her men folk." And they all laughed. "Have you heard from Seth?" Willow asked. "The last we heard was he had joined the salvage teams. He did mention that the city of the dead was almost gone now, the remains they found had all been buried. I wonder if the runners will go out to the prairie or into the mountains now" Willow said. "They will go both ways. The population is growing slowly, but is growing." "What was the last count?" Willow asked. Nimuri spoke up "From Kalvin 1400 or near to it." "Well with some luck April and Daniel will soon add to the numbers." They all smiled. Life was good and they knew it. They shared their thoughts and ideas for the evening.

Soon the gardens would be the priority and with it the hard work.

The following weeks found April and Daniel married; the cabin they built was ready to be lived in and the gardens in Cliffside well underway.

Daniel helped with the ploughing, but then was at his cabin. April and him worked from dawn to dusk to burn out the stumps and get as big a garden as they could this year. They had many gifts from both sides of the families. April's family had given many things from cooking pots to material. Willow gave her spinning wheel and a loom. Carry and West made chairs, dressers, beds and tables. Nimuri had woven baskets and mats. Willow gave her cook book and one on herbs for medicines. She also gave her three empty books to start journals and a family log. They had two bee hives ready for queens. Life was indeed improving, still hard work but that you could live with.

When the gardens in Cliffside were in Willow and Nimuri decided to make a trip to Blackrock to see Daniel's cabin.

When they arrived it was clear to the two women these kids were going to be just fine. It was surprising how much garden had been planted in potatoes. Daniel was chopping wood when he saw them. April was soon on the porch and soon they were all having tea.

"Well I can hardly believe the work you have done here. It's very impressive." "April has been the best" Daniel said. She just smiled. "So what brings you into this neck of the woods?" Daniel asked. Willow pulled a package from her pack. "Dawn sent these for you" she said "more will follow." Daniel opened the package to find 4 panes of glass. A big smile crossed his face and he put the glass on a shelf. "I think Nimuri and I would like to walk around some if you don't mind. I want to see your land here." April smiled "I'll show you" she said. Daniel just looked at the three women and said "I'll go back to chopping wood."

The three women walked down to the lake and Willow starred for some time. "Beautiful isn't it?" April said and Willow nodded. "That it is April. You have all the fresh water you could ever need here." "We get our water from the creek let me show you."

The women headed towards the creek. As they walked Willow pointed out maple trees and walnuts to April.

The coolness of the evening was starting to set in and Willow, Nimuri, April and Daniel sat in the cabin. April made a vegetable soup and some tea. By the time it was done night had taken over Blackrock. With anticipation for the days ahead all slept well.

When Willow got up April was already in the living area, she had the water hot and breakfast ready. Nimuri soon followed.

The day had begun for Daniel; he had already started burning out stumps. While he chopped wood he also tended the fires. April was clearing the brush with the help of Willow and Nimuri. Daniel would burn what was on top after he dug a fire pit around it.

Willow now confident that they were fine and well on the way to a secure and stable life decided to return home.

The summer passed almost uneventfully. A small family moved to Blackrock and the talk was it was the family of the child healer. It never amounted to much other than they moved on past April and Daniel's land almost to the other side of the lake.

The harvest was there before most knew it. April and Daniel arrived at Cliffside to help . When Willow saw them coming she knew right away that April was with child. Willow had the tea ready in no time.

April and Daniel sat with her on the porch. It did take long for April to tell Willow the news. It was a time to be happy. A new life was coming and Daniel was no exception and being a proud father.

Willow didn't let April do any heavy lifting. There was plenty to do without hurting herself. The baby was due mid winter; its was good the child would come then. The struggle for survival always made spring a hard time of the year. The harvest was brought in and again there was plenty for all.

West and Daniel filled the wagon to be taken to Blackrock for the winter. The new year would be a year for April and Daniel. They would have a child and they would have enough land cleared to grow their own food. West helped with the wagon home.

Willow sat on the porch and watched them go. The sun was still warm, but she knew soon the long winter would set its cold icy tendrils into everything. She watched Nimuri separate that last of the wheat from the chaff. The motion of the wheat and Nimuri's skilled hands using the round woven disc to do this was a rhythm Willow knew all too well. The hum of the bees doing the last harvesting of their own was in the air. Willow sat there and wondered if April and Daniel's baby would be a boy or girl. How proud Jo and Zack would have been.

The afternoon passed quickly and just before dusk Willow saw West come back with the wagon. The tiredness showed on him, West was getting older; Willow too felt her age. By the time he had the wagon put away and was cleaned up he was ready for bed. Sleep did not take long to find them.

Winter was not long taking over from fall. The snow soon piled up and the passes for the runners became impenetrable.

April and Daniel should have the baby soon. Willow wanted to go see her, but the snow had blocked the way. The weather turned really ugly for the next week, the temperatures dropped and the cold bit their skin when they went out.

It was during this week that April had her baby. The night was extremely cold. Daniel stayed by her, but he knew that something was wrong. April writhed with pain for hours. Daniel did not know what to do. He knew April was failing, he was beside himself. What was he to do? He was going to lose them both. It was the first time Daniel was helpless and it terrified him. He sat beside her and each time the child tried to come April screamed in pain and Daniel could do nothing. When things got too much for him he almost let his despair overwhelm him.

It was at that moment a banging came to the door. Daniel almost panicked; who could be there and at the same time he was relieved he had some help. Daniel opened the door to find a young man and a young woman. "Please, Please come in" and it was the moans of April that drew his attention from them. "It's my wife" he said "She's having a baby, but it won't come" Daniel said.

The young woman looked at Daniel "I know" she said. "Boil some water" she told him "and make some tea. Ray, help him please and ease his mind." Connie had her heavy clothes off and was at April's side. She felt April's child and soon the fear left April. Ray reached out with his mind and with waves of soothing, calmed Daniel. Daniel realized who Connie was; she was the child healer. He looked at Ray and wondered who he was. How could they have known April was having a baby and they were in such dire straits? "I heard you calling out" Ray said "Connie had a gift to heal and I can feel and hear thoughts. We moved to the far side of the lake because the thoughts of so many people were taking its toll on me." Daniel wondered why they had moved so far away from everyone. "You must love her a great deal, your thoughts screamed as did hers. We had to come."

Daniel then realized that April did not cry out in pain anymore. He went to the bedroom to see Connie sitting beside April with her hand on April's raised tummy. She looked over to Daniel "The child is weak as is April. We could lose them both if she doesn't help now. Ray, tell her."

Ray touched April's forehead and soon April helped Connie and Jerod was born. Daniel was stunned by what he had witnessed. Ray slipped April into a semi conscious state and Connie held Jerod. She lent her strength to him to help him breath. When she was confident he would be okay she cleaned him up.

With Jerod in his bed she turned her attention to April again. She looked at Daniel "If she has another child she will die. I can repair her insides, but I warn you now of this." Daniel looked at her. When Connie was finished with April she changed the bed clothes and April's nightwear. "Daniel wash her everyday and fresh linen and nightwear too. She will be fine." Ray took Connie's hand and the two left Daniel with April and Jerod.

Daniel sat with his wife and child for some time when he heard the cabin door open and close. He yelled in his mind "Thank you, thank you knowing Ray would hear him.

The next week was busy for him, keeping the laundry washed and caring for April and Jerod. He almost lost them both and then like angels in the night Connie and Ray came and saved them. He would have to do something for them in the spring. Help them in some way.

The cold snap lasted about three weeks and then it was gone as quickly as it came. April never spoke of Connie and Daniel wondered if Ray had done something so she wouldn't remember. Whatever they did he would be grateful for the rest of his life. They saved April and Jerod.

April improved everyday and Daniel found the time he spent with Jerod wondrous. When April slept Daniel rocked him in the chair and he looked at the tiny fellow wondering who he would be when he grew up. He was going to teach him everything he could about plants. Jerod would be his partner. Daniel's thoughts changed to the warning gave about April having another child. Did he dare tell her or maybe she knew.

The winter held fast to the land and spring was not showing its signs yet. April was out of bed and well on her way of recovering. Jerod was as normal as any child. He cried when he was hungry or needed a change, but other than that he was contented. Daniel watched April and Jerod. Never would he forget how close he came t losing them. He often held Jerod and look into his eyes. The child was special he thought and then laughed to himself. All parents think their children are special. He watched April her movements told him she still wasn't back to normal. Daniel had no problems changing Jerod or washing his soiled things. He catered to Aprils needs when he could. She spent her free time spinning flax and knitting, sewing what she could.

She had started the family journal. She talked of her mother and father, how they grew up at the fort. She wrote what she could remember about her grandparents. Willow was right she thought the history of people should be kept. She often looked out the window at the frozen lake and marvelled at how large it was. She vaguely remembered Connie and Ray and wondered how they were doing. It was strange to her that they never spoke of them coming when she was having Jerod.

"April come look at this" Daniel said to her. He had been reading some of Zack's books. April went over to the chair beside him. She took Jerod from him and looked at the drawings on the page. "What is it?" she asked. "It's a boat for floating on the water" Daniel told her. "I am going to build one" April looked at him "It's not really a necessity and there are many more things that need to be built" she said to him. He looked at her. The boat was not that important "Yeah, maybe you're right" he said "but one day I want to build one. Maybe when Jerod gets older he can help me." He smiled. April smiled too. With the home land needing so much work yet it was hard to justify making a boat to float on the water.

The now small family spent the winter days and nights in the cabin waiting for the spring thaw. They planned a trip to Cliffside to take Daniel's pride and joy to his folks. They would have to see her family as well. April's family was not as close as Daniel's. Her mother had children too young and too many. She had worked herself almost to an early grave. He father was not a well man; he had worked hard on the land to make a life for his family. The children, most of which were boys left home as soon as they could. April felt sorry for them in many ways, but now they had a nice piece of land and were self sufficient. Her father was part of the council now and would be part of what would happen in Blackrock. Her mom was contented to be at home. So for them it was good, they seemed happy, but April still found it sad somehow. She had felt so different since Jerod was born. When she held him she knew he was going to be different. Just how or in what way she didn't know, but he was going to make big changes in the world.

The weather changed over the next week and Daniel went to tap the maple trees Willow had pointed out to him in the fall. It would be a little syrup and the fresh air would be good. He had been cooped up so much this winter. The workshop would be the next building, he smiled.

The pass would soon be open and the runners would be getting through. He wanted to take Jerod to April's folks then down to Cliffside. He always had so many thoughts when he was out alone. He set up several buckets and headed back to the cabin.

He arrived to find April with a hot meal and tea for him. "I saw you coming" she said and he smiled at her. He would go back later for the buckets. "How about we see your folks first before we go to Cliffside?" he told her as he ate. "It sounds good to me. I don't want to be gone too long. I would like to get at the stumps in the far field this spring." Daniel smiled. "You just make sure you are okay before you start any heavy lifting. You really scared me when you were having Jerod. I thought I was going to lose you and it terrified me. April I love you and Jerod. Don't do anything that would hurt you." April was kind of stunned, it was the first time he had spoken of the birth. "I'm okay I don't really remember a lot of it, just Connie the young woman that soothed the pain. I don't know how but she did." "It was frightening I can tell you" Daniel said to her. "Had they not come I would have lost you both." "Well" April said "we are going to be fine." She rubbed his shoulders and he patted her hand.

"Come on Jerod let's get you some clean trousers." April smiled and cleared the table to wash the dishes.

It seemed that the days warmed up quickly. The snow was almost gone when they decided to go and show off Jerod. He was going well and April was feeling herself again. They had burned out half a dozen stumps already. The ground would be turned over and potatoes planted in the new area. It seemed potatoes added something to the soil for future crops. They would have to leave some of the fields in fallow for a season too. For now the journey to visit the grandparents was the big event this spring.

April's mom had sewn and knit many things for them all. Her dad made a few storage trucks for them and had managed to get Daniel a detailed map of Blackrock. Someone had the sense to make a good one of the small village.

Jerod delighted April's mom and dad it was funny to watch them talk to Jerod and get him to smile. Although they had to cut short their visit it was enjoyed by all. They returned home and unloaded the things they received from her family. The following day was the trip to Cliffside.

Again the trip would be cut short so the work at home would get done. The garden would be the one thing that kept them alive in the following winter. Daniel always realized this and never shirked his responsibility of it. April was his partner in this as well. Jerod was adored by West and Willow. Willow fussed completely over him and West found being a grandpa a real pleasure. April and Daniel beamed that Jerod was the joy for Willow and West as he was for them. They stayed a bit longer than expected Daniel found he didn't want to take Jerod away from his mom too soon. The ground was thawed and the garden was a priority for all. They had to return home.

The trip home was not long and the work outside was not going way. Daniel fenced a small area under a tree for Jerod to watch them. April and Daniel spent as much time of the following days as they could, burning brush and stumps, digging and planting. The garden for vegetables was big enough but the wheat and flax would be a few years away yet.

Jerod grew quickly, by summer's end he was standing at the fence watching his parents work. He had toys and was contented under the tree in the shade. Daniel and April spent what time they could with him and were thankful he was contented with the things he had under the tree with him.

Daniel often took a walk by the lake in the evening and Jerod went with him. He often looked out and wondered how the young woman healer was. Jerod looked intently at the lakes end as well. Daniel found it odd it seemed as if Jerod knew there were people there. Daniel was surprised how this small boy had claimed such a big part of his heart. He wish April could have more children, but after the last birth there would be no way that would happen. Her parents had been to visit and Daniel wished that West and Willow would come before the snow flew.

April now had most of the vegetables in, the turnips dipped in wax, the carrots all packed in sand, the potatoes in bins, the herbs dried and tied as well as the mushrooms. The bees had made the hives their home and there was plenty of wax and honey. Willow had made sure they had apple trees. Dawn had sent stems from a grape vine found after the bees had returned. Daniel had no trouble getting them to grow. The rose bushes did very well and there would be a lovely supply of hip. April had found ample time to search for mushrooms. She had dried tomatoes and gathered plenty of walnuts and Hazelnuts.

Although Daniel did not have time for building he found time to cut lumber from some of the trees cut down last fall.

April had just finished hanging out the laundry, most of which were Jerod's diapers when she saw West and Willow appear on the path. West was pulling a wagon and it didn't take Daniel long to take over pulling it to the cabin. She had tea ready and the four sat on the porch with Jerod sitting in his play area secured there for him.

Willow had brought reeds and flax for April. There was a stack of wheat was well.

West and Daniel soon found themselves over the land. Willow and April sat talking of many things.

Willow picked up Jerod and held him on her lap at the table. "You have done so much work here April. I don't know how you have found the time" Willow said. April smiled and brushed her hair back with the back of her hand. "It's been a lot of work and we are so lucky Jerod has been such a calm good boy." She caressed his small cheek. "Do you want more tea Willow?" she asked. Willow nodded. "Next year I will give you some Marigold plants, they are good to make a poultice for wounds." "I wished we got more beds made for herbs and things, but clearly the land held the priority this summer and next as well. Did I tell you that Daniel wants to build a potting house and another workshop? He says the winter could be spent making many things that people need. He also wants to plant much more next year." "Well you two just remember to take some time to smell the flowers. You can't work continuously. Small breaks give you family time. Jerod will soon become more demanding and he will need to be taught so many things."

It was then West and Daniel returned, West smiling and Daniel still chatting his ears off. "You know my dear I think this young fellow has some good ideas about things." Willow looked at him "So I take it tomorrow will be the beginning of a busy week then?" and smiled. West nodded. "We are cutting down the trees along the edge. By the time we strip them into logs our time here will be gone, but they will be ready to make lumber next spring. He's got some work to do ahead of him yet to just clear more land. Brings back some memories" West said and smiled at Willow.

April took Jerod into the cabin, fed him and he was soon sleeping. Willow rocked in her chair on the porch. West was right; all this did bring back memories. West worked so hard in Cliffside to make it a home for them.

April soon appeared with bread and jam for them. They chatted into the night knowing the next day would be filled with hard work.

When morning broke April had been up for some time. Jerod had been fed and was playing by the fire. The two women had breakfast ready for Daniel and West. Daniel was quicker to rise than West; the hard work over the years was starting to take its toll. Once he got going though it was tough for a younger man to keep up with him. After they ate the two men dawned saws, axes, shovels, rakes and headed to the edge of the farm's clearing.

In the midst of chopping and sawing noises the crash of trees falling to the ground was the most noise heard outside.

Willow and April cleaned up the breakfast dishes and as April heated water for clothes washing Willow entertained Jerod. He was a wondrous little boy. He found contentment in the simplest things. Willow could not tell if he would be an adventurer like West or a man bound on tilling the earth like Daniel. The day passed quickly and by supper West and Daniel had cut several trees.

It was the commotion at the lake that brought April and Willow out to see what was going on. With Jerod tucked under Aprils arm they made their way to see what was going on.

With their arrival at the lake, West and Daniel both waist deep and soaked looked over and roared with laughter. April looked at Willow and then lifted Jerod up and said "Look at those silly fools. Here it is fall and they are both soaked to the bone." The two women hurried back to the cabin.

"They will catch cold" April said. "I doubt it" Willow answered "but they will be in need of a bath and dry clothes." Willow went over how often West complained about wet feet.

The next week passed much the same without the soaking in the lake. By the time West and Willow left, the logs for the next years building lay ready to be cut after a drying time. Daniel was sad to see them go, but they had things to finish up before the snow came.

Time had a way of falling into a rhythm the next few years passed quickly. Jerod now 6 years old had discovered his own mind, much to the discernment of April and Daniel. He could not be made to do things he did not want to; going to his room or missed meals did not deter his attitude. April and Daniel spoiled him. He was the only child they would have. It was not intentional just things that at first were cute were now becoming a problem. April spent many hours in the garden and Daniel with her, it was hard work. Jerod didn't like working in the garden so he had been given the task of spreading gravel from near the stream on the walkway. He didn't mind this as he could see some progress to his toiling.

It had been a particularly hot and muggy the last few days, Jerod was digging some gravel, when he finished loading his small wagon he lay down by the stream to get a drink. It was then he noticed a small creature in the water. This was something he thought, but what was it? He reached out to grab it and in a flicker of a moment it was gone. He spent close to an hour searching for it but with no avail. Whatever it was it was gone. He decided not to mention it to April and Daniel they wouldn't believe him anyways. He was mad at himself that he had not caught it. It walked on the water in a small pool created when Jerod dug out the gravel. Jerod pulled his wagon to the walkway and emptied it. His mind was consumed by the small creature he had seen. He kept looking for another, but never saw one.

The summer passed into fall and then winter; Along with the cold came the endless hours in the cabin. Daniel had been teaching Jerod to read. In frustration he would pout and cry. It made no sense to him. "Put them away Daniel" April said. "He's not going to learn if he cries all the time." "He has to learn to read, April" Daniel said to her. "I know but this is not the way. In the spring I will take him to your mom and dad's maybe they will have better luck." Jerod smiled now he would not have to endure all this.

His self satisfaction would come to an end and this spring it did. April took Jerod to Willow and West's. She had to go home to help with the planting. Jerod now thinking he was on some grand holiday and soon started doing what he did at home which was as little as possible. West didn't take long to see the trouble. Jerod was spoiled, let to do what he wanted to do.

West soon had him in the workshop and Willow had a cushion for him to sit on. Jerod was learning new things and it seemed that doing what he was told right away was smarter than standing or sitting on a cushion for a day or two only to have to do what he had been told to do anyways.

Willow helped him to learn his letters and numbers. It had all been so trying. Then one day it all clicked and he was starting to understand words and then sentences. It was like a flood gate had been opened and the more he learned and read the more he wanted too.

The spring and summer had been one of the hardest for Jerod, but it was the beginning of life for him. After the first few trips to the wood shed his stubbornness waned and he settled down to life.

April couldn't believe the change in him. He was almost a little man now. It was then the friendship with his mother and father started. It was slow at first because April and Daniel spent many hours in the garden. Jerod was starting to understand that the garden was life, without it they would starve. He helped this harvest although a child his help was welcomed. There were so many jobs he could do.

Jerod still had time to daydream and he did that a lot when he and April picked mushrooms. He found ample things to think about in the woods. Jerod's world was getting bigger. He didn't know it yet, but when he could read more he would find out things he never could have imagined.

"Jerod" April called to him. He looked up and April waved for him to come. It was time to go home again.

They walked out of the bush and onto one of the trails Jerod made. April praised him for his hard work. "Did you know that long ago there were roads all over and people had wagons that moved with engines?" "Oh give over mom. How could a wagon move with an engine? There's no such thing" Jerod told her. "This is true, not any more, but at one time it was true. You must spend some time this winter and read some of Zack's books. I think you would find them interesting." "Great grandpa Zack he lived in the old world didn't he?" he asked his mom. "Yes he did" she said. "He has some interesting things to say about it too. I'll be glad when I can read better." Jerod smiled at his mom. "Come on" she said "I need you to haul some water for me."

Jerod wasted no time in getting the buckets. April laid out the mushrooms to dry. A soft breeze was blowing and April could feel the coolness in it.

Fall was upon them and after harvest the snow would settle them into the cabin till spring.

April heated the water to wash clothes. She gave Jerod another bucket and asked him to pick some rose hips, hazelnuts and walnuts were next for him. April and West had their hands full with the garden things. Jerod liked picking rose hips and getting nuts. He had the time to himself.

He wandered to the trees nearby and knew where the walnuts were. The leaves were starting to turn colour. He looked up and watched as the breeze blew the leaves. Soon he had the basket filled with nuts and headed home, then decided to go sit by the creek. He listened to the water rushing down over the rocks. He thought that one day he needed to see where the water came from. He looked out over the lake and wondered what the people did there. They were the healers. They stayed away from everyone. Jerod always felt drawn to them for some reason. He did not know why.

Winter would soon have its hold on the land; the trees would loose all their leaves, the ground would freeze and as the snow came the lake would freeze. He looked back at the stream and he knew he would find the time to follow it next year. Grandpa would come with him. He knew West had been far beyond where most had been. The healer's cabin was about the farthest human occupation in the valley that there was now. The people would not venture further until next spring.

Jerod picked up his bags of nuts and baskets with the mushrooms and headed back to the cabin.

Daniel and April stayed in the fields until dark. When they finally made it to the cabin Jerod had hot water and Jerod was looking through Zack's books. There seemed so many things he knew nothing about.

"Mom" he said "Can I go see grandma and grandpa before the snow flies?" April looked at Daniel and it was agreed he could go. "So, what's on your mind Jerod?" April asked him. "Not much mom I just want to visit them." April looked at Daniel and let the matter drop.

So many hours ahead yet; the candles all had to be made and all the dried herbs put into their clay jars. The flax would have to be spun, paper would have to be made, ropes, buckets and any furniture would now take over the workshop for the winter. The never ending wood piles would have to be replenished. A trip would be made to the healer's cabin to see if they had enough food to last out the winter. The same thing over and over, Jerod was like West he needed more. He was feeling trapped even now at his age. April could see it and Daniel too.

For April she wished him more time to explore and Daniel couldn't understand the wanderlust and was firm to keep him working.

April spent the last warm afternoons preparing the flax on the porch. She watched Jerod chop wood and stack it. When she had the pile of flax done she had been working on she called to Jerod. "Go pack a bag" she told him then she went to the workshop to see Daniel.

She opened the door to see him involved in the project he was working on. "I'm taking the boy to West and Willow's he needs more than just work on the farm here" April said. "He needs to stop dreaming and get his nose to things that need to be done here" Daniel said not looking up from the piece of wood he had been shaping. "Daniel!" April said "You have to remember he is just a boy. If we keep him locked here he will grow to resent us. Not everyone had the work ethic you do. I would hate to think we might be the source of him wanting to leave the farm forever." Daniel looked at her "As you wish take him then." April shook her head and left Daniel to his project.

It would take a couple hours to take him there and she should be back before dark. She grabbed the lantern and some candles as they left the house. The lantern was new, Willows sister Dawn had sent them up from Fort Reed. If it did turn dark she would be able to see her way home. Jerod was more than happy to carry everything to get away from the farm to talk to different people. Maybe hike with grandpa was filling him with such pleasure each step closer to Cliffside.

Jerod wasted no time in bending West's ear over the complex. The stories that grandpa told him were always full of things he wanted to know more about.

Willow sat in the rocking chair as the two men chatted away and they both enjoyed themselves. West had always wished that Daniel had taken some interest in the world beyond Cliffside, but he didn't. Jerod was different he could see beyond the small valleys they lived in.

It was during one of these conversations that passed over the next few days that Jerod remembered the water bug he had seen. West asked him all kinds of questions as did Willow. "Grandpa I never seen another one" Jerod told him. "Next year we are going to follow the water. I never went into that pass I went more north" West said. "But now that I think of it, dad said west not north."

"Come look here Jerod" West opened the maps he had made. Willow's curiosity had her glancing over the papers as well. "This is where I travelled this valley and this one" West told him as he pointed on the map. "Your home is here and this water comes from the mountains here" West was excited. Willow smiled. He had stopped looking to have Daniel in his life, but the desire was still there. After all these years, West would at the drop of a hat search for the complex.

"Grandpa" Jerod said "Dad will never let me go hiking with you. He will want me home to work in the fields." Jerod was becoming a big help to April and Daniel, another man even if he was young; meant 2 more hands and in time a lot more strength.

West knew Jerod was almost right about Daniel not wanting him to go adventuring, but the information about the new creature was something that should be looked into and see if it was let go by the complex or if it was a survivor. "Grandpa do you think there are people alive in the complex?" Jerod asked. "Yes Jerod I do and they are the holders of the past and our future. Well, it's very late and we have burned enough of grandma's candles. Off to bed with you" West said as he started putting things away. Willow hugged him and Jerod headed for Daniel's old room. His mind was full of adventure that grandpa was going to take him on.

Willow had made a last tea for the evening and her and West sat at the table. "Jerod is right Daniel will never approve of me taking Jerod into the mountains" West said to her. "Yes, but let me talk to him I'm sure he will relent." Willow smiled. "You always could get him to do what you wanted" Willow smiled. "Do you think it was let go by the complex or a survivor" Willow asked. "I don't know, but I do know it's the first sighting of another living thing and once again it's here in this area it was noticed. The bees have just made it to the towns south of the fort. Had we not sent the queens I wonder how much longer it would have taken? Going west further might be where my search went wrong. Staying further west then north might be the answer."

Willow finished her tea and patted West's hand as she passed on her way to their room. West didn't find it easy to shut down his mind. The news of the bug relit the desire to search and find the complex. This time Jerod would be with him to share the adventure. West gathered up the last of his mess and went to bed.

The next weeks passed quickly and as usual West and Jerod were never far from each other. He had gathered nuts for Willow as well as reeds for her basket weaving. Willow wondered if the reeds had been a diversion to look the small pond over for bugs. When the two were satisfied that no bugs were to be found the reeds were the reward for they spent there.

Willow could see Jerod had brought the spark of adventure back to West and she decided that she would never again try to diminish it. Daniel was a grown man with a family of his own and he would have to live with the fact that he and West were different. He would also have to give Jerod room or he would be in danger of losing his own son forever. Yes, Willow thought she knew how to handle Daniel on this point.

At weeks end she took Jerod home. April was pleased to see them coming down the path. It was a good visit as it was written all over Jerod's face. He was happy. Daniel's face broke into a big smile when he saw his mother's face as well. After the welcome they headed for the cabin.

Willow had brought paper and wax for them. Jerod would need the extra for his school work. April would spend many hours with him reading this winter. Willow had convinced her into the tour of the farm so she could see the progress they were making.

When they reached the lake Jerod stood throwing stones into the water. Daniel told her of the water wheel he wanted to make and the clay was pointed out. Daniel had the plans made for the new potter's house. Willow was drawn to the small smoke wisps at the end of the lake. "Have you been to see the small farm there to see if they are in need yet?" Daniel looked at the ground "Not as yet" he told her. "I thought I would take Jerod this year. He gets so cooped up all winter. If he learns the way he can check there on his own" Willow looked at Daniel. He didn't like anything that switched their lives from the farm. "Let's have some tea" Willow said and she and April headed in.

"Well Jerod did you have a good visit?" he asked. "Yes I did dad" Jerod replied. "Dad, is it true grandpa at one time was a runner?" Jerod asked. "It was long before I was born" he answered. "It must have been something seeing all those places" he said. "He went to the city of the dead when he was 16 years old. Is that true?" Daniels good mood was turning "All this talk of gallivanting, if grandpa told you then its true I'm sure" Daniel said. Jerod knew his father's good mood was going and changed the subject. "I was going to cut up the wood from the far field, well as much as I could before the snow flew." Jerod smiled at his dad. It was the right thing to say as Daniel's temper was curbed. He rubbed Jerod's hair soon they joined Willow and April in the cabin for tea.

Willow didn't stay long but the walk home wasn't far, but it wasn't a walk for night. Jerod was always sad to see grandma go. Jerod planned to make as many trips as he could. Even with his father's distaste of travelling. It would be his eleventh birthday this year. He rolled all the imagined trips over in his mind. Where he be ten years from now? Would he have his own land or would he be an adventurer?

April and Daniel shared the last tea of the evening. Their lives were so entrenched in farming. What happened beyond was of some interest, but not like the focus on the farm.

Willow, now home found West reading Zack's journals. He tried to picture the great wall, the heli- pad was on and the circular valley over the rise. Even after all this time the wall must exist. Willow smiled to herself as she watched West. He was himself again. Willow loved him, she always had. It pained her so often that Daniel had been so against his father. He was never satisfied to give him the room he needed. Daniel was the new generation; most of the old were gone if not all that lived through the great end.

Willow noticed the grey hair and knew her time on earth would be over in know time. Daniel never had the ability to look beyond today and into the future. The world may never be the same as before that was obvious, but it would change more and more as the people populated more area. Maybe Daniel did see that is was that in his way, but he saw his way before everything else.

She remembered something that had been told to her long ago that everyone there was another half, like two peas in a pod, yin and yang; she never did understand some of the things that Jo told her, they were things of the old world long passed when she was a young woman.

It had been a strange fall this year; so many things from the past that surfaced. West and Willow went to bed and sleep soon found them.

The first winter storm came in a flurry. The wind howled and so much snow fell. Daniel and April thought about the flood in the past years. Daniel spent many hours in the workshop and Jerod was there with him, but every chance there was he would be found reading. Daniel was after him a lot this winter, displeased he spent so much time at what he felt was a waste of time; day dreaming. It didn't get the work done. Jerod couldn't wait for spring, everyday that passed brought spring closer. He was almost depressed when new storms came and brought big snow falls.

It was close to spring when Connie came. The knocking on the cabin door was such an unfamiliar thing. Daniel was a bit shocked to see her there. Willow wasted no time in making tea.

Jerod found Connie so calming and strange. She rarely came near the village. Soon Connie called Jerod over; as she looked at him he found it startling and seemed to know her in a way he had never known anyone else. What was it he felt? Connie smiled and it was a comfort to him.

"What has brought you to us Connie? Is there something you need?" April asked. "I'm here to tell you of a thought or maybe a vision that Telly has had. He has been terribly upset. He sees beyond what we see" Connie told her. Daniel just looked at her. "Are you trying to tell me that this Telly can see the future?." Daniel couldn't handle this, it went against everything. He thought it was crazy. Connie now knew it was a waste of time to come to them. They would never understand. Jerod listened to her and deep in his being her words rang true. He didn't know why or how, but they rang true. She looked at him "Hold close to the things you value the most. There will come a time you will need them. I must return to the others." Connie got up and left the cabin.

Jerod went out after her "What did you mean" he asked her. Connie looked at the boy that not so long was a babe near death. "I have seen you as you, but never mind that. Telly had told me of a coming danger. Keep close to you the things you value most" and with that she covered her face from the blowing snow and was soon gone from sight. Jerod could feel the bite of the cold and returned to the cabin.

He found Daniel and April in a heated argument. "Why did she come here to start trouble I tell you" Daniel said. "Daniel, I don't think she would have come out in a storm if she didn't feel there was some merit in what she was doing" April said. "I don't care" Daniel replied. "They should stay in their village not come out and stir up trouble." "Daniel how can you say such nonsense? Had she not come before neither Jerod nor I would be here right now." With that statement Daniel stopped, it was true they both would have died. Daniel grabbed his coat and started for the door. It was then they saw Jerod standing there. Daniel pushed passed him and headed for the workshop.

April looked at Jerod. There was a kind of softness in her face. "What were you talking about mom? Why is dad so angry?" Jerod asked. April tried to evade answering him. "How does she know who I am and why do I feel like I know her?" Jerod persisted.

April sat down "Jerod come it here." He did. "When I was young I had an awful time having you. I was dying and so were you. Some how Connie came here and she well…she healed us. I don't know what she did or how, but I will not let your father's fear or unwillingness to accept change ever hurt her. I can't explain it" April told him. "Well enough, your father will be fine. I know he would never wish harm. He just prefers things he thinks he has control over." Jerod had so much more to think about.

He rarely in his life heard the harden words spoken like that between them, The strangest thing of all was that he could feel her too and he didn't know how that was possible.

April spun flax for the rest of the day. Daniel came into eat and then went back to the work shop. Jerod read some of Zack's books on the way the world was, his family farm and the schools he had gone too. It truly was such a different world to what they had now.

They days slipped by into each other and when the snow finally started to melt Jerod couldn't wait for West to come and get him. It was at least a month after the snow was gone that grandpa and grandma appeared on the path.

It seemed that Jerod had gown over the winter. He was on his way now to being more of a man than a child. It didn't take long for the women to find things to do. Jerod still had wood to cut for the fire and Grandpa went between him and Daniel. As Daniel started preparing for work in the fields Jerod wondered how they were going to make his father relent in his travelling into the mountains with West.

It was Willow at the dinner table that started. She asked Jerod what he would do in different circumstances. When he couldn't answer she reprimanded Daniel on him not teaching Jerod even the most basic survival skills. Daniel just puffed "There had not been the time ." April could see Willow handle Daniel and start to put him in the position where he was asked something and he would not be able to say no. Before nights end that's exactly what happened. West was going to take Jerod for some survival training and Daniel accepted it as a part of everyone's life. Even Daniel was taught how to take care of himself in the bush.

Jerod was beside himself with glee. He was going for an adventure and it was actually okay. "Just remember that the wood will be waiting for you when you get home" Daniel said to him. Jerod didn't mind at all.

Grandpa helped him get a pack together and Willow, April and Daniel talked of the gardens. "Grandpa I can't believe I'm going with you" Jerod said. West just smiled "You get your rest tomorrow will be a long day." Jerod took forever to fall asleep.

West, Willow, Daniel and April talked about the letter she received from Dawn. They started making things from the scavenged glass. They had found more people after all this time. Word has it they had, about 2 weeks walk away. It was a small settlement of about 30 people. Willow was glad they had been found. "Are they on their way back to the fort?" April asked. "No, Dawn says they wish to remain where they are, but runners and a few folks were going to take them , new crops, trees for fruit and bees." West looked at Willow "It seems more have survived. I hope their lives have been better than Nimuri's was." "They wish to stay where they so they must have had something that saved them." "Well" April said "That brings the population to nearly 1500 now. I am happy there are more people. Dawn mentioned they had gifted with them." "Well that most likely why they survived" April said. "Great more freaks" Daniel said.

Willow turned on him "How dare you Daniel. Since when have you decided you are above your fellow man? How dare you presume that it is the world you think you should be the way you want them. The differences are what makes each of us special. Your own wife and child owe their lives to one of those Freaks, you put it. Daniel I am ashamed of you. I never raised you so you could criticize others." April never said anything but it was true, had Connie not come that evening they both would have passed away.

Daniel felt his face heat up. He knew what he was saying was wrong, but he didn't like them.

For the first time she could see that her son had a flaw and it was not a good one. The subject was dropped.

Daniel said nothing further. It was now and uncomfortable quiet in the cabin.

April broke the silence by asking Willow about paper making. She finished spinning the flax and knew the scrap made the best paper.

West took his tea and headed out for some fresh air. Daniel followed him. "Well son don't worry so much your mom will be over it soon" he said to Daniel. "Whether she is or not I don't care, I don't like them" Daniel told West. "Is it you don't like them or are you afraid of them?" West asked him. "They are just weird. How did they know April was in trouble? They appeared out of no where and they slipped away again. She's been back talking some nonsense to Jerod about keeping things he valued close to him. Is there going to be a thief going to come and steal his books? They are too cryptic. They hide down there at the end of the lake and make people distrust them by their absence." West looked at his son "Did you ever stop to think that they maybe they think the same about us? Seeking them when we are hurt or in trouble. We never include them in our lives. I don't believe for a moment that they are hiding there. They have a small village they feel safe at. The distance makes the journey to them only one of necessary. Had they not come in Aprils hour of need and she died, then how would you feel without you or Jerod?" Daniel never said anything. "You must learn to accept things as they are now" West told him. "With the ending of the world a new beginning has been put upon us. It was up to us to make it better for all who are left, remember that you will be no different the old world people you have been so repulsed by your entire life. Is that not just what they did never let folks be what and who they were. People tried to destroy them because they were different" West said.

Daniel felt like he had been slapped in the face. He never thought of it like that. He was acting like the world he so hated; the ones that nearly took the future of everyone away.

"I'm going to bed son. You think about things and get this sorted out. You are hurting yourself with your stubbornness. West put his hand on Daniel's shoulder and then went back into the cabin. With the journey with Jerod at hand West went to bed. He certainly was not the man he once was, age was creeping up on him.

Willow soon joined him. She would leave for home in the morning. Seeing how petty Daniel was nor becoming and was not something she was all that happy about finding out.

April cleaned up and waited for Daniel to come in. After an hour or so she too retired.

Daniel stayed out; he looked into the night sky and for the first time in his life he had to admit he was wrong about a few things. He went to bed and sleep finally found him.

The morning brought Jerod almost jumping for joy about going with grandpa. Willow helped April with breakfast. Daniel sat at the table and when everyone was there he told them he was wrong about the people at the end of the lake. Willow put a hand on his shoulder.

The conversation then turned to the two adventurers ready to head into the wilds. Daniel told Jerod to learn his lessons well they may save his life. Even if Daniel didn't adventure he could build a shelter, find food, build a fire for warmth and knew something to do if he was injured.

Willow produced a small book and a charcoal for him to write things he needed to remember or just his thoughts.

Mid-morning found West and Jerod at the creek and ready to start their journey. Willow saw them off as did April and Daniel.

The attention was then turned to the gardens. Willow and April prepared the small herb beds and Daniel worked on the bigger fields.

West and Jerod walked most of the day following the creek. By days end they reached the source of it and the summit of a small mountain. They decided to make camp there. Jerod watched as West methodically cut poles and branches. He gave Jerod the job of building their fire pit and collecting enough wood for the night and morning meal. Jerod watched his grandpa make rope from bark to tie the cut branches to form the lean to. West cut evergreen bows to secure the make shift walls.

The two men soon had the sleeping area done and some water was heated and filled with veggies and herbs. Flat bread was shared . West opened his maps to show where they were and then filling where they were going.

Morning gave them a better look at the valleys below and which would be the best one to follow. The mountain was so dark and West soon had Jerod looking into the sky for satellites. He told him the same stories his father had passed to West. Daniel was not interested, but Jerod's eyes sparkled at the idea of what had been before. "Grandpa why is dad so angry at adventuring?" Jerod asked.

"I don't think it's adventuring Jerod I think it's the hours lost that could be used to better our lives here." "Doesn't dad ever wonder what's over the mountain?" Jerod asked. "He might well think of it, but making sure there is enough food for you and your mother is more important to him. His concern is for the well being of us all. He is so hurt over the destruction of the world he is too live in and how they killed off so much. I tell you of the folks from the old world I'm sure did not have any idea of the damage that would be done by their actions." Jerod listened to his grandpa and tried to imagine the old world.

"Do you ever think what might have been grandpa?" ""I did more of that when I was young. I was born not long after the sickness wiped out most of the people. It was very hard to listen to the old folks talk of a world I would never see, but we are here and it can only get better. It's been like the old world never was, Mother Nature reclaimed so much. Once around your age I travelled to the city of the dead. I was so sad to see all the skeletons of so many people. Piles of bones left to the elements." "It must have been a horrific thing to witness. I'm not sure I could see most everything I knew and had known be washed away from my life in the matter of a week or two. Did grandpa Zack know it was going to happen? I mean did he know it was going to all end?" Jerod asked. "No. I don't think so. I'm almost sure he never knew what was going to happen. My father tried in vain to go back to the complex. His accident and being crippled after that made cir so he would never find it. I searched many years for anything out here and have found nothing.

Here let me show you what he told me" and West proceeded to tell Jerod of the wall and the mountains that formed in a circle behind it. He told him of Dee and the fact they had family there.

Jerod listened intently when grandpa had finished the story Jerod knew he would also be one to try and find the complex. West banked the fire and soon followed Jerod in sleeping.

When Jerod woke, West had bread and honey, dried apples and porridge for them. Jerod was happy. This was the most exciting thing he had ever done.

West soon had the maps out and pointed out the different spots on the map, then where they were on the land. They chose the path they would take into the next valley and both hoped the signs of the complex would be in the valley beyond. West always marked his way on the land as well as on the map.

By the time the week had passed Jerod was making the lean-to at night. He had learned so many things from West about survival. They had been lucky the weather was warm and the forest dry. "Well" Jerod told West "Do we go for a few more days or start our way back?" "Let's just look in the next valley then we can go back" West said.

They travelled most of the day then they made camp. West filled in his maps and Jerod made the lean-to. When the work was done the fire was kept going for the heat and light. The sky was not clear this night and the stars were not shining. West looked at the sky then noticed the flashes in the distance. He did not like the storms and after the heat there was one coming. Jerod too watched the flashes in the distance. It didn't take long for the wind to pick up and the rain started falling. They had stock piled some wood and covered it well to keep it dry. The storm raged till almost morning and when it was over the two slept well.

It was nearly afternoon before they woke and ate; today they would start back. West knew he would have to travel this way again soon.

They started the climb p the hills and when they reached the summit they could see the black smoke before them. West just said "Oh my goodness Jerod we have a problem here." West loo and could see the river below "Hurry we must get to the river and quickly."

They wasted little time reaching the river. "Jerod whatever happens you stay here in the river until the fire passes." Jerod nodded. A small bucket was soaked in the water by West and he held it over them from the smoke and ashes now surrounding them. The heats soon reached them and it came in waves. Had they not been in the water the heat would have killed them. Jerod had cried several times and West comforted him. All West could think of was Willow, Daniel, April, Carry and Nimuri. He hoped the fire break held in Cliffside, but he knew Daniel had not completed it in Blackrock.

It seemed the fire raged forever; West held Jerod firmly in the water. The time seemed to pass now with infinite slowness. The sound of it was almost deafening. Jerod held onto his grandfather's arm and tried so hard to be brave. Several hours later the intensity died down.

West uncovered them and looked. The fire had consumed everything in its path. The question now on West's mind was did it go through Blackrock and Cliffside? They would have to climb to the top of the next mountain to see.

The ground was still smouldering when they climbed out of the water. The heat still intense had them dry in no time. It was then that Jerod looked at West and said "Grandpa do you think mom and dad are okay?" West just looked at him "I have no way of knowing my boy so best pick up the pace and see." The ground was still hot and there were still hotter spots that still smouldered.

The closer they got to home the more extensive the blaze had been. West now moved quicker and quicker; his heart raced with each step closer. He knew it was going to be bad. "Please, lease" he thought let them be okay.

"Grandpa, grandpa" Jerod hollered "wait up, wait up." West looked behind to see Jerod trying to keep up. He was black with ashes and soot. West knew he had to slow down for Jerod's sake, but getting back was of top priority. He waited for Jerod to catch up and then they sat to catch their breath.

Everything was gone when they crested the next mountain. They would be able to see the lake below. West prayed the wind had shifted and set the blaze back on itself. The uneasy silence between Jerod and West became more deafening as they climbed the next ridge.

When they reached the top West's knees gave out from beneath him. "Grandpa, Grandpa!" Jerod hollered. He turned to see the whole valley was grey and black. The place that Jerod had called home was gone. It was then that Jerod realized what had driven Grandfather on so hard. Where was mom and dad? West's mind flittered from one thought to another not being able to hold onto any thought long.

The valley was devastated; the green lake looked so alien with the charred surrounding. West pulled himself together best he could. The closer they got to what at one time had been home the more the terror climbed for fear of what they would find.

It wasn't long before West caught movement closer to where the cabin had been. The hope they were alive quickened his strides. It was Connie that went to meet them. She stood in his path. West now grasped the fact they were gone. He sat down right where we was. Jerod had clued into what was now going on and tried to pass Connie, but she held him. "They are gone. It will be no good to see them as they are now." Jerod cried and went to his grandfather.

"How bad" West said to her? "How far did it go and how many are gone?" "A few from Blackrock made it. The fire swept to the river in Cliffside. It didn't jump the river" she told him. "Is Cliffside gone?" The look on her face spoke volumes. West knew it was all gone. All he had was gone, Jerod was all he had and West was all that Jerod had. West just wept. Willow his sweet Willow and Daniel, April; his best friend Carry and Nimuri. Seth had escaped being a runner.

Connie sat quietly beside West, she let him grieve. Jerod too cried, but being so young the magnitude of what had just happened was far from being realized by him. He would realize it in his life.

Jerod soon noticed that there were several people here. It had escaped him at first. Jerod had the strangest feeling about these people, like he knew them but he did not. He looked at Connie "You knew the fire was coming" and the anger welled inside him. "You told me you knew." Ray seemed to appear from no where and was beside Connie.

"It's alright Ray he doesn't understand. Sit here Jerod, Ray help him sleep. It's what will do him the most good" and she pointed to West.

Ray walked over and sat beside West. Soon he led West to where the others were and West lay down on some blankets.

Jerod was not really sure what was going on. "Now Jerod, yes I knew or had a vague idea that something was going to happen. Telly told us" She looked over to Telly and he turned to look at her. His eyes were bright blue with blonde curls surrounding his face. He had a twisted arm and hand. "What happened to him?" Jerod asked Connie. Connie paused for a moment "He's gifted Jerod and the people in his family that should have protected him, hurt him. It was Ray that heard his cries and we found him hidden in a shack away from everyone. They were afraid of him and what he could see." "What do you mean, what he could see?" "Hmmm" Connie said "Telly has the ability to sometimes see things yet to happen." Jerod's mouth fell open "How can he do that? No one can see into tomorrow. I don't believe you." Jerod crossed his arms and looked at her.

Connie just smiled "We all have a gift of some sort. We say together this is our family. People can't accept some things and instead of being given the chance just to live, all of us at one time or another have been in fear for our lives at the hands of the people in the towns." "Is that why you lived there at the end of the lake?" Connie nodded. "My dad said you were to be stayed away from" Herod told her. "He was frightened by what he didn't understand. I saved your mother's life and yours long ago." "You did ?" Jerod said. "It was long ago now." "Why didn't you help them this time?" Jerod asked her. "I didn't know what was going to happen. You have to understand Telly. I could repair some of the damage done to him and sometimes he can't relate what he sees. Ray is with him more now. He will try to help him deal with what he sees. Telly is not as old as you and he had great suffering for one so young." "Is grandpa going to be alright?" Jerod asked.

"We will take him and you to our home and then we will see." Then as if a silent messenger had been sent all were standing by Connie. "They are all buried Connie" One of the young boys told her. "Then come" Connie told them.

West was on a makeshift cot that they pulled along. Jerod was concerned that West did not wake up. Connie put and arm on Jerod's shoulder and he instantly relaxed. He knew her and didn't know how or why.

The day passed quickly as they rounded the lake to their village. Jerod was surprised to see they had a large cave under the waterfall that ran into the lake. Jerod knew this was what kept them safe from the fire. The cave was fairly extensive and went back a long ways. Connie looked at Jerod " We will be safe here for a while, but with no lumber we will have to move."

West was placed on a straw mattress and let sleep. A fire was started and food prepared. Jerod was amazed at how they had this cave stored with everything they needed. He was given some porridge and soon found himself near West. He hay beside him and slept.

Jerod was awakened by West. "Come on boy" he said. It took Jerod a few minutes to gather himself together. Connie gave him a tea and bread. The strain was showing on West's face. Jerod thought he had never seen him look so old. "Grandpa" Jerod said. West never spoke just patted his hand.

When Jerod finished his tea and bread West gathered their belongings together. He thanked Connie and Ray for their hospitality and he and Jerod started out for Cliffside.

When they reached the place which had been Jerod's house, little remained. The graves of three laid there. Tears welled in West's eyes and Jerod cried too. They didn't stay too long before heading to Cliffside. The ash was powder and each step into it raised clouds. There were still some hot spots smouldering. West's steps were slow, but steady.

When they reached the top of the cliff West told Jerod to remain where he was. The cabins were gone; everything was gone. Jerod looked down at the grey and black. His life now would never be the same. West was all he had left in the world. West walked through what were the remains of his home then he went to Carry and Nimuri's. There was little left. Where were the bodies West thought? He would have to bury them. He then remembered the root cellar.

After making his way there he opened the trap door, not sure of what he would find. There in the back corner was Carry and Nimuri resting in his arms. They had not been burned, but they had passed away. West sat on the stairs and cried again. How was he to go on? Everything was gone almost, just Jerod was left. How would he live out his life without Willow? How could he rebuild?

Jerod climbed down and was beside West. He put his hand on West's shoulder. "Grandpa, I will help you" he said. West wept some time still.

Jerod knew they would have to be buried. He could see a spade and went to fetch it. West never felt as old as he did then.

Jerod took the shovel and went to the area that was once the spot they all were to lay. Jerod started digging and he cried the whole time. West son was there and took over. Jerod never said anything at this point. What could he say or do to ease the loss they both felt?

When they were both buried West and Jerod went to what was left of the cabin West had built. It was gone almost. Jerod found a pile of rubble and in it some melted things that he had no idea what they once had been. It made him cry again.

It was then Ray appeared on the path. "Connie says I'm to bring you back" he said to them. West knew that it was the best idea. They had shelter and food. He took Jerod's hand in his and the three men walked quietly back.

It seemed like no time had passed and they were with the gifted again. Connie and the other girls and women made food and soon had blankets and beds made for them. West did not feel good it all had been such a great shock. After being in Connie's company he soon found sleep and he did that.

Jerod stayed by his grandfather. He had several burns that he fussed over. Connie came over and placed her hand on them and then they were gone. Jerod looked at her "You do the others?" she said and again Jerod looked at her. Connie came over to him she placed his hand on the blister then her hand on his. She closed his eyes with the other hand and just said "Feel it away." Before Jerod knew what was happening he was with her, a part of her, but he was himself he could see the burn and the damaged tissue. He knew how to start to repair it. In what seemed an instant Jerod was once again himself and know looked at his burn realizing it was gone. "How did" Connie smiled "You always had the gift didn't you know?" Jerod shook his head. Then he seemed to be overwhelmed with tiredness. Connie took him to lie down beside West. It wasn't long before he was asleep.

Telly stood beside Connie now and smiled. "He is going to be a special man I think" Connie said to Telly and he just smiled.

It was a few days later that the folks started coming. Greenmeadow had escaped the fire and many donated things for the few that survived the blaze. A couple families made it to a place of water and survived but most of Blackrock perished.

West would not leave the small band of Connie's people. He sent a runner back to Greenmeadow to ask for rooms for all. The answer was received back in no time. They would be welcome to live in the school house until arrangements could be made for them elsewhere.

Connie and her family such as they were had never been welcome anywhere. She was hesitant to accept the offer. West looked at her "I give you my word all will be well. It will be a safe haven until you can find another area to live in." Connie finally agreed. With no gardens they would die this winter. They had to take the offer.

West and the men soon had everything packed and ready to go.

The journey to Greenmeadow had started. They were a rag tag bunch that was covered in soot and ash that headed down the path and up the other side to Greenmeadow.

They arrived at night to find themselves welcomed with tubs full of warm water to bathe in. The school had been turned into a room for sleeping and the families had brought food for them.

West was proud of Greenmeadow they had pulled it all together in a time of great need. Blankets, dishes, furniture, toys for the young all filtered into the school house. Connie was afraid that when they found out they were gifted it would all change. West told her they knew already.

Jerod spent most of his time with Connie and her bunch. They worked in the fields and did everything and anything they could to help.

West spent time alone. His grief was almost too much for him to bear. One day Telly came to where West was sitting and in his small crippled hand he had a flower bud. When he was sure he had West's attention he put it into West's hand and stared intently at it, in what was a moment it bloomed. Then Telly insisted that West follow him.

Telly took West to his mom and dad up on the hill and when he took the bloomed flower from West and placed it on Jo's grave. West cried. Telly never left him, his crippled little hand rested on his leg. West knew he was not as alone now as he thought he had been. "I'm too old for this" he thought. He couldn't help smiling at Telly.

It was Connie that came in search of the two guys. She found them, Telly sitting in West's lap and leaning against him. From such great loss came grand closeness. Connie would never have believed that people could have been so kind; so many had already treated her so badly. She went over to West and gathered Telly from his lap. West stood and asked where Jerod was. "He's with the other children in the park" Connie told him.

West left the graveyard and went in search of Jerod. He was in the park area watching the kids play. Most of the adults were still in the field. Kalvin was there teaching something to them all and they seemed to be enjoying it whatever it was.

Brad and Gary made West feel more at home, but his life would never be the same again. How he missed Willow and he longed to see Daniel and April. How much of a shame it was their passing. Willow lived for a while, but they were just getting started. He felt the tears well in his eyes again. He had to get it together for Jerod's sake. West was all the boy had in the world.

West went to the school house and lay down. Connie was there and Telly was already sleeping. "Can I bring you anything West?" Connie asked him. "No I'm fine" he told her. "I just want to rest my old bones." He smiled and Connie went back to the mending she had.

West lay down and sleep found him easily. He was emotionally tired and that he found far more draining than having worked all day. Connie was worried about West he was getting older, the stress and stain that had been on him aged him even more than spring and summer.

Soon fall would be here and the harvest, after that long winter to have to endure. It would prove to be a very long one for them all of them.

Through all the sorrow of the lost, hope filtered in. Connie and Ray kept West busy talking of what was beyond Blackrock and Cliffside.

The children of Connie's family were given flutes and soon music filled the school house. So much had happened. The bug that began the journey up the creek that day was all but forgotten.

Come the early spring they would all leave Greenmeadow and journey west. West and Jerod would join them and it seemed that now the family would now include them.

The first snow came and the cold with it. The school house was well built and kept warm. Food had come all the way from the fort to help those that suffered in the fire. Everything came to help them get started again. Connie had more now than she ever did, but was saddened at the price that had to be paid for it. West never spoke much at all. He found it overwhelming. Jerod still somewhat being a child adapted, but he would find many times in the future the emptiness of being alone.

West tried to make a map of what was beyond Blackrock from memory, it covered the basics, but it was nothing near the one he lost in the fire. Most of Zack's words and Jo's; each life span put the old world further away, something being lost with each generation. Willow and Jo had been so adamant about keeping records only to have it lost all in one moment. West knew for Jerod's sake he must tell him so much before his time was up, but for the present getting things ready to start the new living area and other things took priority. Tools, blankets, furniture, seeds, and cooking items the list was long; two wagons of things came from the fort. New tools, lanterns, dry goods, material and seeds they had to find an area with water and enough wood for cabins, etc…

The burned area was huge; clearing it now would not be as hard as before. The water issue was different; a stream that ran year round without the flood threat was not easy to be found. Connie had been lucky to find the cave under the falls. Not all falls came with that convenience.

West had thought a lot about the fires. Twice now it happened in his life. He was bound to find a safe place for his new found family. The memory of the fire would never leave him. The loss had been too great. He still was not sure how the life he had left would be endured without Willow and Daniel.

Just then he heard Jerod talking. "What do you mean you don't know how to read or write?" he said. West looked over and smiled as Jerod sat down and said "Well, I will help you." He still had Jerod and that was what kept him going.

Connie, Ray, West, Jerod and all but the smallest helped in deciding about their future. What a strange bunch of people; extra ordinary and extraordinary at the same time. They were so much the same as everyone and yet so much more in many ways.

Telly was the apple of the bunch. He had been mercilessly beaten almost to death from fear by his family and he now bloomed. His little crippled body never held back his ability to make you feel better. No one heard him speak yet he spoke volumes. His blue eyes were bright when ever he was near you. He spent hours with West following him when West did not carry him. It was as if he knew the pain he felt and somehow eased it. No one knew the extent of each others gifts, but then it didn't matter; it was not often talked of. If the need arose those that could help just did.

Jerod liked Ray the best. He watched him as he heard people's minds talk. That was so awesome to Jerod. He had asked Ray once what he heard. Ray said "It's like static almost, but then voices of pain or sorrow called louder. Here the voices are not too bad; not many people. When I grew up at the fort the sound was deafening. I always went away from them all." "Is it like words you hear?" Jerod asked trying not to sound impolite. Ray smiled "No just the noise, but I know what the noises mean." Jerod let it go he would never understand that, but Ray seemed to and that was fine.

Jerod had the smaller children learning their ABC's before too long. It made West laugh. He remembered Jerod and how the trip to the wood shed opened his mind to new things and closing his ability to sit for long, helped immensely. He had been such a spoiled child; cry and if you cry loud and long enough and his parents would relent and they did. West often thought of Daniel. How he hated West going, maybe somewhere in his soul he knew he would be gone young. West missed so much of his son and the time they could have been together, but then in some way he was just punishing himself.

West looked down to see Telly leaning against his legs. He bent down and picked him up. "Well young man" West said and Telly's face lit up.

Connie still could not believe how calm and peaceful it had been here in Greenmeadow. She had calm in her soul for one of the few times since she had been born.

The winter had firmly gotten its grip on the land. The cold outside was tempered only by the beauty of the snow on the trees and the cabins. The men had all the paths cleared to each house and work shop. The women all worked on weaving and anything they could to ease the work of the coming seasons.

Sara had invited Connie to help her weave and although she had now idea how to weave, she went. Many of the women took part in weaving cloth. Connie wept tears of joy when they made things for her. It was a time of happiness for Connie. Most talked of the coming spring and Sean and Amy's baby which was due. Many times Connie had been included in making things for the coming child. It would be the first baby to be born in Greenmeadow in such a long time. The arrival was anticipated by them all. Amy of course beamed, but her time grew closer and she was found getting around and doing her work was much harder to do.

It was a few weeks later that the melt of the spring began. All the cabins had long icicles that grew and dripped as the days got warmer and froze again at night.

Amy had just finished her dishes and she felt tired tonight she thought as she took the water out to dump. Then in a blink of an eye she fell; she slipped on some ice. She lay there in the snow and spiralled down into unconsciousness.

At Connie's the children sang and played; it was Telly that came to Connie pulling at her dress. She found Ray putting on warmer clothes

"Come" he said to her. "Telly" she said as she kneeled down "Bring West" and Telly nodded. The look on Ray's face told her they had to hurry.

They followed the paths to the cabin where Sean and Amy lived in. There on the ground was Amy. "Get Sean, Ray" Connie made haste to Amy. She placed her hand on her and in an instant knew what needed to be done. The bucket was still firmly gripped by Amy as she lay there. She was wet and cold. Sean leaped off the porch to her. Connie looked at him "Get blanket, Ray help him." Sean moved quickly and now West was there. He put his hand on Connie's shoulder "Will she be alright?" "I will do my best, but the child is in danger she has gotten so cold."

West, Ray and Sean carefully placed her on a blanket to bring her in. When she was on her bed, Connie told them "Heat water, I will need hot water. Who are your midwives?" Sean spoke instantly "Sara and Lily." "Get them" Connie said " and bring me Jerod." West looked at her and she looked back at him. She then turned her attention back to Amy. She had her undressed and in warm blankets.

When Sara and Lily arrived "The child is coming, but she will not be able to help" Connie said to them. Sara and Lily knew she was gifted, but to what extent they did not know. "Can you help her?" they asked. "I will try. She has hurt her head, the bone is soft. Her mass insides are swelling."

She got up "Ray let no one in." She looked around and saw Jerod "Come in Jerod." Jerod was not sure what Connie wanted, he followed her. Ray sat by the door. Sara and Lily looked at Jerod. Connie held both of his hands. "Jerod, now you listen to me. Don't fight it just follow me and we will help Amy." Jerod nodded. Connie placed his hands on Amy then hers over them. She looked at Sara and Lily "Help the child be born or they will both die."

Then almost like a dream Jerod was with Connie travelling like a sledding on a hill; then like explosions, sparks in a fire and colours, blue, red, black and pink. It seemed to go on for a long time then just as quickly as it started it was gone. Jerod now said nothing.

Connie let go of him and called for Ray. He opened the door and went to Jerod who was now wet with sweat and wrapped him in a blanket took him out of the room to West. He held him close and relinquished him to West. "He will be fine, but will need a rest." West nodded and took him back to the school house.

Connie looked at Sara and Lily "I have done what I could with Jerod's help. It's up to her now. The child is fine, but it will be born this night."

Sara and Lily knew she was right. Connie held Amy's hand as her body contracted with the child. By morning the child's cries could be heard.

Sean sat quietly all night waiting for something, anything when Sara appeared at the door holding a small bundle. "It's a girl Sean and Amy is doing okay. She is far from alright, but we believe all will be well." Sean let out a great sigh. He got up and without hesitation took the child from Sara. He smiled at the sight of her and looked at Ray. Tears fell down his cheeks.

Sara soon had hot water and clean linens for Amy. Connie and Lily had the bed fresh for her. Amy still had not woke up so Connie said "She will not know what has happened. When she wakes comfort her, talk softly to her and let the child touch her skin."

Sean wasted not a minute and was seated beside the bed.

Ray took Connie's arm and before anything else was said was gone. When they arrived at the school house Connie went straight to bed. Ray sat at the table and told the children that Connie and Jerod needed rest and quiet.

West thought, whatever bond was between these people it was something completely unknown to him the surprise was that Jerod not only understood, but was one of them.

West made Ray a tea and sat at the table with him. Ray looked right into West's eyes "Jerod is gifted and I will tell you now it is a blessing and a curse as well. Most people don't understand and that fear can drive them to do awful things. I had to endure Telly's pain with him. His family did that to him out of fear. I heard every scream, every bone that broke I felt it. His mind found mine, for him it was sanctuary, for me it was horror. It took months for Connie and me to find him, but I was much younger then. Most do not have such strength. Amy's thoughts did not hurt me as she called and I heard it. Telly hid in my mind as they smashed his small body. He could not have done that without the power of his gift." West was not sure what to say. This is something he did not understand at all. Ray looked at him "Keep Jerod's gift a closed part of his life to others. Not all people are like these here in Greenmeadow." West knew Ray was warning him and it was a warning not to be taken lightly.

Ray finished his tea and went to lay down.

Telly appeared as if he knew what was going on. He had never spoken that West had known of. Telly looked right at him and said "Don't tell, keep him safe" and West almost couldn't believe he had heard him talk.

He had known this child for months and it was the first time he had heard him speak. Telly returned to the children and West to Jerod's bedside.

He watched him sleep and found himself amazed how much he looked like Willow and Daniel. Tears escaped his eyes. West crossed his arms and sat back in his chair. His mind wandered over his life and soon he had fallen asleep.

The following days passed uneventfully. Sara and Lily did not pass around what they had seen and Sean never saw anything. The two old women decided they had witnessed a thing so wonderful that it was up to Connie to speak of it, not them. Jerod had been taken aside by Connie and he knew the gift he had might not be seen the same way by all.

The snow soon was gone and with it came the time to think about leaving. Connie was surprised at all the things they had been given. Even the wagons to transport it all. It was a sad time and a time of adventure for all of them. Some of the younger men volunteered to help get them to where they were going. West, Jerod, Connie, Ray and all the children now a family all bid farewell to Greenmeadow.

The decision was made to go back to the cave and retrieve what they could from there. If anything had to be left behind it would be safe there until they could come back for it. Sean had given West a special gift for Connie, but she would have to wait until they found a place to live.

With the chance of still more snow they would have to go slowly to the new timberline left by the fire. Each night a suitable place would have to be found.

When they finally reached the cave the young men from Greenmeadow stayed the night and by morning were on their way home.

Ray, Connie and West discussed about Ray and West going first to see if the way was clear for the others. Jerod would stay with Connie and help her there. It was the wisest decision.

Ray and West left the next morning. They could see the tree line; it was a question of the best route to take.

Jerod stayed with Connie and found talking with her a relief "How did you learn to use your gift?" Jerod asked her. She smiled "I was very young. I think I healed my mom, a burn or something. From there everyone wanted everything healed. I can't heal all things; Telly is proof of that and it's people that couldn't e helped drove me away" she told him. "How did you know I could do it?" Jerod asked. "I was there when you were born. You helped me save your mother that day." A smile crossed his face, and then it was gone. "I miss my mom" he said. "I would think something was wrong with you if you didn't" Connie smiled again. "If the great fire never happened you would have discovered your gift it was really just a matter of time" she told him.

Jerod sat back and watched her unpack things for the children. She looked over to him "Keep your gift quiet. I mean keep it a secret. Don't let many know of it. It changes how they see you and what they expect of you." Jerod was contented with their talk and then started to help her. He went for wood and bring back more things into the cave. He didn't know how long grandpa and Ray would be, they might as well get comfortable.

West and Ray reached the timber line and soon found a good water source. The fire had been stopped by a small river. West wondered if it was flood prone and looked for signs of a high water mark. Ray followed and listened, anything he could learn to help keep them alive was a bonus. West was like a father he never had.

It was the following day that they discovered the area that would be their new home. The burned area would be the new field and the wooded area the beginning of their small haven. Satisfied the two men started back to collect the family. The next few years would be hard work, but it was not feared by any. The reward would be home and this was going to be protected from fire and flood. It was an awesome find; a small river that joined a larger one was on two sides, a rock cliff with no trees on the third side and the entrance into the area could be kept clear as a fire break. The rivers were down below close enough to get the water needed, but the good land was up higher than anything that looked like a high water line.

Rebuilding their lives now consumed them all. It would be three years before Jerod would suffer his biggest heartbreak. He was sitting in the park area watching the children playing and listening to their flutes. The gift of the bee hive was one favoured by most of them. Gilda was new to their family and was having trouble fitting in. She seemed to be aware if people were being truthful or not. Although her family loved her they had been afraid of what might happen if it was revealed she was gifted. Jerod always wondered what the problem was over that. Why were people so afraid of them? It made no sense to him. Jerod still felt it was nonsense; had anyone ever been hurt by someone with a gift? He knew they had not. Why be afraid he thought. That being the case Gilda had to learn how to live with and control herself until she could conceal her gift.

It was near the afternoon when Telly came and sat with him. This in its self was not odd, but Telly shadowed his every step. It was not long before Jerod twigged that something was not right. He had a fair idea where everyone was and they seemed fine. He scanned the bush line to see if anything was there; he saw nothing. Then he sat down and Telly was right there. "Tell me" Jerod said to him. Telly looked at West and back to Jerod. Jerod looked West over and could not see anything amiss. He was old but in no way showed signs of pain or absent mindedness.

By dinner time Jerod concluded what ever was the trouble it would pass. After dinner Jerod would take the smaller wagon and work on the pathways. It was too hot to do in mid day. It was best to do first thing in the morning or before twilight. The work was too hard for West now, but he over looked many things that were taking place. He helped design the area to get the best production from areas to grow food, etc...Ray and Connie both learned a great deal from him.

Jerod spent a few hours everyday teaching the children to read and write.

That night after the small children were in bed, Ray and West discussed the new people that had come to Blackrock. It would be ideal to log off some areas to build fire breaks. West was determined fire would never be the killer it had been.

After tea, the evening was enjoyed for a little while, but as always the work would be there for them in the morning, so they all went to bed early.

Jerod was awakened by Connie "Come with me Jerod." He rubbed his eyes. "Here" she said and gave him a hot tea. "How come you are up so early?" Jerod asked her. "I wanted to talk to you alone" she told him. "Today is going to be a long day for you and I just want you to know we all care a lot about you. I have bad news, West, your grandpa has passed away." Jerod just sat there. This couldn't be right he was just with you all just last night Jerod thought. Connie never said much more. "He didn't suffer, his passing was easy" was all she added. Jerod just sat there and then cried. He was the only one left now. In the space of three years his whole family was gone. What was he going to do now? He thought, as he whipped his tears that didn't seem to want to stop.

"You can stay here; you know we are all so very sorry." Connie was telling the truth his mind just couldn't get around it all. Connie gave him a new cup of tea and just sat quietly with him. Jerod cried for about an hour then wandered around the small community areas. What was he going to do now? He thought.

The next week or so he was often by himself not wanting to talk to anyone. It didn't seem much sense talking about it.

West was buried there and Jerod had to decide if he was staying or going. He had become part of this family and it would be hard to be alone. He had never been alone. He thought about his mom's sister, Dawn at the fort. If ever there was a time to adventure it was now. He couldn't make any decisions about his life yet. He did just plain not know what he wanted. He had talked to Ray and Connie about it and they both agreed that the decisions were his to make. If venturing to the fort brought him closer to making a decision about his life the he needed to go there. They were adamant about him keeping his gift a secret. Jerod needed to get away after the great fire and grandpa's passing this part of the world held no comfort to him. Everything he knew was gone.

The next few days found him packing for his trip. He was to visit Dawn and maybe work there for a time. He had never been alone.

Connie didn't want him to go, but knew his life was his own. He knew where they all were and he knew that he was always welcome there.

Jerod never felt lonely, nut now as he started towards the fort loneliness crept up inside him. He missed his grandpa, his grandma and mom and dad. How was he going to face life now that he was alone?

Each village he passed on the way to the fort held nothing for him. He was on one of the greatest adventures of his life and all he wanted was to go hoe and see his mom and dad working in the gardens.

It took the better part of a week to get to the fort. There were a lot of people there compared to the small settlements that had fanned out into the surrounding valleys.

It wasn't long before he made it to Dawn's house. It took her a few minutes to realize who he was, but soon she had him in the house and feeding him. "You look like my mom did" Jerod said to her. She smiled "I will miss her more than you know" she said. She looked over to Jerod "How are you Jerod? You will stay here with us. You are more than welcome. You do know that?" Jerod nodded. "I guess I will look for some work around here." "I will not stand for that" Dawn told him. "You are much too young for that" Dawn told him. "I think, hmm maybe you could help at the library we have here, or" she smiled "let's not think about all that just yet. You must relax and I'm sure you will decide what's best for you." It was good to know he had some time to try and sort some things out.

He was too young really to live completely on his own. Too young to think of marriage, but too old to be thought of as a child. Nothing had prepared him for this. He always thought his mom and dad would be around.

Dawn showed him his room and he set down his stuff. "Would you mind terribly if I looked around the fort a bit?" he said to Dawn. "You go ahead, dinner will not be before dusk." He smiled and after a quick wash he went to see what he could see at the fort.

Jerod still held great sadness in him. Watching all the people in some way just brought out the fact he was alone closer to home. Jerod had never seen so many people in one place. His visits to the common house were his best distractions. He heard all the stories there of the surrounding land and what was going on. People knew of the Blackrock fire and it was the talk of many to go and build the farms again. The heavy clearing had been done by the fire. Jerod never said anything. He best like the tales of the new people. Dawn mentioned a wagon train was going to them and they were looking for the strong and able to help with the wagons. The wagons were not large and were pulled by one or two people. They were also making new trails into the mountains south and west of the fort.

There was an opportunity here for adventure; Jerod just couldn't get past the sorrow yet. Dawn knew how he felt for she too was suffering the loss, but she did have Chad and the hope of children.

It was a week later that Jerod told Dawn the news that he would be joining the wagon train to the new town east. The first trains would set stations and goods would be transported further via the other stations.

It would be mid summer before the people there would get the benefits of the work that had to be done along the way. Jerod had been told of the people that first came from the prairie and how bad off they had been. These folks faired better; whatever the reason they managed to survive the trials that had all but destroyed the others. Jerod concluded it was the leadership that had done it. The men and women like his great grandparents, Zack and Jo. Dawn was happy that something had sparked Jerod's will. If he never found anything there, the travelling and the people would keep his mind active and not dwelling on things past that nothing could be done about.

The fort was buzzing with things when the first wagons went out. They left in intervals of three days. This would go on for most of the summer. Volunteers had to be found to man the message and resting stations along the way.

Four stations had been decided upon; all near a source of water. Each station would have sheds for storage and homes to provide the station folks a place to live other than the public station. Gardens would be made and each would have fire barriers and wind breaks. Fruit and nut trees were started for each station as well as bee hives.

It was a new world now, the old was long gone. The trials of survival faced and now their world was in its infancy.

Jerod often thought of Connie, Ray and all the others. Where were the gifted in this new world? What happened to Telly was cruel, but not like it would never happen again. The old fears were not far from the surface yet, many people harboured thoughts they got from their parents. Thoughts like greed and the hostility to people over skin colour was gone, but fear of people that could do what others could not was still there. Jerod never spoke of the gifted to anyone. Even Dawn, the closest people left in his life did not know.

When the wagons started going, tents had been made were the first shelters. Every wagon emptied was sent to the fort to be refilled with any needed goods. Three days later the full wagons met empty ones going back. It went on for a few months before you could really see the difference. The life line across the land had been established and now the goods moved much more quickly. Jerod felt he was part of something, not just anything, but a piece of getting the world back.

Many days he sat watching the young men pull the carts. He would think of his grandpa telling stories about animals and how they had done the work these men now struggled to do. Animals and birds, it was indeed a strange world.

By the end of summer the life line had been completed. Jerod entered the small hamlet that had survived all this time on its own. The people were leery of them, Anna, a dark haired woman approached Jerod "Hello, I am Anna" she said. Jerod smiled "I am Jerod." "Looks like you could use a drink. Come to the well and I will fetch you some water." Jerod followed her. She wasn't a very big woman, but she showed no fear of the new people, not like the others. She gave Jerod a drink and soon they were walking and talking as Anna showed him everything in the hamlet.

They had plum and apple trees, grapes and cranberries, as well as hazelnuts and strawberries. They grew squash, sugar beets, pumpkins, potatoes, carrots, spinach and the list went on to items like wheat, oats and canola.

"Who told you how to keep the crops going?" Jerod asked. "The old elders as we call them. It's our duty to pollinate for as long as each of us can in the spring. It would be our death if we did not." Jerod soon found all of them could read and write. For such a small community they survived well.

There was a big commotion at the wagon and soon everyone was there listening to the bees in the boxes. A lot would not get too close they had never seen another living creature. Anna was not one of them she wanted to see the bees. The buzzing noise was thrilling her.

Jerod never had seen the likes of that, people that never saw bees. Wax was given to all the families as well as candles.

There were meetings all winter to explain the use of many things that had been brought from the fort. The tools were of great interest to most. The few tools that were here were almost the most valued item they had.

That evening Anna tasted honey on the bread that Jerod gave her. It seemed that the people here were losing their fear. The laughter and merriment were proof of that. Soon a few of the girls brought out stringed instruments and played them for everyone. The soft plucking of the strings made a music that the people from the fort had never heard. Jerod brought out his flute and soon played along with the melody. It was a night all would never forget.

The bond of music drew Anna and Jerod together. After playing many folks had tears in their eyes. All applauded those that had played the tune that would forever remain in the hearts of those there that night. The talk then really became relaxed. The music had opened something that had been missing for far too long.

Jerod was asked everything about his flute; where he learned to play and if all the people at the fort played?

Anna now found any and every reason to be with Jerod. Jerod opened a box from the wagon his aunt had given him and withdrew cloth, pottery and wooden looking things. He told Anna these were donated by his aunt and he would be so happy if she would accept them. Anna was not sure what to say; she took the gifts and from that day on Anna would be with Jerod. She knew that even if he didn't.

Many things came over the late summer and fall to Silvercreek. The lumber was one thing that had been missing for so long. For winter heat a kind of presto log had been made from a mash of wheat shafts. These people had utilized everything they could to survive. Bags of salt were given to each family. It was a treat; the salt they had was always rationed only a small amount was harvested by them from the small salt area they had. Maple syrup was relished and walnuts found their way into everything they could be in. Rose hip tea was their favourite so many rose plants were on e of the first things that made their way into the ground after the long journey. If they died over the winter new plants would be brought in the spring. Dried mushrooms and herbs were welcomed by all the women.

The small creek in the valley was the only thing that broke up the flatness of the prairie here. Winter was coming and the harvest would be in full force soon.

Jerod helped Anna in everyway he could. She had lived with her mother until a few years ago when her mom passed away. The folks in Silvercreek tried in vain to marry her to one of their young men, but Anna showed no interest in them. She knew of the fort and the runners had told them soon the way would be made for many to come here and for anyone to leave and go to the fort. Anna wanted to leave. She had always wanted to leave from the moment she knew there were people and life somewhere other than here. It wasn't bad to live here, just the same thing day in and day out. An opportunity had come and Anna was taking it.

Jerod had spent many hours in Anna's company. He knew she wanted to leave, but the responsibility to the harvest held her here in Silvercreek until next spring.

Jerod stayed in Silvercreek offering his help where hw could. The bee hives had become his project. He knew more about them than most. This year the hives would be left, any honey now collected would have to be used to keep the hive alive through the winter. They had arrived in time to pollinate. Next spring would be the beginning of their work, honey and wax would be the bonus.

Many crates of candles had come and light after dark was thrilling to them. Jerod enjoyed the curiosity they showed with anything new. Plans and supplies came to make candles and to build almost anything they needed. Jars and pots for cooking so many long needed basic supplies.

Anna had taken the material Jerod gave her and made travelling clothes similar to those her wore. This would be her last winter and spring here. Jerod knew she was leaving and offered to trek with her. Trekking alone anywhere was never a good idea. They still had to get through the winter. Food was really not an issue there had always been enough, but now there were many different foods for them. Weaving baskets and cloth took much of the time in the winter for everyone. Paper was being made now as well as presto logs. Winter would soon closed down many things.

The white blanket spread over the land and would soon cover everything to protect all from the bitter cold until next spring.

Jerod stood on the porch of the house he was staying at and looked out over the vast prairie. He wondered if more people were out there or if an animal might one day be found. He thought about Connie, Ray and the children. Thoughts and memories of Blackrock and Cliffside filtered through his mind.

He felt a hand on his shoulder and turned to see Anna. He smiled. "You were so far away" she told him. "Are you alright?" "Yes and no" he told her. "I was just wondering how it must have been for all of you here alone all this time" he smiled at her. He did not wish to talk about things that hurt his heart so much.

"Well" Anna said "We always knew others must have lived through the sickness that came, but with each passing year hope for that was getting slimmer. I can remember when I was really young thinking people would come and our lives would be fun and carefree like a child's dream" she said and smiled. "I always wondered what was beyond that line of the horizon. Most here just called me a day dreamer. I guess I have always wanted just more, of what I'm not sure. I did once pack a bag and walked for a day. I only saw the same as here and came back. With all these people sometimes I think I feel lonely, if that makes any sense?" "Where is you family?" Jerod asked.

"They left long ago in the wind storm. The house we lived in blew apart and they were killed. They tell me I was dug out of the rubble with not even a scratch on me. Funny to think what killed them left me unmarked except in my heart. Oh don't get me wrong everyone here has been more than kind to me. Where is your family?" she asked him. "Back at the fort?" "No, no" Jerod told her "I too am alone. A great fire swept over the mountains and they were lost in it." "I am sorry to hear that" she said to him. "It seems we share many things in common. It's too bad they are such hurtful things." Anna looked at him. "Not all are hurtful, some are lovely; take the music or our friendship or our love of life" she smiled. Jerod smiled too "Yes you are right there." "So when you go back to the fort what will you do then?" Anna asked Jerod. "Oh I don't know I thought about going west. People are starting to go that way it will open to the ocean one day so my grandfather told me." "Oh did he live in the time of the great sickness?" she asked. "No he didn't, but his mom and dad did. That was one of the things that were such a loss. All the books they wrote and the maps they had." "Hmmm" Anna told him.

"Enough about me, why do you want to leave here? Seems you all have a good life here, not much want and now with things coming regularly from the fort. It seems a good place to live."

Anna bit her lip a little. She stood up and looked around. "Stand up" she said to him. "Tell me something you see as you look over the horizon that is different in any 2 spots." Jerod looked and turned in a circle looking. "I never believed life was like this, always the same other than the weather being different nothing changes. I guess I want to see if it's different somewhere else. If I don't like it I can always come back." Jerod had to agree wither. It seemed the clock of time clicked over and the first snows were blowing in.

The people gathered in one place or another. This was the time of togetherness. Weaving was done with sewing, music and hand carving. There was always music, Jerod enjoyed that. Anna always sat near him, it was obvious to everyone that Jerod and Anna were a pair. Unfortunate for Jerod he was not getting the fact that Anna was getting more infatuated with him. They talked of leaving the village in the spring, but Jerod had not clued in that Anna meant leave with him.

The winter seemed to pass so fast. Jerod still had a few jobs to take care of and getting the hives functional was one of them. It was still too cold out; although the snow was almost gone the frost in the air let them know that winter still had its grip on the land. It was during this time that Anna let Jerod to understand without a doubt that she would be leaving with him when the weather turned warmer. Jerod was still a young man and to take on the responsibility of Anna he was not sure he was ready for. The idea was not all bad to him because he did enjoy Anna, they got on famously. The back lash was Jerod was just afraid to feel anything too strongly for anyone. Losing his whole family in the fire had made him build walls around himself. Anna had a way of getting around them and although he was unsure the comfort he felt from her soon would outweigh that fear.

It was a few mornings before Jerod was about to leave that he and Anna walked over the little village. "Anna" he said. "I want you to look at everything here; the house, the people and even the horizon." Anna wasn't really sure why, but she did. They walked for most of the morning and then headed in for something hot to eat and drink. "I am leaving in a few days" he said to her. Anna went to say something, but he stopped her. "I don't think I will ever be back here. It is my intention to go west when I return to the fort. I want you to be sure that if you leave with me it's what you want."

Anna looked at him. She had longed for a way out of the village and here it was. She had no idea what lay ahead for her, but it was a chance she had to take. Now that the road was to the fort she would leave, anyways it would just have been a matter of time. "Jerod thank you so much for your concern, but this place holds nothing for me. If I stay I will be expected to marry, have children and live out my life working in the fields. I can't help feeling there is more, much more out there. I have nothing against the work, but this life is the only one I have. I want to see, do and be part of it something more than here." Jerod was not shocked he too had the same thoughts. He had come to them because of tragedy, but they still were the same. The thoughts of leaving with Anna wasn't something he felt he would mind too much.

As soon as he had the bee hives up and they were doing their thing he packed and was ready to go. Anna packed with his help. She had to remember she would carry what she brought and it might not be heavy now, but in 10 miles it would feel much heavier.

Jerod had learned so much from West and now he was thankful for it. He had the feeling he and Anna would be together for a long time. First things first though there was a wagon that needed to go to the first rest stop, from there they would see if anything needed to go further on.

Anna said her goodbyes and her being the first to leave Silvercreek since the great sickness caused tears in more than one family.

Anna and Jerod took turns pulling the empty wagon. The path was not too bad when the rains came it would be worse. They slept under it at night and after two days they arrived at the first rest spot.

This is the furthest Anna had ever been. She stuck close to Jerod still a little shy of strangers. They got a hot meal and a hot tub of water. Jerod let Anna bathe first then he climbed into the water. When he was done they washed out what they had worn and hung it to dry in the cabin by the fire.

The keeper wanted them to keep taking the wagon it would be better to get it closer to the fort.

Jerod asked if any news had come from the fort and the keeper just mentioned that they had started working on the fields there. The weather was still cold at night, but warmer times were their way.

"Do you think the bees will be of great help?" Anna asked Jerod. "I think when the blooms come and the bees find them there will be things that no one even realizes are there. When the fruits and berries growing wild happen it will surprise even the oldest in Silvercreek. They will get all the wax and homey too." "Oh honey is so good" Anna said and smiled.

Jerod brought out his flute and played a soft melody as Anna listened. The keeper even sat and listened to the soft tune. When Jerod stopped the old fellow smiled "It has been so long since I heard music." He got up and tended to things around the cabin.

"Do you miss Silvercreek yet?" Jerod asked her. "No" she said "Not really, I may feel differently in a few months, but for the moment I'm glad to be away from it. I'm kind of excited to see what's at the end of this road." "Fort Reed is at the end." Jerod smiled. "Tell me again about Fort Reed" she said. "It's the first settlement when the sickness came. The people gathered her and spread out from there. My grandfather started the trek north then west from the fort. They settled in Greenmeadow and from there my grandfather settled in Cliffside. My dad went to Blackrock after the fire. It was in the next fire that my family perished in. My mother's sister lives at the fort. We can stay there until we decide what we want to do." Anna smiled at Jerod.

Both were so young and to brave the new world it would take all their courage and strength.

The following days of their journey met with rain and mud. It made travelling tiresome and hard. They still had the empty wagon with them. The only consolation was that in two or three days they would be at the fort. Jerod never imagined that he would befriend a young woman, but she was turning out to be more than a friend. Anna was his confidant, he told her things he never told anyone else.

The first day after the rain stopped and the path was thick with mud Jerod told Anna how he cried and carried on when he had to do something he didn't want to do, his mom and dad always gave in. He thought he was being so smart until he visited his grandma and grandpa. Grandpa West fixed him right up. He lit his rear end on fire a few times with a switch and it amazed him how heating one end made the other end interested in what was being told to him. How he wished his family was still with him and how much he missed them.

Anna always listened to him. Her story was simple, she lost her mom and dad and grew up working; no family and no say in anything. She was the charity case of the village. She hated it there and when the opportunity came for her to leave she did. The two had a lot in common. Anna and Jerod didn't know it but would live life together for sometime.

When the fort was in sight Anna was so excited, but also afraid. She had know everyone where she was, now she would know no one. Jerod assured her everything would be fine. It was good that Jerod had someone; he had been worried for her.

Dawn spent many hours showing Anna the fort and helping her adjust to life at the fort. Jerod found a job at the smithy and Anna tried several jobs from getting salt at the flats to helping build the new road to the prairie town. She finally found working in the weaving house the most enjoyable.

The spring wore into summer and then fall. Anna loaded the apples and fruits here; the honey and maple syrup too. It was an adventure everyday. The flax was being harvested and Anna was kept busy. Jerod had been to the library a lot. He looked over the maps made of the area around and beyond the fort. He copied several maps out and had shown them to Anna. She was not sure moving away from the fort was what she wanted yet. It was much better than the small village she had come from. They would be bound there for the winter in any case.

Anna was a joy for Dawn. They worked endlessly on things for the fort and for themselves. Chad had started making furniture for Jerod and Anna. They were just friends and that was never an issue. Jerod talked to Chad about many things. He was the only father figure Jerod had.

While Dawn and Anna worked on the harvest, Jerod and Chad worked on Jerod's ideas for a new cabin.

"It seems like you have some good ideas. You remind me of Zack and West" Chad said to him. "I wish I could have saved some of his work, but it was lost in the fire." Chad looked up from his project. "You know, maybe there is some left. I will write my mom and dad." Jerod smiled "That would be awesome." Chad just smiled.

"So are you going to marry Anna" he said. Jerod just looked at him. "Marry her. Gee I'm too young to think like that." Jerod had thought about that but it was a big, big step. What if Anna didn't want him that way? "Well my friend" Chad said "You had better take some action, Anna has a few suitors since she has been here" Chad told him. "Oh give over" Jerod said "I doubt it Anna has been with Dawn." "Jerod my boy Anna is a delicate pretty young woman. Do you think that has gone unnoticed here?" Chad teased him. "I never thought about it" Jerod said. "Well that's obvious" Chad said. "Are you telling me that Anna has other men seeking her had?" Jerod asked. "Well I am not sure about that, but I have heard comments about her beauty and capabilities." Jerod had not thought about anyone being interested in Anna that way, but maybe he should be thinking about it. The subject was dropped and the two men worked on their projects in silence after that.

With the first snow came the awe from Anna at the trees donning their winter blanket. They would be fort bound now until spring. Anna was intent on learning everything about the new home area. Her life was so changed. She had grown accustomed to all the new people. The fact there were others in neighbouring valleys and that information was passed along with runners. Her world had grown ten fold in a matter of months and sometimes it was overwhelming. She had learned so much and still had more to learn. Dawn and the other women soon had her cook book full and she would learn more about the new foods here. Everything from knitting patterns to dripping candles was put in her book.

Anna had no doubt that her life would be shared with Jerod. That was of course if he wanted it. Dawn had welcomed Anna as part of the family already. It was this atmosphere that held over the winter.

The spring came into being in what seemed to be overnight. The men and women filled the fields ploughing and planting. The work was hard and the hours were long. Shifts were taken to keep up the other jobs that needed to be done. When the planting was completed Anna most often found Jerod in the library. Jerod often showed her maps and areas in which he wanted to live. Anna would have followed him anywhere.

Jerod had one book compiled of the things Greenmeadow had sent that Zack had written about the complex. Jerod was sure that he had gone north too soon and wanted to go west from the fort. Small settlements had started to pop up on the way he wanted to go and Jerod was sure he could get some land further in. Chad had agreed to help with the first clearing. If they went before the harvest, the wood would be dry by next spring to cut for a cabin.

Anna work continuously making whatever she could for a home. There was actually a light at the end of the tunnel for her. Her worldly goods had become so much more then when she started walking with Jerod bringing back the empty wagon.

Jerod finally picked the area in which he wanted to live. He invited Chad to go with him to look it over before he claimed it as his own. Chad was delighted. He had a few adventures since coming to the fort. Now that Dawn had Anna to keep her company it would be a good time to go.

Jerod and Chad packed up light packs and made ready their journey. Dawn still had Anna under her wing so to speak and found helping her what she needed to know, a pleasure. Jerod and Chad had to be back before the snow came, so little time was wasted.

Dawn and Anna would work on the harvest. Many of the herbs and mushrooms were dry now. The wheat would all have stoked yet and the flax prepared for spinning; any vegetables that could be dried were and potatoes were put into the root cellars along with turnips that had been washed and dipped in wax. The children gathered the nuts. It was made into a festival for them and apples were done. It was a happy time for a lot of people.

The hard work that all had been done was starting to pay off in knowing no one would hunger. The endless chopping wood was for the teens. Although many disliked it they all knew it would be very cold without it.

Anna had brought her knowledge of making a false log made of straw and many were made.

The smithy was kept busy and the worry of new metal sources never went away. The teams that went to the city of the dead had salvaged what they could, but every family needed things made from it. Life was stable but far from secure. Jerod knew all to well how fast families could be wiped out.

When Jerod and Chad reached the area that was on the map it wasn't what Jerod thought it would be. The valley was shallow; the walls of the mountains were steep and looked unstable. He knew this was not a place he wanted to live. Back to the library he thought and back to the maps. It was while they ate a light lunch that Chad had suggested looking over another valley a little further south but still west. Jerod agreed what did they have to lose?

It would take them two more days to reach it. When they crested the top Jerod smiled. This was more like it. A small river ran to one edge of the mountains and the valley was large and looked almost like meadow then forest. They climbed down into the valley and Jerod knew it was here he would live for a long time. One side was mountains almost sheer and solid rock; the other a river winding down the full length of the valley.

The danger from fire was minimal, floods might be another story, but if he built higher that would not be a problem. He even knew what it would be called, Riverside.

They made camp and they discussed the work needed to be done now. Chad was pleased that Jerod had picked this place, but he didn't like that he was really still a long ways from folks. That would change in the next ten years though.

"So now you have to marry Anna" Chad smiled at Jerod. "Do you think she would have me?" and they both laughed. "I know she wants to marry" Jerod said. "but until this cabin is built I won't ask her. She also likes the fort with all the new people. When she lived in Silvercreek she was not happy maybe she will not want to live out here with just us." Chad put a hand on Jerod's shoulder "She will I have no doubt she loves you and will follow you anywhere." "Well that remains to be seen. Tomorrow we head back and I go city hall and claim the land, we will see" he said.

After some more talk about all the land he would claim they made camp for the night.

Anna had spent many hours in Dawn's company and for all the time in and around all the people and the commotion of life, part of her still yearned for the quietness. She missed the hours she had alone with her thoughts. It actually surprised her because when she left Silvercreek it was one of the things she wanted to leave behind. One thing she did enjoy and was learning how to live with was the forest. There were so many trees each sounding different when the wind blew through them. The walnuts and hazelnuts were just an added bonus and the maple syrup was such a treat.

Dawn told her how she hated living so far out in a small village of Greenmeadow. The fort was where to be.

Anna was finding it hard to cope with all the people and everything that went with them. She was discovering that sometimes the things you want are not the things you really want. She did not want to go back to Silvercreek that was for sure. It wasn't long after Chad and Jerod returned.

Jerod was full of enthusiasm about the place he picked out. Anna was attentive to him and listened to everything.

Within the next few days Jerod had his name put next to the land. They want people to spread out into the surrounding areas. It was the only way to get things going again; safety was factored in there as well.

When Blackrock burned for the second time people from further away were able to send relief. Jerod was sure that more people would move that way if a road could be established. When his excitement died down some over everything he took Anna aside.

"Anna" he started "I want you to come with me to the place I have picked out" he said to her. Anna just smiled she would go just about anywhere with him. She loved him and had no doubt about that fact. "I want to marry you Anna" he told her. "Next spring I want to marry you." Anna didn't need to talk about it. She just looked at him and said "I just want you to know I will go anywhere with you, but I want a family and I don't want to be old before I start one. I don't want more than three children." Jerod just smiled "That's fine by me" he told her.

Here were two souls brought together by fluke circumstances; both had endured great sadness and loneliness. I was a match that had all the things two young people needed to get along. Fate had brought them together and a good life lay ahead for them.

The harvest was brought in and winter settled the fort down to a dull roar.

Dawn and Anna worked to get the things she would need in her new home. Chad and Jerod would build what they could for the cabin. Come spring they would cut the logs they would need for it.

Jerod spent a lot of time now in the library looking at the maps there. Most of the valleys had had runners making maps as they went. His valley had little, but he would change that. He would map it out and then it would be added to the great map in front of him now. He was nearly 20 years old and already had taken the steps a man 5 years old would have taken.

Chad, Jerod, Dawn and Anna shared many laughs that winter all of them worked hard to do what they could before Chad and Jerod left. It was agreed the trees would be cut and would be left to season until mid summer. The gardens at the fort would have to come first. When they finished that, they could work on the road there. A good solid path would not only be an asset for them, but would encourage other young people to consider that land there when looking for something of their own.

They had small gravel wagons and after the gardens were planted the wagons would be put to work.

Anna sat looking at Jerod and wondering what gracious hand of fate had seen fit to bring them together. She had made an agreement to weave cloth and baskets for the smithy in exchange for spades, saws and a sleigh. Dawn chattered endlessly about the wedding; Chad and Jerod stayed fairly clear of the women. Both had work to do and each day shorted the time in which they had to do it.

The winter seemed to drag on forever; the cold winds blew and the icicles hung steadfast to the cabins yet. Anna watched the drifts get higher and higher. Dawn often made her tea when she saw her longing for spring. "It will get here when it gets here" she told her and Anna just smiled.

She sipped her tea and thought how different her life had turned out. A year ago she was in the prairie trying to avoid everyone especially the men folk, knowing soon she would have to pick someone she would have to spend her life with. To live alone with so few people they would have almost banished her. It was her duty to marry and have children, now everything had changed. She was free to make her own decisions about everything in her life. With all the people here at the fort and the surrounding villages having children was no longer a duty, but a choice. She wondered how many more people survived out there. It was possible that there were small bands of folks waiting to be discovered again. They may just have been lucky, to the others that had been found did not fair as well as they had.

"My goodness Anna you're deep in thought today" Dawn said to her. "I was just thinking about how lucky we were you found us" Anna replied. "You must have had to work hard to survive?" Anna said. "I'm sure it was not their intention to destroy everything. In any event it was the consequences of their actions. No one is left now to tell the story. Jerod's great grandfather said it was an accident spurred on by greed and a lust for power, but we will never know for sure. All we can do is make sure it never happens again; a new beginning, one where no one has power over another." "I was just thinking about that in a way how my village almost did that to me. I had to marry and have children. I didn't like that it was always hanging over my head" Anna said. Dawn smiled "I think they were afraid of dying out more than holding things over you. If the population does not increase faster then it depletes then all is lost. Do you think it was more along that line? Dawn smiled. How young Anna still was.

Anna sat quietly. Dawn was right they just wanted to save themselves. She wondered why it had not occurred to her before?

"Come help me finish this blanket" Dawn said to her and the two women sat by the fire and sewed the blankets.

Jerod was in the workshop with Chad. He was being teased over the bed he was making. "You wait and see" Chad said to him. "She will be ruling the roost before what's even happened. They all do." Chad looked very serious at Jerod and said "It's a good thing too; we would run amuck if they didn't keep us in line." Then smiled a big smiled and they both laughed. "You know" Chad said "I might tease you, but it would be an awful sorry place without them. I can't imagine life without Dawn." Jerod smiled. His mind drifted to his own mom and dad; the memories of them together and how they stove for the same things, anything to help people in the new world. He would not be where he was today had they not perished in the fire. How different life had turned out for him.

His mind wandered to Connie and Ray. He wondered how they were doing and the children. His mind then focused on Anna; her soft manner, her strength of will and her fearlessness. For such a tiny little person she had such large dreams. One day he would sit her down and tell her of the complex; everything he knew.

Chad let Jerod alone with his thoughts and soon found himself immersed in his own project. He had made two travelling trunks for them and now was on the third one. They would need them for their future.

Spring seemed not to want to come. Winter's hold on everything was as tight as it could be. It was not only Jerod and Anna that waited, but all at the fort. Winter had its place, but spring was always longed for even with its work it was awaited by all.

Another week passed before Anna noticed dripping of the icicles; spring was coming. Folks all over the fort had their garden plans ready. Chad and Jerod would soon be off to cut the timber for their cabin. When he returned Jerod and Anna would be married.

It was surprising how fast the snows could melt with a bit of warm weather. It seemed almost over night the drifts had dwindled to near nothing. The ice was gone and the cold evenings could not refreeze things.

It was then Jerod and Chad headed out. They would be gone for as long as it would take to cut the lumber.

Anna and Dawn helped in the syrup gathering and the fort came alive with the work of the spring. The fields had to be ready for planting, a new year was upon them.

With their packs laden with tools it took three days to reach Jerod's land. The two men had a temporary shelter made in no time and began to cut the trees. Jerod burned out the stumps that he could. The rest he would have to wait until he returned with Anna. Satisfied that enough trees had been cut down they returned to the fort.

It was then Jerod and Anna were married. There was no big fan fare just Chad and Dawn. Anna had no family nor did Jerod other than Chad and Dawn.

The ceremony was lovely. When Jerod could finally kiss Anna it would be more than a dream come true for both of them.

The four left the town hall and Chad and Dawn went and stayed with friends in the next village. Jerod and Anna were alone for the next few days. By the time the gardens needed to be done both were ready to settle into their new lives.

In the beginning of the summer that they finally found time to go to Riverside. They took a small wagon and the journey began. The makeshift shelter was still intact and with a bit more work it was stable. They needed a place to keep dry and safe from the weather.

Jerod although young soon had the cabin started. Anna was amazed at how easy he made it look. It did take both of them with the help of ropes to get the logs stacked on top of each other.

When Jerod worked to prepare the next log for the building, Anna would split wood for the shingles on the roof. By the time the harvest was ready the cabin stood there with the fire place made and their home was ready for them. One more winter at the fort and they would move. This fall they would come back and clear more land, chop wood, burn stumps, dig the well and work at whatever they could.

This winter would drag on forever Anna thought. Jerod just wanted the super heavy work to be done.

The harvest was upon them and it seemed the cold was nipping at their heals the entire harvest. The fort got the wheat done just in time for the frost came in with a vengeance and not long after the snow hit hard.

The first snow fall measure about two feet. Many people thought they would be flooded in the spring, but winter still had not shown its true colours yet. Things can change quickly from one week to the next in the mountains.

The flax was prepared and the women gathered together for the spinning and the weaving. The wheat shafts were turned into brooms and the scraps into new fire logs. Paper was made and wax was made into candles. This was happy time for many. The arduous work that had been done all summer was now replaced with things that took time. The hobbies, crafts and art work began to come out.

Anna was surprised when from her village of Silvercreek came her stringed instrument. Jerod played his flute and she strummed her strings. Together they made tender tunes for all to listen too. She was so surprised to see the box come with her name on it.

Dawn listened to the music and remembered how Jo often said how she missed the music and the birds' songs. Dawn often thought of Jo and she did miss her. Now here was Jerod and he was married now; time kept slipping by. She missed Willow too, more and more as time moved on. Tears were not one of Dawns emotional shows, but she did feel the loss maybe more than most.

Anna was right this winter was beginning to drag on. The snows had let up though that was a bit of a consolation.

Dawn and Chad went to the common house, but Jerod and Anna stayed home. Anna made tea and they wrapped themselves in a blanket as they sat on the porch and watched snowflakes slowly drift down. "Anna are you ready to move to the cabin?" Jerod asked her. "I don't think I will have time to be lonely Jerod" Anna said. "It will be a while before people will venture that way" he told her. "Jerod, It's not like it's Silvercreek in a few days we would be here Let's go in" she told him. "There are many things I need to tell you" Jerod said. "What things?" Anna asked. "Oh just stuff about my family. My mom was writing it all down, but it was lost in the fire." "Then you must keep track again. When I make paper we will start the family story again" she smiled at him. "I would like that" Jerod said. "There is so much I have to tell you." Anna smiled. "We will have much time to talk. How about we join everyone in the common house? We best enjoy the company while we can." Jerod took his flute and Anna her stringed instrument. They played for everyone and the evening slipped by quickly.

The winter storms came and went. When spring finally showed signs that it was here to stay Jerod and Anna loaded the wagon to go to their cabin. It was the first of many trips they would make this spring.

When they reached the cabin Anna was thrilled to see it. "This is ours?" she said as she looked at Jerod. "Yes it is" he said and opened the door. "It still needs a lot of work, but it's up and after I get a fire going it will be warm."

Anna stood on the steps and looked out over the small area that had been cleared. She would have it cleared in no time and then she could start the garden. She had saplings of fruit trees that needed to be planted soon; rose bushes and herbs as well.

Soon Jerod had a fire going and started to empty the wagon. Anna found her brooms and soon had the place clean enough to put up the pieces of furniture they had. A home of her own and a man that she loved; how different her life had turned out from what she thought it was going to be. Jerod too was happy, it was the first time he had real joy since his mom and dad passed.

It was a week before they had enough area cleared around the cabin to plant their trees and herbs. The well would be the next to dig and as Jerod did that Anna would plant the vegetable garden. A trip to the fort to get the rest of their things was planned.

The water was not far down. Jerod had a well he hoped would last even through the driest years.

Anna had a large garden going, no wheat or flax, but ample for food to last out the coming winter.

The sun was warm now and the mornings no longer had the fog in them. Jerod burned out the stumps and expanded the gardens for next year. He cut down the trees for the other buildings and Anna helped him with what she could. He had a work shop built by summers end. Anna had the garden in and the last trip to the fort was made. Wheat was at the top of the list and then flax. The next year would really show the progress at the farm.

The fall found them hauling gravel to the paths around the cabin. Anna was so tired of the mud. There just didn't seem to be time before this to get it done, but now next spring no more mud she thought and another scoop of gravel went into the wagon. She wiped her forehead and stood up straight. It didn't take long to drag the wagon to where she wanted it dumped. With great satisfaction she dumped the gravel.

Jerod watched her do 2 or 3 loads before he decided to help her. "It looked like you were having such great fun so I had to join you" Jerod said. "It's not that much fun, but it is wonderful to have the path" she said to him. "Well I have to wait for the clay of the fireplace in the workshop to dry and saw you, so here I am." They filled the wagon several more times before night came. The path to the garden and workshop past the cabin was done. Jerod had been taking water into the cabin as this was going on and now they had enough for a bath.

Anna was the first one in the tub and the heat felt great. Jerod waited until she was in the water and he made tea. He lit candles around the room and served her tea in the tub. Anna felt so spoiled. She soaked for quite a long time before she got out.

Jerod put on more water and then climbed into the tub. Anna sat by the fire and combed out her hair. When he finished he threw in their clothes and had them washed in no time. It was something he watched his grandpa do so often he just did it. Anna now almost completely dry hung the clothes. It seems this was the daily tasks until the ground froze.

At that point just stumps and brush was burned. For two people it was surprising how much work they did get done.

Winter soon blew in with plenty of snow. It wasn't as cold as some winters, but it still was freezing outside.

Anna wove her clothes and hand made everything from candles to paper. Jerod's hands were never idle. He carved many things like combs for her hair, spoons, cloth pegs and so many more items. He like to work in the shop during the day. There he made whatever was needed. Anna wanted more buckets and flower pots for herbs.

She planted the rose bushes against the house and the boxes kept each herb separate from the others. Anna wove baskets and mats as well as shades for the porch. Making paper was a bit more work, but when the flattened pulp finally dried they had all the paper they needed.

Jerod had decided a basic family tree was the first thing to make. He could remember right back to Zack. Anna only had her mom and dad, but it would be a good start for their children. So the book of family was started.

Jerod tried to remember things that Zack wrote of but all he could remember were a few animals and things like airplanes and cars. What a shame he thought was lost in the last fire. Anna added her knowledge of plants and Jerod his. The book grew as they entered as many things as they could remember.

The paper was all but used up when they realized it would now be put on hold until new paper was made.

The winter was passing quickly. They found late winter was a pleasant time to play music. It seemed spring answered the tunes and brought warm winds and soft rains.

Jerod and Anna harvested what maple syrup they could from the few stands they had. It would be the gardens that would take the priority over everything else.

Jerod had told her of the complex what he could remember. Anna never skipped a beat. "I'll help you look for it" she said "But promise me that the next 5 years will be devoted to our farm here." Jerod agreed it would be so.

Anna asked him everything she could think of about the complex and why he felt it was there. "I don't know if it is for sure, but my grandpa never lied to me that I know of and he searched for it for years. He said that his father told him to look for a great wall on the side of a mountain that appeared to go no where, if that makes any sense" Jerod told her. "It's been such an awful long time do you think they lived through the sickness?" Anna asked. "From what you gathered they live inside a mountain" Jerod told her. "Well if that's the case we may never find them. If they have been untouched by the sickness they might never come out" Anna remarked. "I haven't really given that much thought, but I think you might be right. It's either here or there because of yet we have found nothing." Jerod smiled and Anna continued to cook down the sap from the syrup. Jerod was true to his word and for the next five years he was steadfast and worked hard as he could. Each year that passed he loved Anna more. The complex was like a fairy tale, some long story. People had moved into the valley near Anna and Jerod and some beyond. It was amazing how fast people had tamed the wilderness and started making it their own.

Jerod looked out over his fields and for that moment everything seemed right. He smiled to himself and headed for the cabin. He found Anna rocking in her chair and knitting. She smiled when she saw him. "Hi there dear" he said to her. "I thought you were going to help with our new school house" he said. "Next time" she said. "What's wrong?" he asked. "Jerod have you noticed anything for the past few years?" "No not really" he said. Anna just sat knitting. "There haven't been any children born. None, I have asked." "Don't be silly" he said. "There are children every year." "Not this year or the last years either" Anna said. "Jerod I'm worried I should have had a child by now" she said. "Well my grandma always said it happens when it happens" Jerod smiled.

It was the following months that Jerod noticed it; no new children. If children were not born the people would die out. The consequences of that affected everyone not just him and Anna.

He took time to write to Connie. He had not talked with her for years and hoped his letter would find her well.

It was nearly a month later and in the midst of harvest when her reply came. "Jerod, my sweet boy what you fear is true. There have been no children born for nearly 2 years, the sickness has damaged the women. With all my skills as a healer I van not right this wrong. I can not fin the problem with them. I am afraid our race may be on the verge of collapse. Telly says that we must wait that's all, no reason, nothing just we must wait." Jerod was stunned when he read the letter. He didn't want to show Anna. She so wanted a child and Telly said wait, then that's what we will do. Telly had a sense that Jerod didn't understand, but he knew that whatever it was there was far more to it then most knew. The next few years had started people to be concerned. More than one household knew the children had stopped. Fear started taking hold of the people. I drew them closer in some ways; the sickness was taking the rest of them now. They thought they were lucky all the work kept going, now it seems they too would just live the last of life then die, mankind would be done.

Anna and Jerod decided to see as much of their world as they could before they left it too for good.

Their garden work did not take much of their time and allowed them the time to search for the complex. Jerod was sure they had travelled further and over more terrain than most had.

Then it happened, a young girl at the fort was with child. Great joy was felt through every household. Everyone waited to see if more became with child and that the child was born safe and sound of mind and body. The children didn't come, but only to the young born in the previous 2 decades. Seems all over 20 years old could not conceive. This broke Anna's heart. She had wanted Jerod's child; their own, the bond of love for each other. A child to nurture and share the rest of their lives with; to grow old with and sharing the worst and the best with. It was clear to her this was not going to happen. Jerod worried about her. It was at his suggestion they leave the valley and move to the farthest valley. They could take over the runners' station. With less people around the pain of not having children might lesson he thought. At least she wouldn't have to watch all the girls with children. Anna declined the offer. "Don't be silly Jerod, running a way never solved anything" she said. He took her into his arms "Anna, I just want you to be happy. I love you. I don't care if we have children. I have you and that's all I need and want." Anna smiled at him. She knew he spoke the truth. Just getting over the fact she was barren was what was hard, but she would have to that was obvious.

A few more years had passed and things seemed to be back to normal. It was then there was a rumour of a new insect being found; one that skittered across the top of the water. When Jerod heard this it brought back all the memories of the bug he had found. With great excitement Jerod wasted no time in sharing the news with Anna. He told her of his discovery as a child. Anna suggested a trip to follow up on this discovery.

Fall was upon them now, with the harvest done winter would soon claim its time on the earth. It was a perfect time for planning it all out. They spent hours looking over maps and it was a surprise to Jerod that the valley beyond theirs was where the water came from that fed the creek by his childhood home of Blackrock. Big changes were happening, new insects and babies being born; a new age was upon them.

With the coming of spring the garden was planted and Dawn had some young folks watch over it. They would receive a share of what was produced for the care of it while Jerod and Anna adventured.

The biggest surprise for them was when they reached the last village and noticed how many people lived there. They stayed in the common house and made plans to venture up the mountain pass all around. Anna knew that Jerod loved to travel in the mountains and if she had been asked she would have admitted that she liked it too.

They were about three days out of the village; sitting in a meadow when on the wind Anna heard it. It was startling at first and she was sure she was mistaken. Then it came again, louder then quiet again. Anna looked at Jerod, he heard it too. It was crying on the wind and not just any crying. It was the cry of a child. "Who would be way out hear?" Jerod said. Then it was there again. "Something is wrong Jerod, that's the cry of a very small child, a baby, a newer baby."

They followed the wind and the sound. They found the source of the crying near the tree line; a man, a woman and a baby. Jerod approached and it didn't take long to realize they were no longer part of this world. He retrieved the child and gave it to Anna. It was so frail; how long had they been there? The baby was in soiled clothes and her skin was sunburned raw.

When Anna removed the swaddling the child wailed and writhed in pain. Jerod looked over the man and woman, they were not like them. They wore different clothes, even the material was different. Where did they come from? Where were they going?

"Jerod we must get the child back to the village. There are two mothers there she needs them or I fear she will meet her parents fate." Anna looked down at the two people on the ground. Jerod knew that she was right.

Anna wet the child's lips with water and had cool moss to cover her bottom. She could wash her better at the nearest stream. The child was not well and she was losing the battle for life. Anna did everything she could think of to keep her going.

When they reached the small village the new mother did not hesitate to nurse the small baby. Anna never left the child for a moment.

When Jerod told them how they came to find her a group of men went to bury them. Although it was not spoken aloud, many worried that there were more people and they would come looking for the child. Jerod couldn't deny this might be true and Anna dreaded it coming to pass. Anna named the baby Kate. Jerod built them a small cabin on the outskirts of the village.

Jolina never missed a feeding; she had a bond with Kate. If they did come for her she would be in good health.

After abut 5years the people of the village stopped worrying about people coming for Kate. Jerod and Anna made a home there and had moved most of their belongings long ago. They were a happy family and Anna was even happier, but Jerod noticed about her. She tired easily and was short of breath. Jerod knew something was wrong, but Anna would hear of it.

Kate was growing and everyday becoming more of her own person. Anna was getting worse. Kate was about 8 years old when Anna passed. Jerod wept for weeks. He had promised Anna as she lay dying to care for Kate, love her and protect her. As far as Anna was concern she was a gift. Before Anna died he tried to heal her. He did everything that Connie had taught him and it was nothing, just one big nothing, she died and he couldn't help her. Kate understood his pain, how he wasn't sure, but she always seemed to know what he needed or wanted.

As time slipped by the pain of losing Anna grew easier to cope with. Kate often would have him take her for walks and she enjoyed them. He often slept after dinner and it was then Kate found reading most enjoyable. She read everything. She most enjoyed the books of their family.

When Jerod woke up she would always have questions for him. Jerod was surprised that one so young would have so many questions. She had endless questions about their journeys and why they went. She had concluded they were looking for something, but Jerod never told her what. She was not unlike Anna even though there was no blood tie between them. They had the sense of adventure and the same sense of wonder of things around her.

Jerod watched her read and wondered how his life had become so far from what from what it started out as; how his dreams had to be changed completely by the circumstances of living.

Kate had an uncanny ability to know what he wanted before he asked her. By the time she was twelve the two often trekked through the mountain passes. Kate was a seasoned hiker by the time she was fifteen.

It was on a summer hike that they discovered the wall. Jerod had heard from some hikers it was there and after checking his maps and rereading West's writings he was sure this was of importance.

Kate of course was always with him. As they headed to the place the hikers told them they had seen the wall. Jerod's mind was going over many things. What if this was the complex maybe he had finally found it. To bad his grandpa never would know. What wonders awaited them? His mind worked over all those thoughts, but then what if it wasn't the complex just a support wall for something the old world had built.

He looked at Kate trudging along behind him. What would they do if they ever found out she was one of them. She never searched for her people. After they buried what must have been her parents the men that were with him were afraid. These people were strangers not from their world, but from where. The clothes they wore were different from anything that Jerod had seen. How he wished that Anna had survived.

Just then Kate hollered to him "Wait up dad" she said and Jerod slowed his pace. When Kate caught up he suggested that they make camp. Kate was for that as they had been hiking for hours. She gathered some wood and soon had a small fire going. Jerod was wrapped up in his papers. Kate knew he was lost to them while he figured things out. She made a filling soup and some dried bread and tea, it was a good meal. Jerod put down his papers to eat and after he made a small shelter for them to sleep under.

As night crept across the sky and the stars became brighter. They both watched the shooting stars and satellites cross the sky. Jerod thought about telling her how they had found her and actually it wasn't far from this spot. Anna's face flashed into his mind. How concerned she was when she found them and how tender she was with Kate. How she washed her blistered sore body carefully and gently giving her water. Just a little at first then wetting a small cloth for Kate to suckle on. She almost ran back to the village carefully holding Kate to her chest and stomach to keep her warm. The concern she felt while Jolina nursed her back to life; at that point to tell her that she could not keep the child was not going to happen.

"Dad" Kate said. "Yes sweetie" he replied. "Are you okay?" she asked. "You seem to be so far away. You haven't spoken very much tonight" Kate said. "I guess I'm excited about this wall. It's two days hike from what I gathered from the hikers. We have a long journey best get some sleep. I want to make good time tomorrow" he told her. "Alright dad you get some rest too" she said and Jerod smiled "I will now, too sleep with you."

Jerod rolled back to the fire that had burned to coals now and let the heat sink into his bones. He missed Anna. "Night dad" Kate said. He just smiled; he couldn't shut down his mind, so many things drifted in and out of his thoughts. He would have to tell Kate. The prospect was not to pleasant for him. He had raised her from a baby, how would she react, but then things were as they were.

His mind drifted to the wall and then to West's book. In the book he remembered it saying that if you find the wall you have found the complex. It was an immense wall; one that time would have a hard time removing. It was built as a landing pad for a flying machine.

Jerod's mind then went to flying machines. He imagined what it would be like to have them now. He tried to shut down his thoughts, but it just wasn't happening. He thought about the hikers that had seen the wall. From what the said it was on the far mountains from them. They never went right to it. Maybe it was nothing and maybe this was just another dry run.

The mountains were high and steep. People didn't go over them, they traversed the valleys. As of yet no maps of this area had been made. He would have to make some. He rolled over several times. Now he watched the embers and listened to the crackling embers of it with the smell of the smoke finally sleep consumed him.

It was Kate that was up first. She had the fire going and porridge made, water boiling for tea and most everything packed for their journey today. If they pushed hard they would make it to the wall they had been told of.

Jerod was sleepy, he ate quietly and drank his tea. It didn't take him long to get going after that and Kate was hard pressed to keep up. Jerod had to get to the wall, he had to know.

"Dad, dad, wait up" Kate yelled. Jerod stopped, what was the matter with him? His anticipation of the wall was making him absent minded of Kate. He had to get himself under control. It was late afternoon when they reached the base of the mountain and before him stood the great wall. He wasted no time in climbing up what he could. Kate watched him and tried to keep up. She was tired and starting to stumble.

"Ouch! Stupid ruins! Why we have to come to these old forgotten spots is beyond me" Kate thought. Always adventuring, her father was chasing some old notes his father had given him.

Kate!!! Kate! You okay my dear? You must be more careful. We don't want you hurt out here. There are too few doctors since the great beginning.

Great beginning, Kate thought some think it should have been called the great ending. "I'm fine father" she hollered back.

Jerod had arrived at her daughter by this time and studied her bruised knee and scraped skin. He had his hand over them and with a thought they began to heal over.

Kate glanced at him and smiled "Why did you never tell me of your gift?" He smiled and said It's just a small gift, that, that's all I can do."

Jerod stood staring at the walls of the old building almost like a fortress. He thought this has to be the place his grandfather talked of.

Glancing back at Kate he thought how small she was when he found her. He had often wondered if he should have told her, but it never seemed to be the right time.

His wife couldn't bear children. The spread of the viruses' man let loose on the world had made it impossible. It had changed the very essence of the people. So many died and the ones left lost so much. Some lost the ability to have children; some gained special talents such as he had, bur for all its worth it couldn't save his wife. He tried to save her, but the virus had changed her too much.

He lingered over the memory and then rubbed the stubble on his face and realized it was time to rest. They had been travelling since dawn and now poor Kate was stumbling around. She must be tired. Well at least the had finally found it. Now the real adventure would begin.

Kate and Jerod had travelled often in the forest far from others. It was pleasing for her to be away from the small village of folks. It always depressed her to be around them. Many talked of those that passed and news travelled fast if one was found with a gift. No one was sure if it was the food, air, or water that changed them.

The cities of the past had fallen into ruins as Mother nature began reclaiming them. Big empty towers of rocks and broken bits of everything one could dream of laying everywhere. From the stories she had been told, there was great panic as folks passed on in vast numbers. The dead laid everywhere and a great sorrow had filled the world. Some say there were billions of people, now just a few hundred were left. It seemed life would prevail as the women alive now were having children.

She was wandering gathering wood for s fire. Jerod had come back from the edge of the mountains where the wall of this old fortress ended.

He smiled at her and thought she was a survivor. She had the gift even if she never knew it.

They sat across from each other at the fire. Jerod looked at her small fire and watched her play with the soft ends of her honey coloured hair.

He had debated to tell her, but thought there was time yet. She looked at him and stood up abruptly.

She turned quickly to the fortress wall and thought she caught a glimpse of someone "What is it my dear?" Jerod asked. "I thought, well I mean we were, oh never mind, just must be the woods and I'm tired." Jerod nodded "Aye, it has been a long day." "Seems to be a fair evening and night will be falling soon." "Tomorrow we will find out more about these ruins if the tales may grandfather have any truth or not."

"Father, why do you search these old place? What is it you hope to find? The old world is gone and with what happened some might say it was a blessing. The memories of the people and the wars. The total disregard for others. Maybe they were right; maybe its better that it's all gone and things have changed."

Jerod gazed at Kate. He transfixed on her face and the wounds started …"Well my dear, it was near here that we found you. Yes my dear Kate, its true I'm not your true father nor Anna your mother, rest her soul. Your parents were dead and you were bawling your head off. I thank everything Holy and good that there were no animals left. They would have made a grand dinner of you."

Kate couldn't believe her ears. She was shocked! How could this be true? There were no people here and the village as well. It was no more than 15 years old. How could this be? Anna had told the story of a group that travelled to the mountains away from the settlement. Even there, with its two thousand, it was days away from the nearest encampment. She stared at Jerod snapping he mouth closed and listened.

"You see, it was my father and his family, along with his best friend that left the settlement to look for a new area to farm. You were not the only one that was found. Others were too, but no one knows where you were from. Your parents were dressed in fine clothes and had trinkets strange to us all. Many searched for your people, but to no avail. My father had told me f these ruins and his father told him this must be the key. So many have come and found nothing."

Kate stared at him. Could this be true? Every bone in her body told her it was, but something…something. She glanced to the fortress and this time she was sure there was something there.

Jerod spoke quietly "Get some sleep dear. Tomorrow will come soon enough and we will have a look around in the light."

Kate followed his advice and set up the bedrolls. They settled down near the fire and the crackling of the wood and smell of the smoke comforted her. Her thoughts travelled far this night…she wondered…her people, Jerod was her people. No one could take his or Anna's place. They were everything to her. How could there be people here in the middle of no where? What was the connection to this old place? How old was it anyways? Who built it and why?

The thoughts consumed her and in all she could feel a tugging at her mind. It was as if someone was sensing her, touching her thoughts.

She sat up in a start and stared at the ruins. Bah! She thought this being jumpy was because she had just had everything she thought was true and safe changed for her. Go to sleep, she told herself as she settled down and pulled her blankets up around her neck.

Jerod was near sleep now and was relieved he had finally told her. She took it well, he thought, but then Kate took time to roll things around in her mind. Tomorrow, yes tomorrow. A new beginning let us hope, a new beginning let us hope…

Chapter 38

*I*t didn't take long for the complex to be buzzing for Dean and Nedera's child's birth and Dern and Tamara's wedding. Great jubilations were felt in more than one home. Life would continue and it gave the young new prospects for the future.

Dana and Todd sat together in their dorm and talked endlessly on the adventures they and their children would have. Life was finding a way to continue as Dana as well as Todd had to agree things never work the way you might think they should, but they do work.

Dana looked up from her fancy work "What do you thing about Rose saying Dean and Nedera talk with the child yet to be born?" Todd looked up from his papers and remarked "I can't begin to understand how their gift works or why they have it. My best bet is that mankind was forced into an evolutional phase and it's now progressing accordingly. June and Philip have the gift as well. Will they be able to talk to the unborn child as well? I don't know that will happen when they have their own children if that's what they intend to do. I never really understood Dern's gift. I don't think any, but another healer might and then it is the same for both?" he smiled at Dana and went back to his papers. Dana continued her fancy work. How different their lives would be because of their gifts she thought.

Dern and Tamara were always together, like two peas in a pod. Most people thought that they would live such different lives because of their gifts, but that wasn't the case at all. They were no different from any young couple. Dern found peace and tranquility in the animal tunnels and Tamara sought out the library for her thinking time. Dern loved the outside and Tam still felt uneasy.

Dern and Tamara met for lunch everyday in the open area. They ate together and found pleasure in many things they talked of. "Dern, do you want children right away?" Tamara asked him. He looked at her watching the children in the play area. "Maybe not right away, but soon." Tamara smiled. "Oh it's so good to be alive" she said. "We are on the threshold of great change and part of something so much grander than this, all of this." Dern smiled "Change doe not happen over night" he said. "It might be still a very long time before we see a lot of change. Going outside has to be voted in, but there were those that did not feel the same way about the world beyond the closed doors."

Drake was born to Dean and Nedera that winter. He was a beautiful baby, so pleasant. He never fussed much and if he did it wasn't for very long. Dana could often be found with him in her arms. He loved to be rocked by her in the rocking chair.

Dern's wedding to Tamara soon followed the birth of Drake. It was soon known that several babies were now being expected in the complex. Dana always told Drake he was the special one. He was the first after so long. Dana never missed an opportunity to care for him. It was strange to watch Dean and Nedera around Drake. The bond between them was uncanny. Nedera never had to be alert to Drake's needs. With a cry she would just get up and go to him. Dean was the same.

The expeditions continued outside in the spring. Dern and Tamara rarely got to be on the same scouting teams. Their gift of healing always put them in different groups.

Dana always worried while they were gone. Todd always reassured her things would be fine. This trip would be different. They would spend some of the time alone in the valley. Although it was enclosed by mountains there was still plenty of room. It would take weeks to cross from one side to the other, Still they found no signs of people. The teams soon started scouting in the opposite directions.

Dern loved the outside he often stood in the meadows looking at the tall trees; sentenials of time gone by. They were tall, straight and proud. If a tree could be proud these were. The meadows filled with all kinds of flowers in the spring and summer. He wondered how long it would be before birds would be reintroduced, but would they survive. The world is a huge place.

They had finished the journey assigned to them and were almost back to the complex. He was looking forward to being home with his wife. The complex had opened a few tunnel. The young needed their own homes. The population was growing life had found its way.

With the healers and the med lab folks at the complex expected to live long and fruitful lives.

Tamara had already arrived back at the complex a few days before Dern. She had gone to look at the new dorms and was just waiting for Dern's approval before she chose one.

After his debriefing Dern soon found Tamara in their dorm. A hot meal and bath was the regular routine when he returned from a scouting trip. Tamara sat with him while he ate. She was always glad to see him home again. "The new dorms are done want to look after you clean up?" she asked him. "What's wrong with our dorm?" he asked her. "Oh nothing, but these are new" she said. Dern wasn't too keen on moving again, but if she really had her heart set what harm could there be? He smiled "Yeah why not? We can look later" he told her. Tamara smiled. She liked the new dorms, the old ones were too rustic or something. She preferred more stone than wood. It was nice to have some wood, but the old dorms were full of it. Clean lines and fresh painted walls suited her better.

When Dana and Todd heard they might move it seemed a bit foolish since they had a dorm already, but they were young and if a new dorm brought them happiness then why not?

Drake was their first born after so long a time, but soon was followed by Jason, Sheri and Jasper. Many more came after that.

The scouting trips had been cut down. The council had decided that if there were survivors they had to be miles away. The repopulating of animals in their own valley now stood as their main focus. From there the extra could be set free into the open world but would not be for a long time yet. The food chains had to be as complete as possible for them to have a chance of survival and that wasn't going to happen overnight. It was not a little undertaking. They had cared for animals for nearly a century; repopulating what was lost would take so many more centuries.

Dern and Tamara found the dorm they wanted and had their own style before too long.

Dana and Todd realized that their lives were on the way to their close. The years had slipped by so quickly. Dana has so wanted Tamara to have children. Having just had Dern, new lives in the family after all this time would be such a blessing. Todd felt the same way. He often thought of his father and the bond he shared with Dern. Yes children would not go unloved as far as they were concerned.

Winter had come to the outside world. To those in the complex some found the snow exhilarating others still stayed in and away from the world that had been lost to them so long ago. Most people enjoyed the comfort of the complex. Hot chocolate was the favoured drink in the winter as was apple cider.

Dana had been to the animal tunnels and they had been discussing freeing some of the seed eating birds in the spring. She had secretly letting loose many insects through the secret tunnel. How many would survive she did had no idea. She did know the bees had, the scouting teams had brought back the news. It was presumed that they had been blown over the mountains or maybe sheer determination of the queen leading her drones on.

Dana had let the moths, spiders, ants and flies, some aphids, some lady bugs the list was of anything that had mated and she could sneak out. So often she pondered, a few sets of finches maybe this year. She wanted to see how ell they fared in the enclosed valley first.

The work was endless for them all in the complex. Not only did they not have to think about themselves and their needs but they had to think of the outside world as well.

The spring came and with it life seemed to renew itself everywhere one could look. Drake now was almost walking and had not trouble stealing everyone's affections when they saw him.

Dana had their lunch in the open area. She once again beamed when she saw the toddlers playing. Todd had taken to carve stone again. His love of it never left him although it might be long breaks between his projects now. He still had the eye for it and any item he carved was done to the best of his ability before he claimed it finished.

Dana had been weaving the cotton harvest from the fall. The need for clothing for everyone was growing with the amount of people. Anything that could be recycled was.

Dana's coworkers had discovered the joy and beauty of making quilts from any scrap pieces of material. It was a gift from the founders quilt making. The women had used it as a tool to make a useful item from nothing and to pass away the endless hours after the virus outbreak. So many people had worked so hard that those here now would live on.

"Hey there beautiful" Todd said and sat down beside Dana. She smiled. "I knew you would be here" he told her. "So have you finished your project?" she asked him. "Almost" he answered then got up to get something to drink.

Dana watched him standing at the counter where people got their food and drink and noticed how old he was. His hair was grey on the sides and he didn't have the energy in his walk he once had. What was the matter with her? Spring was here and instead of enjoying it she just saw it as more time slipping by. Todd made his way back to her table. He had hot chocolate and one for Dana. "Let's go for a walk" he said to her. They took their mugs and headed to the atrium.

There they watched the birds, smelled the flowers and just enjoyed being quiet together.

Dern and Tamara had been in the science labs. Everything they brought back from their scouting trips had to be studied and catalogued. The vegetation was as far as they could had escaped the effects of the virus and many micro organisms still survived. It was still uncertain as to why insects had suffered as bad as they had. Dern was occasionally called on to heal, but that wasn't to often.

The science labs were kept busy with the specimens brought back. Tamara enjoyed adding what they found to the books for the complex. She felt the work would be a benefit for all those that were to follow them in the future.

"Dern" she said. He looked up over his papers "What is it Tams?" he said. "Do you think we should start thinking about a family? I mean I'm not getting any younger and I don't want to be old for the child." She seemed to falter on the words. "Tams" Dern said "When you are ready we will have one not until. I'm not worried about it. It will happen when it does." He smiled and went back to his papers.

Tamara had decided that the time to seriously start preparing for a child had come. Over the spring and summer she started collecting things needed for babies. By late summer she was getting worried that maybe she couldn't have a child. It had been over a year that she and Dern had been married and no hint of a child. She had gone to the med labs and had it confirmed that she was able and she had convinced Dern to do the same. Both were capable, but still no child.

Drake and the other children flourished. His charm was not missed by many in the complex. He managed to win the hearts of all he came in contact with. The gift of thought was never really understood. The doctors in the complex tested his abilities extensively. He was never harmed and could leave the testing at any time he wished. The full ability he had was never found. Without too many others to compare to him, other than his parents it was not sure just what he could do with his mind. Drake always wanted to please everyone, did all that they asked if he could. One of his parents always came to meet him without being sent for. The doctors concluded that unless you had the ability he did then you were not effected by his gift. He could sense you but could not communicate mentally with you. Of course he was still a baby yet and what he might be able to do one day was yet to be seen.

Dean and Nedera along with June and Philip had long joined forces with Dana and Todd. They too worked endlessly with them to have the doors opened. Being younger they took far more of an active roll in the adventure outside. It always seemed so crazy to Dana that there was still many that feared the opening of the doors. Some were open about their dismay over it. Other complained at home behind closed doors, but as time moved on so did life in the complex.

The news that Tamara was finally with child brought great news to Dern, Todd and Dana. Tamara was beside herself with joy. She had waited nearly five years for this.

Drake never missed anything it was he that told Tamara that there were two minds inside her. Dern and Tamara were dumbfounded to be told she was carrying twins. Drake was right there were two mind.

It was early summer when Dean and Nedera headed out to do research for the complex. Drake had to remain in school. Dana promised to care for him while they were gone. June and Philip went with them. They took Maylan with them as she was still being nursed. It was going to be a long journey 5 days was the expected time for them to get the samples they were after.

Dana and Todd enjoyed Drake's company very much, he was caring and thoughtful. It most likely was because of his gift.

Tamara and Dern were never far away now that she was with child and Dana enjoyed having everyone together. She had a family; she had grown up so alone and now she had Dern and Tamara.

With twins expected in the future and Todd her steadfast partner through it all, a tear escaped her eye. Drake was at her side and put his small hand on hers. He looked at her so tenderly she could do nothing but hug him. "It's quite alright Drake, I am happy to have those closest to me here now and that includes you too" she told him. Drake smiled and went back to his colouring pages.

By weeks end everyone waited the return of Dean, Nedera, June and Philip. Everyone started to worry when they were still not there after three more days.

Dana was having trouble controlling Drake "I can't hear them" he said. "I should be able to hear them." He was near panic. Dana took him to the med labs in hopes they could do something to help him.

They had two teams ready to look for them. Dana watched them go and with Drake at her side she leaned over to him and said "They will find them Drake." She rubbed his shoulders as he stood staring out. "Auntie Dana, I can't hear them they are not there, they are gone."

Drake turned and walked back into the complex. Dana followed him to his home. She went inside and then to his bedroom. He lay down on his bed and started to weep. Dana was right there, she picked him up in her arms and again said "They will find them Drake don't worry so." He just wept louder. Dana didn't move she let him cry himself out. When he had exhausted himself Dana let him sleep.

Todd didn't take long to figure out where they were and joined her at Dean and Nedera's dorm. "Oh Todd I don't know what to do for him" she started to cry "How alone he must be feeling. He has heard them all his life, even in the womb and now just silence. The deafening sound of silence. I am afraid for the child." Todd just hugged her.

When the scouting team returned a week later with nothing. Drake withdrew into himself.

More teams went to search and they too returned with no sign at all. It was so horrible Dana cried on Todd's shoulder and he held her tight. "Well, he has us. We aren't his mom and dad, but I will not let him be alone. I might not be able to talk with my mind to him, but I can certainly talk with my heart." Dana knew he would too, just like he did when she was alone in the complex. "I do love you Todd" she said. "But they might not be gone just lost."

Then Dana was consumed with an awful thought, what if they found people and were hurt by them? It was not possible, the scouting teams would have found signs, but where did they go and why?

The search carried on for a month. After which time the council meeting was held and the doors were once again closed. No one was allowed to leave. It appeared that Dana was not the only one that thought of violence from others that had survived out there.

Drake was to stay with Dana and Todd. He had retreated into himself. He spoke little and showed no emotions. Dana tried to never leave him. She took him everywhere with her. Just before Den and Tamara had the twins Drake was sitting near Tamara and looked at her and said "They are healers like you." Tamara smiled.

She took Drake's hand and placed it on her belly "Talk to them if you can and want to. I'm sure they wont mind." Drake closed his eyes for a moment "They can't" removed his hand and looked at Dana. He got up and went to his room at her dorm.

Todd followed him and closed the door. He pulled a chair over from the desk and talked to Drake that was sitting on the bed. "Did you know that Auntie Dana was alone for the first part of her life?" Todd told him. Drake never spoke. "Her father was locked outside when the virus was loose on the world and her mother died in here bringing her life. She never saw them. She was alone until I met her." Drake turned and looked at him. "She know better than anyone what it's like to be alone. When and if you need to talk about things it might be something to keep in mind. She might be able to help in some way if you let her." Drake nodded. "I'm going out to visit with Dern and Tamara. Join us when you are ready" Todd told him. Drake just looked at the floor. Todd left him to his own thoughts on things, but knew he had struck a cord in Drake's heart.

The following weeks were hard for Drake. Somehow this young man had to come to grips with the fact that he was alone and the comforting noises as he put it would be silent forever. That alone would be hard for and adult let alone a small child. His work at school suffered. Drake found no interest in anything. He was swimming in a void so vast and it was all in his own small brain.

Dana could see Drake withdrawing into himself. She knew that unless she did something they would lose Drake as well. What was the solution to accepting that everything that you loved and held dear was gone? He life had been so different; she never knew her parents. She had been alone from the beginning.

It was Drake's appearance at the dorm with the teacher that started his life again. After the teacher left, Dana took Drake by the hand and said nothing. They walked down to the atrium. She sat him on a bench and sat beside him.

It was almost an hour before she poke to him. "Drake" Dana said "I can understand what you lost better than most, but I weep for you still. I have always been alone with my thoughts where you have not. It must be lonely." After a few moments Dana took him by the hand and walked him to the animal tunnels.

Almost all the animals that had mated last fall would this spring give new life. Dana stood looking to each of the pens with him. They stayed there a few hours more. Then Dana took Drake to the open area and got them something to eat and drink. Drake still had not said anything nor did Dana.

Dana sipped her chocolate and then pointed to the statue of Zack. "That statue represents my father" she said to him. "He helped build this whole complex. That one there is my mother. She did all the wood working you see. That's all I have of them now. They have been gone for a very long time." Drake looked at her "How do you like being alone? Aren't you afraid?" he asked her. Finally he said something Dana thought. "Yes and No. Yes because I don't know what tomorrow would bring and that made me fearful. No, because I realize no matter how close you are to anyone you are in fact still alone."

Drake thought about what she said. He was so very young. Dana never pushed him to talk. They enjoyed their drinks and went home.

Drake went back to school and seemed to start to take part in the things there.

Dean and Tamara gave birth to the twins.

Todd still searched the libraries for information on the outside world. Dana went to the agro tunnels and the insect labs to see what insects did what and were what. She learned so much about them.

With the food chains being restarted, it was surprising to her how many insects ate each other in comparison to vegetation. Dana knew she would again release things into the new world and with luck some might survive.

It was mid winter when the news of Dern and Tamara's twin's being born spread through the complex. They were named Tanner and Naomi.

Drake took to them right away. He told Dana they were special. They do what Dern and Tamara can. Dana wasn't surprised that he would have some insight into them that others would not have.

The twins were beautiful and very contented babies.

Dern cared for Tamara so lovingly he treated her after the births. She had had a hard time having them, but was recovering well.

The twins now a few weeks old were taken to the med labs to be checked over by the doctors for any signs of being gifted. Drake was always near them when he could and for them being in the med labs gave him a chance to be protective of them.

Dana and Todd were making dinner Dern and Tamara as a surprise for them. Dana went in search for Drake and found them with the twins. He looked up when she came in. "We are going for dinner with Dern and Tamara. I want you to be there too" she smiled. "Oh, can't I stay with the babies I like them so much" he asked her. She agreed that he could stay until the last minute, but then he would have to join them. Drake ran over and hugged her. Dana ruffled his hair and hugged him back. She got up "Remember 5:30 sharp Drake." He beamed at her and then focused on the babies again.

Dana had been gone about an hour when the whole inside of the mountain shook. With that came the noise, the deafen noise. The doctors were immediately put on alert. That noise and the shaking of the mountain meant only one thing; a cave-in and a very large cave-in.

Drake heard people screaming that that horrible quiet. He went to the twins and saw they were fine. When he went to leave the doctors asked him to stay and be mindful of the twins. They knew there had been a cave-in and the news was that it was in the new dorm area. Drake realized that this was where Dern and Tamara's home is and Todd and Dana were supposed to be there.

It didn't take long for the first of the wounded to arrive. To the doctors dismay the few wounded were followed by the dead.

Drake knew it was bad. He never left the twins for a moment. After he sat with them and they slept and he fell asleep too. The doctors let him sleep.

It would take hours, maybe days before they would have the tunnels clear to know the extent of the damage and the death toll.

Drake woke to the cries of the wounded. At first he didn't know where he was, but then it all came flooding back to him. He got up and the first thing he asked was where is Dana, Dern and the nurse cut him off "Drake, we have a lot of work to do. Would you please help by changing the twins?" He just looked at her for a moment and went to the babies.

He used his gift to sense anything but there was nothing. Drake changed the twins and then fed them with the bottle the nurse had provided.

It was a few hours before Drake was told about what had happened. The news was awful; the new tunnels with the dorms had collapsed. It was a great loss for them. Most of the dorms were housing the young people.

The twins now were as was Drake. Dawn and Tyler, Andy's descendants took in Drake and the twins went to Danny, Dirk's descendant to be cared for. It was all temporary, but they all had to be cared for.

By weeks end the dead had been recovered from the rubble. They had funerals all week. Drake withdrew into himself again.

The whole complex mourned the loss of so many. The procession to the tombs were heartbreaking. Each tomb was sealed and the grief was felt by all.

It took several more weeks for all the rubble to be cleared. The found the fault that caused the cave-in. No one could have predicted it would have caused such an awful cave-in. Tears were shed by many for a long time.

Drake had been present for all the words spoken about the ones passed, but he heard little.

By spring Drake rarely spoke to anyone. His school work was suffering and it was that that brought Tyler to speak to Drake. He had taken him to the library. "You know Drake; here all around us are all the people we have known and lost, many we never knew." Tyler took him to the section that held Simion's writings. He left Drake there.

After about 20 minutes Drake took one book from the shelf, the title was journal one. He started to read it and before long he was totally absorbed in it. Several times he asked Tyler how to pronounce some words and what their meanings were. This was a story of a young woman whose husband was a stone mason. It told of his life in the country which Drake found out was in the old world country named Italy. She described the country, food and flowers, but her main topic was her husband. She was very happy and he seemed to be as well. He got the job here in the complex because of his skills and she was so proud of him. Then that all changed when the virus was let loose. The woman wept for her family that was locked outside and feared what their future would be in the complex. She talked of all the meetings and the fear that gripped all those inside.

"Drake, Drake" called Tyler "It's time to go home my boy." Drake looked up over the edge of the book. "I see you have found something to read" Tyler smiled. Drake just nodded. "You can bring it with you just make sure you don't lose it or dog ear the pages" Drake smiled.

As they walked to Tyler's dorm, "Drake" he asked. "It has occurred to me that you may want to keep your mom and dad's dorm." "Yes, yes!" Drake replied. "I mean yes I would like to keep it." "Well you are far too young to be on your own, but Dawn has come up with a solution. She has a class she is teaching on housekeeping and if you agree to let them use the dorm to practice on then I see no reason that you shouldn't be able to stay there on the weekends, if you want. Of course you have to keep up your studies." Drake looked at Tyler and hugged him. That was the first affection that Drake had shown to anyone since the accident.

Mush of the complex mourned for the losses. Drake and the twins were almost cared for by the whole place. Drake worked hard in school and Tyler, true to his word let him stay in his parents dorm on the weekends if he wanted too.

The twins were a big part of his life. He sensed something with them mentally, more of a bond. The twins shared it between themselves, but Drake could sense it too. He found it a great comfort and the twins never seemed to mind.

So that was his life over the next few years; staying with Tyler and Dawn during the week and in his dorm over the weekends. He shared so much of his time as he could with the twins and always in the library.

As his reading ability improved so did his choices of what he was reading.

The council was called together to hold a meeting about reopening the doors. After the loss of Drake's parents, his aunt, uncle and cousin it was voted that they stay closed. Scouting parts would once again go out, but for only three days at a time. This is how the next three years passed. Other than animals being let out into the enclosed valley, no one was to leave the complex.

Drake pursued letting Dana and Todd' dorm be held for the twins. As they were not old enough to speak for themselves. Drake spoke for them. He managed to have the dorm saved for them until they were old enough to decide for themselves.

The bond between the three of them grew with each passing year. When the twins were about seven years old they asked Drake to take them to the dorm. Drake had not trouble talking to them. The twins had been told many things about their parents and grandparents. Dana, like them had been orphaned as well. Drake opened the door and the three went inside. Dawn had brought what was salvaged of Dern and Tamara's but the majority of the things were Dana and Todd's.

Drake sat at the book shelf and glanced over the covers. The twins told him to feel free to read what he wanted to. He smiled. Tanner and Naomi went through the dorm picking up pieces of personal belongings and trinkets as if they felt something from them. Drake pulled out Dana's journal and after permission decided this he would read later.

They stayed there for a few hours until finally the twins decided it was time to go. Drake looked back into the dorm as he closed the door and knew he would have to thank Dawn for keeping both places so well looked after.

Drake knew soon he would be living in his own dorm. Tyler and Dawn have been wonderful people and so kind to him, but he knew he would have to find his own place in the complex. He thought about what kind of work he wanted to do and each time his thoughts brought him back to the animal tunnels. He would have to see if he could get some kind of work there. Animals were always so much simpler than people. Their lives weren't so cluttered up like people. They ate, mated, grew old and died. Not so much frustration that went with humans and all the carrying on.. From the tip of their toes to the tops of their heads people made more problems for themselves.

Drake was the oldest of the gifted children born after the time of the childless years. Jon, Tanner and Naomi looked up to him. He always made time for them and listened to their woes and triumphs of their gifts. Drake realized that Dana and Todd had way more going on then met the eye. References to things subtle yet there were everywhere in their journal. Dirk, Andy and Simion were linked in their words. It seems that it started with the discovery of the open caves.

Drake went to the view point and looked out over the cave. Dana and Todd mentioned their work and their studies here. It wasn't until Drake was about to leave that he found what Dana and Todd had hidden so well.

He followed their research and retraced their steps. He always came up bland. How could they have these things to study, there just wasn't any or very little.

Drake was down in the cave and after following a lead, he lost it once again. Whatever Dana and Todd were doing down here they hid it well. He had brought some sandwiches with him and found a spot against the wall to sit and eat. He sat opened his bags and pulled out a sandwich and Dana's journal. He opened the book and with that in one hand and a sandwich in the other he leaned back against the wall to get comfortable. To his amazement the wall moved. Drake jumped up fearing a cave-in. When he realized the wall moved and no cave-in was happening he pushed harder on it. Slowly the wall opened. Drake couldn't believe what he was seeing, a secret passageway. Todd had to have done this. The carving of the door was ingenious. Drake went in and with his lamp realized he was in a fairly large room. He spotted torches and lit them. He stood now looking at the room. There were books, maps and dry clothes. Drake sat down and opened a book. It read:

"Dirk is dying: Todd and I have decided to show him our secret and to let him know that he was not responsible for the virus outbreak in the complex. I hope he likes our surprise."

It stopped. The next entry read: "Dirk cried in the sunlight. The meadow was like a land born. Oceans of grass flowed with the wind as it caressed over it. Dirk never spoke much nor did we. We just looked over the land." Drake looked at the doorway it was a passage to the outside.

He picked up his light and began to follow it. Ha passed through the cave of crystals and realized this is where Dana got decorative stones she had in her dorm. He followed further alone the passageway and met with a creek. The trail followed it then the whole room became light and the brightness spot, Drake knew led outside. His curiosity drove him towards the light. He climbed up and then out and for a moment he was triumphant. He felt the fresh air blowing around him. He could see clouds and watched them float across the sky. The air was fresh and clean. He looked over the same meadow as Dana, Todd and Dirk had looked over.

Drake sat there for what seemed for ever. He had to grasp what this meant, if it meant anything at all.

Dana and Todd had been coming outside for a long time. The hours just to construct the passageway amazed him.

Drake climbed back into the tunnels. It took a few minutes for his eyes to adjust to the dimness. He followed the tunnels back to the first room. He sat there and he could almost see Dana and Todd as a young couple here. He took the first few journals left the room and went back into the cave. He closed the door and was again surprised how well Todd had hidden the door. Drake was still overwhelmed by what he had just discovered. People he thought he knew had secrets beyond anything most people could have imagined. Drake now had a personal mission. He decided to find out everything he could about anyone mentioned in Dana and Todd's journals.

The council met again before spring and the door to the enclosed valley would be opened again. The scouts found no one so it was presumed that some accident had taken the lives of the complex members lost out outside. Drake was surprised how many still were against opening the doors.

His mind flashed back to Dana's words in the journal "I am still amazed how afraid they are of the world in which we came. They have become institutionalized. What a pure shame the interests of such a vast and wondrous world would have almost been lost for most of them. It reminds me what Rose once said to me(Why on earth would you want to go out there. We have everything we want and need right her)."

It seemed Dana had faced an almost ongoing battle that to this day still exists.

"Drake, Uncle Drake" cried Tanner and Naomi. Drake turned to see them with their friend Jon in tow. "Well, what are you rascals up to today?" Naomi giggled. "We want to go see the outside. Will you take us? Please, please Uncle Drake" she cried. Drake smiled "I will in a few days. Let all the lookie loos go first. When they get bored then we really can spread our wings." The answer satisfied Tanner and Naomi, but Jon stood looking at him. "You spoke untruths, why?" Jon asked. Drake looked at the lad. "I have found something I must research and need a few days. Tanner and Naomi know I will take them outside after that." Why didn't you tell them that?" Jon asked. "You have a gift don't you Jon?" Drake asked.

Drake looked at him and pushed him out of his mind. He sensed no ability to communicate and returned to himself. "Will you do me a favour Jon?" Drake asked him. "Sure if I can" Jon replied. "Take this list to Sheri in the kitchen will you please?" Jon nodded and left.

Drake made his way to the animal tunnels. After a few inquiries, he made arrangement to take a pair of canaries for release. Tanner and Naomi would be thrilled. It was going to be their world. Releasing animals was beginning to make it something they could do to improve it.

He had been looking at the fish farms when Mark approached. "They are beautiful creatures, fish. They live in a world we can hardly imagine." Drake looked up "How long do you think before we can release some?" "The question is, are the insects surviving in big enough numbers for them to survive? We will have to get samples soon to see how their health is." "I'm going out in a few days I can see if I can catch some for you to study. Do you need live samples?" "No" Mark answered and smiled.

His next spot to visit was the atrium. This was Dana's tranquil spot, her refuge from the world inside and out. Drake stood for a good hour before leaving. He could understand why she loved it there with the birds' songs and beauty of the flowers to go with it. He left there feeling he understood a part of Dana he never knew before.

His journey took him to the agro tunnels where he was met by Ian and Bonnie. They ran the tunnel just as their mother, Petra had. Sheri had no desire for the work and sought a job in the kitchens. "What brings you here Drake?" Ian asked. "I am going out for a few days is there anything that you might want or need while I'm outside?" Ian smiled "No I don't think there is, but ask Bonnie she might have some insects for release." Drake nodded and soon had paper wasps and four pairs of beetles to be set free. He left the agro tunnels feeling quiet pleased with himself. Tonight he was going to devote to reading.

After a shower and something to eat he made his way to the library. He never revealed the journals Dana had written or those by Todd he found in the secret place. He had no doubts they were there to conceal them as the passage was concealed. He brought from his pocket the reference sheet he wished to research.

Tyler was happy to see Drake so involved in something. For so long most thought he would not fair well, but he had the strength of will as well of mind. What ever has him so intrigued thought Tyler. I hope it keeps him busy for a long time.

"So what brings you here again Drake?" Tyler asked. "What have you here?" Tyler reached for the paper and Drake quickly retrieved it and replaced it in his pocket. "So what is so secretive that you won't even show me?" "Nothing, nothing" Drake said. "It's just something I wrote." Tyler smiled. "Well you should write your story it may one day be a great help to someone." Drake had not thought about that, but there might be some truth to his words. Tyler turned and left, he knew if Drake had wanted to share it he would have.

It was the twins' glee that led the way of the party going outside. Jon never said much and Drake never pushed him. Drake was not surprised how few people were outside. "Come on Uncle Drake" Naomi said and dragged on his arm. Drake had the heaviest pack, but the group was not unfettered as they would like to have been. Drake made them all carry something. They walked most of the day and were lucky enough to find a perfect spot in the clearing to set up their camp.

Drake helped them all pitch their pup tents and a small stone ring was made to contain the fire. Lines were hung to air the sleeping bags during the day. Drake had them gather fire wood and after the meal he produced the animals they were to free. He took them to an open field nearby. There he told them the story of the world before the outbreak and the world after. How Simion kept them protected, now it was up to them all to try to make the world home once again. He let them all look at the birds in the small box and Jon to Drakes amazement smiled and took great joy in these small creatures. Drake decided that he could let most of them free.

When he looked at them enough Drake said "We have been the caretakers of you and countless of your family. It is our honour to now to set you free into the domain you once held and will now again become your home." Drake smiled as Tanner, Naomi and Jon set the birds free. They took to the air as if they had always been out there. The birds flew to a nearby tree and amongst songs a new flock had come into being. Drake hoped they would stay in the valley, but come fall they would fly south. Their biggest worry for the time being would be finding food, now it would be revealed if it was enough to help them survive.

The next few days were spent cheerfully. Drake introduced them to the joy of the world outside. It was true what he read in the journals describing the outside world. Although it was just as fascinating to him as the children he didn't let on.

After the few days allotted for their trip Drake took them back to the complex. They had not been too far from sight of the doors.

When he was sure they were back to where they belonged Drake went to his dorm. He stood in the shower for a long time letting the water hit him on the shoulders. He was lost in his thoughts. The pictures of his mom and dad flashed through and around his thoughts. He saw his aunt, uncle and Maylan. Thoughts of this kind had not troubled him for a long time. He collected his thoughts and got out of the shower.

After he dressed he headed for the kitchen and ran into Jason on the way. "Ahhh, just the person I was looking for" Jason said to him. "What's up?" Drake asked. "You're due to start in the communications labs" Jason said to him. "Yeah that's true, but not until the beginning of next week" he said. "Well, do you like to read or have a hobby of some sort, it can get pretty boring in there." Drake just smiled "I'll keep that in mind" and continued to the kitchens.

Drake wasn't sure what to think of Jason. He was pretty much on himself. He had a quick mind and found learning easy. He had no gift, but was very good at most anything he set his hand or mind to.

Drake turned the corner and the smell of baking made his stomach growl. Sheri always liked Drake. He was a loner, while others were all caught up in the mating game. Drake sat back and watched. He was a handsome man, Sheri thought, but as far as a mate he had not seemed interest in anyone she knew of. His gift had something to do with it Sheri thought. It was not a topic that was discussed openly or at all.

The complex was suffering a great loss once again with the last cave-in. So many young couples had their dorms there. The population suffered the great loss with so many young gone.

Drake had a large meal and joked and teased Sheri along with anyone else there. He asked for a package of trail ix and dried food.

Drake was an adventurer. He had found some old books in the library. He wanted to see if he could rough it as it was said in one of the books he read. It didn't take long to get his pack together and went to see Jason. He found him in the communications labs. Drake stared at the wall of monitors that had nothing on them but static on the screens. Each screen had a country from the old world written above it.

"Pretty awesome sight isn't it Drake?" Jason said from behind him. "It would be more awesome if something was on them. Why do we bother after all these years?" Drake said. "Hope my dear fellow, hope" Jason looked up at the screens that were showing the valley. "These are the screens we watch. You know, I don't know what I would do if I ever saw anything on them. All my years here with my father and I think I would jump out of my skin if a strange face appeared on it" They laughed.

"Jason, I'm making a personal trip into the valley. I want to start a week later here if that's alright?" Jason looked at him "I have no problem with that" he said. Drake smiled. "You're a good man Jason. I do believe we will get on famously." Jason and Drake laughed again. "So what's the strangest thing you have seen on the screens?" Drake asked. "Nothing strange really just a few animals and birds . I am still amazed how empty it really is out there." With that Drake made his way to his dorm. He would head out in the morning.

That night Drake had the same reoccurring dreams. He was young and his mom and dad were coming back from the wilderness when things start changing. They realize they have lost their way and start going in the wrong direction. Drake in the dream is calling to them, but they don't hear and they keep going the wrong direction. He can see the sweat on their brows and clinging to each other; they are full of fear. Why did he have this dream? It frustrated him to the end.

He got up and opened Dana's journal. It seems Simion was aware of fear more than most could ever know. He knew the virus got in when the big cavern was opened. How so many survived was a miracle. The losses could have been more devastating. There was still enough to keep the complex going.

When Dirk passed away we found out that he carried the burden of being the one blamed for letting in the virus. He bore the weight of it for the rest of his life. When he sat that day at the edge of the meadow he told us that he knew he was not to blame. He took the blame to give the people of the complex somewhere to vent their anger. It was better that they hate me then to have lost hope in survival. The work seemed less arduous when they had someone to blame for their losses.

Drake closed the journal. He got dressed and got his gear together. He was going to find the entrance outside to the secret passage.

It was still early morning as he walked out the doors. He was soon out of reach of the cameras. When he stopped for lunch he pulled out his map and looked over the mountains that surrounded them.

He started his climb to cross over. The terrain was tough. By late afternoon he stopped, Drake had not come close to reaching the top. He did see the splendour of the valley below him. The trees didn't grow up here just shrubbery. He could see the crest, it was barren rock. Tomorrow he would cross over to the valley beyond.

For now he was getting a fire going. He gathered a small pile of wood to burn. He pitched his small tent. By the time the darkness crept over everything he was quite comfortable at his small camp. The sky was clear and as he gazed up at it he was struck with the immenseness of the sky and how really tiny the world is in comparison. He watched the satellites go by and he wondered if they were holding on to false hope. Thinking others might be out there. Sleep soon caught up with him.

It was the wind that woke Drake the next morning. He was a little shocked at the strength of the wind. There would be no fire this morning he thought as he gathered his things that the wind had tossed about.

With just his trail mix and water for breakfast he hurried to pack his things to continue on. Drake travelled most of the day, moving further up into the mountain tops. The wind had calmed down, but Drake felt the coolness still in the air.

The terrain was now rocks, no trees or shrubs. He would cross in a short while. Drake looked below then turned and kept going. It seemed to happen all at once that he reached the crest and was on his way down the other side.

The new valley was covered with trees other than a small meadow by a creek. Drake knew that the beginning of the creek is where he would find the secret passage. The odd thing was that the wall that had been left by the builders of the complex. It was massive and now although it was overgrown there was no doubt it was a wall.

Drake pressed himself hard and when he reached the wall he made his new camp. With hot tea and warm soup Drake was comfortable there on the wall. He stared out over the trees bellow and tried to image the building of the complex. He could see Simion and Zack and the masons as well as all the people coming and going. Now it was quiet, the passage of time had almost worn the wall down. He noticed ants searching for food. He smiled thinking these might be the descendants of the very ants Dana let loose. He missed them all. A tear crept into his eye and he wiped it away. A good nights sleep, then to see what was beyond the wall.

This was the beginning of Drake's love of the outside world. He never was sure why it called to him the way it did. He found peace in the wilderness far beyond anything he ever found in the complex.

Drake was outside every chance he hw got and the secret passage got well used. He never saw any sighs of anyone and after searching a few valleys beyond Drake stuck closer to the complex.

The valley that held the animals grew his attention more. He followed the deer and watched the birds. His work and journals of what he saw and the species involved were a great help to the management. The valley could still hold more animals. It was far from being over populated. One day they would start letting them go in the valleys beyond. The insects seemed to vanish as soon as they were released in the further valleys. It would be many years before the animal populations could follow.

Drake was proud of Dana's attempts to help do this. She was a woman of vision. She organized the children to run the stations left vacant when the virus got in. She worked her whole life in pursuit to open the doors. From anyone that Drake talked to she had the respect of everyone in the complex. She was missed as was Todd.

He worked along side of her and had many talents of his own. It was the courage of these people in the complex that made it possible for the chance of the world.

Drake had discovered the joys of reading and he learned a great deal of history of man kind. Simion still amazed him with the foresight he had. Drake often wondered if he might have been gifted in some way. There were many gifted children born, but none with the gift of thought. Drake often wondered if he was the only one in the world now with that gift.

Time slipped by and the seasons changed with it. Drake like the cold and the snow, but the complex was the place to be during the winter. The good thing was with winter the spring would come and then the valley was such a sight to see. The trees got their leaves and flowers pushed their way into life with the warmth of the sun. The animals gave birth and it was the world renewing itself.

When Drake used the secret passage he would sit and look out over the meadow and try to image it full of animals like the enclosed valley was beginning to be like. He decided next spring he was going to release the seed eating birds. The birds seemed plentiful now and that meant the plants would be producing seeds again. He hoped they would stay close but with the world waiting for them it would be an awfully long time to fill it up. Several small birds in the world, he doubted ever seeing them again after release.

Tanner and Naomi grew up quickly. It seemed to Drake that it was yesterday he had them camping.

Jon spent most of his time in the agro tunnels now and Drake most of the time was outside. Not many sought the outdoors, most preferred to visit it in the day and to return to the comforts of their dorms.

The council still had not wish to have any signs or little evidence of them being there. Every council meeting Drake came closer to understanding the frustration Dana and Todd felt with the people inside.

Jason had married Kyrie and they were expecting twins soon themselves. Jason pursued Drake and often talked to him about his duty to get married and have children. Drake was not ready nor had found anyone he cared to spend his life with. The eligible girls did chase him, but Drake never used that to his advantage. He knew all to well the pain of personal hurt and would not be the master of it to anyone.

When he chose to be alone Drake used the secret passage. He spent hours sitting up near the entrance gazing out over the meadow. The loneliness grew inside Drake. It was as if he was the only one alive even when he was around other people. The emptiness he felt was a vast void he couldn't fill. He wondered if the people without the gift felt as he did or if it was that very gift that made him so alone.

The wind was calm today Drake thought sitting high above the wall. It was a slight movement below that caught his attention. He watched but could hardly believe what he was seeing, he was seeing people. He hid behind the rocks and his mind was trying to grasp what he was seeing. He looked and there was no doubt it was a man and a young girl. She was a pretty thing what Drake could see. He sent out his mind to see if they had gifts. The older man did indeed have a gift, but it was not the gift of thought. Drake focused on the girl. As soon as his mind touched hers he knew she had the gift. He withdrew his thoughts quickly.

The young girl stood and looked over her shoulder to where he was. Drake froze, he couldn't be seen. Before too long the older man called to her and her attentions now returned to him.

Drake was sure she didn't she didn't know how to use her gift or she would have found him right away. He almost laughed to himself; I am not alone anymore and almost cried. He couldn't leave.

He watched them as the older man walked to and fro on the wall. He seemed completely convinced about it somehow. The girl just shook her head and continued making a small fire.

Drake sat back out of view, people there are people. He wondered how many more there were and where they were. Why had it taken so long to find them? The questions rippled through his mind, one leading to another and then another. He would have to tell the council. They needed to know. The council, Drake shuddered. They would probably close the doors and it would be months or years before any attempt to find out more.

He peered out from behind the rocks and watched them. He never felt her use her thoughts to see, most likely she had been trained to use her gift as he was. Just the fact she had it was more than Drake could have dreamed of. He leaned back behind the rocks and just sat there.

Dana had been right; Simion was right people has survived. They were not alone. This was great. Drake was overwhelmed with it. How many more were there and how did they manage to survive? Drake just sat there. How were those in the Haven going to take the news?

Drake looked over the edge one more time. How strange it was to watch them. What were they doing? Drake watched as the older man walk back and forth on the wall. He was telling the young girl something, but he did not seem interested. Drake smiled and then made his way back into the Haven through the secret passage.

When he reached the area just before going back into the Haven, he rested. He sat where Dana and Todd most like had sat before him. He tried to decide how he was going to tell everyone he had just seen people outside. After all the trips that had been made on the outside in search of people it was ironic that they had found their way here and didn't even have any idea what they had found. He thought about what had happened at the council meeting. This was going to put bees in the bonnets of the best of them. Drake knew they would have to know, but he also wanted to see what Simion had to say on the matter. What different would one day would make at this point.

Drake stepped into the cavern and closed the door and headed for his dorm. Drake's mind was full of thoughts about people. If they were here there had to be more. Maybe some had gifts, maybe even the same as his. He smiled how wonderful it would be to have others like him.

By the time he reached his dorm Drake decided to observe them for one more day before he told anyone.

He had a hot shower then made his way to the kitchens.

The sun rose over the mountains and Kate was the first to stir. She could hear the buzzing. Opening her eyes, she could see the source of the noise. It was the bees swarming making a new colony. How grand she thought.

Since the beginning, there were few things left alive. Bees were one and a few other winged bugs. Flies, the folks called them.

By now Jerod was up and he too watched the swarm. Ah, a new queen, a new beginning he smiled.

"There was a time when there were many creatures alive and the world was full of people." He glanced at Kate. She smiled "And what good did it do?" she said. "They destroyed most everything and left us holding the remnants of it." She was out of sorts and Jerod knew he was the cause of some of it.

"Well, my Kate you know things are getting better. More women are having children and soon the world will be blustering with people again." He knew life was holding on by a thin strand. The future was in the children like Kate.

The village was at least a three days hike away and he was sure Kate was admired by a few young fellows there.

"Is it true," she blurted out "Really true?" she could feel her voice rising.

Jerod stared at her for a moment not sure if he should have told her yet. "Yes my dear. You see Anna loved it out here away from the village. I often thought she would have survived me. She was outgoing and energetic, but she got sick. The virus had adapted. We thought we had escaped the fate of so many. She was young and we so wanted children, but it never happened. Then on one of our excursions into the wild, we found you. Anna was so happy and so sad. Your folks were different and we didn't know from where. It was so strange and you were crying your lungs out. We had no idea how long you had been out here or where you came, but we knew we must find you some food. There were three mothers in the village and getting back was of the utmost importance. We made double time getting home and not a moment too soon. You were listless by the time we got home. Melanie nursed you back and you have been such a blessing since. Anna was so happy having a child she couldn't contain her joy. Of course there was talk of where you came from and fear from some that the others would come looking for you. As the years passed, the fear abated and settled into living. Anna died when you were four. Had you not been with us, I'm sure I would have done harm to myself."

Kate rubbed Jerod's back. She loved him so and the tears glistening in his eyes hurt her. She hummed a mellow tune in her mind and could feel the tension leave him.

Well, she thought, where did she come from and why did no one come looking for her? She felt so alone in a way, but Jerod stood up and said to Kate "Let's go see if we can find out what this place is."

Kate looked up behind Jerod to where the great wall stood. Maybe this is where she was from, but what happened to the others? Were there others? Maybe she was the last of them. Whom ever "Them" were.

Jerod turned and was making his way up the rocks to the wall. Kate followed, her mind twisting over everything. Then there it was again, something soft, slowly caressing her thoughts, soothing. She stopped and looked to the mountain. There was movement up there. She was sure she saw movement.

Jerod was on the edge of the cliff, looking at the wall following it down to the edge of the mountain.

At the panic in her voice, he turned and stumbled. His foot slipped on the moss and was sliding down the cliff. Grasping and clutching for anything he could get his hands on, finally got a grip and stopped falling.

Kate saw Jerod go over the cliff. Her heart was beating rapidly and felt it was in her throat. She ran as fast as she could to where he went over. Her mind raced in panic as she reached the edge.

"Father!, father," she screamed fighting back the tears. She could see he was there, hanging on to life, dangling over the cliff.

What was she to do? What was she to do? He couldn't die. He was all she had. No, no, please no. Her mind was screaming for help. Father! Father, be still, please be still.

Jerod could feel his grasp slipping and could see the terror in his poor daughter's face.

"I love you Kate. I've always loved you my dear."

Kate knew he was falling and panic almost overtook her. Then with a wave of warmth, the strength came. It washed over her like water from a soothing rain. Panic left. She knew what to do. It was like a dream.

She followed the wall to where he was and concentrated on the rock sticking out just below him. Staring at it she could feel it moving, and it was far enough out to give Jerod to give Jerod something to put his feet on.

The heat in her mind was like an oven burning hotter than the embers of last night's fire. The rock moved to give him a foot hold.

He was safe and as quickly as it came, the heat left. She felt like she was spiralling down a tunnel. Kate was exhausted and knowing Jerod was safe, stuck, but safe, she relaxed. She couldn't keep her eyes open. Her mind had to rest and she fell into deep unconsciousness.

Sheri was there as always and soon she had a plate of food and a hot coffee in front of him. Her work never seemed to end in the kitchen; there was always something that needed to be cooked. The complex was full of people and more than three quarters of them ate there rather than at home. Sheri had several people that worked for her.

Drake watched people coming and going and Sheri preparing thing for the following day's meals. He finished his food and drank the last of his coffee. He carried his dishes to the counter and walked towards the library.

It was late before he left there. He had not found anything significant to help him. At this point sleep was what he needed most.

Drake slept uneasily, his thoughts even when asleep were consumed by the two outside. The girl and the older man, it took forever to fall asleep.

When morning came he wasn't sure he had slept much at all. He dressed and went to the kitchen for breakfast.

As he sat there eating he suddenly realized that they may not have stayed on the wall or near it. Drake had to get back out there and see. With any luck they still would be there.

He worked his way down the tunnels to the secret passage. He could move quickly when he had to, the trick was to not look conspicuously while in the complex.

To Drake's relief they were still there when he emerged from the passageway. He watched them as they sat by the fire. Drake felt with his thoughts and as soon as he did she looked right to where he was. She stood and he heard her call to her father. Drake could just see the older man and in that few seconds he watched as he tripped and went over the wall.

Drake could feel the panic rise in him, but it was the terror in the thoughts of the young girl as she scrambled to where he fell. There was a moment of relief then her panic nearly overwhelmed him. The total terror she felt, it was then that Drake realized he had to help her.

He climbed down, but still out of sight. He could see the older man hanging on and knew he must act quickly or he would fall to his death. Drake took the extra strength he needed to complete the task. He was in no doubt that she did not know how to control her gift. He felt her going into unconsciousness. The older man was safe, which at present was most important.

Drake felt guilt wash over him. Had he not sent out his thoughts she would not have panicked and the older fellow would not have fallen. Now all he could hear was the man calling to his daughter. "Kate, Kate" he called, Drake thought what a nice name. He glanced over their belongings and found a rope to let down to the older man. When the rope came over the edge Jerod held fast to it. "Kate, tie it off to a large boulder. I don't think you will be able to pull me up."

With that Jerod started climbing up. After about four feet of climbing a large man's hand appeared to help him. He grabbed hold and Drake pulled him to safety. Jerod was almost speechless.

Drake wrapped him in a blanket then went and picked up Kate. Drake could see the concern and without hesitation he told him she fainted. Drake placed her comfortably by the fire and covered her as well. He led Jerod there and soon had him a cup of tea. The older man was non stop with questions. Drake tried to be polite, but shared little to nothing with him. When he knew they were safe and with a promise to return the following day Drake left them there.

He took a round about route to get back to the passageway. Now it was not an option, the complex and all that lived there were about to be reconnected to the people from the outside and Drake was going to be the one to tell them. Drake was surprised how drawn he was to the outsiders. He thought they might have been gone, an almost panic started inside him. Was it about them he thought? Maybe the fact that they were survivors outside. Drake couldn't be sure, but he was going to find out what he could. The council would just have to accept it.

Kate rolled over and stretched. She was warm and comfortable. The crackling fire and smoke was so familiar.

Then it hit her "Jerod", she sat up and her head started pounding.

Jerod put his hand on her shoulder and eased her back. His touch was healing and she could feel it cover her like a blanket. Then it was there again. That caressing on her mind. Rest now, rest.

Her eyes popped open and she saw him. Beside Jerod, He, Him, he was there. He was dark haired he had shoulders so broad. She could see his steely grey eyes and now it was more of an order. Rest and that falling down the tunnel was happening again. She closed her eyes and fell into a restful sleep.

When Jerod was sure she was resting, he returned to Drake and smiled. "She has the gift you know" Jerod said. She saved me today. Drake smiled "Yes"

"Where are you from and how did you get here? Are there others?" Drake was full of questions.

Jerod looked at him. He was dressed in fine linens like, Oh my dear Heavens, like Kate's parents. "Well my boy, I guess I could ask the same", not sure if he should divulge too much information.

Drake spoke first "I live over that mountain." Wasn't much information Jerod thought. "How long have you been here?" Jerod asked. "All my life" Drake answered. This was going nowhere Jerod thought. "Well we are about three days hike from our village. I would say there are about two thousand people there." Drake was surprised. "Really, that many? That's incredible. Three days you say? What brought you so far into our region?" Drake asked.

Jerod thought Ah ha, so there are others. "I have been looking at the ruins of the old world. Do you know anything about this place?"

Drake studied him for a moment "No they have always been there." He stood up "I must go now."

"Wait, wait" Jerod said "I have to thank you for saving my life. You came just in time. I thought I was going to die." Drake stared at him with those steely grey eyes "I will be back. Are you planning on staying here for awhile?" Jerod said "Yes, I want to study these ruins."

With that, Drake turned and started up the cliff. "We will meet again." Jerod was stunned. "Thank you again" he yelled.

Drake raised an arm.

The questions raced through Jerod's mind. Our, the lad said, our region. There are others, but why was he so secretive? To meet people out here after the Great Beginning! Who, where, why? Jerod remembered something his father said, "The people would be just and kind, but the first priority will be to keep safe and no doubt outsiders will not be trusted."

This is it. He had found it. He was sure the place he was told of and Kate was from them. He knew it.

They would stay until their rations ran out. He never even asked his name. That was astounding.

Jerod plopped down. He tried to recap everything that had happened. It was like a story racing through his mind. The cliff, the rocks moving under his feet. Kate, my goodness, poor Kate. How was he to explain this? The rope coming down? The large arm grabbing his arm, pulling him to safety, out of nowhere, a young man standing there, but he was there. He would be back he said, when, thought Jerod.

He could faintly see Drake as he ascended over the last rocks above them. Kate had the gift. She too had saved him. My goodness.

He said and tried to remember the stories his father told. Hidden in the mountains, if you find the wall facing the valley, you have found it. He knew he had found it. After all this time, he was so close now. Found what? Is the question. His grandfather it was a place of security, safe from harm. It seemed like riddles now, but he knew that young grey-eyed fellow was part of it.

"Oh" he said to himself, what was he going to tell Kate?

Drake had to tell the others. He broke the rules, but he could let the old fellow die. There was something about Kate. She had the gift he thought. His family line was the only line with the gift. Some had healing and others could tell if the truth was being told. Some seemed to know how the animals were. He couldn't think of all that. What would he tell the others?

There were people that had survived. Maybe they were of the ones that left, but this couldn't be. These people didn't know of our Haven. Maybe they knew some of those that left and where they went.

Drake entered the hidden entrance and made his way down the tunnels. Soon he could ear the children and sensed their joy. He smiled and made his way to the science labs.

He always checked the TV screens. He dreamed something would be there. It was his job to keep tabs to see if anything unusual was out there. He was hungry and headed to the kitchen.

Before he got there, Jasper spoke. "You didn't report in Drake." Jasper was of Drake's lineage. "You must report in." Drake stared at him "okay, okay, I will as soon as I grab something to eat." Jasper was always following rules Drake thought. I wonder if he would panic if he saw what I did today? He smiled to himself.

Drake was always so assured of himself. He was young and confident, but he was like the others, compassionate and caring. Up until today, it was just them today in the world, but today, he would have to see the council.

"Sheri would you put the word out for the council to meet, would you darling?" Sheri was of Andy's lineage and smiled "Sure thing" she replied. Everyone knew that she and Jasper would soon wed.

The council chamber was filled up. Members from each lineage were represented.

Drake entered still chewing the bread and butter roll he grabbed from the kitchen. He pulled his leg over the chair and rested his arms on the back of it and waited for the conversations to end. Today he would be the one to tell them they were not alone.

He studied each of them before he spoke. "We are not alone" he started. "Today I saw people outside."

The silence was eerie. Then the voices erupted into confusion. It was like an echo. "We must close the doors and maybe they will pass." Drake stood up "Are you crazy? I said there are people alive out there and from what they told me and as many as a few thousand."

There was a silence. You could have heard a pin dropped.

Jasper was the first to speak "You spoke to them? You let them know we were here?" "No" Drake said "They don't know you're here, but I did talk to them. It's a man and his daughter. He fell off the cliff. He would have died. The daughter has the gift of mind. I felt the terror she felt watching him hanging there. I had to help her. I don't think she realizes her gift."

The whole room erupted into conversation.

"Warren's line was the gift of mind. How could she have this? Maybe as you say, thousands or so survived out there and have gifts. This is great Drake" "You have put our lives in Danger. We don't know who they are, why they are here or where they came from."

"Hold it" Drake commanded.

Silence fell over the room.

"These are people like us. We need them as much as they need us. Did we survive this long just to alienate ourselves from our own kind? It is our duty to help them. If we are to walk the earth again, we need all the people."

Again the room erupted in chaotic chatter.

"Look" Drake said "they told me there was a settlement three days hike from here. They are alone. This is what our forefathers told us would happen. The time is nigh, I vote to bring them in. You can cast your votes. I am going to the library. Maybe there is something there to help us."

Drake stood up and headed down to the library. He would hear the voices growing in louder tones as he walked further. He was now far enough away, now the voices were in the distance. He wanted some peace. He wanted to see these people. He didn't dislike it here, they were out there. The need he felt was to see and believe it.

He sat down and opened the books he spent the last hours looking for. Simion the founder wrote these. The answers would be here. He wished he could have met this man. It amazed him that he knew all the answers.

Tracy and Trina peeked in around the door at Drake and giggled. "Well, you two, what's this a double trouble moment?" The girls burst into laughter and ran over to Drake. He picked one up in each arm and gently hugged them. Drake loved children. They were the future and he worked daily to be sure their future would be better then what had been.

Tracy and Trina were of Simion's line. Jason and Kyrie, their parents feared the line would end when these two arrived. They had no gift, but did have an uncanny way of bringing joy to those around them.

Jason appeared next and watched Drake with the girls. "You best be thinking of getting a wife soon Drake. You've been of age for a long time." Drake looked up "Well, I'm not really ready yet, plain as that." Kyrie appeared "There you two are. Let's go, dad and Drake need to talk."

The girls wrapped their arms around Drake's neck and each kissed a cheek. They scampered down off his knee and headed for Kyrie out the door.

Jason was fairly tall and had taken to wearing more robes for dress, than trousers. He always seemed to be searching the computers for things.

Drake, on the other hand, was outdoors all the way. The first chance to venture out when it appeared safe, he was there. Living in this artificial centre was fine, but outside he felt free.

"Well Drake, you kind of sent the council for a loop. Why on earth did you make contact without first having the agreement of all?" "Jason look, I'm going to explain myself to you. There are people out there and we need to make contact as you put it, the sooner the better." "You haven't thought this through I can see. First what would you do? Bring them here? We maintain enough for our populace. How would we feed them? How do you think they would react to all of this? Do you know if they are warring with others? No Drake, I don't think you thought of too much."

Drake never cared for Jason's condescending attitude, but this time he might be right. "Sit down Jason." Jason pulled up a chair. "First of all, I was not intending to make contact. I was watching them. I never would have had the older man not have fallen off the cliff. What was I supposed to do, let him die? There are people out there, survivors and from what I gather, there's not very many. As far as bringing them here, no not yet, but would consider these two. Let's see how they react and take it from there."

Jason thought for a moment "The council agreed, but remember, we will not war. If we have to we will seal this place tightly, if need be."

Drake watched him and thought, he never changes, always thinking he's the person in authority.

Jason got up and headed to the door. "Take them to the valley; see how they react to the animals. I will send Sheri's brother Jon with you. He will know if they are truthful." Well taking Jon might be a good idea.

Jerod was concerned with Kate, she was still sleeping. He kept the fire going pondering over everything. This was it, he knew in his heart. Jerod had found the place his great grandfather searched his life for. What exactly was it? Why did he look all his life for it and begging us to keep looking? He wished his grandfather had told him more. There was a big gap in the information, when great grandfather's dad passed. Now this young lad out there and Kate.

He stirred the fire and made sure the water for the rose hip tea was on the boil. Kate started stirring, she opened her eyes and stared at Jerod. He was fussing with the tea and looked up and said "No dear it wasn't a dream." She flipped off the blankets and was almost standing when Jerod said "He's gone." "Gone, gone where? Who was he? What was he doing here? Where did he go?"

Jerod smiled "Calm down Kate, we are safe here. Have some tea." Kate took the wooden cup from Jerod "Okay, okay, tell me everything." "Not much to tell. He pulled me up from the cliff, carried you over here by the fire, sat for a while and left. I asked him a few things, but it was like prying a tooth out of a tradesman." "Who is he?" she asked. "He never said" Jerod replied. "Where did he go?" "There over the ridge. Just like that he was here and then he was gone. I did manage to find out that there were others. He asked if we were staying and he would be back. I never found out his name."

Kate just starred at Jerod. Then she realized maybe these people were her people. Jerod said they found her near here.

Drake found what he was looking for. "Should people be found, beware for they have not had the privileges we have. They have suffered hardships beyond comprehension. They are most likely uneducated and war for what they can accumulate. Treat them cautiously, but with respect and kindness. They are your fellow human beings. Keep the Haven safe, for here is where we are and where our life is. Remember that. It is a gift to you. Treat it wisely and it will always sustain you." So he did think some would survive. He closed the book.

Striding out, he headed for the kitchens. "Sheri can you pack a trail pack for Jon and me for tomorrow please love." Sheri looked up and smiled "Are you bringing them here?" Sheri asked. "No taking them into the valley, want to get to know them. If they turn out okay will you help me with them? They most likely be afraid." "Sure Drake, bit what's to be afraid of here?" "Think about it Sheri, they have lived through it all outside. It couldn't have been easy."

Sheri smiled he could depend on her. He knew that. He headed for his dorm, he wanted an early start in the morning.

Jerod and Kate talked most of the evening. Jerod agreed to take her back to the settlement. He would be back, he thought to himself. He could understand Kate's apprehension. After all these people had survived just like them. He was interested in the things they had learned, like new farming techniques, maybe a new food source or forestry tools. The messengers travelled from settlements bringing news of such things, but it was not often and big settlements were weeks away. There was only one in the mountains. The valleys here seemed to grew more food and seemed the bees were more plentiful here. Wax and honey never hurt any household.

Kate, of course was lost in her own thoughts as well. I want to go home she thought. Who did this guy think he was spying on them and then vanishing the next minute? Not even so much as leaving his name. What if there were people? What if they tried to take her back? She thought about him. His dark hair and his eyes, the way her mind felt like he was in there. A shiver went up her spine.

She wanted to go now, but it was too dark. First light she thought. She stared up at the sky. Some moved slowly, others raced. She didn't seem all that tired now, having slept a lot. Kate didn't want to think about moving the rock, but she couldn't help herself.

"Jerod" Kate said. "Yes dear." "What is it like when you use your gift?" "Well for me it's like a warm blanket. I just think of a warm blanket over the wound and heat it up." "Ah" she replied. "Thanks father." Hmm, when she called me father she was figuring something out. "Night Kate" Jerod said. "Night" she replied. She stared into the sky for a long time and then fell asleep.

Drake wasted no time, it wasn't even dawn yet. He was dressed and on his way to get Jon. "Gee Drake what's the rush? Jon asked. "You get the lunch packs, I have a few things to get to, meet me in the tunnel."

Drake led Jon up the first hill and over the first crest of the mountain. "They will be over the next rise, you just tell me if they are being truthful, Okay Jon?" "Okay Drake, what are they like?" Jon asked. Drake laughed "Like us Jon, like us."

They passed over the next crest and down below the wall Drake could see them. Jon too could see the whisper of smoke from the fire. "They are still asleep" Jon said. "What do we do now?" "We wait for them to wake up Jon." Again Drake chuckled. He liked Jon. He had the spirit of adventure, but he was still young, not 20 yet. He was studious and honest. His gift had probably something to do with that. "Break out some of that trail mix my young ward" Drake said. Jon looked at him and smiled.

It wasn't long before Drake could see Jerod rise. "Let's go and move quietly."

Jerod stirred up the fire and added some wood, to make tea and something to eat. He looked up at the wall and it was then he saw the two young men coming. He was going to wake Kate, but decided to let her sleep. This might be the only chance to talk to these people and he was going to take it.

Drake raised his arm in greeting as they approached. The air was thick with apprehension. One step at a time! One step at a time!

It didn't take the two men long to climb down the hill, almost like they were fooling a path. As they got closer Jerod welcomed them to share the warmth of the fire. The other fellow was younger, Jerod thought, more Kate's age. He was fair haired, tall and had blue eyes. He had the starting of a beard.

Drake was the first to speak. "My name is Drake and this is Jon." "I'm Jerod and this is my daughter Kate." All the sound of voices woke Kate. It didn't take her a minute to realize he was back. She gathered her wits about her, got up and moved closer to Jerod.

"Kate, this is Drake." He turned and looked right at her. His grey eyes seemed piercing "and this is Jon." She looked at Jon and felt more at ease. His blue eyes seemed more soothing. Kate moved closer to Jerod.

Jon touched Drake's arm and whispered something. "She's afraid, Drake."

Drake spoke first "What brings you here to this valley?" "Well, as I told you yesterday, I'm interested in old ruins. It's really a long story. It is interesting that these ruins were her before the Great beginning." Jon nodded to Drake. Truth was indicated. "Great beginning!" Drake said. "Yes, after the plagues passed the beginning of the healing of the world." "Aw, yes, We never called it that."

It was Kate that blurted out the next comment "Great beginning! Bah, old fools. It was the Great ending and we got left to pick up the pieces." Drake burst into laughter "Well now, the little bird has a voice."

Kate just looked at him, little bird? Kate moved closer to Jerod. She had made a fool of herself and now had to endure the ridicule for it.

Jerod seeing this "You have some strange ways my friend. Have you ever been away from this valley?" Drake spoke now "No, we have been here for many years, we had all needed and stayed."

Kate looked at Jon, he never said much except to Drake. He didn't seem to fear him at all. That comforted her.

Jerod spoke next "Could I interest you in some tea? It's the best Rose hip tea around" he smiled. "Kate grows the prettiest roses in the settlement." "Sure" Drake said and Jon nodded in agreement.

Jerod was preparing the tea, when Jo offered Kate some trail mix. She accepted it more out of courtesy than hunger. She watched him take some and eat it before she tried it. "Mmm" she said "What are these?" she pulled a cranberry from the mix. Jon looked "It's a cranberry" he said. "They are good. Where do they grow?" Jon looked at Drake. Drake picked up the question "In our valley, not far from here. We can show you later if you like?" Kate smiled and Jon smiled too.

"What are you using to weave your cloth with? I've never seen such cloth." Jon nodded to Drake. That she was telling the truth. "In our valley there is a plant that grows a white puff ball and we weave it. We call it cotton." "Ah" she said "We grew flax." Drake nodded. The tea was ready.

Drake pulled two cups from his pack. Kate stared at them; these are fine clay cups, porcelain. They had strange things painted on them. Drake saw her looking and offered her one. She refused and took the wooden one Jerod had gave her.

Jon and Drake drank their tea and all shared the trail mix. Kate asked, "What are these?" she held up a nut. "Walnuts" Jon said. "They are good" she said. "We are lucky to have them in our valley as well" he said.

Drake looked at Jerod "You seem to be a well spoke man." Jerod looked at him "My grandfather taught us all to read and write and do figures. He was a good man." Jon nodded to Drake, truth.

"Well our new friends might I interest you in a small hike into our valley? Maybe my young bird, we will find a walnut tree to take seeds and cranberries too." Kate smiled "We will come with you." They cleared camp.

Drake looked at Jerod "No more cliff hanging, okay?" Jerod and Drake laughed. Kate didn't see the humour it was terrifying.

Jon spoke little but his presence was soothing for Kate. He was not much older than her and he seemed kind.

Drake couldn't wait to see what they thought when they reached the valley. It took them a few hours to climb down and still there was a ways to go.

It was well into the afternoon before they reached the valley. Tired, hungry and hot Kate plopped down. Jerod, Drake and Jon joined her.

It was about that time she heard it. Song, sweet song, "twitter, twitter, twitter, tweet' she turned on a start, looking for where the sounds came from. She saw them, a flock of yellow finches. "Jerod, Look! Look!" she pointed to them. Jerod was as amazed as she was.

"What are they? Where did they come from?" Drake looked at Jon "Those are birds, Kate." She watched them with glee, as did Jerod. "Birds! How wonderful." "There is a creek up here, we will camp there" Drake said.

Kate couldn't soak in enough listening to the birds and watching them. Then they flew away as quickly as they came. "Have you always had these birds?" Kate asked. "Yes" Drake replied "We have always had birds."

Jerod stared at Drake. "It seems there is more to you then meets the eye." Drake looked ahead "Near here is a good place to camp."

They set up a fire pit and laid out the bed roll. "Tonight try our tea" Jon said. Kate and Jerod nodded. Drake said "Jon fill the canteens please." Jon stood and Kate said "I will fill ours too." She was feeling far more comfortable now.

They gathered up the water containers and headed for the creek. Kate looked back at Jerod and Drake; they seemed so relaxed in each others company.

As they neared the creek Jon said "You go first Kate" trying to be a gentleman. Jon was of age, but found working in the agro tunnel more fascinating than girls, but there was Kate, she was as perfect as a blossom on a cotton plant. Kate squatted to fill her water jugs and caught a glimpse of something. A silver flash in the water. She remain motionless and then there was another. Jo was close behind her waiting for her to finish. His mind was on how golden her hair was and small her hands were.

It was about then, she jumped back so fast she knocked Jon over. The canteens and water jugs flew into the air. Jon who had been standing two seconds before was now firmly planted on his rear on the ground. Kate was scrambling on all fours trying to make some distance between her and the water.

Jerod and Drake could see something was amiss. They were now standing, looking their way. It was Drake that yelled "What's going on Jon?" He was concerned for them both. Jon hollered back "Not sure yet."

Kate by now had stopped. She could hardly get the words out. "There's something in there, in the water! She finally said.

Jon stood and went to the creek to see. All he saw was some fish. "Where?" he said asked Kate." There's nothing here."

Kate collected herself and started towards the creek. As she got close to Jon, she grabbed his arm, not sure getting close was such a good idea. "There!" taking a step back "and there!" Jon suddenly realized she meant the fish. "It's okay Drake" he hollered.

Drake and Jerod sat down.

"Kate they are fish, they will not hurt you. They live in the water." She liked Jon, he made he feel not so unknowing. "You have fish all the time?" "Yes" Jon replied. "They make a good meal" he said with a big smile. "You eat them? Yuck!" "Hey wait till you try them. How do you know if you if you like them?" He chuckled to himself. "Here, give me the water jugs. I will fill them for you."

Kate was keeping her distance, watching him fill the canteens and jugs. When he had finished, he handed hers to her and rubbed his shoulder and neck. "Remind me to keep clear when you are in an escape mode will Ya?" And he laughed. She had to laugh too, it was really funny when she thought about it.

"When you two finish fooling around over there we could use some water here. A tea might be nice." Jon and Kate looked at each other and laughed again. They settled back down by the fire and Jon was happy making tea.

Drake and Jerod were talking of food resources here and how as people moved up and down the valley, food was becoming more plentiful.

It was about then a fish jumped in the stream. Jerod saw it this time, he stood up. Drake watched. It was Kate that spoke "It's just a fish father" with a look at Kate he said down again. Jon and Kate burst into laughter. Drake looked at them both and Jerod shook his head and smiled.

"Well I see, what is so funny" Jerod said. He kind of felt ignorant and sat back down. "How is it you have creatures here that the plague never killed?" Drake said "Not sure, they have always been here."

Jo looked at Drake, he almost said something but didn't. Kate of course had watched this and knew something didn't fit.

"Maybe it's the location of the mountains that protected them" Drake replied. Jerod seemed satisfied with the answer, but Jon looked at Drake and knew he was lying. Kate never missed the glance passing between them either. She was starting to feel uneasy when Drake said "hurry with the tea! I will be an old man before its done." Jon smiled.

Jon wanted to see Kate's reaction to a real cup of tea. He waited in anticipation as he handed each of them some. He had given Kate his cup and this time she took it without hesitation. As they drank, Kate almost purred. "This is so good. Where did you say it grows? I must have a plant to take home." She was looking on the patterns on the cup, marvelling at how pretty they were.

Jon smiled over her enjoying it so much, but when she said a plant to take home, he felt pangs of sadness pass through him. He thought when Jason told him he was to interpret with the outsiders it would be boring, He wanted to stay in the tunnels and make sure things were running smoothly. Now he felt happy and glad he was picked to meet them. Everything, that most found ordinary, he was seeing through Kate's eyes now; it was exciting. They would leave and he wasn't sure if it was a good thing yet.

Jerod asked "How long till we make it to your village? With spring, there are always storms and shelter is always a comfort." "A week" Drake replied. "We will follow this range" pointing to the mountains that held the Haven. Drake had failed to contemplate on how to get them to his village. Jon again glanced at Drake knowing he was lying again.

Light was falling quickly, the enclosed valley seemed quiet and peaceful. They had travelled all day and they still had a week to go she thought.

Jon was settling into his bedroll, "We will catch a fish tomorrow" he said to her. She climbed under her covers and smiled. "I'm not going to eat it!" Jon laughed. Jerod said "I will try it." He too was ready for rest.

Drake just smiled, his mind was trying to improvise how to keep them here and what could be the village. This had gotten a little out of control, but he would figure out something.

"Night father and Jon" Kate said. "Night Dear" Jerod said. "Night Kate" Jon smiled. "Night little bird" Drake said, as he looked her way. "Night" she replied softly. Kate was still not sure of him. There was something about him that shook her soul, but what was it? Jo seemed perfectly at ease around him and Jerod too. Tomorrow would arrive before she knew it and she wondered how he was going to catch a fish. She smiled and pulled up the blankets.

The day started with bird songs, the finches were back. Kate was delighted, she just lay there with her eyes closed and cherished the sounds. She thought how the world needed these sounds. Her thoughts lingered to the settlement and how the children would be so enthused. The fire crackling and the sweet songs, she smiled.

Then Drake broke the moment "You better get up my little bird or Jon will have caught all the fish."

She opened her eyes and smiled. As she got up, Drake handed her a tea. She looked to the creek where Jerod and Jon were sitting. She smiled and headed that way.

Drake was thankful for the moment alone. How was he going to take them to a village that didn't exist? He had to improvise something and quickly. Think man, think! This was turning into more than he thought it would. All he could hear is Jason's voice, "You haven't thought this through, have you?" He was right, he hadn't. In his hurry to meet them he had not considered a lot of things. But had Jerod not fell, this could have been worked out with help from the council. Drake wasn't going to second guess himself on that score. He knew he did the right thing.

"You got it, you got it!" Kate squealed and clapped her hands as the fish flipped around at the end of the line. Jon looked up at her and beamed. "Hrmph" came from Jerod even though Jon had shown him how, he was having no luck.

Kate watched as Jon pulled his knife out and hit it. She carefully observed him scrape off the scales and then gut it. She didn't like it much, but seemed to know what he was doing. He vigorously rinsed it clean and handed it to her. She took two steps back and Jon laughed.

It was Jerod's turn now; he carefully watched the cork bib and pulled on the line. He had it, he had it. In his delight and panic instead of winding the line, he just kept backing up until it was flip flopping on the shore.

Jon waited no time in rescuing the situation and hit with his knife. Jerod watched as he scraped the scales. Jon stopped and handed Jerod the knife. Jerod took it. Jon was feeling pretty pleased with himself "Let's cook these up."

Kate and Jerod followed him like a pair of children waiting to see what to do next. Drake had sharpened a few sticks and handed them to Jon when they arrived at the fire. Jon smiled "Thanks Drake."

It wasn't long before the fish were cooked and Jerod had to admit they tasted pretty good. Kate couldn't get past the first bight. Fish was not for her. Drake and Jon enjoyed them too. Jon reached into his pack and gave Kate some trail mix, she was content with that and smiled. He was so nice and she noticed more and more about him.

Drake was drawing the mountains in the dirt, giving Jerod an idea of where they were travelling.

It was then when Jon said to Kate "Want to see if we can find a walnut tree or cranberry bush? I can show you other good ones as well." Kate glanced at Jerod "Yes you can go dear, I want to see what Drake is showing me, just don't go far." She looked up at Jon and smiled. He held out his hand to help her up.

It wasn't very far when they came to a small field with a rock slide of stones on it from the mountains. Jon was looking at the vegetation seeing what was growing when a butterfly landed close by a flower. Kate gasped. Jon held his finger to his mouth "Shhhh" then slowly walked over to it and cupped his hands quickly over it. He captured it. "Come here" he told her. She cupped her hands over his and opened them slowly, just enough not to let it go but enough for her to see.

"Its beautiful" she said. She stared in amazement at the tiny creature, then at Jon. He opened his hands and it fluttered away. She watched it until it was gone. Jon watched her. "It's a butterfly" Jon said. "It's beautiful!" Kate replied. "Yeah they are kind of neat."

"At the edge of the small field was a woodlands" Jon told her. "If we are going to find a walnut tree we had better look in the trees" they laughed.

They had not gone far when they came across a fawn. Kate stopped, she was mesmerised. She could hear Jon in the background, "Don't move, be still, it's a fawn, it won't hurt you, but will run if it's startled." Jon moved closer to her. "Talk to it" he said. "Come here little one. I mean you no harm" They slowly moved closer. Then with a flip of its tail it trotted towards the stones. "Let's follow" said Kate. "Okay" Jon replied.

They carefully moved closer and it ran a bit more. It was heading to the hole in the mountain wall. A few more steps closer and it darted ahead and into the hole.

Kate followed; Jon now said "Don't go in there, come back!" Kate was inside now, it was an old mine shaft. The fawn was gone and it was dark inside. Jon standing at the entrance said "Kate come on, let's go." She was still looking for the fawn. "Kate come back" he again told her. "What is this place Jon?" "I think it's an old mine shaft." "What's it for?" she asked him. "There are a lot of them in these mountains. They are from before, not sure." He hated lying to her, but realized now why Drake had not told the truth. They just wouldn't understand.

Then just a ways further, they heard a cracking of wood and the fawn bawled in pain. Kate rushed ahead. "Kate! Kate!" Jon yelled and the sounds started the rumbling. He raced ahead and grabbed her. He was forcing her to the entrance he could see ahead and the cave ceiling collapsed. The beams rotten by age gave way. "Jon!, Jon!, Jon!" No answer, "Jon, Jon" she cried, panic was getting hold and in her mind she was screaming.

Drake immediately stood up "Come now" he said to Jerod. Drake knew where they were by the calls in her mind. He was at a full run, Jerod couldn't keep up but followed.

It seemed like an eternity since the cave in. Sobbing, she was on her hands and knees trying to did the debris off him. There was a big beam on him and another on that. She tried to lift it, but couldn't. "Jon, my beautiful Jon!"

By now Drake had arrived and it didn't take him long to assess the problem. Jerod was there now and he knew this was bad. Kate was still sobbing. "It was my fault."

Drake turned to Jerod "We have to lift these beams." Down the tunnel were more rumblings. "Hurry, we must be quick before the entire shaft caves in!"

Drake was a big man but Jerod was stronger. He was heavier through the chest than Drake. "Okay, let's lift" Jerod and Drake heaved but nothing. Kate was almost screaming now through her sobs. Drake grabbed her. "You have to help my little bird, you have to help me!"

She stared at him "How?" "With your gift like before" "I don't know how" then she felt him in her mind. "Quiet little bird, let it go, let it go." She could feel the heat, it was so hot, like an oven. Drake held her arms. He now moved to the beam in his mind. He knew what to do and the energy flowed. It was so hot she could feel the beads of perspiration flowing on her.

The beam slowly came up. Jerod immediately saw it and pushed it with all his strength and it moved out of the way.

Kate was beginning to feel like falling down the spiralling tunnel again and Drake was there, "Not yet, I'm too tired" he said. "Not yet" he said again. The heat came back, hotter and hotter, it was unbearable, her knees buckled under her, but Drake kept on. She spiralled down, down, down in her mind.

Drake now had to finish alone. Jerod could see Kate was unconscious and Drake was soaked with sweat. The beams began to rise, Jerod was right there. He pushed for all he was worth and it fell and they fell away from Jon. Drake collapsed, he was unconscious.

Jerod was Jon's only hope. He saw the blood and knew he was in peril. He put his hands over the deepest wounds to stop the bleeding. He concentrated and as the warmth passed from him to Jon, the bleeding slowed. Jerod kept it up until the bleeding stopped. He knew Jon was still hurt badly, but the bleeding stopped it gave him more time to help him. Now it was like reliving his past with Anna. He couldn't save her, but he was going to save this young man. He followed the meridians flow of energy in Jon's body, healing what he could. Jerod was sweating profusely when Jon opened his eyes.

"Thought I lost you young man" Jerod said. Jerod needed rest. He was so involved in saving Jon; he never considered Kate and Drake. "Oh my God!" he crawled over to them. They were alive, but unconscious.

It was then he heard Jon's voice "You must get help Jerod. You must go to the Haven."

Jerod knew they needed help, but from where and from whom. "Drake said the village was a week away." "No!" Jon said "go to the Haven. Listen to me." After about twenty minutes, Jerod had a good idea where the haven was. Jon was lingering between consciousness and unconsciousness. Hurry was the last thing he said.

Jerod got up slowly, he was so tired and needed to get help. From what Jon had said the Haven was not far away, about three hours. Jerod knew he would have to leave the three of them there. He was so tired but he dragged himself up and left the cave. It wasn't noon yet, so with help he could be back before nightfall.

He walked as fast as he could, stumbling and falling. Each time he well he thought of Kate, Jon and Drake and dragged himself up again.

The directions were good. He could see the points Jon had told him to find, leading him to the Haven. Slowly he made his way up. He could see the passage Jon told him to find. He was so tired. He entered the tunnel and followed it down. It wasn't long but to Jerod it was endless. He heard children. He found it, he found it.

He followed the chatter of the children's voices. He met Kyrie. "Help me please!" he begged. Kyrie stood like a statue; this was an outsider she thought.

"Help me please, they are hurt!" Just then Tracy and Trina bound from a room. "Help me" Jerod begged.

Without skipping a beat the girls went to him, each taking a hand. "Father will help you." Kyrie realized what was going on and went to Jerod. "Tracy, Trina get your father!" "It will be okay" they said and bounded down the hallway. "They are by the creek, a cave-in, Jon's dying. I don't know if Kate and Drake will survive." Jerod fell to his knees. "Calm yourself" Kyrie said and put her hand on his shoulder. Calm yourself, we will help."

It was not more than a few minutes and a crowd was starting to form. Sheri had brought him a drink, then out of no where Jason arrived.

He was walking fast and his robes out behind him. Now he looked at Jerod. He knelt by Jerod and asked "What happened?" Jerod relayed the story to him. "Get a team together" he started calling out names. "Get the healer and stretchers. Sheri you get some water. Jasper, organize a search team. Get those familiar with the area." Jerod was tired, but his strength was slowly coming back. He got to his feet "I'm going with you, my daughter is there." Jason looked at him "Okay" he said "But we must move fast."

"Naomi and Tanner give him some strength please." They placed their hands on Jerod's shoulder and face. He could feel the warmth cover him and his strength return. "Enough" Jason said "the others may need more help." Naomi and Tanner stopped.

It was Tanner that spoke "You have the healing gift too?" he said. Jerod replied "Yes a little." With that the team was ready and Jason put Jasper in charge.

Sheri near tears stood by Jasper. Jerod overheard Jasper say "Don't worry we will bring them home." With that they made their way out of the tunnels and back outside.

Jon was awake; here and there, moments at a time. He tried to see Kate, but every movement caused him excruciating pain in his legs and shoulders.

He called to her but no answer. He called to Drake too, but nothing. How could this have happened? He thought. He knew the danger. How could he have let this happen? His heart sank as he thought that Kate and Drake , his confidant and friend, might die. All he could think was how could this have happened? And he slipped away again.

It took the team just under two hours to reach them. Naomi and Tanner instructed them to take Drake and Kate outside. It was not their bodies that needed mending, it was their minds.

Tanner moved to Jon, it didn't take him long to assess the troubles. He looked at Naomi and said "His arm and shoulder is broken as well as both his legs. His insides are still bleeding. Help me!" They joined their hands with Jon and each other. After a few minutes which seemed forever for Jerod, they opened their eyes. "The bleeding has stopped." Tanner examined Jon's legs and set the bones. He set his shoulder and arm.

Tanner looked at Jerod "Could you help, bones are hard to mend?" Jerod sat down and joined hands with them. It was wonderful; he followed them through Jon's body to the broken bone and healed. After the legs he released their hands. "Help him" Naomi said "He needs rest." The team laid him on a stretcher and Jerod now spiralled down a tunnel in his mind.

Naomi and Tanner finished with Jon and stumbled out of the cave. The team had Jon on a stretcher and out now too.

After examining Drake and Kate, Tanner spoke "Drake has gone far beyond his mind. He will need strict bed rest. All we can do is wait. As far as Kate is concerned she is lost. I can not bring her back. She has gone too far in her mind. We will make her comfortable and seek the council as to what shall be done." Jasper had the team take them back to the Haven.

When they arrived, all of them went to the medical station. They were bathed and put into dorms.

The council was called and decisions were passed.

Jon now awake and Sheri was sitting by his bed. "So you finally have decided to bless me with you company" she said. She placed her hand on his face. "I thought I had lost you my dear brother." He looked at her and tried to roll over a bit. "Argh! I feel I have been beaten by a mob." "You rest you need it." "Sheri" Jon said. "How are they?"

Just then Naomi and Tanner came in. "You look like you will survive." Naomi went to his bed side and placed her hands on his shoulder, after a moment, his stomach, his arm and legs. "Looks like you are going to be just fine" she smiled.

Tanner then said Let me speak with him, take Sheri for something to eat." The women left and Tanner stood there. "It's bad isn't it Tanner? Tell me." "Jerod will be fine, he needs rest. Drake over extended his gift. He might come back, but it's up to him now. The little girl Kate, well..." "Tell me" Jon demanded. "She's gone too far into her mind. I don't believe she will come back." Jon moaned, "Please go. GET OUT! GET OUT!

Tanner looked at him "I'm sorry Jon, Drake is the only one with the gift of thought, our gifts can't help her. Jon could feel the tears welling up in his eyes "Go, Just go" he said again.

Tanner left the room and stopped outside to talk to Sheri. "Keep him in bed today and tomorrow. After that if he can get up let him. Sheri thanked him and went into Jon's room.

Jon was crying openly now and Sheri felt awful for him. "Tell me what happened Jon, maybe I can help." "Sheri, it was my entire fault, my fault" he sobbed more. Sheri sat down, she listened as he told her of the days they had had together and how he felt.

Patiently she sat there. When he was done, she looked at him. "Sounds to me you are feeling sorry for yourself." Jon just stared at her. "I think you have love for this girl and if that's true then don't you give up, don't you dare give up. Help her back and Drake too. Naomi and Tanner don't have the gift of though. They can't be sure. You must rest now and when you can, help them.

Sheri tussled his hair and said "I know you and I know you will find a way to reach them. Now get some rest" Sheri smiled. Jon closed his eyes and soon he was sleeping.

By now Jerod was awake and lying in bed, not really sure what to do. His clothes had been taken and the room was so strange, light but no candles, warm yet no fire and the comfort of the bed. He stared at all the things in the room, the painting of creatures and the desk with trinkets of some sorts.

Tap, tap he heard. "Excuse me Jerod are you awake? It's me Tanner." Not really sure what to do Jerod said "Come in." Tanner opened the door and closed it behind himself. He pulled up a chair and sat near the bed.

Tanner inspected him for a moment. "Do you mind if I help you some?" Jerod was bursting to speck. Tanner spoke slowly and precisely, "You are in what we call The Haven. I'm sure most of the things you see here are not familiar. Please don't be afraid. I will explain all. No one here will hurt you in any way. I'm actually surprised that you here at all."

Jerod stared at him and blurted out "Kate my daughter how is she? Where is she?" Tanner knew he must tell him "Kate is sleeping in the next room. I can not tell you her condition is not serious. You must prepare yourself for her not pulling through." Jerod starred at him "Can you take me to her?" Tanner looked at him for a few moments and agreed. "These clothes here have been provided for you while yours are being cleaned. Get dressed and I will return in a few minutes."

Tanner Got up and looked back at him "We have much to discuss." He left. Jerod got dressed. Kate not going to make it? That's impossible he thought. She wasn't hurt.

In his mind he raced back to the cave-in. He saw her collapse. It was her gift, he knew Drake had done this.

He hastily pulled on his clothes. He headed for the door and opened it. Tanner was waiting there. "Take me to her please." Tanner nodded and extended his arm directing him in what way to go.

There were few people few people, but at this point it was Kate he wanted to see. Tanner was beside him stopped and put a hand on Jerod's shoulder "We must talk; you may see her for a short time understand?" Jerod looked at him and nodded his understanding.

Tanner opened the door. The room was similar to the one he was in. Kate was laying in the bed. Naomi was there and Tanner said "Let's give them some time." Tanner said to Jerod "Talk to her, she may hear you even if she doesn't respond," Naomi and Tanner reached the door and as they were leaving, Tanner reminded Jerod "Just a little while." Jerod nodded.

He pulled the chair close to the bed and picked up her small hand. "My sweet Kate, please don't leave me, please." He knew the tears were running down his face. He kissed her hand and stared at her small face. Her whole life seemed to pass before him. She was such a bright, happy child and all the memories of Anna; the laughter, all the happy and sad times. The joy he felt when he remembered how Anna dotted on her and Anna' plea to protect her. Now she just lay there. "Kate please don't leave me alone, I can't bear it." He sobbed softly still holding her had.

Tap, tap "Jerod" It was Tanner "Please come with me. You can come see her when you like. I promise. We will do what we can." Jerod asked "What's the matter with her? She doesn't look injured." "Come " Tanner said "I will try to explain as much as I can."

Jerod gently put Kate's hand down and pulled up her blankets. He leaned over and kissed her forehead.

Tanner patiently waited for him. He knew he was in shock and things would take time. He brought Jerod to the sitting room. He motioned him to sit down. There was a tray of food and drinks and Tanner encouraged him to eat something. "Hmm" Tanner said "This might be easier if you asked me some questions." Jerod took a sip of tea. "I can see her whenever I like?" Tanner replied "Yes. You can have the room right beside her where you are, but let me remind you not to be upset when you are with her. I'm not sure if she can hear you or not. My gift is to heal the body as you are well aware. Drake is the only one here with the gift to use thought. Naomi and I can't help her nor you with your gift." Jerod could feel his anger rising. "Where is Drake?" Jerod asked. "I want to know what he did to her." "Jerod" Tanner began, "Drake saved Jon's life with yours and Kate's help. He's going to be fine by the way, but he is in the same condition as Kate."

Jerod almost forgot that Drake and Jon were of the people here. He began to feel embarrassed at his outburst. He looked at Tanner "Please forgive me. I am lost at the moment and at my time of life. It's not that great a feeling." Tanner smiled "It's really quiet alright. I can understand a lot of how you feel." "How is Jon?" Jerod asked. "He will be okay, he was hurt. I did what I could for him." "This is like a bad dream." Jerod said and held his own head in his hands. "This place is so strange, what have I brought Kate too?" Tanner knew it was too much too fast. "Come with me" Tanner said and showed Jerod the way to the outside. It wasn't too far and maybe being outside might help.

They sat outside for a long while. Tanner, not saying anything was giving Jerod time to sort things through. Jerod just starred into the valley. "Did you know I have been looking for this place most of my life?" Tanner listened. He looked at Jerod. "Well now that's interesting. How did you know the Haven was here?" Tanner wasn't sure exactly what Jerod meant by that. "Oh, I never knew exactly what it was I was looking for, only a place. It's been a family quest of sorts, goes back to before the beginning. It's what brought the people to the mountains and valley, my great grandfather."

Tanner was intrigued, "You say this mission, quest as you put it brought the people here?" Tanner knew there was more to this, but let it lie. "So how many people survived out there? Your settlement, tell me about it. There might be something to help Kate" Tanner smiled.

Jerod needed to talk and having joined with Tanner in healing was more comfortable enough to tell him. "The settlement, well it's really a group of people helping each other survive. We have homes, children and work to find enough food to make it through the winter months. A lot has changed in the last years. Seems to be more food in these valleys then in the valleys further away. Father worked hard and he, like myself pledged to look for it; the ruins in the mountains. He taught me to read, he was adamant that I learn. His father, my grandfather taught him. Times were very much harder for them. They survived the first plague, so many died. I know people fought for and killed each other for food, but in my life there has been no such fighting. There are so few people left, joining together was the only answer."

Tanner sat listening. "When the communication stopped everyone in the Haven believed they were the only ones left. There was always hope that some had survived, but to find Haven would have been impossible for them, due to its remoteness." Tanner never told Jerod he wanted him to talk. He knew it would ease him and also give him something to adjust to the haven.

"You say that it was your grandfather who set you on your journey into the mountains to find us." "Yes" Jerod said "From what granddad said, he always thought he was going home. Does that doesn't make any sense does it?" Jerod said.

Tanner smiled "Not really", but then Tanner knew this might not be some chance meeting. Tanner asked "How many people at your settlement?" Jerod replied "We have a nice settlement of about six hundred now. The people are happy now. It was not so pleasant when they first came, life was hard. We lost a few people from old age and some from the plague. Some women stopped having babies, but it has passed we found new hope with the first births."

"Ah" Tanner sad "We had deaths." "Kate was born to your wife in the settlement?" Tanner asked. "No, no" Jerod said "She passed when Kate was four years old." "That must have been hard for you" Tanner said. "Yes it was, Kate was all I had left. Anna pleaded with me to protect her after we found her; Anna changed so much, her whole life was different." "You found Kate?" Tanner wasn't sure he had heard right. "Oh yes" Jerod replied "It was on one of our mountain trips, maybe a day or two from here. I was looking for the ruins, it wasn't so much the quest my family had, it was an interest as well. To see things of the past interest me and anything to help our future is a value."

Just then Naomi appeared "Excuse me Tanner, Sheri was asking if she could speak with Jerod, she seems concerned with Jon." Tanner looked at

Jerod and thought this might not be a good idea at this point. Jerod stood, "I would like to see the lad if I might. I've come to enjoy his company and he and Kate get on so." Tanner said "You need your rest my friend, I'm concerned for you" and he smiled at Jerod.

Jerod looked back at him. "Well mooning around and feeling sorry for myself will not help Kate and sitting idle will not help me either. I would like to see the boy." Tanner realized that Jerod was a strong man in spirit. He didn't want him to push himself too hard, but at this point holding him back would not be good either. Tanner gave the okay "Not for long" he said.

Naomi left Tanner outside and escorted Jerod to Jon's room.

Tanner had heard an amazing story. How could anyone know of this place? Found Kate? He needed to see Jason and returned inside.

As he walked along he thought that the library with some of history of the Haven might be a good place to take Jerod. Drake was the one with the mind for books, but he was still unconscious. Drake, Drake what have you done? Thought Tanner as he made his way to Jason's living quarters.

Naomi was a gentle woman not far from Jerod's age. She began to express her concern for Kate and Drake. She assured Jerod that they would do all they could for them. She talked of Sheri being Jon's sister and how his recovery was coming. Jerod enjoyed her company. Around the next corner and Sheri was there. Naomi introduced them and headed for Drake's room.

"I want to thank you for all your help with Jon. He is my brother you know?" Jerod smiled "It's perfectly okay, I am glad he is okay." Sheri took Jerod's arm. "Please walk with me for a moment." She looked at him and he nodded. "I am worried" she began "Jon is blaming himself for everything. Can you help me?" she asked. "I know your daughter is in a bad way, but I believe Jon can help her. I know Drake and he surely help, but at present it seems that we must help them."

Jerod was surprised how this woman surveyed the problem and was on her way to try and repair things. "Just what do you think we should do?" Jerod said. "Well" she said "I know Drake, he's strong, always has been, but my Jon doesn't have his strength. Jon has the heart of will, just to say he's got more compassion than anyone else I have ever met." Jerod through in "Yes he is a grand lad." Sheri smiled. "Now it seems to me that the problem with Drake and Kate is they over extended their gifts. We must help them find their way back to us. Jon would know things, emotional things, you know. Things most would not notice." Jerod stopped, he looked at Sheri. "You see, humm, let's say we can help Drake back and he can help Kate. I'm not sure, but they have the gift of the mind. Now I have no gift, but from what Tanner and Naomi have told me, they are kind of locked inside themselves, deep in their minds." Jerod was beginning to understand what she was saying. "I believe you are right, but do you think Jon could help?"

"Well now, that's the trouble, Jon has to get over his guilt. I'm not sure he is to blame, but to him he is. You see Jon isn't like most people, he has a gift too, you know? He can tell you if you are telling the truth or not. I think that's why he spends so much time alone, but that's neither here nor there." Jerod looked at Sheri. This is a remarkable woman. Maybe she was right, maybe; maybe she was right.

"Slow down" Jerod said "I'm not sure what it is I can do." "Talk to him, talk to Jon. He has talked much of the last days and well I think." "Talk to him and then tell me what you think" she smiled at Jerod. "I think he is in love with Kate" Sheri smiled at Jerod. "Don't tell him I told you" Sheri smiled.

Jerod looked at this woman and thought, I think I like her. "This is Jon's room" she said and she patted his arm. "I will let you alone with him. I would like to go and see Jasper for awhile. I'm sure he will want to know how Jon is coming along."

She opened the Jon's door "Knock, knock" she said "you have a visitor Jon." "I don't want to see anyone" then Jon saw Jerod. "Okay I will be back soon, going to see Jasper" and she took her leave of them.

Jon was sitting up in his bed. "Here, here" Jon spoke "come sit." Jerod walked over and sat down. Jon looked straight at Jerod and said "Thank you for getting help". "It's okay young fellow, I was almost neck deep into it there. I'm glad you sent me in the right direction." "Thank you for healing me Sir." Jon was having trouble looking at Jerod now. "Well now" Jerod spoke up. "Seems your sister thinks we can help Drake and my Kate." Jon blurted out "I'm sorry, it's my fault. I should have been more careful." "Just hold on there" Jerod said. "You don't know Kate like I do. She's a pretty independent sort. I really don't think you are fully to blame. Kate has a knack for getting into and out of scrapes." Jon was a bit relieved.

Jerod continued, "Does your sister always talk that much?" as he leaned over to Jon. "Yeah she sure knows how to talk" Jon said and they both laughed. "I think Jasper is going to have his hands full there" Jon said. "I think that if anyone gets with Kate will have the same trouble" Jerod said. "Oh, I wouldn't mind" Jon said. "She reminds me of a cotton flower" Jon smiled. "Ahhh and what do you think of Drake?" Jerod asked. "I like Drake, he has always been there for me and others. I like how he is so independent and adventurous. He likes the outside, always hiking, kind of a loner, but that's okay. I like him" Jon replied.

"You feel okay?" Jerod asked. "Yeah I guess so, I'm pretty sore, but Tanner and Naomi said that it was normal" Jon answered. "Well, I must admit, this village is some village" Jerod remarked. "Sorry about that" Jon said. "No, no don't be sorry. I have been looking for this place for some time now."

Jon just stared at him. It was the truth and of any of the people in the Haven, he knew it was. "I just didn't expect this" Jerod smiled. Jon knew that was the truth too. "Well, young man, I think you need some rest" Jerod said. "Thank you for coming. Umm, have you seen Kate? Is she okay, I mean does she look okay? "Yes, yes, but you had better get well yourself before you worry about others." "How can you help take care of them if folks have take care of you? Your sister is worried about you" Jerod smiled. "Tell you what, I'll go check on Kate and come back later and fill you in." Jerod patted Jon on the shoulder and left his room.

Jerod headed to Kate's room. Kate was alone in her room. He pulled the chair closer to her bed and sat down. "Hi there sweet face" he softly whispered. He sat there and looked at her. She looked so peaceful, just sleeping.

Jerod now started to think of Drake, maybe he could help. He wasn't angry at him anymore. Maybe Jon's sister, Sheri was right. He just sat there rolling around in his mind everything that had happened in the last week. He remembered first meeting Drake and it dawned on him that it was Drake that had helped her save him. What a foolish old man I have been. I have to go see that young man later he thought. I just want to sit with Kate a while.

Tanner at this point had been with Jason. "That's impossible" Jason said. "I know" said Tanner, "but that's what he did say." "How could he know of the Haven. No one knew from the outside, that's impossible." Tanner looked at Jason "Well when Jon is up to it we can see if he speaks the truth." Everything was getting too complicated Jason thought. He knew id this settlement decided to come to the Haven it could mean chaos. He would have to research the archives. Drake would know more, he spent hours searching the library about the outside world.

"Thank you Tanner, I'll look into this" Jason finally replied. "Check on Drake would you?" Tanner nodded.

Jason wouldn't say Drake was his best friend, but Jason knew everyone needed to keep the Haven going. No exceptions. He did have things to thank Drake for. He was the only one that convinced him to open the Haven doors. After the last virus episode, Jason feared they would never be able to venture into the world again. In some ways it seemed more important to him now that Tracy and Trina arrived. He wanted more for them. They deserved more in their lives. It was Drake that started to let some animals out, to see if they would survive.

His was the family that braved it first too. Jack and Gwen, Drake's parents took to hiking the hills and soon had Nicholas and Heather hiking as well. It was awful when they never returned from their journeys. The council had closed all adventuring. Only animal checks in the valley were permitted after that. Jason wondered if Drake had searched for them. He had to learn to use his gifts so he wasn't with them when they left and never came back, He knew Drake would be an asset to the moving out when the time came. Now when he wanted to know anything he would look up some information. He preferred the computers. Anything written in journals would not be there. That was Drakes, he was always reading them. Jason made his way to the communications tier.

Drake had not stirred much from when the accident happened. Tanner and Naomi checked on him several times a day. Jerod was given permission to visit him. Jerod talked to him of his journey there and thanked him for saving his life when he was hanging on the cliff. He talked of Anna and Kate, but nothing seemed to get through.

Tanner suggested to Jerod to go with Jon now. He was up and about to see some of the complex. Jon had been told not to show him too much. Let him absorb what he was seeing before moving further into the tunnels.

Jon spent more time with Kate than he really should have, but he couldn't help himself. She was so perfect he thought as he walked into her room. He was trying to think of things that might have triggered her emotions. Jerod didn't mid him being there. It eased him to know Jon cared too.

One of the first places Jon took Jerod was the school. Jerod was astounded at the things they had and how well the children learned. Tracy and Trina wanted him to sit with them and he did. He would visit the school more he thought.

Jon also took Jerod to the main living area. This was something Jerod had not expected. The grandeur was overwhelming; the high ceilings, the statues and the water fountain. He never imagined such wonders could exist.

As they strolled around Jerod noticed a statue of Dee and beside her one of Zack. Jerod couldn't believe what he was seeing. "Oh my dear Lord!" he said. "That's my great grandfather" he told Jon. Jon knew he spoke the truth. "That" Jon stated "is a statue of one of the founders. He was lost outside when the viruses hit. All here believed he perished. Dee, his here is of the lineage to Tanner and Naomi. If this is fact what you tell me is true, then Tanner and Naomi are relatives of yours." Jerod couldn't his ears. This Dee was not his great grand grandmother, her name was Jo Anne he thought. Pieces of his life were falling into place. He had no idea that his great grandfather had been married before. That's why he wanted them to keep searching for this place.

Jon said to Jerod "Are you okay Jerod? Maybe we better go back and see how Kate is doing?"

Jerod never spoke much after that. He followed Jon to Kate's room and sat quietly with her.

Jon went to see Jason. He had to tell him what had transpired. He found Jason in the library. He had been looking for any clues about people outside, but there wasn't much. For two days now he had searched and wished Drake was well to help him.

"Jason" Jon called him. "Yes Jon what's the trouble?" Jason asked. "No troubles, but I think you should know what I just learned from Jerod" Jon told him. "I took Jerod to the living area and he recognised a statue of one of the founders" Jon told him. Jason looked at Jon, "How could that be?" "He said it was his great grandfather. It was the statue of Dee and Zack. He spoke the truth Jason."

Jason sat down "That makes sense now" he said. "Zack was out there when the viruses were let loose on the world. When they never heard from him all presumed him dead, but as Jerod is in his line, it seems he did survive. That's why he knew of the complex. This needs to be discussed at a meeting. Thank you Jon."

Jon made his way to Drake's room. There had still been not response from him. Jon talked with him for a while.

When Tracy and Trina arrived they just sauntered over to the bed. Each of the little girls placed a hand on his face. After giggling a bit they looked at Jon and told him "He will wake up now." Then they left the room. Jon knew they spoke the truth but still Drake did not stir.

Jon went to Kate's room. Jerod was not there now. He must have gone to his dorm, Jon thought. He sat with Kate and thought of her in the valley, her excitement of seeing the animals. Then it struck him, that's it he thought. The canaries, she loved the bird songs.

Jon got up and made his way to the animal tunnels. After a brief conversation with them there, he had a few canaries in a small cage for Kate's room. He returned to Kate's room and placed the birds on the desk. Jon looked at them and said "Sing for Kate." He went and sat beside her bed. It was not long before the birds started to sing and Jon saw Kate's eyes move beneath her eye lids. She never opened her eyes, but that was the first movement he saw since she was brought in.

Jon went to find Naomi and Tanner. They were with Drake.

After telling them what had happened. Naomi went to see her. After a few minutes, she looked at Jon. "I just don't know Jon, but it is encouraging. Keep them with her." Naomi placed a hand on his shoulder "Don't give up" and she left the room.

Jerod was in his dorm. He could believe what was happening. Zack had been here, this was the place. All the time had passed and they were here, amazing.

The council had its meeting and there was much chatter. Jason explained how Jerod was of Zack's line, the people were astounded. He had the gift of healing like Tanner and Naomi. They too were of Zack's line. All this time Zack and his children survived. They had searched for the Haven, trying to get back. They agreed to let them stay and would open the entire Haven to them.

Jason was astounded that Zack had survived outside. Things may get better. The outside was opening up after all these generations. It was almost to much to handle. They would have to ease Jerod and Kate into the Haven and then the folks here to the outside.

Jerod lay on his bed and just pondered everything he saw, it was unbelievable. Just wait till Kate sees this, my poor Kate she has to e alright, she has to be. He sat up and decided to go see Drake. He just had to help, but first he had to wake up.

He made his way to Drake's room. Naomi was just leaving as Jerod arrived. "He has not stirred yet" she told him. "That's okay Naomi, I will just talk with him" he told her. She nodded and left. He went in and sat next to Drake's bed.

He began telling Drake of Zack. He told him how he was his great grandfather. Jerod chattered on for about an hour when Drake stirred.

Drake opened his eyes and looked at him. Jerod could see Drake was in pain. Jerod put his hand on Drake's shoulder and told him to rest. Jerod wasted no time in finding Tanner and Naomi.

He went to Kate's room. Jon was there. He told Jon and he could see the relief on the young man's face. He told Jerod how good it is if Drake is back, he might be able to help Kate. Jon was soon on his way to find Tanner.

He found them talking to Jason. They were excited by the news that Jerod was related through Zack. This was the biggest thing to happen in the Haven in a long time. Jon interrupted to tell of Drake's awakening.

Tanner made his way to Drake and Naomi was not far behind. They found Jerod first and got the details of what had happened, before asking him to join them.

The three went to Drake's room. He held hands with Tanner and Naomi and stepped over to Drake. Tanner told Jerod to relax and go with the flow of the energy. They were going to follow the paths through Drake's energy meridians in his body. It would help with the pain in his head. They followed Drake's energy paths. Jerod could not only feel, but see the flow. They followed the paths through Drake and eased the ones in his head to a more synchronized order. They directed Drake's tangled energy into smooth ribbons throughout his body and eased the pain. When they were done they left Drake.

Tanner, Naomi and Jerod returned to their own selves and the healing was done. Drake opened his eyes "Thank you" he said and closed his eyes again.

"Let him sleep now" Tanner said. "Might do us some good too" Naomi said, "We'll see you t your dorm" she told Jerod. He was very tired and made no effort to say no. He needed the rest too. He didn't look at them and said "That was amazing. How did you learn to do that?" Jerod asked. Naomi replied "We have had training, just as you saw, we too learned. We need to talk soon you get some rest. Tanner will check on Kate" she added. "Hopefully Drake can help now he's back, but not for a few days. To alter a flow of ones energy taxes not only us, but whom ever we help. The three of us carry the burden, Drake carries his own." Jerod nodded and thanked them again as he entered his dorm. He climbed into bed and slept.

Drake woke to find Jon sitting beside him. "How long have I been unconscious?" Drake asked. "A week Drake" Jon stated. Drake sat up. His head throbbed but not too bad. "Glad to see you are okay, you had me worried" Drake told him. Then the realization of where he was hit him.

"Jerod, Kate where are they?" Drake asked. Jon looked at him "They are here" he told him. "They okay?" Drake asked as he eased himself out of bed and stretched.

"Jerod is fine, he's adapting, but Kate…" Jon stopped talking. Drake looked at him "What about Kate?" Drake was beside Jon now. "She is in a bad way Drake" Jon told him. "What happened?" Drake asked. "She couldn't be healed by Tanner and Naomi" Jon looked down "No Drake it's not her body that's wounded, it's her mind. Tanner says she is dying and he can't reach her" Jon said. "Where is she?" Drake asked. "She's in the next room" Jon replied.

Drake dragged his clothes on and as soon as he was dressed he headed to Kate's room. Jon was hot on his heals. Drake stopped Jon at the door and said "Stay out and don't let anyone else inside." Jon nodded and Drake went inside.

Drake pulled up a chair beside Kate's bed and put her hand in his. As he sat there, he slowly started to caress her mind. There was nothing, Drake continued further. He realized she was deep into her mind and she had no avenues back. It was then he notices the flock of birds in her mind, then a butterfly. He felt the soft delicate warmth she held them and it was gone. Drake slowly left her mind.

When he returned to himself, he was drenched with sweat and Kate lay there unmoving. He should have not joined with her. She did not know how her gift worked. She did not know how to build pathways back to reality. He held his head.

Jerod made his way past Jon, the sight of Drake holding his head made Jerod panic. "Drake, my daughter can you help her, can you help me?" Jerod asked. Jon was there trying to get Jerod to leave. It was then that Drake spoke "Get out, both of you, now!" The silence echoed in the room. Jon took hold of Jerod's arm and escorted him to the door and tried to reassure at the same time.

When the door closed, Jon looked at Jerod "he will do what he can Jerod" Jon told him. "We must wait. I know Drake will not leave her now. I'm not sure, but they are bonded now. I have no gift other than knowing if people are telling the truth or not." Jerod understood the bond he felt when he joined with Tanner and Naomi. He looked at Jon "Yes my boy I understand" Jerod told him.

Tanner and Naomi soon were there. After talking with Jon, Tanner and Naomi decided to take Jerod for a walk outside. They knew that Jerod was a relative and it was important for them to discovered how he managed to survive. Tanner told Jon "It may take a long time or short, but we must leave them." Jerod was still reluctant to leave, but it was Naomi that took his arm and said "We must prepare for Kate. If Drake can help her, she will need all of us to make the Haven and how it came to be, easy for her to understand" Naomi smiled. Jerod was starting to relax and he knew she was right.

"Jon you need to find something to pass the time" Naomi said. "You fretting and worrying outside the door will not help her." Jon knew she was right. Jon turned and told Naomi "Yes, you are right. I will be in the agro tunnel." Naomi grabbed his arm "We will let you know right away of any progress Jon." He nodded and walked down the hall.

Naomi still had Jerod's arm and smiled "I think a breath of fresh air is in order. We have much to talk of Jerod and I think you might find it all interesting." Tanner looked at Jerod and said "I do believe you will be interested." Jerod knew that these two were related to him in some way and he was about to hear how.

He looked at Kate's room. It was Tanner that said "If she is to get well, it will be Drake that will help her. We must let him have the piece to do what he needs to do." Jerod accepted the situation and the three made their way outside.

They stopped at the kitchen and asked Sheri for a lunch for them and to have it brought outside. Sheri nodded.

Jon was beside himself. He almost went to talk to his sister Sheri, but decided to be by himself. He went to the agro tunnels. He found much solace in growing things. He found himself checking the grade wheat and thinking it would have to be harvested soon. Samuel was his man help in the tunnel. Soon they were discussing the harvest and replanting of the crop.

Samuel could see something was troubling Jon and asked if everything was alright. Jon soon related the situation to Samuel. Samuel listened carefully to Jon and said "You know the outsiders should have been left to there own fate." Jon was a bit stunned by that comment. "Why would you say that Sam?" Jon asked. "We have been safe here for many years. Every time we have opened to the outside it has come to no good" Sam looked at Jon. "It caused great sorrow when the virus was here. We lost many dear to us. Then after we regained our lives, the virus mutated and left the women barren. Now again we are opening ourselves to danger." Jon could understand his feelings, but pointed out "the Haven was built to protect us from the worst of the outside and it is time for us to re-enter the true world."

Samuel looked at Jon "I don't find the harm in staying here and I think that the outsiders will do us harm." "I think you are wrong Sam, we were meant to be outside. The Haven was not supposed to be our home forever, just until the turmoil of the outside settled itself." Sam told Jon "I am not the only one that feels threatened by the outsiders or by those that push us to go there." Jon knew Sam was being truthful and it was a shock to believe that there were some that never wanted to leave the Haven. "Sam do you know I have been outside and I think it's wondrous? You should go out it is safe now" Jon told him. Same shook his head "Not me, I'm content here" he smiled. "Well Sam, this is not getting the work done."

Jon was still rolling around the fact that there were others that never wanted to leave the Haven as he checked on the rice fields. As he looked at the rice field, his mind wandered to Kate and when she first saw a fish. He smiled. He could then feel the dread come over him. She had to come back, she just had too. Drake please help her, he whispered to himself.

Drake was still with Kate. How could he help her back? He racked his brain and remembered his father and mother joining with him. They taught him and how the teachers instructed him from the notes left by his uncle and aunt. Life was so different when he had family around. He thought how they stood almost alone in front of the council and dared to venture outside. His father was sure it was safe. The animals were alive, even thriving. They would eventually have to go out and he would be the first to go if that would convince them. They made a few trips and it was on one of these trips that they never returned. His aunt and uncle had gone too.

The council again closed the outside world out. Drake was the one that changed it again. He went out often and even though he looked for signs of them, he never found anything. It was on his last adventure out he found Kate and Jerod. Now through his parent's actions, Kate lay here. He pulled himself together. Although he was tired and hungry, he wanted to try again to reach her.

Again he held her small hand and slowly caressed her mind. It was like travelling in a clouded mist. He felt like he was walking knee deep in mud. As he struggled, looking for anything that would connect them he saw the canary flock. He called to her in her mind. No images that he could make out. Slowly he left her again. He found himself once again sitting beside her. He let go of her hand. His head was throbbing and he was sweating profusely. Time had no meaning when he was joined with her and now he needed rest. He got up looking at Kate "I will find you, rest now" he told her and made his way to the door.

Jerod was waiting outside the room. The day had been spent talking of many things with Tanner and Naomi. They were indeed related and the group of them told each other the basic history of how life had been for them. Jerod was astounded at the wonders they told him of the Haven. Tanner and Naomi admired how Jerod and the others managed to survive outside.

When Drake opened the door, Jerod stood up. Drake looked at him "I haven't reached her yet." "You have been all day" Jerod said. Drake just repeated that he hadn't reached her yet. "I will try again, but I need to rest Jerod" Drake told him.

Drake went to his dorm. He took a long shower. After his shower he went to the library. He needed to read the journals his aunt and uncle wrote.

Jon finished in the agro tunnels and head to see how Kate was. He brought some roses t put in her room. Jerod said she grew roses. When he entered Kate's room Jerod was there. "Where's Drake?" Jon asked. "I don't know" Jerod replied, he left. He said he was tired and he would try again Jon. He said he couldn't reach her. I can't lose her now Jon, he has to help. He just has to" Jerod said almost in tears.

Jon knew how Jerod felt. He too felt the same way. Had she not helped Drake, Jon knew he would not be here. He loved her and there were no doubts in him now about it. Jon asked Jerod if he had eaten and Jerod said he had. Jon told him that he would sit with her later and he should put the roses near her, maybe she would know the scent. Jerod left and went to talk with his sister and get something to eat.

Jason was there and invited Jon to come and sit with him. Jon decided to join him. He would talk to Sheri after. Jason inquired after Kate and Jerod. He was glad that Drake was finally awake. He would have to speak to Drake later.

Jon talked of crops and their progress. Jason looked at Jon do you mind if I ask you something?" "Go ahead, feel free" Jon said. "You know I have always been cautious about venturing outside. I do realise that we will eventually have to...well can you tell me, I mean did you like the outside? Do you think we should work toward building outside? If Kate and Jerod survived, let me get to the point Jon. I want my children to live outside in the future. The Haven was built to protect us from war, but it appears to me we should start thinking about living more out there."

Jon was stunned that Jason was asking him about this. "You should really talk to Drake. You know he knows far more than I do or talk to Jerod, he is a wise man" Jon told him. "I just wanted to know what you thought Jon. I will of course look more seriously into this" Jason replied. "Well" Jon said "I think you are right. We should be thinking more about being outside, but there are people that do not want to leave." "What do you mean?" Jason inquired.

Jon proceeded to tell him of his conversation with Samuel. Jason never thought about never leaving the Haven. He knew that sooner or later the people would. The fact that some never wanted to leave struck him as odd. "That's interesting Jon I will have to bring this up at the next council meeting. Well I have to get the girls, thank you Jon it was an interesting conversation" with that Jason left.

Sheri was now pouring coffee for her and Jon. She knew him well enough to know he was troubled about something. She was soon sitting across from him and he told her about Kate and Drake. Sheri said "If anyone could reach her it was Drake. He did not say she was lost to us, just he could not find her." Sheri smiled "It will be fine. Soon you two will be roaming all over the place. You go get some rest" she told him. "I told Jerod I would go site with Kate later" he said. "Don't make yourself sick, that won't help her" Sheri said as she picked up the empty cups and went into the kitchen.

Jon got up and went to Kate's room. Jerod was not there now and he sat with Kate. "Kate please come back, let Drake help you please Kate. I need you" he said softly to her. Jon sat there for quite some time. Kate lay there unmoving. Jon bid her good night and went to his dorm.

Drake was in the library and found the journals. He was intent on finding a way to help Kate back. Had Kate been able to stay joined with him he could have eased her back. Her collapsing was like dropping her off the edge of a cliff and Drake didn't know how far she had fallen. The next thing he realized was Tracy and Trina near him. They climbed on his knee and each placed a hand on his face. He could join with them through the material bond they shared with each other.

Jason was also in the library "Drake we must talk. Girls give me some time alone with Drake." They climbed down , Drake hugged them and they were off to the children's section of the library. Drake rubbed his eyes and stretched.

Jason sat across from Drake "There are some things you need to know. Jerod is of the founder Zack's line" Drake looked at him. "How do you know this?" Drake replied. "We have talked to him extensively and after reviewing Dee's, Simion's and Warren's journals. Zack was locked outside when the virus hit. They all thought he had perished, but he did not. He and his family have looked all this time for the Haven. Jon can attest to Jerod telling the truth. Now come the interesting part which concerns Kate." Drake looked at him and raised an eyebrow. "Jerod is not her father, he found her" Jason told Drake. "Found her! What are you talking about?" Drake asked.

"It seems Jerod and his wife had no children. They loved to hike in the mountains and on one such trip they found her. Her parents were dead so they rescued her" Jason told Drake. "So what's so interesting about that? From what I have seen with them, death wouldn't be uncommon for them outside the Haven. They struggle for survival. The fact they made it at all was a miracle" Drake answered. Jason looked at Drake "Let me finis please." With almost a huff Drake sat back in his chair.

Jason continued "Jerod told me that Kate's parents were not of his village. They were people none had seen before. They wore clothes similar to ours. They had strange items with them." Drake suddenly realized what Jason was saying. It was his aunt and uncle and their baby Maylan. "Are you saying Kate is Maylan?" "There is a strong possibility it is so. They found her about two days hike from here" Jason told him. Drake couldn't believe what he was hearing. Jason stood up "If it is true you have family again. I would like to do a blood test to be sure." Drake said "No, no, not yet I don't want her to have any pain, it might set her further away." "She is unconscious it won't hurt her" Jason said. "No! Just because she isn't conscious she still feels. Promise me nothing will be done yet." Jason nodded his agreement.

He left Drake sitting there. Drake ran everything through his mind. Could Kate really be Maylan? Could there be a chance he had family after all this time? She had the gift of thought. Drake needed to eat, he was starving. He left the library and headed for the kitchen.

"Sheri Love, got something to feed me darling?" She smiled "be a minute Drake and will be right out."

Drake sat at the table his mind on Kate. It wasn't long and Sheri brought him something. She could tell he was troubled and asked "How are things going with Kate?" "Sorry Sheri I just need to think for a while" he said. Sheri put a hand on his shoulder. "It will be okay, you will find the way" she told him and headed back into the kitchen.

Drake finished his food and headed to Kate's room. He met Tanner on the way. "Tanner make sure I'm not disturbed today with Kate, no one understands." Tanner nodded. Drake went into Kate's room and closed the door.

Jon soon arrived at Kate's room and Tanner refused him entrance. This is going to be a long day, Tanner thought.

Jon knew Drake would not have refused access to him if it was not in her best interest. So he returned to the agro tunnels.

Sam was there. "You're here early" Sam said. Sam just told him he was working on something. Jon asked if he needed a hand and Sam told him "No, no I can manage." "Sam have you checked the alp alpha. The animals will need a fresh supply soon" Jon asked. Sam left the counter he was at and said "I'll do it now Jon." "Thanks Sam" Jon replied.

Jon wanted to check on the bean plants, fish food would have to be made soon and the protein from the beans was a good part of it. As he walked past Sam's counter he noticed that he had been mixing some things together. He would ask if he was making a new fertilizer. Sam was older and Jon always learned things from him. Sam had been offered head supervisor in the agro tunnels, but had declined. He did not want the responsibility. Jon took the position and the two of them got on great.

Sam soon returned and told Jon all was well. Jon asked "What great thing are you concocting Sam?" "It seems that Carol's flowers are not doing so well. She sent her young fella down to get something to perk them up. She never leaves the tunnel much. Did I tell you, she has woven the nicest cloth rug I've seen yet. That woman has talent I tell you." Jon smiled "I would like to see her work sometime, maybe get something for Sheri and Jasper's wedding." "I will tell her you are interested" Sam told him. Jon felt tired today. He had been worried to much and the strain was taking its toll. "Sam I'm calling it a day" he told him. "Go get some rest" Sam replied.

Jon left the agro tunnels and went to the kitchen. On his arrival he found Jerod. Jon marvelled at Jerod and his ability to adapt to new situations. He reminded him a lot of Drake. Jon asked to join him, Jerod was glad to have his company. "It seems that we have been locked out of Kate's room" Jerod told him. "Don't worry Jerod" Jon said "Drake is a good man." "Yes I know, but Kate is so young, so small. I just couldn't handle it if she doesn't pull through."

There was an awkward silence before Jon spoke. "You up to seeing more of the complex? It's really large, much larger than you realize." Jerod agreed, he needed something to take his mind off Kate.

"I'll take you to the agro tunnels. I think you will be quite amazed." Jerod agreed it would be interesting to see how they grew the food here. They had so many different foods that he had never seen before. Jon explained how the hydro phonics worked and how they grew some things in the soil.

When they arrived Jerod could hardly believe his eyes. The tunnels seemed endless and all the different crops. Jon took him through many of them, explaining how it all worked and what each crop was for. The fruits and vegetables Jerod marvelled at, some he knew and some he never saw before. Jon was like a proud father showing Jerod everything. Jerod couldn't have been a better subject to share it with. Jon was amazed at the questions Jerod asked, how long do the plants survive? What is the harvest ratio? What the fruits and veggies could be used for? Could they be preserved? Jerod told Jon all this could help so many in his settlement.

Jon listened and then told Jerod "Do you think it is a wise decision to tell them of the Haven? It has been a shock to you, what do you think their reaction might be? People here are a little afraid that if they find out they might come here and take things in haste." Jerod knew Jon was right; it had been a shock to him. Had he not had stories in his family it would have been a greater shock. "You are right my boy, you just might be right" Jerod told him. "We have a council here where everyone has a say. We must one day re-join the ones living outside, but I think we should be moving slowly."

It was then when they noticed a young fellow standing there. It was Carol's son looking for Sam. Jon sent him in the direction they had last seen Sam. The young lad stared at Jerod and then hurried on his way.

"Do you want to see if we can get in to see Kate?" Jon asked. "Yes, yes let's go" Jerod nodded. They left the agro tunnels and headed for Kate's room.

Naomi was there when they arrived. They could tell by the look on her face that no one was going in. Jerod suggested they go get something to eat and Jon agreed.

Drake was with Kate, he decided instead of him trying to find her let her find him. He joined her in thoughts and led her into his past. To the time of losing her parents and the sadness of her heart and mind. He could feel her reaching through to him. Find me little bird he thought.

Just as he headed into the midst of her thoughts he saw her, felt her. He reached for her, but couldn't pull her back. Come to me let me show you how. He could sense great sorrow and sadness. He knew she was trapped there within herself. Slowly he brought the images of the canaries, the butterflies. He shared her thoughts of the fawn, but then she was drifting away. My little bird, this is the way. He sent her pathways for her to follow. If she didn't follow them, she would stay trapped. Drake sent images of Jon; he could feel her gentleness for him and then the pain. Then she was gone. Drake called to her, but she had recoiled back in her mind and shut off the avenues they had just built.

Drake was back beside the bed now. He could not leave her now. She had almost made her way back. She did not know Jon was safe and well. The canaries were singing and Drake could see more movement of her eyes under her eye lids. It was a sign to Drake that Kate wanted out. He slowly joined with her again. This time he would start her journey back to reality. Drake sensed that she was stronger than before. He thought of Jon and Jerod. He could visualize them to her and he could feel her get closer. Come on little bird, then he felt her strong pulling. He let her pull him to her, it was a joining of his mid to hers. He felt her fear and soothed it. He felt her pain and Drake eased it with images of comforting things. She was with him now and Drake encompassed her in his energy. He could feel her slowly relaxing. He sent her images of the journey back to reality. She followed the pathways. Drake sent her vivid mental images of him and her to make it easy for her to follow. They were almost there, almost to the last bridge out. Drake surrounded her with his thoughts and carried her over the last bridge.

They were back. Kate opened her eyes to see Drake there. "Thank you" she told him. "Rest my little bird, rest" he told her. Drake never let go of her hand. He just rested his head on the bed beside her and he slept too.

Tanner that entered the room. He placed his hand on Drake's shoulder. Drake lifted his head and left Kate's hand go. Tanner motioned for Drake to follow him out of the room. Drake complied.

He sat in a chair outside Kate's room and told Tanner and Naomi "She needs rest, but she is back." Naomi hugged Drake and Tanner smiled. "I was getting worried. You were in there for two days" Tanner told him. Drake looked exhausted "I need a shower, Tanner let her rest" he said.

Drake left and headed for his dorm. After a long shower Drake flopped on his bed and slept.

Jon and Jerod, for the last two days had waited for word from Naomi and Tanner, were together when Naomi appeared at Jon's dorm. She knocked and entered "She is back" Naomi said. Jon said "Thank you Drake" and looked at Jerod. Jerod was crying, the reality of her being okay overwhelmed him. Naomi said "She well have to rest, but you can see her briefly. Please don't wake her, let her wake on her own. Do you want to go see her now?" Naomi asked. Yes they both said in unison and smiled at each other.

Jon said "Jerod you go see her first, I will see her after you" Jerod nodded and Naomi and Jerod left for Kate's room. When they were gone Jon cried now. "I have her back now, thank you Drake" he whispered, as the tears flowed down his face. He would go tell Sheri but first he needed to collect himself.

Jerod quietly entered Kate's room, silently went over to her bed and sat down. He was there for sometime when she rolled over. It was the first real movement he saw from her in the last weeks. He felt tears flowing down his cheeks. Jerod thought now of Anna and how he told her that he would protect Kate. After all the things he had learned in the last few weeks, he wished Anna was there for him to talk to. He felt so alone in that moment. Then Kate moved again. Jerod decided to leave her and let her sleep. After Drake's help, she would need as much rest as possible.

He must find Drake and thank him. He was the man that brought his Kate back. He knew that he would forever be in his debt, first his life and now Kate's.

Jon was with Sheri and Jasper. He was beside himself with joy. Kate would be okay now. He had always respected Drake, now he felt he would never be able to repay him. Sheri and Jasper were happy for Jon. They teased him on his feelings for Kate. Sheri gave Jasper a look to stop teasing him. Jon and Jasper laughed.

It was late when Jon went to see Kate. He didn't stay long, he just sat beside the bed and looked at her. When she tucked her hand under her chin Jon got up and left. Seeing her move was the confirmation to him that she would be okay.

Drake and Kate both slept. It was everything Jerod could do not to wake Kate or Drake for that matter.

Jon was just as bad. Naomi and Tanner took turns in Kate's room. They didn't want her to wake up here and be frightened.

Jerod was in the library and got some of Dee's journals to read. He sat quietly beside Kate reading them. Jon brought fresh flowers for her and the canaries sang. It was two days later when she stretched and opened her eyes.

There was Jerod she smiled and closed her eyes. She moved, almost stretching. She was sore. Then it came back, the cave-in and her eyes popped open. "Oh Jerod!" she said. "Jon, where is Jon?" Jerod reached over and held her hand. "It's okay, he is alright Kate" Jerod told her. She realized that she was not outside. She was in bed; she looked around, where was she? Then she looked at Jerod "Where is Drake?" "He's fine dear, you must rest. Do not excite yourself okay?" Jerod told her. She pulled the blanket up. "Where are my clothes?" she asked.

It was Naomi that spoke "they are being cleaned. You rest for now. You are in no danger, but you sure gave us a scare. Would you like me to have Jon come see you? He's been worried sick" Naomi told her. Kate said "He was hurt I saw him." Naomi placed a hand on Kate's forehead and she started to relax. "Jerod" Naomi said. "She will need time to adjust. You must explain things, but let her ask you." "Alright" Jerod nodded. "I will let Jon in for a visit after she has had something to eat." Naomi told Sheri "Just liquids for today, tomorrow gelatine and maybe toast." Sheri got up and went to the kitchen. Naomi looked at Jerod "I'll leave you here and get her calmed down. Her muscles will be sore, a bath will help her later." "Thank you Naomi" Jerod said. Naomi smiled.

Kate had been watching all the conversations, what was going on she thought. Jerod sat back down an looked at Kate. She was about to say something and Jerod said "Listen first then you can ask me, alright?" Kate nodded.

"Let me see, the first place to start. Okay" he said. "The cave-in, do you remember Jon being hurt and Drake joining with her and me to move the old timbers?" "Yes" she said. "Well Jon was hurt very bad. I healed him the best I could, he knew as did I he needed help. Drake and you over extended your gifts to move the timbers. We almost lost you my little girl and Drake too." Kate was about to ask and Jerod told her to listen. "Jon lay there and told me to find this place. It's called the Haven. I had to leave all of you and find my way here. Jon gave me very good directions. The folks here followed me back to you. They brought you and Jon here in no time. It was Naomi, the lady that just was here and Tanner her brother that healed you. He is well now. That was, let me see at least two weeks ago. Okay Kate there is much to tell. Things here will be unbelievable, but you are quite safe. Do you understand ?" Kate nodded. "Now before you start. You have been in great peril yourself, so you must rest. Had Drake not saved you I don't think I would have cared to live." With that Kate started to cry. Jerod held her hand and let her cry. Through her sniffles he assured her that Jon was fine and Drake was fine also. The sobs subsided, it was then she noticed the flowers and then the birds sang. "Jon brought them for you" Jerod told her. She wanted to go see them, but she found she was stiff and sore.

It was then Sheri rapped at the door. "Come in" Jerod said. "It's just me Sheri" with a tray for Kate. She brought juice, tea and broth. She placed the tray on the table. Jerod thanked her and she left "That was Jon's sister."

Jerod placed a napkin under Kate's chin and gave her some juice to drink. She drank it slowly. Her throat was sore and her lips were dry. It tasted so good she thought. Jerod told her it was apple juice. "It's very good" she said. Jerod smiled "This is one of many new things you will see." "What is this place father?" Kate asked. "This is what I have been looking for. We found it Kate. We found it at last. I have so many things to tell you, but first we must get you up and about." After some broth and tea Kate felt very tired. Jerod could see her fatigue and tucked her in. He kissed her forehead "Sleep Kate you need the rest."

It was Drake that Kate woke to. She watched as he paced the floor. Then he saw that she was awake. "Aw my little bird is a wake" he smiled. Kate sat up a little. "I wanted to see for myself that you were with us again" Drake smiled. She reached out for him and he took her hand. "Thank you Drake, thank you." Drake sat in a chair. "I should not have sought your help with Jon." He patted her hand. "Could you have saved him Drake?" she asked. "Probably not, but it was my life only then would have been at risk" he said. She smiled at Drake "You are a good man." "When you are stronger we will talk." He let go of her hand and headed for the door. At the door Drake said "Get well my little bird" and left the room.

As Drake left Tanner and Naomi entered. "Looks like she's with us again" Tanner stated and winked at Kate. Tanner came closer and placed a hand on Kate's head. After a few minutes he said to Naomi, "Let her try some solid food and get her up. She needs to walk a bit, her muscles are stiff. I'll come see her tomorrow Nomi. Keep the visitors down, she still needs rest." And Tanner left.

Naomi looked at Kate "Don't mind him. He can get a bit bossy, but he is right. There is water here beside you. I want you to drink, Okay?" Kate just nodded. "Oh Jon is waiting outside. Would you like to see him or should I send him away?" Naomi watched. "Oh might I see him, just for awhile?" Naomi smiled "Sure but not long."

She helped Kate sit up. She had a basin of water and a wash cloth and placed it beside her. Kate washed herself and Naomi brushed her hair. Naomi stood back" Okay I will let Jon in, but just for a little while" Kate smiled.

Kate was relieved to see him walk in. He had more flowers for her. "They are beautiful Jon." He put them on the counter. "Are you okay Jon?" Kate asked. "Yes I am, Tanner and Naomi and your Jerod healed me." Jon was sitting beside her. "Oh Jon I was so worried for you" Kate told him. "No more than I was for you" he told her "We thought we had lost you, but Drake brought you back" Kate smiled. "It's funny I was so afraid of him and now I don't know why" she smiled. Jon poured her a drink of water. He could hear her dryness of her voice. "Jon what is this place?" Jon looked at her "We call it the Haven. There's plenty of time to see it, just get your strength back and I will show you everything alright? Jon smiled.

It was Sheri that arrived next. "Okay my dear brother she needs to eat, out you go." "I will come see you later Kate" Kate smiled.

"Kate I brought you something to eat. Tanner was pretty strict about it" Sheri said. Kate smiled. Sheri brought the tray over to Kate. There was toast, gelatine, tea and juice. Kate looked at the jello and after she tasted it, she said "Oh I like it." Sheri smiled cherry gelatine. Kate ate the rest of the food and lay back and closed her eyes. She was sleeping before Sheri left.

Tanner was outside Kate's room with Jerod. "Try and get her up some today Jerod" Tanner told him. Jerod nodded. Sheri closed the door "She's sleeping again." "I will sit with her" Jerod said. "She still really has no idea about it here. I would like to have her a bit better before she sees the wonders here" Jerod told them. Tanner agreed. "Oh if Drake wants to see her, please let him" Tanner added. Jerod went in and sat beside the bed. He started reading to her again.

Jon was in the agro tunnels, it was Carlo's young son there again. "Are you looking for Sam?" Jon asked. "No, I guess I'm looking for you" Jon turned, looked at him and smiled. "What is it I can help you with?" The young fellow sat on a chair. "Is it true you have been outside?" "Yes" Jon told him "I have." "Did you like the outside?" "Yes I did like it" Jon told him. "Haven't you been outside on a school trip?" Jon asked. "No, my mom won't let me, she says never go out side or you will die" he said. Jon walked over and sat beside him. "Well I'm alive and I went out" Jon smiled. "My mom said if they go out, my dad will make sure you don't bring danger back." Jon raised an eyebrow, "Just how was your dad supposed to do that?" he asked him. "My dad died, but mom says he made sure they didn't come back." Jon knew he was telling the truth. "I got to go home. Mom gets scared when I come here. Bye" he said and jumped off the chair. Jon wasn't sure he heard what he heard. He sat there for a few minutes. I have to go tell someone he thought and he left the tunnel to look for Jason.

He found Jason in the living area. "Jason have you got a minute? I have something important to tell you." "Sure Jon, mind if we walk and talk?" Jason asked. They walked along and Jon told Jason what the boy had told him. Jason stopped in his tracks. "Do you realized what you are saying Jon?" Jason asked. "Yes I know" Jon said. Jason crossed his arms and brought a hand to his chin. "Leave this with me Jon, I have to check out a few things." Jason told him. "I need to see Kate. She's awake now" Jon smiled.

Jon realized that he had nothing for Kate. He stopped off at the kitchen to see Sheri. Sheri wasn't there, but Jasper was. Jon asked Jasper "Do you have a few minutes Jasper?" Jasper told Jon "Sure sit down." "Jasper I'm off to see Kate, but I get all flustered like." Jasper laughed "Looks like our Jon has finally found his other half." Jon smiled "I do care for her more than you know."

Then Jon stopped talking and looked at Jasper "Well maybe not" and they both laughed. Jasper told Jon "Don't worry Jon the uneasiness will pass. Then you will grow together, it's a wonderful feeling. You will see, just be yourself" Jasper told him. "Now go and see her." "Jasper" Jon said. "She has no idea what the Haven is. She has lived outside all her life. I never saw such wonder as hers when she first saw a bird. It made me feel proud that she was with me when she first saw them" Jon told him. "Hmm" Jasper said "Maybe you could spend more time outside where she feels more comfortable." "You might be right Jasper, you might be right" Jon replied. "Thanks" Jon told him and headed towards Kate's room.

Sheri was there sitting in Kate's room. When Jon arrived she picked up her hand work and left. Jon sat beside her bed and took Kate's hand. Kate opened her eyes and smiled at him. Kate couldn't believe he was there and he was okay. She sat up and looked t him. Jon started first "I'm so glad that you are okay. I thought I wouldn't have been able to live with myself had you been hurt. I should never have let you go into that old mine shaft. I knew the danger." Kate stopped him "It was you that got hurt Jon. You were so hurt," "I'm fine now and now you are too." "What is this place Jon?" Kate asked. "This is what we call the Haven" Jon told her. "There will be many things here you will not understand, but you are safe."

"Father, where is father?" Kate asked. "He's exploring. He has more time to adjust. I think he likes it here" Jon told her. "Yes that sounds like father" Kate smiled. "I want my clothes" Kate told him. "Some of your clothes were torn in the cave-in. Would you mind if I picked you out something to wear?" Jon asked. "I just want some clothes Jon. I want to get up and move around" Kate told him. Jon smiled "I will get Sheri to help me pick out something for you to wear then." "Jon, do I have to stay here?" Kate asked. "At least until Tanner and Naomi say it's okay, yes. They may seem gruff, but they are good healers so listen to them Okay?" Jon said. Kate nodded.

"There is so much you need to know about the Haven. Do you want me to tell you?" Jon asked. "Yes please" Kate replied. "Let's see the best place to start is at the beginning. Simion the founder built this place. It would be before the virus was let loose on the world." "It's true then" Kate said. "What's true?" Jon asked. "Father's stories of a place his family has looked for all these years." "Yes, it seems that Jerod is of Zack's lineage" Jon said. "So these are his people here?" Kate said. "Yes" Jon told her. At that moment Kate felt so alone. All this time and he has found them. She was happy for him, but where were her people, then she thought.

"Jon, I'm getting tired" she said. "I will leave and let you rest then. I want you up and about" he smiled. Kate didn't want him to go, but she wanted to be alone for a while. "You will not go away for long Jon?" she said. Jon smiled and said "No, not for long. You rest now and I will be back later" Kate smiled. Where was her father Kate thought as she watched Jon leave?

When he was gone, she rubbed her legs. She flipped back the blankets and eased herself onto her feet. She felt so woozy, her legs hurt and she was so stiff. She edged herself along the bed. When she reached the other side, she went back the way she had come. She was exhausted. She was leaning on the bed trying to muster the strength to get back into bed when the door opened and there stood Drake.

He was to her in about four steps and lifted her into bed. "Not yet" he said. "Tomorrow Nomi will help you." Kate looked at him while he fussed with her blankets. "I don't want to be here any more Drake. Nothing is right, everything is so strange" she said. Drake straddled the chair as he sat and said "You want to go back to your settlement?" "Yes I do" she replied. "I know it there Drake." "What about your father? Do you think he wants to go back?" Drake asked. I don't know" Kate replied. "I see" Drake replied. What about Jon then?" Drake could see that he had hit a soft spot. "I don't know" Kate said again. "You seem determined to go. You don't know where, with whom and you don't know who or what you are leaving behind. Sounds like you have a good plan."

Kate started to cry. Drake stood up and went over to her bed and held her. "Listen my little bird, get well first. Open your mind to new things. If you really want to go back after you're well I will take you myself, Okay?" Drake told her. She could feel him caress her thoughts and she found it comforting now some how. After awhile she was overcome with tiredness. Drake laid her back and covered her up. "You sleep, it will be okay" he said. "I don't like being sick in bed either" and she smiled. Drake got up and left. Kate slept now.

Drake stopped at Sheri, who was waiting outside. "Stay with her, she is feeling very alone. You might have Jerod spend more time with her." Sheri smiled and said "Jerod was just here. I will see that she is not left alone too much." Drake turned on his heals and headed to the main living area. It was there he ran into Jason.

"Drake" Jason called to him. "Join me for a moment will you?" Drake sat hat his table. "What do you know of Agoraphobia?" Jason asked. "Not much, why what's up?" Drake asked. "It is possible for people to be afraid of the outside. Most have never left the Haven. You know, now that we know there are more people out there, we will have to start venturing out." Jason looked at him "Yes, it seems so to leave here and join the world again after all this time" Jason said. "I've had some ideas about that, to ease the people into the outside" Drake said.

"That brings me to tell you of a conversation brought to my attention about the fear of going outside" Jason told him. "Spit it out man, spit it out" Drake said. Jason looked at Drake "First you must listen and do nothing until I get to the bottom of it." Drake now knew something was up. "Tell me Jason."

Jason continued. "The conversation was about some in the Haven making sure that those who left never came back to bring harm." "Just what are you saying Jason?" Drake was starting to see what he was saying. "Are you telling me that my parents and aunt and uncle were murdered Jason?" "I'm not sure, but I plan to find out" Jason said.

Drake stood up "Tell me who Jason." Jason stood up "Drake sit down do you hear me?" The two men faced each other. "If they have done harm to them Jason, I'll..." Jason cut him off. "You will what Drake?" "IF, IF! It's true they are sick. Do you kill sick things or do you try to help them?" Drake sat back down.

The days of when they left ran through his mind. Drake had wanted to go with them so bad, but he had to stay behind. To think someone killed them was beyond his thought process.

"Drake, Drake" Jason said to him. "Let me look into this. If it's true the council will take action." Drake looked at Jason, he got up and headed outside. He found solace there. There was a rage building in him. He needed to get away for awhile.

Drake stopped off at his dorm and grabbed a few things. He put them in a pack and made his way to the kitchen. Sheri was there as always. "Sheri love, can you find me some trail goods, about a weeks worth?" "What's up Drake?" she asked. "Nothing, just need some space is all" he replied. Sheri went and got what he asked for. He took the food and headed outside.

The wind was blowing fairly hard, but Drake barely felt it. He hiked hard for a few hours, soon he was at the ridge and into the valley Kate and Jerod came from. He had travelled a fair distance and it started raining. Drake knew he had to find shelter. The rain was less intense in the trees and he found a clearing. Drake built a lean to and made a fire. He leaned back and looked at the stars through the opening in the trees. His mind wandered to his mom and dad. He remembered how adamant they were about leaving the Haven. People should live in the world, not in tunnels his dad would say. His mom agreed as did his aunt and uncle.

Drake could understand them. He knew the freedom he felt when he was away from the Haven. He spent countless hours in the valley watching the animals. How could anyone kill them for that? Agoraphobia Jason called it, fear of the outside. Fear this, all the fresh air, the sunlight, the wind, the stars. He thought of Kate, could she really be Maylan? He would not be alone if she was. He started to smile, Kate did have spunk and he would give her that. She soon would be a woman in her own right and one that no one would push about.

He left his mind wander to Jon and Kate. They were a good pair, he decided finally. Jon was smart and steadfast; Kate would bring out his nature to enjoy things more. Jon would make Kate think about thinks before putting them into action. Yes he decided he was good for her and she was good for him. His mind rolled back to his parents and the rage was once again there. He had to get a grip. He had no outlet at the moment for it. It was better that he was alone out here until he had it under control. He had stayed up all night, at day break he let sleep have hold of him.

It was afternoon when he woke up. The fire was out and the rain had stopped. He stood and stretched. He gathered his gear together and started walking. He liked this valley, he thought. He had ventured here some but never this far. Today he would cross the next ridge. As he hiked, he checked his bearings.

Later that night he set up camp. He was just into the next valley. It would be in this valley where Jerod found Kate. His parents and his aunt and uncle had been here. Drake laid back on his bedroll, he was tired.

The dawn was there with the sun shining on his. Soon he was awake. Drake gathered his gear and started walking again. He thought about them and walked more. Soon the rage was too much. He picked up a thick pole and hit a tree, he was next too. He hit it again and again until his hands hurt. The fury was over, he was drenched with sweat and exhausted. He fell to his knees and Drake cried. He cried for them, he cried for himself and he cried for everyone that was snatched away from him that day. He cried for the loneliness he felt deep inside since then. Drake knew he could go back now, but he would spend a day or two thinking about the people that had done this.

He dragged himself to his feet and started walking again. He could hear water near and followed the sound. As he got closer he could see the creek, it had a water fall. Drake wasted no time stripping off and going in. After he felt clean he dressed and headed to the clearing where he had spent the night. Soon he had a fire going and was sitting back with some tea. Drake was a complex man as most had found in the Haven. He had many of the young women chasing , but until now none had interested him, not for any length of time. He was honest about it and he would never use them for his own pleasure. Drake just had found her yet.

Kate and Jerod had presented a whole new world to him. When he got back he would have to spend some time with Jerod and he was going to the council meeting. What happened to his family must never happen again. People in the Haven had to start going out more. It was time. He would have to read what Simion said about it and the others that lived outside.

Jerod and Kate would be a great help too, if they decided to stay. Drake again thought of Kate, she wanted to leave. She did not like it there. For one so young she had some shocks in her life. When he joined with her there was sureness, he felt. It had been a long time since he felt that.

Drake slept well that night. The morning sun found him. He made tea and ate. He decided to head back to the Haven valley. After packing up, he looked around and knew he would come back.

After a good days hike he could see the wall. Just over the next ride he thought some fishing was due. Drake made his way to the river in the valley and set up camp.

Jon had been to the tailor station and with Sheri's help picked out some close for Kate. He was going to see her and hoped she would like them. Jerod was sitting with her when he arrived. "I brought you something to wear Kate" Jon told her. "Oh thank you" Kate replied.

Naomi soon appeared and sat with them. "Oh Kate" Naomi said. "As you know we have some very different things here." Kate nodded. Jerod told me he found you when you were a baby. Is this correct? Naomi asked. Again Kate nodded. "Well this place we call the Haven was built many years ago. The man that built it was called Simion. He knew the world was in peril. So he used his resources and built this place so people would survive. When the viruses or plagues as you call them were let loose on the world, Simion closed us in here. We lost many, but not like the people on the outside. We even had animals stay alive." Kate glanced at the birds. Naomi watched her, "yes like these birds. There are many more, anyways, when the virus had done its damage we again shut out the outside. Fear of other sickness kept us closed up in here. We continued letting animals go from here and when none had died, we opened the doors to the outside again. We had no idea that others had survived this long, with no animals for food or bugs or bees for pollination we believed mankind had to have perished. It was Drake's family that made the moves to start going outside. Drake had to remain in and do his studies. His family went out and never returned. His uncle and aunt had a baby girl with them."

Kate was beginning to understand what she was saying. "Are you saying I might be that girl? Kate asked. "Yes" Naomi said. "There's no way of telling. I might be from somewhere else" Kate said. "There is a way we can tell for sure" Naomi stated. "You can?" Kate said. "Yes" Naomi replied. "Can you tell with me as well, just to put any doubts to rest?" Jerod asked. Naomi replied that she would.

"How is it you can tell?" Kate asked. "We have the resources here that will help, but we need something from you" Naomi asked. Kate pulled her legs up under her chin. "What do you need?" Kate asked. "We need a sample of your blood." Kate was now shaking her head, Jon was sitting beside her. Jerod took control, "How do you get this blood you need?" Jerod asked. "We use a needle which is hollow and we take it from your vein." Jerod looked at her. Now it was Jon that spoke "You can take some from be. It's completely safe" Jon told them, "and it hurts so very little."

Jerod looked at Jon, then Kate and then Naomi "Okay Jon that would be a great help" Naomi said.

It was Tanner at the door with a tray. He had a white coat on with surgical gloves. "Have they agreed?" Tanner asked. "Take mine first, so they can see" Jon said. "Ah, that's a splendid idea." He went to Jon "Roll up your sleeve" Jon said. Tanner tied a rubber tubing around his arm and drew a vile of his blood. He released the tubing, gave him a cotton ball and bent his arm. "Hold it there for a couple minutes please" Tanner told him.

Jerod was fascinated. "Here may take mine" he said. Tanner took Jerod's blood too. Kate looked at them "From my blood you can tell where I'm from?" she asked. "No Kate, not where you are from, just if you are related to Drake. If you are then it proves you are from the Haven." "It's okay Kate, I will hold your hand" Jon told her. She agreed. Tanner soon had her blood. After checking to make sure the blood had clotted and they were all fine. Tanner picked up the tray to leave. "How long will it take to find out?" Jerod asked. "Give it two or three days and we will know" Tanner stated.

Jerod turned to Kate "Are you okay dear?" "Yes, I'm fine" she replied. Jon was still holding her hand. "Naomi" Jon asked "Might I take Kate for a small walk" Naomi looked at him and then Kate. "Humm let me talk with Kate" that was their queue to leave. When they were out Naomi said to Kate "You don't have too and you can stay here. It's really soon for you to be up." "I want too" she smiled. Naomi told her "I think you might be too weak yet." "Please" Kate said "I'm so tired of it in here." Naomi put a hand on Kate's forehead and then she touched her legs. After a moment she said "Okay, but not very long."

Naomi helped her dress. The clothes were soft, comfortable and fit well. Jon even got her some shoes. After she was dressed, Naomi brushed her hair "There now, you look better." Kate like the clothes. "Okay" Naomi said "You hang onto Jon's arm or Jerod's arm until you get a bit steadier on your legs." Kate nodded.

Naomi left and it was Jon that came in. He stopped and looked at her. "What?" Kate said. "Nothing, just looking how lovely you are" Jon smiled and Kate blushed. Naomi was behind him, "Not very far you hear me and give her your arm to hold onto. Do you hear me Jon?" "Yes, yes Naomi" and he stepped to Kate and offered his arm. She tucker hers under his and walked slowly. "So where do you want to go?" Jon asked. "Not far okay, my legs are sore." Jon smiled "We will go and see my sister Sheri. She runs the kitchen." Kate agreed.

They walked past the school and Kate heard the children laughing. Then onto the kitchen they strolled. Kate was wide eyed with the things she was seeing. The kitchen was strange, the tables and chairs were made of metal, not wood and the food she saw. Some things she knew and some she didn't.

Sheri soon appeared "Ah there's our little wounded one" she smiled. Kate smiled back. "What would you like?" Jon asked. "I don't know" Kate replied. "Hmm let's see" Jon said "Sheri how about a caramel sundae and tea?" ate smiled "I like tea, but what is the caramel sundae?" Jon smiled and said "Trust me." He escorted her to a table and helped her sit. Jerod sat beside her and Jon sat on the other side. Sheri soon had her tea there and wondered how she boiled the water so fast. Then she brought out the sundae. Sheri added a cherry on top and some whipped cream. Kate smiled, she had never seen anything like it before. After the first mouthful Kate smiled. "This is wondrous Jon" she said and Jon just smiled.

Kate gave Jerod a bite. "My, that's good, what is it?" Jerod asked. "It's ice cream" Jon said. Kate ate every bite slowly to savour the taste. "Maybe this place isn't so bad after all" Kate said and they al laughed. Kate watched as the people came and went. They ate so many different things. They all took time and chatted. Kate thought they all looked happy. After they finished, Jon got up and got her a damp napkin to wipe her hands and face with. He was so attentive. They sat there about an hour.

"Can we go outside?" Kate asked. "Sure" Jon said and got up and offered her his arm. She gladly took it and again tucked it into his. Jon smiled. They walked down the tunnel and soon Kate could see the outside. She felt relief. For some strange reason Kate thought they would not let her gout, but it appeared that she was wrong. Soon she tired and was looking for somewhere to sit. Jon escorted her to a rock out crop and she sat down.

The fresh air was nice. She felt the soft breeze blow against her skin and it felt good. "So you have been here all this time?" Kate looked at Jon. "Yes we have lived here for many, many years." Jerod said "you should see the wonders they have it's marvellous." Jon sat near Kate "There are many things you will find are strange, but we just use them as tools of survival" Jon told her. "We work and grow food, make clothes just different then you is all. The people here are just people." Jon smiled. Kate liked his smile, it made her heart go pitter patter. They stayed outside chatting for about half an hour.

It was Kate that said "I would like to go lay down. I'm feeling tired." Jon was instantly up and at her side. Kate stood and felt woozy. Jon saw it immediately and swept her up in his arms. Kate smiled. "Thank you" she said. "No problem" he said and carried her back to her room.

Naomi was there "Okay what happened?" "Nothing, it's just easier to carry her" Jon said. Naomi gave him a stern look "you wore her out. You should have brought her back sooner! "Oh no" Kate told her. "I felt a little woozy is all." Jon laid her on her bed and removed her shoes. Soon he had a blanket over her and had her propped up with pillow. Jon looked at Naomi "We should get them dorm rooms." Naomi put her hands on Kate's forehead and legs. "We will ask tanner, but for now let her rest." Jon and Jerod took the hint.

Soon Kate was warm and it didn't take her long to fall asleep. Naomi had helped her get into her sleeping garments and now Kate was resting, she folded her clothes and laid them on the counter. Naomi stared at her and hoped that she was indeed of Drake's line. He had been alone so long and unlike the others in the complex she knew how it affected him. She will never forget the days when his family did not come back. She watched Drake build walls around himself, more of a protective function on his part. He was not the same since then, joy had left him.

She looked at Kate, if this was Maylan, how fate had saved her. How it was a descendant of Zack, her own line. The odds were phenomenal. Naomi smiled at Kate and thought. Even if you are not from the Haven, you have brought hope.

She left the room and found Jerod and Jon sitting outside. "She will be fine, but you must let her heal. She has been unmoving for nearly three weeks. It will be a few days before she regains her strength. Please don't over tax her." Jerod and Jon nodded.

Naomi had a way of making even older men feel like children. Jerod liked her. She knew what she was doing and took no guff from anyone. He did not want to have her displeasure. For a small woman he feared the consequences of making her angry.

"Well Jon" Jerod said as Naomi walked away. "How about showing me some more of this place?" Jerod smiled. Jon smiled too. "How about seeing the stockades where we keep the animals?" "Lead on Jon" Jerod replied.

Jon was happy to show Jerod around as strange as things may seem to him. He had an insatiable curiosity. They first came to the atrium with the butterflies, the plants and the variety of bugs there astounded Jerod. They passed through there to where the fish farms were and then onto the animals. Jon having been around them all his life showed no fear. The people taking care of them walked among them with no problems at all. Jerod couldn't believe the variety and size of some. Jon took him to the waste management and explained how it worked. Jerod was stunned at the ingenuity of it all. Everything worked together. This Simion had brought the whole place into a functioning unit. He was amazing.

They soon found themselves in the living area. Jerod still marvelled at the beauty here. The world must have been a wondrous place before the virus. How could man have been so stupid?

It was Jason that appeared next and asked to have Jon for a few minutes. Jerod was content to look around and watch the people for a bit.

Jon walked with Jason. "I've been looking into what you told me. It seems there are many more here in the Haven." Jason said. "What do you mean?" "I seems there are many more here that have a fear of the outside, agoraphobia, then I would have first imagined. Have you seen Drake?" asked Jason. "No I haven't seen him for a few days" Jon replied. "Okay than you Jon, thank you for bringing this to my attention." Jon just nodded and Jason went on his way.

Jon returned to Jerod. "Jerod" Jon said "I think it's time we got you two a dorm." "Okay my boy, lets go see what you have" Jerod said. Jon smiled and led Jerod through to where the dorms were.

Drake relaxed by the stream. He was getting to prefer the outside to the Haven. He had been running everything over in his head, from his mom and dad to meeting Kate and Jerod. He smiled when he thought of her. Kate did remind him of his aunt. Why had he not seen it before? Then her gift, it was familiar somehow. He remembered Maylan, how tiny she was. How could someone do this? His rations were gone and he was hoping for a fish for breakfast. Jon was the better fisherman. After not having any luck, he packed his gear and headed for the Haven.

Jason should have found out something by now and Drake wanted to get to the bottom of this.

Jason had to get to the bottom of things. He had been to see the boys mother Carol. She confirmed the boy's story. After Jason was satisfied she had no part in the murder, he took her to the medical station.

Jon, who was with him never dreamed that people in the Haven lived in such fear of the outside world. Jason also proved without a doubt that Kate was indeed Maylan and Jerod was a descendant of Zack. His present course of action was to see to it that anyone in the Haven having fear must speak up and get the offered help.

Jon wanted to tell Kate, but Jason told him no. He wanted Drake to know first. Jon could understand that. Jason called a council meeting.

It was about an hour later that people gathered in the council chambers. Jason got up and called them to order. He started by telling them that it was time to start considering moving out into the world. The danger they feared had passed and through the Haven all would still have what they needed.

A shout came from the crowd "It's the outsiders that have caused this." Jason immediately took hold of that comment "The outsiders as you call them are people just like you and me. They are the proof that we can live out there once again." Another shout came from the crowd "What if we want to stay here?" Jason then told everyone "No one has to leave here if they don't want too. All I'm saying it's time we started making more effort to start settling out there. Only those that wish to live outside. Anyone wishing to stay here is welcome to do so. The Haven will not be closed to anyone. We must vote on this, but think carefully before you cast your ballet. Simion, my great grandfather built this place as a refuge from disaster, he knew it would happen and we all know it did. This refuge was not to be made into a prison either. It was his hope that we would again live in the outside world and I believe this is the time. I want more for my children then tunnels and artificial lighting. I want them to enjoy the sun and fresh air. So you all think on that for your children and theirs when you vote." With that Jason cast his ballet and left the council chambers.

He went to speak with Tanner and Naomi. It was Tanner he spoke to first. "What do you think?" he asked Tanner. "She does have Agoraphobia, but the boy seems well enough." "Tanner" Jason asked "maybe we better make sure that any that suffer with this are brought to our attention." "Jason, this is a sickness of the mind. Her fear of the outside has been instilled since she was very young. I'm not sure we can help her. Her son is fortunate that we discovered this now or she would have instilled that fear in him. I dare say that there will be others that suffer as well." "I understand Tanner. We must find them and help them. I need to pick up the girls. I will speak to you again soon on this Tanner." And Jason headed to the school.

Jerod had been with Kate all morning and had a surprise for her. After she was dressed and was ready, Jerod tucked her arm under his and slowly took her to their dorm. When he opened the door Kate couldn't believe her eyes. It was a beautiful room. Jerod escorted her to the couch and she sat down. Jerod lifted her legs up and she put them down. "Gee father stop fussing, I'm fine." "How do you like it?" "Oh it's nice father. Do you like it?" Kate asked. "Yes" Jerod told her "You have not seen the wonders that this place holds. As soon as you are better I'm sure Jon will show you around." "Father don't you miss home at all?" Kate asked. "What's troubling you dear?" Jerod asked. "It's just so strange. Oh I don't know. I just miss home."

Jerod sat beside her. "Kate you do understand that this is what I have looked for all my life and my father and his father? Tanner and Naomi are my family. We are not alone anymore Kate." "But you are my family" Kate said and started to cry. Jerod hugged her "Now you listen to me. I will never leave you. You are my daughter. If after I have spent some time with Tanner and Naomi, you want to go back to the settlement. I will go with you. After all now that I know where it is. I won't have to search anymore." She smiled, it was then she noticed the flowers and the birds.

"Jon brought them for you. I dare say the boy has fallen for you" Jerod said. "Oh father I do like him, but." "But what?" Jerod asked. "Oh father I would have to stay here." Jerod sat down beside her "Kate what's the matter? You are not yourself. What is troubling you so?" "Father what if I am Maylan? What if they won't let me leave?" "They as you put it would be your family and they can not hold you nor would they." Kate seemed a bit more relaxed. "Would you like to go for a walk later Kate?" "Maybe later" she said "I think I will go lay down for a while" she said. "Alright dear." He helped her to her bedroom. After she was comfortable Jerod left and closed the door.

Drake was back in the Haven and was looking for Jason. He found him in his dorm. The girls of course bounded over to him. They each placed a hand on his face and after a giggle or two they were off to play. "Jason, what did you find out?" Jason told Drake to sit down. "No thanks I'm covered in trail dust. Just tell me" Drake said. "The woman's husband did murder them. He poisoned their water. Drake she was not involved Jon was there" "Where is he? Where is he?" Drake asked. "He's dead Drake. He died a few years ago" Jason told him. "Jerod is a descendant of Zack. His blood proves that and Kate is indeed Maylan." Drake just looked at Jason "Thank you Jason. I will be in my dorm" and Drake left.

Drake took a long shower, dressed in clean clothes and headed to the kitchen. He asked Sheri to make him something to eat and asked her where Jerod and Kate were.

Drake ate and went to their dorm. He knocked and waited. Jerod opened the door and invited Drake inside. "Where have you been lad?"

Jerod asked. "No where really. I just had to go and sort through my thoughts. Is Kate here?" he asked. "She's resting" Jerod told him. "Good" Drake said. "It seems that you are related to Tanner and Naomi" Drake said . "Yes I am happy. I have been alone most of my life. Kate has been my only solace." Drake nodded. "I know the feeling" Drake said. "Then you know that Kate is my cousin that we all feared dead?" Jerod looked at him. "I have not told her yet. She's having troubles Drake. She wants to go back to the settlement." Drake asked "How far is the settlement?" "It's about four days from here" Jerod told him. "Does Jon know she wants to go back?" Drake asked. "I'm not sure she has told him" Jerod said. "What's your settlement like Jerod, the people there?" Drake asked. "The people" Jerod told him "moved into the valley about fifteen years ago. It took us about five years to get the field ready for planting. The past ten years have been clearing the trails, passes and just living. There is much work to do and most never leave the valleys. We have noticed that there are more bees coming west and I know why now." Jerod smiled.

"How many people do you think are in an area of a circle say five hundred miles across?" Drake asked. Jerod rubbed his chin "Humm I would say 1000 people maybe 1500." Drake to Jerod that when Kate wakes up, he would like to take her for a walk. He was not going to tell her. He said he would be back to get her. Jerod agreed. Maybe Jerod would find out what was the matter.

Drake went to the kitchen and had Sheri make up some ration packs for an evening meal. Drake headed for his dorm and ran into Jon on the way.

"Jon" Drake stopped him. "Drake it's good to see you back. Have you talked to Jason?" Jon asked. "Yes I have Jon thanks. I just wanted to tell you that I will be spending the evening with Kate" Drake told him. "Drake just be well" Jon said to him. Drake put a hand on Jon's shoulder "It will be fine. You worry to much for one so young" Drake told him. Drake continued on to his dorm. He grabbed the items he needed and headed on to Jerod and Kate's dorm

When Drake arrived at Kate's dorm, she was there and dressed. "So have you come to tell me I can't leave now?" she asked him. "Not at all Kate" Drake replied. "I have come to ask you to accompany me outside and well…talk of some things I think you might be interested in knowing" Drake told her. Kate walked around the room a bit. She looked at Drake "If I choose to leave I can?" she asked. Drake smiled "Yes indeed, you can leave anytime you want. You don't have to stay even now, but please let me ask you not to reveal the Haven. The people here need time to adjust to the outside" Drake replied. "Okay" Kate agreed. "I have taken the liberty to pack some things. I will take you to your settlement after we talk" Drake told her. Kate looked a bit dumbfounded "My father is not coming?" she asked. "No he wants to stay for a while" Drake told her. "Where is he? I want to talk to him."

Drake opened the door and asked her to follow him. Drake found Jerod in the kitchen and Kate walked directly up to him. "Father" Kate asked. "Yes dear" "Are you coming back to the settlement?" she asked. "Not at the moment Kate. I want to stay here for a while. A lifetime of searching has brought me here and I have much to see yet. I have talked to Drake and he seems willing to take you back if you wish to leave right away." Kate just looked at him, then to Drake ""Alright you can take me back Drake. I want to go home."

She stopped at her dorm and felt there was nothing she wanted, so they headed out to the Haven Valley.

"So tell me about your settlement. It must be a wonderful place. You are in such a hurry to get back" Drake said to her. Kate didn't want to talk, but she told him "It's not that it's so great, but it's home. I know my way there. Here everything is strange" she said. "Strange is not bad just different. We do have our good points. Take Jon for instance" Drake stated. Kate stopped in her tracks "I didn't get to say goodbye. How could I not say goodbye?" Kate said. "Okay, let's sit for a minute." Kate sat down and Drake sat across from her.

"We can go back and you can tell him if you wish?" Drake smiled. "Kate may I share something with you, I mean join with you again? I you to know something and I can only show you what I mean."

Kate was hesitant. She was a bit afraid of joining with Drake. His gift was unnerving to her. She thought, since she was leaving and maybe after she used it more she could help the people at the settlement, if she knew how to use her gift better. "If I say yes" Kate asked "Will I be able to use my gift better?" "Every time you use your gift you will learn to command it better, but it takes time. I could teach you but you are going" Drake told her. "I want you to share some of my memories. They might help you." Kate realized that Drake was trying to help her. "You mean how you helped me back?" she asked. "Yes like that" Drake told her. "Okay what do I do?" she asked. Drake smiled "Here hold my hands and just think of nothing." Kate held his hands and tried not to think of anything.

It took some time , she drifted to several thoughts of Jon and her settlement; the bird song she heard even the sounds of the wind. Then it was there, that soft caress of Drake's mind. Then like waves of water he joined her mind. She could see him. He was a boy, she called to him, but he didn't answer her. She saw him with his parents, then others. They looked like they were going somewhere. She saw them hug and then Drake was in a learning place. It was interesting to her; she didn't understand what he was doing. It then drifted to someone talking to him. His anger and fear almost overwhelmed her, then it was sorrow and despair. The essence of loneliness was clear and vivid. She felt it close over her. Then she felt the existence of life without the care and thoughtfulness of loved ones. The thoughts carried her through his life. She watched him watch her and Jerod, everything he felt. It followed to Jon and then shifted to her and who she was. She knew Drake was her cousin, that she was Maylan. She then found that she was sitting holding Drake's hands.

"Why didn't you just tell me?" "You had to see to know" Drake replied. Kate hugged Drake. "These are my people?" she said. "Yes" Drake told her. "Drake there is something you need to know. I was leaving because I was afraid of them" Kate told him. "I know" Drake told her, "but we need you, I need you. Please don't go Kate" Drake said to her. "We need yours and Jon's help to get the people to adjust to the outside. Will you stay and help? I'm sure Jon wouldn't be upset if you stayed. He thinks very highly of you." Kate blushed "I like him too."

They had stayed joined in thought for hours. Dusk was starting to fall and Drake asked her if she wanted to go back or stay outside for the night. Kate looked at him and said "Well cousin, how about we stay out tonight. We have so many things to catch up on." Drake just smiled, he was no longer alone. He rolled out their bedrolls and got a fire going to keep them warm.

The rest of the evening was spent talking of their lives and thoughts of things. Drake was happy for the first time since he was young and Kate was happy that she too was no longer alone.

Drake watched the stars overhead. Kate was family and she had the gift. For so long his only use was with twins and they were too young to understand it. Drake looked forward to teaching Kate how to use her gift. Of all the gifts, the power of thought could be dangerous. He almost lost her, but now they joined in a way no one could understand or break apart. Jon was a lucky lad, Drake smiled. Kate would be a good woman for him.

He looked over to her sleeping. You were lost and now you're found, he thought. He was very interested in the other people, through Kate he had mental images of them and how they lived. It was remarkable they had survived.

Drake was almost too content to sleep. He wanted to pick Kate up and continually hug her, he smiled. Her mind and his were now joined as it should be. The last emptiness now had light, he sighed. He watched her and his mind drifted to Jon. He liked the lad; it would be a good match. The two complimented each other. She had the softness of soul that suited her, yet he was strong too, that suited Drake. His mind was at ease now. He thought about the women that had been in his life. Maybe it was time that he thought about a partner. He had contentment now he thought he had lost forever. Kate had given him back his life. She didn't know that, but in any case she had. He closed his eyes and let sleep take him.

He woke to Kate stirring the coals to the fire and added more wood. "It's about time you woke up" she said. He leaned on an elbow "It is, isn't it?" he said. "What's my little bird got planned?" Kate looked at him. How strange that she felt so much a part of him now and before she was so unsure? "You can start by explaining to me about our gift and tell me about my parents. They had the gift too didn't they?" she asked. "Yes our line carries the gift of thought. My father and his brother, you and me, had there been more children they too would have it as ours will." "You mean if we are married to those that are not gifted?" she asked. "Yes the bond does not break, ever." "How come I never felt you before?" Kate asked. "There was too much distance between us, but when we got close enough you felt me as I felt you." "It was our bond from birth. When we all thought you lost, my mind ached daily with loneliness. It's hard to explain. I had the comfort of my father, my uncle and you all my life. We often talked with our minds. Then it was gone, silenced for what I thought was forever. When I felt you in the valley I had to come and see, it was an overwhelming desire drawing me. You will understand that now as you use your gift more" he told her.

Kate watched him as he got up. "It's a good thing you were there or I would have lost Jerod" she said. "You were already saving him. I just helped you. Your screams were so terrifying I had too." Drake smiled. "You heard my screams?" she asked. "Loud and clear, your mind was grasping for anything and everything." Kate sat beck "This is really a scary thing" she said "what if I get angry would I hurt anyone?" Drake raised an eyebrow "You could, but human nature and your compassion for life wouldn't let you. Just because you think it doesn't mean it will happen." Kate sighed. "That's good to know. How did we move the rock then to help Jerod?" she asked. "We created a bridge for him. Our minds used kinetic energy. We forced the stone to move with it." He knew she didn't understand. "I will show you later. You will understand" Drake told her. "Let's have something to eat they are probably wondering what happened to us at the complex." Kate looked towards it. He was right and the rest of the time there, they joked and laughed together.

Drake told her stories of the people in the complex and Kate told him of the people in the settlement. They were really not that different.

Soon they had their gear packed and were on their way back to the Haven. Kate stopped in her tracks. She stared at the ground "What is it?" she asked. Drake looked to see "It's a snake" he said "They keep the rodent population down. The foxes help. Although we haven't let many faxes go yet." Drake was so nonchalant about it she felt more at ease. "Have you been letting these animals go for a long time?" she asked. "More in the last decade, but there have been many in the past 40 or 50 years. They don't seem to leave the valley, but I'm sure they will" Drake told her. "We have bees and flies and that's about all I've seen" Kate told him. "They would seek out solitude on the most part going to where there are no people. There's a lot of country out there." Drake told her. "It will be a long time before there is enough to populate any given area to become noticeable." "How is it so many survived in the complex and none outside of it?" Kate asked. "The virus or plague kills on a genetic level. If you have a certain sequence in your DNA you are immune, if not then you get it. The animals we started with were the top breeds and we did lose many." Kate didn't really understand, but Drake's explanation seemed to be the right answer.

They arrived back in the complex. As they stood outside, Drake asked her if she was ready to really see what was there. She smiled and told him "I'm not afraid anymore." He smiled "Then let's find Jerod and Jon and get something to eat." Kate had no objections. She was hungry too.

They found the two men already in the kitchen. Jon stood when he saw them. Kate went right over and hugged Jerod, then stood beside Jon. "I'm staying for as long as you will have me here" she told them. Jon's face brightened up as he smiled. Drake pulled up a chair and at the look on Jon's face he smiled. "Seems the trip solved some things" Jerod said. "Oh father, you have no idea, I'm not afraid anymore." She smiled at Drake. "Did you know we are related to each other?" she asked. "Drake is my cousin. I was born here" she told them. Jerod smiled he was glad she knew the truth about herself. "What has brought out this comment?" Jerod asked her.

"It's kind of complicated. Drake just joined my mind to his and showed me what happened is the best way I can explain it" Kate told the. "So you are going to stay then?" Jon asked. "Yes if it's alright?" she replied. "More than alright" Jon stated. "It's wonderful." He placed his hand over hers. "You offered to show me this place. Is the offer still open?" Kate smiled at him. "You bet" Jon said and he just beamed. "Thank you Drake you seem to know all the time to fix things, I won't ever forget this." Drake winked at Drake.

Sheri, who had been near knew a great change just took place in Drake. He was different. His tension was gone and he looked more at peace. Whatever happened made both of them contented. She was happy for Jon and Kate. She hoped the new additions to the complex would transfix the notion about living outside as the best for all.

Jon and Kate soon found themselves deep in conversation about the complex and Jerod smiled. He was home as was Kate. This new life was about to begin and he wondered where it would take them. He looked over to Drake and he too saw the change in him. The hardness of soul was no longer there. Whatever took place out there had changed them both. Jerod added it to the list of many things he had seen since they had arrived at the Haven, as they call it.

Jon and Kate spent most of the time together. He spent hours showing her the Haven, telling her the history. She liked the animals and was amazed at the different foods. Jon and Kate shared a bond that only existed between a man and a woman. Drake often took Kate to the library. There they read and she learned about her gift. Often Jerod was there reading about something or other. She was happy. It didn't take long before she relished hot bathes with bubbles and cookies with milk.

She met so many people and often shared conversations with Sheri. She always had lots to say. She told stories about people there that Kate couldn't believe were true. They laughed and had good times together. Sheri was always doing some fancy handiwork on things and Kate with her nose in some book.

Jerod was the one to come and talk with Kate. "Kate I would like to talk with you. I'll meet you in our dorm, okay dear?" he asked. "Sure dad" she answered. She bid Sheri goodbye and headed to their dorm.

When she arrived Jerod was excited about something. "What's the matter father?" she asked. "Oh there's nothing really the matter, but do you realize what exactly this place is? It's a self contained nursery. They have the ability to replenish all the animals, birds and bugs. Do you know what that means? It means they can give the people back so much that was lost" he said "I think what Jon has told me they have been doing just that" Kate said. "Every year the surplus animals are set free to the outside."

Jerod stopped for a moment. "Then why is the enclosed range the only place we have seen them, why not anywhere else?" "We have Jerod, we have bees and flies. Without them letting them out for so many years we would not have those." Jerod rubbed his chin "True" he said. "I just think that the people of the settlement should be able to share in this wealth." Kate looked at him. "I will talk to Drake and Jon. You talk with Tanner, Naomi and Jason. It's run by the council so maybe a council meeting is where we should be talking." "I believe you are right Kate. I believe you are. I will go see Tanner and Naomi. See if you can find Drake and Jon" Jerod said. "Alright, I'm sure the council has been planning to let more animals out." You are probably right, but then I think of the people of the settlement and what this would do for them. Just think of the animals to pull the ploughs, to feed them and pull wagons. How much easier life would be?" Jerod couldn't stop his mind from wandering to the benefits for the people. They each set out in search of people they needed to gather a council meeting.

Kate, Jerod and Drake all stood in front of the council. Drake as usual had no fear in addressing them. He had always been of the opinion that they must rejoin the outside world.

Jerod presented his ideas about helping those still outside. The council did not share his excitement with his idea. "We must proceed carefully and with caution. If they were to discover us here they may fail to work for themselves and put the expectation of caring for them on us. A few people would not present a problem, but too many would jeopardize ourselves and them as well."

Jerod understood exactly what they were saying. He had to admit they were right about it. Yet Jerod all too well the hardships they faced and how much could be eased with the help of the people here.

The debate went on for hours, some things had been agreed on and others had not. By the time supper rolled around the council adjourned to the following day.

Jerod, Kate, Jon and Drake retired to Jerod's room. They would wait until the kitchens emptied some before they ate. Jon did get a tray of coffee and tea to tie them over.

Jerod talked of the people outside. His thoughts passed to the gifted and decided to tell Drake and Jon of them, how they were treated, if any should be given access to the complex and that they should be first.

Drake was stunned to hear the stories Jerod told about them. Gifted people Drake thought He knew at that moment they would be needed someday. Jerod painted a broad picture of life beyond the Haven and by all accounts his opinions were the truth about them. The council would have to hear what he had to say.

The evening passed quickly and the next week was filled with council meetings. The end result was that the gifted were to be the first to be offered the Haven as a refuge. Then from there more decisions would be made. They requested the group of Drake, Jon, Kate and Jerod travel to them and present the offer. Life was about to change again and this time to all the people.

Insects and birds would now be released outside the protected valley.

Jerod turned to Kate, Jon and Drake "So it begins" he said and the four had no doubt what meaning that statement carried.

It was another week before they readied their gear to start their journey to the gifted outside. Jerod, Kate, Jon and Drake stood at the doors to leave and knew that the world was going to get larger for everyone. Simion's vision and dreams had brought them to this point. They had survived and now their journey was to gather the people together, bringing the people back from the brink. They had made it. Jerod, Kate, Jon and Drake now faced what could be the joining of them all.

They said goodbye to those there to see them off. Their journey began as did the hopes of all the Haven. The outside folks were about to get a long over due surprise and many gifts they couldn't have imagined.

The day was warm as were the hearts of the four that journeyed out to the others. All Jerod could think was "So It Begins."

9 781426 958878